White Wool and Yellow Gold

Effie Sutton

Cover design by Judy Hudson
All photos are from family collections except the John Scales house in Wagontown, which was found on AccessGeneology.com

As with any work of fiction, the characters, incidents, and dialogs in this novel are products of the authors' imagination and are not to be construed as real. Any resemblance to actual events or to persons, living or dead, is entirely coincidental, except for the reference to Joe Monahan, a noted character of the time who ranched in the Owyhee Mountains.

ISBN: 978-1-7362365-3-6
Independently published

10 9 8 7 6 5 4 3 2

Praise for White Wool and Yellow Gold

- *...I became engrossed in the story line and could not put the book down... I was impressed by now much local history and life at the time Sutton was able to pack into her story.*

- *...a wealth of detail...from how sourdough biscuits are made and what remote communities did for entertainment, to how WWI affected even remote mining areas such as Wagontown...*

- *...loved the vernacular of the time and often felt that I was living in the Snake River flats of the early 1900s*

- *...I wanted it to keep going...it was great reading*

- *...I am loaning my copy out continuously. It was great*

- *I seldom read a novel written from a woman's point of view...I like it and what it was about. I even liked the language...which is typical of some people at the turn of the century.*

- *I would recommend to everyone for a great historical and interesting story...made me feel like I was there and living it myself.*

Forward

Effie Proud Sutton (1887 – 1978) came from Michigan to Idaho as a 15 year old in 1902. She and her family arrived in Caldwell by train, then travelled to the Snake River valley by horse drawn wagon, crossing the mighty Snake River on a cable ferry. Her

parents soon purchased *The Rocks,* a remote half-way station in Owyhee County that provided lodging, meals, and livery to travelers. They expanded the business, building a three-story stone structure with eleven bedrooms and extensive holding pens for stock.

With Effie's new life in this rugged country, her formal education was left behind as she embraced the family business of providing meals and lodging to the many sheep and cattle ranchers, stage coach passengers, and freighters traveling between Caldwell, Idaho and Jordan Valley, Oregon.

In 1907, Effie married nearby rancher, Conrad Sutton. They started their family on the Squaw Creek Ranch where their first daughter was born at home. At least one season took them to Wagontown, a mining town near DeLamar and Silver City, where their eldest son was born at home. While their sheep grazed on the mountain, they lived in the historic John Scales home. This house

v

and Wagontown, with its intriguing mining, resort and racetrack history, is the setting for much of the story for *White Wool and Yellow Gold*.

Eventually, Effie and Conrad moved their family to Homedale, Idaho, where Conrad served as County Commissioner. Effie partnered with him in community leadership.

When the cattle market fell in the 1920s, the Suttons lost almost everything. After selling their stock at a great loss and paying their debts, they were left with their furniture and a matched team of horses. They relocated to Leona, Oregon, where Conrad logged until his death in 1926.

Effie was then a widow with five children ranging in age from 9 to 17. She moved back to Idaho and eked out a living during the Great Depression by cooking or sewing for others. In later years, she kept house for her bachelor son and nephew, answering the call for help in times of crisis, sickness, and births for her extended family. She was a gentle, loving soul; a voracious reader, master quilter and seamstress; she gardened, hiked, fished, and wrote numerous short stories.

The story of *White Wool and Yellow Gold* had its beginnings with a fountain pen outline on one page of a discarded ledger from her family's Poison Creek half-way station (see cover image). As early as 1935, she tried to arrange time to *work on her book*, but it was not finished until the 1950s. During that time, she taught herself to type on an old black manual typewriter.

Effie's spelling was *creative*, but her memory and observation of geography, world events, cost of goods, and other details were incredible. Her innate ability to craft an intriguing story, draw the reader into the scene, and present the way of rural life have left us with a treasured window into the early 1900s.

The main characters in *White Wool and Yellow Gold* are fictional, although she makes mention of historical events and sites in the Owyhee Mountains.

The one time Effie submitted her manuscript to a publisher, it was rejected. Discouraged, and without the profusion of publishing avenues we enjoy today, her *book* was shelved, but never forgotten. Few people read the lengthy manuscript with its faded, irregular print, but Effie's family longed to publish *her book*, if only to honor her memory. Finally, twenty-nine years after her death, granddaughter Judy Hudson edited the manuscript, and was astounded by the richness of history and intimacy of reading her grandmother's presentation of a 19th century woman's life and struggle with relationships and quest to provide for her family.

Edits made were primarily of spelling, punctuation and sentence structure, retaining Effie's manner of writing and choice of words to the extent feasible. In the original manuscript, Effie had given pseudo names for the geographic locations, other than Boise City and the Snake River, but because of the historical significance of her book today, the actual names of the rural and ghost towns were used.

Effie's youngest daughter, Bertha Sutton Hudson, and Judy Hudson published *White Wool and Yellow Gold* locally in 2007, getting it into the hands of Effie's descendants. Not surprisingly, there was great interest outside the family system, and numerous copies of the book were sold by the Owyhee County Historical Society Museum and Library.

By 2021, Judy Hudson had become an author in her own right, and made more grammatical edits of the book prior to publishing it through Amazon. Again, she retained Effie's style of writing, and it is with great hope you will enjoy the historical treasure of *White Wool and Yellow Gold.*

--Judy Hudson, granddaughter and editor

Chapter One

THE WEST BOUND TRAIN arrived two hours late on this hot September day. A thick haze covered this small railroad town in southwest Idaho. The setting sun was a mere red globe one could gaze at without squinting or shading of eye.

The railroad depot was the busiest place in town at this hour. Still, many idle people hung about to see the newcomers. Among the few passengers alighting was a middle aged mother and two daughters. Anyone could see they were thus related with the same clear complexion and smooth brown hair, each watching everything about them with the greyest of eyes.

"Mama, what we going to do if Daddy isn't here to get us?" the smallest of the trio asked the instant her feet touched the ground. "However is he ever going to find us, Mama?" Six year old Annie hovered near her mother, hesitant to branch out in this new strange place, yet clearly did not miss seeing a thing as her gray eyes took in the depot set in this dusty town of Caldwell, Idaho.

"There now, you and I will wait here," her sister Mary told her as they edged out of the crowding people. Mary could feel a small hand tremble in hers. "Stop your fretting, Annie. See, Mother is going to ask that man at the desk which way we go to the hotel."

"Will Daddy be right there when we get there?" There was near panic in that question.

"Don't you remember, dear? Mother, you and I are to go to the hotel and rest until Daddy gets here."

"I guess I 'member," the child said, half doubting.

"In no time at all, we will have a nice room where we can rest and eat supper. There might even be a bathtub. Wouldn't a nice bath be fine?"

Annie was not much interested in a bath, and not much hungry since she frequented the lunch that Mother had brought with them on the train. Impatiently, she stayed beside her sister until her mother reached them. "The ticket agent says there is only one first class hotel in town, and it is generally well filled up, so we'd better get over there as soon as we can. He says it is two

1

blocks from here. Do you think we can carry all this luggage?"
she asked as Mary picked up both heavy suitcases.

"I can manage these all right, if it is but two blocks. Can you
make it with that awkward lunch basket? I know it's much lighter
than it was three days ago, but it is still awkward." Mary had set
down one of the heavy suitcases to hold open the street door. Her
mother attempted to exchange the light basket for the heavy grip,
but Mary's nimble fingers got the handle first. "No you don't,"
laughed her daughter. "These two balance up real well."

"How you sound like my mother, my sweet daughter," sighed
the weary woman. She watched her footing closely as they
proceeded along the uneven boardwalk. A fine light-colored dust
lay thick everywhere, necessitating that she lift her skirt with the
one hand that Annie still clung to.

They arrived at the Pacific Hotel with faces beaded with
perspiration. The hotel was a fairly new, yet plain wooden
structure. At a glance, they could see that the ground floor hosted
a saloon and barber shop off from the lobby. The dining room ran
the width of the building, with the kitchen toward the back.

"There are 20 bedrooms upstairs, madam, but they are all
taken," the clerk explained to Mrs. Williams. Noting the weary
droop to her Mother's shoulders, Mary took over. "Mother, you
are just too tired to even stand. Come sit in this easy chair." She
propelled Mother to a big overstuffed affair, and smiled as small
Annie climbed up beside her. Marching back to the desk, she
explained, "My father thought he would perhaps be here ahead of
us and have a room reserved for us. Has there been anyone by the
name of David Williams registered here within the last few days?"

The clerk carefully scanned the names for the past week, then
shook his head sadly. "I'm sorry, Miss, but there seems to be no
one by that name here."

"Of course he was not sure just when he would arrive, for he
is coming with an emigrant car, filled with our household goods,
plus the stock and farm equipment. He left Illinois nearly a month
ago."

"In that case, it would be very hard to tell when he would get
here," admitted the clerk.

"I understand that is true. We have been traveling now for
three days and my mother is worn out. I must find some place she
can rest. We were in hopes we could get rooms and our meals

too...."

"Oh, you people can get your meals here anyway," the clerk explained. "Supper is at six, breakfast at seven, dinner at noon. All meals are $.35 unless you are boarding by the week; then they are some cheaper. You are welcomed to wait here in the lobby until you can locate rooms elsewhere. I'm sorry, Miss Williams, we don't have an extra bed in the building. And I know of none liable to be vacated."

There was a stir among the knot of men toward the front. Before Mary had time to ask for direction to some place they might possibly find rooms, a tall well-tanned man stepped forward. Tipping his stiff-brimmed hat to her, he turned and bowed to Mrs. Williams. "Do you people happen to be David Williams' family haling from near Springfield, Illinois?"

"That we are," answered Mary and her mother in unison.

"My name is Max Thorn; perhaps Mr. Williams has spoken of me?"

"Indeed Father has," beamed Mary as she shook his firm hand. "Father told us you were very kind to him."

"I liked your father on sight. He'll make a good neighbor." Turning to the clerk, he told him, "David Williams is the man who came out last winter and bought the Sebren place close to my ranch. These people will be my guests until Mr. Williams gets here and they can get moved out. See to having the bed in Number 17 made up fresh, and rustle up a cot if you have to go out and buy one on my say-so."

"Oh, we cannot let you do that, Mr. Thorn. We do appreciate the offer, but we cannot take your room," Mrs. Williams assured him.

"Nonsense." Max waved the clerk away to do his bidding. "I can find a place to sleep easy enough. I know a lot of people in this burg and one of 'em will bed me down for the night. Now, if you people are hungry and don't mind eating before you go to cleanup, I'd suggest you go along into the dining room now before the grub runs short, as it does sometimes." He led the way, holding the swing-door open for them. "I've already eaten, but I can always handle another piece of pie with a cup of java to wash it down," he said as he turned toward the waitress coming to set up their table. "Maggie knows what a pie face I am."

Mary began to realize how hungry she was by the time the

3

several dishes arrived. A platter of meat held a few slices of roast beef randomly placed; a pat of dressing, and several pieces of broken browned potatoes, but the food was well cooked and tasted good to these hungry people.

Huge cups of coffee were brought in, and one was put beside Annie's place, much to her amusement. "Could this girlie have a glass of milk instead?" asked her mother.

"Sorry Lady, but there isn't one more drop of milk in the kitchen."

"Then water will be all right," Mrs. Williams told her, and handed the cup of coffee to Mr. Thorn.

Maggie brought in their dessert on the next trip -- five wedges of huckleberry pie, which she carried along one swaying arm. As they finished off the last of their pie, the weary travelers told Max of their long journey from Illinois.

Max carried the cot as the Williams family traversed the long uncarpeted hall to their room. The desk clerk nodded toward the red light indicating the fire escape. "That is one thing Mr. Bussa insists on me telling everyone staying here about. When the old hotel burned down, there was no easy way out, and in such cases, people get scared. One man never did get out, while all he had to do was to kick out a window and climb out on the porch. Wasn't a dozen feet to the ground." As Max passed them going back toward the stairway, the clerk explained the door to their left. "As yet, there is but the two bathrooms and lavatories put in. The ladies is at this end of the hall. Rather handy for you." Setting down the basket, he tested the made-up cot with his hand. "I hope this cot will be comfortable for this young lady." He tried to get a smile from Annie with no success.

After the weary travelers were settled in Max' room, Mary came wide awake. She wanted to see this new place, and not through the windows facing the gloomy street. There was one lone light at the corner street, but it hardly pierced the haze in the growing dusk. She could see the dim buildings across the street below with their false fronts in helter-skelter heights and sizes. The few people and rigs passing along the street were but dark shadows. Coming to this frontier town would have dismayed many a young woman reared as Mary Williams had been in a sheltered home and a well-settled community. But to Mary, all this spelled adventure. At eighteen, she was as free and

4

independent in her thinking as the most rugged of her pioneer forefathers.

Her concern for her mother and sister's well-being was the only thing that kept Mary from stepping out onto the dusty sidewalk right now. *I'd like to walk back to the railroad depot and make more inquires. Surely Father is close by.*

Mother removed her soiled dress, while Mary unbuttoned her shoes. Hardly was she horizontal before she spoke. "I can't remember a bed feeling as good to me in all of my forty years. Both of you girlies had better rest too."

"Three days and two nights without a bed is a long stretch," Mary agreed while helping Annie out of her pinafore. "Take off your stockings as well as your shoes; they are bound to be dirty," said Mary as she dusted off the small shoes and rolled the soiled hoes to tuck into one corner of the suitcase. She was amazed to find Annie nearly asleep beside Mother. "See here. If you are going to sleep so fast, I'm going to fix you ready for bed right now and put your gown on." Annie was soon transferred to the cot.

Mary sat there wide awake. "I have just been thinking, Mother. Neither of us put our names down in that book, and if Father should come in the night and the clerk not be there, he would have no way of knowing we were here." She did not tell what else she had been thinking about--no use worrying Mother.

"You are right about that, Dear. Might be a good idea to step down to the desk and sign our names."

"I won't be gone long." Softly closing the door, Mary hurried along the hall and down the stairs. The lobby seemed more cheerful and cozier now that it was fully dark outside. When she told the clerk her errand, he turned the book about for her to read for herself. Their names were written down in plainly legible script. "Why, our names are already down here." She was a little puzzled.

"Yes, Max figured putting down your names was the best way for your father to know."

"Mr. Thorn thinks of everything."

"No he doesn't," retorted Max coming in from the street. "I never thought 'til this minute about going over to the depot to learn what I might about freights and stock trains. Would you like to walk over with me?"

5

"Yes, I would like to very much," she answered truthfully. "I'm not one bit sleepy and I keep wondering how close Father might be to here. I'll go tell Mother I'm going."

"Better bring a wrap," he called after her.

To Mary, there was nothing unconventional about her striding along beside this man she had never seen until two hours ago. To her, he was no stranger. Father had told them much about him; about his odd ways of saying things; how his eyes laughed when his face would be so very straight. She knew too that he must be nearly 35 years old. He wasn't married; he lived on a farm close to their new home, and he owned sheep. *I must remember it isn't farms out here—it's ranches*

"Just how is your mother stacking up anyway?"

Mary suppressed a laugh over that expression, none too sure as to the correct meaning, but guessed it must be an inquiry about her mother's general well-being. "She says she is alright—just very tired. A good night's sleep should put her right again, but I've never seen her so completely done-in as she is now. If Father doesn't get here tonight, I may have to play like I'm head of this family and call a doctor, who will undoubtedly order her to stay in bed to rest for several days."

Max gave her a quick glance under the street light. "You're one nice looking girl with a brain or two; and not afraid to use yer bean."

Mary laughed now. "I'm not pretty, and all your nice complements will fail to make me good looking." Another laugh. "I've never before had my head called a bean. In the East, they are sometimes referred to as a block of wood. I'm not sure but what I prefer to be called a *bean head*. Beans can grow and blocks can't. I feel like I've come west to grow up with the country. There are so many things I want to learn about. I'm liable to ask all kinds of green horn questions. And I'm not going to be miffed if you call me a *bean head*." The light was too dim for her to see that his eyes were twinkling. Through the window, they could see the ticket window was closed. The only stir about the place now was the swing lantern along the tracks.

"Here comes the *brakey--the* switchman. Ten chances to one, we can learn more from him anyway." They moved in his direction. After a brief exchange, Max had the information he wanted. "More than likely your father's car was among those freights and stockcars shunted on that siding up at the loading chutes. I'll take you back to the hotel, then mosey up that way. I would ask you to walk along with me, but the dust is ankle deep in places. The road is so full of chuck holes, it isn't even pleasant to ride that distance."

"It surely is dusty. Doesn't it ever rain before winter time?"

"Oh yes, it can rain here in the summertime, but it's not as apt to do so. There hasn't been enough rain in four months to lay the dust even. But one of these days, it will turn loose and we'll all be praying for it to stop. I just hope it holds off long enough for you people to get all moved and settled."

"I take it that it wouldn't be very good if it rained much?"

"For it to rain and settle the dust would be very fine, but for it to keep it up very long is something else again. See, most of the roads out there have never been graded up, so the water just soaks in. And if it happens to be an adobe patch you hit with loaded wagons, you're in for fun."

"We have clay in the East," Mary told him.

"When you hit clay and it's wet, you will slip and slide every which way, and go ever' direction but what you want. But with a patch of 'dobe, you don't get out at all without you layin' down and rollin' out of it. That stuff will mire a saddle-blanket. Every step a fellow takes, he's going to pack about a half-acre of soil with him."

"There's Father right now," Mary said excitedly as he mounted the steps to the lobby. Rushing in, she hugged the tall gaunt man eagerly. "Oh, but I'm glad to see you, Father! We got here all of two and half hours ago. Did we beat you?"

"Yes, you beat me. It's less than an hour since the car stopped rolling. I spent a few minutes trying to figure out some way of unloading the stock yet tonight into those corrals, but voted against trying it alone. Just how is Mother standing the trip?"

"She's more than tired. She is just plain worn out, and if Mr. Thorn hadn't given us his room so kindly, I just don't know what would have happened to Mother."

"Why, Mr. Thorn, I didn't recognize you." David Williams was abashed. "Somehow you look different." Then he realized Max was no longer wearing a mustache.

"I shaved off the brush lately. Expect that's the difference in my looks. As soon as you've peeked in on the rest of your family,

7

I'll take you down the street where you can get something to eat. They only serve meals here at certain hours."

"Thanks, but I have already eaten supper. As soon as I assure myself as to Mother's state of health, I will need to head back to the car. I don't wish to leave it unguarded for long; but can I trouble you about the best way to hire two stout men in the morning to help me unload?"

"There'll be enough time for that come morning. I'll have my rig ready by the time you are back downstairs. I can just as well run you out to the Flats." Turning to Mary, "I hope you sleep well this first night in Idaho, Miss Williams; you might like this sage brush state well enough to stick around for a while.

Chapter Two

MRS. WILLIAMS AND THE two girls had but commenced their breakfast, when in trooped her husband carrying a tall can of milk, and Max Thorn, with two other men in tow. "Daddy, Daddy! You never woke me up last night," scolded Annie. "I never knew you was here 'til this morning."

"I know I didn't, Annie Child," he said as he kissed her. "You were sleeping much too sound about then. Even Mother was hardly awake." He patted his wife's shoulder. "I'll carry this heavy can to the kitchen for this girlie, then we'll be ready to sit with you."

Maggie Bussa hurried ahead to hold back the door for him, still a bit mystified as to why this stranger should be bringing them all this milk. "Sure glad to find someone to use this milk. Seems such a waste to just throw it away," David Williams explained to her and the surprised cook. "If you have containers to put it in, I'll take back the can and be able to bring you more this evening or in the morning perhaps."

Max Thorn seemed to have brought in the out-of-door smells along with him. He was in working clothes that carried the scent of leather, horses, and sage brush. With one deft move, he brought an extra chair from the next table, making this six-placed table seat seven. By his asking the two men with him what their names were before introducing them, everyone knew they were strangers to him. The slightly built middle-aged man, called Hank Nappier, had thin hair and brown eyes, and appeared to be a slow moving, mild mannered man. The tiny purple veins about his nose and cheek told of his weakness for drink.

The other man was the opposite in looks. John Marcus was tall and as fresh-faced as a girl. He had hair just short of being black, and the bluest eyes Mary had ever seen. As she studied him via furtive glances, she could tell he was not the youth he at first appeared. There was a strength about his jaw and squareness of shoulders that made her want to study him more. His hands showed calluses and lines that were sure signs of hard work. He seemed slender in comparison to Max Thorn, but when her father came in, she could see they were all three of the same height—about six feet. "Let's eat," said David as he sat himself beside his wife. "Have you ordered for us?"

9

"Not much ordering to do," smiled Mother. "We had no more than sat down when here came our breakfast. It's very good too—much more than we could eat ever." She smiled as another platter of bacon and eggs arrived, along with a plate stacked with toast, and another piled high with hotcakes.

Maggie snatched another place setting from the table nearby. "Any of you want mush? I think it's oats."

"I just fed mine to my Cayuses," grinned Max, helping himself to two hot cakes. David and the two other men ate cereal. As Maggie came in with the bowls, Max snapped at her, "Make mine two coffees, Maggie, and don't be slow about it."

Mary was shocked that Max would say such a thing to the busy girl. Then she saw his twinkling blue eyes and the dirty look Maggie mocked him with. These two evidently understood each other well. Mary noticed that those twinkling eyes were all but laughing. Then she glanced toward the man who had been introduced as John Marcus. Their eyes met but briefly, but she was keenly aware of his blue eyes set in an untanned face. A slight smile played about his mouth as he met her eye. She wondered what manner of man this John Marcus was. She knew he must do heavy work to make his hands so rough, but she could tell nothing by his clothes—a light colored shirt; a suit coat with shiny elbows that had seen better days. And instead of overalls like Max and the other man wore, John's trousers were a heavy twill cloth.

Mary's attention was pulled toward her father and Max as they spoke of their plans for the first work at hand. As they finished their meal and plans, she spoke up. "Now I know you two have thought out all the whys and wherefores about this unloading business, but there is one little item you forgot to mention. All this work calls for food. How would it be if I walked up that way a couple hours before noon and had some sort of a meal ready for you?"

"Very good idea," Max answered, taking his last sip of coffee. "Only don't you try walking in this alkali dust."

"Then I shall try running through it," she said as she turned playfully away from Max. She noticed that John Marcus was grinning as he left the table.

"I'll drive back for you along about ten o'clock," Max told her.

"Will anything hinder you from riding out as we go, Mary," asked her father. "You could be of some help in leading the cows and team around a bit. They've been tied up a long time. I suspect Mother needs to stay pretty still and rest all she can. Annie, can you take good care of Mother?" he asked the wide-eyed child, and waited for her nod. He spoke again to Mary, "While we are at the blacksmith, you see if any store is open this early to buy a loaf of bread. I believe my grub box still holds plenty of staples otherwise."

The morning proved to be somewhat cooler and the sun shone less fiery, but every step by man and beast or turn of wheel raised a smothering cloud of the eye-stinging dust about them. In no time at all, Mary took off her hat and tied a silk scarf about her head and face, leaving only a peep hole to see out from. Shortly, she found she could see nothing in this billowing dust, so she held the opening together with one hand and her hat with the other. There was no danger of her falling out of the wagon, for she was wedged in-between her father and Max Thorn.

That one mile seemed twice the distance over the uneven road. Mary was greatly relieved as she descended from the rig. A hard callused, yet gentle hand aided her step down. "Why, there seems to be no dust here except what we brought," laughed Mary as she looked at the gray coating of dust covering the five of them. She stepped away from the men and shed her jacket, shaking the disagreeable stuff from her clothing. Seeing a whirl wind of dust close by, she held her hat edge with her teeth and tied the scarf over her head again. She put her jacket back on, but was at a loss as to what to do with her hat. Seeing no safe place to put it, she pinned it atop her head as she came toward the group. "I must look like a gypsy." She caught John's faint smile. "I don't want this hat to blow away. If it gets as warm as it was yesterday, I'm going to need it."

"You look all right to me," the young man said timidly. Mary noticed a bit of color rise in his cheeks, but he was quickly distracted as Max assigned him a task.

There seemed nothing for Mary to do until the livestock were out of the railroad car. Cinders had been placed close beside the railroad tracks to prevent dust, so she walked along the tracks to the corrals. Climbing to the top of the first heavy gate, she could see a glimpse of the darker rim of foothills on three sides. Toward the north, the rise of ground close at hand prevented any distant view. The town of Caldwell from this distance was less impressive. There was hardly a tree or anything green to break the monotonous drab color. Few buildings were painted, and those that were, seemed graced with gray and brown shades. *I want my house painted white and my barn bright red,* Mary thought as she hurried closer to the train car. Her father handed her halters for the two fine roan milk cows as they came cautiously down the crude wooden ramp.

"I've already picked out the mountain I want to climb, Father," she told him gaily, as if it was easy to do. Her father admired the adventurous spirit of his grown daughter, with no inkling of how that spirit would lead her in the near future. Mary led the two gentle cows in wake of two fine matching Clydesdales led by Max. He took them to an open place free from brush and rocks to let them roll, which they promptly did, stirring enough dust to set them coughing.

Mary laughed, "I bet they're happy over their freedom to roll, even if they don't like the dust. I fail to see one spear of grass or anything green for these cows to eat. They might as well be tied up again somewhere. I'm sure I can be of help at the car." She was petting the two roan heads rubbing against her.

"Plenty of hay to make 'em happy in the corral," Max said as he led them away. "Nothing to hinder them being turned loose in one corral, and these in another, as long as no stock shows up to be shipped."

"Do they ship cattle as well as sheep from here?" was her first question.

"Yes, and horses too. But not large ones like these Clydesdales." He gave each one an admiring rub as he unsnapped the halter rope. "Mostly range horses—they're smaller." Seeing the girl eyeing the bale of hay as if she would be attempting to handle that next, he said, "I'll wrestle that and feed 'em, while you pick out the spot you want your kitchen and dining room so we can set her up." With two clips of the heavy pliers he carried in his pocket, he was flaking apart the pressed hay.

"The north side of the car is the best place," she told Max as she rounded the tall orange colored structure, "but that will mean carrying that heavy grub box and everything so much further."

"Now you should worry about that," he teased, "with four of

us men to get it there." Hank Nappier lifted the heavy-hasped box out of the way of tables and chairs being set out. Not content to be idle, Mary took two of the light weight chairs along with her as she went to the shady side. It was getting warm now. Mary took off her jacket, draped it over a chair shoe, and anchored the troublesome hat to it with the hat pins. "Will you need a camp fire?" Max asked, righting the table he handled alone. "Can you manage that?"

"I think so," Mary answered quickly. "What I am wondering about is what to use for fuel. Do you suppose the Oregon Short-line will object to me picking up any bits of coal scattered along their tracks?"

Max' eyes danced again, surprised at the resourcefulness of this girl. "Guess they wouldn't arrest you. I'll get your father's ax and have an armful of brush for you in much less time. You know where the water is?"

"Do you mean that piped water beside the corral? Is it any good? It has such a nasty odor." She wrinkled her nose in distaste.

"Sure is. Artesian water is pure. It's the sulfur in it that makes it smell that way. Some wells are half boiled, but this one is only slightly warm. When the water gets cold, you don't notice the sulfur taste or smell."

Mary could hardly feature not being able to detect that odor. As she filled a pail with the tepid water, she still hesitated to drink any of it. She set to wash and peel potatoes, and slice them for frying. Max was soon back with a good armload of wood. True, it wasn't stove wood such as she was used to, but it seemed to be burning readily, starting off with a snap as soon as a match was put to it. It had the funny smell of sage, so she guessed it must be the kind of brush called sagebrush. She would not bother asking anyone now--everyone seemed much too busy.

When Mary called dinner an hour later, they still seemed too busy to want to stop their work. "Why, here I thought you men would be starved by this time," she chided as they came to wash in the four basins of water she had ready.

"I see you're used to fixin' for a harvest crew," spoke Hank Nappier upon seeing those pans of water ready, him being the last one to start washing the dust away.

"Mary has helped her mother feed many a hungry crew of

men," Father said as he finished with the roller towel and handed it to the next one. He uncovered the butter dish, sugar bowl and jam, while Mary dished the nicely browned potatoes and the platter of fried ham, with the fat edges crisp and curled. "Fall to," Father invited as the coffee was poured. "At this small a table, there need be but little passing. Everyone helps himself."

"The cream and milk in these small pails seems to be still sweet. But these cookies and nut cake might not be edible—they're so dry. I'll leave them in the cake box to be more room on the table." Uncapping the jar of relish to pass, "This piccalilli is real good with ham."

"All the same as thrashing crew feed," joked Max, helping himself before passing the jar on.

"Not quite," laughed Mary. "No fried chicken, fresh tomatoes, or blackberry pie for this meal. What I'm wondering is, what would there be to thrash out here. All I see is sagebrush in patches."

"You haven't looked closely. There is some grease wood among the sage."

Mary knew by his eyes that Max was teasing. To carry on the joke, she asked, "Would anyone get seed if they were to thrash all the brush?"

"More apt to get wood ticks," Hank Nappier joined in.

Mary could see that this man by the name of Nappier was quite a wit if he were acquainted. Max plied him with questions as to where he had been, the different places he had worked, and if he knew the whereabouts of certain ranches. "You know the country well enough, but the question is, have you ever juiced a cow?" Mary could but laugh over that expression.

Hank Nappier did not laugh. He was slow in answering. "Yes, I've juiced many a cow. Always claimed it was cows that set me adrift. I was born and reared on a dairy farm, but I didn't like the steady routine of feeding, cleaning, and milking at certain hours without fail. The only difference in the season was the mud, snow or rain in the winter time and the heat and flies in the summer to give spice to my life. I know how to milk alright, but as a means of livelihood, I say nix."

"Would four or five days be too long a stretch to trail out two cows as far as my ranch?

The man finished his cake and coffee, but did not answer

quickly. Mary sensed that it was their cows Max was talking about, so she cut in. "Oh, but I'm wanting to lead the cows out. I'm used to walking. If it isn't more than five or six miles between places, I can make it just as well as Mr. Nappier can, and he can help here with the unloading. There must be any number of things I don't know how to do, but I do know how to lead those cows. I'm sure I can do it."

Max' eyes were not twinkling now as he gave her a level look. "Yes, I rather think you could do it, or die trying. But you're new to this country, and it would be a much harder trip than need be. My advice is to save your strength 'til you get to your new home. There will be plenty of work for you there. That place is some run down. Only bachelors have lived in the house these several years. I've found few of them who were good housekeepers." He turned his gaze back to Nappier.

"I guess I could make the trip alright. Quite a walk for man as well as cows. How are you solving the feed and water question along the way?"

"You know where the Shultz Ranch is? That's better than three miles–nearer four. If you start out soon, you could make it by good dark, I believe. I'm on my way to the ranch for two freight wagons and six head within an hour. There is no use of Williams here fussing around hauling this stuff out a load at a time—just as well take it all at once. I'll stake you out a barrel of water close to the road, about half way between here and the Shultz' place. From there, I'll haul another barrel to half the distance to Reimers. Come the third day, you'll be to the rim mid day, and sharp to your right as you start down the grade is plenty of water. There's a patch of grass below it. They can rest and feed a couple of hours there, then you can still make it to the ferry by night fall. If they get too leg weary between there and my place, either one of these ranches will let you stay. Understand now, I can arrange for feed for both cows and you, and a bed. But you see to it that you get a lunch put up each morning. I can get you a fair saddle horse by merely going after him. Do you want to bother with him?"

"Be handy to have one to pack my lunch and water bag."

"Alright. I'll catch up with you within two hours at the most. Say, while Miss Williams isn't looking, you snitch those slices of ham and hide 'em between two hunks of bread. They might taste awfully good before you get supper tonight."

"I surely can put up a lunch for you while you are watering the cows." Mary was covering food and putting it away. "Those dry cookies would only make you thirsty. How would some apples do? I see a few good ones rolling around in here." She fished them out, along with a small cloth sack to put the whole wrapped lunch in.

Mary took the lunch to him as he was ready to head south into the heat and haze. There were many dim roads and paths leading off every which way, and she wondered how he would know which one was the right one to take. He didn't seem to be following any of them. She was not fully at ease seeing those cows led away by a stranger. Then she had to remember, *Max Thorn knows this country, and Father trusts him. He would not send our cows out with someone he didn't think was alright.*

Washing the dishes and packing everything back shipshape did not take long. The half-pail of water remaining doused the fire out. Father and John Marcus were assembling the wagon and she could see no way of helping there. The team nickered to her as she climbed the corral gate. "You old rogues are glad to see me, I know." She rubbed their heads as they crowded close. "I can see less now than I could this morning," she said to them. "Maybe you two would like some more of that half warm water." After watering them, she curried them well and fed them more hay. Watching the two men work for a moment, she asked her father, "Is there anything at all I can do to help?"

"Not a thing that I know of, Daughter. Instead of unloading much today, we've decided the better plan is to get this wagon in to the blacksmith for brakes to be put on. They promised to have it fixed by morning; then we can load the wagons direct from off the train car. We're almost through here, and while I harness the team, you two can hoist the chairs and table back inside here. I'll lend a hand with the heavy box."

Riding back into town on the high spring seat, they were sometimes above the billow of dust and could talk. As they neared town, Mary said "Do you know, this might not be such a bad looking place if they would plant several trees and paint their houses lighter colors." She caught the smile on John Marcus' face.

"It would make a difference," Father nodded. "Perhaps they

16

will do so in time. As I understand it, this town is hardly old enough to vote. That number of years is pretty young when applied to a town. Not so young if attached to a man. Have you voted yet, Marcus?" he asked banteringly.

"I haven't voted as yet," he answered back, "but that isn't because I'm not old enough. I was 25 a few days ago. Just never happened to be at the right place to vote."

Mary flushed as she looked at him briefly from the side. "I would have guessed you to be three or four years younger than that." She was attracted to him and very aware of his clean and muscular body next to her. His nearness disturbed her, and to shy away from that, she talked on. "I wonder what Mother and Annie have found to amuse themselves. Maybe it is a good thing we are going back to town early today. I can look around to see if there are any fresh vegetables to be bought. We really should have some for dinner tomorrow."

"So you aim to come out tomorrow and cook our dinner for us?" her father asked.

"I just as well, if Mother and Annie are making out alright. When I go to the stores, I think I'll buy Annie a new picture book. That might please her."

"Better still, take the child along and let her pick out her own book. That will please her twice. We'll just leave the wagon at the stop now. I believe the team will be safe enough hitched here while I go in and visit with Mother a short while."

Annie had been at the window impatiently watching for them. She danced down the steps to meet them, demanding of Mary, "Why didn't you come back right after dinner? Mama said maybe you would, and you never."

"I know, Chickee. How you been today? Has Mother rested lots?" All of them trooped in and found Mother seated comfortably, close to the window.

"We both took a nap, didn't we, Mama? A nice long one." Annie was happy now with all her family around her. One small hand clutched her father's; the other held on to Mary's dress while she tried to back into the chair beside her mother.

All three grownups smiled over Annie's head at this trick of hers. "That sign says it will be six o'clock before we can eat supper here," Father remarked. "Will that give you girlies time enough to do your shopping?"

"Can I buy something, Daddy? I have my very own money I saved all the way on the train." Annie was dancing about again.

"If you can find a book you would like, surely you can." David Williams beamed with pride as he watched his two daughters pass through the door John Marcus held open for them. "Are you getting rested, Mother?" He pulled up a heavy chair close to hers.

"I'm not half as groggy now as I was this morning. Another 24 hours, and I'll be rested."

"I hope so. The trip out to the ranch is not going to be an easy one for you. The cows are already on their way. Max Thorn learned that Mr. Nappier was used to handling cows—grew up on a dairy, in fact, and he agreed to lead them out. I believe that is much better than Mary havin' to do it. She was a bit disappointed, I know."

"I expect she was. I doubt she realizes just how hard a trip that would be in this heat and dust. I am pleased to know that a man who knows this country is making that trip. Have you learned what manner of work the younger man follows?"

"He said something about mining and prospecting. He's a willing enough chap when you show him what you want done, and the way to do it. It's plain he's never been around a farm or ranch much. I believe Annie could come nearer knowing how that wagon should go together than he did." Father sighed with weariness. "I'll say this much for John Marcus: He don't talk a man to death. Hardly talks at all. That could be because I know nothing about mines and he knows nothing about farming."

Mother Williams glanced out the window and caught sight of Annie dancing about on the opposite side of the street. "That child has her new book, I see. She looks in it one second, then the next she is circling Mary and that young man." Mother's eyes crinkled at the corners. "He may not be much of a talker, but from here, it doesn't look like our daughter is doing all the gabbing."

Both chuckled. "We must remember to draw that young man out in conversation at the supper table to see just what manner of man he really is. You'll have to be the one to do that, Mother. I need to eat in rather short order and get back to the car. Max Thorn assures me there are few people in this country that would bother things left unguarded, but I'm uneasy about doing so."

Chapter Three

"WHOA," CALLED MAX THORN sharply as he set the brake and sprang to the ground. "Steady there, Nelly," he spoke to the horse as he brushed past to reach bits of the black leaders. The small gun in his right hand was at ready, and he neatly severed the head from a rattler coiling in the dust of the road, not more than a dozen feet ahead of the team. One kick of a booted foot sent the head into the sagebrush beside the road. With his boot on the body of the reptile, he pulled off the rattles, then sent the rest of the dead snake after the head. "No use leaving that varmint in the road even if it is dead and harmless. It still can scare a flighty horse," he explained as he holstered his gun and climbed back into the seat.

"How did you ever see that snake in time," asked Mary Williams. "I only saw it just as you shot it."

"Have you seen many rattlers?"

"No, I've never even seen one."

"That's why you didn't see it. You would hardly know what to look for. I'm always on the lookout for 'em along here. Seems to be a favorite stomping ground for 'em. That's why I bother to pack this gun handy."

"Your eyes must be pretty sharp at that," Mary said admiringly.

"I depend a lot on that black leader. When I see his ear prick up and he commences to crowd the chain or swing out, I know in which direction to look. That bugger sure hates rattlers, and like most range horses, can smell 'em or something." He held out the rattles to small Annie, but she shrunk away from them. Then he proffered them to Mary. "So, you want to keep a memento of your first rattler?"

She accepted them readily. "Are they supposed to bring good luck or something? I have read about people collecting them."

"Can't say what ideas different people attach to them. I always figured the keeping of 'em was about like the keeping of deer horns and such—just to show people you seen or killed 'em." He gave her a puzzled look. "Now you, with all your common sense, wouldn't happen to be superstitious, would you?"

"Me be superstitious? I see you don't know my father very well," Mary laughed. "The one thing that will make him furious is

19

for anyone to say such things. He wouldn't even allow ghost stories to be told at home. He feared some child might believe them. No, I truly believe I'm not one bit superstitious.

"Glad to hear that," was Max' odd comment.

"How many miles is it 'til we can see the river?" Annie was getting restless. She had asked that question at least once every mile since they left Caldwell at day break.

"Well, let's see," drawled Max. "What was the last number of miles I said we had traveled?"

"Nine," whispered the child.

"That's right. And I would say perhaps we have come another mile. That would make it ten. That's half the distance to the ferry, but we are going to see that old river three miles before we get there, remember? From the top of the grade, there will be things to see. The distance won't seem so long."

Annie wiggled around to find a more comfortable position, now leaning heavily against Mary. She sighed, "I don't think they measure the miles right out here."

"You might be right about that, young lady," Max' grinned.

Mary was getting pretty weary herself and wondered how Mother was faring in the other rig. They lost sight of them more than five miles back. Max had said her father had undoubtedly dropped back a few paces so as not to eat their dust. They were stirring up plenty of it. There were a few short stretches where the soil was a different color, which produced little dust. Max called those granite formations. One wheel track would be worn down, making the wagon tip at an angle. About the time Mary would consider getting out some apples to eat, they would be over that darker patch of soil, which Max called *ash*, and they would be in the dust again. When a slight breeze whipped the dust away and Mary could see ahead, she saw that the ground seemed to be creased with many parallel roads. Few crossed over the wheel tracks that were cut deeply in the white ash soil. "Why so many roads?" she asked.

"That is called *The Thousand Roads*. I wouldn't say there is that many, but there is more than I've ever taken time to count. The wagon wheels cut down too deep in this light soil. Some of these roads have holes in 'em more than hub deep. It's possible to break an axle on a heavy loaded rig. That's why we are going to swing left here and make us a new road just like hundreds of people have before us."

"Will Father be able to follow our tracks?" She was a bit worried.

"I think so, but he understands the reason for all these roads. He asked about 'em last winter. Then it was mud instead of dust."

"Surely this kind of soil would not grow very good crops."

"On the contrary, it grows some very good ones. Might be rather hard for a tender foot to handle right off at first. It will sub-irrigate fine."

"Then all it needs is water? But how would they ever go about getting water on this land?"

A grin came to Max' dust-covered face. "Some guys in the know claim this can be made into one of the biggest artificial lakes in the world. There are some survey stakes along this road. See, this is like a shallow bowl through here--lower than most of the surrounding ground. And if they build a dam about a mile west of here, it would make a pretty good-sized pond."

"It would take more than a pond to do much good, wouldn't it?"

Max grinned even broader. "Well, they figure it will be some 27 miles around it. If they ever build it, we'll have to travel a different route in to town."

"Would that make it a longer distance?"

Max shook his head. "Very little if any. Of course, they haven't built it yet."

"You sound rather skeptical about their doing so."

"They may build it alright, but I wonder if this ground will hold water. It's pretty porous in many places. Might be that good-sized streams get lost. Along the rim toward the river, there's lots of cracks and crevasses—even caves that no one has explored."

"Would the water feed from the Snake River?"

"The plans are to use the flood waters of the Boise River. See, that is higher than we are here, while the Snake River is several hundred feet lower. From the Boise River, it would be gravity fed, and not more than fifty or sixty miles of canals would be required to bring the water. Wait until you see the Snake River, then you tell me how they'd go about getting the water up here." His eyes were twinkling again.

Mary tried to smile, but found her lips painful in their dryness. Annie was sound asleep and heavy to hold, making it all but

impossible to turn around to see in other directions. The ground
had a bit of an incline, and nothing to see but the sagebrush on
either side of the road as far as her eye could travel. "I fear I'm
getting as impatient as Annie to catch sight of the river."

"Just to the top of this rise—two to three miles, I'd say, and
you'll see it; unless there happens to be a dust storm along the
Flats. Those pesky winds can obscure the river and Flats, but I
don't believe there is enough breeze stirring to indicate a dust bath
down below."

Mary wondered why this man kept referring to the Snake
River as being lower and never once calling this a valley. Always
the Flats. The dust was not so troublesome now, but she was
thirsty, hungry, and the noon sun was almost too warm to be
wearing her dustcoat and scarf. Another mile and she reached her
hand out impulsively. "I'm going to have to trouble you to hand
me the water."

As he handed her the canteen, Max said, "This road is a new
grade. The old one angled off up the river a ways. Even the ferry
site was at a different place than now, but the road out from
Caldwell to the rim follows the old trail pretty close."

"Can I see our new home from here?"

The whip was now pointing south across the valley floor and
to the west. "You can't quite see your place. A ridge coming
down from these low foothills intervenes, but it is in that
direction. You can see the road that angles back to the river.
Where that green alfalfa field is, is my place."

A puzzled look came to her dusty face. "It looks somewhat
like a checkerboard. I see gray, green, almost white, rust, and a
few patches that are all but red. What would the red be?"

"That's Russian thistle, or tumble weeds as it's called here.
It's sure a pest. Some guy, who's supposed to be smart,
introduced that weed into this country thinking it would make
food for stock."

"Won't anything eat it?" Mary might be weary, but she was
very alert.

"Yes, they'll eat it in the spring if there's nothing else, but
generally there's plenty of browse, so the stock eat the grass and
leave the tumbleweeds to grow unchecked all summer. When they
are dry, and the wind breaks 'em off and fills every ditch and
fence row with 'em, all one can do is burn 'em." Max now

released the brake as a signal to the teams as they started down the steep grade. The brake was shot back into its last notch and his foot held it there. The grind of blocks against the sliding wheels awakened Annie. The noise was deafening. There was no talking now. Mary was much too busy hanging on and holding Annie to keep her from sliding off the tilted seat. Annie could not reach anything to brace herself with her short legs. The wagon jolted over the steep rocky grade, terrifying Annie and making Mary none too easy as they swayed in the wagon seat down, down. The only respite came at the sharp curves—switch backs, Max called them.

The screech of the brakes was not as deafening now, and the wagons were more on an even keel. Mary could smile at the off horse in the second team, neatly hopping over the chain as soon as it touched his legs. Slowly they pulled the two heavily loaded wagons around the hairpin curve. Just as expertly, the same horse hopped back to his right side, and his mate even followed him for an instant. The touch of the long whip Max carried would make this horse get back to his own side the very second the chain straightened out. "That cayuse hardly savvies the chain yet," said Max.

"I was wondering why you carried that whip when you never seem to use it." Mary tried to smile, but it came out as a grimace. She did not know if her comment had been heard, for the brakes were again howling. The team traveled at a faster pace on down the slope to the water's edge. The ferry already nearing the approach was being poled into place, thudding ever so lightly against the dock. Nimbly, the lone, deeply tanned man made it fast, with one hand waving them on with the other.

Annie leaned into her sister, more afraid of this wide stretch than the steep grade they had just traversed. She half-cried, "What'll we do if we fall in?"

"Why, this ferry boat is made flat so we won't fall in," Max told her while he wound the reins about the brake rod and sprang to the wooden planking, flexing his arms as he talked to the ferryman. The ferry glided smoothly through the water—a dramatic contrast to that hellish road. As they passed mid stream, they could make out several children atop the bank watching their arrival. She could see the upper story of a tall unpainted house and wide shed-like barns. As they approached the opposite bank, nothing could be seen but the steep road hemmed in by a solid wooden wall. Max was ready, and released the brake the second the chain barring their way was dropped.

The wagons rolled free from the ferry as the plunging horses pulled the wagon up the steep grade. They never stopped until the top was reached. Again, the setting of the brake was the signal for them to rest. "That trail wagon sure lugged," Max said. "I should have dropped it and made the extra trip back for it." As the heaving sides of the animals ceased, the brakes were released and rolled easily the short distance toward the buildings. "Three here, Mrs. Leach. And two more coming," Max called to the woman in the doorway with a babe astride her hip. "We need dinner for ten—we're that hungry," he joked as he helped the two girls down.

"I'm wondering if our team can make it up that awful steep climb," Mary questioned before her feet trod the hard packed, windswept ground.

"I think they can. That team has a powerful lot of pull in those stout legs of theirs. But to be on the safe side, I'll mosey back to the chute with one of my teams as soon as they are watered."

Mrs. Leach called to the group of towheaded children, telling one of them to come mind the baby while she got dinner on the table. She now spoke to Mary and Annie coming to the house. "Better come in out of the sun. It's a mite cooler in here. Make yourselves to home. You may be tired of setting after that long ride out from Caldwell, so walk around or rest on the couch or whatever you like. We were sorta looking for you about now. Some of the younguns' seen you as you topped the rim." She deposited the restful babe on a folded quilt in the middle of the floor, going about her work as the five children sidled in. They were like stair steps as to size—three boys and two girls. Never a word did they say as they eyed Annie curiously.

At first glance, Mary judged them to be dirty and unkempt. As her eyes became accustomed to the gloomy room, she saw they were not dirty at all, just very tanned. Their nondescript clothes were faded by sun and many washings. The girls wore their sun-bleached hair unbraided and loose, which gave an untidy look. All seemed too bashful to talk to Mary when she spoke to them. "What do you say, Annie, if you and I go out and watch Father and Mother cross the ferry like we did?" Annie was eager to do this, and they were no more than out the doorway when out trouped the bashful children who raced ahead of them to a knoll— a very good spot to view the on-coming boat. A creaking noise was close at hand as the cable swayed with the movement of the boat. Not noticing any such noise when they had crossed, Mary looked sharply about and found this end of the cable was anchored a few feet from where they stood.

Annie was frantically waving her hat to their parents, although neither one seemed aware of it. "Mother didn't see you, Dear. Father is much too busy driving the team up that steep grade. He couldn't wave back to you. Let me tie your hat back on or you'll get a blistered face yet before we get home." There had been no need of the extra team waiting to give aid with this loaded wagon. Father and Max both helped Mrs. Williams down. Mary guessed her to be more than tired and offered to lend a hand. Max gave way to let her take over.

"Mama was you scart of that big river? I was. But we never once fell in."

"No Child, Mother wasn't frightened. I'm just too tired now to talk much," Mother told the excited girl. She tried to sip the water slowly and kept the wet cloth to her head, for it felt good.

The meal was dished and on the table the moment the two men came in. Father seemed too concerned over Mother to think about eating. Sensing this, Mother struggled to a sitting position with his help. "Now you two just help me over to that table, please. I'm just too famished to make it under my own power." Once at the table, she bothered Mrs. Leach for a cup of tea to be made for her. This she sipped while eating a small amount of food she had allowed Father to serve her. Seeing the questioning look on the woman's face over her turning down the serving of dessert, "I'm just as hungry as the rest of my family, and would so like to eat my fill of all this good food, but from past experiences, I know I better not if I want to finish this trip sitting up instead of stretched out on a bed." She was feeling better and managed a smile. "I know that bread pudding must be good with the nuts and raisins showing through it. Annie, perhaps, wants my share and is too shy to ask for it." She noticed that Father and Max were both taking more slaw and green onions, along with another slice of boiled ham. "Tell me, how do you keep green stuff so crisp in this hot, dry climate?"

Max grinned. "Wait 'til you see their garden patch. Those youngsters make quite a bucket brigade to water that garden at sundown."

"Would trees have to be watered that way too?" Mary asked. She had been wondering why there was not a tree or shrub about the yard.

"Yes, and they'd sometimes have to haul it most of the year. There's not always enough rain or snow to keep 'em growing. We've had several trees started. First ones we didn't have protected good enough, and they got girdled by porcupines. One hard winter they froze out—not having water, Pa said. The younguns planted whips of willows, but they haven't made it either."

"I'm feeling almost normal again, Mrs. Leach," Max told her as she filled his coffee cup.

"I too am feeling better by the minute," voiced Mother Williams.

"No more grades; not so much dust; and not too many hours of sunshine left," said Max. "Do you think you can make it on in, Mrs. Williams, or do you prefer to rest here and one of us come for you in the morning?"

"Goodness me, no one needs to make any extra trip for me. If the worst is over, I can manage the last ten miles."

"Then do a bit more resting until the teams are hitched and ready," Father advised. About an hour passed before the teams were ready and the loads were shifted about.

When Mrs. Williams was carefully hoisted up to the wagon seat, she saw that the bedsprings and mattress were anchored just behind the seat, covered with a blanket. "What under the sun made you go to all that trouble?"

"That was Max' idea," Father told her as he climbed up beside her from the other side. "And a pretty good one, I believe. Only wished we had thought of it in the first place—then you would not have gotten so weary." He released the brake now to follow in the other wagon's wake across the barren ground. Heat waves danced, giving the appearance of water at some distances. "Let me help you back to that bed before you get tired now. In that way, you can stand the five miles we still have to go."

"Five miles" questioned Mother. "I thought it was ten from here."

"Max says the teams can hardly make it with the wagons loaded this heavy. It'll be late supper time by the time we get to his place. He has room enough to bed us down. I think it'll be better to wait 'til morning daylight for that last five miles.

"Annie should have rode back here with us and rested on this bed you have fixed." Mother was always thinking of others instead of herself.

"Oh, there is a nest fixed for her on the other load. Max figured she was wearisome to Mary this forenoon when she slept."

Chapter Four

THE SLOW MOTION OF the freight wagons soon made Annie drowsy again. She let Mary fix her into the snug nest just back of the seat. Now relieved of her wiggling about, Mary began to enjoy the trip. She could move about in the seat and look in all directions. There wasn't nearly as much dust. In spots, there seemed none at all, and she asked about that. "Is this a different type of soil in these places where it isn't dusty?"

Max shook his head as he spoke. "I can't see that it is. My theory is that these patches are just closer to water. Notice how the ground is lower? And with this road running parallel with the river, there is bound to be more moisture seeping closer to such places than to higher ground." His eyes took on their twinkle. "Have you figured out how you would go about getting water out of the river and onto the land?"

Mary smiled as she scanned the rim-rocked bluff to the north. "No. I will leave that question to others to figure out. But I'm beginning to understand why you refer to this place as *down* while we were coming from Caldwell. Just how much lower is this anyway?"

"A couple hundred feet is all. The climb was so gradual all the way out from Caldwell until we got to the rim, one don't realize they are climbing more than a thousand feet. So it's a good drop down from the top."

"I'll say it was," laughed the girl with almost a shudder thinking about the tilted wagon over that rocky downgrade. "Does anyone dig wells in these low places? If water is that close, it looks like that would be one way of getting water."

"Sure, one can dig a well and get surface water in these low places, but then comes the question of pumping and raising the water to a higher level to get it on the land. About three of the ranches on the Flats have drilled artesian wells like I have to water their ground. A few places along the foothills, like the place your father bought, use the spring runoff of the small streams to grow their crops. Along the river itself, some have tried out water wheels to hoist the water out into ditches."

"Doesn't that work out well?"

"Not too well. See, the river can raise and lower several feet, and a wheel big enough to do much raising of water is a heavy thing; not easy to raise and lower. They are expensive to build, but they sure can be undermined by the water and washed away in a hurry."

Mary glanced down to see if Annie was sleeping before she asked her next question. "I wanted to ask you how deep the water was at that ferry, but I feared to frighten some small person the more." She smiled as Max met her gaze.

"Right at the crossing, I would say it's not more than a dozen feet at low water, but this mile below there, the river channel is something different." He pointed the whip toward the small willow covered island mid stream." The channel on this side from here to the island is about five feet deep about now. But from the other side to the north bank, it's 300 feet deep. I understand they have located plenty of holes 600 feet deep. That's what gives the water such an under tow. Makes swimming dangerous, and accounts for the loss of life."

"Would that be why the river was named the Snake—if it's that treacherous and doesn't look it? The name could imply that instead of its twisted course, couldn't it?"

"Now that's a thought," grinned the pleased man. He liked talking to this young woman. "Can't say whether the Indians named the river or if white men coming in later named it. I wasn't here then." His eyes were dancing now.

"Oh, I know you are not that old," laughed Mary. "Do you mind telling me just how many years since you came here? If you liked this country at first or did you miss the timber like I do?"

"Nearly 15 years since I landed here by accident. To be truthful, I did not like these white flats and barren hills at first. And the lack of trees was the most noticeable thing at first."

"You say *accidentally* you came here. Were you headed further west?"

"That's right. When I left Kansas, I aimed for the tall timber of the coast country; but I fell in love with it along with another young fellow who was coming here. I changed my plans and stopped off with him to give this country the once-over. I stayed and he didn't. Before the year was out, he was back in the Blue Grass State."

"Were you ever sorry you didn't go on to the coast?"

"Always figured I'd go there before putting down roots, so to speak. Nearly four years before I found myself without a job, and I took off for the tall timber. It was midwinter, and for a few days, I sure enjoyed that mild rainy weather. Everything was green. It was sure some different than near zero, like it was here when I left. I was thinking about getting a job and staying there—just waiting for the rain to let up sorta. Then when I learned it had been raining for four or five months and could be another three months before it would think of stopping, I changed my mind. I like rain alright, but I want it to stop sometimes and give the sun a chance to take over."

"I understand the continual rainy season is the reason for the big timber. The lack of rains here must be the reason for no trees in this state."

"Say, you haven't seen much of this state yet," the man cut in. "It may be rather young, but she isn't small. Don't you believe it if anyone tells you we haven't trees. We have some of the biggest untapped forests of pine of all the states. Why, some places the timber stands so thick you can't see the hills for trees."

"How far is it to the nearest timber?

"I'd say fifty to sixty miles up beyond Boise City a few miles, and you get into timber."

"That is in the opposite direction of DeLamar and Wagontown isn't it?"

Max had been expecting her to ask questions about those places, knowing that was where John Marcus hailed from, and guessing that John's talk of mines and prospecting had interested Mary Williams.

"Yes," he answered, and fell to wondering what her next question might be.

"John Marcus mentioned there was timber up there. He said something about some people trying to put a stop to the mining companies cutting the timber to put in their mines."

"Yes I know. The mining interests think it's a slap in the face for anyone to suggest they even pay for the timber they cut and use because it is on public domain. To most people, that means they have a right to do just as they see fit—cut down all the timber that's taken hundreds of years to grow, foul up the streams, kill all the fish. Some of them are running short on water, and when all the trees are gone, there will be less snow to cling to those higher hills to furnish water. I wonder sometimes why people don't get *hep* to all this."

"Do you know where the Mills place is? It's at that place called Wagontown, I believe, and I think it is near DeLamar."

"Yes, I pass the old Mills place perhaps a dozen times a season. It's on the main road from Reynolds to DeLamar, and it's less than half a mile from the sheep trail my sheep travel to the summer range, fifteen to twenty miles further on."

"Yet you'd never seen John Marcus before until you hired him to help us?" This was a half question.

"Can't remember ever seeing the man before. Not being interested in the mining game, I wouldn't be apt to meet him."

"But he said he knew you, or about you, I believe that is what he said."

"Lots of people in these hills know me by sight. To them, I'm that crazy headed sheepherder by the name of Max Thorn, who lets his sheep run over the best mining ground in the country. Lets the *varmint* get into every test hole dug in the hills and leaves the stinking critters there."

Mary laughed heartily, but she did not tell him those were almost the very words John Marcus had used in referring to Max.

"You are not crazy; nor are you a sheepherder. You own and run sheep. Isn't there a difference there?"

"Not to some people. But then I was a herder to begin with. Most sheep men start out that way."

"John Marcus said he and his pardner bought the Mills property last spring. They think they can get some capital to develop it with as soon as they get a better showing. That was what he was out to Boise City and Caldwell to see about. Do you consider that good property or *ground*?" Mary laughed at herself. She was not sure that she used the word *ground* in the right way.

"What I know about mines and prospecting could be put in your eye and you wouldn't feel it. That old Mills tunnel may have the richest kind of a vein, I wouldn't know. Ever since old man Mills died, there has been someone in there digging. Never heard of anyone finding anything yet, but it's like I say, I know nothing about the game. All gopher holes look alike to me."

"You have called tunnels and mines gopher holes before. Why do you?"

"I guess it is because there are so many of 'em all through the hills. Prospectors dig holes here and there, never find anything; go

31

on to another hillside and dig some more holes. They never do anything about the ones they dug first. Never cover them over. The deeper they have dug them, the more of a trap they are for sheep to fall into."

"Don't they ever ever find anything in all their digging? Just how do mines get discovered?"

"Yes, it's true some mines are discovered that way. But it seems a bigger share of 'em come to light accidentally like. A pack mule may kick over a rock, or a guy digging a grave to bury his dead pardner might notice the different colored ground and investigate." Max grinned at Mary's tense serious look. "That is not saying there hasn't been plenty of gold and silver taken out of these hills, for there has. But I do believe if every dollar taken out was stacked up in one pile, and every dollar in labor or cash that's been sunk into all these mines and worthless mining stock was piled up into another heap, those two stacks would just about equal."

"Then mines don't mean much to this state?" Mary was confused.

"Oh, but they do mean a lot to this state. Part of the wealth of the state comes from the mines, but according to the last statistic published, a like amount comes from the sheep industry." Max knew his remarks were puzzling to this girl, so whimsically he told her, "Like I said before, Idaho is a good sized state. Not all its wealth comes from white wool, or yellow gold. There are quite a lot of cattle here. Dairying is blossoming out. They raise a lot of hay and grain here. In a few places, they are trying to grow sugar beets, and I look for that industry to keep growing. Lumbering ranks high on the list too." He pointed out with that useless whip to a cluster of unpainted buildings and small trees a quarter of a mile from the road. "One of our near neighbors by the name of Barnes lives there. Pretty nice people when one gets acquainted with them."

Mary had been turned looking south to keep the setting sun from annoying her eyes and had been appraising that scene. "If there is lumber to be had for building, I wonder why they don't build good sized barns out here."

"They'd be rather ornamental instead of useful here on the Flats. All hay is put in stacks. Cattle, sheep and horses are fed in the open. Seldom is it stormy enough for stock to hunt shelter.

Dairy cows would need a barn of course."

"A coat of paint might be ornamental too," smiled Mary, "but wouldn't it also preserve the buildings?" She was sure Max' eyes would be twinkling, but he didn't turn so she could see.

"That's true enough both ways. I rather think most of these settlers are not thinking of their small house as their permanent homes. They expect to build bigger ones. Those they would paint and make attractive, while these they just endure. A few of these homes are right comfortable on the inside, but like my place, it looks like heck on the outside. Max' eyes were not laughing. Not even a twinkle, for he was thinking how his ranch, with its unpainted buildings, were going to appear to this discriminating young woman.

"Do you know, about the first thing I want to do is to climb that mountain." She said this to cover up the blunder she felt she had made. Her eyes were sweeping the darker foothills, honing in on the Flats toward the south. "What would be the best way to go about such an adventure?"

The man's eyes could twinkle now. "First things come first in this country, and the very first is to be well-used to a saddle horse. You'd be sadly out of luck without that four footed friend in these hills. By spring you might be able to rope and catch a wild bronco, saddle him, and ride him. Then you would need to learn to hobble him and be prepared to make camp, sleep in the open, and go on from there if you are going to climb a real mountain. These are just foothills."

"I know you are poking fun at me when you talk about me roping a wild horse, but I do intend to learn to ride just as soon as we can afford a saddle horse. Tell me where you draw the line between mountains and foothills, as you call them. To me they seem like mountains."

"When you get to the top of those, you can see nothing on the other side but more hills to climb. It's more than a good day's ride before you would get to the top to get a view all ways of the compass. That peak might be called a mountain. Rightly, of course, those are all mountains, but you'll never hear them called anything but hills by the people who live here. I doubt the highest point in this corner of the state is more than ten thousand feet high."

"That would be high enough for me to climb." She said this

33

airily as she helped Annie to climb back in the seat. "My, wouldn't that be exciting. Have you ever been on the tip top of any of them?"

"I've skirted close to the top of several of 'em looking for stranded sheep, but can't truthfully say I've been right on the tip top."

"What was the most exciting thing you did when you first came here?" Mary wanted to keep him talking. The distance did not seem as long then, and she was learning lots about this country from Max Thorn.

"I guess the most exciting thing was being on the tail end of a cloud burst, only it didn't seem so at the time. But when I think of what might have happened, cold chills sorta creep up and down my spine." He paused to steady the teams and wagons through a rough low place.

"Do tell me about the cloud burst. John Marcus said how he was nearly washed away in one. They must be dangerous. I don't understand how they come up so quick without warning."

"Oh, there is generally warning enough if one knows how to interpret it. A tenderfoot, or new comer not wise to them, can sure come up missing. That was what I was—the greenest of tenderfeet. Hadn't been here a month before I was out on a trail with three other men trying to hustle a band of lambs down to Murphy to load 'em by a certain date. More than a week earlier than now. And talk about it being hot weather this past week— that year it was several degrees warmer. Those lambs wouldn't budge more than half of the daylight hours, so we trailed 'em by night. Letting them go just as far as we could see to keep some sorta tabs on 'em, then camping right there 'til the first streak of gray in the morning. It was to be the last night on the trail for us, and we were pushing 'em. We wanted to get in as close as possible, so to be first in the morning to load out. The day had been a scorcher. Come night, and she clouded up like a storm, though none came our way. Soon it was dark, so we just had to camp right where we were—rolled our beds off the pack animals and crawled in. The whole bunch of us, being so dead for sleep, we slept like the dead, expecting the sheep movement and noise of the dogs to awaken us. Neither did. Those lambs had edged away gradually sometime around day break, and the dogs along with them. What had been a dry streamed the night before when we flung down our bed rolls on the bank, was now running brim full. Water was wetting the foot of our beds."

"You mean it hadn't rained there, but a cloud burst came close enough to send all that water down the stream?"

"That is just what it did. Somewhere close to the head of that stream, say fifteen or twenty miles distance, a small cloud burst had occurred. By the time it reached us, the force of the water was dulled perhaps, but even then, it was rolling boulders that weighed several tons. What gave me the shivers was learning that it was only an infant of a cloudburst. Had it been bigger, or that small canyon more of a boxed-in type where the water could not spread out, we would have been bowled over alright."

"Then it is dangerous to camp close to a stream in the mountains?"

"No, only where it's boxed-in like. If it's a narrow canyon or gorge, then the wisest thing to do is not camp or build a cabin within the natural wash of that stream. The one thing that makes me hunt higher ground along about dusk on a hot threatening day is to see any stream with no willows or young twigs springing up. You can be pretty sure a cloudburst has swept that stream clear of willows in not too many years past, and could happen so again about now."

"Then they do happen in the same place more than once?"

"They seem to favor certain areas. Some claim it is that special formation of hills that cause them in the first place. I don't understand all I know about 'em either, but I have known one little creek to lose its fringe of willows three times since I've lived here."

"Was herding sheep the first work you found to do?"

"Yep, that's right. By any chance, you thinking of starting out in that line of work?"

"I wouldn't know the first thing about herding sheep. Now if it was milking cows, that would be different."

"One doesn't have to have much savvy to start out wrangling the woolies."

"Please be serious and tell me just what that word *savvy* means anyway. I have heard it used several times since I've been here."

"The Basque herders always say, *Me no savvy English* when they can't speak it well, or pretend they can't. It's a known fact they can understand it long before they will speak English."

"Do you have any Basque herding for you?"

"Not now."

"I take it that you have had. Were they good herders? Did you like them?

"They are generally good at handling sheep, for they are mostly herdsmen in their own country. To me it isn't a question of not liking them—let's say I like it better when I can talk to a guy and explain to him a little bit about the rights of other people, as well as myself."

"What nationality do you find are the best herders?"

"Now that is a question hard to answer. In this part of the country, Scotchmen are favored, for they, like the Basque, have sheep in their own country and seem to be natural herdsmen. You can find about the widest range of nationalities herding sheep, and men from every walk in life—men with all the degrees any college can bestow upon them, down to those that cannot write their own name. There is one failing many have in common, I'm sorry to say, and that is the weakness for drink. I have come to the conclusion it was drink in the first place causing them to tackle the lonely life of a herder."

"You mean they want to be off in the wilderness so they cannot get it?"

"That's the case with some of them surely. But looking at it from another angle, men who drink too much and too often are going to go broke, lose their jobs, and drift west. Being down to their last *frijoles*, last bean in other words, they are going to take the first job they can get. And around here, that would be herding sheep."

"I see what you mean. But I want to know, do women ever herd sheep?"

"I've never known of one doing so, but there was one herding the woolies out from Reynolds 'til a few years ago. Now she has squatted on a piece of land and has a few head of cattle. At least several people say she is a woman. None of 'em actually know if she is a woman. They just think so because she never mingles with the other ranch hands all the different places she's worked. True, her voice is more feminine than otherwise. Not long ago, someone tried to tell me what a great desperado Little Old Joe Morgan used to be. That is all pure *bunk*! Joe Morgan, man or woman, has never gone out of the way to bother anyone. She might have flourished a gun at someone, but I'd say it was to make sure they let her alone."

"What odd people inhabit these hills." Mary laughed in spite of her weariness. "You still haven't told me who you consider the best   herder."

"I think that honor would have to go to Wong, a Chinese. I have never known another of that nationality to herd sheep; not around here at least. He was an old hand with the Bale's sheep outfit when I first came here and went to work for them. It was summer time and all the bands were out in the hills. They gave me a band of wethers to start on. I didn't know the first thing about sheep and had a lot to learn, believe me. I didn't know how to cook, so nearly starved the two dogs and myself before I learned."

The sun was now in the west, but in the afterglow, Mary's eyes twinkled at thinking of his meeting with Wong. "Like I said, I was green when it came to looking after sheep, and about the very first thing I did was to mix my herd with Wong's band. He was herding bucks, so there was no great damage done, but we had to go to a corral to separate them. We came together near dusk, so couldn't make any corral that night, and being about half way between Wong's camp and mine, we were discussing which camp we would head for. Wong could talk fair English—enough to make me understand he was all for going to his camp. I wasn't so in favor of that. What I knew about Chinese had not been good. Then he commenced in his lingo asking me if I liked *lice-um* that he had *heap lice-um* at his camp. I, not knowing that Chinese could not sound the letter *r*, told him in no uncertain terms what I thought about him and his lousy camp. I called him a dirty so-and-so and stalked off. Then he caught my arm pleadingly, telling me he wasn't dirty, he was clean. And for a fact, he did look clean. Then more of that same talk about *lice-um,* telling me over and over about him *eat-um lice-um. Heap good lice-um. You come see. Me cook'um good.* That settled it for me if he would cook, for I was near starved. And how that smiling face beamed when I headed to his camp with him! He was as pleased as punch to show me his camp, and could that Chinese cook! I have never eaten better sourdough bread, or tastier lamb chops. And still, I can hear his pleased chuckle as he turned that fluffy cooked rice into bowls, nodding his head as he said, *Nice lice-um. You eat-um lice.*"

Mary laughed heartily, much to Annie's wonderment. "That must have been amusing. Do you think Wong caught the humor of the mistake?"

"Oh yes. I'm sure Wong saw the funny side to it all. But it being my mistake and I was his guest, so to speak, he was taking extra pains to not embarrass me."

The weary team commenced to quicken their gait to almost a trot. "You crazy Cayuses, you don't need to try galloping from here on in," he pulled sharply, "just to let us know you are glad to get home. We're glad ourselves to get here. I see a light in the kitchen. Hope Jake has supper ready for us."

Chapter Five

MARY STEPPED DOWN FROM the stepladder and to the doorway to better view her work. "Just think, Mother, I've been at this painting and papering for three weeks now. It's sure taken me a long time to get this house livable. A month tomorrow since we landed in this state. My, what a lot of different things have happened since then. I keep hoping it will rain and settle the dust. Father isn't in favor of me trying to paint the outside of the house since there's so much dust swirling around." She moved the ladder to start on another window casing. "I'll have this all finished before night. What would you suggest I start on next?"

Mother Williams, prim looking even in her oldest house dress, wrinkled her nose at the strong odor of fresh paint. "It's a wonder the smell of this paint in here doesn't get to you, keeping those windows closed against the dust coming in," voiced Mother from the doorway. Before she could say more, Annie left her school work to add her plea.

"If you get done before it gets dark, will you take me horseback riding? Mama said you might if I did my lessons real good," her brown head nodding to emphasize each word. "Don't you 'member when Max gave you Blacky, he said he was the kind that let me ride right back of you?"

"Max didn't give me the horse, Child—just loaned it to us until we can buy one," admonished Mary. "Now I might...just might be through this smelly mess before dark and we could see how Blacky likes to carry two girls instead of one," she said slow like, then grinned at Mother when the child scampered back to her slate. "Not much sewing to tackle outside of piecing quilts. And that's better work for stormy weather, don't you think?" She was prompting Mother to get some suggestion.

"You have more ambition than I ever had, I do believe. You've cleaned this whole house, as well as papering and painting it; now you are hunting more to do. We should have the goods to start on your winter's dress. It would be a good time to make that. How about you and Annie ride in to Caldwell tomorrow when Max Thorn goes in? He's asked you, Girl, to ride in with him, thinking you might want to go to the fair. You could take in a day of the fair at least, and then pick out your own dress material. I'm not in favor of sending for it sight-unseen. Annie should have a dentist look at that tooth of hers."

"Now Mother, how about you being the one to go to town? Surely a rig like a buckboard with a fast driving team would be much easier riding than atop the loaded wagon."

"Any riding, no matter how comfortable the seat or rig, seems to set me back. Going with Father after that load of sagebrush last week was almost more than I could stand. And that was a very short trip."

Mary knew this to be true, and was sure she was going to have to be the one to take Annie to the dentist, for Father to drive in with their own team of heavy horses would be a much slower way of going. Mother went back to her work of baking, not pressing the question. *I want to go, and I don't want to go* was the girl's thoughts as she painted away with no more interruptions. *John Marcus didn't come right out and ask me not to go anywheres with Max Thorn in his last letter,* was her next thought, *but that is what he meant when he wrote that he hoped I wouldn't go with others, but wait until he came down and took me places.*

By noon, her head was weaving about with the fumes of the paint and so much thinking. *I have to go, and that's that. I believe I won't write anything about it. I'll wait to tell him when he comes down next month to visit. I know I can explain it much better than I ever could write it.*

Mary was counting on that planned visit. *I want Father and Mother to know John better. They sometimes act as if they are not too favorably impressed with him, but they will be when they know him better.*

It was evening, just at supper time, when Max stopped on his way to his ranch from the hills. He needed no urging to accept their invitation to eat with them. He and David Williams talked of many things—plowing, burning of woods, digging of ditches, and the ever pressing need for rain.

"This scarcity of water is sure playing havoc with the range. With little feed left anywhere, streams dry, and springs not much more than mud holes, owners are afraid to start trailing out their herds. Luck was with me—I bought a pasture with plenty of water, so the one band is in clover for a week at least. I'm hoping, along with dozens of others, the good Lord sends us some rain pronto, or there is going to be a big loss in the sheep business." The meal being finished, he rose from the table. Stretching up his full height, he could just touch the ceiling with his finger tips. "Nice job of painting you did on this. Funny how much difference a can of paint and a roll of wallpaper makes in a house. I believe I'll try it out on my bunk-a-lation one of these days. Might need some pointers at that. Say, did I hear any takers on my offer of a ride into the fair?"

Annie's braids bobbed in her excitement to get the words out. "Sister and I can go. Mother said we could. I's to get a tooth pulled...maybe?"

"Fine. Fine. I hope that tooth don't hurt a bit getting pulled. Now if we get started almost before day break, we should be in town before too late dinner time." He was watching Mary, who had said but little all during the meal. Catching her eye at last, he asked, "Would five o'clock be too early?"

"No, that isn't too early. We'll be ready then."

"I'll need to cook breakfast early for these girls...how about you come a few minutes ahead of time and eat with us," Mother wanted to know.

"That is a kindly thought that should make Old Jake very happy, he not having to get up before his usual getting up time. Thanks. I'll be on hand. And thanks twice for this good meal." With a half salute, Max left.

***

"We made pretty good time at that." Max squinted at the sun as they neared Caldwell. "Not much after one. I have drove it in less time when I was in a hurry and there wasn't so much talking going on." His face a blank, he eased the sweat and dust-streaked team around chuck holes in the road.

Mary could not help smiling. She knew that jibe had been for her. She had not asked her usual string of questions. Before she could think up a lively retort, Annie broke in, "We never seen even one little rattlesnake today."

"Have you been worrying about one waylaying us? Now maybe that is what's been preying on other minds." He was sure he'd get some action now.

"I'm not half afraid of rattlesnakes as I thought I would be after killing three of them in our own door yard. I think I could do battle with the general run of them." Mary made her face as passive as the one glancing her way. "There could be other

41

worries, and a little one that keeps popping out at me is this: How does this small town manage to sleep this crowd of people milling about the streets, when hardly a room was to be found a month ago?"

"That question worried Caldwell a few years 'til they come up with a pretty good answer. Now, at fair time, every home in town that has an extra room, bed, or cot lists them with the few hotels. After they have their rooms full, they give the address of rooms in private homes. So all one has to do is to apply at the hotel and they'll send you some place. Or better still, do as the rest of us from the Flats do...go out to Mrs. Bishop's home."

"Oh but I wouldn't think of that," Mary stated, "never having met the lady."

"All the introduction you'll need to Ma Bishop's home and hospitality is living on Snake River Flats. She and her husband were among the first to settle there. They sold out a few years back when his health got bad. They had just gotten their new home built when he died. Their youngsters are all grown and gone now, and she lives by herself. Her place, being a little ways out of town and she being rather independent, she won't list her rooms. But then she don't need to to have them full, for there is about enough people from the Flats during fair time."

While waiting for their steaks to be cooked at the restaurant, Max passed the time with talk. "I'll have to tell you a joke that happened last year over this sending people to private homes at fair time. Lantz Steele was herding for me then, and I brought him in for medical care. I had to go on to Boise City then, just like I'm having to go this time. Lantz stayed here. Long near bed time, one of the hotels gave 'im an address, and he moseyed out there. Now Lantz has one of the best educations of about anyone around, but he does like to use big words. With every glass of beer, he'll think up bigger ones. So when the woman of the house answered the door, he asked her if there was any chance of him hibernating there for a few nights. The woman slammed the door in his face. She might have thought Lantz was drunk, and she could have been half right on that score. Again, she might not have known what the word hibernating meant. That word has sure had a work out around the ranch for a year." Max broke off his talk as their steaks were brought in, for they were hungry. And they ate in near silence, the quicker to get away from this stuffy room.

"Now, I'll take you out to Ma Bishop's," Max told Mary the instant they were on the street. "It's better than two o'clock, and that train leaves for Boise City about four, if it should happen to be on time for once, which is seldom. Sure as shooting if I was behind, it would be early." Handing the two girls into the rig, he urged the tired team into a good trot. "I know you Cayuses are weary, it's but a short stretch. "Don't know as I explained about Ma Bishop not liking to cook. Like I say, she has all that big house and is more than glad for any of us *Flatters* to come stay, so we do. And pay her for the rooms just like we would at the hotel. But we eat our meals in town.

In no time at all, the two were made welcome, given the last empty room, and were spending the next few hours chatting with this new acquaintance on the cool east porch. To Mary, this little white haired woman was a source of amusement the way she chirped about every kind of subject under the sun. As the early dusk approached, and she became aware of the two going back into town just for their supper, she remonstrated, "Not a mite of use of you doing that. I don't like to cook, and everyone knows it, so I don't pretend to fix meals for all comers. I'm not cooking tonight either, it's just too hot. But there is plenty of cold roast for the three of us. Green stuff out in the garden if you want to gather some. What, with milk, bread and butter, we can get by without building a fire. I'll get a jar of fruit from the cellar. And remember, you two just as well eat your breakfast with me before you start out. T'aint going to hurt me a mite to add another handful of oats to the mush pot, or a bit more coffee. T'aint right for youngsters to have to wait around to all time of the day to eat when they are hungry."

After a full day at the fair in the heat, Mary didn't care for more of it. Neither did she like to refuse taking Annie this afternoon when she had been so good about having her tooth pulled—not crying once. "Alright, we'll go out to the fairgrounds after we eat something," she stated, being hungry herself, but forgetting Annie's sore mouth for a second. "Maybe a dish of ice-cream would not hurt your mouth." Annie brightened to the thought.

The main road leading to the fair (one could not call it a street) led past the school house. Here, the milling crowd blocked the way. Instead of trying to push their way through the throng,

43

Mary led Annie out around and wound up close to the school house steps, the only uncrowded spot. Then she remembered this was to be children's day at the fair. The school, marching en masse, was to be admitted free. The lines of students were forming now. The tired and exhorting teachers were having more than their hands full getting them in better order as to size than to age. A very strident voice commanded their inattention, "Now once again we will line up," said that shrill voice above the hubbub, "and learn if you children know your left foot from your right or can count to two."

"Oh, I see Max," Annie, on the step above Mary, leaned down to tell her. "And he runned away so fast." She looked again. Mary climbed up beside Annie and could see nothing of any familiar face.

The long wavy lines were hardly in motion to the loud "one-two" when Mary caught sight of Max Thorn dashing back, with his long arm swung out and above those in front of him. Bits of metal glinted in the sunlight. What had been marching lines close at hand one second, was now a medley of scrabbling children, grabbing at nickels and dimes at their feet.

The teachers who, at a distance had not seen the cause of the broken line, were tried beyond their patience. They now all took a hand at pushing the wiggly scholars into some sort of order. "You children may like standing out here in the heat, but I fail to," came that disagreeable voice. "We either march or we do not go. Suit yourselves." Again they started on their march. Max' sinewy arm got in a better swing this time, scattering money over a wider area. One of the teachers spotted him this time. "Marshall, Marshall! Arrest that man," screamed a pedagogic voice above the uproar.

"I don't like standing here all day," lamented Annie, not liking all the confusion and not understanding the reason for it.

"Alright, we'll go. But let us walk away from all the people; we can go faster." The dust was thick in the air wherever they went, smarting their eyes. A hard press of people was at the gate. Mary kept tight hold on Annie's hand as they were swept along with the crowd. Mary heard comments on all sides of her. "More fun than I've seen in a month of Sundays," came from one giggling woman. "I call it disgraceful," a very pompous man voiced. "That marshal should have been there to keep order. He is never around when he is needed."

"I'd give a cookie to know who it was," a smiling young woman spoke from the other side of Mary. "I guess Miss Holmes would give more than that," her companion retorted. "Yes, I know. That teacher is mad enough to eat ten penny nails!"

Annie's choice of amusement was the merry-go-round and rode alone very well. That left Mary much free time for thinking, while watching out for Annie. It would be very easy to get separated in this crowd. *I wonder what fun Max found in plaguing those teachers,* she asked herself. *I doubt I'll ever have the nerve to ask him.* She was fast learning the most lonesome spot in the world was in a crowd of strangers. Her spirits lightened for an instant when she thought she caught sight of a familiar gray, stiff-brimmed hat, but the tanned face beneath it was not Max Thorn's. All this might be fun, she reminded herself, if there was someone to talk to. Seeing others chatting and enjoying the events with companionship pressed that truth home to her.

Annie, at last out of pocket money of her own and found she could not wheedle any more from her sister, consented to call it a day. During the walk back to town, Mary rolled over in her mind which was the better plan: For she and Annie to take their chances at getting a meal downtown, or for her to buy a good steak and take it out to Mrs. Bishop's and cook supper for the three of them. *I just don't know how she would like that, and I wouldn't hurt her feelings for anything. She has been so good to us.* Then came the thought of buying some bananas, pears and oranges ready to take home on the morrow. The better grocery store was beyond the Pacific Hotel.

"Hi there! You two are just the ones I've been looking for," Max Thorn greeted them from the hotel steps. "Did you know the dining room opens at five instead of six during fair time? That means in five minutes, we can eat. Have they been starving you, Miss Annie?"

I's as hungry as anything!"

"Good. I'm glad to hear it. Do you know my mother used to say she would rather feed ten hungry people than one who wasn't hungry?" His eyes were twinkling as they met Mary's. He seemed to be in very good spirits as he led them into the half-filled lobby.

Mr. Bussa, as well as the clerk, was behind the desk. Both spoke and acted very friendly. Mary was cheered and forgot her lonesomeness. Once in the dining room, Maggie, with a very flushed face in her mad rush, called, "Hi!" They needed to share a table with others—an elderly man and two women. Max seemed to be acquainted with these people and introduced Mary to each— a Mr. and Mrs. Greer and her sister, Mrs. Phipples. Soon they and Max were talking about other acquaintances and places.

Naturally this was not of much interest to Mary until she heard them mention the places Silver City, DeLamar and Wagontown. From the conversation, she could see that all three of them had at one time or another lived there.

"I was talking to Cap Summers and his wife last week," Mr. Greer told Max. "First time I've seen them since they came back from California. Cap's beginning to show his seventy-odd years."

"If you ask me, I would say he's still going strong," chuckled his wife. "He thinks he can drink just as much whisky as ever."

"That's it—he just thinks he can. A doctor or two has tried to tell him in a nice way that he can't." This came from Mrs. Phipples. "Greer, did you notice if Cap still wears his diamond stud or stick pin?"

Mr. Greer chuckled before he answered. "I never thought to look. Do you suppose Mrs. Summers still has her diamond rings and watch?"

"You can rest assured Molly Summers still has those rings." Mrs. Phipples was positive. "They were her insurance against starvation—the reason why she held Cap to his promise to buy them for her in the first place. And that's why she always wore them, even though she was scrubbing her dirty floors—she was afraid to take them off. Cap would have pawned them in a minute if he had ever needed to, and could have got his fingers on them."

"I guess she never had to pawn her rings," was Max' comment. "Must have been about then, Cap made his big strike."

"That's right," Greer nodded his white head. "Cap finally made a swag of money. Enough to last him out his lifetime, even if he lives to be one hundred. But that man was a speculating fool a good many years."

Mary had heard the name of Cap Summers somewhere and was trying to connect it up in her mind with what these people were talking about. *I must remember to ask Max so I will get it straight.* She found but little chance for conversation with Max until morning on their way home. It was much cooler—really pleasant, when they could travel fast enough to keep ahead of their own dust. "Do you mind telling me if this Cap Summers…you and those people last evening were talking about…was all truth or partly fiction?"

"Every bit was truth. I must admit he was rather a famous character—quite a mining tycoon in his day."

"But that about someone biting the diamond out of his shirt stud. That must have been fancy instead of fact?"

"That was what I thought for several years, for no one would verify that yarn. See, after Cap made his big money, about the time I first landed here, people began to forget all the ornery things he had done and just tell the better things, like him helping to build railroads and hotels and such."

"Oh, now I can remember where I heard that name," cut in Mary. "He is the man who made such a rich strike up above DeLamar and built the railroad out to Murphy to take supplies out and the gold in."

"He started to build it on his own hook, maybe, but a sheep man with a woolsack of greenbacks helped pay for it. That might have been the reason why the road has always been classed as a public carrier. Anyway, no one has stopped us from shipping our sheep over that line."

"But for anyone to want to steal a diamond by biting it that way." Mary was puzzled.

"Larry Wilson wasn't stealing Cap's diamond. By foul means or fair, he was just getting the wages that Cap owed him. I'll have to tell you the whole story so you will understand it. It's the one I said I doubted so long, then I met this Larry Wilson. He's quite a guy. I was having a couple of beers with him, and as it turned out, he had had several before that. He was getting pretty well oiled; quite talkative and I ups and asked him about biting that shiner out of Cap Summers' shirt front. And he admitted he had done so, and told me how it came about."

"Not sure what year Cap Summers came to Silver City and DeLamar. Mr. Greer said last night he landed there in 1860. Could have been about then when Cap came, for they knew them well. There was no lazy bones in Cap's makeup. He was always working, even while he was working the other fellow. He'd lease ground, hire men, and every now and then, he'd make a little money. But he always forgot his men needed paying. I guess

Larry had worked for him off and on for years, 'til he had about a $1000 coming in wages. He wanted to collect some of that in the worst way, for he wanted to go east to get married and bring his wife back." Max paused to pass the water sack to both girls, then took a long drink himself. In one of Cap's flush moments, he had bought or traded for this fine diamond. From then on, it always flashed from his shirt front. The men he had never paid must have resented that fact. Seems Cap's mind often run to diamonds, and he had promised to buy his wife diamonds as soon as he made a strike. To the merchants and just about everyone, that was galling, for he owed them all. It got so bad, he couldn't get a sack of flour on credit. That's where the pawning of Mrs. Summer's watch came in. More times than she cares to remember, that Mrs. Phipples loaned her $20 on it to buy food for her and the children. She would always manage to redeem it sooner or later. But Larry had no luck getting any money out of Cap. He was getting mad enough to try most anything. Larry was a short small man, and Cap, taller than I am, so he decided fighting wouldn't do any good. Then he set his mind on a plan. Every time he met Cap, he would dun him. The bigger the crowd and the more fuss he could stir up, the better. One day his chance came. He had badgered Cap long enough. He was mad. It happened right in front of the store and Post Office. Of course, the fight didn't last long before others were stopping it, it being so one-sided. But Larry had stepped in close, had even landed a punch or two."

"Then what happened," questioned Mary when Max stopped talking.

A one-sided grin creased Max' face. "Not much of anything happened for a short while, 'til Cap missed his diamond. Then came the tall hunting. He was sure he must have lost it in the scuffle, so that is where he commenced to look. When he posted a $1000 reward to anyone who found it, most of the town was out looking. The teacher couldn't even hold school for lack of scholars."

Annie wiggled around to look up in his face. "Didn't they ever ever find it?" Max and Mary exchanged glances, both were surprised.

"Not in the gravel and dirt where they were looking. It wasn't lost there. None connected up Larry's leaving town with the missing stone, for all knew he was intending to leave. In about ten days, or as soon as Larry could get to New York and a letter get back here, the mystery was cleared away, for the letter had a pawn ticket for a $1000 diamond."

Annie was getting drowsy in spite of all the interest she displayed. Mary waited until she slept before asking more questions. Then she started in a round- about way, "This Cap Summers was undoubtedly an odd man. Not many like him, I expect. But I ran across a man with a rather odd sense of humor yesterday—one that throws money around just to torment frustrated teachers."

"How did you know that?"

"I wouldn't have believed it if I had not seen it. Some people seemed to think it a good joke. Others thought it anything but a joke. I'm just curious for your reason." A sideways smile robbed her words of any criticism. "Those teachers had more than their hands full already."

"Sure they had," Max nodded. "And maybe those youngsters needed some know-how about marching and keeping in step. But they don't need all that drilling in one day when they are all excited and *hepped-up* up about getting to the fair. Not when it's ninety-nine in the shade and there was no shade. Now you tell me, did you ever hear such a voice on any human being?"

"It was rather raspy for sure," Mary laughed.

"That woman might make a good hog caller, but I fear such a screech would scare the porkers away from the feed trough."

Chapter Six

MARY WAS IMPATIENTLY TRYING to finish this job before dusk. This making a Christmas tree out of sagebrush was not to her liking. The reason for it was Annie's disappointment over John Marcus' failure to get her a promised tree, and here it was Christmas Eve. Annie was close beside her, watching her every move. "Sister, you are making it look most like a real tree. If you get it all done 'fore Daddy gets in the house, maybe he'll think John already comed, maybe."

Annie chatted on. Mary said but little. She was more disappointed than she cared to admit over John's failure to come; nor had there been a letter from him for two weeks now. His last letter had told her of it snowing there while it had been raining here. She looked down at the grotesque creation under her hand, more dissatisfied with it as she twisted the last frill of green tissue. But Annie was delighted with her tree. When it was carried into the living room, she commenced to put her small horde of presents about its base.

With an effort, Mary tried to enter into the merry spirit of the season. "After supper, perhaps we can pop some corn and I'll help you string some. That might look nice on your tree—like it was snow." Back she went to the kitchen to clear away the mess she had made and to finish the supper. She was not fooled about Mother leaving her all the cooking to do these last few days. She guessed it was to keep her busy so she would have less time to be unhappy.

She liked to cook, but there wasn't much more to do now. A pot of dried corn had been simmering on the back of the stove since noon. Into this, she poured heavy cream. The roast loin of pork in the oven and its dressing was sending out its savory smells. Applesauce was cooking on the back porch. Peeling potatoes and putting them to cook took but a moment. She still had time to spare, so she set the table with care, gracing the center with a bowl of red apples, a few oranges mixed in for color effect, and a handful of nuts for good measure. Father spied that the instant he came into the kitchen with the pale of milk. "Ho ho…so we are going to have Christmas after all."

"What is that old saying," asked Mary, "if you haven't turkey, eat goose; if you have no goose, eat chicken? Our meat tonight is

50

roast pork, but we have nice fresh applesauce to go with it and plenty of other food, so why not be happy? This being merry at Christmas time must just be up to the people themselves, don't you think?

"You are so right about that, Daughter." David Williams' heart was heavy too for this eldest chick of theirs. He sensed her disappointment. Experience told him that Mary would have many such disappointments to live through…bigger and sadder ones perhaps. His biggest sorrow was seeing Mary's growing interest in John Marcus.

Annie, hearing him come in, hastened to the door. "You can't come in here, Daddy, 'til after Santa Claus has all the presents fixed."

"Do you think Santa can find us this year out here on Snake River Flats?"

"Course he can," insisted the child. "'Course, I know there is not a real Santa. Mama told me all about him being just the good spirit inside of us, making us give nice things to other little boys and girls that might not have much. And maybe surprise 'em."

"You understand quite a lot for a young lady of six going-on-seven."

"Mama told me lots more things," boasted the child. "She told me what Santa is going to give you and what he is going to give Sister, and to Max Thorn. You never never can guess what Mama is putting on the tree right this minute." She turned her head to watch Mother fasten the tinfoil star to the top most branch. "Oh, it's making my tree look so pretty. I won't tell you 'cuz that's a surprise too."

"You and that mother of yours have lots of surprises, haven't you?" He had no time to say more, as there was a rap at the kitchen door. He opened it to Max Thorn. "Come in, come in. You're just in time for supper. I hear Mary putting it on the table this minute."

"Not so fast, Williams. I haven't come for supper. In fact, I should not stop a second, but being close here at the sheep cab, I run over to let you know I can't make it this evening after you good people going to all that bother of getting an invitation to me."

"But you are here now." Father closed the door. "Won't take a moment longer for you to eat your supper with your feet under this table, than it will at your place. We promise not to detain you after the meal if you cannot stay, but you know we would like for you to."

Mother came out to add her welcome. Annie danced about telling her, "Max is here, Mama. Can we open our presents right after supper? 'Cuz maybe he can't stay long."

"Quiet, Child. We'll see."

"Goody goody," chanted the girl, happy in the thought that now she would not have to wait until later for her presents.

The gloomy day was ending more cheerfully. The most unhappy person couldn't remain glum around Max Thorn when he chose to be gay, and he was exerting himself to be cheerful this evening. He had expected to find John Marcus here and promised himself he would not have stayed, had he been. A full hour they stayed at the table visiting. Mother and Mary, scraping and stacking the dishes very quiet like, turned a deaf ear to Annie's hints about going in to see her Christmas tree.

Max, catching the impatient child and rough housing with her for a second, asked, "Why are you in such a hurry? I bet Santa hasn't been here yet."

"Oh yes he has. We have the presents right under the tree this minute!"

"Not all of 'em. I met the Old Boy himself as I was coming along. There being no snow here for him to come the rest of the way in his sleigh, he let me bring some in my buckboard."

Annie excitedly climbed from his lap. "An' you never once brought 'em in?" This was unbelievable. "Can I help you carry 'em in? And can I guess what mine is?"

"One question at a time, Dearie," reminded Mother.

"I'll tell you what." Max stood up. "You're just the one to carry a lantern for me while I pack 'em in. They might be much too heavy for you, but you sure can have all the guesses you want," he added seeing her crestfallen look.

In and out the door, the two made three trips. The first time, Max brought in a large rectangle slab of shale rock, partly covered with paper on which Mary's name was written. The next trip brought what looked like a short length of wood, a broken limb from some tree. But Max was not carrying it like it was wood, leaning over as he carefully put it on the floor without much of a thud. Small Annie hurried to look at the name and spelled it out.

"This is for Mama, I know." The last trip in, Max brought two packages. They were better wrapped, no part of them to be seen.

"The biggest one is for me," crowed Annie, "an' I'm the littlest!" She tried pinching the bulky thing, which was mostly hard and unyielding.

"How about those guesses?" Max teased.

Annie wrinkled her small brow in thought, not knowing what to guess. "I guess we better wait 'til Mama and Sister is through with the dishes." She fell to pinching her father's presents. "This is for Daddy and I can guess what it is." Then she whispered *turkey* in Max' ear to have him nod that she guessed right.

Mother and Mary found a very thoughtful girl when they came in. She was neither chatting about her make-believe tree nor the two strings of small pearls that festooned it. Mother was sure the child had not seen her put them there. One strand was much shorter than the other and could easily be assumed it was for her. "How many guesses have you made?" Mary wanted to know

"I can't guess even one." She was trying to crowd into the easy chair

"Then we'll just have to unwrap it so you can see what it is." Max tore away the paper, exposing a sturdy foot stool. "Jake made this for you with his pocket knife. He's always whittling on something, and this gnarled juniper log I brought down to him last summer ended up looking like this."

Annie, rubbing her hands over the smooth wood that showed the grain of the wood so plainly, half smiled. "I never never could have guessed it."

"That is what makes Christmas so much fun," remarked Father. "Getting a present you never can guess."

"I guessed your present right off quick." She was eyeing Mother's and asked, "Did Jake makes Mama's present too?"

"No, Jake had no hand in fashioning that. Old Man Nature did that; no telling how many thousands of years He was doing it." He lifted the petrified log and took it where Mother could feel it.

"Why, it feels like stone, yet it looks like wood," said the surprised lady.

"It is stone. Or rock now. Once it was a tree, but it is petrified. I thought it would make you a good door stop. Even the strongest wind on these Flats could hardly blow your door slam-bang with this against it. Then I wanted you to know there really were trees growing in this country at one time."

"Some of those trees must have had leaves too," he told Mary as he held the slab of shale so the light showed the imprint of a large leaf, very perfect and symmetrical. "It can be either a door stop, hearth stone or out-of-doors seat."

Mary traced the outlines of the leaf with her finger tips. "Such thoughtful and enduring presents. Would not walking on this spoil this leaf?"

"It might in time. Shale has a tendency to crumble. The head of the house gets nothing but perishables. All of you will have to help him get away with it. And I've got to high-tail for the rancho, or they'll think sure I fell in a badger hole and broke my leg."

"Santa brought you some presents too." Annie hurried to get them.

She placed a small limp packet in his hand first. "That's from me. I made most all the stitches myself. 'Course Mama helped me a little bit." On top of the handkerchief, she placed another soft package. "That is from Mama. She knit your gloves most in two nights." Next she got down on hands and knees and brought out two items: A wrapped fruit cake and a small cloth bag tied with a length of binding twine. "Do you know why Daddy fixed this up funny this way? He said he didn't know what to give you, but you never never could buy these kind of nuts in a store. They are hickory nuts. Auntie sent us a great big sack of 'em."

"I bet I can guess what this is," pretending to smell the cake. "It smells just like good fruit cake."

Annie's head bobbed. "Sister says it hain't good like Mama's is, but Daddy says it's most as good."

Max made his getaway soon after that. Now the Williams family settled down to look at their other presents and then to bed early, for they would need to be up early to get that big turkey roasting if it was to be done for dinner anywhere near noon.

Christmas passed quietly; likewise New Years. Two days later, in walks John Marcus. Annie caught sight of him first as he turned into the lane. "But he never brought any tree," cried the girlie. "'Course it's past Christmas time now, but maybe I could of planted it and it would grow for next Christmas."

"No Dearie, it would not have grown after being cut down. See, the only ones that could grow must be dug up with the roots left on. And the ground must be frozen up there, so one couldn't be dug up now," answered Mother while she watched Mary rush to meet John. "Remember, Annie, John had said he would bring you the tree if he could. Ten chances to one, they were all buried deep in the snow, so I wouldn't ask him too much about it."

"Why Mama, John kissed Sister. I seen him do it."

"I know, Child. You and I kiss those we like very much when we haven't seen them for a long time, don't we?" She hugged the little girl. "That's another thing I would not say anything about."

Annie could forego asking about the kiss, but she had to find out about the Christmas tree. "Mama says maybe all the little trees was buried down in the snow," were her first words to John.

"That's what they were—all that were small enough to pack on my back. And the snow wasn't crusted good enough so I could get close to a big tree to cut the top out of it."

"Was you just buried in the snow too, so you couldn't get out for Christmas?"

"Just about buried," smiled John. "Christmas day we could not get out of the house until we dug our way out. Took half a day to get a path made to the tunnel so we could work. It was New Years day before the road got plowed out so we could get to town. The only way we could have traveled anywhere would have been on snowshoes or skis and I had neither. I thought I knew all about snow too, living in Colorado most of my life." That was a very long speech for John Marcus to make.

John stayed a week. The days flew by for the two young people, so busy making their plans. From the first day of John's arrival, it was more than plain to these anxious parents that Mary was very much in love. Far into the nights, the lovers talked in the cozy living room. David Williams tossed beside his wife, keeping her awake. "I don't like it, Mother. It just don't seem like John is the man for Mary."

"There we go again," Mother tried to be reassuring. "We can't just up and tell Mary she isn't old enough or wise enough to choose whom and when she wants to marry. The law gives a girl that right when she is 18. I'm beginning to think we two just would not like to see our oldest chick leave the nest, no matter who she chose as a life partner."

"Of course we wouldn't urge her to leave, but my mind would be a lot easier right now if it were possible to take her up into those hills so she could see the place and country. According to what I can learn, the higher places are much different to live in than here on the flats. Winters are long; much colder. They cannot grow crops there like we do here. And if ever there was a farm woman, Mary is one. She is just not seeing the picture as a whole."

"That is true, I expect," whispered Mother. "And it's all through those rose-colored glasses of love the both of 'em are looking right now. But then, the mountains are where Mary wants to be and I fear that is where she'll be living, for John and his line of work would naturally live in such places."

"The many places he has worked and prospected, he must have led a rather roving life. Sometimes I doubt John has the faintest idea of responsibility."

"If he hasn't, he'd better be finding some ideas. A few years from now, there will be a family to support. I've heard tell of several young men who didn't stay put in one place long until they married; then they had to settle down. Any roving life would pall on Mary shortly. She is pretty level headed in spite of her talk about climbing mountains to see what is on the other side."

David Williams was not worrying about that part of Mary's adventurous nature. He had had that same urge when he was her age, but fate had said nay. A widowed mother and two younger sisters had needed him at home through those years. When released from the need to care and support them, he was ready for his own marriage. "Mary has plenty of courage, we know."

"Sure she has," voiced Mother wearily. "And the ambition to go along with it. If we are wise at all, we'd better get to sleep and not try crossing all the bridges that aren't yet built in this state or in our imaginations.

By now Mary was a fair horseback rider, enjoying the canters she took about the Flats. The idea of borrowing another horse for John's use while he was here had been hers. She little guessed John's reluctance on that score, not realizing his unfamiliarity with riding or handling of horses. Noticing how awkward and uncomfortably he still rode this morning as they started after a week of short trips, her heart smote her. "It might have been selfish of me to plan this ride to take you half way to Murphy. I was thinking how we could be together just that much longer. We don't have to ride fast, starting this early. We'll have plenty of time to go 15 miles. But the long part of the trip is the other 15 for you to walk."

"Don't worry about me walking that short a distance," John told her. "I really believe I prefer to walk any day than to bother with a horse."

"Don't they have horses to ride up there in the hills?" She was not aware she had fallen into the habit of speaking of the mountains as hills.

"Sure. Most of the ranches have horses, and there are horses to be hired from the livery stables, I guess. Winter time, they use more tams for their sleighs and snow plows."

"Down here there hasn't been enough snow to even think of needing to plow out a road this winter. I understand it can snow plenty here though. It might come yet, but it is mid-January and not a speck of snow on the ground now."

Riding slowly and conversing, these two seemed in perfect accord. Not until they reached the half way point did any rift enter their pleasant dreams. "This must be the turning back point for me." Mary viewed the dry creek bed, a broken flume close by, and willows a few rods above denoting water holes. "There will be water for the horses, I'm sure. And it looks like there is plenty of brush for a fire to set beside while we eat our lunch. I hope it isn't all squashed carrying it back of the saddle this way." Mary was already untying the leather thongs holding the wrapped package securely to the cantle. This she dropped beside a good sized sage brush and led her horse to drink, noting that John did not take the bit from his mount's mouth. She removed it and remarked, "He can drink so much more comfortably, I think."

When John would have picketed his horse, Mary said not to do so. "Both these horses are trained to stay put by just dropping the reins this way. Max explained that is the way most horses are trained." Mary laughed as she saw the scowl come over John's face. "You don't need to try making me believe you are jealous of Max Thorn. You know it as well as I...there is no reason for you to be jealous."

"You may know a lot about horses, my dear, but there is a lot you don't know about men. Why shouldn't I be jealous of Max Thorn? He lives down here right close so he can be doing many things to make you like him, while I'm still stuck up there in a snow bank for the next few months. It's plain as the nose on his face—that man would like to cut me out. I believe he'd do most anything to do it."

"Now that is silly." Mary tried to shake him by the shoulder. "Don't my wishes enter into the picture at all? I love you and have promised to marry you the first day of June. I don't love Max Thorn, and if you knew anything about the man at all, you would know he would be the last person in the world to be making love to me or to anyone where there was none in return."

"Your folks don't seem too keen about me as a son-in-law. Perhaps they would like Thorn better. Why else were they trying to get us to wait a year?"

"That was because they thought you might be better fixed in your work so you would know just where you stand in your tunnel work. You notice they didn't insist we wait any year's time. They want me to be happy. They would never put stumbling blocks in the way of that. I will be 19 the day we are married. That is the age Mother was when they were married and commenced their life together without much money—just a bare farm and a house to live in. Like you say, you have a house and can make a living for me, so I'm not afraid to start out on a shoestring."

"It's a much bigger house than theirs. But remember we are not going to stay holed up in any such a place for very long. When we make our strike, we'll be long gone from Wagontown. You have heard that saying, *All trails lead to California*?" John was breaking brush over his knee for their fire. He well knew how to make a campfire. Then he scouted about for three of the flat boulders for seats and a place to spread their lunch.

Mary could smile with him over that grand dream castle he was building. She had dreams of her own, but being practical by nature and upbringing, she was sure they would fulfill those dreams only by a lot of years of living and hard work. The glory of this hour they had allotted themselves was tinged with sadness over their soon parting. Although John's display of jealousy was a minor thing to the young lovers, it had not added to Mary's peace of mind. Neither did it convey to her a side of his nature that she might find hard to live with.

The last kiss given, Mary turned toward home alone, leading the other horse. Once she waved to John, then he too started on his way, east by south. Before many miles, he would leave this road, taking a dimmer one directly south. It was the one he had traveled coming down, the same distance as it would be to

Murphy if he kept right on this road. Taking the shortcut, he would come out a good ten miles above that place. To find a place to stay at Murphy all night, without a cent of money in his pocket, might prove hard to do. He did not know anyone in that small place.

This being broke did not often bother John Marcus. He had been in that state most of his life. Being so now was the one thing he had not confided to Mary. As he trudged on, his long legs ate up the miles as fast as they had ridden their horses in the slow walk. His one thought was of their tunnel work. How much rock Tim had been able to move in the time he'd been away, and would Tim be waiting for him at DeLamar by tomorrow evening?

Not a worry where he would be sleeping this night, he was sure that would be in the barn at the way-station. His bed would be horse blankets and feed sacks. He patted his bulging coat pockets. The rest of the lunch Mary had insisted on him taking with him would be both his supper and his breakfast.

It was full dark when he reached the snug barn. No one had challenged him sleeping here before; nor did they this night. He took pains to be up and outside when the hostler came to care for the stage teams, this being the place the mail and passengers were transferred from wheels to sleigh on the way up. The wheels came back on on the way down. John climbed the snowy hill along with the few men passengers this day. Ed Wheeler, the driver, knew him by sight, and at his bidding, John rode from the first summit to the next station atop the loaded sleigh. Ed, noticing him not coming to dinner, went out to bring him in. "Good God, Man, if you are broke, why didn't you say so? Come on in and eat. I'll stand you a meal. From the looks of the weather on top, you may well earn your grub before we get in tonight. We may all be packing mail sacks on our backs."

The storm over the top was but a light powdering of fresh snow. The wind whipping it up into their faces was the worst to combat. Mid afternoon, when the stage swung downhill to Jordan Creek, John hopped from the sleigh, calling his thanks back to Ed. There was no use riding up the creek the four miles to Silver City, even if the ride was free, when the like distance would take him to DeLamar, down the creek.

Tim Nichols was there waiting for him, just like he hoped he would be. After a hearty supper, which Tim paid for from his small horde of money, the two of them trudged homeward. Tim packed beans, coffee and a side of bacon. John's load was a fifty pound sack of flour. That weight rested light on his strong shoulders. The lure of gold, ingrained into their very beings, was stronger here where all the talk was of prospecting and mining.

Tim did not ask John about his trip; he would learn that by bits of talk later. Tim did not approve of John's notion of getting married. "Dam foolishness, if you ask me," had been his comment more than once. No, he was not expecting John to do much talking. In this he was not disappointed.

Chapter Seven

MARY WAS FEELING RATHER lonely as she started home. *This week of John's companionship has sure spoilt me for living without him,* was her thought. She urged her mount along at a faster gait. The bay horse she had to lead was not so inclined. After half a mile of that discomfort, she stopped. "Well, I know I can change saddles or shorten the stirrups. Blacky, you lead well, I know that." In a matter of minutes, she swung into the different saddle and tried the stirrups as to length. Much to her surprise, as she rode on, the bay horse was much the easier gaited of the two.

Freed of the awkward tugging on the rope, she could ride at ease and as fast as she wished. "All I want to do is to be home before dark," Mary spoke aloud. There was no one within miles of this lonely road. "You two are nice horses alright, but you sure could take off on most any of these angling roads leading toward your own home, and I not be the wiser until too late." She would need to return this borrowed horse back to the Thorn ranch tomorrow. *But that is another day. I don't want that extra ten-mile ride tonight. And besides, tomorrow will be mail day.* Twice a week the mail was brought to the Flats. *Funny that I would be looking forward to mail day. There will be no letter from John this week.*

Most of her thoughts were of John and how lonely he looked as he trudged on foot. By his own account of his life, as far back as he could remember, it was of that order. He had been born in Denver. His father had died before John even saw the light of day. His mother had made a living for the two of them until he was 14, just ready to start in the higher grades of schooling. Her death had left him without kit or kin, he thought, until an uncle showed up unexpectedly. It was Wesley Marcus, his father's brother, who had settled up the few accounts, paid for the burial expenses, and took John to live with him. "Uncle Wes had prospected all his life. He always seemed to have plenty of money for grub, good tools and bedding, as well as clothes when we needed 'em," John had told her confidentially. "I just naturally expected he had money stashed away some safe place, but when he was caught in that slide and died from the injuries, I found less than $80—hardly enough to pay to have him decently buried." John had sounded unconvinced, as if he still thought there might have been a nest egg of his dead relative hidden some place.

Piecing his story together from what he had said at odd times, she could see him starting out alone for sure now, doing the only work he knew the first thing about: prospecting. *He was not quite 19 then. That was the age I am now,* was Mary's thought, and she could feel more compassion and understanding for the lonely youth roaming the mountains most of the year. He only worked the mines in the winter time to get money to grubstake him for the next season.

And John now having this good start, he is the more determined to stick to it until he does strike it rich, as he says, was Mary's thought now. In her own way, she was just as determined to help him, so that wish of his could be fulfilled. *I'm never going to nag and be a burden to him, I can promise that,* Mary was telling herself. *As long as John furnishes us with a comfortable house and the necessities, I will let him dig all he wants to. I know I'm marrying a prospector.* In her inexperience, she did not know how far or over what rough-going this unselfish way would lead.

For one sure thing, I'm not going to plan any expensive wedding, was her thought in regard to her parents' modest means. *We'll just be married right at home. All the people on the Flats will no more than fit into the two big rooms, so we won't need to limit our invitations. All I mind is that there is not one girl near my age to have as bridesmaid. But then, I don't have to have one,* was her practical solution. *I'm not going to have any fussy or expensive wedding dress either. But it is going to be white.* She fell to figuring just what pattern she would use and the most sensible type of material to buy. She would make her own dress, with Mother's help of course. *I'm going to be busy these next few months if I get those last two quilts finished and last comforter tied off. Yes. And I must put that bedspread back in the frames and finish that tufting, even if I did make that mistake on it and can't well take it out. I will have only the two spreads and am sure to need them.*

Mary was trying to get back her happy thoughts while going over her wedding plans. *I could be a lot happier if I wasn't so hungry.* She was just aware of her need as she spied a sheep cab in the distance. *I'm almost starved enough to rummage through that wagon, no matter who it might belong to, and see if I can find something to eat.* She had eaten but little breakfast in their hurry and less lunch, she remembered. *There will surely be some dried prunes in that grub box.* Thinking how good those would taste, she rode gaily on, not once expecting anyone would be about that cab.

As she rode closer, she could discern horses beside the rig, and smoke whipping low, away from the stove pipe stuck through the canvas top. Max' favorite saddle horse was tossing its head to get the last grain of oats from the nose bag. No one was in sight except Mike Ryan, washing dough from his hands. "Grub is about ready," he told her as he gave the murky water a toss from the pan. "Better hop down and eat."

Max stuck his head out the doorway to see who Mike was talking to and the dogs were making such a fuss about. "Hi," he said, and his hand came up in that half salute as he stopped at the wagon tongue. He grabbed up two nose bags, dipped a measure of feed into them, and brought them along as he came toward her. "Those two look like they could do with a feed." In a lower voice, he said, "How about you putting on the feedbag along with us? Mike will be pleased as punch if you'll so honor his cab wagon." Patting the horse's neck, he added, "I see you learned this bay doesn't lead good. I should have thought to tell you that."

"I learned it pretty quick, so swapped horses coming back. I was surprised to find the bay a much easier riding horse, only I have a feeling he might leave me setting in the middle of nowhere if he got the chance. He seems to shy easy."

"That is right," Max told her, loosening the cinches on the last saddle. "That's the reason why I didn't wish him off on you in the first place. That cantor of his is a pretty easy gait, but he does like to spook at every jack rabbit or screech owl."

Max' head would have brushed the smoke-begrimed canvas had he stood straight in the highest places in his cab, so he bent slightly forward, pulling out the honored seat for her, the only bench with a back on it. Mike had already set out another tin plate and cup. Rummaging in the small drawer beneath the table, he brought out knife, fork and spoon for her. "You've never eaten a meal in a sheep cab wagon?" At the negative shake of her head, Max continued, "Then you have never been properly introduced to the west." Max might talk about Mike being honored to have her eat with them, but it was he that was doing the honors in serving her.

"For the last three hours, I've been trying to figure out why Mike insisted on trailing his sheep to this road before stopping so we could cook a meal for ourselves." He was putting a huge spoonful of food onto her plate right from the skillet. "And he made his special mulligan stew too. You have to try some of that. I know it is heck for looks, but it really isn't so bad." He served himself, then turned the handle so Mike could reach it after he had dropped the hot biscuits on everyone's plate.

Mary smiled at the food being called mulligan, for it was potatoes fried with sliced onions and bits of ham, then a can of peas added, and cubed cheese allowed to melt through it. "Very good. I would say you are a very good cook, Mr. Ryan." Mary tried to make herself eat more slowly

"Mr. Ryan," winced Max. "Mike, when was the last time you were called Mister? This sure is a red letter day for you."

Mike did not seem to mind being the butt of Max' jokes, or foil for his wit. The same easy grin played about his unshaven lips. His hazel eyes might be rimmed and somber most of the time, but still a glint of humor shone there too. When the meal was finished, he moved with deftness in spite of his hard years of work and drink, putting the jars of pickles, jam, honey and butter away. In no time at all, the cab was made shipshape and ready for rolling.

Mary glanced back at the interior as she left and thought how convenient it all was. The wide bunk bed in the back end; the small table with the cupboard above and against one side; the diminutive stove on the other. "Do you know, this must be rather handy when you have to be in different places."

"Yep. All the comforts of home without room for a family quarrel." Max' firm hand came up to steady her as she stepped to the wagon tongue. Before he had the nose bags slipped from the horses heads and the saddle cinches pulled taut, Mike was ambling out to the brewing herd, the two dogs tight at his heals. Mary looked at that sight when Max spoke again. "No use of you bothering with this extra horse. I'm headed home now and can just as well load two instead of one. I'll leave the cab just short of the ranch. You choose which horse you now prefer." He held up the reins of the first one then the other.

Mary laughed at the antic he was going through. "Why it doesn't make much difference to me. I feel safer on Blacky, but this bay would be harder for you to lead."

"Don't worry about that. He'll do better beside another horse anyway. You seem to be very happy this day." His eyes were questioning her.

"Why, I am happy this day," she told him quickly, then hesitated, not sure if she wanted to tell him the reason for her happiness. Nodding toward Mike in the distance, she asked, "Do you think he is as lonesome as he seems to be?"

"I expect he is at times." Max spoke from experience. "I rather think most people without a home or any family ties get lonesome. I know that I do, and I keep pretty dang busy. Mike just goes on another bender to cure his lonesomeness. That cure to me is just plain poison. I don't forget a thing. Just come out of it with the awfulest headache, worse off than I was before. I'm lonesome enough today that I wish you were going my way, or I yours, so you would keep me company."

His eyes, so intent on her face as if to read her thoughts, and the things left unsaid made her aware of the true state of affairs. Somehow she must set herself right. "A moment ago I said I was happy. And you being the good friend you are to all of us, I want you to be the first to know. I am to be married the first of June. John and I made our plans while he was here." She had hurried to tell this much, now there seemed nothing more to be said. She had not expected him to be swift in any congratulations perhaps. Neither had she expected he would make this long pause before saying something.

"Thanks for telling me." His voice sounded as drab as the winter scene about them. "I guess there is no law against me wishing you all the happiness this old world can afford." His hand did not come up in that half salute as she rode away at an angle from the dim road he was headed on.

The slanting sun's rays, shining at last from under the clouds, bothered her eyes facing it, but that was not making the tears come. *And all I ask of life is to be happy.* Somehow she was anything but happy. *Seems that I make everyone unhappy along with myself.* A feeling that she had betrayed Max, as well as her parents, clung to her mind for several more miles.

Getting into some sort of happier frame of mind by the time she reached home, she was bowled over by small Annie's accusing eyes. "Why, whatever is the matter with you, Chickee?"

she asked the too still child.

"You going away just made my stomach sick all day."

"It would have been much too long a ride for you, Dearie. Three times as far as from here to the ferry. You shall ride with me every nice day from now on," she answered, thinking the trip today without her was what mattered.

"I'm never, never going away and leave Mama and Daddy and make 'em feel bad. I's not going to get married when I get big," came out in unchild-like tones. "That's what made my stomach sick."

"Oh you funny little sister." There was a catch in that voice as she picked up the child and hugged her, cradling her in her strong arms one minute, the next carrying her kitchen-ward atop her shoulders. "Here, Mother, is your spinster daughter, age seven. What's the cure for a sick stomach?"

"No home remedy has helped." Mother tried to smile, even if it didn't come out as blithely as she wished. "The treatment might be a long drawn out affair. Many little tablets of wisdom, much too old for a seven year old; daily rubs in the oil of loving kindness might help more now."

"You hear that?" Mary tousled the brown head. "You and I love Mother just like anything. What do you say you and I help her right this minute? You want to set the table, and I bet I can find something to do.

"Supper is cooking, but we do need a salad of some kind. I'll let you do that—you're better at those than I am."

"Now I wouldn't say that," laughed Mary, a bit wispy. "Just fess up that you don't care much about salads, but Father does, so you try to make them on that account. You ate some of that salad I made the other night with the grated apple and cabbage mixed together. Tell me honestly if you liked it any better?"

"Yes it wasn't half bad. I could almost eat that with relish. Did the ride tire you?"

"Not too much, but I did get hungry. About half way home I suddenly realized I was starved. I guess at noon, John and I were talking so much, I failed to eat much lunch. Was I ever glad to see a sheep cab loom in sight. I was thinking this once, I'd rummage in someone's grub box and see if I could find a piece of bread or a handful of prunes, and there was Mike Ryan and Max Thorn with a meal already cooked. So nothing to do, but I had to eat with them. I sure did not need any urging. In fact, there was need of holding myself back from eating too fast and too much." While she was busy shredding cabbage, then a firm red apple, she told them about Mike's mulligan stew. Father, coming in with the milk as she told the tail-end, had to hear all of it. So it was a happier family that sat down to their supper.

"Let's see. That will be Max' last band of sheep to bring in," remarked Father. "Did Max say if he was putting them in the feed lot?"

"No, Father, he didn't say that. But I'm sure they were headed for the ranch." She had no intentions of saying too much about Max Thorn.

"I expect it will be the feed lot for them in that case." David Williams was thoughtful for awhile. "It has been an open winter so far, but with the rain holding off last fall 'til so late, grass didn't get much of a start."

"Father, with this kind of weather I could paint the house, just as well as not. I can choose the sides the wind doesn't hit, and stop if it comes up a storm."

"It wouldn't dry the best, is the main hindrance. Aren't you trying to bite off a pretty big chunk?" He was trying to smile as of yore. "Why all the hurry? Are you thinking I will be like the Arkansa'r Max was telling about—who couldn't mend the roof in his house when it was raining, and when it wasn't raining, the roof didn't need mending?"

"Oh, you are not that way at all, Father," Mary scolded. "But you have so much to do. Come spring, you will be just that much busier. I'll be busy too, I know, with all I need to do, but I'm much younger than you. I know I can climb that ladder easier than you. This house needs another coat of paint. One can hardly tell it ever was painted. If you can afford to buy the paint now, I'll promise not to waste it. Then I won't feel so bad to put you to all the expense of paying for the goods for my dress and what few things I have to have."

"Don't feel that way, Daughter," Mother hurried to say. Father couldn't say anything for a short while. Neither parent wanted to show feelings before Annie. Both had figured that out in their own way. "Are you wanting to make your own dress, Dear? Have you forgotten Aunt Sylvia promised to make your dress when you wanted it? She would feel she was just paying in part for all the fine hand hemming you did for her when her girl, Sylvia, was getting ready to be married last spring. Auntie, being a dress maker, it would be a much nicer one than either you or I could possibly make." Mother's voice was getting calmer as she talked.

"That is just the trouble, Mother." Mary was very sure about this. "It would be much too fine. Auntie's mind runs to silk, lace and long trains on wedding dresses. Gowns, she calls them. What earthly use would I have for such a dress as that up in the hills? That is where I expect to live and I want something practical. A dress I can wear and wash and get some good out of. My mind is settled on a white Irish linen. I could use the yoke of that nice Cluny lace I already have. I know I could make that, with your help of course."

Father had master over his voice now. "Your wishes should govern your wearing apparel at such a time. Just don't think you must skimp just because we happen not to be flush at this time."

"I'm not thinking that, Father dear." A catchy laugh. "You don't know what expensive cloth Irish linen is. We might have to pay $.75 a yard and it will take more than five yards. I already have all the under things I need, except hose. There will have to be a new pair of shoes, though." Annie, feeling she was left out of all this talk, edged her way onto Mary's lap. "Getting sleepy, Chickee? Do you want me to fix you ready for bed before I do the dishes?"

"My stomach is getting sicker." Her nose was partly buried in Mary's soft blouse.

"Did you know Daddy is the best stomach rubber there is? He used to rub my legs when they ached—it always cured them. You just set on his lap here by the fire while I get your gown. Remember, you must get toasty warm, for I want you to warm my bed ready for me." This was the usual evening ritual. "And there is just one more thing I want you two to understand," commenced Mary the instant Annie was asleep and tucked in bed, and she and Mother had come back to the cozy living room. "You must not think of getting me any expensive set of silver. I know how you have always planned to do so. Just like Grandma Blatchey gave you two when you started out in your own home. You cannot afford it. Just think of all the table linen and bedding you've been helping to provide for me. That big old trunk is more than full. I was reading the other day about how young ladies now are talking about their *hope chests*. That trunk is mine surely. Why, there is enough to set up housekeeping right now with all the odd spoons I have been collecting and dishes given me since I was knee-high." Mary picked up a bit of sewing as she sat down.

"You have no curtains in your collection, remember?" Mother was practical too; not one of the three guessed what little use there would be for curtains in Mary's new life.

"And that is one thing I'm not going to plan on getting until I see the house, measure the windows, and plan out what would look the best." No one seemed to have much small talk. After a long pause, she said, "I do not know how many windows there are even. I never asked John. I know he mentioned there being six big rooms, besides a shed room on the ground floor. Now a house of that size would have several bedrooms upstairs. I won't try furnishing all those right off." She could smile over all the promised space.

"That would be several windows. They could be various sizes perhaps, but a set of kitchen half curtains would not come amiss."

"No you don't, Mother." Mary wanted this to sound like a joke. Tapping her on the shoulder, "How do I know yet if I want white, green or sky blue? But there is one thing I do want, and that is a few seeds of every kind of vegetable that we can figure out will grow up that high." She shook her head in much seriousness. "I received no help when I questioned John as to what would grow up there. He admits there is a fenced garden plot, and that it is good soil. But that is as much as he knows about the growing of a garden. To hear him talk, sometimes, one would think he thought all food stuff grows in the tin cans; dry beans in sacks; and bacon just happened to be already smoked from the first." A wry smile.

"Beans, I fear, would not grow or do well that high," Father bestirred himself from his sad thoughts to say. "They, like most vine stuff, would frost too easy. But the hardy vegetables, all those that grow underground might do well. Cabbage and peas can stand a light frost and are short growing time. Onions from sets come quick. Did I hear right...that the elevation is forty-five hundred feet?"

"Something like that. I know DeLamar is more than five thousand and Wagontown is down the creek from there two miles.

John never talked as if it was any steep grade within that distance, so I think it must be just normal grade." She was thoughtful as she took down her long braids, brushing her hair well, then again plaiting her hair for the night. "There are so many, many new things to learn. I feel like Annie says so often, *I just never, never can learn it all at once.*"

Chapter Eight

TWILIGHT HAD DESCENDED INTO night over the hills. Tim Nichols, watching from the east doorway of the old Mills House, could no longer see the road as it twisted between clumps of willows along the rocky point of the bluff, or even as it crossed the small gulch by a wooden bridge close at hand. But his keen ear was attune to every sound. Leaning against the paint-peeled wood of the door casing, he smoked continuously, pausing only to do some tall cursing every once in awhile, a habit he had when alone. Here he was very much alone. John Marcus, his partner, had been gone five days. The closest miner's shack was at least a mile distance, so all the sounds the night air carried were of creek and birds. There was hardly enough breeze to make a noise in the sparsely scattered trees on the steep hillside hemming in this narrow valley on the south.

The screech of a night owl broke the stillness. Tim spat over the edge of the unroofed porch, cursing again fluently, winding up with his pet peeve, "All prospectors are fools. Some are crazy fools. John Marcus is the most crazy of all fool prospectors. I'd say he was a double damned fool, getting married and not one dollar to his damned name." Tim spat again, then listened. A faint sound. That could be a slide of wheels against brakes. Then all was still again. "Expect that's them coming down the steep pitch," holding his face toward the north that his ear might be more apt to catch the faint rumble of the rig as it crossed the nearest bridge. This he did not hear, it being too far. All was still for a moment, then the ping of metal on rock floated down stream. "Yep, that's them." Tim turned back into the kitchen, putting match to a stub of a candle stuck to the high shelf running nearly the full length of the gloomy room. Moving the pots and pans about on the stove, he built up the fire, then pushed most of the cooking vessels toward the front again. He paused at the door for a second, but he didn't expect to hear much, knowing the travelers would now be on the race track. That quarter mile, set like a crescent between creek and bluff, was not marred by rock or stone.

Now he put match to the wick of the lantern he held ready. The globe needed washing. The creek of the wagon came clearly as they rounded the rocky point. He ambled out the west door to the barnyard, along the picket fence to the big gate. This he swung

71

open. The hollow sound as the rig rolled across the gulch bridge set his teeth on edge. "Another minute and I will see which is the bigger fool: John Marcus or that fool woman he has fooled into marrying him." Tim now cursed under his breath.

"We are here, Tim, because we are here," John sang out. The tired team managed a half trot through the gateway. "Did you about give us up a-coming tonight?" The noise of the brakes being set would have interfered with hearing anything that Tim might have answered, and John was not expecting an answer. He lost no time in getting to the ground, then called up to Mary, "Come this side, I'll help you down."

"I can't," came in a dismayed tone. "My feet are asleep. I can't stand on them yet. You go ahead and unhook the team. I'll rub my feet and get some feeling into them."

Tim was leading the team toward the barn by the time Mary dared trust her feet on the wheel to be helped down. "Put me down, John. I'm much too heavy for you to carry me this way." He never paused in his rush to carry her. The three steps to the porch was almost his undoing. "You silly man, wrecking your back carrying me." Mary patted his shoulder as he let her prickly feet touch the floor.

"I didn't carry you," John panted. "I packed you over the threshold of your new home." Mary was still clinging to him, trying to make her feet work. "Set down in a chair, Honey. Let those feet get limbered up easy like. I should go help Tim put up that team."

"I forget—nothing is carried in these hills. Everything is packed." She would have laughed, had she not been so weary. The faucet was dripping above the big wooden sink. "Running water, John, oh, how glorious! I don't remember you telling me about that." She made toward the water, unsteady at first, needles and pins prickling her feet at every step. It was he that reached for the dipper and handed her the drink. "And what good water. So cold," were her first words as soon as she had downed the first drink. "I must have been dry clear to my toes." She handed John the dipper as if she would have more.

"Don't get water logged now," he teased. "I had you sized up as not much of a sand lizard, liking to live down on the hot dusty Flats where the water is warm like dishwater. You alright now?" he asked as she flashed him a smile. "I should go help Tim."

Tim, coming in through the first room that instant, demanded, "When did I get so dang lazy I couldn't put up one team of Cayuses alone?" He started to blow out the lantern, thought better of it, and hung it from a suspended wire in the middle of the room. The candle was about burned out. Reaching for a fresh one, he lit that from the dying one, dripped a drop of wax in a different spot, and pressed the tall one there before pinching out the gutted one.

John smiled. "Tim, forget your grouch long enough to meet the best little woman that ever hit these old hills. Mary, this is Timothy Nickles. You'll perhaps never hear his full name again, so I tell it now. But don't you let his growl scare you. He really isn't one bit cross."

Neither Mary nor Tim gave answer to John's sally. Very gravely, they shook hands, said the usual words of greeting, and meant every word they had said; for these two seemed to gauge the others' worth. Tim had not expected John's bride to be quite like she was. Soon he was putting the belated meal on the table, covers of each pot serving as hot pads as he scouted those to the bare table top. Coffee, black and strong from its long standing, was poured into huge tin cups. An unwashed flour sack, wrong-side-out, covered the pan of biscuits he took from the warming oven.

Mary helped herself to brown beans; speared a slice of bacon from the tin pie plate of fat it swam in; and took a mound of rice cooked with raisins. She made no move to serve herself bread. John, noticing this, broke apart a biscuit and put in on her plate. "Don't you let Tim see you turn up your nose at his sourdough bread. I know it looks like heck, but it tastes pretty good."

Tim snorted, "John, you dang fool. Ten chances to one your wife has never seen sourdough bread, much less tried it."

"That's right," smiled Mary, "but here is where I do try it. I have heard a lot about this kind of bread. A friend of my folks down on the Flats, Max Thorn, was always telling about sourdough bread." As soon as she spoke Max' name, she saw that same look spread over John's face. This time she laughed. "John thinks he doesn't like Max Thorn, just because he happens to own and run sheep."

"Don't know as owning sheep is the sin," Tim said, "but running the stinking varmints where other people want to live is what's wrong." His lopsided grin looked comical in the dim light.

His bright blue eyes, his most noteworthy feature, seemed hooded in the flickering light.

Gingerly at first, Mary tasted the bread alone, then with a bite of bacon. "Tastes good," she approved. She would have liked to have tried this new kind of bread with butter, but she refrained from asking since it was not in sight. She started to put condensed milk in the cup of coffee, but seeing its strength, she stopped. "There is no need of me fixing this coffee, I so seldom drink it. This nice cold water is so much better to me." Gracefully, she arose and helped herself to the dipperful of that.

"See, I told you—you were no sand lizard," teased John.

Mary smiled at him, but said nothing. She was still trying to decide if she really liked this sourdough bread. It was rather heavy and tough of crust, perhaps from its long standing, she thought. But still it was satiable. Putting some of the tomato sauce from the bean pot over the bread made it very tasty. With her hunger hardly satisfied, she commenced to get drowsy. "Why, I'm getting so sleepy I can scarcely keep my eyes opened to see to finish my meal."

"The high altitude does that to some people," Tim told her.

"But the joke is on you," laughed John. "You can't go to bed until we get that wagon unloaded and get a bed made up."

"In that case, let us get at it before I do fall asleep." Mary hopped up from the table. "Excuse me. I should have asked if you two were through with your meal before being so bossy." No one said anything. It was Mary, who took down the lantern and carried it as well as a few small things under her other arm, lighting the way to the northeast bedroom where the men took the large trunk.

This room opened off from the front hall; also from the dining room. It seemed the smallest of all the rooms. It showed signs of being lately swept. Dust was thick on the sturdy furniture of a light-colored wood finish. Mary, testing the lumpy looking mattress with her hand, explained to John which of the packing boxes contained the feather bed. "I believe that is the only other box you will need to unload tonight." She was sure that she heard a very apt expression from Tim as to what he thought of feather beds in general. As they went to do her bidding, Mary thought, *I'm not going to quarrel with that funny man. I'm much too weary right now and besides, I think he doesn't even know that he is cursing; maybe he has done it for so long.* She hurried to wipe away the dust from the dresser top before the men should be back. *That was sure a filthy thing to do, using my nice handkerchief for that,* she scolded herself.

It was not long before the household slept this night. Mary's eyes flew open to early morning light, with a whiff of frying bacon and coffee coming to her. "It is morning, John. Tim must be cooking breakfast already. Let us get up right now. There is so much for me to do—so many, many new things for me to see this day." Mary was wide awake and soon up. Not so with John—he was more than half asleep and meant to stay that way as long as he could. Mary dressed and slipped out the room by the hallway and on out the door, and looked about her. Coming well after dark, she had no idea of what this new home of hers looked like. Her eyes turned toward the east, the direction she was sure they must have come from last night. A short distance of road was soon lost in the green of willows. The craggy hills everywhere still held their shadows, except the higher ones to the west. The sun was glinting away the morning dew. What took Mary's eye the more was the small steep mound to the north. The road along the front yard fence skirted this small hill. In no time at all, she was crossing that road and scrambling to the top of that knoll.

Breathing in great gusts of pure air after that quick climb, she surveyed her home below her. From this vantage point, she could see it as a whole. The house, with its white peeling paint, looked smaller from this height, but she knew it was neither low or small. The unroofed porches did look odd. The yard on all sides was green. On either side of the house, it was wider than in front. It all seemed to slope toward the back. A few trees and bushes lined the east yard fence of white pickets. They, like the house, needed paint. A good sized rock building half filled the space between house and fence at the lower corner of the house on that side.

To the west were unpainted fences, gates and the outbuildings, barns and corral—all drab and weather beaten. Mary's eyes did not dwell long on these, but the steep rocky hill to the south took her eye. Every tree, big little and indifferent, scattered among those crags held a special meaning to her. *That is the first one I want to climb,* she told herself, little guessing she never would do so for pure pleasure. The small valley opened out wider before the barns, making a small field. *Now who was it that said, "If one would fain win the mountain, win the valley first?"*

And here I have won both at once.

Mary was very happy with her new domain. She was wondering about that tall rusting smokestack nestled between hill and creek when a faint *moo* of a cow carried in on the still air. It was then that she could see the stir of a roan back in the pole corral. Another long *moo* sent her flying down the steep ground and toward the corral. "Why, how under the sun did you get here, Roany cow?" asked the happy girl. Hugging the familiar head that rubbed against her, stepping away to look her over the better, she could see the swollen udder. "Why you poor thing, you are aching to be milked." Giving her another quick pat, she raced to the house and barged into the smoke-filled kitchen. "Good morning, Mr. Tim." She couldn't remember his last name. "Can you tell me where I would find a pail to milk my cow?"

Tim seemed slow in answering, so she went on to explain, "I haven't the least idea of how my cow got here, but she needs milking. Any kind of pail, or bucket, as you westerners say, will do. I can wash it right here." She was busy washing her face and hands. The warm water with soap felt good, then came the dash of cold water.

"I don't know of a doggone thing that looks like a bucket around the place except this bean pot. Better call that sleepy headed John or he'll sleep all day. As soon as we eat breakfast, that bean pot will be emptied."

Mary wanted to laugh over the idea of beans for breakfast. She hurried away so Tim would not see her smile. Shaking John awake, she commenced to hand him his clothes so he would dress the faster. "The faster you can dress, the quicker we will eat breakfast and that bean pot will be emptied. Then the sooner I can get our cow milked."

"What under heaven are you talking about?" demanded John.

"I don't understand it all either," Mary told him. "But Roany is out in the corral asking to be milked. I never dreamed Father was doing any such thing as sending her up here, and he must have started her all of a week ago. She never, never could have come all that distance in less time."

"How do you know it's your cow? She may be a stray."

"Oh, she's Roany alright. She knew me. Before I even saw her, she was mooing to me. I was up on that knoll in front of the house looking around."

76

"What in Sam-hill are we going to do with a cow?" lamented John as they came to the kitchen.

"Why, we'll milk her of course. She'll keep us in milk, butter, cream and cheese. I know Father always considered the cow was mine, but I never thought he would do anything like this. True, I haven't been doing any of the milking these past few weeks—I was so busy getting the outside of the house painted.

"Do you know how to milk?" John seemed surprised.

"Of course I know how to milk. Don't you?" Mary was the one surprised now when John shook his head. Mary expected Tim would make some comment about the cow, but he didn't. This meal was the repetition of the meal before, except the coffee, being freshly made, was less black. Mary was sure it would be just as strong, so declined having a cup. The bread was more crisp and easier to eat, but it was light enough now to see the faint yellow streaks from the careless use of soda. She found herself eating two slices. "Can you shed any light on how or when my cow arrived here?" she asked Tim. She thought since he was sleeping on that side of the house, he might have heard someone leaving her.

"She must have come early last evening about dark. I was up to DeLamar then. Coming back, I noticed a rig coming from this way and headed Jordon Creek way at the fork of the road. Wasn't close enough to talk to 'em."

"And to think Roany has been in that corral all this time without food or water." She hurried to wash the bean pot, knowing this would not hold a third of the milk. She scurried to hunt up other containers, unearthing a small crock in the dim pantry, and a deep four-gallon crock in the stone cellar. *Now for a strainer,* she thought, being sure that neither one of the men would be any help with that. Unpacking her trunk of prized household linen, she grabbed the first plain dish towel. Tying that over the freshly washed crock, she was ready for the milking of Roany.

Both crock and bean pot were full before she was through. *But how am I to carry that heavy thing to the house without spilling it?* Then she laughed. *Silly me. I can take this gallon to the house, empty it and come back for more.* This she did.

Tim was putting the last washed breakfast dish away as she sailed into the house. "Oh, you men are so used to having to do dishes, you forget there is a woman about," she bantered.

Tim grinned that funny grin of his. In the morning sunlight she could see the intense blue of his eyes. They were almost on a level with hers, for Tim was short for a man. *Rather I'm tall for a woman,* was Mary's thought as she remembered her five feet and seven inches of height. The men seemed ready to go to work. John consented to helping her bring in the rest of the milk. Now as the two tramped down the steps in their heavy shoes, Mary called to them, "I forgot to ask you if the fence is safe enough so it will be alright to turn the cow out for water?"

"Don't know how good the fence is all the way around. Seems okay to turn out horses. Maybe cows are different." Tim seemed as indifferent as John.

"Roany isn't breechy," Mary defended hotly. "She needs to be out to eat grass and to get to the creek for water."

"She better not get to the creek or she'll be a dead cow," stated John. As he kissed his bride of two days, he could see the troubled eyes. "Come along, Honey, and see the creek. Then you'll know what I mean."

Tim tramped on ahead of them. John held back the willows from brushing her face. They grew thick here, and she caught no sight of the water until they walked the length of the approach to the foot bride. "Oh, what is wrong with the creek?" Mary was horror stricken. "What makes the water so milky? It even smells terrible." She was offended by such a sight and odor. Gone was her dream of a pure mountain stream.

"It's the cyanide in it," John told her.

"But why do they put it in the stream?"

"It is used in the milling processing up at DeLamar. Helps catch all the fine gold that used to wash away from 'em."

"Surely fish can't live in such a stream, for cyanide is a poison?" It was a half question, and she had answered it herself.

"No, fish don't seem to thrive on cyanide. Bye now, I have to hot-foot it over to the drift and put in a round of shots for Tim."

Mary was detaining him with her hand within his arm. "John, tell me true. All the animals drinking this water would die?" She was suddenly fearful, this country seemed alien.

"I guess they would. What I think is, most animals won't drink it if they can get other water. Never see much dead stuff along here. See, Honey, there is lots of springs and seeps all along here. Any stock can drink there instead of this water." Seeing her fear, he spoke more considerately, but he was in a hurry to be gone, so kissed her again.

"Will you and Tim be back for dinner at noon?" she managed to ask.

"Nope. I see Tim put himself up a snack. I'll be back within an hour. I have to take that team home today. I promised Kirt I'd have 'em home by noon." In no time, he was lost to view among the rocks and willows.

I can't see how even willows can grow close to this stream. Then she could see that where the water touched them, they were nearly dead. Now she understood what Max Thorn had meant when he talked of mines fouling the streams. She did not tarry beside the offensive stream, hurrying to care for Roany's needs. Spying her halter and rope hung by the gate, she led the cow first to the grass in the yard and watered her with dishpans of water from the faucet in the kitchen. That took several trips. Knowing the many, many things she should be doing, her busy brain began to plan as to the best course. It would not be nice to keep the cow in the dooryard—this she knew.

Bright green spots on the hillside north of the barn took her eye. Those must be the springs and seeps John spoke of. Leading the leg-weary cow to the first one, and picketing her to a sage brush, she was thinking about finding a shovel. She thought she could dig out any spring there might be when she saw water about the cow's hooves as she cropped into tender grass.

Mary raced back to the house to commence her work. The dark pantry was fairly cool. There she placed the milk and washed strainer and bean pot, and put those to air. Now came the bed making. The room was full with the packing box and trunk, so she pulled these to the dining room and looked over the possibilities of this room as a whole. It was large. Two windows let in the morning sun. The door between them, she propped open to let in more light and the fresh air. The big table and chairs, the only furniture, were of dark wood—heavy and massive looking. *I won't unpack things until I get everything cleaned. By then, I will know where I will want them,* she told herself while finishing the bed and hanging up their clothes. *No real closet, this.* She viewed the curtained corner of the room.

Thinking other rooms might have better closets, she opened

the door across the small hall and peered into those rooms. The first one was real large with only a worn couch in it. This had evidently been a parlor by the looks of the wallpaper and half of a window drape still hanging—a rich brocaded cloth in wine color. Dust was everywhere, but no real dirt. The next room, opening into this by a wide archway, must have been a sitting room in the distant past, was Mary's conclusion, for she found no closet or clothes press of any sort. A heating stove stood in the corner closet to the opening between the rooms. The bedstead, dresser and commode were of the same dark massive wood as the dining room furniture. This was Tim's room.

Clean, but unironed clothes draped the dresser. Dirty work clothes hung over a chair. Muddy shoes and soiled socks were tossed in another corner. The fetid smell of feet was everywhere. She found she could not open the windows, so she flung all the doors open. The one leading out of this room opened into the first room she had entered last night, and it joined the kitchen. *My, what a nice big washroom this is,* she thought. *But why don't they have the water piped in here?* Many cobwebs were draped from the high ceiling. Lines stretched the width of the room. They must have hung their clothes to dry here in the bad weather. Her fingers itched to get at sweeping down those cobwebs, but she would need some sort of a step ladder since the ceiling was so high.

I'd better go see how Roany is doing. The thought of that poisoned stream was ever with her. While tying her in a different spot, she saw John coming to the barn for halter ropes to catch the horses feeding further up on the hillside. *Why am I worrying this way? Those horses have been loose all night and they are alright.*

"What the heck is this?" John called out, staring at the crate set just inside the barn door. He had nearly fallen over it.

"Why, it is a crate of chickens," Mary said, peering in beside him. "Whoever brought Roany must have brought them." She was looking the crate over to see where it should be opened.

"I wonder how many more surprises that dad of yours has up his sleeve."

"That would be hard telling," Mary said, lifting out one of the fine barred rock hens. These, her father had not sent. The chickens at home were white rocks. Max Thorn had the only barred rocks that she knew of on the Flats. John, thinking Father had sent them, might be better, she decided. "I wonder what kind of a chicken house there is here?" she asked. On looking up, she saw John striding away toward the horses. Putting the hen back into the crate, she went unerringly to the right building.

It did not seem too dilapidated. The wire netting about the yard seemed chicken tight. *I really would like to clean this all and whitewash the inside and make new nests before I put them in here, but they shouldn't be left in that crate longer.* Kicking over a battered water pan, and seeing it was without a leak, she took it to the house and filled it with water. Back again to the barn, John helped her move the crate to the hen house to get it out of his way. "How many miles do you have to go?" Mary asked him.

"About four, I'd say. If it wasn't for that walk back for you, I'd ask you to go along with me." John yanked out the last few things from the wagon not unloaded last night. "It would be lots nicer with you along to talk to.

"Phooey on you if you think I can't walk four miles," laughed Mary. I will have to run and close those doors and get my hat." With that, she raced back to the house.

Chapter Nine

"I KNOW, I SHOULDN'T have come with you," voiced Mary as John gave her a hand to help her climb into the wagon. "There are so many things I should be doing." She made herself comfortable on the spring seat. Knotting the scarf she carried about her neck, "I don't need this about my head. There seems not a bit of dust here. Isn't it a beautiful day?"

"Generally pretty nice here in the summer time."

"Nice," laughed Mary. "I would say gorgeous!" After several minutes, she remarked, "This is a real good road, but it doesn't seem to be traveled much."

"No one down below here uses it much except Kirt, and he seldom comes up this way. He says he does his trading at Reynolds." John swung the whip in an arch to the north. "The main road to Reynolds is up there along the ridge."

"You mean the road that climbs the grade right from our place?"

"Yes, that's the one," John told her. "It's headed northwest there, but after it gets out on top, it angles more to the west in that direction."

"Then do we hit that road later on?" Mary was trying to see all around, turning first this way and then that.

"We don't hit it between here and Kirt's ranch. Have to go a mile due north from there to strike it." A teasing look came to John's face. "You want we should walk back by that road? It won't be more'n three miles further."

"No thanks." A smile flashed, "I believe the four mile walk will be all today. So this way is like a short cut from here to there," she mused. "Is this your west line fence?" she asked as John climbed from the wagon to open a three-strand wire gate. No answer. She deftly released the brake and drove the team through, stopped until John climbed back in the rig, and repeated the question.

"I expect it must be." The wagon was tilting as the road curved up and over a rock strewn point.

"Who owns the ground on this side of the fence?" Mary viewed the rough serrated ground, running like miniature ridges toward the evil smelling stream they were soon following again.

John caught the joke. "No one would want it but Uncle Sam.

He's just stuck with it!" The road was getting rougher. In spots, brush crowded close to the creek bank.

"What smells so spicy like?" asked Mary, sniffing the new scent. "It is strong enough in places to kill the foul smell of the stream."

"Don't know. Might be those service berries up on the hill above us. I see they are in bloom; or the choke cherries. Don't see many of 'em down here, though."

"It must be something right close to the road. I note it more when we ride through brush like this." She reached out for a branch of the dry looking stuff. She found that it didn't break off. Only a few leaves, both yellow and green, and shreds of fine bark came away in her hand. Sniffing this, "Yes, this must be it. But what a queer shrub it is with both colored leaves."

John broke off a small twig the next close brush and handed it to her. "The yellow leaves come out first, then the green ones."

Mary, looking at it closely, then exclaimed, "Those yellow leaves must be the blossoms. The leaves are just coming on now. There are plants like that I know–one is called forsythia."

"They call this buck brush around here."

"Do sheep eat it?" Mary was noticing the hills were more barren the further they traveled.

"They might. They are that much like goats. They tell me they eat most anything." John glanced her way.

"Are there many sheep around here?" Mary was very serious, not heeding his joke.

"There better not be. This is cattle country. Kirtland might take a potshot at any showing up close to here."

Mary nodded her head in understanding. "That is it, this Kirtland, or Kirt as you call him. He's a cattleman. Does he have any cattle?"

"Several, maybe a thousand. I really don't know."

"Then he must be fairly wealthy. What will his wife think of me calling first this way?"

"Kirt has no wife," John grinned broadly. "He is a confirmed old *bach*. At least he was never married that anyone around here knows about. But everyone seems to know all about the time he thought he was going to get hitched."

Mary knew *hitched* must mean married, so asked, "What happened? Did she die or one of them change their mind?"

"Don't think she changed her mind. She just had other intentions than Kirt thought she had. She must have been a slick one."

Mary patted his arm, "Are you going to tell me the joke so I can smile with you?"

"Guess it was anything but a joke to Kirt about that time, for he was dead gone on the woman. She was new to these hills, and that was quite a few years back when Kirt was not as well fixed as he is now. But he showered her with a fine diamond ring, a watch and good clothes, and he had collected together a few hundred dollars for their wedding trip. She was the one packing the money for him. He wanted 'em to get married before they started. She wanted to go to Portland, so that is where they headed. Just before train time, she developed a terrific headache, and sends Kirt over to the drug store to get her some pills." John, not much on talking, stopped now.

"And she was gone when he got back?" Mary was trying to piece together what must have happened.

"Yep. She was gone. Left a nice little note for Kirt telling him to take the medicine. She was taking the train."

"Why, that was a terrible trick to play." Mary could hardly believe anyone would be that mean. "Did he ever see her again or get his money back?"

"He never got his money, that's for sure. He had her arrested, but they found no money on her. That is why I say she was a slick one. I believe if I had been Kirt, I wouldn't have had her jailed. That is how everyone come to know about it. He must have had to stand some ribbing."

"No wonder he has never married. Perhaps he thinks all women are like that. Will he be afraid of me?"

"Oh, you're not dangerous now." He gave her a tight hug. "You are married. He has sense enough to know you won't be trying to marry him for his money."

"We won't be apt to be asked to stay for dinner?" Mary was getting hungry already, and it still could not be near noon.

"Sure, we'll be asked to eat if Kirt is home. If he isn't, we'll just go in and cook our own meal."

"Why, we couldn't do that and him not be there?" Mary was doubtful.

"That is the law of these hills. Houses are never locked.

Anyone happens along about mealtime or bedtime is supposed to cook themselves a meal or stay all night if need be. Just don't leave any dirty dishes or use up all the dry wood and not cut some more."

"That is so different than it would be in the east," Mary told him. "There, we wouldn't go into a friend's house unbidden and they not home."

"Guess friends and neighbors don't live so far distant either. Here, if you want to see someone a dozen miles away, you'd dang near starve before you got home if they weren't home. Most of the old sourdoughs will cuss you from hell to breakfast if you don't stop and eat with 'em. And curse you worse if you offer to pay for it."

"How you do talk," admonished Mary with a smile. They were climbing up over one of those endless ridges. When on top of this one, the ground fell away, leaving a view the Kirtland ranch. It stood two miles below in all its early summer greenness. "Oh, what a pretty place. Please stop for a minute, John, so I can see it from here. What a beautiful picture it would make--just like a big jagged-edged bowl—so green at the bottom, with faint gray green all around the sides; the broken rim rock of several shades of black, brown, gray and light colors at the top. I wish I could paint. This would be one picture I would do."

"Are you thinking about starting that said painting today?" John teased.

"I regret to say I couldn't paint a picture if my life depended on it, so you need not worry about your wife traipsing off down here to paint this scene." The grind of brakes made conversation impossible. After going through the last gate, the road hugged the creek bank, spoiling but little of the tillable land. "This field is so green, it looks almost blue," Mary puzzled.

"You easterner," smiled John. "This isn't a field...this is a meadow."

"Why is it called a meadow instead of a field?" John did not answer that question, so she amused herself by watching the different shading about them. "I know now why this is so blue looking in some places. It is a flower growing thickly in the hay." The road turned at a sharp angle and crossed the creek; the house, barns and corrals stood close to the bank on this side. "If I owned this nice a ranch, I would want my house further away from this evil smelling stream."

"Guess this house was built here long before they ever used cyanide for mining." Even when John set the brake and the team stopped, he made no move to climb down, but continued to scan the hillside. "I see Kirt coming. Now we'll see how good your eyes are. Can you see him?" He dropped his eyes to look at her with a grin.

Long minutes passed before she could discern the moving speck weaving its way in and out of a jumbled mass of rock fallen from the rim in ages past. "Fie' on you! That was hardly fair, for I bet you saw him as he came over the rim and you could see him against the skyline. Isn't that true?"

There was lots of fun in not admitting the truth, even if she had guessed right. "Don't know if Kirt wants to use this team or not," he remarked, hitting the ground and unhitching. "We'll leave 'em harnessed 'til he gets here." Mary had unhooked the tug on her side and dropped the neck yoke the same as he. "Sure is nice having a pardner to work right alongside me." Their hands met and clasped as they took the team to the barn. It was a low, rather small building, like most of the barns found through the hills.

"This barn is not in keeping with that nice new corral."

Mary admired the double corral of bright peeled poles. The shrill screech of a horse rent the quiet air. She now hurried toward the enclosure. She peeked between the horizontal poles of the gate at the milling animals kicking up the dust. "I'm sure I've never seen so many different colored horses in my life," Mary told John as he came to stand beside her. "You said this man raised cattle, but from the looks, he owns horses."

"Yeah, he has plenty of horses. Guess he never sells a one of 'em. Can't see what he wants with so many of 'em myself." Kirtland was cantering into sight now, and his horse answered the piercing neigh of a dark cream colored horse, proudly tossing his mane of white.

"What a beautiful horse that is." Mary was enthralled. "I don't blame anyone for not selling such animals as that." The horse coming close now was every bit as spirited and of the same color. Man and horse seemed of one piece, so well did Kirt sit; even to the same light color, for Kirtland wore faded tan clothing. Once on the ground, he looked short beside the tall mount.

"About time you got here, Kirt," laughed John. "This wife of mine is all taken up with these horses of yours. I want you to meet her and set her straight that none of 'em are for sale." Another laugh.

Very courtly, Kirtland bowed, with his hat in his hand, while he shook hands with Mary. "I'm mighty pleased that John brought you down, Mrs. Marcus, so I can see just what a fine wife he picked for himself." While he congratulated them warmly, he little guessed Mary was using every effort to keep from laughing. Kirtland, in the saddle or with his hat on, was a very ordinary looking man. He was deeply tanned up to his hat band. Minus that hat, his pink scalp and thin white hair gave him the oddest *night cap* appearance. "I see you two young people are the happiest folks going. And I'm glad. That is the way it was meant to be. Come on in and we'll pile on some grub." He put his hat back on and squinted his light blue eyes skyward. "Must be about that time."

"Please, Mr. Kirtland," Mary implored, "will you first tell me what all these oddly colored and marked horses are called?"

Kirt was in no hurry now that someone would talk horses. Folding his arms along one of the poles, he explained, "You know the ones called pintos?"

"I thought I did. It was a bay spotted with white and generally a bald face and white eye. But there is a black with dashes of white. Is that a pinto too?"

"Yes. Now those light colored tans, or creams, with the white mane and tail, like I rode in on, are called *palomino*. Sometimes their manes are not white, but lighter in color than the rest of them. Take for instance that young filly there by herself." He pointed his gloved hand toward an all tan animal—mane and tail as golden as wheat straw.

"But when they have a black mane and tail, they are called something else?" Mary asked.

"Called just plain *buckskin* then." He singled out another. "See that sort of bay roan with the blotches on the hips? They are called *appaloosa*. But that flea bitten one next to him with no special color, but has light colored legs and bald faced? They are called *sabino*."

"What queer names," laughed Mary. "Almost as odd sounding as they look. Are those Indian names? Come to think of it, if they are, those names mean something."

"Pinto means spotted," cut in John from the other side of her.

Mary laughed at him and leaned on his shoulder. "That is the only one I do know."

"Some of them are pretty apt to be Indian, but some of them are Spanish names. For instance, that two year old black with the gray dapples showing." He indicated one close by. "They are called *rabicano*. And I know that is Spanish. One of these days, that one will make a fine saddle animal." He turned away from the corral gate now, all three walking house ward. "Quite a bunch of Spanish cowboys coming up with the long horns from Texas. Some years back, they had saddle horses of Arabian stock. I rather think that was where those names came from."

"Did the Spanish cowboys, or vaqueros, stay in these hills?" Mary wondered if she would get to see one.

"No, they drifted south again. Guess they didn't like the cold winters here any better than the longhorns did." Kirt opened the yard gate to a perfectly barren yard, graced only by a mammoth lilac bush just bursting into bloom. The top most branches were higher than the house.

"You mean the long horn cattle wouldn't stay?" Mary was curious.

"Oh, they stayed alright. 'Til they drowned or froze to death." To Mary's questioning look, he explained, "See, up to about 1888, I believe it was, quite a lot of those cattle had been brought into these hills. Most of them were wintered down along Snake River where the Bruneau runs into it. Used to be lots of tall grass there. No one thought of raising hay or feeding their stock. That was the year of the worst storms known in the history of this state. There was deep snow and the rivers froze over. The cattle, and horses too, would just drift with the storm. Horses froze to death standing up. The cattle would bunch up in the lee of the river banks until they would break through the ice. Thousands of them drowned in a short while."

"My, what an awful loss that must have been," voiced Mary as they entered the house.

"It was. Just about wiped out several cattle outfits." He placed chairs for them. "Make yourselves at home. I'll start a fire." He rattled the stove lids back on the rusty looking cook stove. "I see she's burned down to a few coals." Carefully, he raked these together, broke off a few small pieces of wood here and there from the uneven wood piled high in the wood box. Back on went the lids and in no time, the fire started off with a snap.

None of this was lost on Mary. "Would you please tell me what kind of wood you burn? It must be good—it burns so readily."

"Mahogany," Kirt answered while he scooped potatoes into a pan from a bin built right in the kitchen wall. "I guess it's rightly called mountain mahogany. Never grows too big, but it is good wood. Only thing about it, it's so crooked it won't burn straight ashes. So hard you can't chop it once it's dry. You have to use a buck saw." He handed John the potatoes to peel. As he passed the stove, he poked two pieces of the dark wood into the firebox, and handed one to Mary to heft.

She nearly dropped it. "What heavy wood! I'm sure I never saw anything like it before."

"Lots of oil in it. Guess that's why it burns out stoves so fast. Now look at this stove of mine. It looks like it has been used forty-fifty years, yet it's not more than five since I bought it." He turned the drafts to heat the oven and slow down the roar.

"Let me peel those potatoes, or do something to help." Mary felt idle.

"No, you are the honored guest today." The man went about his work of meal-getting as handy as a woman. "John sure ought to be able to get the jackets from those spuds while I cut some ham." With that, he brought out a big wrapped cured ham; evidently a screened outdoor cooler on the north side of the house was this handy cupboard. Next went two heavy skillets onto the red topped stove, dripping melted fat into one. He commenced to slice the washed, peeled potatoes as fast as John got them ready, keeping up small talk while doing so.

To the coolest spot went the covered pan. Into the other went thick slices of ham. Mary noted how he overlapped those just like she was taught to do, with the fat edges down. Rewrapping the meat and putting it back in the cooler, he brought over a covered granite kettle. Now he washed his hands well under a drippy faucet, much like the one at her new home. Out came the molding board. Flour was scooped by handfuls into a dough pan. Not until he had hollowed out a deep well in the center of that flour did he uncover the kettle of sponge. With a few deft moves, he flipped balls of soft dough over to coat them with melted fat. The oven was red hot as the pan of biscuits was slipped in.

"You, knowing where the dishes are, John, you can put 'em on the table. We'll be ready to eat right soon." He measured coffee into the pot before washing the dough from his hands. He added the heavy silver coaster set to the table along with a small pail of honey before dishing the hot food.

Mary was ravenous, not trying to talk now. The food was so good; biscuits so light; coffee clear amber. Again she noticed the lack of butter. Neither were there the canned milk or fresh milk and cream. That seemed odd, knowing this man had hundreds of cattle. She would soon learn that the one place they did not milk cows was a cattle ranch. "I do believe these are the best tasting biscuits I've ever eaten," she complimented with her third.

"Yes," answered Kirt. "I think sourdough is the best bread."

"You call this sourdough bread too?" questioned Mary. "It isn't one bit like the bread Tim makes and calls it by the same name."

Loud laughter came from John. Kirt smiled. "That is the richest joke yet." John could not talk for laughing.

"Stop your laughing and tell me the joke so I can laugh with you."

John patted her hand. "That is the best one yet. You see, Kirt here, is noted for making the best bread in this country, while Tim is noted for making the poorest."

"I can well believe that," smiled Mary, "having sampled both kinds."

"For the life of me, I can't understand why some men persist in spoiling good bread. It's just a waste, I say," Kirt complained.

"Would you mind telling me what the secret is to making it good instead of poor?"

"No special secret I know of. There may be as many different ideas on the subject as there are bread makers. Each one seems to have a new twist. Some make their dough so stiff they never can get the soda mixed through it. Others go the other extreme and leave the dough so thin it runs out of the bucket. Wastes a lot. And besides, when you have to mix in a lot of fresh flour as you make bread, it never is going to be as light unless you let it stand quite awhile before it is baked."

"You speak of dough. Do you mean the sponge you had in the kettle?"

"Yes. It's called dough, or starter. Remember, you always want to save some back to raise the next batch you stir up. Some guys never seem to learn even that. They'll use nearly all the dough and wonder why the next batch isn't light. Summer time you need to keep it where it's fairly cool. Winter time, you'll want it where it won't be getting chilled."

"That sounds just like the starter we used for buckwheat cakes in winter time in Illinois," Mary told him.

"I wouldn't know about that, but I'll show you right now how you stir it up so it will be ready for the next baking. He dumped part of the flour remaining in the pan into the kettle, added a cup of cold water and beat it vigorously a moment while Mary looked on.

"And that is all you add to it now? What about when you make up the bread?"

"That is all I put in now. Some think canned milk and sugar makes it better. All I could ever see it did was to make the dough sour the faster. You noticed how I handled the dough, making it into bread? Keep it soft; don't work in a bit more flour than you have to. The salt and soda goes in easier. You, being used to baking, will know it takes but a mighty little soda to do the trick."

"You don't add any baking powder?" Mary was asking this innocently, not knowing this was one thing sourdoughers never admitted using.

"No need to if your dough is as light as it should be come time to bake."

"I do thank you for all this information. When I can make sourdough bread half as good as yours, I hope you will come and eat dinner with us."

Chapter Ten

"I BEGAN TO THINK I never would pry you away from talking to Kirt," John bantered as soon as they were out of hearing distance. "He'd keep talking 'til night if we'd of stayed." John was in a hurry to be home and to work. His long legs were striding along, with Mary nearly at a trot to keep up with him.

"He really is interesting to talk to. One learns so much from old-timers like him. How old a man would you say he is?"

"Hard telling." John was not thinking along that line right now.

"Looks like a man of sixty nearly, but he can't possibly be if his parents settled here in the fifties, and he said his mother planted out that lilac bush the year he was born." Mary walked fast for awhile. "I wish he had not been so generous with these flowers. They are getting heavy."

"Here, give 'em to me." John stopped short to take the huge armload of fragrant branches from her, and her light jacket she carried instead of wearing. Wrapping the bundle in the jacket and tying them with the sleeves, he now flung it over his shoulder, holding only the cuff with one hand.

"I can walk so much easier now," giggled Mary. She felt so free that she stooped and plucked a blue flower close to the wheel track. "Hey, this is wild iris making the whole place look blue. We children in the east called them flags." Even that slight pause made her trot faster to catch up with John. She slipped her hand into his free one, thinking that might slow him in his walk. Once through the gate and on the steep upgrade, he did notice her laboring breath.

"Walking too fast for you?" He was puzzled over her dropping to the ground exhausted. "I forget you are not used to hiking in this higher air."

"You–don't–have–to–run, do you?" Mary was still out of breath.

A smile played about his mouth as he sat down beside her. "I wasn't running, but guess you must have been keeping up with me. Sorry. You'll have to call a halt to me. When I get my mind on the work in the drift, I forget everything but the need to get at it."

"Looking back from here, I can see it all has been uphill."

Mary took a last look over the Kirtland ranch. "Do you think he would come to dinner sometime if we sent him word?"

"Hard telling. He might though. You must have made quite a hit with Kirt. I never heard tell of him giving anything away before, and he gave you all these lilacs."

"That is hardly fair, John Marcus," she scolded. "He loaned you his team for that trip down to the Flats and back and didn't expect any pay for it. I think that was very generous."

"Maybe so. Most people think he's stingy when it comes to money. I think myself, one couldn't borrow a dollar off him if you had half this state for security." That was as near as John ever came to saying he had tried to borrow money from Kirtland and failed.

"If one had even one hundredth part of that much, they would not need to borrow. Maybe he looks at it that way. I know I don't like this idea of borrowing money. One just has to work that much harder to pay it back." Some of John's talk was not lost on her, but she had no intention of interfering in his and Tim's business. Letting him help her to her feet, and feeling so much better for the rest, "You and I are young and able to make our way in this world. We don't want to start out saddled with any big debt."

John kept silent. He could not spoil the beginning of their life together by telling Mary they would not even be married now if he had not borrowed to make this year's payment on the place, as well as to pay for the ring on her finger and the suit of clothes he wore that day. He was still peeved over not being able to make that $40 to include a new hat for himself.

"I'm sure I can walk up this steep road if I walk," Mary laughed. "And don't try running. I'll not talk. I believe that will help. Will we rest for a little while at the top?"

John grinned at her, reminding her she said she would not talk, and the next breath asking a question. "Now if you can hold your nose so you can stand to walk close beside the stream, we won't have all this uphill and downhill. That would be just a waterfall grade."

"Let's try it." Mary panted from the top of that little ridge, for she could see many more just like this one ahead to climb if they kept to the road. "I'm going to try to keep my shoes from getting wet in that water. Mr. Kirtland might be right about it spoiling shoe leather." Going downhill was so much easier, she needed to watch her step going through the scrub brush to the creek. "Now look at that path on the other side of the stream." Mary was disgruntled over none on that side.

"Hang on," John commanded as he made the descent down the embankment and balanced her on his shoulder the next second. "Now your nice new shoes didn't get wet," he teased as he let her down. The short distance was not even telling on his wind. As they started up the stream, only Mary's hand tugging on his slowed his long strides. In some places, there was a fair path through the brush; then crumbling banks made them take to the whitened rocky edge again.

"This is much better," she said once, then she saved her breath. Even a waterfall grade can be a climb in places if the fall is several hundred feet to the mile. Mary had no intentions of detaining his hurry more than need be. For that reason, she did not talk until they came to their fence. The respite, while John opened the gate, was welcomed with a comment, "Mr. Kirtland seemed so surprised when I told him we had a milk cow." She was wondering how Roany was fairing.

"No more surprised than I was this morning." John did not sound pleased.

"That was a funny story he told about how that family down near Reynolds got their start in cattle," Mary laughed a bit in disbelief. "Do you think he meant it for the truth?"

"Guess so. I never heard of anyone saying Kirt was given to tall tales." He had the gate closed now. "Seems to me, I've heard that yarn told for the truth before."

"But for them to start out with just the one cow and in a few years to wind up with a couple of dozen head just because the cow would go steal another cow's calf the minute they shut hers away from her?" Mary shook her head. "I expect there are cows like that, but I've never seen one. She scanned the arable land as they walked. "Do you know, I think Mr. Kirtland is right when he said this field would raise enough hay to feed our cow. You notice I said field instead of meadow?" She was trying to tease now.

"Thanks to Mr. Kirt, I learned that meadows are those that are sodded so they can leave the water to run on them 'til near hay-cutting time." She was getting no conversation out of John. "Ranching up here in the hills is some different than down on the Flats. There, if the water was left running that way, great holes would be washed out, or boggy places would appear. I am still laughing over the reason Mr. Kirt gave about why he didn't want a ranch down on the Flats—saying, he would *never be working the same ground twice—what the wind didn't blow away, the irrigation would wash away.* John, what are those mounds of odd colored dirt along the edge of this field?"

"Those are the tailings that were left when the mill closed down. Remember me telling you about Mr. Mills, the man who first owned this place? He was the one that built the tailings mill across the creek."

"Is that what those big rusting smoke stacks belong to?" Mary cut in.

"That's it. When he died, they just naturally closed down for awhile. About that time, the mills at DeLamar commenced to use the cyanide in their processing, so there was no more tailings coming down stream that was worth working over."

"I'm not sure I understand what you mean when you talk about tailings."

"It's the leavings—the sediment that the fine gold washes away in. Come. We'll walk by those slump ponds and you can see what I mean."

All Mary could see when they reached that side of the field were shallow depressions in the ground, some square, others oblong. All were half filled with dead weeds among the new green. "Are these low places what you call slump ponds, and why?"

"They were dug much deeper than they look now, of course. It was into these places they turned the stream until they were full. Then as soon as the water evaporated, they shoveled up the tailings into those heaps and worked it over at the mill." He pointed to the broken wooden framework. "That was the conveyer they used to carry it to the mill—sort of an endless belt business."

"And does this have gold in it now?" Mary kicked at one of the mounds.

"Sure it does. Enough if a man worked hard, he could pan out $5 a day."

"Then why don't you do just that, John? You could be making some money while you were getting this off the field, so it will grow more hay for our cow."

For an instant, John was angry. Then he caught her to him,

and roughed her cheek with his hand. "Who wants to be bothered with a cow or the growing of hay? This isn't a ranch. It's mining ground. Besides, these tailings don't belong to us. I tried to buy 'em when we bargained for the place. In fact, I thought I could talk the heirs into selling 'em, but they wanted $5,000, and most of that in cash. As soon as we get that drift opened up better, we'll be making more than any old $5,000. Then we'll be long gone from here. He hugged her, then started on toward the barnyard. "It will be sunny California for us."

Mary made for the cow the first thing, tying her in a different spot. *I think it is lucky for this family that one of us is practical,* Mary told herself while watching John tarry in the yard just long enough to get a drink from the hydrant before hurrying toward the tunnel. Now her own feet were hurrying to go see how the chickens were faring. They needed more water. This she gave them, spying two fresh laid eggs in a nest, and another rolling about in the crate as she moved it.

"Three eggs!" She washed the one from the crate very careful like. "I can see a very different breakfast for this household than beans." She was still amused over that, little guessing there would be many a morning when she would be glad to have beans.

The house was cool, but it was also gloomy after the bright sun, so she flung open the doors, the better to see what she was going to find in the way of food to cook her first meal in this new home of hers. *This range, being so big, I bet it will take a long time to get hot. I'd better start a fire as soon as I look over the supplies. Then I want to go upstairs and at least peek into those rooms.* Mary was planning while looking over the shelves of the cellar. There seemed no food kept here at all.

With a stub of candle lit, she made the rounds of the dark pantry: a parttial sack of flour, dry brown beans, rice, coffee, and half a slab of bacon; a small amount of rolled oats in a sack. A cheap grade of baking powder was tucked well out of sight, with only a few spoonfuls remaining in the can. The package of soda and salt sack were handy beside the flour. No sugar or shortening did she find here, as they were on the long shelf in the kitchen. A nice red can held the sugar; the lard pail contained bacon drippings.

Four o'clock now. That means we will have to have rice for supper. She feared beans would scarcely cook in two hours. *I fail to see any raisins, so it will be just plain rice.* That was not worrying her, but the lack of soap was. *I want to scrub that table right off before I commence any cooking.* Only the tiny slivers of hand soap could she find, and no scrub brush. *Oh, but there is going to be soap aplenty tomorrow,* she told herself as she brought out nearly a full can of lye from below the wooden sink. *I'm sure I haven't forgotten how Mother made all that nice hard white soap last fall from all that stale fat we found left in the house.* In her mind, she estimated how many pounds of grease there must be in those pails.

Oh, but here is something that will cook quickly. She brought to light two cans of tomatoes—one she put back; the other she set up in sight.

I remember now, there are directions right on this can of lye on how to make soap. She was busy with her reading when a thought came to her. *It says here any stale fat with salt in it should be boiled up in water first to get the salt out of it, cooled, then skimmed off. I'd better do that the very first thing and let it set overnight where it is cool.* She stopped short for a second. *Some of that fat is rancid and won't smell very good. But I have to have soap to make things clean around here.* So the first thing she put on the new hot stove were the pails of grease to melt so she could strain it into the dishpan of hot water.

While they were melting, she dashed up the steep dusty stairs. *My, what nice big roomy bedrooms all four of them are.* She pummeled the mattresses on all three beds. *I do believe any one of these is much better than the mattress we have on our bed.* She flew back down to the kitchen, sure there would be shifting about of mattresses very soon.

Blithely, she hummed while doing the disagreeable work first, carrying the awkward pan of hot fat and water to the shed that opened off the kitchen. *Now I hope the odor will be gone by the time I have supper cooked and the two men get here.* She found the rice very dirty. It took several washings before it suited her. Spreading clean papers over that grimy table, she proceeded to slice bacon and assemble things for biscuits. *Tim or John sure know how to sharpen knives.* It was a joy to use them. *I will need to fry that bacon a little while beforehand to have fresh shortening for these,* she told herself as she sifted flour, salt and baking powder together.

She hadn't found anything that resembled a kettle of sponge or sourdough. *Not sure I would dare try making them, had I located it.* She was just as well pleased to be making biscuits with baking powder. These she patted out on paper and cut them out with a small tumbler. Molding board and rolling pin showed no signs of being used for a long while. *They are needing a good washing first,* was her way of putting it.

Mary added a few broken pieces of bread from their lunch box to the tomatoes, which were simmering on the back of the stove. At odd moments, the table had been set. Her first thought had been to use the dining room and that big table. The table cloth she had unpacked would not cover that sized table. *I don't want to scare those two off my first meal.* The red checkered cloth gave the kitchen a homey look. A single spray of lilacs in a low vase graced the center. A loaf of nut cake and part of a pat of butter came from the lunch box too. The small jar of pear preserves she emptied into a fancy compote dish. "Supper is already to be dished," she called to the men as they came in. "I'll have it on the table by the time you are washed."

The first dampening of her spirits came when Tim refused one of her dainty biscuits. "I don't eat poison when I know it," he told her with a sly grin. To Mary's puzzled look, he asked, "That bread is made with baking powder, isn't it?" When she nodded that it was, he explained, "Some people that stuff don't seem to bother. They eat it all the time. But to me, it's all the same as poison." Without another word, he got up from the table and found two dried out sourdough biscuits. These he dipped in his coffee to be able to eat them. When first the rice was passed, he set it down without taking any. Seeing John flood his rice with rich cream, he changed his mind. "Never was much of a Chink, but with honest-to-God cream, it ought to taste pretty good." He then ate rice with a relish.

To Mary's asking if he would care for a dish of tomatoes, he shook his head. She then asked him if he ate tomatoes in any form.

"About the only thing I've found 'em good for is to season beans, and to clean a frying pan."

"To clean a frying pan with? I don't understand." Mary was baffled.

"Haven't you ever noticed how bright a frying pan will look

after you've cooked tomatoes in it?"

Mary stayed the angry retort on the tip of her tongue. She was determined not to quarrel with anyone in her new home. Not until she saw his funny grin did she lose the desire to tell him she cooked tomatoes in something more suitable than an iron frying pan.

John did full justice to her supper, finishing off his meal with another biscuit, butter and preserves. Tim dished himself some of the rich sweet fruit, spooning sugar over it, then covering it with rich cream. Mary dared not look up for fear of laughing while this was going on. Cutting the loaf of nut cake, she passed it first to Tim and then to John.

"I'm full already." John patted his lean stomach. "I know that cake is good—maybe I'll eat some before I go to bed, but biscuits and jam is where I shine. I bet I ate a dozen of your little biscuits."

"In that case, I'll have to eat your slice," Tim grinned, helping himself to more cake. Then he reached for the coffee pot, draining it of the last drop. "I have to have my caffeine. The weaker the brew, the more I have to drink."

Mary could safely laugh at that. "A gentle hint the coffee was not strong enough, I would say. I'll let one of you two make the coffee from now on. I so seldom drink it, I'm not at all sure I would get it the right strength." She was beginning to see through Tim's contrary talk. "Will you please tell me if it is better to soak those dry beans overnight before cooking them?"

"If you expect 'em to be done by noon, you better," was Tim's answer.

"Does it take that long to cook those kinds of beans?"

"It does up here. For every thousand feet above sea level, you have to add an extra hour," he informed her, pretending to swipe the last slice of cake that was cut.

"You just go ahead and eat that slice." Mary tumbled it to his plate, "and I can slice more if you wish." She saw his hand rise in protest, so she carefully wrapped up the cake while conversing. "I found three eggs, so that means bacon and eggs for breakfast. Did John tell you we found a crate of nice hens just inside the barn door?" she asked Tim. Seeing his surprise, countered, "So that rules out the thought that the cow was brought last evening."

"Yup, it does that. Of course, I don't lay awake listening for prowlers about the place." Another grin. "And besides, this house is pretty snug built. Be damned cold if it wasn't. A lot can take place on the outside, and you never hear it in here if the doors are shut." He was stacking the dishes ready to wash them when he noticed their fragile look. "I don't know about washing these. Afraid I might break 'em."

"Never mind about the dishes. I can easily wash them as soon as I'm through milking, but there is something I'm wanting you to do, and that is to show me how to mix up that sourdough sponge; and where you keep it."

"Nothing to mixing it up," Tim told her as he reached just inside the pantry doorway. "About the coolest place I know of, in that corner. Sorta hidden there for sure. All you have to do is add flour and water." He lifted the cover and the sponge was nearly to the top. "No need to mix more. Plenty here for morning, not using it tonight. Might be a good idea to put it out of doors for the night—she won't be getting too sour then." He put back the cover and hung the kettle from a stout spike outside the kitchen door.

Mary hurried through the milking, petting and rubbing the cow but a second. "You are not going to be tied up for very long, Roany-cow. I'm going to make sure that fence is up tomorrow so you won't get to that poison water." She had been relieved when Mr. Kirtland said that stock that were used to the stream, and know where to find good water, seldom drank the murky stuff. She just wouldn't take any chances.

In the privacy of their own room this night, Mary asked, "What hour do you have breakfast, and what do you generally eat?"

"Oh, Tim is always up with the birds," was John's answer.

"I mean, what do you generally cook for that meal?"

"Anything that is handy." John never cooked if he could find someone else that would do it.

"Do you have beans?"

"Not always, but if they're cooked, Tim heats 'em up."

"There being no beans cooked, would you eat rolled oats? That seems to be the only cereal I found."

"Hard telling if Tim will eat it or not, but with cream, that would taste good. You cook it any way you want to. Don't you pay any attention to all Tim says. A lot of his talk is just for fun. He is notional about his eating, but he is so doggone good every other way, there isn't a mean hair on his head. He never holds a grudge, and he'd give a friend the shirt off his back."

"I believe he would at that," Mary stated, "but tell me why he thinks anything made with baking powder is poison."

"That is just one of his queer notions. I think it's because he likes sourdough bread better."

"That nut cake was made with baking powder, and he ate three slices," Mary chuckled.

"And you'll see that it won't hurt him a bit," cut in John. "I've seen him eat things raised with baking powder before, and it never hurt him—as long as he don't know it. That is why I say it's just one of his funny ideas.

Mary chuckled again as she snuggled down in bed. "The cake might not hurt him, but I should think those sweet preserves would."

"What was wrong with them? I thought it extra good."

"It is good, but I know of nothing more rich and sweet than pear preserves. Did you notice how Tim piled the sugar on top of his dish? And then rich cream over it all?"

"I didn't happen to notice that," John laughed. "I bet Tim never knew the difference—that it wasn't dried fruit cooked without sugar. That might be one joke Tim would not grin about."

"You needn't worry about me telling him about it," confided Mary. "I'm just going to learn how to make sourdough bread so good that he'll have to praise it. And I will never tell him when I use *poison*."

Chapter Eleven

"OH MY, OH MY, what sad looking biscuits," lamented Mary as she stooped to take the pan from the oven. "Here I've practiced five days on making this kind of bread, and these are the worst yet." She continued to pile them on a plate. "But the saddest part is we have to eat them, for there is no other bread."

"They are alright," stated Tim with vigor as soon as Mary placed the plate in the middle of the table. He helped himself to one, split it apart and slapped on some of the fresh churned butter. "They taste good, no matter how they look. Can't anyone make 'em lighter than these, unless they use *poison* in 'em."

"Those Mr. Kirtland made that day were much lighter," defended Mary.

"And do you know something?" Tim speared another flattened biscuit. "I've heard more than one of Kirtland's hay men say he uses poison in 'em. Of course, he never admits it, but it's like one fellow said, there is a hell of a lot of empty baking powder cans about the place for a guy that never uses the stuff."

Mary had no intention of pursuing that subject further. "John, someone must go to DeLamar for groceries. We are just about out of everything to eat. And I want some yeast cakes. Then this bread question will be solved, for I know how to make good light bread."

"Never cared for the stuff myself," Tim said with a grin. "My old mother sorta bragged that she never baked light bread in her life."

"Then you must have been reared in the south." Mary had wondered what part of the States Tim had called home, for he'd never said.

"Just over the Mason Dixon line."

"How would buttermilk biscuits do? They are made with soda instead of *poison*. I'm sure I know how to make those."

"Now you're talking," beamed Tim, filling his plate with beans and cottage cheese. "Buttermilk bread is the real thing. Sourdough is just a make-shift when one doesn't have milk."

"We have the milk, alright." Mary's voice took on a determined ring. "But there is mighty little else in the food line: Flour for two more meals; coffee for only one more pot, but I guess you know that. No more beans or canned tomatoes. The last of the sugar went into this custard." She was serving this very carefully to not break it up. She wanted some kind of answer from John.

"Why, all you have to do is to send your order up by the first timber hauler that stops for water or passes toward town. They come back empty. No trouble to them to haul it down." John went on eating as if the getting of food was all settled—nothing to worry about.

"Do you realize your wife might not know which store to write out the order to?"

"Those haulers know. We have sent up by them before. There really is only one store in DeLamar—the company store. That other one in Lower Town is the junkiest looking place, I wouldn't buy anything from them on a bet." Never would John Marcus say he had been refused credit there.

Mary was busy thinking while the two finished their meal. She didn't like the idea of asking strangers to do her shopping for her. Nor did she know for sure where she would find a good milk pail. "If you two are so busy you cannot go, what's to hinder me going? Surely I wouldn't get lost. It didn't seem a very large town when we came through it that night."

Tim snorted, "You sure can't get lost in DeLamar. There is only two roads in the place. One runs uphill. T'other runs down."

"I think I'll go this afternoon. I'll have to have one of those haulers bring down the heavy groceries. If I can't get lost, there is nothing to be afraid of."

"You better watch out for those Cousin-jacks that infect that camp," Tim told her as he left the table.

"Now just what are Cousin-jacks? I have heard both you men mention them, and I want to know what to look out for." She looked toward John, but he only grinned. This being Tim's joke, he didn't intend to spoil it.

"I know I'm green, a tender foot and all that, but I want to know what they are—if they are something to be afraid of. If you two wise guys won't tell me, I'll have to stop the first person I meet and ask them." She was thinking Cousin-jacks might be some harmless bird. She had heard tell of a bird called a whiskey-jack.

"You be sure and do that." Tim was enjoying himself. "I'd give a buck to know the answer you get," floated back as the two left for work.

Now they do think they have some joke on me. I'm not sure what a buck is, but I rather think it is money. I'll just fool those two, I'll find out the answers to those questions on my own, thought Mary as she hustled to finish her work.

The day was warm and pleasant, with only occasional dusty spots. She was enjoying this walk, not having to trot to keep pace with John's long stride. Having kept so busy cleaning and then putting in that small garden of peas, beets, carrots, spinach, radish, and lettuce, her morning had been taken up. She had not once walked this way from the house, so this was all new to her eyes. Once past the willow clumps, she could enjoy a nice smooth road. Then she realized this must be the *race track* John mentioned. Once over that fourth mile, the road was anything but smooth.

As she picked her way over the rocky point now, the unmistakable smell of sheep assailed her nostrils. She watched her step because of the loose rocks, and could see there were sheep tracks everywhere. There was a bridge ahead, and she realized this must be the sheep trail Max Thorn had told her about. It was plain that sheep had crossed this bridge, a few dead animals were left about, adding that putrid odor to the stench of the stream. She held her nose until she was across the stream and had climbed a short steep grade. The road led along a north slope, and the offending odor vanished as the road veered away from the stream.

Flowers and green shrubs abounded. The road was still damp and spongy, as if snow had clung along here until recently. This was an every year occurrence, making this mile of road impassable during the winter months and spring. *It is beautiful along here,* Mary thought. The idle machinery, left here and there rusting in the weather, was puzzling to her. *I suppose it is because it is so big and heavy, is the reason they don't move it away,* was her thought. She had seen no buildings that looked like a dwelling house until the road swung back across the creek. Ragged tents and dilapidated shanties came into view first, then tin roofed huts glinted in the sun.

It smells of cows and horses. Mary could not mistake that odor, like it could be corrals and lots of cattle, yet hardly a hoof was in sight. She was not aware that DeLamar's only dairy was just above her head, filling the niche of bench land. To have seen it, she would have needed to turn and look back after getting well past this place. This she didn't do; too many new sights were opening up ahead. True to Tim's prediction, there seemed to be only the one road. The row of false-fronted buildings that lined the wooden sidewalk seemed to be mostly saloons. On the opposite side of the road, there was only a foot path. Crowded between the foot path and the stream was a blacksmith shop, livery stable, and farther up the steep road, a butcher shop perched half over the vile water.

Mary had passed through Lower Town, only she was not aware it was so called. The noisy vibration was louder here, deafening as she rounded this point. She could look with awe at the huge red mill and its sprawled tramways against the hillside. So unpleasant was the noise that she hurried on by some distance, then turned to gaze at the scene. *Looks like some huge red dragon clinging there, but it slipped and reared its head high.* People were coming and going here, rigs passing and raising a thin sprinkle of dust. She gave the other hillsides, with their hodgepodge of homes, but a fleeting glance before continuing on her way.

The sidewalk was more even; the buildings larger. Many of them were painted, with a few window boxes of flowers in bloom. The most imposing structure held a hotel sign. The space between bluff and stream was wider here, allowing buildings on both sides of the road. Then she saw the town was coming to an end in this direction, but opening wider across the creek to the south. A short stout bridge spanned the stream; a road showed here and there. Large ricks of wood studded the depleted wood yard. To one side of that came the school house; a small church building next. Neat homes dotted the steep ground as far as she could see. Looking back to the buildings at hand, she noted the U.S. Post Office sign hung from the last one on her left. Climbing the few steps, she could see the DeLamar Company Store with the Post Office occupying one corner of the building. Into the letter slot went her fat letter. She felt better now that it was on its way to Father, Mother and Sister Annie. She asked if there was any mail, but not too disappointed when told there was none. "I hardly expected a letter this soon," she told the kindly face eyeing her.

The store proved to be larger than she expected, with well stocked shelves—not so gloomy now that she was in out of the bright sun for a moment. There were not too many customers about. A fresh faced youth came around the counter and extended his hand. "I'm Jim Burch." His smile was friendly, "and you must be Mrs. John Marcus."

Mary nodded. "I am," she told him with a shy smile, for she still was not used to the name.

"I want to be the first to welcome you to DeLamar." His handshake was hearty. "The news leaked out that John was bringing home a bride. Now seeing you, I can surely congratulate John. He is the wise one. Here's hoping you like these hills and want to stay."

"Oh, but I love the hills," Mary assured him. "I have no intention of leaving them."

"Good. Good. That is what I like to hear. Did I understand right that you also are new to this state?"

"Less than a year since we came from Illinois," she told him.

"Then we must shake hands again," this young man was beaming, "for I'm another one from the Sucker State." Soon these two were talking away like old friends. Mary was giving him her order, which he wrote down, but she chose to pick out the different items.

"This seems to be the very smoothest of milk pails," she told him after rubbing her hand over each seam. "I will take that with me. Also the scrub brush. Yes, I want soap, both toilet and laundry. I made soap the day after I arrived, but really, it's too new to use; I should let it dry. If I can borrow the use of that knife, I will cut off a small piece of this bacon to take down." The next second, she was tucking one end of the slab into the pail and then folding the wrapping paper well about the cut side. "I'm also going to take down a few of those potatoes for supper." She fitted those in. "Oh, I should carry down sugar also." She just remembered there would be none for the men's coffee. She added a one pound package of coffee to her load, and a ten pound sack of sugar.

"You're filling that pail mighty full," the dapper young clerk told her. He brought a small paper bag and poured a couple cups of sugar into that, folding down the top very neatly. "Much more than you should pack," he said as he saw her eyeing the bulky sack of rolled oats. "Here is a new kind of cereal." He handed out a small packet. "These are really samples. You take one and try it out and let me know what you think of it. I believe it is made entirely of wheat. By the way, how is John and his partner, Tim, doing in their developing work?"

Mary laughed. "You must not ask me any such questions, I'm so new to all this kind of work. I hear talks of drifts, sledges, wedges and ledges. I'm not sure what they all mean."

Jim Burch laughed with her. "Plenty of time for learning all that. It's quite a game—quite alluring and fascinating to some people." While he was talking, he was giving heed to the Post Master signaling him. "I believe Mr. Lyons at the Post Office wishes to speak to you Mrs. Marcus."

By the time Mary could walk the length of the store, several men had stepped to the office window and she needed to wait. It rather surprised her to see how much those men looked alike. Each of them medium build with dark hair, yet the bluest of eyes; pink cheeked, and as tanned as John. *These must be miners, and from their speech, they must be from England,* was her thought. As they drifted out of doors, and it was her turn at the window, she surprised herself by asking, "Are all the miners here English?"

"Pretty much all Cornish," was his answer. "Cousin-jacks, they are called here. Mrs. Marcus, I overheard you asking Jimmy for a milk pail. Now that must mean a milk cow, and wherever there is milk, there might be butter. What I wanted to learn, will you have an extra pound or two of butter that you would sell me? The wife and I are both butter eaters, or rather I should say, we are if we can get good butter."

"Why I hadn't thought of it, but I'm sure that we will have more butter than the three of us will use. And I would be glad to let you have some." She smiled, amused. "But aren't you taking a chance on ordering butter before you know if I can make good butter? My father always claimed a big percent of people don't know how."

"One glance is enough to tell me you are clean and particular, Mrs. Marcus. You making sure your milk pail was without roughness tells me that you are used to the care of milk. I'll take a chance on you making good butter. And it will be fresh. That is more than I can say for the butter finding its way here. I will gladly pay 50¢ a pound. Do you think that will be a fair price?"

"I think that will be very fair, and I promise you, I will bring you a mold of butter in a very few days. I found both a churn and butter mold at the house, and we have the nicest cool cellar for keeping milk. I never dreamed I would be so lucky." Mary was happy as she hurried home. The pail was heavy enough to make her change hands often. Now she caught sight of the dairy herd high above the road. *I'm going in the dairy business too,* she was telling herself, *but I won't interfere with you, whoever you are. I understand you sell just milk. Mine will be in the form of butter, and maybe cottage cheese. But until I can get some grain for those chickens, most of the curdled milk will have to go to them.*

She smiled to think of learning the meaning of the expression, *Cousin-jacks* so easily. If she kept her ears opened, she would learn what a *buck* was perhaps. Another smile came as she caught sight of the knobby end of a potato as she changed hands again. *My, won't it seem good to eat potatoes again. Beans may be alright, but I miss potatoes so. I must be half Irish.* Then she fell to planning on cutting the seed end of every one of those tubers when they arrived tomorrow, and spading more ground to plant them. *I could gouge out each eye and plant those,* she reminded herself, *but Father never thought they were as good as the seed end. I must think about getting these turnip, cabbage, and parsnip seeds in yet tonight if I can. At least the cabbage seed must go in.* Mary Marcus might be living in mining country, but she was planning to plant every kind of seed that would grow in the short season.

***

"My, my. Here it is September, and I haven't climbed one mountain yet." Mary laughed over that fact, while testing the green peas for doneness.

"I haven't noticed you twiddling your thumbs." Tim was drying his face and hands at the sink.

"Oh, I haven't been too idle," laughed Mary. "Just think, this is our last meal of green peas." She poured in rich cream to stretch the meager amount.

"Glad to hear that," John paused his splashing of water to say. "Now we might have some beans again." His voice sounded out of humor. Mary did laugh over that fact. She knew that John preferred beans to potatoes and all other vegetables.

"You'll get your beans and often, I fear, in the months to come. Our potato crop isn't going to amount to much. Not much more time for them to grow. A light frost covered the ground this morning. When should we be thinking about getting hay for the cow?

"What you worrying about hay for?" John was not worried and could not see why she should be. "Do you mean to tell me she's eaten all the grass around here already?"

"You know there is such a thing as preparing for winter?" Mary said lightly. She could see John was not in a happy frame of mind, and she would not add to his burdens if she could prevent so doing. She had come from DeLamar all primed with excitement over going to the Labor Day celebration, but this was a poor time to mention their going, so she would let that ride until morning.

The men were eating a leisurely breakfast. For some unexplained reason, they were not going to work this Sunday. Mary was happy over this. *It will be one day I can get a meal and not be expected to carry it over to the mouth of the tunnel.* This was so the men could eat in a hurry and lose no time from their work. When first she had planned a picnic meal, there had been no thought of having to keep it up better than two months. Carting hot food that distance was sometimes a problem, and she would need to make two trips. Picnics had lost their appeal to her. "Did you know DeLamar is planning quite a big celebration tomorrow?" she commenced.

"They generally go all out on Labor day," John told her.

"Jimmy Burch said yesterday we should by all means come. I would surely like to see one of their celebrations. Did I hear you say you would consider taking this wife of yours?"

"I can't do it this year, Honey. Haven't the money for it. Another year we hope to have plenty of *prosperity* to celebrate right." John went on eating the fresh pan cake she brought him from the griddle.

To say Mary was disappointed would be putting it mildly, this being the first place she had asked to be taken. She hurriedly pulled the hot griddle to the corner of the stove and went to milk, hiding her disappointment. Tim had given her a very penetrating look. She didn't think he saw much, so quickly had she turned her face away. She was never to know the conversation going on in the kitchen she had left.

"Of all the dam-fool men I've run across, you take the cake," Tim flung at John, still busy eating. "The only time or place that wife of yours has asked you to take her, and you turn her down."

Tim got up from the table in disgust. "I wouldn't blame her if she up and leaves you one of these fine days." He poured himself the last of the coffee and stood drinking it down before giving the next blast. "You with your dam-fool head stuck in that tunnel. You are not thinking of her at all. Can't you see she is wanting to go in the worst way? Which is only natural." His cup clattered to his saucer.

"How can I take her without the price of our meal in my pocket?" John demanded, stung into retort. He was wondering if Tim would fork over a dollar or two.

"Don't think it's any fine meal or money you haven't got that she's wanting. It would be seeing the crowd, the races, and fun." Tim quit the kitchen for his own room, coming back in working clothes.

"I thought you really meant it when you said we wouldn't work today." John was puzzled.

"Nothing to hinder me resting tomorrow, is there? I guess the good Lord can forgive us working this one Sabbath along with all the rest of those days of rest we've worked. I'm not at all sure He's going to forgive you if you don't wake up and think some of what your *frau* wants." With that, he stalked away to work. John, in work clothes, was ready to leave the west porch as Mary came from milking.

"Why, I thought you two were going to rest this one day," Mary commented.

"I thought so too, but Tim changed his mind. Wants to work today and rest tomorrow. Do you know something? If I had the price of our meal, I'd say we would go up to DeLamar to the blowout tomorrow. Did you spend all the butter money on stamps?"

"There was only the one pound yesterday," she hurried to tell him, "and I did get that all in stamps. But I can just as well fix us a lunch. I'll think up something real good," she assured him as she hurried away to strain the milk.

A good lunch means sandwiches, she was telling herself for the sixth time. *Those few young chickens are really too small to kill. I wonder if I could be lucky enough to find a sage hen or cotton tail.* She had learned to shoot the twenty-two very well, and sometimes added a rabbit or bird to their menu. She liked to hunt, but when coming back empty handed, it seemed a waste of time. *And I'm going to have to make every minute count this day to get both bread and cake baked. I can pull beets; the tops will make good greens for noon. I'll pickle some. They would go pretty good in our lunch.* On she planned, then a sudden thought made her smile. *John never once mentioned me bringing the meal over to the tunnel. I'll just pretend I expected they meant to come to the house.* She knew that would give her a bit more time, so she set forth with the rifle to see if she could find something.

Knowing by now how the sage hens always hung about the springs and water holes during the heat of the day, she circled those first. No luck. The morning was still too crisp. A young snow shoe rabbit bobbed up to look about him. *I think this must be a snow shoe,* examining the kicking animal before carrying it home. *I know it is no jack rabbit; nor is it a cotton tail. Now I do have to hurry to get this all dressed and to cool out of sight so it will be a complete surprise to both those men.*

Chapter Twelve

LABOR DAY DAWNED BRIGHT and cool. No frost this morning. Soon after sunrise, the rigs commenced rattling down the grade from the northwest on past the place and up the creek toward DeLamar. Each was filled with gaily dressed people— some singing, some shouting; the hills echoing back their merriment. "If we hurry along and get started," John stated as he pushed back from the breakfast table, "some of these rigs are bound to pick us up."

"Oh, but I prefer to walk," Mary told him, "than to be so crowded. Every one of those passing rigs has been loaded." Never the less, she hurried with her work. Their lunch was already packed in a shoe box. Tim's dinner she would leave here on the table, well covered. He had made no move to fix any snack to take with him to the tunnel, so that meant he intended to come to the house at noon.

"Climb in," called the driver of the first rig overtaking them as they left the yard gate. He saw Mary hesitate because of the already filled wagon. "Always room for one more," he said jovially. There was a shifting about in the load and a place was made ready for her on one of the seats.

Knowing she was taking someone else's place made her uncomfortable. A small girl stood in front of her, hanging onto the front seat for dear life. Mary put her arm about the thin mite to draw her to her lap. "I have a little sister about your size. Her name is Annie. Will you tell me what your name is?" She soon realized the child had no intention of sitting on her lap, nor talking either.

"She's terrible bashful," said the mother, half turning in her seat. "We don't get to see strangers more 'n twice a year maybe."

"Then you people must live further away from a town than we do." Mary wanted to be friendly, no matter how uneasy she felt.

"Ya, we live quite a ways yonder. Pa says it's more than ten miles. Our nearest neighbor is five miles distance."

Mary tried to visualize being that far away from another habitation. She did not mind the two miles distance; she could walk to town.

While the road was good, she tried to carry on a conversation with the woman, but found that hard to do, so gave up trying at

112

the first rough going. Before they neared the second bridge, rigs with unhitched teams and saddle horses lined the road. "Looks like it's going to be a pretty good size crowd," one of the standing men announced. "Guess about all of Reynolds must be here." Slowly, the wagon crept on up through Lower Town. The throng of people opened up the way for them, then seemed to fill in right behind, dust or no dust.

In Upper Town where the road forked, people en masse did not give ground. John stepped from the stalled rig and helped Mary down. "Thanks ever so much for the lift," he called loud above the noisy crowd. "Someday I hope to return the favor." This last perhaps was not heard, for the rig inched its way toward the bridge to cross over into the wood yard. Mary held tight to John's hand so as not to get separated from him in this press of people. She had no idea where he was taking her until they were on the inside ring of spectators around a large granite boulder.

Mary had noticed this gray rock there beside the road before, never guessing its purpose until now. Now she was close enough to see the innumerable drill holes. All these preliminaries for this contest interested her. Some of it she didn't understand until the signal was given. The two men who were pitted against each other in this test of skill were as far apart in looks, size and smoothness in handling the drill as any two miners could possibly be. Chris Johnson, a wiry little Cornishman, the holder of the championship the past several years, was about half the weight of Dan Rivers, a husky young giant. Both men were stripped to the waist, as were the two men with cans of water suspended from short poles. These they held above those straining arms, water dripping down through punched holes.

The very tenseness of the crowd told of the interest. Also it spelled out the large wagers that were made on the outcome. This year, there was an added spice to this contest. Chris Johnson was well liked; not so his new opponent. It was Mr. Lyons, the postmaster, who signaled the start, standing with watch in hand to count the minutes and call time. But it was Mr. Orchard, the mine superintendent, a very dignified Englishman, who measured those drill holes. When it became known that Dan Rivers had drilled a fraction of an inch deeper than Chris, all bedlam broke loose. Brawn and strength had triumphed this once over finesse and skill. There seemed to be more cries of dismay over Chris losing than cheers for the winner.

No real jubilance was heard, just noise of several hundred people talking and shouting at once. "Too bad it was Chris to lose," someone close beside Mary said.

"It was at that," another answered, "but one man can't remain champ forever."

"A second more and Dan's arm would have been a crackin,' I'm telling you." Mary tried to see who said that, but John was moving her through the crowd too fast.

"My, what a crowd," Mary said the instant they paused on the fringe of the mob. "I wonder where so many people come from?" John seemed not to heed her question. Strangers to her were greeting him, and insisting on his going for a drink. This he did, after assuring her he would be right back. And he did come back after half an hour of waiting, flushed of face and more jolly. This was repeated several times within the next two hours until there came a time when John failed to return. She edged more on the outside so to keep watch for him. It was no trouble to find a higher spot to look down on the milling throng, but no familiar spiffy gray hat appeared.

She still carried the box of lunch under her arm, and was getting tired and thirsty. Everyone below her seemed to be having a good time. *But I wonder just how many of them are wishing they were home.* Mary wished she was. Acquainted with so few people, there was no one to talk to. All she could do was watch the crowd. She wondered again where all these people came from in such sparsely settled hills. She had yet to learn that all of Silver City was here this year. It was an easy task to spot the rangers and cowboys among the miners, with their deeply tanned faces and different hats. The miners seemed to favor the bowler type instead of the stiff brimmed Stetson. A sprinkling of peaked hats of the variety known as ten or five gallon hats moved about. The different colored neckerchiefs below those hats were interesting. Some were as bright as any dye could make them; others were black. The white ones were fast losing that purity with sweat and dust. The day was getting warmer by the hour.

"You are just the one I've been looking for, Mrs. Marcus." Jimmy Burch was close at hand when he spoke. "The ladies' nail-driving contest is about to start. You must get in on that." He was already assisting her down to the sidewalk level and along the short distance to the store's loading platform. "I would say you should be able to hammer in more nails than the best of them!" He urged her along, took the box from under her arm, and stood holding it while someone else pressed a hammer into her right hand and nails into her left.

Mary was given no time to back out on this contest. She no more than hefted the heavy hammer to get a good grip on it when the signal was given. Much to her surprise, she came in second best. The three round, hard silver dollars soon grew warm in her hand. There seemed no one but Jimmy to be elated with her over her winnings. He, being so much in demand this day, could not stay and talk to her long.

Again, she edged back to the hillside and found a flat rock to use as a seat. Knowing now that she was hungry and with no sign of John, she opened the lunch and ate her share. The jar of milk was tepid, but she drank it anyway, trying to find water to drink. The money she so carefully tucked away in her blouse pocket seemed unreal. Never once did she think of using it to buy herself a meal. Yet she was thinking about John, disliking the thought of him having no money to pay for one. *If he shows up soon, I can surprise him by giving him part of my winnings.*

The crowd now shifted across the creek to the wood yard. No sight of John anywhere. She tagged along in the wake of the mob. Jimmy Burch had said the sack race was to be first on the program after noon. That might be fun if she could find some place from which to see it. People were climbing to the top of the ricks of wood dotting one side of the yard, while the rest went to the higher ground about the school house, church and tiers of homes.

One lone woman had perched herself a-top the first wood rick. Mary nimbly climbed to sit beside her. "I hope you don't mind my coming," she spoke first. "This being the one closest to the bridge, I can see my husband when he comes looking for me."

"I like company," the woman told her with a shrewd look. "Never turn down a chance to talk to people, sane or sober." She cackled a humorous, but not pleasant laugh. "You must be new to DeLamar. Can't remember seeing you before."

"Oh, I've lived below here at Wagontown for three months now."

"Then you must be John Marcus' wife. I heard he got married." She gave Mary another appraising look. "They tell me it isn't proper to congratulate the woman on marrying. It's the men you say that to. I doubt very many women want to be congratulated on hooking up with some of the selfish mortals anyway. They are pretty much all cut from the same pattern. Some have it over others in looks. Some are born with more sense than dollars." Another disagreeable laugh at her own joke. "I must say, you picked one with plenty of good looks. Here's hoping he has some sense too."

Mary was sorry she had climbed up here or spoken to this woman. She did not like her stare or anything about her, yet was puzzled as to why. The small dumpy woman was dressed in a loose other-Hubbard dress. The material was the very finest. Her iron grey hair was pulled to the top of her head in an unbecoming knot. *I just won't think about her. I'm up here to see the sack race,* Mary told herself, and looked to where half a dozen men lined up, half enveloped in loose gunnysacks.

Mary knew none of the contenders, but it was laughable to see their funny hobbling antics. Soon after that, many men came dragging out the fire hoses. The water fight was a fierce wet and cold battle while it lasted. Not for long could either side stand up to that blast of icy water. The slanting ground was running rivulets of muddy water in no time.

After the jumping and pole vaulting contest came the miller and the chimney sweep. This was slow getting under way. At last, two men strode out of the knot of men, each carrying a sack at arm's length. Very carefully, they managed these sacks until they neared the long smooth pole suspended between two stout posts, also peeled. Other hands held the sacks while the two men shimmied up the posts. Once seated on the pole several feet above the ground, they inched their way along toward the center, sack at the ready. One of the contestants was much smaller than the other. The woman beside her was pointing him out to her. "That Ted Sweeney is as nimble as they come. But he, with that sack of soot, and no weight to it, will be no match for George Hambly should that big ox get a good swipe at him."

Instead of the crowd being tense with excitement, they were shouting at the top of their lungs. With each swing of the sacks, the roar of laughter was deafening. Back and forth the length of the pole, those two fought. Each had a generous sprinkling of flour and soot until they were a blotched gray mask. Hambly seemed not to mind the slaps of the soot sack, it never quite landing in his face. He was only waiting for a good swing at Sweeney, but that acrobat was never where he expected him to be. He could round that slippery pole out of harm's way so very easily. His blackened sack was limp, with not much soot left. Hambly, crowding him close, at last got his chance. It was Sweeney's leg over the pole as he rounded it. That took the force of that swing, breaking the sack of flour. Sweeney seemed to float to the ground in the gray cloud.

Mary found herself laughing until tears rolled down her cheeks.

"Dumb fools," grumbled the woman beside her. "Work like dogs every day in the year but Labor Day, and work ten times harder on this day at their celebrating."

Mary made no reply. The crowd now surged back across the bridge and she could see they were lining both sides of the road through the town. Men on horseback appeared, pressing back the crowd, leaving the road clear. "I thought the race track was down close to Wagontown," Mary surprised herself by saying.

"It is. They always use it if there are real race horses. This is just a saddle horse race." A shrill female voice could be heard above all the noise. "There is Jean Keller again on Bailey. I expect she'll win; she always does."

Mary thought the string of curses and rough talk came from one of the riders, and surely there was no woman or girl among those. She had yet to learn that Jean Keller always dressed as a man, and could out curse the best of them if she was riled. And this must be one of those times. Mary commenced to climb down from her tall perch, not that she expected to get any better view. Her head was beginning to ache and she concluded it would be near supper time by the time she reached home if she started now. There was no use looking for John in this jam. She wondered if she could possibly squeeze along the creek's edge, past those people. This she found she could do without getting her feet too damp. *There doesn't seem to be much cyanide on these rocks above the mill,* she was thinking to herself as she picked her way down stream, climbing back up the steep bank to the road before reaching the butcher shop.

It was odd for it to be so still along here—no rock crusher vibrating the ground and air with its din. It took long minutes for her to worm her way through the press of people between here and the end of Lower Town. Half the crowd was here to see the finish of the race. That didn't interest Mary at the moment, but she heard again that same shrill voice, a tone of triumph edging it louder. *Sounds like Jean Keller, whoever she is, has won.* Now being free of the crowd, Mary could make good time on her trek home.

Tim was just finishing his meal, sipping the last cup of coffee as she came in. "Do you mean to tell me you lost John in the big city of gold?" was his greeting.

"I either lost him or he lost me in that crowd. I'm still wondering where all the people came from. Instead of hanging around looking for him until dark, I thought I'd be wise once and come on home. He'll surely guess that is what I would do." She was tying on a big apron. "I'll go feed the chickens, then I might eat some supper before I milk."

"I fed those biddies some of that curded milk. Is that what you use?"

"Yes, that is what I feed them. It makes pretty good feed when you have no grain."

"I didn't see anything else, so took a chance on it."

"Thank you, Tim. You are always so thoughtful. I'm not too hungry." She considered the rest of the lunch in the shoe box, but pushed it aside and fixed a bowl of bread and milk. While eating that, she re-read the letter from her mother she had gotten this day. "Mother writes that Father is now cutting the third cutting of hay, and he's wishing they had some way of getting a few ton of hay up here to us for the cow this winter." Mary was refolding the letter. "I wish it were easy to do. Hay isn't selling for very much as yet down on the Flats."

Tim said nothing, picked up his dishes and washed them under the faucet. Putting the food away, she remarked, "Mother is busy drying fruit and sweet corn. Not having too many jars to can all she wants, she's drying it. She even hinted that she would be sending us some. We as a family like dried corn—have you ever eaten it?"

"Can't say that I ever have," Tim told her, putting away the last dish.

"It really is pretty good, but it is like dried beans. It takes lots of soaking and long cooking." She soon realized Tim was not much interested in what she was saying and she didn't care about talking either, so she pulled an arm full of turnips that were warty. These she took to the cow as she went to milk. When she came back to the house, Tim was nowhere in sight. She knew he could have gone to his room and to bed, but he was not in the habit of retiring this early, so she guessed he had headed for DeLamar.

Mary didn't feel like reading this evening, so did not light the lamp and soon made ready for bed. Then she found she couldn't go to sleep without John beside her. The bed seemed vast and unfamiliar, but she did rest, and sleep overtook her near midnight, only to be rudely awakened as Tim helped John's unsteady steps along the front walk and into the house. "Can you make it now on your own?" Tim asked.

John's response did not sound natural, but he made it into the bedroom well enough; even got most of his clothes off and into bed.

Mary could not see this disordered spouse of hers, but there was no mistaking that odor of vomit. She knew but little about drunkenness, or the effects of alcohol. Father Williams did not drink, and she had not encountered it elsewhere. John had not drunk before. *It could be because he has had no money to spend for such,* was her first thought. There was no getting to sleep now with that stench beside her. It was she who lit the lamp and brought warm water, soap, wash cloth, and towel, and insisted that he wash and make himself clean. She did most of the bathing herself and got him into clean underwear. She carted all his soiled clothing out of doors, only to be greeted by his retching as she entered the room again. He had leaned well over the bed, so only the floor was befouled this time, but it took much scrubbing and changing of water to make it clean. Now she put down many papers. Feeling so unclean herself, she bathed and put on a fresh gown in the not-too-cold kitchen.

John snored loudly part of the time. There was no sleep the rest of the night, no matter how many sheep she counted. She built a fire at daybreak, and decided to sew after starting rolled oats to cook. When Tim made his appearance, she folded up the sewing. "Must be about light enough to see to milk; I'll do that while you make coffee and fry the bacon. There is plenty of bread for toast instead of biscuits, unless you are tired of toast."

Tim put on coffee and had the bacon done when she came

back in, but left the toast for her to make. She peeked in to see if John was still sleeping when Tim called to her. "Better haul that sleepy head out by his heels or he'll sleep all day." His loud voice awakened John as he expected it would.

John dressed and came to the table. His meal was coffee. Evidently that did not taste good from the wry face he made. "That damn beer I drank must have been half spoilt." He held his head with his hands.

Tim gave a snort of derision. "Free beer mixed in with give-away whiskey on a Labor day is bound to get spoilt. Did you keep tabs on how much of the rotgut you downed?"

John shook his head very carefully. "It wasn't the amount I drank. It was not being used to the stuff lately that throwed me for a loop."

Tim was skeptical, having heard this many times before in his checkered life. "I can still do a bit of mucking 'til noon. Do you think you'll be up to working by then?"

John answered that he thought he would, but he acted none too sure about it the way he looked. When noon rolled around and Tim came to the house for dinner, he found that John had gone back to town; he voiced his disgust.

"Oh, he hasn't gone to drink more," Mary assured Tim. "He promised me he wouldn't. He has gone to buy blasting material."

Tim, knowing that John had no money, was wondering where he made the touch, but it wasn't like him to ask any questions, so he didn't now. Silently, he was eating the meal Mary dished for him.

She was getting a bit uneasy herself before John came loping down the road. A small shot of whiskey, and caps and powder to make their work go faster in that drift, was the tonic he thrived on. "I'll be right over, Tim, just as soon as I can grab me a bit of dinner," he called out.

There was no staying miffed at John when he was optimistic as he was now, but she had been the least bit hurt when he had taken it for granted that she meant him to use those three precious dollars. She had naturally told him about winning that silly nail-driving contest. Then she tried to reason herself out of her hurt. *Why wouldn't he think it was right for him to use it? He thinks every dollar the butter brings in is for him to use. Caps, powder, or fuses, one or the other he must have.*

Mary had hardly thought this was right at first. There were many things she needed about the house, and some of them she couldn't buy at the store on credit—for instance, curtains. And she really would have liked to have saved a little bit every week for the time she might need it. Now, as the afternoon wore on and she set about cleaning and polishing her walking shoes, she could see the sole was breaking. *That means I'm going to have to have these resoled before I wear them hardly once more, or they won't be able to fix them.* From this hour, she commenced to plan.

By Friday noon, she had the churning finished, the butter wrapped and ready; only three pounds to spare, but there were four quarts of cottage cheese to take along. *I'm going to ask $.40 for those,* she was telling herself. *The wisest thing I can do is to get myself another pair of shoes and leave these to be half soled. Then I'll be fixed for the winter.* She well knew her kid shoes would not last walking in these rocks. She delivered the two molds of butter to Mr. Lyons. He also took one of the jars of cheese. Before she could move away from the window, Mr. Orchard had bought the last pound of butter and two of the cheese on Mr. Lyons' recommendation. Another man quickly paid the $.40 for the last jar.

Jimmy Burch was busy fitting shoes on another woman. Mary found a seat on a nail keg and took out Annie's letter to read. The childish printing was very well done, easy to read, and Mary was not giving it all her attention. The shrewd Cornish woman close at hand was not satisfied with the fit of the shoes. Again Jimmy climbed to bring down more pairs. At last she sounded pleased. "These are just the fit," she beamed as she stomped about. "Now tell me the size of 'em," she said, taking them off to look in one while Jimmy found the size in the other.

"These are fives, Mrs. Heer. You want to wear them or shall I wrap them up for you?"

"Oh, indeed, I'm not wanting to buy 'em. You are much too dear on your shoes. I just wanted to know what size to be sending for."

Mary dared not look toward Jimmy as he squatted there putting the scattered shoes back in their right boxes. The woman was well out of the store before she could safely keep her face straight. "I came to buy shoes, but I fear this is a poor time after you had such a session as this with one female." Her laughing eyes took in the innumerable boxes. "What is that old saying about it taking all kinds of people to make a world? There's no way I would no more send away for shoes—I want to try them on before I buy. I believe I wear a five, and I would like a walking shoe, something like this type."

Jimmy looked inside the shoe she had taken off and handed him. "We do have a good English walking shoe, something of this order. It sells for $3. I know that is about a third more than some shoes, but the sturdier built ones seem to stand up better in these rocks. Would you like to try on a pair?"

"I would like to. I need to leave these I'm wearing to have them resoled. Why, this shoe feels fine on this foot. Now if the other is as comfortable...." It was.

The next minute, Jimmy was buttoning them for her. "Do you know, Mrs. Marcus, you are a very wise woman. Mrs. Heer will send for her shoes and be paying postage half a dozen times before she is fitted."

Chapter Thirteen

TWO WEEKS PASSED BEFORE Mary again walked to DeLamar ahead of schedule, loaded down with more jars of cheese than pounds of butter. *I believe it brings in more money that way,* she was telling herself as she walked along this nice autumn day. *The amount of cream it takes to make a pound of butter will make two quarts of cheese, extra rich. There is the difference of $.30 there to pay for that curdled milk. But I must not rob those hens of their food. I wonder if I can find any cheap grain to feed them. I'll have to pretty soon—cold weather will be setting in soon.*

She had many thoughts as she hurried along, not all of them pleasant. One of the most unpleasant was John's attitude over her paying for her shoes. She could have put them on the bill, that is true, but she had not needed to buy any wearing apparel for herself until then. And disliking to buy on credit, she just naturally had paid for them. She had not yet paid for or gotten the other shoes she left at the cobblers. They were the reason for her trip this day. Last week, John had delivered the butter and cheese, and had promised to pay the $.50 and bring down her shoes. This he had not done, claiming he had forgotten about them.

I must get those shoes. They'll save the good looks of these new ones in my tramping over the hills picking chokecherries. I will not spend more than a half dollar, and maybe he will be happier over my trip up today. Her sharp eyes spied the large clusters of purple elderberries just taking on their dusty sheen of ripeness. *Now there is something I'm going to pick on my way home, if someone doesn't beat me to them.* She marked the spot well in her mind. *They'll mean a pie for supper.* Sorely she missed the fruit and fresh berries.

Just at the outskirts of Lower Town where wagons often camped, she noticed a queer mound of something nearly white at the base of a sheer rock on the hillside. *I never noticed that before. What can it be?* Stepping over to see what it could be, she found it was egg shells. Smashed eggs by the hundreds had streaked that smooth rock face and fell in this heap. *They do not smell like they were spoilt ones. Why all this waste?*

It was to Jimmy Burch that she put the question as soon as he was free to take her order. She liked Jimmy well. He was by far

123

the best clerk—always so courteous and helpful.

"You are right, Mrs. Marcus, in thinking there are hundreds of eggs wasted there. A full eleven cases were smashed." Jimmy smiled broadly at her.

"What I can't understand is why were they smashed?"

"At least six boys in this town thought it lots of fun to have a great target practice with those eggs when they found Pete Closen's wagon unguarded. He is one of the peddlers that bring in produce pretty regularly. He used to come of a Saturday, but because of those boys botherin,' he took to coming weekdays when they were in school. Only this time, they were not in school."

"But what can they do about it?" Mary was appalled at all the waste.

"Pete did something about it alright." Jimmy seemed to be happy telling this part. "I have to hand it to that Swede. His having had trouble before with that same bunch, he had them pretty well spotted as to names, and he made a round to each of their parents and told them he's suing them for the price of those cases of eggs."

"And he really made them pay for those eggs?"

"He did just that. Of course, there was quite a howdy-do over it. Most of the parents were going to prove their young hopefuls were in school at that time. The teacher and the school's daily record proved they weren't. So this mining town holds several unhappy couples right now. How many boys are eating their meals from a shelf, I haven't heard. But I do believe a few more times like that, and it should put a stop to a lot of the pranks they have pulled and have gotten away with."

"I take it they have sometimes been worse than mischievous?"

"It would be easier to tell what they won't do than what they will. They haven't as yet cost a life, but last spring they came near doing so. That was when the creek was at its highest, and that gang caught Lou, the Chinaman that does laundry, just as he came along the sidewalk where it hangs partly over the stream. They twirled the two heavy bundles of clothes he was carrying suspended from his neck yoke until he toppled over into the water. If men at the mill hadn't seen it, Lou would have drowned." Jimmy needed to leave for the next customer, but he called back humorously. "They never did find those bundles of clothes."

Mary needed to hurry home and not stay to hear any more exploits of the youth of DeLamar. She had her shoes to get and those elderberries to pick. *I'll have to half run if I'm to get a pie baked and cooled enough to eat for supper,* she was telling herself.

The month of October ushered in with a nice rain, then another frost, but the days remained bright and warm. Mary perspired freely as she hurried to the tunnel. Carrying the kettle of hot beans, the basket with dishes, bread and butter was awkward. "I'll have to go back for the rest," she called to the two men coming out of the dim opening. "You two commence eating. I'll be right back." She wanted them to be through their meal as soon as possible this day so she would have the longer half-day to go further a-field to look for Oregon grapes, chokecherries, and elderberries.

The men had eaten their first plate of beans and were dishing the second when she came toiling up the steep path with coffee pot and pudding. "My, I'll be glad when you two decide you've time enough to walk over to the house to eat your noon meal with your feet under the table like white folks again," she said in a joking manner, only she was not jesting. She poured coffee into their waiting cups.

"But think of the time you are saving us by bringing our meal over here." John was very much pleased with this arrangement. Tim said nothing.

Mary often wondered what kind of thoughts went on behind those eyes of intense blue. Mary had eaten her own dinner at the house during a few minutes wait, all except her dessert. She had not wanted to disturb that nicely browned rice custard until she served it now to all of them. Eating hers in jig time, she now poured the last of the coffee. "Will you men put your dishes in the basket and bring them when you come home tonight?" she asked, covering the bean pot and wrapping up the bread. "I'm in a hurry to get to picking chokecherries."

"What do you want to tramp the hills all day long for?" questioned John. "There isn't cherries or berries enough anywhere to pay for the shoe leather you wear out. Besides, there still might be a rattler out yet." He knew there were no snakes out this late.

"Sure we'll bring the dishes back," Tim answered when he saw that John had no intention of doing so. "Run along and pick your berries, an' no need to look out for rattlers. Any self respecting snake has hunted up his winter quarters 'ere now. They are that much smarter than we humans are."

"Seems there is a difference," Mary playfully pinched John's ear as she got to her feet. "Whether one wears out shoes looking for something to eat or just for an outing." She didn't tarry to see how John took her jest, but she heard Tim's funny snort.

Night had already fallen when the two weary men opened the west door. "I see you found some berries," was John's greeting. The fragrance of a fresh baked fruit pie filled both rooms.

"That isn't all I found." Mary was happy. "I have one big surprise for you two, and I bet a cookie, neither one of you can guess what it is." She made quite a game of the guessing. All of John's guesses were wide of the mark. Tim never guessed at all, continuing to eat his meal.

"I'm nearly full enough, so I don't care what your surprise is. Just bring on your berry pie." John was through with his guessing.

"If my nose tells me right," drooled Tim watching Mary reach for the cooling pie, "that pie is made with apples instead of berries."

"Did you go to town today instead of berrying?" John was huffed.

"I did not," Mary told him firmly while cutting the small pie in equal thirds. "I picked these apples off a tree, and not too far from home either. I know I must have passed that tree a dozen times and never once noticed it until the apples took on a yellow tinge."

"Why, there isn't orchard trees within miles of here." John was skeptical.

"I didn't say a thing about orchards or trees," laughed Mary. "I said a tree. At least that is all I could find. And it is not very big, but it had seven apples on it. It undoubtedly is a seedling, but thanks to someone dropping apple seeds along that abandoned ditch up above the race track, we can eat fresh apple pie tonight." She brought out the last slivers of cheddar cheese to eat with it, then she showed them the two lard pails full of chokecherries she had picked. "So that means more jelly as soon as we get more sugar," she explained. "John, if you will get more twenty-two cartridges as you go to DeLamar tomorrow evening, I can easily kill some cottontails or sage hens. I saw several today."

"Sage hens would be mighty poor eating this late," voiced John, not saying if he was going to town or not. Mary had already set out the cream so as to churn it in the early morning. She disliked spending her time going to town when there were still cherries and food stuff to find, but feared they would never get the cartridges if she didn't go.

Carrying in the milk the next morning, she remarked how Roany was going down on her milk. "John, just where and when are we getting the hay for the cow?" She never once questioned but what he would get some when the real need for hay came.

"I haven't the least idea. Looks like she is pretty well fed." He and Tim hurried to their work, and she rushed to put cheese to drip on the line.

Mary couldn't understand John's indifference to the cow's need. *He seems to think those few dollars the butter and cheese brought in were a godsend to buy blasting material, being how it's not possible to buy that on credit.* She continued to churn impatiently, the thud of the dasher beating time. *If this butter would come quickly, I could go to town this forenoon and have the whole half day to go berrying.* She smiled a bit over the difference of picking the wild ones here and in Illinois. *There, most berries were sweet and good to eat. Here, I've not found any that are fit to eat until they are made into pies or jelly and jam.* Then she remembered the few ripe gooseberries she had found earlier and had eaten. *That handful was good, but for the life of me, I can't see how anyone can like chokecherries to eat out of hand. But I do like the jelly made from them. Even better than elderberry and Oregon grape. And those are not bad tasting if one can make it up right quickly and not let the cooked juice stand on the berries over night.* A wry grimace came to her mouth at the thought of the bitter tasting jelly she had made the one time, being much too weary to fix the juice to drip after cooking it at night. *I will never ever do that again,* she promised herself.

The butter was long in churning, so her trip to town was after noon. At meal time, she had tried to learn for sure if John intended to go this evening. Another thing she could not understand—his not saying *yes* or *no* to such simple questions. *I suppose those cherries would not spoil if I didn't get sugar by tomorrow. But we do need some kind of fresh meat. And the only way I know to get*

*good meat is to go to that butcher shop myself and give him to
understand I want no more spoilt meat.* Mary disliked going in
that smelly place. *One reason I must remember to get those
twenty-two shells today—cottontails are plentiful. I didn't think
that last sage hen was too bad cooked in that Dutch oven. No
matter what John says, he seemed to enjoy it too.*

As the days grew shorter, Mary found herself doing her work
by lamp light, spending most daylight hours on her jaunts—none
of them to the hill tops for the view, but she visited every nook
and ravine that held shrubs and plants that might yield to her store
of filled jars and jelly glasses.

"Where's the jam?" John looked up to ask while still
buttering his bread. "Are you going to be so Scotch that you'll not
let us eat jam for supper the same as this noon? Why do you go to
all the trouble of making it if we are not to eat it?"

Mary smiled through her weariness. "You can have jelly or
jam for the morning meal as long as it lasts. That will mean about
40 breakfasts unless I can find more cherries than I have the last
few days. I made you a custard pie for noon, remember, and this
evening it's a nice prune whip. I won't let you starve for the lack
of something sweet." Another smile. No answering grin from
John, but Tim gave her one. She at first had put jelly on the table
for all three meals and was soon appalled at the amount they
would eat. At that rate, there would be none put aside for winter.
She was still hoarding those dozen jars of elderberries for pies.

This last day of October had started out nice enough. She had
stayed at home this morning to wash, but by afternoon, had
decided to go to those highest hillsides toward the north, having
caught sight of colored shrubs in several indentations. *This might
be my last day out this way,* she told herself as she bent against the
strong wind. All signs pointed to a storm brewing. She spent
much time in lea of those higher hills, finding an odd cherry tree
here and there. Stripped of most of their leaves by now, they were
hard to see at a distance, but the half dried chokecherries still
clung in a sparing number. As the afternoon waned, and she came
out to a knife-like ridge the better to climb higher, she was
surprised at the force of the wind. *Why, I can't stand upright
against it.* She buttoned her jacket up snug. *Feels like I have no
clothes on at all.* With face turned partly from the blast, her eyes
saw the bright red seepods swaying on a wild rose bush close at

hand. *I believe those could be strung like beads for Annie's doll.*

She fought her way toward the bush. It was slow work, picking those bobbing pods from the prickly stems. So intent was she on gathering them that she was startled when she heard a voice close at hand.

"I see you are gathering rosehips for jam like my mother used to." He saw she was startled, and hesitated as he came closer. "I have always claimed they make about the best jam of anything I know of in these hills. You haven't by any chance seen a small bunch of sheep straying over this way?"

"No, I haven't seen a single sheep." She had to keep her back to the wind to be able to speak. "Or stock of any kind. I wasn't out this forenoon. They could have passed then. Excuse me, but did I understand you to say these seedpods make jam?"

"They sure do—about the best to my way of thinking. Mother made lots of it when we lived on the homestead. It was high up in the hills where lots of wild roses grew."

"Do you have any idea how she made it or what she would be adding to it?" Mary knew she would not dare stay longer this day to pick more, no matter how good that kind of jam might be. Her washing was on the line and the storm was getting closer.

"Not much idea, but I know she cooked those pods before she rubbed them through a pan sieve. I doubt she had much else to add to it except sugar. Guess we are in for a storm for sure." With that, he turned and rode back with the wind helping him along.

Mary scurried downhill as fast as she dared. She was much further away than she had thought. It was all but dark before she reached the house. The lighted kitchen seemed good to enter. John was building the fire. "Oh, I thank you so much, Tim, for bringing in my clothes. All the way home, I pictured them whipping to pieces. It's a wonder I didn't fall head over heels, I came so fast when this storm came up."

"What under the sun made you go out a day like this?" John was hungry and peeved knowing supper would be delayed. "I've heard tell people from Kansas are never as happy as when the wind is blowing. Didn't know those from Illinois are the same way."

"I've seen it blow there too, but never any harder than it is doing here right now." Mary had lit the lantern. "Put two kettles on with water in them. I'll go pull those last turnips and the hill of small potatoes. They'll cook quickly." She didn't wait to hear John grumble over that delay. It was long minutes before she came back in, half frozen, and dumped the vegetables into the sink from her apron. "I couldn't keep the lantern from blowing out, so I had to get these by feel. I believe the ground is freezing right now." She washed the marble sized potatoes, and would cook them with their skins on. "If one of you want to slice the bacon while I get the peelings off these, our meal will be ready that much quicker." She was making short work of getting the young turnips cooking.

It was snowing when she went to the barn to milk while supper cooked. The storm seemed to come from the east now. Facing the storm as she headed back to the house with the milk pail and lantern was a struggle. "My, what a night." She shook the snow from her clothing in the washroom before coming in to the warmer kitchen where Tim was dishing up the food. "I pity any man or beast that has no shelter tonight." She started to say she pitied the cow with no hay in front of her this night, but refrained–John was edgy enough. To make amends, she reached down a small cup of jam. No dessert was ready except cookies.

In the morning, she opened the door to a solid wall of white. "John," she called, "you'll have to come and shovel a way out so I can get to the barn to milk." She set down the pan of peelings she had fixed for the cow, and turned to finish the meal she had put on to cook. Both men tunneled and trampled snow until she called them to come and eat. They were still only part way to the barn. Her own meal would hardly go down, worrying about the hungry cow in the barn. She wondered if the small store of corn meal and rolled oats would keep her from starving until hay could be brought down from DeLamar. *I can't see through the fast falling snow if there are enough willow leaves left to gather.* She had no idea the depth of the drifts that had piled up until she watched the men shoveling and realized it was over their heads in places.

It was Tim's hand that helped her up the steps as she came back to the house with the milk. "Take it careful on these steps. Snow is still falling so fast, not much use of trying to clear them good."

"What do you want to stay out in the barn freezing this way?" John was worried over her being gone so long.

"It isn't so cold in the barn," she told him in a quiet tone while she strained the milk. "It's really a snug barn. I'm not worried about that. What I want to know is how long will it be before they snowplow the road so we can get hay down here for the cow?"

"Might be spring before they plow her out if the company has plenty of wood and timbers, and I rather think they have—they been hauling lots."

"But the cow will starve to death in a few days." Mary was frightened.

"Why let her starve? She's in fair shape. Why not let her feed us for awhile?" John asked. Tim had left the room.

"Of course Roany has about half fed us all along, all the milk, cream, butter and cheese we can eat."

"I mean make beef of her." John was blunt. The cow meant nothing to him.

"Oh, no–not that," wailed Mary.

"So you would rather let her starve?"

"No. I don't want her to starve to death. How many days will this storm be apt to last?" She was trying to figure some way out.

"Might be another day at least, but this can go on for a week. Don't think for a minute you can get hay down here from town. Hay means cash. Have you got $25 for a ton of hay?"

Mary knew then she was licked. "It would be more merciful for you to kill her," she told him while yet in command of her voice. On through the cold dining room she went to the front hall and up the steep stairs. The one back bedroom with the chimney warming the floor was not too uncomfortable. Dejectedly, she crouched beside the rough brick, still wearing her warm jacket, so the cold was not acute. After the first flood of grief had passed, *I should have foreseen this and saved every cent the butter and cheese brought and bought hay,* she told herself, then found her mind busy figuring up how much that would have brought in. *Most weeks, it has been $3 or a bit more. That is $12 a month, and for four and a half months. That would have bought more than two tons of hay even at that price.* Another flood of tears, for she knew that amount of hay would hardly winter a cow in this cold climate. *I guess it would barely keep her alive.*

Then bitter thoughts crept in. *I wonder if John will miss that $3 a week to buy his blasting material?* She well knew what a difference it would make in their daily food. Long and bitterly she wept, feeling responsible for failing to care for the cow. She had failed Father, who had given her the cow in the first place, and went to all that trouble and expense to send her up here when first she was married. In her misery, she lost count of time and the cold. She even dozed in sheer exhaustion. The heavy tramp of boots on the stairs aroused her. As John came near her, the smell of the butchering about him, a wave of nausea assailed her.

"My God, Mary, what are you doing up here sick this way?" He was frightened by her retching. "Can't you talk to me, or tell me what's the matter with you?"

"We gotta get her down out of here," said Tim. They picked her up bodily between them and carried her down those steep steps. She was violently sick every step of the distance. "You wait now, John, 'til I spread a sheet or something over the bed before you put your end of her down."

John, not knowing what to do after getting her shoes off, attempted to take off her soiled jacket. She pushed him away. "Go wash," she managed to say. "Go change."

"Man, get away from her," thundered Tim from the doorway, pulling the baffled man out of the room. "She said go wash and change clothes. Might be the smell of the fresh blood on us that made her sick. I've heard tell of it affecting people that way." Both men stripped to their underwear in the kitchen and scrubbed up well. Tim went to his room and donned clean shirt and overalls. Back in the kitchen, he noticed John's soiled shoes. "Take off those damned shoes of yours before you go after your clean clothes," Tim said while unfastening his.

Mary lay spent and pale. No more nausea troubled her when John helped her off with her jacket. All her clothing needed to be changed. He put a gown on her and covered her up to stop her teeth from chattering. After carting the soiled clothes out to the hallway, he sat beside her, holding her hand. His callused fingers tried to find her pulse along her wrist. His awkwardness was piteous. "Don't look so scared. I'm alright now," she told him.

"But what made you sick in the first place? That's what I can't understand."

"I'm not sure that I know." Letting all the bitterness and rancor seep away, she pressed his hand against her cheek. "I guess we'd better count ourselves lucky. Some mothers-to-be are dreadfully sick every morning. And here I've never been sick once before."

"John," called Tim, "did ya learn where your wife hid the tea?"

"There is no tea," Mary said. She also could have told them she never drank tea, but did not feel like talking just now.

"Tea is supposed to be good for sick folks," muttered Tim. "What kind of a damned household is this?" He was so relieved to hear Mary speak good naturedly that he said the first thing that came to mind.

Chapter Fourteen

EARLY THE NEXT MORNING, Mary awoke to the smell of frying liver. She dared not move in her fight against nausea, speaking just enough to make John understand she was alright, but wanted no breakfast. So still did she keep, that she went back to sleep.

The bright sun, blinding in the dazzling whiteness, greeted her as she poked her head out of the west doorway. The porch was shoveled clear of snow, and walled paths led toward the barn and chicken house. The men were now headed toward their foot bridge and the tunnel with their shoveling. She reached for a coat and came out onto the steps to look about. The men caught sight of her then. "Sure is a different looking place, isn't it?" called John.

She nodded, and commenced her descent of the steps and the path to the chicken house. Tim's shout stopped her. "You get to hell back in that house!" He guessed where she was headed and remembered he had dumped the offal in the hen house.

"I am just going to see how many of those chickens lived through the storm," she told him.

"I still say get back in the house. Those biddies are okay. I've fed 'em and watered 'em. Get back where it's warm before you freeze your feet."

"There will be nothing to feed the chickens now, so I think it's better if you two will chop their heads off for me. I'll dress them out and let them freeze. They'll keep that way until we use them up." She was feeling a bit wobbly, so retraced her steps.

"How about later in the day?" called Tim. "We'll be needing plenty of boiling water you know."

By dusk, the last fowl was minus its feathers and drawn. Tim was still fussing about the washroom, cleaning up the mess he and John had made picking off the feathers. He had cursed under his breath all the time they had separated the coarse feathers from the soft ones.

Mary smiled over Tim's talk. It wasn't bothering her in the least. "I don't know how I can thank you two for doing all this work for me. The only way I know to repay you is to cut up this youngest fowl and fry it for supper." She was testing the beans while talking. "I finally came to enough to put beans on to cook this forenoon. They may be edible by the time the rest of the meal is ready."

Fried chicken, pan gravy, hot biscuits and jelly was their supper; the beans still not done. "Do you know it is just five months tonight since I first ate a meal in this kitchen?" She expected no comment, so continued. "And this is about the third time you two haven't worked over in that tunnel. How come?" She wanted to joke.

"Just too damned lazy to shovel snow coming and going yesterday," grinned Tim. "Snowed enough during the day, we'd had to work just as hard to get back to the house. That would never do."

For two weeks, Mary was house bound. The snow was getting settled and a crust to it, so she had hopes of getting out. "And here comes more snow on top of that." She was watching the big flakes sail through the air. As the men came in, they shook the lose stuff from their outer clothing in the washroom. "Lucky for us you two put in part of your time getting wood." No comment. At the table while she carved the roasted hen, she remarked, "A week from today will be Thanksgiving. I'm saving the largest hen to roast for our turkey on that day."

"You better," John told her. "I don't look for any wild one to fly over, seeing how none was ever known this far north. But a goose could do so. As soon as the new snow gets crusted, we might get out enough to get a snowshoe or two."

"Are they really as large as people say?" Mary asked.

"They are not small. Neither are they as big as a cow," Tim said in ready wit, then cursed himself for his thoughtlessness.

"I ought to know how doggone heavy they are," he hurried to say. "Last winter, that week John was down on the Fats, I shot three of 'em and packed 'em in on my back. I swore they weighed a ton before I got here with 'em. One was all I got away with in a week's time. I was hopping around here like a hare myself by then."

As neither John nor Mary took up the conversation, Tim continued after a pause. "I like grouse or pheasant the best of all. The next place I git is going to be a place where there is a grouse in every tree top and a quail under every bush."

Tim was getting restless—both John and Mary were aware of it by the little things he said. He and John worked only sporadically in the tunnel now. With no powder and caps, the work was going slower. John seemed discouraged, not liking the idea of Tim leaving. Mary was surprised he had not thought of trading off the beef for blasting material. Tim was also thinking the same thing, but said nothing about the scheme he had in his mind until he had finished the sled he was fashioning this evening.

Three pair of crudely made snowshoes were hung above the stove to dry. "There. Let her snow. Who cares," boasted Tim, rubbing his hand over the fairly smooth runners of the sled. The next morning, he tested out walking on those webs, and drawing the sled loaded with wood. He found it could be done.

"The sled don't cut in too deep, but what I can make it," he told John who was watching from the wood house. "What do you say I haul a quarter of that meat up to DeLamar and trade it off for other meat and grub? Your wife isn't eating any of that meat and you know it."

"She doesn't get sick any more when we cook it though," John hedged.

"Maybe so, but that isn't giving her grub she should eat. Remember that."

"I guess maybe that would be the best way." John did not like the idea.

` Tim was in a sweat to be on his way before John changed his mind. It was supper time before he returned with his bulkier load—a sack of flour, a slab of bacon, coffee, twenty-five pounds of rice, and a box of raisins the same weight. "Now you can have Chinese grub mixed with California Nectar," joked Tim as he carried these in and pointed to the printed label on the box of raisins reading, "California Nectar."

"How good you are, Tim," smiled Mary, "but how did you ever manage to haul all this down? If I would have known of your going up to town today, I would have had you mail a tiny package for me. I have my Christmas things to send to my folks. It would never do for Annie to not get her doll clothes by Christmas."

"Rather thoughtless of me to not mention I was going, but if tomorrow is as good a day as today was, I'll go again and can mail your package then."

The thermometer registered ten below zero the next morning. Tim made light of that, "Don't worry, I'll be warm hauling this load to town." He set out with another quarter beef. His load back this day was beans, sugar, dried prunes and apples, salt, more bacon, half a case of canned tomatoes and a dozen cans of milk wrapped up in his sheep-lined coat.

When Mary noticed this, she scolded him good. "What made you take off your coat and freeze yourself to bring down that milk?"

"I can thaw out and be damned near as good as before," Tim grinned at her, "but this milk isn't worth a tinker's dam after it freezes." He took off a mitten and set out one can of milk, another of tomatoes. "Maybe you better tote the rest of this canned stuff down to the cellar, John, where it won't freeze. It's fixing to crimp down tonight. Might hit thirty below before morning. And you and I know things will get solid right here in this kitchen when it gets that cold."

While still at the table, Mary remarked, "I've never experienced thirty below."

"Don't expect you have," Tim said between his last few bites of food. "One has to be up north or higher up in the air like we are here. I well remember once when I thought I was going to freeze to death in March walking along the lake front in Chicago. I felt like I had no clothes on at all, the wind was that cold."

"I know," admitted Mary. "It can get cold when that lake breeze hits you."

"Breeze hell! That was a gale," snorted Tim. "I'm never going to that windy city again unless it's August. It will be south for *Yours Truly*." That was as near as Tim ever suggested where he was going, but still not a word as to when he would start out.

Thanksgiving Day came, and Mary spent the early part of the day getting the half frozen hen thawed out so she could stuff it and get it to roasting. "It sure is going to make dinner late this day," Mary told the two seated men, idly talking.

No comment was heard from either one about the postponed meal, both full of breakfast yet. "I wish you were staying 'til spring, Tim," John said. "As soon as Mary is able to travel, we're liable to be on our way out too if things don't look up around here."

"When the grass is green, this pasture will look just as good as the one over the fence," Mary spoke lightly, fixing to roll out pastry for the pie.

"You might be right about that," Tim nodded to her, not replying to John's hint about his staying. His bundle of clothes, just a change, was already tied together. All he had to do was roll his two blankets in the morning. This day of feasting was as happy a day as Mary could make from their limited store.

At three, and all three hungry, she pronounced the roasted hen ready. "Sure seems odd to be learning to make sourdough bread all over again," she said while dishing the hot biscuits from the oven, "but I can't seem to keep the sponge warm enough to make good bread. It's bound to get chilled at some stage. I have tried every way but putting it in our bed."

"What are you talking about?" John made a grimace of distaste.

Mary laughed at him. "I know just how you feel about the thought of bread sponge being put in a warm bed to keep warm so it will rise. I felt the same way when first I heard about it. We had a little old English lady for a neighbor once, and that is what she did. And how those people around the country thought it was such an unclean habit—even her daughter-in-law thought it about the dirtiest trick imaginable. Those two didn't get along very well on that account." Mary now talked while carving the hen. "Child like, I liked the poor old soul, and she told me all about how she fixed that covered pan of sponge—wrapping it first with a special cloth, a worn out table cloth; then it was covered with papers, and into the warm bed it went just as soon as she could beat it up and get it wrapped in the mornings."

"Don't you try making me sleep with any pan of bread," John told her as he took his place at the table.

"Oh, she didn't sleep with it. She just put it in that warm place until the house would get warm and cozy. But if the day was a windy raw day and didn't heat up to suit her, she would heat a brick, and put that in the bed to keep it the right temperature for the second rising. Seems in England, it is often damp and cool and they haven't got stoves like we do here. Some of them even do their cooking in an open fireplace. The bake ovens are big out-of-door affairs with several families using one."

"Maybe that's why Cousin-jack lives on pasties," joked Tim.

"I'm not sure that I know what pasties are," Mary smiled. "Do you two remember when I didn't know what the expression *Cousin-jack* meant?" To their grins, she added, "And you both

138

got such a kick out of that joke. I did learn that very day that Cornishmen are called that, but I was some time learning a *buck* meant a dollar." After she had poured their coffee, she asked Tim, "Do you know what a pasty is?"

"Sort of a meat pie business. The Cousin-jack I worked with once packed one of 'em for his lunch each day. He was more apt to be a-bringin' it wrapped up and inside his shirt. Claimed that was the way they did it in the old country."

"Now that would be a fine lunch," John said in derision.

"He seemed to like it. Of course, I just as soon have two hunks of bread and a slab of meat between 'em, but their saffron cakes, or *nubbins* as they call 'em, are pretty good eatin' if one has plenty of coffee to wash 'em down."

"A guy can eat most anything if you have the coffee to go along with it," John concluded.

"I can remember the little old English lady making some small cakes. They were very, very yellow, and she put raisins or currants in them. I believe she called those saffron cakes. I liked them well, but I didn't care for the tea so black and strong. She always made it to drink as we ate those nubbins."

Dusk made the warm room shadowy before they moved away from the table. "Here it is five o'clock. We are not liable to get any supper in before bedtime. There's enough food cooked should either one of you get hungry," Mary told them as she cleared the table.

"The way I'm feeling right now," said Tim, "supper will be in the morning."

The men were astir early the next morning, eating a hearty meal of steak and sourdough hotcakes. "This chokecherry jelly sure goes good on these," Tim said as Mary came to the table. "The reason why I'm eating so much this meal, Mrs. Mary, is the fact that I know I won't be getting any such good grub as this from now on."

"Then you are going to leave soon?" There was regret in her voice.

"Yep. Just as soon as I can jiggle the rest of this coffee down in the chinks." He was standing now, pretending to shake his body. "Oh, maybe I better help John saw a cut or two of that wood first, or I might not be able to bend over to fasten on the *webs*."

With dishpan on table close to the stove, Mary was finishing up the work when Tim came in with a huge armload of wood, dumping it beside the range instead of in the wood box. "This is sure wet and sappy. You'll need dry it out some in the oven before it will even burn. But a stick of it, along with your dry stuff, will make your woodpile last longer." He laid a layer of sticks in the oven to dry. He fumbled in his pocket with an unmittened hand, bringing out a worn bill, which he placed beside her dishpan. "This isn't much, but it will take you out of here and home if..."

"No, Tim. No. You must not do that," Mary protested. "We'll manage. And remember, you're going to need every bit of money you have starting mid winter this way." She tried to put the bill in his pocket.

"Don't worry about me." He deftly put the money under the pan. "I'll get by. But you're not going to unless you wear the pants in this family. Keep 'em on, and buttoned up tight. Kick John out and make him chase down the dollars." He gave her a half salute as he put on his mitten, going on into the wash room.

Mary did not realize Tim had already left until John came in with his load of green wood. Dumping it down, he went to the wash room and then to Tim's room. "I didn't know Tim was leaving. Why didn't he say good-bye?" he asked as he came back to the kitchen.

"He didn't tell me good-bye either." One hand covered the bill as she moved the pan, slipping it to her apron pocket, then emptying the water. "I guess he doesn't like farewells. It is going to seem odd with Tim gone." She was not liking Tim leaving the money, and had not figured what to do about it. "Do you think he will write ever?"

"Never seen him write a letter the three years I've known him." John was blue and discouraged. "For the life of me, I can't see why he would start out this way. I'm sure he hasn't a cent of money. Work might be hard to find in the middle of winter."

As the day wore on, it became warmer. "It's almost comfortable out of doors," was John's verdict as he lugged in the last cut wood.

Soon, the steaming teams and shouting men came into view with a snowplow. "Just think, if Tim had waited another day, he would have had easy walking."

John went out to where they made a wide circle to turn around in the barnyard. They paused for only a moment of talk, then were on their way back to town. "Didn't you ask them in?" was Mary's question as John came in.

"Sure I asked 'em to come in. They seemed to be in a hurry to get back before dark. Some kind of big doings—dance or something tonight."

"Now if tomorrow is as nice as today, I believe I'll try walking to town, just to get out of the house."

"Another day like this," John told her, "and I'd say that fresh plowed road will be chuck-a-block full of snow again. Of course, I'm not a tenderfoot, nor a real old timer." He hung up his coat and cap.

"What has a tenderfoot or old timer got to do with it?"

"They are supposed to be the only ones that predict the weather."

"I heard it different than that," smiled Mary. "It was only *new comers* or fools that dared predict the weather." She noted John's surprised look. "I fear Tim's cussing must have been contagious."

True to John's expectation, the road was filled with new snow within two days time. "I really am not minding being snowed in," Mary informed him, "but I do hope they will have it plowed out by Christmas time so those singers will be able to come down in their sleighs. I would like to hear them sing their carols. Jimmy Burch says they have a few with very good voices. Then too, I look for Father and Mother to be sending us a box along about then." She sighed, "I just wonder what Sister Annie is busy making about now."

"If it's very much of a box, it might not get here 'til spring," was John's pessimistic comment.

The short days went fast for Mary as she kept very busy. While John was at work, she divided her time between reading and sewing on his present for Christmas—a soft warm rug with all the worn out woolen socks she had found about the place. She held it up to admire her handiwork. *Now all I have to do is bind it all around.* She glanced at the clock. *My goodness, no wonder I'm famished. Here it is past three. I will have to hurry to get it all finished before John gets home. But first, I'm going to have to eat.*

The rug was now spread beside their bed. Night was here. No plow had come to clear the road. *That means we will not hear carols sung this year,* she told herself. *I'm getting a bit worried about John. It should not take him so long to make it to town and back again.* She commenced to count the hours since he had been gone. *This being alone and worried on Christmas isn't funny.* Candle in hand, she marched to the dining room to find a book to read. *Not sure that I can keep my mind on what I read, though.*

More and more, Mary was grateful someone had left that box of books in the attic. At first she expected someone to be coming to claim them—they were all so nicely fit into a stout chest, as if overlooked. *Whoever they belong to won't mind me reading them, I'm sure.* She had unpacked them to get the heavy box downstairs, then put them back in it. *It is one safe place. No mice can destroy them in that.* It's a bother to hunt out a book quickly. She was still looking when she heard John thump his snowshoes against the house to free them from loose snow.

Mary was in the wash room by the time he got the door open. "I've been worried about you ever since you left—wishing you had not gone. Here, let me unfasten those overshoes. You act as though your hands are numb."

"I'm not so cold; just dead tired." He dropped the gunny sack and its contents to the floor with a thud, stood still while she unsnapped the buckles for him, resting his hand on her firm shoulder. He kicked off first one boot, then the other. "Lucky I didn't tackle hauling that sled up there."

"You couldn't have hauled any box back if it's that bad traveling." She helped him make it to the warm kitchen.

He dropped into the first chair. "It isn't there. They've only brought in the letter mail the past two weeks—on their backs. There are two letters for you in my pocket." He made no move to get them for her. She was taking off his shoes now, and putting his feet into the felt slippers she had made for him from old hats. "You're waiting on me like a baby. But to tell you the truth, I'm not sure I can even make myself get up and wash for supper. That is how worn out I am. Soft snow is hell."

Mary giggled in her relief that he was home safely. "You just sit still. You don't have to move." She brought water, soap and towel to a chair close at hand. "I'll put your supper on the table and move that right up to you."

"Aren't you going to eat with me?" he asked, seeing only one plate.

"I have to tell you the awful truth. I ate my dinner less than three hours ago. I was so busy finishing your Christmas present, I never noticed what time it was. So I'm not one bit hungry now."

"It's no fun eating alone." Weariness was making him cross; he had gone beyond the hunger stage. Slowly he picked up his fork as if in doubt he wanted food at all. "I don't like you making me a present when you wouldn't let me buy you one."

"Oh but Darling, this is different. What I made you never cost a cent. For you to buy me something fancy and on credit is what I balked at. We must buy only what we need to live, you might say. Did you bring the soda?"

"Yea. An' half a dozen cans of tomatoes. They are liable to be frozen."

"Did you say tomatoes? Oh, that is the best Christmas present of all." She hurriedly brought in the gunny sack and lined up the icy metal cans, choosing the one with the biggest bulge. "I've been hungry for tomatoes."

"I heard you say you were." John was eating with more vigor now. "That was all the load I wanted too. Every step, I'd sink down a couple of inches." Mary came to the table now with a dish of half frozen tomatoes. "I thought you weren't hungry," he said teasingly.

"This is my dessert," she smiled, "all the same as ice cream."

"I would think they would give you a stomach ache, bein' that cold."

"Oh, I'm eating them slowly so they won't bother me. Are the letters in this coat pocket or the other one?" She was a bit impatient to hear from the outside world, pretending to rummage in the pocket closest to her.

Slow like, he drew out the two from an inside pocket, holding them just beyond her reach. "Am I going to have to wait 'til morning for my Christmas present?"

"You can have your present any time you can find it. I haven't wrapped it or hidden it, and it is right in plain sight about the house."

"Holy gee, that isn't fair." He gave her the letters. "And me tired enough to hit the hay this minute."

Mary patted his shoulder as she poured him more coffee. "You can go to bed just as soon as you like, My Dear. That still won't hinder you finding your present."

"Is it a nightshirt? Are you going to make me wear one of those things?"

She smiled while opening her letter, knowing his dislike of getting into a sleeping garment this cold weather. "Stop your fretting. It isn't a nightshirt, but I'm not giving you any other hint." Mary was now reading Mother's letter while John finished a prune turnover with coffee.

"Mother wrote this the fourteenth and says they started our Christmas box the week before so we'd be sure to get it by now. But her post script says not to worry if it is delayed, as there is nothing in it that will spoil or freeze." She made short work of reading the other letter, but laughed, amused. "Cousin Sylvia has some of the oddest ideas about these hills. She seems to think they are peopled by Indians still. And here I've never once seen an Indian yet."

"Haven't you?" asked John. "A few of 'em comes through here once in a while, fishing or hunting. Guess they all winter on the reservation south of here." He was not much interested.

Chapter Fifteen

NEW YEARS PASSED, AND it was another week before the road was plowed free of its drifts. "Too late in the day to make the trip yet today," John told her on coming back to the house, "but I'll go up tomorrow to see if that Christmas box of yours has come."

At the supper table Mary was giving voice to her thoughts. "I really would like to walk up to town with you. I'm without sewing material. I'm not sure just what I would find suitable for baby clothes, but surely they should have baby flannel." She was soon aware that John did not favor her tackling the trip.

"If that box is there, I can't haul it and you back on that sled."

Before the dishes were out of the way, the sound of sleigh bells was heard the instant she opened the door. "Someone's out riding. They're stopping here, John."

John was striding through the house and opening the hall door. "Pretty heavy box this. John, how about some help with it?" Jimmy Burch called. Mary brought the lamp to light their way as they carried it in. "Evening, Mrs. Marcus. We were just out for a spin this fine night, so thought I would do my good deed for the day by bringing down your belated Christmas box. Must be something extra good, as heavy as it is." He and John took it to the kitchen.

"I know there are good things in that box. A fruit cake, I'm sure. How about you and your friends coming in to sample a slice of it? I will make coffee." She so hoped they would come in. This not seeing anyone but their own two selves for more than a month was a bit monotonous.

"I would like to, but doubt I can talk those girls into being away from town that long. Laura has a taffy-pull planned as soon as we get back. Thanks for the invite anyway. I hope the rest of this new year will be happier—each day better than the one before." With that, he bowed himself out.

"My, that father of mine was afraid this box would come apart." She viewed the well-roped box to see where the end of the rope was.

"Don't cut the rope, John." She stopped him as he had his pocket knife out. "I'll help you up-end it. This is new rope—must

145

Effie Sutton

be better than fifty feet of it."

"I thought you were in a hurry to get this opened." He closed the knife.

"I am, but not that anxious as to spoil this good rope. Father is a good one at tying knots too." She tugged knowingly at one now. "But I generally could untie them. If I can't soon, you can use the knife. Looks like you'll need a hammer too. Not only is this roped well, it is nailed stoutly."

"Not only a hammer, but a cold chisel, wedges and pry bar." He was trying to joke, but did not like the thought that he might have to go to the tool shed. "Must be gold bricks in it, and he was afraid to lose 'em."

"Not gold, Honey," Mary told him as she conquered the knot, "but things gold can't buy." The rope now loose, the next knot was easy. "Maybe that screw driver on the shelf would help to pry up one corner so you can use the hammer."

There was much prying and hammering to the tune of ripped boards before the top was off. Mary was on knees, folding back layers of paper, pinching each sack as she lifted them out. "This is dried corn. That light weight one is pumpkin. And these must be hickory nuts; and these butternuts. And here is popcorn."

"How do you know what is in all those sacks?"

"By the feel. Oh, this must be a fruit cake all tied up pretty this way. I can't figure out what this is." She pinched a big firm package. "Will you lift it out for me, Honey? It seems pretty heavy." Not until John had it out and resting on the corner of the box where she could tear away a bit of paper and sniff did she say, "Its butter! Oh, how glorious, and what a lot of it. I know what that next big package is without smelling or pinching," she laughed. "It's a cured ham with all the bones taken out. I have seen Father fix those for Aunt Sylvia many times. Auntie could not handle a meat saw well, so Father would bone the ham and tie it up tight so she could just slice it off easily. These two last sacks must be dried apples and peaches." These she piled on the floor beside her. Then came flat paper boxes; these she shook. "This one doesn't rattle at all, so it may be dried strawberries or fudge." John's hands were waiting for them. "Open them and sample some if you want." The next box rattled as well. "This must be nut meats, home-made candy and dried cherries. Now we're getting down to the presents," she said as she lifted out soft-wrapped parcels with names on them.

"Two for you and two for me. I bet I can guess what you'll find in that small one from Annie. It will be a nice white handkerchief she has hemmed. Oh, I thought she would be sending me the same and here it is a white apron. Mother must have helped her with this, it is so very well made." She glanced to the bright blue flannel shirt John held up. "What a pretty color of blue. That mother of mine has been more than busy. Look at these two fine nightgowns she has made me. And a short dressing gown too. That is a French flannel, I do believe."

It was John who spied the shoebox. "Is this a present you overlooked or don't want? It has your name on it."

"That will be bedroom slippers from Father, I know. He always said he never knows what else to buy. Aren't they pretty? Almost the same shade of blue as your shirt. I expect he picked out that material too. Mother doesn't try to ride that long distance to Caldwell. You'll have to help me up, John, I'm so weighted down with all this love and bounty." There were tears in her eyes. She smiled through them as she saw John digging out a mouthful from one of the boxes. "You would be eating those dried strawberries the first thing. They always were what I went for first as soon as Auntie's box would come."

"I thought this was candy," John told her. "It's good, whatever it is."

"Sure it is. Only I like it better than candy. And it is easy to make. All you have to do is dip the whole berries in a thick boiling syrup for half a minute, then put them out on plates and platters to dry in the sunshine." She was quiet for a little while with her own mouth was full. Later she opened the other boxes, sampling nuts and candy nibbles, a tart dried cherry. Then she fingered dry flinty shavings from one of the sacks. "I see where we are going to have a pumpkin pie."

"Not out of those shavings, I hope." He could not think of them being anything else.

"Dried pumpkin makes pretty good pies. Of course, it needs to soak and cook quite awhile. The only thing I can wish for is a couple of those eggs the boys in DeLamar smashed and wasted last fall. I could make a much better pie with eggs. I wonder if those young imps have wished they didn't do it."

"I doubt such a thought bothers them." He ate a handful of

nut meats. On seeing Mary arranging the sacks back in the box again, he asked, "Where do you want all that stuff stored?"

"Just draw the box into the washroom for tonight. We'll want some ham for our breakfast and butter for hotcakes. I'll put some of the dried fruit to cook tomorrow and dried corn too. I don't know just how good that will be without cream, but butter will make it edible I'm sure."

"What's wrong with canned cream?"

"One thing wrong with it is the fact it isn't cream–just milk. And there are but two cans left. I've never made a pumpkin pie with that kind of milk, but I understand it works very well and I'm game to try it. Oh, no. I can't make a pie soon—we have no lard or shortening. I just remembered."

John pointed to the can of bacon drippings. "Plenty grease there, looks like." He was not going to be robbed of the promised pie.

"And that is the one kind of fat that will not make good pastry." She was fitting the covers to the right boxes on the cluttered table, thinking all the while. She knew butter made the very best of pastry, but was determined not to use that precious butter for anything but table use and seasoning, it being impossible to buy butter or eggs in these hills in the winter time. "If I can chop some of the fresh suet fine enough, I can make pie crust with that. These cherries make wonderful steamed puddings. Have you tasted those?"

"Don't offer me anymore this night. I'm heading for bed."

***

"What a strange sounding wind." Mary was waiting for John as he came from work in the tunnel at noon. "Here it is the middle of January, and it feels almost like spring. The trees and rocks are showing up on that hillside fast, like the snow is melting there, but it doesn't seem to be here."

"It's a Chinook alright," John told her.

"I've heard that word before, but don't understand what it means. Can you tell me?" She followed him in, closing the door on the stiff breeze that seemed warm, but still so penetratingly cold.

"Guess it means warm wind or something like that." John

148

was busy at the sink. "Sometimes comes along in mid-winter from the west or northwest, and it will take the snow off in a hurry from any place it happens to hit. Like that hillside. I'm hungry—what do we have good to eat?"

"Lots of good things. Beans cooked with the shank-end of the ham. Dried corn, and an apple brown-betty. Say, wouldn't it be wise to get more wood if the snow melts on that side hill before it gets buried deep again?"

John admitted that might be a good idea now that she mentioned it. But by night fall, and with the band of dark earth showing naked of snow, he forgot it. He was making big plans for the work in the tunnel on the following day. Mary eyed their depleted wood supply with concern. It took much urging the next morning to make him change his plans. "I'm sick and tired of this house," she told him. "I want to get out while it's decent weather. You don't fancy me walking to town on snowshoes," she teased him, "so I'll go help you get wood instead. I can even put us up a lunch if we can make a little fire to make coffee and keep it warm while we eat." It took plenty of urging before they set out with sled, rope, axe, and the basket of lunch.

As long as John stayed busy cutting wood, she carried the sticks to the sled at the edge of the snow. When it was piled high and roped tightly, she carried armloads back to the house to keep busy, bringing back the basket for chips. "Laugh all you want to, but these chips and twigs will dry out fast and make good kindling."

The tired muscles in the calves of her legs were kicking up a fuss as she carried home the last basket and the axe. The piled-high load on the sled was hard to manage on the uneven path, giving reason for his grumbling. Not one word would she say about her discomfort. When supper was cooked and on the table, she could not sit to eat her meal because of the cramps. "That's what I get for sitting about the house for three months." All the rubbing she could give them herself was not taking away the kinks. "You go ahead and eat your meal. I'm going to get these feet of mine in hot water and see if that will help." In too much misery to lift the foot tub from the sink, she stood gripping the wooden frame.

"See. You had no business trotting all over hells bald acre the way you did." John was slow in coming to help her. "We should never have went after wood today." As he lifted the shallow tub down, a thought came. "This isn't deep enough to get the water up where it will do the most good. Wouldn't the wash boiler be better?"

Mary nodded her head, not able to speak and keep from crying. It was long minutes before the pain eased away, thanks to the warm water, and she could smile through her tears. "Stop your scolding. They are letting up and I'm hungry enough to eat my share if you can push that table a little closer this way so I don't have to disturb my underpinning for a little while longer."

"Don't you know enough to quit when you're tired?" he asked in poor grace as he inched the table closer so she could eat.

"Perhaps I'll learn in time. Look on the bright side. Think of all the wood we brought in today." Giving no time to the cooking or baking any dessert this day, she had set out the last of the fruit cake and the last of the dried strawberries. They were getting dry and crystallized now, but John ate them.

"I wish we had more of this kind of candy." He persisted in calling it candy.

"There's no reason why we cannot grow all the strawberries we want to right here in our own backyard. And I know how they are dried."

"You trying to kid me into thinking strawberries will grow here?"

"Sure they will. Don't you remember Mr. Kirtland telling us what a nice patch his mother had?"

"Remember, that is several hundred feet lower than here."

"Yes, and DeLamar is a few hundred feet higher than here and I saw berries growing there. It's later in the summer when they ripen."

"Strawberries are not enough," boasted John. "You and I are going where bananas, oranges and apples grow on trees—where all we have to do is pick 'em off."

"If you get far enough south for bananas and oranges, good apples won't grow," she pointed out.

"Who said so?"

"I read about that just yesterday in one of those books left here. There is so much I'm learning from those books. After you spoke about it being a Chinook wind, I looked that word up and learned it is an Indian word, and they have a legend about it. But the real reason is caused by the Japanese current of warm air, and when it swings in close to the western coast, we get the benefit of it in these higher hills." She did not like to hear John talk of leaving this place. To her, it was home—the place she expected to make more *homey*, like with paint, paper and curtains. The bare windows were a reminder. Several times she had been tempted to send for curtains with the $10 bill Tim left. To her code, that would not be right. Now she was faced with the thought she might have to really use it, whether she wished to do so or not. *The Marcus family can live without curtains up to our windows, but our baby arriving in the middle of the month of May will have to have clothes.* The samples of cloth Jimmy Burch had sent down by John at her request had proved rough and unsuitable for baby clothes.

From the catalogue, she was sure she would be able to order a fairly good layette for the sum of $10. But the question was getting the order mailed, or the arrival of the package without explaining to John the source of that money. *When I haven't seen fit to tell him about it all these months, it would be hard for him to understand me doing so now,* never once admitting there was a fear that that bit of money would go for caps and powder like all the other cash.

While drying her swollen feet just out of the cooking water this night, she worried over the problem. *I should have that material soon to be sewing on them now.* The only way she could see was to send the money to Mother and let her do the ordering for her. *The quicker way would be for them to buy those things in Caldwell and mail them to me, but that would mean Father would have to do all that shopping. Mother doesn't try riding that long trip,* she reminded herself. *But if I do write out the order very plainly, the quantity and grade as well as price, he might not have too big a job.* This she would do, and have the letter ready to be mailed the first time John went to town. She had little hope of anyone passing by to mail it. Luck was with her, though. She had but finished and stamped the envelope when three youths came half walking, half gliding on the now packed and crusted snow. Their snowshoes were pieces of thin smooth boards, not webbed at all. She was curious about those, as they slipped their feet from the straps and came in for a drink of water.

"Yes, they are a different kind," they told her. "Sorta like short skis. They are pretty good for going downhill. We'll better be able to tell how they are going uphill by the time we get back to town." With a laugh, they accepted cookies, but declined to wait for coffee to be made for them. They would gladly mail her letter for her. Their pause had been short, just time enough to swallow two molasses cookies, another drink of water before they picked up their slim sticks, propelling themselves along the icy porch.

Three weeks later, when the package came, Mary was dismayed at the size of it. *Surely that cannot contain enough clothes to keep the smallest babe warm and clean.* On opening it up, she found only blankets, stockings, shirts, and a few yards of fine nainsook for dresses. Fingering through them, she could see there was twice the number of blankets than what she ordered, both large and small. This was disheartening. *How could I have written that order so poorly that Father failed to understand it?* Seeing John looking on, she brightened and held up one of the tiny shirts. "Aren't these the cutest little garments the folks have sent? And the nicest lot of blankets?"

"I thought you weren't going to let them know anything about the baby until it arrived?" There was a slight reproach in his tone.

"I know. I did feel that way at first. And I didn't want to have them worrying about me, but then I got to thinking there is nothing to worry about. Look at the hundreds of babies born every day; and maybe they would like to look forward to having a grandson."

"Would you be afraid to stay alone, day times of course, if I were to get a job up close to DeLamar?"

"Goodness no, I wouldn't be afraid. Whatever gave you that idea?" She was so happy at the thought of John with a job, she laughed. "Now, tell me how much further away would you be than way back in that dark tunnel?"

"I just didn't know if you'd be scared. I heard in town today that Guy Belcher is wanting a man to help him sink a shaft deeper on his claim up above town. It's only supposed to be about two months work. I didn't go see him. Thought I better talk to you first."

"You just go right ahead and see that Mr. Belcher and get that job. You really should have seen him today while you were in town." She had stopped reading Mother's letter to say this.

"Mother writes that she is doing the machine stitching on all the baby things before she sends them since we have no sewing machine, so all I'll have to do is the hand sewing. But that will be plenty to keep me busy so I won't be crying and lamenting while you are at work." Her cheeks were blushed and eyes shining as she hugged his head and shoulders against her. "Oh, I'm so happy. We must get up real early in the morning so you can be up there by daylight. I'll even stick a lunch in your pocket so you could go to work right tomorrow," she told him with a lingering kiss.

John did not seem so much enthused over the prospect of a job. "Do you know, living up here in the hills must agree with you. You are prettier than you were the first time I saw you."

"Not prettier, but clearer complexion perhaps," she told him. "I was just reading about that today—how some mothers-to-be have such blotchy skin, while others have better color. It seems there is no explaining it really."

"You read a lot in those books." He let her right herself to put the meal on the table. "I suppose you've learned all about how to have that baby all alone by yourself?"

"Yes, I've read all that too. Of course, I can't say I want that to happen, but it's good to know what's to be done and how to do it in case of emergency."

"Well, you sure are not going to be alone. I'll be through with that job, if I get it, along about the first of May."

"Oh, you must get it. You'll be through with it in plenty of time. Come and eat supper now." She was thinking how needless it had been for her to send that money for the baby clothes, bothering Father and Mother with the order when soon she would be able to send her own list and have it filled. She would not have been so happy this night had she known that a job for John Marcus did not always mean money.

***

"What a glorious first day of May." Mary opened wide the kitchen door to the morning sun. "Spring has really sprung, as you say, even if the air is still a bit nippy. After it warms up, I'm going for a ramble. I want to get out of doors so bad." She smiled at the skeptical look John gave her as he made ready for this last day of work.

"You better not ramble too far. It will be night before I get home to pack you back to the house should you topple over and not be able to get up." He did a lot of teasing lately.

"You don't need to worry. I won't be traveling far, even if I do have the urge—just along the path and around on level ground. I'll be sensible." She did not stand to watch John out of sight. *I'll hurry through my work so I can get out of doors that much quicker. That will cure this touch of spring fever.* Then she grimaced at the thought of hurrying. That was one thing she was discovering she could not do.

It was noon before she had the work done to her liking— floors swept; the dining room dusted; their bed made up fresh; herself bathed; and a clean housedress slipped on. *I have to go in my bedroom slippers, for I cannot fasten my shoes. But then, I'm not going far. I would like to see if there is one dandelion showing any place. Mother always claimed dandelion greens are about the best spring tonic she knew of.* Then came a dampening thought. *If I do find any, I can nowise get down to dig them. Oh, I can get down alright by falling down, but it's the getting up again that I fail to manage.*

She took it slow and easy like to make sure of her footing. At the bridge across the gulch stream, she stopped and watched the tumbling water. In a few months, this would be a very small stream, but now it was running bank full. On she walked between the willow clumps, past the point of the rock and out on the level race track. *I know I must turn around and go back.* The first twinge of new discomfort came then. *I'll say, I better get back to the house.* The going now was slower. *I can't walk fast to save me, but I can still keep going in the right direction,* she told herself. She had no intention of letting herself panic, even though she often had to stop for a moment's pause. *That's the third one of those nasty twinges.* When she stopped on the bridge this time, it was not to admire the rushing water, but to wait until that keen pain eased away. The sound of the water deadened other sounds, so she did not hear the rumble of the rig following her. The instant she stepped to the earth again, she turned in astonishment.

"Hello there," called Max Thorn as he drew rein. Taking in the situation at a glance, he vaulted from the rig. "My God, Mary, you're in labor and trying to go for help."

Now free from that tearing pain, she answered freely. "No, Max. I went for a walk and I guess I shouldn't have. I was just trying to get back to the house." She could do no more talking now. She could offer no help or hindrances as she was boosted into the rig and driven the short distance to the gate. All she could do was to cling to the seat of the swaying buckboard.

Max kicked a rock against the gate to prop it open. Instead of aiding Mary to the ground, he hoisted her to his shoulders and bore her into the house, thankful the door stood ajar. As the next pain came, he eased her to her own bed. She realized Max was frightened, and as soon as she could speak, she assured him, "I'm alright now. You sure helped me to the house in a hurry."

"I'm going for a doctor," he told her in no uncertain terms. "Is there anyone else you want me to bring?"

"Don't know as there is need of getting a doctor now. I feel fine. Baby isn't due for two more weeks at least. I think I just walked too far." Her voice trailed off key. When she again took stock of her surroundings, she saw that Max was gone. The welcomed feeling of knowing help would be coming was steadying to her now.

Chapter Sixteen

DR. MATTROCK, SO NEW to DeLamar, was not enjoying this May day. *Why oh why did I ever leave Ohio,* he said to himself with his teeth all but chattering. This business of building his own office fires to keep from freezing was not to his expectation. Steam-heated buildings had been his habitation since entering medical college. His internship, while not all rosy, had at least been more comfortable than this. *Not sure I want to sign up with the DeLamar Mining and Milling Company for any lengthy stay. If it is as disagreeable as this in May, what will it be like in winter time?* He had no one to question. Jimmy Burch at the company store was the only person he felt well enough acquainted with yet. *What good is there in asking him? That little guy is sold on these mountains. Just because he likes them, he thinks I should too.* He sure did not care to be hemmed in long by those half barren snow-capped peaks.

It was a week last night that he had arrived to fill this emergency. The company doctor had been forced to give up because of failing health. There had been some correspondence over this coming vacancy. DeLamar Mining and Milling Company naturally had wanted a doctor with more experience, but failing to find one, they had wired Dr. Mattrock. With distaste at leaving the now warm rooms for the bracing outdoor air, he turned dampers to hold the fire better while making his round of morning calls. The sun was out in all its force, and fast melted the frost, even warming the crisp air. The small two-room office was much more comfortable as he unlocked the door after his noon meal.

If I'm no more rushed with patients than heretofore, I can get in some badly needed reading, he told himself. The first thing he picked up was the company's contract. He might sign, and again he might not. Some of the clauses in it would bear thinking over. *Naturally, I would be bound to this town only and none of the outlying communities, being hired and paid by the DeLamar Mining and Milling Company.* He understood all this, and could see the need of his not leaving without their say so. With this all fresh in his mind, he hesitated an instant when the door banged opened and a tall man boomed at him, "Grab the satchel you need when a baby arrives. There is one on its way at Wagontown."

Dr. Mattrock's one-second delay in complying to this emergency maddened the frightened man who, at his hesitation, pulled out three bills and flung them to the table. "There. You are paid. Now move." Something small, round and of very hard metal poked Dr. Mattrock in the back, propelling him right along to the door and into the rig standing ready. With one scoop of his other hand, Max Thorn picked up both bags and tumbled them in at their feet as he picked up the reins.

The doctor was without hat. He might not have been able to keep it on had he worn one. Never had he experienced such a wild ride—both hands were needed to stay seated. Not a word was spoken the two-mile distance. Max was bent on getting topmost speed from the team and still keeping them in hand. He well knew they would run away if given half a chance. The gate in the white picket fence was still propped open. Dr. Mattrock took the short walk at a run, with Max Thorn right at his heels carrying the satchels. The wail of a new born infant filling his lungs for the first time greeted them.

Mary, half sitting, nodded to them. "Am I glad to see someone more versed than I in caring for this new son of mine." She had been trying to wipe the tight shut eyes just like the book had instructed. Now patting the small blanket about him, she smiled as Dr. Mattrock took over. "He doesn't seem too happy in this rough old world."

The rattle of the stove in the kitchen told plainly that Max was building a fire. His hand on the tank told him the water was still fairly warm. He filled the teakettle from that faucet, and commenced to fill other pans until the top of the range was covered. He might not know what else was needed, but he was sure of the hot water question. Without talk, he poured water from these into the white wash bowl for the doctor as he came for it. He anticipated the need of drawing the table closer to the warmth when the small bundle arrived.

Dr. Mattrock, busy giving the babe a good oiling, guessed by this man's watching that he had never before seen the youngest of the human race getting its first initiation to oil, soap and water. "Nice healthy boy this," he said as an opening to conversation. When the tanned man with those intent eyes said nothing, "I'm sure he would have been none the worse had we not arrived—that young mother of his seemed to know what to do."

"Did she say who was to come in to care for her and this young fellow?" Max' voice had taken on a sharp edge.

"She seems to think she and her husband can manage, this being his last day at his work." Dr. Mattrock was puzzled by the man's hasty departure. He could hear the rattle of the rig as it crossed the bridge, and guessed he must be headed back toward DeLamar. Later, taking the dressed mite back to his mother, he asked, "Is this man Thorn always so unpredictable?

"In a way he is unpredictable." She tried to smile. "I doubt Max knows where to find Mr. Marcus. He never once stopped long enough for me to tell him. Max should never have rushed away this way and not taken you back to town. Baby and I will be perfectly alright here by ourselves until my husband gets here, and I'm sure you need to be back to your office."

Dr. Mattrock's first opinion of this patient was what a sensible woman she seemed. But as the minutes dragged along to an hour, and she was still talking and asking forty-eleven questions, he was not so sure. He even took her temperature, knowing a slight rise in that could account for this steady flow of talk. He had yet to learn he was about the sixth person she had seen in the many months to talk to.

Max Thorn came down the road and across the bridge at a much more reasonable gait this time. Very carefully, he helped a little old lady out of the rig and carried in her ancient valise. "Mary, this is Mrs. Blatchey. Where shall I put her grip?"

"In those rooms across the hall, Max," she told him, then turned to the slight gray-haired woman taking off her black bonnet. "I'm truly glad to see you, even though Max should never have gone for you. For it is this way, Mrs. Blatchey, goodness only knows when we will be able to pay you."

"I'm Grandma Blatchey to half a dozen of my own, and Grandma in name to about all of DeLamar," cut in the quick moving woman. "I might as well be Grandma to you too. I've heard about you, but I've never met you before." She was of the gossipy kind. She started in on more talk, giving Mary no chance to speak one more word with either the doctor or Max Thorn before they left.

As Mary lay listening, she could but think how she had wished for some woman to talk to, and here with this one, she could not get a word in edgewise. Some of the talk was not very interesting. When at last she could say something, it was along the line of her thoughts. "Did Max Thorn scare you with his fast driving? "

"Maybe I'm not of the scaring kind," beamed the old lady. "After more than twenty-three years in these hills in all kinds of rigs and weather, it takes a lot to make my hair stand on end. Now that young doctor, maybe he's never rode on roads all on a slant. They're either up or down and always sideways." Grandma had finally taken her wraps to the other room and come back tying on a big white apron. "Now would you be caring for a nice cup of hot tea?"

"I am hungry, but I do not care for tea. I doubt there is any in the house anyway. If you care for tea, I'll have my husband get some tomorrow up town. Do you suppose a dish of the cold cooked rice could hurt me any?"

"Heavens sakes, Child, it won't hurt you. Do you want cream and plenty of sugar on it?" She was already leaving the room to get it.

"Just some of the raisin sauce dipped over it, please," Mary called to her. "I care so little about the canned milk," she added, then stopped talking as the woman was out of hearing range of her voice.

***

The team started out at their fastest clip to the dismayed doctor. Max remarked, "I take it you are in some hurry to be back in that office of yours."

"I am," was the clipped answer. "It is the one place I'm supposed to be at this hour, and not leaving the territory of DeLamar without first notifying the Mine and Mill office.

"Damn small territory you have, is all I can say." Max was not too sure just how much trouble he could get into, making the doctor come away against his will.

Dr. Mattrock did not like the mockery in that taunt. "How about looking at this from my side of the fence. I'm in this mountain fortress but a week. How am I to know Wagontown was only a settlement? Remember, you never said it was but two miles distance. To me, it could have meant a distance of twenty-two miles. All your small burgs with *town* or *city* tucked on to them is very misleading." They hit the rough and rocky part of the road, so there was not much conversation traveling at such a speed. Not another word was said.

The doctor wondered if he would have liked this silent man beside him if they had met under more favorable circumstances. Idly, he wondered what the man's opinion was of him. There was no reading that grim face, or any thoughts going on behind those blue eyes with their faraway look. If he had been but slightly acquainted with Max Thorn, he might have known he rated well the instant his bags were deposited inside his office door.

"This joint don't seem to be overrun with the sick or maimed. How about coming next door for a drink on me?" His face had lit up on seeing the empty room.

Dr. Mattrock nodded toward the money on the table. "There is all of $10 more there than the regular charge, which is $25. Pick that up and I'll go have a drink with you."

"I'll be damned if I will," snapped Max, moving toward the door. "So I did take you whether you wished it or not. I paid you. But God help you if anyone else knows I did so." With that blast, he was gone.

Smoothing out the wrinkled bills to put them in his cash box, Dr. Mattrock was nowise sure he would even care to tell of this episode. *So this man, Thorn, doesn't want it known he did the paying for this trip.* He thought about this, and the reason there could be. *Might be a jealous husband. Might be any number of reasons. But Mrs. Marcus spoke as he had just happened to find her trying to make it back to the house, aided her and came for help. Evidently these Marcus' have no money, and this Max Thorn is a friend of her family's. So why all this howdy-do?* There was no way of knowing the answer to that question.

Chapter Seventeen

MAX THORN WAS NOT whistling this day as he rode his swaying buckboard. As he started down from the top of the Wagontown grade, it was like a turning point in his mind. *I sure am a softy. Had no business agreeing to come this way in the first place,* he was scolding. *I like Williams, and I see how they are feeling about their daughter having to leave this home she likes and expects to keep. But hang it all, they might as well learn they are not going to be able to be the soft cushion all along the rough road she'll be traveling to keep pace with that guy.* He did not name John Marcus by name. He did not care to think about him, much less see him. *If there is any indication that he is around the house, I'll hand him the letter, but stick around just long enough to see that he hands it on to his wife. In that way, I'll have fulfilled my word.*

David Williams and his wife had been very much perturbed over Mary's nice newsy letter. She told of a planned departure of the Marcus family for parts unknown. Mary's only concern was over leaving this home she liked so much, and rather feared that John would someday be sorry they had ever left it. She felt there was no way of holding on to it, even though two years payments had been made on it; and even that amount seemed a lot to waste. She'd said she believed the place was worth all and more of the $600. John and Tim had agreed to pay for it in the first place, but apparently fell behind in payments. Father Williams, fearing the mail would be too slow to reach Mary before they left, had driven to Max Thorn's place and asked him about the value of the property.

Damnit, I had to tell him the truth. To my way of looking at it, the place was well worth that amount. Of course, it won't be to Williams if he has to be saddled with it and can't sell it. How in the heck is he going to get that fellow to turn it over to him after it's paid for? All these thoughts were running through his mind as he caught sight of the top of the Mills House. Another thought edged in, *I can well get my throat cut if I don't watch out.* On down the last steep curve, he careened. *The place looks deserted like they might be already gone.* No wagon. No team in sight. And the front door was closed. The only sure sign they still lived there was the flap of white clothes on the line, a baby's wash. No one answered his knock. *Ten chances to one they are in town right now.* That thought did not cheer him much. *If there was any legal way for me to buy this place, I'd sure do it. Williams wouldn't have to be burdened with it.* Max knew there was little chance of him buying it. Since he owned sheep, the heirs would not sell to him. *All those interested in borrowing around underground seem to stick together,* was his rueful way of saying it.

A little flap of the reins, and the team picked up speed for a fast trot along the smooth race track. At the far end of this bow, Max pulled up sharp. Mary Marcus, babe in arms, was walking just ahead. "Whoa there. What do you mean out walking again when you shouldn't be?" He held out hands to take the bundle she carried so carefully. "You headed toward town? That is where I'm going. What's the use of wearing out shoe leather when horse shoes cost so little?"

"Yes, DeLamar is where David and I are headed," Mary said with a smile as she climbed into the seat beside Max and took the sleeping boy again." He isn't a very big boy yet, and he didn't seem to weigh much when I started out, but he was getting heavier all the time," she laughed.

"So, David is his name—named after his grandpap, I dare say. Well, he couldn't be named after a finer man to my way of thinking. By the way, I seen your folks just a day or two ago. They are sure wanting to see this new addition to the family." Max had a thought on how to handle the question of the relinquished place differently.

"I know they are," said Mary with a trace of sadness. "I was so in hopes we could go that way, as we leave tomorrow."

"Oh, you folks are leaving these hills? I thought you liked it here."

"I do like it here. But John is very discouraged—trying to do so much development work with no capital. Right now other pastures wave greener." This last was spoken humorously.

"What are you doing with your place here, selling it?

"No, we couldn't sell it, it not being paid for. But I do believe there are others that might want to take it over where we left off; maybe pay us for what we have in it. But John seems to think the waiting around to find someone interested in doing so would only be a waste of time."

"Did you ever think about leasing the place?"

"I'm sure John hasn't tried to do that. Neither am I sure it would rent or lease for enough to keep up the payments on the place."

"I'd be willing to lease it for $100 a year. Would that be enough to cover your payments?"

"That would be more than enough. But I'm not sure John would consider it."

"I know. He don't like sheep men." Max said it in a funny tone. "But if you're leaving the place for a year or two, someone else can be buying it. You'll have no strings on it and could not hope to keep it. To lease it, you would always have it until you wanted to come back to live here. Or failing that, when it is once paid for, it could be sold for perhaps more than you've sunk into it in the first place. Maybe it would be best to let your dad handle the payments while you're away. I could easy turn the money over to him."

Mary's smooth forehead wrinkled in thought. This was a great temptation to hang onto the place. She was sure John would not approve. That $40 above this year's payment might look big enough that he would make the deal. But how about next year's, and six more years after that until the place was paid for? She was not sure of those, John not being one to look ahead at such business deals. "Would my say so on a lease be enough?" One part of her mind was hoping it wouldn't be.

"I believe it would," Max assured her. "I'm not anticipating any trouble. I won't be bringing sheep in close to here—only I might swing a band in over the top of the ridges from the sheep trail, both spring and fall."

He drove carefully over a rocky place. "What I want the Mill's place for is a sorta headquarter camp for the camp tender— a pasture for the pack string. It'd save me having to give him a cussing several times during the summer for letting them get away from him." Max' eyes were twinkling now.

No answering smile from Mary. She was seeing all sides of this question. "I would like Father to be the one to handle the money and the payments, but it is already due and I fear it might be too late by the time he could get it mailed back here—someone is sure to know we are leaving."

Max nodded his head. "Might at that. If I were to hand you this year's money this very day, could you make the payment?

Then there would be no question about it."

"I know of no reason why I can't. But I will need to give you some kind of written word that you have leased the place."

"That might be better. While we don't look for trouble, some nosey guy might want proof I had a right around the place." He stopped the team, holding the reins between his knees while finding a stub of a pencil, which he handed Mary. He opened his time book to a clear sheet. "The simplest worded lease will be enough."

"You know better how they are worded, Max. You write it out and I will sign it." The die was cast. *I don't dare tell John the place is leased until it is paid for, or he'll get homesick for it and want to come back,* was her thought while watching Max' tanned hand write out the few words that were easy to read. Still, it weighed heavily on her conscience. She carried no purse, for she had no money. As the bills were counted into her hand, her thought was for a safe place to carry it. "It will have to be here," she spoke as she slipped them into the small breast pocket in her dress.

A weight seemed to roll from Max' shoulders with this attended to. He appeared more carefree. "You never have said how you came to be walking, and you people the owners of a team of horses now, I understand."

"Yes, we have a team. They are *Cayuses.* John patched up the harnesses that came with them, so it would be safer. The wagon was at the blacksmith's for repair, so he has been busy doing those things and hasn't tried out the team until today. I mentioned this morning how hungry I am for fish. I've lived here almost a year and never once had trout to eat, so that is where John is this minute—over on Deer Creek to see if he can catch a mess for our supper." She said this rather proudly. "Of course, I was in hopes I would get a ride and the chance to go fishing too, but John wasn't sure just how that team might perform. Thought it best that David and I not be along."

"So you are to meet him in DeLamar? Max was again uneasy.

"No, he won't be coming back that way. This trip to town is on my own. I wanted to make sure my letter was on its way to the folks. I addressed it to Annie this time. She is getting to be quite a good letter writer for a child of eight. I expect she is more than thrilled over the thought she might have a school close enough to go to next year."

"Oh yes. That is her big topic of conversation, along with this boy she hasn't seen," Max told her while holding the babe until she was safely on the sidewalk at the store and Post Office. When relieved of that small bundle, his hand came up in his usual half salute.

"I'm never going to try thanking you for your hurried trip after the doctor that day," Mary said, but he would have no thanks. Another turn of his raised hand brushed it aside as he hurried away. Mary started up the steps to mail her letter the first thing, then remembered, if she would get the payment tended to first, she could send along any information as to Father making the further payments. Writing down the right address to send to Father, she also sent him today's receipt of payment as a safeguard against her losing it, or John seeing it.

"Oh yes, Mr. Lyons. We'll be back some day," she told him as she bought stamps and asked him to hold any mail coming for them until she could send him their new address. "At least I'm sure we will. I really like it here."

Jimmy Burch wasn't busy for once. She asked him for their bill. She wrote down the staggering amount of $321.92 in her neat script on the back of the new writing pad she had just purchased. "I have no way of knowing when we will be able to pay this, Mr. Burch," Mary said with great earnestness, "but we will pay it as soon as we can."

Jimmy Burch peeped in at the sleeping infant. "I don't suppose you would trade this fine boy for the best mine in these hills?"

"You are supposing right on that question," smiled Mary. She would have liked to have visited for another moment, but she had several things yet to do and wanted to be back home if possible before John.

Dr. Mattrock was not in his office, so now she climbed the hill to Grandma Blatchey's small home. It was several minutes before she could get in a word edgewise, with that happy woman's admiration of David's growth and gain in the past ten days. "I think myself he is gaining. Not having scales to weigh him, I could not be sure of just how much, of course. The doctor was not in when I stopped there just now. I so wanted to weigh David, and

I wanted to pay Dr. Mattrock. I can also pay you now for all your good care of me."

"Why, Honey, I got my money from your folks in a letter just yesterday." To Mary's blank look, she reassured her, "That good looking husband of yours pulled a surprise on you, did he, paying me and not saying a word about it?" The pleased woman produced the envelope with a slip in a scrawled script and the $10 still folded inside.

Mary noted the hand writing and the date on the envelope. John had not sent this, she was all but certain of that. Without giving another indication of this fact, she took herself back to the still empty doctor's office. *That was not John's writing. And besides, he has no money. His two months work was the price Mr. Belcher asked for that team and their patched up harness.* She had not been happy over that transaction. The team meant they were leaving. John called it a *stroke of luck* the morning before David's arrival. *I promised myself I wouldn't nag or butt in on his work, just because I don't understand his way of doing things,* she reminded herself now, as she had several times while spending those days in bed.

The joy of this precious babe beside her had taken off the raw edge of her disappointment. Now she carried the small boy proudly as she headed toward home. *I guess that money is burning a hole in my pocket,* was her thought as she resolved to stop and pay the bill at the butcher shop. She would much prefer to pay any of the other bills than that one. Thirty-nine dollars would be such a little dent in the store bill. The doctor wasn't to be found and Grandma Blatchey already had her pay. *But where from,* was the unanswered question.

"Better hop in," called Max as he stopped beside her. "Just as well ride. The forks of the road are better than half your distance home." He held out hands for David.

"I would be glad of that lift, but I need to stop at the butcher shop for just a moment." She handed over her boy and hurried into the smelly place, expecting to be but a few short seconds to pay that bill and be rid of any obligation to this surly man she so detested. He was taking his own time in thumbing through his grease stained ledger, figuring again the bill Mary was remembered by heart. "I know you claim the bill is $41.50," Mary explained for the second time. "That is what it would have been, except for those times you sent down spoilt meat. You agreed then you would deduct that $2.50 from this bill."

"I no sell spoilt meat," thundered the outraged man. "You pay bill–$41.50, you hear? No spoilt meat, I say." If looks would have daunted Mary Marcus, she would have paid the amount she held ready in her hand and let that mollify his anger. Instead, she slipped the bills back in her pocket and marched from there with head held high.

Max said not a word while she climbed into the rig and again took the babe. There was no point in trying to talk as the deafening noise of the rock crusher filled the air. It wasn't until they reached the more quiet end of Lower Town before he spoke. "So, you had a run in with Butch? I pretty near came in and gave him a good punch in that fat nose—that's what he needs."

"I went in to pay him the bill we owe him." The indignant red was leaving her face, "which should have been $39.50. He claims it is $41.50. Several times last summer, he sent down meat that was not fit for food, and when I raised a holler about it, he agreed to deduct the amount from the bill. I see he never has. That makes me more than riled now." A half humorous smile creased her face. "I fear he'll never know how near he came to being $39.50 richer his day."

"I don't blame you for not paying him. I wouldn't pay the old so-n'-so one red cent 'til he makes it right." A sudden thought crossed his mind—*that money would be all that was left from the lease money.* "Let that devil sweat off some of his fat waiting for his money. My advice to you is to hang onto the few dollars you might have. Starting this way on a trip can be uncertain at the best. Remember, you have more than just yourself to think about." He noted the squirming of the babe and his mother arranging his blankets so to nurse him. He drove slower and spent the time in talk. "You know, to keep that young fellow's bread basket filled, you have to fill your own."

"Don't worry," cut in Mary. "I have a very healthy appetite. Also, I have a great big deal of curiosity. When is the guilty person going to admit sending Grandma Blatchey money through the mail, pretending it was the Marcus family?"

"Not guilty, Your Honor," Max said sternly.

"I was sure it was not your handwriting. Neither is it Father's. Besides, it was mailed right here in DeLamar. Leaving tomorrow this way, how am I going to track down who paid her?"

"Can't help you on that score." Max' response was firm as he redirected her attention with more questions. "If I have to make another trip to town, all on account of Pete Nickel's fun, that guy is going to have to find himself another job."

"He is one of your best herders, isn't he?" Mary brushed aside her own troubles enough to ask, "What has he done so terrible?

"He and one roan bull have had about three run-ins already this spring. This last time, Pete decided to see just how tough that critter's hide was—used him for target practice with that light 22 rifle he packs."

"Of course I never saw Pete but the once, but I never thought he was of the cruel type."

"Can't say as to just how cruel Pete is, no one having caught sight of that bull yet. Maybe he is still going; I hope so. I'm not going to pay for any more split tents. This one I got today is going on Pete's account. I can already hear him beefing over it. But daggone it, the last thing I told both him and Titus, the camp tender, to snake up some poles and make a fence about Pete's tent there on the head of Pole Creek. There's always salt hungry cattle around there. It wasn't a quarter of mile for them to get all the poles they needed, and they had the pack string to do the work of snaking 'em downhill. Still they were too lazy to do it."

"Will cattle just go in and destroy a camp?" This was news to Mary.

"That they will. It's the salt they smell and are after. The sack of salt, bacon and cured ham are the first things they go for. Of course, they'll eat flour, potatoes, and most any vegetable. What they don't eat, they'll sure spoil. The first visit that roan made to Pete's camp, he was very calmly eating the last spud when Pete showed up on the scene. Pete whoops and hollers, and that beast managed to go right through the tent, getting out of there in a hurry. Titus happened out the next day before Pete got too hungry and took him out more grub and another tent. A week later, the same thing happened again. After that, Pete was pretty mad and packed the rifle with him. Three days ago, when he saw that familiar roan rump sticking out of the tent flaps, Pete just up 'n whams away. That tent is in two pieces."

"That must have been funny," Mary laughed heartily. "No

wonder Pete was ready for vengeance. I bet he was mad."

"Pete mad? I'm the one that was mad. He just might have to pay for a tent. I'd almost bet he talks Titus into paying for half of it, being he was half to blame."

Mary chuckled again. "Do you remember saying you pitied the camp tenders? How they had to tolerate all the cursing of the owners and beefs of the herders?" As Max made no move to take up the conversation, she went on. "Their lot might not be the most pleasant. I have just been thinking how unpleasant a doctor's life can be at times. They never know when they are going to be called out, summer or winter, nice weather or foul. I expect many times they don't get paid. I went to Dr. Mattrock's office twice to pay him, and I didn't know where to leave it and…"

"Why worry about paying that saw-bones?" snapped Max. "He's paid good by the mine company. Besides, he never got there in time. Maybe he can't collect for work he didn't do. Your boy had already arrived, you know. Put that money down in your sock until you need it. And speaking of money in a sock, you should hear what happened to Mike Ryan this spring when he put money in his sock."

Max paused for a moment, his eyes holding a slight twinkle as they met Mary's. "Mike took his lay-off the week before shearing. As he commenced a spree, he put a ten spot in his sock so he'd have something to sober up on. He was in a bad way when he came back, and we were at the shearing corrals. We put up with him for the whole week, so as to have him on hand and ready to take the band out once they were shorn. It did plenty of raining about then, so it was pretty miserable for those sleeping outside. Neal Ramsey, the young fellow who did the cooking for them this year, is a soft-hearted chap and he let a bunch of 'em unroll their beds in the dining room and sleep there. The only thing is, Neal would have to rouse them up to get out of there so he could set the table for breakfast. Mike was one of this group. After the meal, about the last day of shearing, when Neal swept out the joint, he finds a ten spot, and at noon he asks if anyone has lost a $10 bill. No one seemed to think they had. Mid afternoon comes, and Mike says it was his. He remembered putting that bill in his sock to have when he sobered up. So Neal, the softy that he is, gives Mike the money, and at supper time, there is no Mike. He walked that five miles to the stage road and went on in to Caldwell to spend his last cash on drink." Max shook his head as if angry even thinking about it. "Come morning, there was no Mike to take out his band of sheep. I sure cussed Neal up one side and down the other. Gave him to understand hereafter, any money he happens to find, he's to put it in his own pocket and keep his dad-blamed mouth shut about it."

"Max, you know you would have done the same thing as Neal did. You'd try to find who the money belonged to."

"No I wouldn't have if Mike Ryan or anyone like him was around. Tell me what earthly use is money to them more than it takes for them to get good and soused on? Kenny Larson was a good example of that. I believe you met him once. He herded for seven years, never spent a cent for clothes, picked up other herder's castoffs. He went in to Caldwell with $21, and it didn't last him three days."

"Was he the one whose money was stolen from him?"

"That's the one."

"Couldn't they have done something about tracing who stole it?"

Max shook his head. "What would it have benefited Kenny if they had restored him, say half of his wad? Just another few days and he would have been rolled again."

"And is it a hopeless task to get them to save even part of their wages? All this seemed so sad to Mary.

"I tried to do that once," Max grimaced at the remembrance. "A hell of a good worker made me promise not to give him all his money. I saved some of it back for him always. I stood his abuse just the once, and as soon as he sobered up, paid him in full and kicked him off the ranch."

"It must be like a form of insanity," Mary suggested. "They might be sane in every other way, until they get to drinking."

"An' the more they drink, the crazier they get. But I heard a new reason why sheep herders go crazy. It is trying to find the long ways of their boughten quilts." Max' face was blank of expression.

"There is no long way to them. They are made square." Mary could laugh over that joke.

"But then, I have been thinking, herders are no more balmy than some others living way off by themselves. You have two prospectors living not more than a couple of miles from here that sure aren't the most sane…"

"Oh you mean the Wilbur brothers?" cut in Mary. "They are twins, and I can't for the life of me tell them apart."

"So you have made their acquaintance. Don't you agree they are a bit off?"

"They surely don't talk sensible about their claims. Telling about the millions of dollars they have right there in the grass roots. Why, if they had that rich a claim, they wouldn't have any trouble getting money to build a mill would they?'

"That is the way it looks to me. Every year they tackle me, wanting me to build 'em a mill for ten percent. One hundred thousand dollars they figure it will cost. I sure got rid of their pestering me this spring. I told them I'd build their ole' mill if they'd deed me the ranch they have in Boise Valley. See, they have a pretty good ranch—must be worth thirty, forty thousand."

"What did they say to that?" Mary wanted to know.

"They were outraged, as I expected they would be—asked me if I wanted them to starve to death. See, the rent from that ranch has grub-staked them every year since the gold bug bit them."

"And to think they have that good a ranch, yet they're off up there living like they do." Mary still could not understand such behavior. "John says they live in a make-shift cabin. Do you consider them dangerous?" She felt a bit uneasy, for each of those men had come for dinner with her and John this past week.

Max shook his head. "They would be to anyone monkeying about their claims. Pretty sure they would shoot first and ask questions afterwards."

"Aren't you afraid to have your sheep camp so close there?

"Oh, they know sheep men and herders are crazy, but just for the grass. Besides, they like mutton." Max' eyes twinkled now as he cramped the buckboard as she could step out to higher ground easier.

Chapter Eighteen

THE STILLNESS OF THE autumn day was broken by the creak of the loaded wagon, the whine of two cross children, the click of metal—on rock one second and in deep dust with the next turn of the wheels. Even the thud of the horses' hooves was muffled in dry roadbed. In places, the dust billowed up about the slow moving rig, adding discomfort to the occupants. "Oh, but it is great to be back home again," Mary Marcus said as she carefully wiped the stinging dust from her eyes. "Just down this grade and we'll be there." She saw the odd look Dick Palmer turned to give her. "Oh, you cannot see the place until you are right there." She could laugh now, a great lightness of heart was spreading all through her. And it was not all due to hunger either. She was thankful they had made the trip back safe and sound. She had feared neither wagon nor harness would hold together that long.

"I'll be good and glad to get out of this dust," John said as he spat out the last mouthful.

"How many miles did you say this grade was?" Dick was witty.

Mary's laugh this time awoke David. As he came up from his nest at her feet, she kissed his cheek. "Mother's boy hardly has a bit of dust on him." She had taken extra pains to keep the bit of canvas right to shield him, yet allow him air to breathe. This trip had taken a great toll from her strength, for the two squirming mites taking up part of the space between the two seats needed much tending. With pity, she looked at those two dirt streaked faces. "I don't blame you two children for crying. I'm tired and hungry enough to cry too. But that would not get the dust washed off, food cooked and beds made up so we can get into them tonight."

Dick turned again on his hard board seat, a grin creasing his dusty face. "I have yet to see you when you didn't come up with more sense than the rest of us put together." The thought of food and rest was all Dick Palmer was craving just now. Two weeks of this traveling on short rations had not been pleasant, but he had not complained.

Mary said nothing. She never did take note of any compliment Dick handed out. Mrs. Palmer, on the spring seat beside her, only glared. Mary tried to distract her, "Look at those chokecherries,

172

will you? There's just so many this year. And the wild rose bushes are nearly red with rosehips. I see where you and I can be busy until snow comes, gathering them for jelly and jam." Her own mouth was rimmed with dust, and she was much too weary to wish to talk, but a shout went up when she caught sight of the roof peak. "We are here, John! We are here!" She did not heed the rough jolting of the wagon on the loose rock for the entire descent to the very foot of the grade."

"David and I will get out here," she said to John the second he stopped for Dick to open the gate for him. "We'll go in the front way to unlock the doors," Mary's feet were already on the ground and reaching up to two-and-a-half year old David. *Even this little respite from that ever-lasting crying and whining is grateful.* She led David through the front gate and up the short walk. The key Father had so lately sent her was in her hand. She knew there was another key above her head on the door jam in case she should lose this one. *That was more than thoughtful of Max having this lock put on,* she thought as she turned the Yale lock on the inside.

The house had that *shut-up* smell, but she found no litter of any kind. She had not worried about this home of hers, or in what shape she would find it. Lighting the first stub of candle she found in the gloomy kitchen, she set about building a fire the first thing. There was plenty of dry wood and kindling in the wood box. After water was run into teakettle and two wash pans for the top of the stove, she gave David a drink and quenched her own thirst. "Isn't this the best cold water, Sonny Boy?" there was time to say before the noise and crying came on to the room. Lighting another candle, she explored the dark pantry. David clung to her skirts, but walked with her, not making a sound, while she peered into flour can and other containers on the shelves.

The flour can was light weight, and she carried it to the kitchen. Seeing Dick bringing in the grub box, she motioned for him to set it on the table. "It will be safe there." The two small gleams gave light enough to see. From the dusty grub box, she brought out the last clean dish towel. "Here is a clean soft cloth to wash those poor kiddies' faces and hands. They might feel better." She tore the thread bare cloth in two parts. Dick took the one she offered him after his wife only stared at it, instead of accepting it. Dipping the other half in the now warming water, she handed it to David. "Make your face and paddies clean, Sonny." She set him on a chair in the nook between stove and table so as to protect him. Off came her dusty coat and scarf from about her head, washing her hands well, but with no towel to dry them on, she commenced to fix supper. There could be no talking above the howls filling the air.

Their meager supplies were unpacked from the box, along with the battered tin dishes. She was ready for John to set the box down. Wiping the dust from the table, David's food came first. That was easy to fix: Two tough health crackers were soon broken into his bowl. Malted milk was dissolved in hot water, part of which was poured over the crackers. This diet had kept him well and happy the whole trip. *But I'm glad there is going to be dried fruit and other food for him from now on,* she thought. "You feed him tonight, Daddy." She pushed the bowl into his hands, unmindful that he had not yet washed.

None of the weary group gave heed to what Mary was cooking for supper. They were used to her planning and producing edible food under the most trying circumstances. She had measured out half the flour found in the can. A pan of biscuits she now slipped into the fairly hot oven, then half of the coffee from their own supplies went into the pot, and on to boil. Into the skillet went a small amount of precious flour, with a like amount of bacon and ham drippings. "John, you stir this and finish the gravy while I get this boy to bed." She took the sleepy boy over her shoulder with one arm, the other hand carried one candle. With dismay, she looked at the bedroll dumped just inside the bedroom door. "Can Mother's sleepy boy get his shoes unbuttoned while Mother gets our beds made up?" She set down candle and boy and tugged at the dirty, dusty rope.

It was long minutes before she had the stiff tarp unrolled to get at the bedding. Her hands by now were covered in dust. She vigorously rubbed them free of soil on her heavy stockings. *There is no need of me doing that trick now.* She knew there was plenty of water for washing away all soil. This once, she had no intention of going to the kitchen until her sleepy boy was safe in bed. "God love him," she whispered, picking up the sturdy chap and tugging away at his shoes; his eyes were closed in half-sleep.

Two dining chairs against the side of the big bed made a very good bed for David. He was tucked in quickly. The hubbub in the kitchen had not lessened, and she well knew that it would not until food stopped their cries. "John, you lift the pan of gravy to the center of the table," she said above the noise while placing a bent cover to set it on. "Dick, you get your children eating," she called as she placed hot biscuits right from the oven on each plate. These, the men broke apart and spooned gravy over them. It took much blowing before the two plates of food were cool enough to let the famished children wolf it down.

Coffee was poured, John and Dick both were serving themselves from opposite sides of the pan. Still, Mrs. Palmer sat unmoving. "Aren't you hungry?" asked Mary as she sank onto her chair. "You'd better move your chair up; there doesn't seem to be another out here." To have that crying stopped was heavenly. She could even smile while dipping the browned pan gravy over a biscuit. "I've been hungry several times in my life, but tonight tops all those." She made herself eat slowly, sipping the hot coffee between bites. Mrs. Palmer at long last moved up to the table. No bread was left on her plate by now—the two children had snatched them at once. Mary served her more biscuits and placed two more at each place.

"I thought you said we didn't have flour for bread," John was coming to life enough to ask.

"We didn't have—I found this flour here. I divided it, leaving half for breakfast." She kept count of each biscuit she doled out to make sure each had their share, but mainly to keep the two children from wasting one morsel more than they would eat.

"There." Dick mopped up the last bit of gravy from his plate. "I'm beginning to feel well fed again." He held out his cup for more coffee. Mary divided the amount left in the pot between his and John's cup. Both men turned down the last crisp round of bread, seeing Mrs. Palmer's plate clear of food. She let it drop from the long fork to her plate and commenced cleaning out the frying pan so she would have gravy to eat with it. "You damned kids quit yer fighting." Dick cuffed them smartly, but that had no effect on their snatching and clawing to get that last bit of bread from their mother's plate. It was wasted, most of it going to the floor. "You damned heathens aren't hungry—you didn't eat a speck of that. Just wasted it so others can't have it." Again he rapped the both of them to stop their fuss, but got more howls for his pains.

"They need to be in bed, Dick." Mary had to raise her voice

above the uproar. "Never you mind about these dishes—John and I will get them done. You take the bigger bit of candle, for you have your bed to make yet. Those rooms on the west used to have a good bed, and there's a couch that opens out to a bed."

"When did the Palmer family need more than one bed?" Dick demanded as he herded his wife and two offspring ahead of him through the wash room.

"My, what a relief when that noise is two doors away." Mary was much too weary to move. "John, are you able to get hot water into the dish pans for me? I can manage to wash them if I can do them seated here. Oh, that's right, there isn't a clean towel to dry them anyway, so just put water in one pan. After they are all washed, I'll scald them with the boiling water from the stove, and tip them up to drain. Never have I appreciated a good bed and springs like I'm going to this night." The candle sputtered out as they finished this small task. Undressing and getting into bed in the dark was nothing new.

"Morning has come much too soon," Mary said as she stirred to let David snuggle between his parents. There could be no time lost this day in cuddling and loving him. Dawn was graying the skies. She kissed him and tucked the bedding about him as she got up. "You keep Daddy warm for a little while."

I wonder if I will ever get enough of this good water, she thought to herself after getting the fire built and drinking her fill. Still too dark to see well, she spent the time while the stove was getting hot in combing her hair, walking out to the east porch, and sniffing the fresh air as she plated her long braid. *It's such a wonderful feeling to be home again after being gone for so long.*

This burden with the Palmer family had not been her expectation or wish. The only reason she consented to ride in the same rig with them was the fear that John would balk and not come at all. *How he could be so unreasonable, I sometimes wonder.* She did not want to think about the unhappy times, so hurried to get breakfast underway. There might be more unhappiness this very day, but she was determined to start the ball rolling come what may.

While still at the table, and the whining children had their mouths full of food, she asked, "Which of you two men volunteer to go to DeLamar for food and which to cut wood?"

"Looks like you have plenty of wood in the wood box to do

you today." John did not like the idea of being hindered one more day in getting at the tunnel work. "We two need to get right in there and see just how much work Tim has done. I know your dad wrote that Tim had come and did the assessment work each year we've been gone, but we gotta see for ourselves how she looks."

"You have to eat to work, remember." Mary was not going to back down.

"Sure, but isn't there anything about the place you can feed us with today so we can take a look-see? We might have to go up tomorrow anyway."

"There isn't even a bean to cook. One cup of rolled oats is all. I doubt that will make gruel enough to go around for one meal." Having stated the extent of their food supply, she left the table and the two men to talk over what they would do this day. She hurried to bathe David and let him splash happily in the water while hunting out clean clothes for him. She was sure the two other children would be busy fighting over the last biscuit for a minute or two. Another thing that made David fairly safe was their deadly fear of water. "Here Daddy, you dry your son with this small linen towel I found, while I steam the wrinkles out of his velvet suit."

John was good with David, but she always had to suggest the things for him to do. Her mind raced with things she must remember to do this day while in DeLamar. Moving the small garments slowly above the spout of the teakettle, she thought: *I must get plenty of malted milk and more crackers if possible. I need Castile soap, baby oil, sweet oil or olive oil, whichever I can get. Safety pins. I need to see Dr. Mattrock so he'll know we will be calling on him in about another month. I can pay him for when David arrived, but I won't have the full amount to pay him next time.* From snatches of talk, she caught that Dick would be the one going to DeLamar to ask for supplies on credit. She figured he would be the one—John would not have the nerve to do so. She must have herself and David ready to go, so she really moved fast to have the dishes out of the way and herself dressed in her only presentable dress and lightweight coat. It, being of a loose fit, was all concealing.

"You are not going lookin' like that," Dick snapped at his wife as she moved enough to pull on her jacket. "Look at you. Your hair isn't even combed. The kids need washing as well as their heads combed. And I'm not waiting for you." With that, he left, followed by Mary and David.

I knew this would happen, Mary thought. Being honest with herself, she was not sorry that bedraggled trio was not along. *I can't blame Dick for being ashamed of them. I am myself.* Then she fell to wondering why it was that Dick himself always appeared neat and tidy, even though his clothes were of the poorest quality and stiff with soil, like they were this moment. Dick, a trim built man of medium height, could buy clothes to fit his sparseness. And fit, they did. A frayed cuff or raveled seam, he trimmed smooth. Mary noticed that he always kept shaved, his dark brown hair trimmed, and she had yet to see him with it uncombed. *How can he stand that slack wife is a mystery.* That she was not really bright, and their two children less smart, Mary had been sure of before starting out on their trek from central Nevada, having lived more than a month close to their makeshift camp. John and Dick had formed a partnership working together. Dick was a very good workman, and John liked him.

Can't blame John for liking Dick. I do myself, but I can see the other side of the question. Ah yes. Mary had been seeing that for these past six weeks. The money she had earned over a washboard had paid for the food both families had eaten all that time. This trip to town was not only to get food for David's wellbeing, but it was to pave the way to rid herself of responsibility for this family.

"There's sure been a lot of action around here at sometime," Dick interrupted her thoughts as he took in the scattered machinery rusting away. "Looks like we come to the right spot— must be plenty of work to be had."

"They hire a good sized crew in the mines and mill here at DeLamar," she told him. "You being a good workman, Dick, you should have no trouble getting on."

"Oh, I'm satisfied with my job, Mrs. Marcus. John and I get along very well together."

"But remember, John has no money and no credit in this town. We already owe more than we could pay in a couple of years working for good wages. You are the one having to buy on credit, and my advice to you is to tell them you are a miner and looking for work, even expecting to go to work, or you might come back without a dry bean to cook."

"I know John has no cash. I'm willing to take the team off his hands."

"That is the part you'd better not mention. Don't say a word about working for John. You would stand a much better chance."

"You being acquainted in this burg, where would be the best chance of me getting grub on jawbone?"

"At the store in Lower Town. I'll point it out to you as we drive through. You'll need to drive on up into Upper Town to be able to turn around in the wood yard. David and I will be close to the Post Office then. That's where we need to go first. Don't wait for us, we can walk back to Lower Town." She pointed out the store to him, but did not try talking more. The noise of the rock crusher filled the air with its din. David clung tightly to her arm holding him.

"That's quite a mill, that," Dick stated admiringly after getting on past. "So this is the famous DeLamar I've been hearing about."

"Yes, this is it. Make sure you don't get lost," she tried to joke. "We two will get off here. The wood yard seems pretty well filled with wood, but they always leave a turn around." She took care in climbing from the wagon. David was leaning far forward. "Be careful, Sonny, wait until Mother reaches up for you."

"Well, well, the wanderers have returned," was Jimmy Burch's greeting with a hearty handshake. "Are you glad to be back?"

"I surely am. They can have what I saw of Nevada and Arizona, or give it back to the Indians for all of me. I like these hills better. They seem like home."

"Glad to hear that. And how is this young man?" He proffered David a huge stick of peppermint candy, and smiled as the serious little fellow hesitated about taking it. "Don't tell me you don't like candy."

"The size of that stick would scare most any small boy not in the know," Mary smiled back at him. "Shall we break off a piece?" David understood this and was soon munching away. "I see you have some of those health crackers. I want several packages of those. Have you malted milk?"

"Only this one small jar, Mrs. Marcus." Jimmy handed it up from below the counter. "And the cap cover seems to be damaged, so it might be hard to open, but I believe the contents are perfectly alright. I understand the drug store is out of malted milk also. As for these crackers, I'll be glad to let you have the lot of them at half price. No one in this camp buys them—they prefer the soda crackers."

"And they have been David's main food this past year. They keep well, and where we have been much of the time, that has been quite an item; the same way with this kind of milk," tapping the dented top. "He likes it better than the canned kind, and it keeps without spoilage. Oh, yes, I want several cans of lye. There is so much waste fat left at the place, I can see where we are going to have plenty of soap this winter. But I do want two cakes of Castile soap." She sorted out three clips of safety pins while Jimmy tied a stout string about the cans of lye.

"Are you going into the soap making business?" Jimmy asked with a smile.

"I'm going into the laundry business instead. So if you know of any single and hard working men who want their clothes washed and patched, will you give them the word?"

"I will be glad to. You know, you might do very well at that. Lots of them don't like to peddle out their clothes."

"I found that out at several small camps we were close to. Wherever I could find water, I could find all the dirty clothes I could manage to get done. I charged $.25 for each change of underwear, socks and handkerchief; shirts were $20 extra. Some of them needed starching and ironing, of course. Others were woolen and needed the more careful washing and hardly any pressing. Do you think that is about the right price?" she asked while counting out the money to pay for what she had just bought.

"I think that's a very reasonable price. And let me wish you luck in this business venture." He continued to visit until Mr. Lyons interrupted to hand Mary a letter.

"This came two days ago, marked to be held until called for; so you see we were expecting you home, Mrs. Marcus." Mr. Lyons seemed to be glad to see her too.

"Thank you very much. This will be from the folks. They were the only ones I let know we were headed back." Gathering up her purchases, she found them quite a load. Taking David by the hand now, they headed to Lower Town to where Dick waited for them.

The closer they came to the vibrating noise, the more frightened David became until she could not walk for him clutching her about the legs. Forced to pick him up and carry him, she was in a bad way for a short distance until Dick saw them coming and loped up the hill to relieve her of the packages. David was not about to turn loose of her neck.

"I got everything you had wrote down on that list, Mrs. Marcus," Dick was told her as she and David climbed into the wagon, "except that case of canned milk. I wondered if there was any use in getting it—your boy on the other kind, and my young ones won't drink any kind of milk."

"I know Dick, they don't drink milk, but they will eat all the different kinds of food cooked with it, so they do get it whether they know it or not. And they really should have milk to grow right. By the way, did I have dry beans written down on that list?"

Dick scanned the slip of paper. "Guess not. And we have to have beans." Off he trotted, coming back with a case of milk under one arm and a twenty-five pound sack of beans under the other. "Now we're fixed for eats for awhile." He was happy as he climbed in and they went on their way. "I thought for a little while that guy wasn't going to let me have grub. Then I remembered what you said about me hinting I wanted work. He said they were putting on men every few days."

Mary sighed from tiredness, but more from the hopeless task of making this man see where he should take a paying job with real wages so as to support his family.

"I learned about the same thing at the Post Office and the Upper Town store," she told him, but did not press the point. Jimmy Burch had promised he would phone down and let her know the first time he heard there was an opening at the mines. Mary was sure Jimmy thought she had been inquiring for John's benefit. She did not see fit to correct this. *If Dick gets work, with John disliking to work alone, he might take the hint and go to work at the mines too.*

She was dismayed to learn that Dr. Mattrock had left DeLamar. *I don't know how I'm ever going to get him paid. It being another doctor, a stranger too, we'll be calling down in about a month or so. I'll need to have twenty-five collars on hand. I know I should have waited and seen him today, but Jimmy said he was seldom in his office until afternoon. That was too long a wait for David. Besides, I might not have any home left if we don't get down there soon.*

A big house might be harder for two destructive children to tear apart than a camp. All they seem to know is to smash or scatter things. She was sure she would be much happier when she did not have to put up with them or the sullenness of their mother. *That woman is going to be worse than ever, now that I rode to town with her husband this day.* No, Mary Marcus was not very happy as she rode home. As the house came into view, "I see the house is still standing. I believe the best thing to do, Dick, is for us to take all this food to the cellar. I'll unlock it the first thing. In that way, the kiddies cannot get at it to waste one bit of it."

"Pretty good plan." Dick hopped down to open the gate. Mary drove the team close to the other yard gate. "You get it unlocked, and I'll pack it in there as soon as I put this team in the barn. We won't unharness them—John might want to haul in wood this afternoon if he's got enough cut," he told her as she and David made their way through the yard gate.

Chapter Nineteen

"MY, ISN'T THIS ANOTHER glorious autumn morning?" asked Mary of the two men as they came to the west porch ready for work. "Not a killing frost yet, and here it is the middle of October." She came out here to be free from that everlasting squabble of the two children. Breathing in the fresh crisp air, "I want to go pick cherries and rosehips, such a morning as this, but I have to wash instead. You two will have to guess when noon comes, so I can have a long afternoon for my gathering."

Neither man answered, but Dick waved a hand. She turned to enter the house to be about her work. Mrs. Palmer stood in the doorway, unmoving as usual, a sullen stare on her face. "I guess that wave must mean they heard me," Mary didn't expect an answer, or for her to move out of the doorway so she could enter. She stepped lively, in spite of her bulk, along the porch to the front of the house. She came in quietly so as not to disturb David, should he be sleeping. *How any grown woman can be so ignorant as to stand in a doorway and not move out of the way when she knows someone is wanting to come in.* Mary was very tired of always having to ask her to move, and waiting then for her slow response. *Sometimes I'm afraid she won't comply even when asked. I do wish Jimmy Burch would telephone down to me this very day to say a man could get on in DeLamar.* She tiptoed to the telephone nailed to the wall, back of the swinging door that led to the kitchen. The morning sun, peeping over the hills, lit up this dim corner and she wanted to be sure she understood how many rings meant this place. Mary was not too familiar with using a telephone, and this being a *toll line*, she was less sure she understood it. Father had written about it when Max had it installed for his convenience, having one at his ranch on the Flats at the same time. It helped that the new lines were going in so close to his place, and the fact that he bought so much stock in the company.

"As I understand it, we don't have to pay anything for having this telephone here," she had explained to John when first he spied it. "It's called a *toll line,* and you only pay when you use it."

"We won't be using it, and for all of me, they can come tear the thing out." John would have liked nothing better than to have done it himself. The small posted on it gave him pause. It stated it

183

was the property of the Bell Telephone Company, and anyone damaging it was liable to prosecution. He let Mary know he wanted nothing to do with anything Max Thorn installed.

The biggest flare up had come when he learned Max had leased the place. Any joy John Marcus might have felt in knowing they still had some ownership in this property was swallowed up in his jealous ranting. Mary wanted to put all thoughts of that unhappy time far from her. *John was so unreasonable to think Father had done the leasing—what would he have done had he known I was the one?* Mary had not told untruths; neither had she explained. John had assumed David Williams made the deal, and that the lease money had been the amount of the payment. *I'm paying through the nose for all of my deceit,* she told herself as the swinging door bumped her hard. The two screaming youngsters hit the door, and tried scrambling into the dining room.

She collared both of them and took them bodily back to the kitchen, but the noise had already awakened David. She fixed his food, and while he ate hemmed in between stove, table and wash tubs, she went about her work. "Now you two stay on that side." She pushed them beyond her piles of soiled clothes and scouted the toy box after them. She knew she would have to resort to flips of water every now and then to keep them there. *I'd better be glad they are scared of water,* was her thought as she rubbed away. She was not going to let those stares cast her way bother her. The dishes were unwashed, but never once had Mrs. Palmer washed them. *I wouldn't care to eat from them if she did,* was her feeling on the question.

Mary had hopes that the woman might be able to pick chokecherries or rosehips, but after the first try at that, she gave up any such idea. *But I sure bless Dick's sharp eyes for seeing that old baby buggy up over head in the barn.* With that, she found it easier to go further distances. David could nap in it and then she could push both he and the pails of cherries back home.

The last piece of clothing was ready to hang on the line, all piled in the basket and foot tub atop the table out of harm's way. David, with his handful of play dishes, was still content on the floor beside her. Long ago she gave up trying to let the three play together. David could not understand those two just snatching everything he might pick up to play with. Tubs of rinse water were now emptied. Those two seemed to sense there was no water there to hit them and tried to crowd past the bench. The dipper held a teaspoon full from giving David a drink. That amount sent them howling out of the way. Building up a better fire, she now spent the time to make a dried apple pie and slip it into the oven before putting David to nap. With a safety hook high on the door, she felt he was safe while she hung out her wash. Half way through, she unlocked the cellar door and brought out the bean pot to put on the stove to heat, turning the pie while there.

When she mounted the porch, she spied the men as they stepped from the tunnel. *I'm glad for once they are a few minutes late.* Coffee was on and bacon frying, and she was washing dishes by the time they reached the house. "Warm plates to eat on is the style around here," she told them, as she set the dishes she was wiping on the table. John was the first one washed. "You dish some beans onto the children's plates to cool while I cut bread." As Dick finished drying his hands, Mary nodded toward the coffee pot. "You can pour that." She was not sure he could hear her above the noise. Neither bread nor bacon dared she place on the table, but served it a slice at a time to each as ready for it. "Almost afraid our pie will be too warm to eat," she stated as she went for David so he could eat his meal and be ready to go with her.

"You know, there are only two kinds of pie I like," grinned Dick as he cut the pie to serve himself a wedge. "That's hot pie and cold pie." He rapped the grimy hands with the knife as they tried to get at his pie. "Leave it alone. It's hot." The word was understood enough to stay their hands as to that one serving of pie, but they dived into what was put on their own plates. Howls of fright came once their hands stuffed the still-warm pie into their mouths. "You dumb kinds," thundered Dick. "I told you it was hot." The two men did not tarry over their meal.

I can't blame them for hurrying away. I'm doing the same. Mary had taken the food stuff back to the cellar in jig time, the used dishes were again piled to be washed while supper cooked. Night was already falling when she pushed the buggy through the gate. John met her.

"Don't you ever know when to quit?" He picked up the tired and sleepy boy and carried him into the kitchen. Mary followed with the full pails of cherries, setting them down on the table for one instant to pick up one at a time to put them up on the high shelf. That space of time was enough for four clawing hands to send cherries bouncing to the floor.

"Get out of those, you damned kids. They are not fit to eat!" He swatted both soundly. Dick had no patience with his children. Chucking them both through the washroom door, he now pushed his wife after them. "Keep them in there 'til I can sweep those things up."

In the uproar, David puckered up and commenced to cry. "Now don't you start in bawling too." John was out of patience trying to get him out of coat and leggings.

"No, David Boy isn't going to cry," Mary spoke soothingly close to him. "David is going to have a nice warm bath, and then some supper. Just as soon as Daddy can get his clothes off, Mother will have that bath ready." She drew the water into the foot tub and peeled off her jacket to test the water with her elbow. David's catchy giggle, half laugh and half cry, greeted the sight of his bath. Draping the worn blanket about the chair to shield him from the draft when the doors would be opened, her hand went to her pocket. "Dick, here is the key. Would you bring the food from the cellar while I get David's gown from the line?"

Mary slipped out the same door instead of going through the washroom, and walked the longer distance to the line. She was back in time to open the door for Dick as he came with his hands loaded. Into the warm oven went the gown to air and warm. "Just wrap him up in the blanket, Daddy, until I get his food ready. He might need a little help to eat tonight, for he's one very tired boy." All the time she was talking, she had been fixing his bowl of warm milk. Part of it went into his mug, the bread broken into the rest. "This will be easier to eat and quicker to fix."

John aided in getting his warm gown on midway of the repast. "I believe he is asleep now, but still eating."

"I know," Mary said while hurrying to get the clean, dried dishes onto the table. "The second he stops eating, get him into bed. I fear we'll all be going to sleep over the supper table tonight." She wondered why Dick was watching every move she made this meal, but she had not long to wonder.

"Ma, why don't you have sense enough to do like Mrs. Marcus here?" he asked his wife. "When her young one cries, she bathes him, feeds him and pops him into bed. Why don't you try that?"

"An' make 'em cry more?" demanded the dull woman.

Mary hid her smile. *That's the first sensible thing I've heard her say.* "Has either one ever liked a bath?" she asked the mother and received only the sullen look again.

"They've always yelled their heads off," Dick told her. "Some folks say kids like their bath. These two never have." His eyes held a puzzled and defeated look as he watched his four year old son and year younger daughter mow away their food like little animals. He knew this was all wrong, but had no success in making them use a spoon or fork.

"I'm sure most children like a bath," Mary said in a normal voice. The howls would soon be tuning up. "Some, not at the very first, perhaps, but if the bath is made pleasant, neither too hot or too cold, they soon enjoy it." She stopped talking as the crying got louder at the mere mention of a bath.

This night, she insisted that John help her with the dishes instead of letting Dick help. As the big gloomy room became quiet and peaceful, she said, "I know you don't like to wipe dishes, John, but I'm tired enough. I cannot stand any more of that noise."

"Why doesn't that woman put those howling brats to bed where they belong?"

"I doubt she could make them stay in bed if she was able to get them there in the first place. She can't handle them to wash them. Just when I am sure that woman is without common sense, she comes up with some smart saying like she did at the table."

"I can't see where that was smart," grumbled John. "Sounded pretty dumb to me. For the life of me, I can't see how come Dick, as smart as he is, could hook up with any dumb cluck as that."

"Perhaps women were scarce when Dick took a notion to get married." She tried to speak pleasantly, though she was very weary. "Why I say that was a smart observation of Mrs. Palmer's is because if she attempted to handle those two, it would only mean more crying. Have you ever watched her try to wash Daisy's face? She never gets the job done, any more than she can get all the tangles out of her hair. That small tot fights like a little wild cat. I know, for I still have scratches. That is why they can go with hair uncombed for all of me." She sighed as the last dish was finished. "You think Dick is smart, and he has the appearance of being smart, I must admit. But he must not be, or he could see that his wife cannot handle those two. He can't make them mind with all his swatting them."

"They need more of it to my way of thinking."

Mary caught hold of his arm and stopped him as he was about to leave the room for bed. "You know and I know—they are not going to get more spankings. They are not getting any better—worse if anything. They are turning our home into a nightmare, John. We can't have it."

"Trying to go back on your word, are you?" he taunted. "You know Dick is a good worker and he wants that team. I sure as heck don't want 'em." With that, he went on to bed.

How can he be so blind, she questioned the dark as she snuffed out the candle. *How can they feed that team? Come deep snow, they'll starve to death unless they are smart enough to head for the Flats ahead of the storm.* John knew all about the deep snow here, but Dick would not be wise to it. *How can John be so unfair?* Still no answer to that question, so she went to bed too.

Weariness of body brought sleep in spite of a troubled mind. "John, wake up. Father has come." She sat bolt upright in bed. John thought she was dreaming and made no move to stir. "Father is here. I heard him." She piled out of bed onto the chilly floor in her bare feet as the tramp of heavy feet came up the walk.

"Anybody home?" called a voice following a smart rap.

"Yes, oh yes! We are home, Father." Mary opened the hall door by that time. David, rudely awakened out of a sleep, began to cry. John, slipping into his pants, wrapped the boy in the first thing handy and carried him to the hall also. David's whimpering and the chilling of her bare feet brought Mary to her senses and checked her emotional upheaval. "Come in, Father. Poor witless me, keeping you standing out here freezing and scaring my boy, was I?" She would have taken him in her arms, but John moved toward the rest of the house with him. "Let's all go to the kitchen. It will be warmer there." Her voice was not yet steady. The flare of John's match lighting the candle made her aware she had nothing on but her night gown. "You go on to the kitchen, Father. I'll put on something more." With slippers on her feet and tying the sash of her dressing robe, "Did you have trouble finding us in the dark?" David was already snuggled in his Grandfather's arms, trying hard to look up at his face so far above him. "Oh, and David went right to you. Not one bit afraid." She was happy over that.

"I would have had trouble had not Mr. Finch, the dairyman above here, put me wise to the one road leading off to the left. But I would have been wiser had I left the cow there 'til morning. Leading her is what made me so late getting here." He patted the boy eyeing him.

"Oh, Father, you haven't brought us another cow?" That was almost a wail.

"Surely I brought a cow, and the hay to feed her. How else is this fine boy going to get milk to grow on? Now I would like nothing better than to cuddle this grandson, but I best give you to your mother while your father shows us where to put my tired teams, as well as the moo-cow."

Mary could not speak as she accepted David into her arms. All the fears of another hungry cow rushed to mind. That team of horses without fodder would surely eat up most of the hay. This was a worse calamity than three years ago. David snuggled down for sleep, wrapped in nothing but her petticoat. She took him back to his own bed and hoped he would settle down, for she must go put the tubs and wash boiler against the yard fence and get the bucket to water those horses and cow. They must not be turned loose this night.

Father Williams swung his lantern about and caught sight of her darting about in the dark. "What are you doing out in this chilly night?"

"You need to water the team and cow here from this pump, Father. They must not be turned loose tonight. They might go to the creek for water, and that water is full of cyanide." She was sure she would never get over her fear of that poisoned water.

"Then John and I will see to that. You go back to where it is warmer." He worried about this daughter of his, Mary heavy with child, yet tripping about in the night. What if she should fall?

Mary went back to the house, but spent her time going to the cellar for food and had a lunch set out by the time Father and John came in. "Do you care for coffee, Father?"

"Not this late at night, Daughter. I have some sleeping to get in this night. Just dump that roll of bedding down for now, John." He washed at the sink, carrying on a conversation all the while. "You see, this is only half a pleasure trip. I loaded the wagons with baled hay coming up, but I'm lookin' to take back good

189

juniper posts. And what a time I had getting that hay baled. They don't seem to do much of it around this country yet. Don't you fix any more food for me to eat—that is more than plenty. I shouldn't be hungry at all. You know what lunches Mother puts up— enough to last you a week when you are only to be on the road for 48 hours."

"Is that all the longer you were? But how did you get the cow up here this time?" Mary was eager with questions.

"The same as last time." Father smiled as he commenced eating. "Only this time, Tom Ewing walked all the way. He was bringing up the pack mules that got away and came to the Flats. He wouldn't ride them on a bet, Max says. I believe that is one man who would rather walk than travel any other way."

"That was the way my uncle was," John surprised them both by saying. "He always had a burrow or two for packing our beds and grub, but he wouldn't ride one of 'em."

"Father, I know you should be eating and not answering questions, but tell me how Mother and Annie are, then I promise to keep still." Her eyes shone with tears.

"They are fine, Daughter. Just fine. Annie is sure happy about going to school now that one is close enough for her to go to. She seems not to mind the four mile ride twice a day. She has grown tall...you would hardly know her. Mother looks well, and I believe she is, but on a long trip like into Caldwell, she would be down in bed for a few days afterwards." He stopped talking, not as much because he was hungry, but because he had no intentions of telling Mary what he had learned from the doctor. The news—a heart infection, and the most they could do about it was to keep Mother from getting overly tired.

"There never was such a wonderful surprise as when I heard your call. Did you call more than the once before coming to the door?"

"Just the once at the gate, then at the door," Father answered.

"Here I said I wouldn't ask you any more questions," she smiled as she said this and pushed a small jar of jam toward him. "I want you to try this on your bread and see if you can guess what fruit it is made from."

Dutifully, he sampled some on his bread, then some of it alone. Smacking his lips, "It's mighty good tasting jam alright, whatever it is. There is almost a raspberry twang to it, but I'm sure it isn't made from those."

"No it isn't raspberries. It is made from wild rosehips. There are lots of them around here. It takes a lot of work to make it, rubbing it all through a pan sieve, but where fruit is so scarce, it is well worth all the trouble, we think. You shall have some of your favorite jelly for breakfast," she told him as he pushed back his chair.

"You mean elderberry jelly? That will be a treat. Been a long time since I've ate any."

"Mary's been hoarding this jam, so we couldn't eat it," John helped himself to bread and jam before she could get it put away.

"If I didn't keep it out of sight, they would eat it up faster than I can make it. Father, I hate to have you climb those steep stairs to go to bed this night."

"I have my bedroll and I've used the ground for a mattress one night. It won't hurt me a mite to just unroll my bed right here on the floor."

"Oh no, you'll do nothing of the kind," Mary scolded. "Not with three bed springs and mattresses upstairs. I know everything must be covered in dust, for I haven't spent even one day cleaning house since we came back. I want to get every chokecherry, elderberry and rosehip gathered before winter socks in. I know I can clean and scrub to my heart's content after then. John, you'll carry up the bed roll for Father?"

"I won't carry anything, remember, but I'll pack it up there," he said as he shouldered the heavy roll.

Mary handed him the lantern she had just put a match to. "I do believe the back bedroom, where the soap is drying by the chimney, has the best set of springs of any of the beds," she told John, then bade her father goodnight.

Early dawn found the household astir. Father came in with the pail of milk; Dick had a wooden crib bed on his shoulders; John munched a donut from the sack he carried. Father beamed with pleasure at Mary's surprise. "I found that crib selling for $1 a week ago at a sale, so I upped the ante $.25. Didn't know if David had a bed of his very own or not, but figured you could use it perhaps. It's one of those kind you take apart and put together easy like. Annie tried doing so several times until she was sure it worked. She helped Mother make the pad for it, and she made the pillow. So we'll say it is Annie's gift to David."

"My, won't that boy be proud to have such a nice bed all his own. You men all get about the table for breakfast as soon as you can," she told them above the noise. She took the sack of donuts from John's arm and set it on the high shelf. Then she dished rolled oats for the grownups. The children's oats were already dished and cooling. She handled the pitcher of fresh milk, pouring a small amount into the cooling cereal and doling out the right amount of sugar to keep it from being spilled.

The meal went well, Mary handing out biscuits as needed; likewise, bacon and the glass of jelly. With the men's second cup of coffee, she served the donuts, placing one on each child's plate, two on each man's. One, she broke in two for David and herself, then held the sack for Mrs. Palmer to help herself. She was a long time about taking only one of the two remaining in the sack. She might as well have taken both of them, for the sack was snatched from Mary's hand. Dennis, the four year old boy, got his hands on the last one. Daisy, not to be out done, snatched half away from him.

"Stop your fighting, you damned kids." Dick yanked them back into their chairs. "You haven't eaten the one you already have," he yelled above their howls. "You fight over everything, just like a couple of dogs over a bone.'"

"Mary wondered what Father must think of such behavior and talk. He kept his eyes on small David as if to see how he was reacting to all this hubbub. As the worst of the noise subsided, Father asked, "Would it make unloading that hay much easier if I back each wagon right up to the barn door? If you have a plank about the place, we could just slide the bales down it."

John nodded instead of speaking, his mouth full of donuts just then.

"Let us be up and about it." Dick was already on his feet, draining his coffee cup standing. The three men were soon out of the room. Mary put away the food stuff out of reach. Next came the crib bed to be put under lock and key. Both Dennis and Daisy were in on the clean pad with their soiled hands and dirty shoes.

The dishes can wait again, she told herself as she and David fled the house. "We'll go see David's moo-cow." Going toward the barn where the men were busy unloading hay, and on to the corral was the leg-weary cow. The other cow was roan, but this one had dark markings. "But you are one beautiful cow," Mary said around the lump in her throat while she petted her. David was timid and would not touch her.

Now as they walked back, she saw the boxes and sacks piled against the fence. "Father, you said you brought up hay for the cow. It looks to me like you brought a year's supply of food for this family." Father did not stop the up-ending of bales to talk. The two Palmer children raced from the house as they spied those boxes and sacks, and the next instant, they were clawing at the broken side of an apple box. Bright red apples spilled out.

"Stop it," Mary called sternly, knowing anything she said would have no effect. She hurried to them, grabbed them by the back of their clothing, and forced them through the gate and hooked it. Both clawed a big apple in each hand. *Maybe these will keep them busy for a little while.* Mrs. Palmer was taking it all in from the porch, making no attempt to stop them from racing through the other gate and coming in from the back yard by the chicken house. Mary was ready for them now, holding the thin board from the side. She wielded it against first one then the other as they tried to snatch more apples. Howls and screams rend the air. It was Dick who saw her predicament and came to the rescue.

Paddling them soundly, he carried them to the house, forcing his wife inside with them. "You keep these damned kids inside, do you hear?" His angry voice carried as far as the barn.

The first wagon was now unloaded. Father came with the empty wagon, ready to hitch onto the full one. Mary asked, "John, can you and Dick take all this to the cellar so it will be safe, while Father gets that wagon in place?" She slipped the cellar key into John's pocket as he shouldered a sack of potatoes. From the sound of things, those two were out again and would soon be back. Gathering up the hem of her apron, she gathered the scattered apples as fast as David could hand them to her. Not until the last squash and the broken box of apples were being carried to the cellar did she leave her post.

"Plenty of them all over the yard," John said as he came back. "Do you want me to help you pick 'em up?"

"David and I'll manage." She still had the thin board and made a swing with it to let him know she would use it. "I do want the key, though." Their very life depended on that bit of metal.

Chapter Twenty

FATHER WILLIAMS WAS MORE than worried. While Mary seemed well and able to cope with this disjointed household now, he thought, *There is coming a day when she won't be up and able to do so.* As the Palmer family left the warm kitchen for their quarters, and John pulled off heavy shoes ready to think about bed, he bestirred himself to learn what he could about her plans. "Shall I put another stick of wood on the fire, Daughter? You and I have hardly had time for a chat."

"Yes, do that, Father. We must get in a little visiting this night. I'm not pleased for morning to come and to see you on your way. I know that is just plain selfishness on my part with Mother and Annie waiting so anxiously for your return. You've been here five whole days, yet it seems like I haven't seen you at all." She dried her hands and came to sit beside him.

"Neither one of us has been very idle," he gave her his whimsical, but understanding smile.

"I know," Mary said nodding her head. "And there is no talking with those two ill mannered children around. I'm glad you have those posts to take back." What she was really glad about was John and Dick helping Father out and loading them.

"Just how are you going to handle those two imps of Satan when you'll need be in bed? Their mother seems worse than useless in caring for them."

"Useless is the right word. I have been experimenting these last few days with a long keen willow switch, and found they are afraid of that. I have found no way to control them except through fear. The morning after you came and they scattered the apples so, I used that thin board on them. I was so put out at their snatching apples right from David's hands as he tried to put them in my apron. I had to whack them very hard to make them stop—I was actually afraid I might injure them; so now I have a willow switch on that shelf. Of course, I can't stop the whining or howling, and when their father is about, I let him take care of them. I doubt Dick is teaching them anything. It seems that he isn't going about it in the right way. Maybe they cannot learn. At first I spent a lot of time trying to teach them to play like ordinary children so David would have playmates. I could get nowhere." She leaned close to say quietly, "The Palmer family may think they have

194

settled down for the winter, but they haven't. I'm only waiting now until the word is telephoned to me that a man is needed at the mines. I learned there are houses of a sort to be had in DeLamar. Dick always listens to what I have to say. I believe I can convince him he should take that job."

"Then John and his partnership isn't of the lasting kind?"

"It just can't be, Father. Dick wanted to buy the team from John, but he doesn't have a cent, so he agreed to work for six months to pay for them. All this took place about the time John and I were so homesick to get back here. I was unaware of their agreement, and I told John of the lease and our still having this place to come back to. I know John must have been glad, but he was also very unreasonable over the fact a sheep man had been the one to lease it." She didn't mention that John's jealousy of Max Thorn was part of the trouble. She spread her hands in an attitude of resignation. "If John let the team go without payment, our chances of getting home was slim. That is how we came to be saddled with the family as well as the team."

"Tell me, which one should I ask about borrowing the use of that team to help me down with my load?

Mary brightened at once. "Oh, Father, here I've been worrying my head of what I could do about that team. I thought I would have to turn them loose some dark night and chase them away to get rid of them. But if you do get the use of them, you'll be saddled with feeding them all winter."

"That isn't too expensive down there. Ten chances to one, they could run in pasture most the time and do very well. How about you and David coming down home for the next two months and let Mother and Annie have the pleasure of caring for you while you are in bed?"

"That would be all very fine for us, but that would be for only a few days. The return trip in winter with two little ones would not be easy. No, it just would not do. Besides, I wouldn't be getting rid of the Palmer family were I to leave."

"Daughter, I fear that woman is not going to be a mite of help to you when you need it." This was almost a plea.

"I know she won't be. But John and Dick are both handy when I tell them what I want done. Both of them can cook, and they are going to have to help me a lot these next few weeks, so they'll know how and what to do. I have them pretty well trained about keeping the cellar locked so our foodstuff will not be wasted."

"How are you fixed for money? You'll need some for the doctor at least."

"I have more than $35 of that last $40 you sent me from the lease. And several men's washings are being sent down every day or so now. I took up ten little bundles day before yesterday when I borrowed one of your teams and drove to town. That meant $3.50, for each man had an extra shirt to do up. I spent the whole amount for sugar so this family will have jelly and jam this winter. Like John says, I'm guilty of hoarding it too. Father, I have three small glasses ready for you to take home. One is elderberry—that's for you. The chokecherry can be for Mother—I believe she will like that odd tartness. The rosehip jam will surprise Annie."

"I'm not sure I like the idea of you taking on that extra work when you have more than enough to do without it."

"That is what John is always saying." Mary smiled at her troubled parent. "You don't need to worry about me overdoing it. Those washings are easy to do. I like to wash. And they bring in a fair return for my trouble. Water was not always to be had for washings in the places we camped in Nevada and Arizona. But where there was water, I had all the laundry I could do. A few days, I made as much as $5 a day. That was as much money as miners made in a day. One of the mines needed a cook and they offered me the job, but John objected to me taking it. I fear it wouldn't have been good for David. I couldn't have given him much time, and then all the men made so much of him, buying him all kinds of presents. He could have been made selfish without anyone realizing it."

"You know my old saying, Daughter—about never selling yourself short? Now I'm suggesting that you not sell your husband short. Let John, in other words, shoulder his own responsibility, and have the satisfaction of supporting his family."

"Oh, he will, Father. Just as soon as he sees where this digging around in that tunnel won't make him rich." She did not want to pursue that line of talk, or say that John wasn't aware he was suffering too. "It is nearing nine o'clock, and I should let you get some sleep for the long day ahead of you, and I need to be up reasonably early to have your lunchbox ready. So I think we better go to bed."

"Yes, six o'clock comes early these mornings." David Williams was tired.

At the breakfast table, as soon as the worst of the noise had subsided, David Williams asked, "I've been wondering which one of you men I should ask for the loan of the team to help me over the hill? Those posts are pretty heavy, and I might have more than my two teams can manage."

"That's right," John spoke. "I don't know which one of us would have the say so. Dick here wants to buy them, and I bargained to sell 'em to him."

Father turned to Dick. "How about it? Have you need for them that will pay to keep them through the winter?"

"No work that I know of for 'em, except to get some wood, which we'll have to get pretty soon." Dick went on with his meal.

Father thought for moment. "As I understand these hills, the getting of that wood needs to be very soon. It is nearing November and snow can be too deep to get about. How much wood do you think the three of us can cut and snake up to your wood house in one full day?"

"A right smart pile, I'd say," commented Dick.

John was slow about saying anything, so Father turned toward him. "Do you think you and I can cut faster than Mr. Palmer can haul those logs? In that way, you would have your pile of wood, and I can be on my way only one day late. I will agree to winter them for their use. Surely there will be some way to get them back here in the spring when you want them.

John was still slow about answering, but David Williams' steady grey eyes pressed him for a reply. "It's alright with me if it is with Dick."

"Then let's get to getting." Dick was already on his feet while swallowing his last gulp of coffee.

"I will have dinner on the table at 12 o'clock for you starved men," Mary called after them.

The day was a mad rush. Dick had changed teams more than once at David Williams' suggestion. Dinner was a hurried affair. Dark came before Father and John made their weary way in behind the last small untrimmed trees. "Those limbs left on made the pile look bigger," joked Father as he saw Mary holding the lantern high to light the way for Dick to unhook the chain.

"It is a nice lot of wood anyway." Mary handed the light to

John. "Just as soon as this team can be unharnessed, I'll have supper on the table. I put feed out for all the horses, and watered the others. The cow is milked already. I know you all must be dead tired. But my, what a showing for your work!" She now made for the house and last minute preparations.

There were no attempts to talk at the table this night—everyone was much too tired. Food did not still the noise of the two children even this once. Dick became angry. "Take these damned youngsters to bed," he yelled at his wife. "They are not eating and won't let anyone else eat for their fighting." The sullen woman got up from the table, but it was Dick who manhandled the two of them, pushing her along with them to their rooms.

The noise was two doors away, so Mary could finally think straight. She spoke to Dick as he came back. "Dick, I was to blame for those two not eating their supper. They acted like they were starved when I fed David at the regular supper hour, so I gave them food then." She could have said she could not stand their crying any longer.

"They need to be in bed anyhow." Dick was still angry.

Mary could now put more hot rolls, the pat of butter, and glass of jelly on the table since there were no snatching fingers to spoil or waste them. *I'm sorry that poor scrawny woman didn't get to eat her meal, but then she might have just sat there not eating the rest of the time anyway. Maybe that is why she is so skinny—just hasn't sense enough to eat when she can.* "I baked more cinnamon rolls today. Do you men want some or would you rather have them for your breakfast?"

All three men voted for the morning meal. Soon, the hushed household slept. Breakfast was a hurried meal. Mary spent the time packing Father's lunch. She served each a sweet spicy roll. David, in his highchair, tugged at her sleeve thinking he was left out.

"Oh, Mother hasn't forgotten her boy," with a kiss on his neck. "I have the nicest little roll up here in the warming oven waiting until David has his last bite of cereal eaten." She helped him to spoon it to his mouth.

"Daughter, you do not need to put in half those rolls you are about to wrap there."

"In other words," smiled Mary, "you are telling me you prefer one of them right now?" She served each man one more roll.

Mrs. Palmer had not eaten the one yet. It was disgusting to see the two small mites with their mouths crammed too full. Tapping their dishes to call their attention if possible, "All this food sticking around must be eaten before you can have more rolls." That might stay them from snatching their mother's, but it was doubtful.

***

With Father gone and the two men back at their tunnel work, the short days fell into some sort of a pattern. Mary, with David dressed warmly, spent all the daylight hours possible gathering the last of the chokecherries. "There's been enough heavy frost to prevent them from making good jelly," Mary remarked as she cooked more of them this evening. "I'm going to try this batch with plenty of apple peelings cooked along with them. The frost doesn't seem to make any difference in the rosehip jam, so I expect that is what I'd better gather the most."

"Are you ever going to quit all the tramping around?" John sounded tired.

"When snow comes," she retorted. "This autumn is different than three years ago. Here it is mid November and hardly a flake of snow as yet. I hope it holds off another day or two. I want to get everything washed up in the morning."

"You are always washing," John grumbled as she made ready for bed. "I thought you just washed yesterday."

"I did." She would not say that it was other people's clothes—that seemed to make John edgy. "This is all the bedding; I want everything clean. By the way, John, I wish you would take time off mid afternoon and go uptown and speak to that new doctor there. You might have to be trotting up there to call him one of these nights in a hurry."

"Why make two trips? When you need him is time enough to go for him." With that settled, John took himself off to bed.

By noon, the last sheet, blanket and nearly every piece of wearing apparel they owned, except what they were wearing, was on the line. The breeze whipped them dry without the aid of the sun, which refused to shine through the overcast sky. At dark, the last one of them was brought in, folded and put away. Floors were scrubbed, with plenty of food cooked and baking done. The house was filled with the good odors of baked potatoes, creamed dried corn and fresh baked bread. The disagreeable noise was going full blast, so there was no talking most part of the meal.

None noticed that Mary was not eating. She was doing her usual, serving the food to their plates right from the stove close at hand, keeping the butter and jam out of the way of darting hands. The rest of the time, her hands clutched the table edge. She did not hop to fill John's cup with coffee the instant he held it out. A small gasp of pain escaped her lips. "What's wrong with you?" demanded John, still eating.

"I think that wife of yours is already in labor," Dick said as he reached inside the washroom for the coat he just taken off. "You better go find out for sure, then I'll hot-foot it up after the doctor." He drank the last of his coffee while waiting for John to come back. John was a long time in coming. Dick had time to eat two more rolls and the last smear of butter.

All of his pleading was couldn't calm Mary. She could not talk for sobbing, acute pain making her more wretched. David, awakened by such noise close to his sleeping place, added his cries to his mother's. John was in straits now. Taking the wailing boy with him, he went to the kitchen. "I guess you better go for the doctor. I can't get her to say anything. She's miserable." John had to step close to Dick to make himself heard above the noise. Back in their bedroom, Mary's wild outburst was spent—there was only a groan as each pain wracked her. In the free space, she held out her arms for the unhappy boy and cuddled him beside her until he went to sleep.

Touching John's bowed head, she motioned for him to move David to his own bed. Now free to move about, she laid out gown, slippers and dressing sack. "I would like the foot tub of warm water for a sponge bath, but I fear the racket from the kitchen would arouse David if you open that door."

"How do you shut off that noise without knocking their heads in?"

"There is no way that I have found." She was a bit bitter and wanted him to have a taste of what she had to endure so much of the time. But she did need to be clean. "If you can make your voice sound as cross and mean as you did twice before this night, you might scare that woman and her offspring into getting to bed."

"Ah, Mary, don't take it out on me this way," he pleaded. "I didn't mean we wouldn't go for a doctor. I didn't even know you were sick. You never told me." He was very repentant. "If I can get that squalling pair and her off to bed, you would be warmer bathing in the kitchen. Dick and that doctor won't be here for maybe an hour yet."

"Alright. You try getting rid of them. Better go out this door into the hall, then down the porch to the kitchen door. In that way, no door will be opened into the dining room to disturb David." Her pain was subsiding, and she wondered if Dick had gone for the doctor when not necessary. Quietly, she tip-toed in to see if David was covered. A slight twinge was her reward for her effort. *So that means I might have to do some more walking before this is through with.* She could hear John's voice pitched high and sounding unnatural as he ordered them to bed. *It seems like he's making it stick,* was her thought while walking about and making sure the warm kitchen was really vacant before venturing out there.

"Why in sam-hill couldn't that lazy woman wash up these dishes? John eyed the cluttered table while water ran for Mary's bath. "Don't she ever do anything?"

Mary could not answer for a moment. "I know of nothing she'll offer to do. And you'll find you will not get very far telling her to do something." *Now I would have been wiser to not have said that last. Let John see for himself how she acts, should he suggest her doing some simple thing like dishes.* "Thank you for getting the water ready for me, John." She was trying hard to overcome her resentment. "Now if you will put a chair underneath the door knob to the washroom so none of them can burst in on me, I'll catch this outside door and pin a paper up to this window." Mary didn't worry about the lack of window curtains tonight.

The kitchen was once again spic and span, every dish washed and put away, the table scrubbed and the floor swept. John had helped greatly at all this. "The one thing you must never forget is to put all food back in the cellar the instant the meal is over. Lock that door, and by all means, don't lose the key," Mary said again before Dick returned. "Just today, Dennis dodged in there when I went for milk to use in the baking. Before I could stop him, he had wormed his fingers into a mended place in that wheat sack and let the grain run out on the floor. That is another thing. In feeding those hens Father brought us, fill the pint can in the sack full once a day. That's enough for the dozen. Maybe you'd better feed them in the morning or at noon, since it's generally dark before you and Dick stop work."

The tall youthful looking man Dick ushered in did not look old enough to be a full fledged M.D. "This is Dr. Thomas," Dick said. "I had a time finding him, Mrs. Marcus." Dick was looked puzzled at her being up and walking about very natural like. "Rest of them have gone to bed, have they? I wouldn't mind that second cup of coffee now."

"Lucky you know how to make it." Mary handed him the key. "You will need to go to the cellar for cream. You might take a pan along and bring back some cookies and that small pitcher of milk." An abrupt twinge showed on her face.

Dr. Thomas asked some routine questions. In-between those and her answers, John tried to make clear the severity of her pains. "Doctor, this husband of mine was not closer than two miles when our son arrived two and a half years ago, so you must overlook his version of such things." Mary told him.

Dr. Thomas laughed. "This being absent at such a time, I have heard is sometimes by design."

"It wasn't in that case. We thought there were two more weeks to wait."

The waiting hours were long, not only to Mary walking the floor, but to John, weary from work and fearful in not knowing what to expect. Dr. Thomas, well versed in such things, did not anticipate any serious complications in this case. *A strong healthy young woman, already the mother of one normal child, born with no assistance whatsoever, according to Dr. Mattrock.* Dr. Thomas had plenty of time for idle thoughts this night. He had put two and two together. This family must be the one Dr. Mattrock had told him about. *Their names were Marcus, the same as these people. She mentioned that they had lately returned here.*

"How many miles do you suppose I've covered this night?" Mary was weary and faint with hunger.

"Several, Mrs. Marcus. I'm sure you must be about exhausted. Perhaps a whiff of chloroform will help you relax a bit." He had come to the conclusion that tense nerves were the hindrance here. The man called Dick had babbled about a crying spell. In this calm appearing sensible woman, that would mean some emotional strain. Dr. Mattrock had her sized up as a well adjusted woman—

not frightened at being alone, but pleased that someone with skill was about to wash and dress her child. That tall tale about Mattrock being forced at the point of a gun—all the same as being kidnapped—Dr. Thomas was not sure he could believe all of that. Dr. Mattrock admitted he was not sure it was a gun poked into his ribs. From all he could learn, the man never was known to carry a short gun.

The gray of morning streaked the eastern sky as Dr. Thomas rode back toward DeLamar, leaving the new baby daughter and her mother asleep. Things sure happened plenty fast once she relaxed. He thought about the odd expression on John Marcus' face as he advised to let his wife sleep as long as she could. *That man acted as if that was something unheard of.* Dr. Thomas was still glad he had given her that sedative. *From the sound of all that commotion in the other part of the house, she'll surely need it.* He flicked his horse for more speed. He was getting used to riding again and enjoying it, but not so much this time of day.

Chapter Twenty One

DR. THOMAS WAS TAKING a fast cantor down the creek to this place called Wagontown. *It'll ease my mind if I know how they are.* It was a routine call, but had occasioned him a good bit of trouble to be away from the office this hour or two.

The gusty wind was neither strong nor cold, but whipped particles of dirt and sand up into his face every few minutes, spoiling the real pleasure of the ride. He rapped at the same door he had been taken through three nights ago. No one answered his rap, and from the sounds within, it was doubtful he could be heard. A dull faced woman eyed him through the glass in the door. At his second rap, he turned the knob to come in. Something was wrong here. This was not the clean orderly room he remembered. "I am Dr. Thomas. I came to see my patient, Mrs. Marcus." The woman staring at him remained mute. In that second, he heard the faint call from beyond the next room.

"Come in, Doctor." A door was opened by a small boy who returned to his play upon the foot of the bed. "Rather I should say come in if you can get in," Mary Marcus wiped the few crumbs from a chair seat as she made a motion for him to close the door on the two tousled dirty children following hard on his heels. "I know this a terribly untidy room and evil smelling for anyone to come into. I think I'm alright once I get rested, but I want to ask you if this foul odor and not being able to bathe the babe properly will harm her. It is much too chilly in here I fear. I oil her and rub her and keep her as clean as possible, but don't dare undress her and do it right." This all came tumbling out fast, like she was afraid she might not get it said otherwise. The noise outside the door was now louder. "If you open the door and can scare them away, it might help."

"Take these two away with their noise," Doctor Thomas spoke sternly to the woman behind them making no move to quell the confusion.

"You may need this persuader," Mary told him as she held out a willow switch. He took it, not sure if he would have to use it. They seemed to understand that limber twig, edging back toward the kitchen. "Now close that door and keep them away from here." He held the switch at a threatening angle, not aware he was doing so until the woman backed away. "Is this all the protection you have against such noise?" His face was grim as he closed the door almost shut. A glance through the crack told him they were on the way back. *Snap* went the switch, and the swinging door was back in place. "Is there any way of shutting them further away?"

"There is no way of locking the swinging door, but if there were, they could go outdoors and come in two other doors. We are safe enough in here. Having the bed up against this hall door, they can't get in, and that one I is blocked off with the two heavy chairs. David is very good about shoving that one close to the door while I wedge this one in." Her weakened state was plain in every word she spoke and the drop of her hand on the chair beside her bed.

Something had to be done, and done quickly. He was none too sure of his ground, not knowing what connection that feebleminded trio had in this household. "While you are busy taking care of your two little ones, who is taking care of you?" "Mr. Marcus does what he can. He brings our meals, but he's afraid to bathe such a small babe." Her eyes wondered over the used dishes and mound of apple peelings on the commode. She tried to smile, but it came out as a grimace. "When John brings our food, I must say it looks like it is plenty; David's and mine all on the same plate. I have to have him eat here with me. Otherwise he is too unhappy with all that noise."

"How much sleep are you doing?" He knew he need not ask that question.

"Not very much, I know. Nighttime, when I should be sleeping, I fail to be able to get to sleep. Daytime, it is much too noisy, and then I have a bit of fear when my eldest is not napping. I know there would be no harm intended toward the wee one, for there is much affection there, but that is the trouble—there is almost too much loving unless I'm alert."

"I would say you need a bite of lunch right now." He did not like that pulse at all. He moved fast, coming face to face with the dull woman as he opened the door. "Mrs. Marcus needs food. Can you get her some sort of a lunch?"

She did not move. "All food locked up," was all she managed to say.

Dr. Thomas did not know what to make of this. He glanced back into the room as the patient spoke to him, "It is true. The food stuff is under lock and key in the cellar." He closed the door and stood against it as if to make sure of keeping them out. "It has to be kept that way or there would be none, you understand. It's too much bother for you to attempt to get us a lunch. Please don't trouble yourself about it."

"Let me be the judge of that, Mrs. Marcus. Part of your tiredness right now is the lack of enough food. Can you tell me where I would find the key?"

"It is right here." She drew the bit of metal on a string from under her pillow to hand him. "Those two children will trouble you, dodging in just the instant you open that door. They always do, snatching apples, potatoes or onions...whatever they can. They don't eat them, they just scatter them and waste them." She offered him the willow again. He did not take it, but thought he might have to resort to its use before his thundering voice carried weight enough to make them move away.

He hunted for dishes in the dim pantry. They felt rough and poorly washed to his touch, so he washed and rinsed them as well as he could in the standing bowl of water. Armed with two bowls, spoons, cups, and a small pitcher, he made for the rock cellar just outside the kitchen porch. A gust of wind rounding the house kicked up a bit of dirt in the short distance. He wished he had brought something to cover the food. By the time he had the door open, two small mites ducked in. The dishes clattered to the broad shelf beside milk pans. "Drop those and scoot out of here." His harsh tone seemed unheeded. By force, he took the bright red apples from their clawing fingers, only to find them snatching another while his hands were reaching for them. He was afraid their scant clothing would give away as he carried one in each hand outside. It would be useless to turn them over to their mother eyeing him from the porch. The half opened icehouse door swinging in the breeze caught his eye. He deposited his human burdens there, and turned the outside catch on the door.

Back in the cellar, he worked fast to collect food, not sure the rotting door would stay shut long. From a covered kettle, he dipped rice into one bowl; stewed dried prunes went into the other. *I have not seen heavy cream like this since I landed in the hills,* was his thought as he dipped the pitcher full, then set the cup with milk atop that. To carry all these in one trip, he set the bowl of prunes atop the cold rice. Folded squares of cheesecloth lay close at hand—one covered the milk; the other protected the bowls. He was glad of this, as he had to set one or the other down to close the door and snap the padlock. He had no intention of crowding past that staring woman. The steps up to the porch in front of the dining room door were clear so he went in that way.

"I had to chastise a couple of youngsters before bringing you food," putting the food close to her hand on the chair. "Can you tell me where I would find sugar?"

"Don't bother about the sugar, please. David and I both like the prunes over our rice. They are quite sweet. Oh, it was nice of you to go to all this trouble." She drank the milk first.

"Leave the milk for this boy; I'll bring another cup. You down all the cream you can manage." He spooned out the heavy cream over the rice as he spoke. "Sugar is quick energy too, so if you have any, tell me where I can locate it. I will bring another dish for this fine chap, so he can handle his own lunch."

"The sugar is in a red can. I keep it on the high shelf right back of the stove, but it could be on one of the pantry shelves." It was an effort for her to talk.

As Dr. Thomas came in with sugar, another bowl and spoon, howls and screams came from the kitchen. "Sounds like they made it out alright." He smiled as he poured cream for her to drink, spooning sugar for her as well as small David. David seemed content sitting on the footstool next to his mother, while using a chair for his table. He very carefully spread a square of cheese cloth for a napkin. "You are quite the boy," Doctor said, admiring his well shaped head and chubby face turned to him with inquiring blue eyes. "Could you enjoy your repast more if I were to scatter that noise further away?" he asked as he saw the woman hesitate over each spoonful.

"I have inured myself to that noise, so it won't quite drive me out of mind—knowing that it is only until I'm up and around again helps me put up with it." She could hardly eat. "That is an awful lot of cream, Dr. Thomas."

"Remember, you're needing an awful lot of food." He tried to coax her along to get as much food down as possible. Taking the spoon from her fingers, he fed her. "This son of yours thinks it's funny to see Mother being fed. Does he talk much?"

"He can talk very well, but it is generally when we are alone, and that we haven't been for more than three months. I'm worried about what affect those three out there might have on this impressionable age."

"Do you mind telling me how you are responsible for that trio?"

"Oh, I'm not. Only we are saddled with them, and as I say, I cannot get rid of them until I'm up and around again. My dear generous father brought us a milk cow. And Mr. Marcus cannot milk. Dick Palmer, the man of that family, can. Mary thought she had not answered his question. "Mr. Marcus likes Dick Palmer to work with him. He's a good workman," she said between spoonfuls. "I fear I cannot eat much more, Doctor. While it is still enough, I want to ask you if there is danger from them to my children or me? I know something is wrong with them. The children cannot seem to learn, and she looks at me as if she would like to kill me." Mary sighed a troubled breath. "I don't know what to think. I had no fear of her while up and around, but now that I'm flat on my back, I feel helpless. I've known all along that she has not liked me, and I know I am some to blame. When first they were camped beside us, and would come to our tent to eat because they had no food, I naturally resented that. I would try to talk to her and at least treat her like a human being. When I couldn't get a conversation out of her, I quit trying to talk to her. Being more than busy, there was no time to stand around waiting for her slow response if she should happen to take the notion to make any."

Dr. Thomas was seeing the whole picture. "Generally speaking, feebleminded, which they undoubtedly are, prove not too vicious. But with insanity mixed in, there is danger. If you cannot send them packing, then you should have someone in to care for you as a safeguard. Do you know of anyone in DeLamar I could take word to?"

"The only one I know is Grandma Blatchey. She is the one who came to care for David and I when he arrived. But she could never cope with that noise and confusion. It would drive her wild."

"I haven't met her yet, but I do know of a husky woman of middle age wanting work. I believe she could handle them. Mr. Olson was hurt and not able to go back to work as yet. The only drawback, Mrs. Olson speaks very little English. I do not know how much she can understand of the language, but the husband can make himself understood well enough. You could tell him what is necessary. With all of the pans of milk in your cellar, I believe Mrs. Olson would take her pay in the butter she would be able to make. They are frugal people. Shall I send them down? " He was determined to find care for this patient.

A great drowsiness kept Mary more asleep than awake after the doctor left. The food and the promise of help soothed away her fears. She was hardly aware that David had pulled away one chair, making it possible for the door to be opened part way. The confusion broke in on her and she set up in bed, willow switch at the ready. "Oh, forgive me," she cried to two kindly faces. The twig dropped from her hand and she covered her weeping face.

Work roughed hands straightened her back in bed, patting the covers about her. A crooning of comforting words came from the woman. Mr. Olson, in broken English, let her know they understood all the trouble she was having. Next he asked where he should take his wife's bedroll and valise.

His stumbling questions quelled her near hysteria, pointing to the hall door so close to the one they had come in. She told him, "Upstairs, just any of the rooms. The one with the chimney will be warmer." In no time, he was back down and asking what his wife should cook for supper. "Tell her to do just like she would in her own home." She handed him the key. "This is for the cellar where all the food is kept. Will you go with her so they cannot trouble her?" From the man's nodding head more than his words, she guessed Dr. Thomas had explained much.

Mrs. Olson had already tied on a big apron and was gathering up all the soiled clothing, taking it out as they went. He had carried out the used dishes. David peered out after the strong people, not afraid, just curious.

Sunday dawned with the promise of snow from laden skies. The threat was still held in abeyance mid afternoon when Dr. Thomas came again to the Marcus home. The smiling Mrs. Olson brought him to the door of the spotlessly clean bedroom, withdrawing after placing a chair for him. "I had to learn firsthand if you were doing as well as Mr. Olson seemed to think you were."

"If being bathed twice a day, fed at least five times each twenty-four hours, and pampered to no end would make one well…I should be well and out of this bed by now. When can I get up?"

"That is the way I like to hear my patients talk. Just don't be in too much of a hurry about this getting up."

"But Baby is almost a week old, and I'm feeling so much better, thanks to Mrs. Olson's care, and to you for sending them down." She smiled up at the pleased woman who brought steaming cups of coffee and a small braid of sweet bread, with a coveted pat of fresh butter, sugar and cream. "See how she feeds me between meals every day?" Small David toddled in with her, gave Dr. Thomas a long look, then went back to the kitchen to eat his lunch with Mrs. Olson at the kitchen table. "Mrs. Olson surely loves David. She must like to see him in that velvet suit. It's getting pretty small for him, but every day she has it all washed and steam pressed for him to war. Does she have any sons?"

"I believe not. I've noticed just the two daughters at their home. By the way, I hear no undue noise. What has happened to them? Has she chloroformed them?"

A laugh came before she answered. "The funny part is, I don't know what she has done to make them behave so quietly. I know she keeps them in their own two rooms except at meals. I hear her going in there and fixing the fire. I'm sure she is the one doing it. And when they get tuned up, I hear doors open and a sudden hush to the noise, then doors close again. It must be heaven to David to have free run of his home." Tears stood in her eyes. "John says he can't see that she does anything unless it is to make a face that scares them. Whatever her technique, I must learn it before she goes home."

"Does that mean you not freeing yourself from their presence?"

"Believe me, I will do that the first day I'm able to get out and milk—and Jimmy Burch at the Company Store phones me that the mines want another man. Will you please hand me that box of handkerchiefs from the top of the dresser?" When it was placed in her hands, she brought out three worn bills from beneath them. "I may pay you for your work, but never for your kindness. We'll always be indebted to you for that. But you haven't said when I can get up."

"So I haven't. Try setting up in a chair tomorrow while the lady makes up your bed. Another twenty-four hour rest and you might make it under your own power. Nothing will be gained by your hurrying back into harness, remember. Let Mrs. Olson stay as long as she will. I'd better be stirring my stumps to make it back to town ahead of the storm."

Snow was falling heavily before bedtime, and by morning, the men needed to shovel a path to their work. At noon, they shoveled again to get to the house for their meal. Sometime Tuesday night, the storm abated. Mary was up and dressed as early as Mrs. Olson. "I do hope they can plow out the road before tomorrow," Mary remarked as John and Dick washed for breakfast. "I'm sure this kind lady will wish to be at home for Thanksgiving."

"Hard telling if they will or not." John didn't worry about such things. Life was again getting back to normal. Mary was up and around. The more subdued noise of those Palmer children hardly annoyed him this morning. Nor were they allowed to stay in the kitchen after the meal. Mrs. Olson had the fire built and those rooms comfortable by the time they were through eating. Without words, she herded those two and their mother into their part of the house. Mary bathed her daughter, Margaret, in peace by the kitchen stove. David was happy to be allowed to watch. *The only flaw is not being able to talk to this good woman,* she thought as she nursed the sweet smelling babe and put her down for more sleep.

My, my. All this work gets done as if by magic. The baby's wash was being hung on the rack by the time she was back in the warm room. As the hours passed, she was surprised how well they understood each other without words. Mrs. Olson set sponge for bread. Mary picked the rocks from brown beans and started those cooking. Mrs. Olson arranged the pans of clabbered milk along the coolest edge of the range. Butter was to be churned. This she would not allow Mary to do, putting the pan of apples into her hands instead, and placing a chair for her. A rolling motion with her hands made known her intention of making pies. All this did not get done before noon. Mary wondered what was being planned for that meal.

She was not worried, nor was there need to worry. Potato soup, thick and savory with onions and cubed bacon, was dished by the time the men arrived. Quick gingerbread was cooling for desert. Every bit of stale bread was crisped in the hot oven and made into croutons. The bright orange of cooked dried peaches, peeled, sugared and mounded high in a dish was very attractive.

As soon as the meal was eaten, there was no mistaking Mrs. Olson's meaning that Mary Marcus was to rest. She escorted her right along to her bed. David, with washed face, was ready for a nap in his crib.

I can think of a dozen things I could do sitting down, but the bed felt good and she soon slept. Margaret, letting her know it was time for her mid afternoon repast, awoke Mary. Mrs. Olson was just then tiptoeing out with David, who had awakened first. "My, my, it must be three o'clock and I have slept two whole hours. How am I going to get back into the groove this way?" Fondling the babe an instant before changing her, "I know you are hungry, Little One. You are dry at one end and wet at the other. As soon as I remedy that, I have to get busy."

On reaching the kitchen, the work seemed to be all done. Floors were scrubbed, pies baked and cooling. A batch of cookies were baking, with loaves of bread ready for the oven. David was eating a cookie and had a glass of milk at one corner of the table. Milk and cookies were being placed for her. Mrs. Olson understood that Mary cared little for coffee. She smiled as she made Mary seat herself and eat the lunch.

It was still a white world outside. No snowplow had carved out a road. Nothing moved in the stillness. Mrs. Olson paused to listen each time she made a trip to the cellar. Mary was sure she was expecting someone to show up. *And that would have to be a snowplow.* There could be no traveling otherwise. Cream was put into her hands. The salt can and huge crock of curdled milk was also placed before her. Mrs. Olson was wanting her to season the cottage cheese. She did this and mixed it evenly while Mrs. Olson bustled about putting the cookies away, turning out the crisp brown loaves and slipping the large pan of rolls into the oven. They were baked and ready to come from the oven when Mrs. Olson's face beamed from the doorway. She held the door ajar for Mary to hear the shouts of men, even before the plow and teams could be seen in the gathering dusk.

Mary nodded that she heard, and she nodded again as the woman made a motion as if asking if she should make coffee. Mary was sure that must be about the last bit of coffee in the house, but knowing how much this woman enjoyed her coffee, Mary would not say nay. Mrs. Olson then did an odd thing. Instead of setting the supper table as usual, she put the plates at one end, along with knives, forks and spoons. The cool food was grouped handy for serving. She opened the door before her snowy husband could knock. They talked rapidly in their own tongue for a moment. The next moment, Mr. Olson was bowing to Mary and telling her as best he could what a fine thing she was doing, feeding those hungry men.

She had no time to tell him they were welcome to a meal—he was gone that fast. In no time at all, six pair of snowshoes were being swept free of snow in the washroom. Only their outer coats were shed as they trouped in. "I was never so glad in my life to hear a dinner bell as I am this once," a short heavyset man said as he came in. "Will you excuse us for not washing?"

Mary nodded to him that it was alright. Mr. Olson introduced them by name. Sullivan was the one that came first. A lean man called Honey came next; Hambly, also a Cornishman; and McBride called Mike. Mr. Johns followied Mr. Olson. Mrs. Olson dipped beans to each plate as the men passed her. There were enough chairs for all of them. Sullivan did not bother with one, but sat on the floor close to the stove, using the opened oven door for this table. McBride used the bracket shelf on the range. Three of them used the one side of the table to eat. Noticing that Mr. Olson had not fixed him a place, Mary moved David in his high chair so there was space for him. She filled his plate while Mrs. Olson poured coffee for all of them, the last cup coming to her husband's hand.

There was no talking for several minutes. Beans in their tomato sauce, cottage cheese rich with cream, warm rolls opened enough to hold butter, was all fast disappearing. More butter was needed, so Mrs. Olson went for that. The jam was gone. Mary reached to the shelf above her head for a glass of apple jelly just made. She was glad it was set and not runny. More beans were dished with mounds of cheese. The rolls were down to the last two. Mary commenced to slice one of the fresh loaves. Not much was needed, as the men were tapering off now.

"I'm beginning to feel human again," Sullivan told them as he helped himself to pie and dripped the heavy cream to cover it.

"Another cup of that good java and I think I can make it back to town." Mike held out his cup for more coffee. Hurried words passed between husband and wife.

Mr. Olson explained there was no more coffee to be made.

"You don't know what you are missing if you don't try some of this buttermilk, Mike," Hambly told him, helping himself to more.

"That is fine stuff. Ice cold on a hot summer's day, or to sober up on." He gave Mary an impish grin. "Right now I'm trying to warm up. If it's all the same to you, ladies, I'll make myself some Cambridge tea. When I was a lad, that was our supper drink." He poured boiling water from the teakettle to his cup, adding cream and sugar to taste. "In fact, that was sometimes dang near all we had for a meal." He dunked cookies in the hot liquid.

"Watch yourselves, and don't founder just because you have the chance," Sullivan told them as he finished and was getting into his coat. John came out about then and got poked playfully in the stomach. "Man oh man, you should weigh 200 pound by spring, eating such good grub. There's no words coined to tell you good people what this hot meal means to this gang. We were darn near starved."

Mary figured Sullivan must be the spokesman for the crew. As he stepped closer to the washroom, Mary said, "I'm sure Mrs. Olson will want to be home with her family tomorrow, being Thanksgiving, but it will be much too cold for her to ride home on the snowplow, I fear."

"No need of her doing so. There'll be someone wanting to get the rust off their sleigh runners this night, now that the road is opened. Someone is sure to be down for her." There were hardy handshakes as they all filed out to the blanketed teams.

Mrs. Olson chopped cold potatoes for frying to extend the meal for the two families. Mary added a little water to the beans in the bottom of the kettle. They were plenty thick. Now she dashed to the cellar for the jar of pickled beets that had come in the box Mother sent. She also brought back a glass of chokecherry jelly. The supper was ample, but Dick was disgruntled because there was no coffee. The rest of them drank milk or buttermilk. The children added their usual fights to the unrest.

Mary was glad to see them all getting off to bed this evening. While the two of them washed the dishes, Mrs. Olson listened at the cold door more than once. At the first jingle of the sleigh bells, she was out of doors several minutes before she came back in with the box of butter from the cellar ready for her to be on her way. Mr. Olson came in quietly and went to lend a hand at bringing down his wife's bedding and valise.

Mary was not sure how many pounds of butter were in her box, but guessed there might be a dozen. *She surely has earned every bit of it.* As the two came back, she fixed cheese for her to carry with them.

Chapter Twenty Two

DICK PALMER WENT TO milk in poor spirits for a Thanksgiving morning. No coffee for supper; that would mean none for breakfast. He thought about not working at all this day, but walking up town to see if that store would have some coffee grounds. When he walked into the kitchen with the pail of milk, John was busy grinding coffee in the hand mill. "I thought there wasn't any coffee."

"There wasn't, 'til someone brought some down," John told him while dumping the small drawer full into the can. "Mary thinks those hungry guys were so glad of that hot meal last night that they smuggled that box of grub into the cellar when they came for Mrs. Olson. For there it was, just inside the door when I went for bacon for breakfast. Several pounds of coffee, a ham, side of bacon and a hunk of beef as big as a turkey. Can you beat that?"

Dick took the milk strainer from Mary's hand and went on to the cellar. When he came back, he asked, "Where do you keep your sack of beans?"

"Why, the small amount left yesterday after I put some to cook, I put in this can here on the shelf. We needed the gunnysack to wipe our feet on."

"Then meat and coffee isn't all they brought down. There is half a sack of beans against the wall."

"We are not going to eat beans this day," laughed Mary as she rinsed the milk things. "Look at that big roast, will you? I believe those men would have sent down a turkey if they could have found one on short notice. My, they must have been more than starved last night. Now I wonder," she was busy turning the bacon, then beating up the hotcake batter, "I fear there is no stale bread for dressing to go along with the roast. But I can roast the potatoes right in with it. And the jar of cranberries Mother sent up with Father will go perfect with it. Also, she sent up a jar of mincemeat. You men missed a pie last night—I promise I'll bake one for you today."

She motioned for them to get to the table. Mrs. Palmer and their two had come to the room howling and fighting in full swing. While flipping cakes, Mary thought, *Might better leave the jar of mincemeat until Christmas. It will keep. Apples need used up first. That last squash shows a bruise. There are just two eggs and there might not be another one until spring!* "How about a pumpkin pie made from a squash?" she asked between howls.

"I thought I heard tell about a mince pie?" Dick was happy with all the coffee he wanted.

"Plenty of apples for a pie," John said when he could be heard. "How about a pie of all three? Then I can tell you which I like best."

"You wouldn't want all the good things in one day, would you?" she teased. Dick grinned at her. Mrs. Palmer glared all the more.

The men worked Thanksgiving Day the same as usual, a bountiful dinner at noon, another at evening. There was so much beef, potatoes, and gravy consumed that there was still pie left. In the early evening, Dick had made a pot of coffee, and he and John were about ready to eat pie, along with their hot drinks before going to bed. "There's been plenty of sleighs coming down this far today," Mary told them as she came from the cellar with the cream, "but this one looks to be stopping out front instead of turning around in the barnyard."

At the knock, Mary opened the door to Jimmy Burch ushering in a dark-eyed lithe young woman. "Mrs. Marcus, I want you to meet Laura Newberry. That's her name now, but I have hopes of changing the Newberry part to Burch in the spring." He held her arm as if he had brought her in against her will.

"Then congratulations are in order," Mary said as she shook hands with both of them, surprised to find the girl's hand as limp as she could possibly make it. "I do wish you two the best of everything, and hope you have the longest and happiest life together." She seated them and offered them coffee and pie. Miss Newberry declined both. Jimmy accepted coffee, then seeing John pile the whipped cream on his serving of pie, relented.

"Look at that cream, will you? Honest to-goodness real cream. I've changed my mind. I will have some pie just to get the cream. I know I shouldn't be one bit hungry—less than four hours ago, we devoured a big turkey dinner at the Lyons' home."

"This household had a big dinner too, thanks to some kind people in DeLamar. I rather expect you are aware of the box of food slipping into our cellar, for I'm sure most of it came from your store." Mary served the pie with plenty of cream.

"You should have seen Sullivan fume because there wasn't a turkey, not even a goose or chicken to be had that late."

John laughed heartily. "That is just what Mary said—that they would have been sending down a turkey if they could have found one. For my part, I prefer roast beef any day."

"My, those men must have been more than starved to appreciate the meal so," Mary added.

"They were hungry alright," Jimmy told her between bites. "And when men get hungry doing such work out in the snow and cold, they get mighty uncomfortable. And grateful, knowing you people gave them the last of your coffee along with that fine hearty meal."

"We didn't deserve any thanks, though. It was Mrs. Olson who prepared it all."

"You didn't stop her or say nay." Jimmy was enjoying this.

"Of course not," Mary assured him. "When I saw she had arranged for them all to eat, I figured snow plow men are like thrashing crews in the east…anyone coming along who is hungry is supposed to be fed."

"You are right about that, Mrs. Marcus. But I dare say, every man of them have at one time or other spent extra hours plowing out someone's road for them, and not been offered even a cup of coffee."

"They tell me it takes all kinds of people to make a world," Dick spoke up for the first time.

Jimmy Burch turned to look Dick over. "Are you a newcomer in these hills? I can't remember seeing you before."

"Been near two months, we've been here. Don't know if that makes us new or not."

"Excuse me," Mary cut in. "I had forgotten you two were not acquainted. This is Mr. Palmer, Mr. Burch."

"Are you another hard rock man?" Jimmy asked. From then on the discussion was of mines and mining.

Mary could see that Miss Newberry had less interest in their talk than she had. The girl was getting restless. "Would you like to see our new daughter?" Mary was lighting a candle. "We think her a very fine baby." She was thinking how glad she was that Mrs. Palmer and those two children were in bed.

"Won't it awaken her?" The girl seemed less interested in this.

"I doubt that it will, but no harm done if it does, for I will need to fix her for the night very soon." She did not speak while going through the dining room. Baby Margaret slept on, not minding being viewed. But David stirred in his crib as they started back through the dining room. Mary snuffed out the candle and let the girl go on to the kitchen with only the light from under the door to guide her, while she covered David and patted him for a moment.

"I would have liked you to have seen our son also," Mary told her once again in the kitchen, "but David is a very light sleeper. If he gets fully roused up, it takes a long time for him to get back to sleep again."

"Yes, Laura, you should see that boy of theirs sometime. He's the type of son a man wouldn't mind having duplicates of," Jimmy boasted.

It was more than plain that Laura Newberry was not interested in anyone's son or daughter. Her only thought was to pry Jimmy Burch away as fast as she could. With lighted candle, Mary led their way along the snowy west porch. Jimmy paused as soon as they were outside the house. "Doc said there was a steel man needing work from down this way. If he would happen uptown along about Monday morning, I'm sure he could get on."

Mary's thanks were hardly heard.

Mary worried about the apparent mismatch between Jimmy Burch and Laura Newbery. John and Dick both made comments about the girl's snooty ways. The more troubling thought, however, was how would Mary get a chance to talk to Dick and convince him he should take that job at DeLamar. *Only three days to work this out.* She went about setting the kitchen to rights before going for the baby. She was not troubled with doubts about her influence over Dick. Simple, unaffected fellow that he was, he looked up to her as if she was very wise. *And I'm going to need all the wisdom he thinks I possess to handle this right.*

Sunday evening came, and she still had not found a workable plan. Busy now chopping the last of the beef to make hash for their supper, a solution came to mind. Seeing Dick prepare to go to milk, Mary said, "John, how about you building up a hotter fire? If you will, I will make hot biscuits for supper. We'll leave the stale bread to toast for breakfast in the morning."

After the meal, she sailed around, not only sponging her

bread, but fixing everything she could for the morning meal. Bacon was sliced, coffee measured, rolled oats put to cook. She set the alarm a few moments ahead of the usual getting up time.

Her plan worked. She was up and out to the barn before Dick made his appearance outside. "What's wrong? Can't I milk to suit?" Dick was hurt.

"You milk just beautifully, Dick. And you have cared for this cow all the time I've not been able to do so. Now I'm equal to the milking again. I should, by all means, get back into harness. I do wish John would learn to milk like you do. He thinks he can't, and just won't try."

"No reason for you coming out in the cold. I can just as well milk."

"I know you would, Dick. And I appreciate all you do to make my work easier. But can't you see? You people won't be able to be here all the time. How are we all going to live when our supply of food runs out? You went in debt for that first order when we got here."

"I'm not kicking," Dick cut in. "I can go get more grub when we need it." He seemed very sure of this.

"You might be able to, and again, you might not. But, say you could, by spring, you would have at least a $100 grocery bill to pay. That is the price of the team you are working to pay for. You might have to sell the team to pay that bill. For all your work, you wouldn't be one cent ahead."

"Again, I say I'm not kicking. We'd be living, wouldn't we? And eating better than we ever have."

"Food isn't everything your family needs, Dick. Not a one of you have the clothes to keep you warm. It is going to be colder than it has been up to now. There is no way to buy those unless you go to work for wages. They are needing a steel man right now in DeLamar. If you go up there this morning, you can get that job. That was what Mr. Burch came to let me know about Thursday night." She could see that Dick didn't like the thought of a change.

"Have you ever thought about who paid for the food for the two families those two months before we arrived back here? It was my work over a washboard. You are not the kind that expects someone else's hard work to feed your family. Nor can I assume the responsibility of more than my own family. Both you and John are very short sighted when it comes to money matters and looking ahead. I believe neither one of you gave a thought as to how both families were going to be fed for these six months while you were working to pay for that team. I'm not objecting to you having the team, Dick. If after working for good wages, you want the team, I won't say a word. But your family must be your responsibility. Your wife is not happy in someone else's home."

"She's not happy anywheres." Dick sounded forlorn. "She won't cook or take care of a house—just let's the younguns waste all the grub that I do buy."

"Then you must keep every bit of food under lock and key, just like I have, so they cannot get to it." She was through milking, but didn't hurry to leave the barn. "If the house you find in town today lacks bed or chairs or things we have extra, I will be glad to loan you those."

Dick had reasoning power to see where a move was in sight for the Palmer family. "I take it John isn't in on this?" He took the heavy pail of milk from her hand.

"No, he isn't, Dick. He will be very unhappy over you leaving, for he likes you; likes to work with you. But I'm putting it to you straight why you must get work with wages coming in. I'm not asking you not to tell John what I've just told you, but it would make my life much easier if you don't." She trotted along behind him toward the house. She had a feeling Dick would not put the blame of his leaving onto her.

John had the breakfast about ready to eat when they entered. "You folks go ahead and eat," Mary told him. "I'll strain this milk first." She was destined to never know the words Dick used to let John know he was leaving. When she came from the cellar, John was more than glum, hardly eating or speaking, but no angry looks were cast her way. The fights and howls of the two children were not stopped. As the unpleasant meal ended, John donned coat and cap, ready for work.

"Going to change your mind and stick 'er out 'til spring and see what we can uncover by then?"

"No." Dick had trouble saying that little word. The lure of sudden wealth was as strong in him as it was in John Marcus. "I think I'll hit 'em up for a job in DeLamar this morning." He watched John clump out alone. It was not long before he left for town.

Mary was glad everything had gone as well as it had. *He must get that job.* David was up and wanting his breakfast; Margaret was asking for her bath and to be nursed. Bread was to be mixed and put to rise. She should get the cream up from the cellar to be a bit warmer, ready to be churned. The noise and confusion had to be borne, as their wood supply was getting too short to keep more fires than was necessary. Quickly pushing the table up to the wall underneath the high shelf, leaving the nook for David to eat his food in comparative safety, she set out the bench and tubs, with a bit of water in one to flip at the two unruly ones when they tried to come this side. "You will have time to wash your clothes, Mrs. Palmer, before I will be ready for my wash. The children's clothes that you might need today, we can hang above the stove here and have them dry."

When she came back with the crying babe who thought she was neglected, Mrs. Palmer still sat where she was, making no move to wash or clean the faces of her youngsters. *This is once I'm not washing one single piece of their clothes. Goodness knows, I have plenty of my own to do. I must remember to put some whole wheat to cook— not much rolled oats left.*

Noon came and she was still knee deep in washing. A disgruntled John helped her push bench and tubs aside so they could eat. She had sliced off the risen bread dough. They baked it on the hot griddle while the beans heated. Applesauce was cooling. "Dinner is ready as soon as I can get these dishes wiped and about the table. Will you wash David's face, Daddy." She paused her work enough to hand him the wet washcloth. Another, she dropped into Mrs. Palmers' lap, but her hands would not accept it. "You make your two clean enough to come to the table."

Dennis came to the table unwashed. A few futile swipes had been made at Daisy's smeared face. This was too much for Mary. Grabbing up another wet cloth, she pinned the fighting boy against his chair and had him clean before he could fight free. Now she went to work on the screaming girl. Not coming out of it so easily this time, a nasty scratch along Mary's forearm smarted before that mite was halfway clean.

Food was at last stopping that unearthly racket. John, who had not spoken, watched David stare at the two cramming food into their mouths. "I wonder, sometimes, what all you are thinking about."

"Whatever it is, my only hope is he'll forget it." Mary was still wrathful, her arm hurting like furry. She left the table and dabbed it with turpentine, the only medication she had.

"I expect he will before he's old enough to tell us what he thinks." John knew it would be more pleasant with these gone, but the thought of Dick leaving him and having to work alone rankled.

The wash was finished, bread baked and cooling, and the house filled with the spicy aroma of cinnamon rolls just taken from the oven when Dick came back, driving a borrowed team. Mary's heart sang. "You haven't had dinner?" she asked as Dick came in unsmiling.

'No, but that don't matter."

"It does too matter. Bread is baked and I left the bean kettle on the back of the stove thinking you might be hungry when you got back. You can start eating. Take a minute or two before coffee comes to the boil. Those sweet rolls might be cool enough by the time you're ready to eat one." She had dished beans for him and was cutting a fresh loaf of bread. The racket of the two fighting to get to the table and that food ahead of their father, was deafening. It was but four-thirty. Knowing she would never learn a thing about Dick's new job if she didn't feed those two again, she reached for more dishes, dividing the cooler beans for them and dipping more for Dick as he slowly sat down. Very carefully, she doled out those slices of bread. "You might as well eat too, Mrs. Palmer. It might be rather late before you get around to supper." Very slowly, she moved her chair to the table.

"Now tell me about your new job and what kind of a house you found," she asked Dick as she poured his coffee, as well as his wife's.

"I wouldn't say it's much of a house. Three small rooms, but it will be easier to keep them warm, I guess." The man renting him the house had pointed that out. "There are two stoves; a table; two or three chairs. That's about all. That steel man they have hasn't made up his mind yet if he wants to leave or not, but they are needing men on the swing shift in the mines. I'll go to work at four tomorrow."

"Then you need to take a couple of these lightweight chairs. And that iron bedstead upstairs will be the easiest to take apart and move. Is there any kind of a pantry, cupboards or storeroom?"

"A cubby hole in the kitchen has a door to it. Couldn't say if it's mouse tight, but a padlock might keep kids out of it." Dick sounded bitter. As Mary served him another slice of bread, the children snatched it. He swatted them good. "Eat the grub you have on your own plates. Won't you ever learn anything?" he shouted at them.

Mary was busy wrapping bread and fitting a cover to the syrup pail of cooked whole wheat. She debated about giving them any of those good rolls. Those children couldn't possibly be hungry. That was why they were setting the way they were. In the end, she cut one in two and placed each half on their plates before serving Dick two with more coffee. She was sure his wife would be slow taking out even one roll. Those grimy hands would get two others, so she placed the roll onto her plate. Now came the snatching and fighting all over again.

Dick jumped from the table with his last swallow of coffee, picked up both of them, calling to his wife to come get their coats on them. She so slow, was still coming when Dick rolled up their bed and carted it out to the sleigh. Both shivering youngsters tagged at his heels. He spanked them good, putting them back in the house. "I said get their coats on 'em. What do you mean letting 'em run out this way?"

All this shouting awakened Margaret so close to that hallway, and she added her cries to all the noise. Mary, going for her, heard the shouting continue. It seems the coats couldn't be found. Putting the babe in David's crib where it was less noisy, Mary marched to the now dim room where Dick was frantically searching for coats. Mary looked in each dresser drawer, under the bed, and back of the couch. Dick opened it up to look, while Mary shook out a pile of dirty clothes from the corner.

Mary tried to collect her thoughts. This could be a trick of that glowering woman standing there not saying a word or helping to look. "Dick, did you notice when you rolled up your bed? Those coats could have gotten into that."

"Why in hell would they be in that?" Dick stamped out to look, slamming the doors to keep the small ones from dodging out again. It was in the bedrolls that he found the coats. Mary was fast poking those evil smelling clothes into a gunnysack. She could hear her small daughter letting the world know she was unhappy. The washroom door had opened and closed. That would mean

John had come in. Going out that way, she followed him into the kitchen and handed him a hammer.

"You go upstairs and get that iron bedstead apart and help Dick load it, while I see what is wrong with the baby." John went, but with poor grace. Dick started to herd his family out. Mary stopped him. "Dick, there is still the bed, springs and mattress to get loaded. And your box of dishes and camping things in the cellar." She now paused in her mad rush to make a light in the kitchen for David's comfort and put Margaret in the buggy so she could see him and be happier.

She had to be out there to see that they came for the box she carried from the cellar to the snowy porch. John did that while Dick came for the box of food she had packed. "One of these pails is milk. The other is cooked wheat. There is bread, butter and bacon, and a package of coffee I ground for you. Not very much sugar to divide with you, but it will be enough for your breakfast. I found this small padlock and key not long ago. The key is so tiny, I put it on this long string. It might help until you can get a better one."

Dick looked down at the box of food neatly packed, then up at her as if he was about to say something. But he didn't speak; he just carried it out. Mary found the gunny sack of clothes still in the hall and handed it to John. *Looks like they are bound to leave those so I'll have to wash them.* No goodbyes were said. John poked the sack in the sleigh and hurried back to the house out of the cold. "They'll be howling worse with the cold before they get to town," was his comment as he closed the door on the noise.

Mary said nothing, but hurried to go milk before it got any darker, there being so little coal oil for the lantern. When she came back from that chore, John looked at her accusingly. "Don't I rate any supper around here?"

"Sure you do. I'll strain the milk right here in the house and set it in the pantry for once. If you want a slice of ham tonight, just bring it from the cellar. It isn't locked. I'll clear this table in jig time. Then you and I can eat in peace for once. David Boy has eaten all he wants from the looks of things, unless it is more milk to drink."

The mad rush to make sure the Palmer family got away this night and with food enough to last until Dick could get more had tired Mary. She ate slowly, enjoying the quiet meal. She hoped

John would say something to indicate that he enjoyed the cozy feel of just their own little family. Instead, his first words were a worry about how Dick was going to make out. "For the life of me, I can't see how he thinks he can better himself any. Even if he does get wages, he's going to have to pay rent and buy fuel. That woman of his won't cook. How are they going to live?"

"Looks to me that is Dick Palmer's worry, not ours," Mary said in measured tones. The irony of John worrying about them, when he never once worried about his own family having food or not, cut deeply. She was afraid to speak. *I'll surely say something hateful.*

Chapter Twenty Three

MARY SLOWLY MOUNTED THE few steps to the west porch, and sat down for a moment's rest. *I like to view my month's work from this vantage point,* she told herself, looking down on the fine garden she had growing. More than half her waking hours for the month of May had gone into the spading, raking, ditching, planting and now weeding and hoeing that garden. The rows of peas showed up well. They were almost ready to bloom. *Another week, we should have lettuce for the table.* Looking down at the handful of radishes she had pulled, *Not very big, but they are sure going to taste good for supper.*

Spinach, turnips, and beets were making long lines of color. *Those tiny carrots can hardly be seen from here, but I know they are there.* Her weary back reminded her of the last two hours she had spent on hands and knees weeding those fine little plants. *They are sure slower to get started than I was thinking they were. And those parsnips are as slow as the onion seed. Of course, I knew they would be, but those little onion sets will give us onions to eat very soon.* In the small fenced plot south of the barn where she had grown her garden the first summer here, she had planted the strawberries that Father had sent. The few roots of rhubarb and asparagus she had planted there along the fence. *I hope they weren't too dry to survive. Those gooseberries seem to be doing better than these older bushes that had been here all the time on the east side of this yard.*

In her mind's eye she could see this yard outlined with all kinds of hardy flowers, but not this year. *It is the growing of edible things I need to put my time in on.* The box of cabbage plants she had started in the window, and lately moved to the porch to harden up, stared her in the face. *Those must be put out this very evening.* She felt as if she should be up and about them right now, but knew the children would be waking up from their nap soon. And it was so comfortable here in the warm afternoon sun. She smiled as she heard David's happy voice talking to Margaret. *I'm sure blessed with good natured children.*

Mary was still thanking her luck over getting rid of the Dick Palmer family. *I have nothing but pity for Dick. Poor fellow, he doesn't know what's wrong; nor would he know what to do about*

Effie Sutton

it if he were told. And surely I'm not the one to tell him. I know so little about feeblemindedness or insanity myself. Her thoughts were a bit grim as she recalled John's reaction when she had tried to tell him her belief of what ailed Mrs. Palmer and the two children. She would not say it was Dr. Thomas who had put her wise, fearing that would not be right to do so.

Well, then, if that woman is off, *that's all the more reason he should never have left here. He can't handle 'em alone,* had been John's verdict. He never gave a thought of the danger or unhappiness to his own family. Mary was fast learning John's indifference to the extra work or cost to feed those extra mouths. *He didn't have to do any of the work and he was foot loose to leave the house the moment the noise got unbearable. Naturally he didn't see the picture in its true light,* had been her charitable summing up of the case then.

And now, I've got to make a trip up town, and one day soon, to learn if Dick Palmer is intending to buy that team. The payment on the place was now a few days past due. John had been working for a man by the name of Smith for more than a month, *but that may not mean money in this family's coffers. It could be just exchange work.* Mary did not want to admit it, even to herself. John might not see fit to make that payment, should he be paid the price of his work in hard cash. She had sounded him out on the question of making the payment, but could get no real answer. *I shall have to pin him down this very night.* She got to her feet, hearing David calling. That would mean the baby needs dry diapers or is hungry. "Coming, Sonny."

After making the roly-poly babe dry, Mary stretched out on the bed to nurse her, with David cuddling against her back. *Might be a good thing his kicking about will keep me awake. I've plenty of thinking to do.* Her trouble was, no matter how she thought or planned, she still didn't have money to pay on the place. She earned a good bit of money with the laundry that kept being sent down, and she would send it back by the first hauler going toward DeLamar, *but it has cost us a lot to live. We have all had to have clothes, as well as shoes and more bedding. There has been but $30 and a few cents to go on that old bill of ours.* She knew this was but half the amount she would need for that payment. *If Dick really wants that team and happens to have as much as $30 for the first down payment, I would be tempted to ask Jimmy Burch*

228

for that amount I've paid on the old bill so I could make that payment. I sure don't like to do that. Neither do I like the thought of having to ask Father to make the payment for me.

"I have our fifty cabbage plants set out," she was proudly telling John as he ate his supper. He was late getting home and was tired after his day's work and two mile walk, and not very talkative. "You say you have but a few more days work. Does that mean you will be able to make that payment on the place then, when Mr. Smith pays you?"

"Smith hasn't much money to pay anyone. We are just exchanging work. I must have told you that." He hadn't.

Mary's hopes would have been dashed to pieces had she been depending on this money. Somehow she had not been. And she was wiser to this exchange work than she had been in Nevada. "And is this man Smith a good work man? I mean, a better worker than you?"

"He's a good enough worker, but I wouldn't say he could put out a bit more work than I can. Why?"

"If his work is no more valuable than yours, then he can't expect us to feed him his dinner. You've carried your lunch all the time."

"Certainly I'll give him his dinner. I'd feel pretty cheap not to. He has no one to cook for him."

"And I would feel lots cheaper to feed the man, and all the same as tell him I didn't consider my husband as good a workman as he." She knew she could never make John understand that extra meal cost her money, so she was going to try a different tact.

"What nonsense. Smith will be only too happy not to have to pack his lunch bucket."

"And were you happy to pack yours every day? Did he once ask you to eat with him? You say you are just as good a worker as he is, and you two are exchanging work. Then why must you pay him a bonus of dinner to live up to your 50-50 agreement? It sounds as though you are not the man he is. I'm ashamed for you!"

"Of all the fool things you can think up, this takes the cake. You never before objected to 'im eating with us."

"Maybe I haven't, but every time I've been ashamed nevertheless on this exchange work. To think how you let yourself be gypped this way. If you want everyone to know you don't think you're as good a man as the next, I can't stop you, but I'm not cooking any more meals that way."

"You telling me I can't give Smith his meal when he comes here to work?" John couldn't believe he heard right.

"If you want to go buy food, as well as cook it, I can't stop you. If you want everyone to know you are a soft snap a..."

"Stop it!" John was angry. He was cornered on this buying point of paying for food, and how little work would get done if he had to also cook? "Maybe you think that is the way to get ahead in this world, but it isn't the way it works." There was no companionship between this couple that night.

God forgive me for being such a shrew, Mary prayed silently. *I'm getting as bad as a she-lion guarding her lair.*

There were no overtures of peace or compromise the next morning before John left. *I don't dare to if I am to make this decision stick.* Mary hurried about her half-day of washing. *He would think I'll soften and will bring Smith his meal after all.*

It was fully dark before John came in that night, and he wasn't alone. "Come see who I brought home with me," he called to Mary. She had just finished putting their own clean clothes away. John sounded happy. "Come out and tell me you won't feed us."

"Why, Tim Nichols." Mary was happy to see Tim, as John knew she would be. "Where have you been these past three years and more? Oh, we heard about you coming both years to do the assessment work, while we wandered about worse mining prospects." She could laugh, even though she felt the prick of John's barbed wit. "I can have supper ready very shortly, such as it is." She wished there was something a bit extra for this meal, but then she remembered Tim liked beans just as well as John did. There was plenty of bacon, and the cow being fresh, there was cream for the stewed prunes and cottage cheese.

The three of them visited until late in the night. Once, John asked Tim if he ever considered coming back and taking up where they left off with their partnership. John felt safe to ask this, knowing Mary would never refuse Tim meals.

"It's this way, John. I'm still broke. I've promised to go to work for that fellow close to Elko, like I told you. But I was so close on my way there, I couldn't pass up the chance to stop to say hello when I heard you folks were here again."

Mary was not worried about Tim becoming a *star boarder.*

She was sure he always paid his way. From what she could learn, it was his money that kept John and him in blasting material the year before she came here. She still believed he had made both years' payments on this place.

Some unusual noise woke Mary from a sound sleep. "What's that racket, John?" She sat bolt upright in bed. "Sounds like an animal walking around the house."

"I expect it is. I put Tim's saddle horse in the yard to eat the grass. He was afraid he would have trouble catching him in the morning."

"Did you make sure the garden gate was fixed so it couldn't swing open?"

"That horse isn't going to bother your old garden with all this good grass to eat." John snuggled down to go back to sleep for another few hours.

Mary slipped on her slippers, and with a shawl over her gown, went out to the yard. The dark colored horse was busy cropping grass just now. Mary was but a shadowy blur. She found the gate leading into the garden unfastened. All the horse had to do was to push against it and walk in. She was full of foreboding as she made the gate secure and went back to the house and to bed. It was too dark to see the havoc already wrought on her fine garden.

That heart sickening sight came with the early morning light as she started toward the barn with the milk pail. The pulled pea vines and half trampled rows spelled ruin to most of the vegetables. How long she wept over this fresh disaster, she never gave heed. John, thinking she had gone to milk and should be back, came to the west porch to see if she was coming. Mary, leaning on the gate crying, was unusual. He went to her and would have hugged her to console her, but she eluded his hands. "What do you want to bawl over a ten cent garden for?" Neither one of them knew Tim had seen this from the washroom doorway.

Fleeing to the barn now, Mary was alone with her grief while she milked. In her busy days, there was no time for weeping and wild lamentation. The children had to be fed, bathed, and their clothes washed; food cooked, and to do this job of living. She strained the milk in the cellar and came to the house only as the last resort. Tim and John were already out on the west porch ready to leave. David wanted down from his highchair. Margaret had tears in her blue eyes, feeling very much neglected. Mary strained some cereal and fed her. *My milk might upset her the way I'm feeling right now.* Mary was more than upset.

Mary's day was much too busy for reflective thinking until time to churn the butter. Margaret, constantly nursing, was soon asleep. With the churn two thirds filled with heavy cream, it seemed a long time in breaking to the impatient woman. *Still plenty work to get out of the way. Those colored clothes should be in from the line so as not to be sun faded.* While hanging out the wash, she had been too heart sick to look toward the trampled garden. Now she thought about it. *I suppose I shouldn't expect a garden to mean anything to John. His mind runs only to the gold that might or might not be found in the earth—never a thought of what food it will grow.*

Moving the dasher slower now to gather the last particles of butter, *I wonder when he is ever going to wake up to the fact he's not one dime richer for all his hard work.* With smooth wooden paddle, she lifted the yellow mass from the buttermilk, carefully pressing out every bit possible before washing the butter under the cool water faucet. Then came the salting and working. This was a familiar routine. She could think and still do it. *I wonder sometimes just what kind of a life John must have had to make him so biased in his thinking. He is so good in most ways, but never a thought as to ways and means for a livelihood. I know his mother worked at her sewing and supported him and herself until her death. Perhaps that was the first strike against him. He was so used to her working—he had no idea that he should be helping to support her. Of course, he was pretty young when she died. Then along came Uncle Ned and he took over the responsibility.*

Snatching in the colored clothes first out of the bright sunshine, *Just as well bring in everything. They are all dry.* That took her down along the garden fence. *There is no doubt about it, some of those smashed plants are trying to spring back to life.* Walking about the soil, *I do believe those cabbage plants are the hardiest of anything.* She stopped to press the dirt about some of them to aid them in their struggle to survive, counting them as she did so. *There is all of a dozen that might make it. I wish there was some way of getting twenty or more plants just like them. I would stick them in every spot where other plants have been killed.* She tried to estimate the number of plants this amount of ground could grow. *There might not be any in DeLamar, but as long as I have to make that trip very soon, I'll just go this very afternoon.*

"Hi, David Son," she called to the busy boy. "Come in and wash good. We will eat our lunch very soon now, and then we might go to town."

"Can I walk?" was the chap's question.

"You can walk back, Sonny, but maybe you'd better ride going up, or your little legs will be too tired to get home." She wanted him to get a short nap. *Besides, if luck is with me and I can find plants, there will be no place for him to ride coming back.*

Seeing Jimmy Burch in his fine black suit, Mary remembered this was his and Laura Newberry's wedding day. Jimmy, with white flower in his coat lapel, was waiting on customers the same as usual. "Have they kidnapped your bride? Or is it not possible for this store to get along a week without you while you take your honeymoon trip?" Mary said lightly, placing the four folds of wrapped butter on the counter.

"The town wants to give us a real wing-ding of a house warming tonight. You folks better come up. The way it's turned out, I'm not going to be able to get away on our trip for another week. The treats are on the house this day. I know you have no special liking for a cigar, but I'll make it candy or fruit for you. Which shall it be?"

"Oh, I prefer fruit any day." She was hungry for an orange— more than a year since she had tasted one, "but we cannot possibly come this evening. John is late getting home from work. What I'm minding most is the fact that I have nothing to add to your house warming. You're always so generous to us." Her hand touched the pounds of butter. "Two molds of this is such a little gift, but if you will accept it in the spirit it's given an..."

"Indeed I will! I don't call two pounds of fresh butter any small gift when money can hardly buy it." He handed David an orange as well as a stick of candy, and tumbled two more of the bright round fruit into the foot of the buggy. "But speaking of presents, I have one for you. A friend of yours left it here for you this morning bright and early." Jimmy brought a folded slip of paper from the iron safe. Inside was a $20 bill. "Tim Nichols didn't say what you had to buy with it, but seemed to think you might want a few cases of canned vegetables to replace the stuff his horse ate up lately."

Mary nodded, unable to control her voice for a moment. "It is true. Tim's horse did destroy much of my garden, but Tim was in no way to blame for that. He didn't even know there was a garden his horse could get into."

"He at least thought this was the only amends he could make. If you are in a hurry, you don't need to pick out the case goods you want just now. But when you do, I'll see to having them sent down by a hauler."

It was an awful temptation to use this money in her fingers and ask for the $30 that she had paid on their bill to make the payment this very day, *But I still would be $10 short,* a small voice cautioned. "Will you let me think about it for a little while?" She moved away from the counter as soon as he nodded and made it plain she was to keep the creased bill in her possession.

David munched his candy, yet still alert to Mother as she scanned her father's letter. *If he has anything to say, he always writes it at the very first,* and there was news in this one. He had written to learn if either John or Dick Palmer wanted to sell that team. The team had wintered fair, and there was a small demand for teams right now. A new neighbor coming in had wanted to buy them and their patched up harness, and had offered $100 for them.

Suddenly the world looked brighter to Mary Marcus. *That may be the way of getting the payment made on the place this year.* She would go right now and learn if Dick wanted to buy the team, or if he had any claim at all on them. *I'm sure John will be only too glad to turn them into cash.* With a wave of her hand to Jimmy, letting him know she would be back, she wheeled the baby buggy along the loading platform and to the ground, and then on up the hill to where she understood Dick and his family lived.

It was steep and uneven, making it hard work pushing that old buggy. David scrambled along behind her. *I wish I could see Dick and not have to go clear to the house.* The thought of that dull woman staring at her from her peculiar eyes was distasteful to Mary. She was so intent on keeping the wheels to the path, she did not see Dick coming down the hill until he was right before her. "How lucky I am, Dick. You are just the one I was coming to see. I just received a letter from my father, and he asked if you were still in the notion of wanting John's team?"

"Can't say that I am." Dick did not act too friendly. "Hay's costing around $25 a ton, and I doubt they would stick around town here very close if turned out to feed."

"Do you feel you have any interest or claim on them?" Mary wanted to be sure on this score.

"Not any that I can see." He had his lunch kit with him as if he was on his way to work, yet it lacked a good hour before time to change shifts. Dick did not ask how the Marcus family was, and only answered the questions Mary put to him as they walked along back down the rough path.

Mary now stopped at the store all primed for business. Hurriedly, she wrote another P.S. to the letter she was about to mail to her folks. Upon learning from Jimmy there were no cabbage plants to be had in town, but perhaps could be shipped from Caldwell, she had another thought. Jimmy telephoned to learn if they could be had. "About how many do you think you could handle?" he asked her while waiting for this connection.

"Five hundred," she answered, then wondered just how expensive those plants might be, having them sent out by rail to Murphy, then by stage the rest of the way. *Whatever their cost, I'm going to have to take them after Jimmy has gone to all this work and expense to telephone for them.*

"Alright, Mrs. Marcus, I have ordered you the 500 plants," Jimmy told her as soon as he hung up the receiver. "They will pack them good and get them to the express office by evening. That means they'll get here on the stage tomorrow night, but that will be plenty late at night. You might better come for them the next morning. I'll try and remember to water them as soon as they arrive. The cost is $.50 a hundred. The packing and wrapping will be another $1, the phone call $.35, and the express and freight is likely to be $1. So that is going to make each one of those cabbage plants cost you a cent a piece. But if every one of them live, you are sure going to have an awful lot of sauerkraut."

Jimmy's chance remark about sauerkraut set her to thinking as she and the children headed home. *Why not make them into kraut? I believe they would bring in more money that way. Might be enough to pay for all the extra work. I'm sure I still remember how Father made it. I did plenty of the trimming and cutting, while he did the most of the pounding and salting of it.*

True to her expectations, John was willing to sell the team for the $100. That night, she wrote another short letter and had it ready for John to mail as he went to work. He offered to go the hour earlier so the letter would go out on the morrow. The quicker that letter got off, the quicker that money would be back here to help him in his work.

When Father's letter arrived a week later with the money order enclosed for $40, John was angry when he saw the amount. He expected the $100. "What kind of gyp is this? You said the man would pay $100 for that team and harness. I won't sell them for no $40."

"John, quit your shouting. The team did sell for the $100, but I asked Father to send this year's payment on the place out of that amount. It would save you or me a trip to town."

He turned on her in all his anger, "Did you ever stop to think you could let me tend to my own business? Here I have a good man coming to work for me the next six weeks, and not even half the amount of cash I was supposed to have for blasting material. Never a thought do you give to how you hinder me in my work," he stormed at her.

"You would find it much more than a hindrance if we lost this place and had to pay rent. You couldn't find a livable house for any $5 a month—that is what this is costing us. Four more years and this will be paid for. We can't afford not to keep the payments up."

John would not stay and listen to her. It frightened her to see him tramp away still so angry. *I would almost be willing to feed this man, Smith, his noon meal to make John feel better,* but John made no overtures. Neither would she. Mr. Smith came each day carrying his lunch.

As the summer days lengthened, the men became enthused in a big way. "If that lead blossoms out the way I think it might, you are going to feel mighty foolish sinking that $60 into this old house, just when we are needing every cent we can lay our hands on for a bit of developing work."

Chapter Twenty Four

THE GROUND WAS COVERED with frost this early morning. Going to milk, Mary felt the crispness under her feet. As she came back to the house, John spoke her thoughts. "About time for your father to be showing up. Remember, he said about the forepart of October was the easiest time for him to get away."

"Yes, I was just thinking the same thing myself. I know in his last letter, he wrote he had the promise of a good man for these ten days." Mary spoke cheerfully. Life was on more of an even keel in the Marcus home. The wild anticipation of early riches of the summer had flattened out to dogged determination on John's part. He would stick to that lead until he unearthed something. "I'm sure glad I had most of the cabbages pulled and covered last night," Mary said as she strained the milk, washed, then commenced to eat her breakfast.

"Looked like plenty of 'em still out there." Coming from work in the half dark, he had walked close along the garden fence.

"Only about fifty head. They are the smallest ones, and not cracked a bit. I hardly think the frost was heavy enough to harm them. David is sleeping late this morning, he was so busy yesterday. As I pulled each cabbage, he would knock all the dirt from the roots that he could." She smiled over those small fists beating away so fast. "I wish Annie could come up with Father, since she couldn't come this summer as she planned. I know Mother could never tolerate that long ride on the loaded wagons."

Knowing Father, she was sure he would come loaded. He had assured her he would bring hay for the cow each year, and take back juniper posts. Her only worry now was getting those whiskey barrels down from town before Father arrived. *If I don't, that will mean a trip for Father after them.* Not liking the idea of going to the saloon herself and asking for those barrels, Jimmy Burch had laughingly said he would do it for her for a sample of the kraut she was planning to make.

The next night, they were hardly through with their supper when John thought he heard a rig. When he opened the door, the creak of loaded wagons came clear. "He's here," he said unnecessarily, for Mary had to have heard it too.

Seeing David nodding in sleep over his supper, "I'd better get this tired boy to bed first," she told John softly. "Light the lantern and go on out." This he did. Later, she just had to dash out to see for herself that Father was alright. A quick hug and kiss while he still watered the teams assured her of his well-being. The beam of the lantern light outlined the barrels atop each wagon. "Father, did I forget to write you that I had barrels promised for us? Good stout whiskey barrels."

Father's chuckle sounded merry on the night air. "You wrote us to that effect, Daughter. But I had a chance to buy these good oak barrels very reasonably. I'm sure you were much too young to remember the once we made kraut in a whiskey barrel—how it was full of the tiny specks of charred wood. Of course, that amount of charcoal did not hurt the taste of it; nor did it harm us, but I fear it might hurt the sale of your kraut."

"You think of everything, Father Dear," she said over her shoulder as she hurried to have his meal ready by the time he came in.

In the morning, Mary and David were on hand when the barrels were edged down the slanting plank to unload. "At first, I was of a mind to fill one of these barrels with apples. That's how we used to ship them in the east. Knowing the road they would be hauled over, though, I feared they would be apple butter by the time they got here." He gave an expert roll of the cumbersome barrel on its edge and had it against the fence. "So I put wheat in it for your chickens. One of them just has flour." He was ready to steady the next one when John started down the incline.

"Yes," scolded Mary, "and I can just tell what is in those other two barrels: Dried corn, dried pumpkin, dried fruit galore; a ham and side meat. Maybe some lard. No telling what else."

"You missed one item, Daughter," laughed Father. "I brought some shelled white corn for hominy. I remember how you liked hominy so well. The dried beans are a new kind to us, spotted like. Your mother doesn't care too much for them, so we are loading them off onto you folks."

"Did...did you bring one apples?" asked David timidly, catching his grandfather's eye. David Williams swung the small chap to the high seat on the lead wagon and folded back the dusty tarp, exposing the boxes of apples fitted so snuggly there. With strong hands, he pulled away one of the thin boards so David could fish out an apple. "One for Mother also."

"Pretty dusty for you up there," Grandfather said as he lifted him down, "or I would leave you there and let you watch this unloading business. Even the apples are coated with dust in spite of the tarps."

"Oh, but they are lovely." Mary rubbed the two red apples briskly on her clean apron. "There is no fruit that can take the place of a good apple...to an apple lover at least." She was savoring the crisp, juicy sweetness as she bit into hers. David had the most pleased look on his chubby tanned face, upturned to hers as he made good dents around his apple. "Come, Sonny, we must go to the house. Baby sister will be asking for breakfast and her bath by now."

The shorter days were altogether too short to get in all the work there was to do. David Williams and John cut posts during the daylight hours, and made kraut each night. This was the fifth night they had worked at it, and the end was just about in sight. They were all three very tired. "It takes a devil of a lot of cabbage to fill one of these barrels." John had done most of the pounding.

"It does indeed," answered Father. "I don't know when I have seen nicer cabbage. We didn't have good luck with cabbage this year. What the worms didn't eat, the grasshoppers did."

"Remember, Father, you are to take home all the cabbage you can, and a keg of this kraut too, if you can make room for it."

"I have no room to haul kraut, but I will take Mother a few heads of these nice cabbages. She might be so pleased with them, she will make me coleslaw for a week," Father teased. It was a standing joke that Mother did not like the raw cabbage, but it was Father's favorite salad.

Mary laughed over that. "Do you think the heads would haul better and bruise less if I pack them in an apple box?"

"I expect that would be the very best way to get them to the Flats. Do you have something to put those apples in so to use one of the boxes?"

"Oh yes, there are still a couple of boxes from last year still intact."

"I always wondered why she wouldn't let me use them for kindling," John cut in. "I suppose now you'll say you knew you would need 'em for just this sort of thing."

"Joke all you want to. I didn't know what I might need them for, but I sure knew they are handy to have around for several things."

Very carefully, Father smoothed down the last bruised shreds of cabbage in the barrel to cover it all with the white cloth Mary handed to him. Then he placed a rock over the top to hold the cabbage down in the brine.

"Father, just how much of these cabbage trimmings would I dare feed the cow at one time?"

"I would say a basket full would be plenty. And it might be well to cut all those hearts lengthwise so she can't possibly choke on them."

John now understood the rest of the talk and wanted to get the mess cleaned up and out of the way at once. "Cabbage leaves shouldn't hurt anything."

"But it has been known to bloat a cow," Father said as he rolled the barrel to the shed where the other barrels and kegs were lined up. "Now that this is all tucked in for the night, I think I will be very shortly. I'll need no rocking to sleep this once." This was his way of saying he was more than ready for bed.

"I know you are worn to a frazzle, Father. Next time you come, I hope you won't find anything to do except to cut your posts and visit each evening. We sure haven't done much of that this time." Mary was washing the cutter and drying it so it would be ready for Father to take home.

"What you going to do with all that stuff if you can't sell it?" John asked as he closed the door between the shed and the kitchen.

"I'm sure it will sell. At least by spring." Mary was almost too weary to talk. She could have told him Mr. Baers at the hotel had already bargained for one barrel and might want more than one. He told her he would be glad to take it as soon as it was cut and pounded, but he had no good place to keep it during the fermentation stage. Mary well knew what a horrid odor the kraut made during that time. *One more barrel can hardly make a worse smell,* was the way she thought about it. *I haven't told John about the odor there will be. He'll learn it soon enough.*

"Can you promise me you won't try to carry those kegs up town on your back, Daughter?" Father kept talking while he washed. John was already trotting off to bed.

"Nothing is carried, Father," she smiled at him. "Everything is packed. I sure had a laugh over one woman's expression in Nevada. She was speaking about the work she had been doing

240

before her baby was born, and said *while she was packing* the baby. I can assure you I have no intentions of moving those kegs or barrels. Anyone wanting to buy them will need to come for them. One barrel is already sold and the possibility of another. My only worry now is setting a price on it. It should be fair both ways. I want it to make the payment on the place."

"I should think it might do better than that. And when you do sell it, remember to ask for the barrels back. Most people will return them if you ask. And this might be a venture that you would care to try again. By the way, you haven't told me what deviltry that gang of boys has been up to lately. Or are the parents doing something about it?"

"As far as I hear, they're not doing anything to stop them. It may be hard to do so. Some of them are wise in getting away with so much. They just won't go to school half the time. It must be easier on the teachers when they are not there. The people they like to torment the most, besides the Chinese, are the Italians, who cut and bring the wood down from the higher hillsides on pack burros. They have a whole string of the animals *tailed together,* as they call it. Seems one man may go in the lead of them, and another might follow after. Sometimes they are let to travel by themselves. Somewheres along that trail, those boys are waiting and they'll loosen the cinch, and soon pack saddles and loads of wood are scattered down the hillside. And by the time the owner is back to investigate, those scamps are long gone."

Father nodded. "The only hope for such boys is good hard work. They can't be hired in the mine or mill; they don't want to go to school; so all they do is make trouble for everyone. If those parents would put those boys out to cutting and hauling their stove wood instead of buying it, that stunt would soon lose its favor, I believe."

"I'm sure you are right about that, but where is the person to make those parents see to that? Most of those people are good, hard working folks. I have met a few of them, and the fathers take pride in the fact their sons have it so much easier than they did. Those men have but little schooling, and their ambition is to be good miners and mill workers. Their boys are hoping to be the same. They wouldn't be getting much incentive for an education at home. Sometimes I think, because it is free and expected of them to go to school, is the reason why they resent it the more."

Father nodded his head again. "When a youth won't go to school or tend to learning anything while there, he might better be doing something he likes to do, if it's no more than trimming dolls' hats."

Mary laughed over Father's alluding to doll hat trimming. He considered that the most useless occupation in the world. "I know I could talk here all night and still not get all said I want to, but you need your sleep and rest the same as I do. I want you to rest assured, when Annie comes next summer, all you have to do is to let us know what day she is coming and either John or I will be in DeLamar that night waiting for the stage."

Again the slow nod. "I feel sure the child will be old enough to make the trip alone safe enough, since she only has one change to make at Murphy, from railroad coach to stage. It could be that someone would be going to Murphy and she could be taken right to the stage, but I rather expect she will leave from Caldwell, for we do have to go there every few weeks. What I want to be assured of, Daughter, just how are you fixed for this winter?"

"All fixed, thanks to you and Mother. But really, Father, you shouldn't do so much for us. You can't afford it. Let us try shifting more under our own power. That might be the only way we'll learn to make a living for ourselves."

Father met her eyes with his steady blue ones probing very deep. "Once the income of this family doesn't come from that washboard under your hands, I can bow out. The price I would have to pay for posts about pays for my trip up here. The hay and food stuff we have.

***

"I never realized how much I've left undone while busy making that kraut, until I try to catch up on my work," Mary told John as they ate their noon meal alone. "I washed all the forenoon; now I must scrub floors, churn the butter, and I've got piles of mending and pressing to get out of the way. What I really should do is go gather those elderberries. If I don't, the birds are going to have them all, or a stiff breeze will come along and send them all to the ground."

"Just what good are elderberries anyway?" John was disinterested.

"You seem to eat the jelly and your share of pie when I make one. I know they are seedy and all that, but up here, it's about our only source of fruit. A pie from them tastes pretty good. I might have to use them for our supply of jelly this year. There aren't any chokecherries—there must have been a frost last spring at the wrong time. There are plenty of rosehips for jam. If I was sure Margaret would sleep for the next two hours like David is apt to, I would rush up the gulch just to see if there are any Oregon grapes this year. That was the only place I found them last year. Do you know our young daughter is getting so she will climb out of the crib? I can hardly keep her anywhere now. What will it be when she is walking?" She hurried about her work while John finished his meal.

With the ending of October and the advent of November, Mary's garnering for the winter came to a sudden halt. "Just like that first autumn I was here. Remember how the first snow came on the first day of November?" She didn't mind the coming of snow this year. The cellar held enough food to last them until well into the spring with careful management. She had a fair-sized bin of carrots in sand, and another of beets. The cabbage hid some of them. She had been surprised at the amount she finally dug up. The turnips and rutabagas were quite wormy, so they would go to the cow. She reminded herself to sort those potatoes again to make sure not one of them wasted. Several had bruised in hauling. Four times she had handled each potato very careful like, to test them for keeping. "I believe this is the first time in four years I've cooked potatoes twice in one day," she was thinking aloud.

"Spuds can fill a guy up, but I prefer beans myself. A man can work all day on a plateful of 'em. Say, how are you going to get rid of all those barrels and kegs of spoilt cabbage?"

"Don't call kraut *spoilt cabbage*, John," Mary scolded. "Not where David can hear you anyway. That son of ours picks up everything he hears. I'm not worrying about getting it sold. It is not quite through the fermentation stage. I do think it will finish alright in the cellar—it being warmer than the shed in this kind of weather. As soon as this snow gets packed down or plowed out, I want to go up town. There's lots of laundry to go up. Do you suppose you could rebuild that old sled or a new one so I could haul it easy like?"

"Why do you bother to wash other people's clothes?"

"For the money they pay to have them washed." She was short with her answer.

"I haven't seen any money coming in for all your work and trouble."

"What do you think has paid for the food we've eaten for the past year, or the clothes we've worn out?" Mary was nettled.

"Why worry about that? We can always get credit."

"How do you know you can get more credit? I doubt you can with better than a $300 grocery bill against your name. Nor would you have the nerve to go ask for more credit." She was getting angrier by the minute.

"What do you bet I can go up town this very evening and get grub on time?"

"I'm not betting on anything." She did not want to put him to the test. The store just might let him have more credit. *That would only mean more for me to pay. It's lucky for me he cannot buy powder, caps and fuse on time.* She was sure that troubled John.

Her anger was short lived as she remembered how he had schemed this very day to get those heavy barrels to the cellar, and the hours on end he had pounded so faithfully. Besides, she did need a sled of some sort. "I have no way of knowing how much we'll get for that kraut, or if I can get it all sold before spring. Last spring, the sale of the team made the payment on this place. You didn't like it, but it had to be. There was no other way. This kraut must make the payment for this year. What is over and above that $60, you can have."

"How do you know it will come to anywhere near that amount?"

"I don't know for sure, but Mr. Baers at the hotel was willing to pay $15 for one barrel. If the others sell, that will be the $60. The kegs, holding only a third as much, won't be worth more than $5 as I see it. We can only sell three of those, for we need to keep one for our own use."

"The fresh cabbage is much more to my liking than kraut," John informed her, thinking they could just as well sell all four kegs.

"There are less than two dozen head left, and they will be gone by New Years. They won't keep much longer than that anyway. Come spring, we will appreciate the kraut."

It was snowing when they went to bed this night. It was still falling when Mary was ready to go milk in the morning, so very light and fluffy. "It's so beautiful," breathed Mary on opening the door. "Just like a fairy land picture, all in white." Seeing that the snow was not of any great depth, she stepped back into the washroom and pulled on a pair of John's overalls that were dry on the clothes line. "The snow is so light, I believe I can just snowplow my way through it without you shoveling a path for me. But do make a path to the wood house so you won't bring in more snow than you do wood. And I will need a path to the cellar. The cream for churning needs to be brought to the house." Mary knew all about shuffling along through the snow with her feet close together to make a sort of path. The distance was not far enough to exhaust her. In a warm and pleasant frame of mind, she sat down to milk.

A week later, when Mary went to the west door to call John to dinner from the shop where he was putting the finishing touches to the hand sled, he hopped over puddles of slush. "Wouldn't you know the snow would be gone by the time I got that sled made."

"I still think I should make my trip to town this afternoon. As warm as it is, it might be mud coming back, but another snow could be on its way. Can you sharpen your steel or find work here in the house so as to look after the children?"

"Guess I could file a saw. It's sure needing it, but the noise will wake them up."

"No great harm done if it does. These longer nights, their naps are shorter anyway. They'll play pretty good most of the afternoon. Just don't let the fires get too low—it gets too chilly for them to play on the floor." Mary was in a hurry to be on her way before John thought of some reason why he couldn't look after the children. He was good at finding reasons, yet she knew he gave them good care when he could find no excuse for not staying.

The trip this day with the loaded sled was no easy task. She was weary when she carried the last of the butter and jars of cheese to the counter. "This six pounds of butter and eight quarts of cheese must weigh ten times more than when I started with them," she told Jimmy Burch. He was lugging in the huge bundle of laundry.

"It must be miserable traveling. But then you just thought of us poor people without clean clothes and fresh butter as well as cheese, and dug your toes in a little deeper and came on. That's how you are." Jimmy was smiling.

"Something like that, I guess." Mary could smile too, now

that she had made it. "It looked for awhile like I would never make it. I wanted to bring you a sample of sauerkraut."

"Oh, is the kraut ready to eat? Several people have been asking if we're going to get any in. I never have tried selling it, but believe I might be able to get rid of a keg if I had it here."

"The hardest part is any buyer will have to come for it."

"That is easy enough done," Jimmy told her. "Might be that Mac can go down yet today. In that case, you would have an easy way home without dragging that heavy sled through the mud and slush. Plenty of dirty clothes have been piling up here for you," he called back to her as he dashed out the door and over to the mine office to learn if MacLean was busy.

Mary had read but part of her letter before he was back again. "Yes, Mac says he can go and will be hooked up and ready in about twenty minutes, so sit down and rest yourself until then."

"I better go down and talk to Mr. Baers and learn when he will send for his barrel of kraut. That is going to be heavy to handle. And to get it up in a wagon will need more than one man. With more snow and a sleigh, it might be easier."

"If he wants it today, tell him to send along another man with Mac." Jimmy started to go about other work, but turned back to ask, "How many quarts do you figure is in one of those kegs, and what's a fair price?"

"A keg is supposed to hold thirty quarts—that's full of course. I believe there are 25 or 26 quarts of kraut in one. At 20¢ a quart, that would make it come to $5. Do you think that's reasonable?"

"The price to me is alright. I'll sell it for two bits a quart, and everyone will be happy." He hurried away with a grin.

Chapter Twenty Five

"I BELIEVE I'M MORE ready for Christmas this year than ever before." Mary gave voice to her thoughts this night as she sewed on the last shoe button eye to a plush dog she had made for David from bits of an old mouse-chewed coat she found in the attic. The doll, dressed in frilly but washable clothes beside her, was all ready for Margaret. Mary was reminded of how many hours it had taken her to hem and make that doll and its outfit, and again spoke aloud her thoughts, "I wish I had a sewing machine. I could sew so much faster."

"Isn't that just like a woman? Never satisfied with what they have," her husband teased, rumpling her hair. "Always wanting something more. I suppose you think Santa is going to put one in your sock for Christmas?"

"Silly." Mary brushed the hair back out of her eyes. "I can wish can't I? Though I know I won't get one unless I should find one cheap enough that I could afford to buy it."

"What you going to buy it with?" demanded John. "And how you going to make the payments on this place like you was so sure of doing? Letting the store have those kegs of kraut and never a cent of money."

"Listen, John Marcus." Mary was determined to get this settled once for all. "The store didn't fork over the cash—that is true. But those kegs paid for that mackinaw you had to have; overshoes for all of us; those work pants you have on this very minute, and such things that we had to have. It all came to around $15. When those last barrels were sold, didn't I divide that money with you—giving you the $15 just like I agreed to?" She stopped talking, feeling herself getting quite wrought. *And I want to feel peaceable these holidays.* She rather expected that John was without caps or fuse enough to use up all that powder he had lugged down from town as soon as he got his hands on that money. *Thank heaven I had sense enough to leave that $59 in Jimmy Burch's safe. Any two pounds of butter I can get up town with now will make the $60. And I must make that payment before something comes up to prevent it.* No, she was not worried about the payment. Neither could she talk it over with John. It would be the same old unpleasantness if she did. He seemed not to realize that the money she earned, she had every right to spend as she saw

247

fit—*and that has to feed, clothe and care for our children.*

John, guessing he had made her sore at him, took a different tact. "You still mean for us to go up town to that shindig tomorrow night?"

"Why of course." She noted his scowl. "I thought you would want to go. We haven't been to any social gathering since we came back here. Those good carol singers came down here to sing for us last year when we couldn't get out, with Margaret so young. This year, it won't harm her in the least, and David is old enough to enjoy seeing Santa Claus, I'm sure. Everyone we know in DeLamar is asking us to come. They're sending a sleigh down for us, and said they would bring us back. How could I tell them we wouldn't come?"

"I could have," John told her flatly as he made ready for bed. He hadn't said he wouldn't go, leaving that possibility open as a way out.

Mary understood him better now and didn't say more, but talked of other things. "The last time you were up town, did you ask how the Chinaman with the broken leg was doing?"

"No, I never asked, and never heard anyone say. If those damned boys were took out behind the woodshed a few times, they might quit such pranks."

"The most effective way, I believe, would be for them to be compelled to do the work he would be doing if he was able—even just these few weeks that he will be laid up with the broken leg."

"Yeah, and when they were loaded down with two heavy coal oil cans of swill for the pigs like the Chink was, someone should run ahead of 'em and dig a hole in the path and fix a trap for them to fall into, just like that unlucky Chink did."

"It just might take something severe like that to cure them."

"A broken neck is the only cure for 'em. I'm ready for bed. Are you going to sew all night?"

"I am through. I'm just wrapping these so there will be a surprise for them to undo Christmas morning."

Christmas eve it was cold. "Must be zero right now," John stated as he came from the tunnel. He came in reasonably early for supper. Mary was sure he would go to the Christmas doings after all, and she hurried to get the meal on the table.

"These two have napped nearly all afternoon, so they mean to be awake to see Santa this once." Mary was gay in her talk, dishing up their food. Margaret was in the high chair now, and David was on a foot stool on a chair, which brought him up to the right height. "I brushed and pressed your suit this afternoon. And you should see how cute that little blue outfit looks on Margaret. I finished the leggings today and pressed all three. The coat and bonnet are big enough that she might be able to wear them another year too, but I'm not too sure about those leggings fitting another season. She sure is a fatty. Mother knew what she was talking about when she sent Annie's outgrown coat and cape for Margaret."

"How you going to keep them warm and your feet from freezing tonight?" John wanted to know.

"I have both soap stones and two flat rocks heating in the oven this very minute. Baby is wrapped so good, she won't be getting cold at all. If David sits on your lap with one of those warm stones in the seat between you and the driver, he can set his feet on that so he'll stay warm." She had everything planned so there would be no loop hole for John.

MacLean came for them in a two seated cutter, deep with robes. His good humor kept up all the way to the lighted schoolhouse. Neither Mary nor John got a word in edgewise. The lights from the tall windows shone out across the wood yard, shoveled path, and deeply furrowed road. As they stepped from the rig, Mary gave the sleeping babe into John's arms, and she led David by the hand. Then she realized he was hemmed in by the crowd and could not see, so she hoisted the heavy boy well up in her arms. The room was filling up fast—most of DeLamar seemed on hand. They were ushered up toward the front so David would be able to see. Mary was on the isle side, and noticed Jimmy Burch escorting a freckle faced chap as tall as he to a seat nearby. *I believe he is one from that gang who likes to play pranks.* Mary smiled to herself, wondering just how that wiggling youth was going to get out. He seemed tightly wedged in where he was. She would have smiled more had she known five more youths were similarly seated and watched over in different places in the room this night.

"And is this the wee boy I once took care of?" Grandma Blatchey came to stand beside Mary and patted the apprehensive David.

"Yes, this is David, Mrs. Blatchey. He has grown somewhat

in the meantime. Have you heard we have a year old daughter too?" She felt more space between her and John. She scooted over now, and there was room for this tiny old lady to squeeze in beside her.

"Yes, I heard about your girl." It was very noisy around them, making it difficult to talk, but Grandma chatted on. "Sure a big crowd here. Too bad a couple of their best speakers are sick and can't come. If I was twenty years younger, I would offer to speak a piece. I used to be pretty good at speaking." She was forced to stop because of the press of people along the isle.

"Why, I could just as well give a recitation if that would help them any." Mary said it almost without thinking, with a strong urge to give something, and to feel she belonged. "I believe I still remember some of them."

Grandma's wrinkled hand went out to fasten on to the dress of a lady passing their seat. "Mrs. Caulkins, this lady here says she'll speak a piece to help you out."

"Oh, would you be so kind?" She was evidently relieved. "We are so short of entertainers this once. I believe I've never met you before. I am one of the teachers." She poised her pencil above a pad. "Your name please? And the subject of your reading?"

"I'm Mary Marcus. I fear the only ones I remember well are humorous ones."

"So much the better. We need something to liven up the program. Do you mind if you were called among the first?" The woman was busy writing while talking. After she had moved on, Mary's doubts set in. She wondered if she could possibly go through with it and not get stage fright. *It has been more than five years since I have stood on a rostrum before a roomful of people.*

John gave her a disgruntled look when she gave him David, and the still sleeping babe to Grandma Blatchey. She indeed was called among the very first to be called. Her knees might be trembling, but with a sure tread, she made her way forward. *The Bewitched Clock* was new to most of this gathering. Mary orated it well, and from the thundering applause, it was well received. Now came the eerie *encore, encore* from sides of the room. She had not counted on this. With a quick thought to all those she knew well, there was not one Christmas ode among them. So the next best thing to do was to give the shortest, and the one that she liked the best. It was also the one she had been the most trained in rendering.

"I's losted, can you find me please?" Mary's flexible voice intoned the quest as appealingly as any small lost child would. The room was hushed all through the short lines, as if this crowd too would like to know the lost child's name. Now came the childish lisping, "I's never bad, 'cept'n when I been a throwing stones. Then my Mama says, "Mehildabell Sophira Jones, what has you been a doing?" Mary's voice rang in realism even to the stamp of foot.

Seeing David's small frightened face, she rushed toward him. The cry, *encore, encore* went unheeded, but still the clapping continued and would not stop. At last she stood out in the isle and bowed. "I beg of you to excuse me." David was clutching her tight about the neck. "It happens that my son isn't used to seeing me in any role but mother."

Later, David viewed Santa in his red suit with very meager interest as he kept a tight hold on Mother. The two red mosquito netting stockings, filled with nuts and candy and oranges showing through, was of passing interest. Many people, whom she had hardly met, stopped to tell Mary how they enjoyed her recitation. Mrs. Caulkins had no time for a word, but squeezed Mary's hand while others were talking.

The soap stones and rocks still held a little warmth as they climbed into the cutter. David still clutched her, so it was he she covered with robes and tried to snuggle down to keep warm. "John, make sure Margaret's face is protected. There seems to be a bit more breeze."

"You sure made a hit with your pieces, Mrs. Marcus," complimented MacLean. "They would have kept you speaking all night if they could have."

"I wanted to help out, but I didn't think about the effect it might have on others in my family." She spoke guardedly because David was just now relaxing a bit.

"Everything went off fine and dandy for once," chuckled Mac. "No red pepper, garlic or limburger cheese came anywhere near the stove this night."

"Is that the usual stunts those boys pull at such a gathering?" Mary shuddered at the thought of the red pepper on that hot stove.

"They never miss the chance. Only this time, they didn't get

251

near the stove. A regular vigilantes group escorted those boys to their seat and then wedged them in to see that they stayed there."

"That was what Jimmy was doing," Now Mary understood his actions.

"Yes, he had Hank cornered. Happy Hank, they call him, and don't you ever let his angelic mug fool you. He may look as innocent as a baby, but I say there is more of that gang's deviltry hatched in that one brain than all the others. Now Doc Thomas took on the bad actor, Slim Leach. He's slim, and might wiggle out some knot hole, but not with Doc guarding him. Guess the boy pretended he got sick. Anyway, Doc took him outside and walked him around for awhile. That might have been when he was relieved of the can of cayenne pepper."

"How is the Chinaman with the broken leg doing?" John thought to ask.

"Alright as far as Doc can tell yet. That's another thing. What that gang of boys won't do to torment those Chinks. When they celebrate their New Years, along about the 6th of February I think it is, they give all kinds of presents. Big fine silk handkerchiefs that come from China, and for a fact, I've seen half a dozen around Happy Hank's neck. Twice as much candy, preserved gingerroot, and leachy nuts will be coming his way. And perhaps the next night, Hank'll be rounding up the gang to smoke 'em out."

"How do they do that without getting caught?" Mary wanted to know.

"The first act in the play is to stretch a wire across the opening on their front porches, just above the top step. Just high enough to trip 'em when they come pouring out of that house where they have gathered for their card or dice game. Chinamen are great for playing games and for gambling among themselves. About the time the game is going good, the lightest weight chap will be hoisted up on the shoulders of the taller one, or a ladder is used— most any old way for 'em to get onto the roof to chuck a gunnysack down the chimney. If they have a good fire going, there is going to be some smoke pouring out of that stove pretty soon. What with those men getting tripped as they come out, that gang has plenty of time to be home and maybe in bed."

Mary laughed, but very quietly so not to awaken David. "I thought we had pranksters in Illinois, but they were tame compared to this gang. There, they liked to go out to the country and swipe watermelons or cantaloupes. Sometimes, they would bother with fruit other than melons. They called it *cooning*–never stealing. While most of them would take just what they wanted to eat, no one minded their fun. But every once in awhile, a gang would pull the vines and destroy all the melons. And then an old blunderbuss would be loaded with rock salt or fine birdshot. Those who got peppered with that weren't fast about trying to *coon* melons again very soon."

At their home gate, Mary stepped out of the cutter with David still asleep. "We surely appreciate you coming for us and bringing us home this way. And we wish you the merriest of Christmas. Oh, I can manage this child if you can take the soap stones and Baby too." She stepped aside to let John go first to open the door for her.

"I'm glad Christmas comes only the once in a year," easing the babe to the bed.

"Shhhh," Mary warned, taking off David's coat, cap and shoes all so very carefully so as not to disturb him. By the time she made her way to the not-too-cold kitchen, John was fixing himself a lunch. "This once, our boy is going to sleep with his clothes on. He never has before, but he has never been out this late before either. I expect Margaret will be waking up pretty soon for her drink of milk, then I can make her ready for bed. I think I'm hungry too. It could be just seeing you eat." It was a bowl of bread and milk she fixed for herself. John lunched on cold ham, applesauce and cottage cheese.

Mary was happy this night. No longer did she feel like an alien in DeLamar. She had entered in and been accepted. Her thoughts were of the people she had met and had seen this night. "There were a lot of people there—just about all the school house would hold. I didn't see a thing of the Palmer family, did you?"

"Nope. I rather think they might be gone. Haven't run across him all summer, in fact. Is this the last of the apples?" He was cleaning out the bowl.

"There are more apples, but no more sauce," she answered with a smile. "I didn't see Jimmy's wife, Laura, either. I wonder if she is one of the sick ones in town."

"Haven't you heard? She's gone to Boise City to live."

"I should think now would be the time when she would want

to be here with her husband," Mary said musing. "She must mean to stay out until after the baby comes."

"Some of 'em are thinking she means to stay there from now on—thinking she'll make Jimmy sell out his interest in the store and move to Boise City if he wants to live with her."

"Seems odd she is so bent on living in a big town—I understand she was born in Silver City. One would think these hills would be home to her." Clearing away the crumbs of their lunch, she continued. "If she didn't want to live in DeLamar, she should never have married Jimmy Burch. He is one person that is very content where he is."

"Yeah, I guess he likes to be the big frog in a little puddle, instead of a small toad in a big pond."

"Not so much that—his business interests are here. Of course, I know Mr. Swan has a good opinion of Jimmy Burch, but then, he has a right to have. Jimmy has a good business head on his shoulders, and has climbed pretty far for one of his years. I understand he is half owner of the store now. Mr. Swan leaves all the managing to him. It looks like Margaret is going to sleep right straight through without a drink of milk. We might as well think about sleep ourselves, but the funny part is I'm not one bit sleepy,"

As they made ready for bed, still in the kitchen as usual, Mary remarked, "I wonder if the carolers will come down to sing some night during the holidays like they did last year."

"Good heavens, Woman, haven't you had enough gaiety for one Christmas?"

"Oh, yes, but I still like to hear them sing. There are several good voices among that group. This year, I will have fruit cake to serve them instead of just cookies."

"I see where Johnny Boy doesn't get any cake if there is as big a crowd as there was last year." He was thinking about all the cookies being eaten.

"Stop your worrying. I made two cakes this year." She laughed at him. "Aren't we the rich ones—Mother sending up that box of dried and candied fruit and peeling by Father? I knew she meant for me to make our own cakes this year, so as soon as all that kraut was out of the way, I made them. They should be good and moist about now. It's been two months, and we have chocolate so to make that hot drink for any that do not care for coffee. Apples are getting scare; I believe I'll just have one around in sight to offer them."

Her saying that amused John. "What you going to do if that same girl, Helen Orchard, ups and asks you for an apple?"

"I doubt she will if none are hanging on the tree or in sight. She really is a very polite girl. The more I think about her asking for one last year, the more I think it was a matter of politeness. She didn't care for milk or cookies and never drank coffee. She didn't want to seem rude in refusing all refreshments. She might be just an apple eater like I am. I think she is very nice from what little I have met her. Dr. Thomas seems to think she is pretty nice too. Wouldn't they make a nice looking couple?"

John was not much interested in Dr. Thomas and his courtship of Helen Orchard, the eldest daughter of the mine and mill superintendent.

Morning came all too soon. Both children awoke early wanting breakfast, so it was late when Mary went to milk. Bright streaks of light in the eastern skies reflected on the snowy field below the barn and corral, though the house and buildings were still in the gloomy shadows of the hills. She thought she saw something moving out in the center of that whiteness. *It could be some sort of a mirage.* On coming back from the barn, she glanced that way and noted an ungainly movement. "John, there is a big bird down in the field. It acts like it is trying to fly and can't. Do you suppose it could be a wild goose? There couldn't be any sort of a trap, could there, holding it fast?" Her questions kept tumbling out.

If she had not been watching and listening, she would not have heard the tiny report of the 22 rifle. John picked up the gray bird and started back. *That means it must be a goose or something edible.* She hurried in now and set to work in gay spirits.

"I might as well have saved that shot," John said as he lugged in the heavy bird. "He couldn't fly because the tip end of one wing is shot away. See? This is where I hit him." John parted the feathers and down to show the fresh blood of his shot in the back. "He couldn't get traction in that soft snow. Don't look like he was touched another place but that wing, so I think he'll be alright to eat. Couldn't be too long ago he was hit. He must have just glided in."

"The Marcus family has no turkey for Christmas, so a goose

falls from the heavens. What kind of a goose would it be?"

"Canadian honker, I guess, from the color of it. How are you ever going to get it dressed and roasted this day for dinner?"

"I doubt that I can, he is such a big bird. Luckily, our oven is big or we never would be able to roast it whole. I think we better just have the snowshoe hare roasted like I planned for today, and I'll take my time getting this bird ready. It will take time to save all those nice feathers and down."

"Why do you want to bother with such stuff?" John could not see the sense to it.

"For pillows. One can never have too many of them. Both children will soon need larger pillows, and I'm going to be one happy woman when I have enough down saved for a whole quilt or comforter."

"Whoever heard tell of such things?"

"Haven't you read about the feather beds that people in the really cold countries sleep between?" Then she remembered that John was not much of a reader, and she tried to explain what she knew about them.

"They must be very warm, not heavy like blankets."

"When it's cold enough for all that trouble, why don't they just go where it's warmer? That is what I'm thinking very seriously of doing."

Gone in that minute were Mary's happy feelings of security. The remembrance of those many months of their nomadic wanderings came back. The hard beds on the ground, makeshift camps, lack of water sometimes; never the comforts of a home. *I tried to be a good sport and not complain, but I want no more of it.* She set her mind to the task of combating John's discouragement and restlessness. "There is still coffee, and it's hot. Set down and enjoy it. I'm still hungry—never half finished my meal. Let us be happy this one day, John. Remember we have never had it this good since we've been married." She could speak glibly about them being happy, but happiness was eluding her.

Chapter Twenty Six

"WHOO-EE," SOUNDED FROM THE road at the front gate. Doors were being opened this fine summer day. Mary heard the rig stop and hurried out; she was expecting more laundry to be sent down. "I've a whole gunny sack of dirty clothes for you," called the teamster. As she reached for the dusty sack, he said, "Jimmy Burch said I wasn't to just dump these off, like we sometimes do, but to tell you there are letters for you in there too. Those miners must think you like dirty clothes."

"I like to see them clean again," she answered spiritedly. "I thank you so much for bringing them down and bothering about my letters. Would you like a glass of cold milk or buttermilk?"

"Not thirsty just now. Thanks anyway for the offer. I might take a *rain check* on that if you don't mind," he said with a pleased grin, then he drove on up the rocky grade.

Mary had never heard that expression before, but guessed at its meaning. There were two letters—one in Annie's slanted hand writing; the other addressed in Father's easy to read script. This she opened first. A special delivery stamp was affixed to this. "Mama, Mama, read to me." David tugged at her apron, wanting to get in on the letter too.

"I will, Son. This letter is from Grandpa, and he says Aunt Annie will be coming up to see us on the 16th of June." She stopped reading and did a quick calculation. "Why, today is the 16th. That means she will be here tonight. My, my, what a lot of work we must get out of the way this day. Sonny, will you take these letters and put them up safe so Sister cannot reach them? Mother will read them to you at noon so Daddy can hear them too." She wanted to get David out of the way so she could shake the sack free from all the dust it had collected on the road down. In no time, she had the dozen small individual sacks of soiled clothing dumped on the washroom floor. As she sorted them out and put them to soak, she soon knew to a penny how much these hours of work would bring. *Nine of these have a shirt in them to do—that means $3.15. The three that are just the change of underwear will be 75¢. That is just 10¢ short of $4.*

John did not receive the news of Annie's visit with much enthusiasm. Late evening, he flatly refused to go meet the stage. "If you think I'm going up town and stand around for the next two

257

to three hours 'til that stage comes, and not the price of a beer in my pocket, you are mistaken."

No more was said, but Mary did plenty of thinking. *I wonder if he has some inkling of that woman coming out yesterday and buying that gallon of milk and quart of cream.* Nothing had been said about it that she knew. Ordinarily, she kept no money about the house, so she could answer truthfully that she had none when he asked. *I wish John would get it through his head that the money I earn is not going up in smoke. To feed, clothe and house this family is my first and last consideration.* She would not offer him the money now to make this trip, to her way of looking at it. *It's all the same as bribery. After refusing him money for caps lately, I'm not going to fork over that needed money to get him to do something I can just as well do myself.*

Moonlight made it possible to see the road well; she allowed herself plenty of time. *I surely must be there when the stage gets in. Annie would not know what to do if I weren't.* As to where she wait from now until then, she had not given much thought. Seeing the stores and most of the homes dark at this hour, she thought, *I suppose I could stop here at the hotel and wait in the lobby.* But several men were collected there. Then too, it was just far enough away that she would not see the stage stopping at the Post Office. *Plenty of waiting space here,* she told herself as she perched on the loading platform.

Across the street, Dr. Thomas' office was dark like the rest of the buildings. Only the drug store in one corner of the saloon next door was lighted. *I suppose it would be perfectly proper to go to the drug store, but I'm not going to do so.* The few times she had gone there to buy necessary items, the door between it and the saloon was always ajar. *I'm sure glad I wore this warm jacket.* She hugged it about her. Well in the shadow, she did not expect anyone would see her, but Jimmy Burch came along the sidewalk from the hotel, passing just below her.

"Hello there. For heaven's sake, Mary Marcus, what do you mean setting out here in the cold? Waiting for the stage, I expect. Come on up to the house and do your waiting where it's warmer and in a comfortable chair." His hand was already steadying her as she hopped down to the walk. "I doubt Laura has gone to bed yet. No matter if she has, you are waiting in here." He held the door opened for her in the neat small house just above the rambling store building. "Gone to bed yet?" he called as the two entered.

"You don't need to yell your head off and wake the baby. I've just got her down and hope she'll stay there for a little while." She was hardly civil to Mary, who wished she was anywhere but here. Laura, in dressing gown and slippers, wandered about the room, restless as a caged animal. Seeing Jimmy prepare to make coffee, she griped at him, "What do you want to make coffee at this time of the night for?"

"To drink." Jimmy tried to make it sound witty. "I see no sense in walking down to Lower Town just to get a cup of the Chink's when I can make just as good a coffee at home." He was not going to quarrel with Laura before Mary Marcus. Neither did he intend to let her have the last word. It was he who ushered Mary in to see the sleeping babe when Laura made no move to do so.

"A very pretty looking daughter you have, Mrs. Burch." Mary tried to make the best of things until she would be able to leave. It surprised her to see Laura drinking coffee after reproving Jimmy for making it.

He was the one doing most of the talking to keep the conversation going. "Have you heard Dr. Thomas is thinking of taking the fatal step? It's rumored he might be a Benedict before another year rolls around." He tried to pour more coffee into her cup over her protests.

"No more, thanks, no. I hadn't heard. He should make a very good family man, having such a knack with children. Did you know David has shortened Dr. Thomas to Dr. Tom? It seems to amuse the doctor."

"And he'll be just like all the rest of 'em," snapped Laura. "As soon as the knot is tied, he'll set down in this tiny crack in the hills and expect to vegetate and go to seed."

"Can't see a thing wrong in staying put where there is enough room to put down roots." Jimmy held a mocking tone. "Now a place like Boise City is getting so many cement sidewalks and paving, the best of seeds will have trouble finding soil to germinate."

Mary would have liked to have smiled at Jimmy's way of saying he had no intentions of moving to Boise City, but knew that would be unwise with Laura in the mood she was in.

"Sometimes I wonder why it is that lots of folks, like me for instance, reared close to a fair sized city, yet never have any desire to live in one. Other people live further away, and perhaps want to live in the towns and bigger cities. What is that old saying about, *what is one man's meat is another man's poison?* This must apply to people's free choice of dwelling places. Now, I have drunk coffee to keep me awake and warm until that stage arrives. I can just as well wait on the store steps instead of keeping you people up this way." She stood up to leave.

"You are not keeping us up," Jimmy hurried to explain. "I have to take in the mail tonight. Lyons isn't feeling too hot these last few days."

"If you ever went to bed at a decent hour, I never knew about it."

Jimmy disregarded his wife's jibe, drinking the last swallow of coffee. He stepped to the front door ahead of Mary and listened with the door held a foot wide. "Can't tell if I hear the stage or not. They make plenty racket across the street."

"If you've got to listen, go on outdoors to do it. I see no need of you keeping the door open and chilling the whole house this way."

Jimmy closed the door to a mere crack, holding it that way with his foot while lighting a cigar. "Funny how one door lets in more air than another." His tone could be jesting.

"You are so smart, Mr. Burch. That back door, being so close to the hill, never made a draft until you swung the front door wide open."

"The stage has arrived." He opened the door with a flourish. A gust of wind caused by the fast rig sent the door slamming against the wall. A cloud of fine dust swirled into the room before Mary could get out and the door closed. "Now she will have something to be sore about."

"Jimmy Burch, you know your wife has every right to be sore about the bath of dust her immaculate house just received," she reproved him.

"I know it, but you and I know that was not intentional. But Laura will never believe that." He stopped talking as they neared the stage stopped at the store steps. "Hi," he called to Ed Wheeler, helping out a tall young lady. Mary would not have known her own sister in this half light unless she spoke.

"I knew you would be here," said that young miss, hugging Mary tightly. "You look very much like I remember."

"And you hardly look the same at all," Mary said as she gave her another hug. "Five years since I've seen you, and you have caught up with me in height. My, how you have changed."

"Yes, I hear that from all sides. Mother thinks I look like you. Father says I act more like you every year. Max Thorn tells me I'm not half as grownup as you were. He still treats me as if I was about six years old." Her heavy valise was handed out. Mary took it. "Do we have to carry that heavy thing down tonight? Father thought it better to leave it here someplace and take down just the two lugs of fruit. Those cherries and apricots might have to be canned the first thing in the morning. Maybe you'll have to make jam out of them if they are squashed.

"We'll ask Mr. Burch if we can leave the valise here." She spoke loud enough for Jimmy to hear, but he went right on locking the door.

"Might as well take it right on down with us tonight." He took the handles from her fingers. "You and your sister are not walking when that team of mine is needing ten times the exercise that they get. Can we manage everything?" he asked as Mary stepped out with the two well tied lugs, one to each hand. "It will save time if we just step down to the livery stable."

"These are not too heavy." Mary kept step with him and Annie. Somehow, she figured Jimmy wanted to be away from the store and his own home just about now. *Can't say as I blame him, but then, I'm sure he isn't any angel to live with either. I feel sorry for both.*

What a mixture of grownup airs and little girl ways this sister of mine is. Mary was still smiling as they entered the house quietly, thinking about Annie telling Jimmy she would remember him in her dreams for being so kind to bring them down so she didn't have to walk. "Goodnight, Sister Mine," she all but whispered as she lit the candle and took Annie to her room. "I know you are as tired as you can be. As soon as daylight comes, we will talk as fast as ever we want to, which will be plenty fast." She kissed her and made her way to the west suite of rooms in the dark. John could easily be awake, but he made no pretense that he heard her as she crawled into bed. *Oh, but this bed feels good,* was her last waking thought.

Annie insisted on doing the dishes while Mary canned the fruit. "This is the last jar." Mary tightened the last hot cover as she spoke. "I've saved out just enough for a cherry pie for dinner and a dozen apricots that seem firm enough to keep until tomorrow. They are such a treat, I believe we'll eat them fresh."

"I have eaten so many of them this year, they are still coming out my ears." Annie made a wry face about it. David squealed with delight and wanted her to do it again. "I haven't time to play with you now, David. I must help your mama. You and Margaret go outdoors and play awhile, then I'll come play with you." She made her fingers fly, pitting cherries. "I could make the pie all by myself if you want me to."

"I'm sure that you could, My Dear." Mary was busy stirring something floury in a bowl. "I know Mother would never let a daughter of hers grow up without learning to bake and cook. Right now, I'm thinking about time. The quicker we can get the pie in the oven, the quicker it is going to be baked and out cooling. I have the pastry ready to roll out if you prefer to do that over pitting."

"I never saw you rub the shortening and flour together, Sister." Annie was puzzled. "That's the part I don't like about making a pie."

Mary laughed. "Then I'd better show you this quick way I have. Once I had a sore finger and didn't want to put my hand into dough, so I tried mixing the shortening, salt, water and flour all at once in a bowl, and mix with a heavy spoon. I find I can really make better pastry that way." Mary already had the pie ready to be filled and reached for a handful of the cherries to help pit.

"My, but you work fast," Annie said admiringly. "I guess you have to or you never would get done all the work you do. What day do we go up to see DeLamar?"

"I was just thinking about that." Mary sugared the cherries. "Perhaps tomorrow afternoon would be a good time. The butter and cheese will be ready, and I think I can have the last of that laundry ironed and buttons sewed on by then. There's really not much more ironing than the dozen handkerchiefs. I've got nine shirts to press, but it's going to be quite a load to take all at one time." She slipped the pie into the oven.

"Do you pack it on your back?"

Mary smiled. "I bought an express wagon this spring, thinking that would haul more and be easier than the old baby buggy, but I cannot say it is. Margaret does not sit still in it, and David walks both ways now."

"If the old buggy will run at all, why can't I take Margaret in it? Can you buy ice cream in DeLamar?"

"I doubt we could find ice cream for sale. If it weren't such a climb up to a snow bank, I would say we could make some ice cream ourselves. It is too steep to take the children and almost too far to go and get back while they nap." Mary did not want Annie carrying down enough snow by herself.

"But you haven't a freezer?"

"No, we haven't, but a lard pail with a good tight cover makes a pretty good substitute for a freezer. I made ice cream Easter Sunday. There was snow around close then."

"But how do you twirl the cream around to freeze?"

"You just turn the pail around by the bail, or part way and back again. One must open it up often and scrape the frozen cream away from the sides."

"It must be lots more work to make it that way than with a freezer." Annie was thoughtful about how she was going to get her favorite dessert.

"Yes it is more work and slower," Mary admitted, then smiled. "But you and I are not minding that just so we can have ice cream. If we can manage to haul a twenty-five cent cake of ice down tomorrow, we'll have ice cream for supper."

"I could pack that much on my back if I had to." Mary laughed, but Annie bristled at once.

"What made you laugh, don't you think I could?"

"That would be a very cold load on your back, Dear. But the reason I laughed was your saying *pack* instead of *carry*."

"The children at school laughed at me when I said *carry*, so I quit saying it."

"I expect they would laugh. John still pokes fun at me when I say it. Or call a ranch a farm. Meadows are still fields to me, the same as a bucket is still a pail. If you have Margaret in the buggy, I can bring the ice in the express wagon."

"Oh goody, goody." Annie was all child now, racing out to play with David and Margaret.

DeLamar as a town was disappointing to Annie. She had expected something different, although Father had explained it was not a city, or even a big place. "Why, there's hardly any sidewalks or nice buildings." Annie was critical of Lower Town. On the climb to Upper Town, she commented, "This is the crookedest street I ever saw. And what a noise." Again came her funny wry face, and she hurried on past the worst of it. Now she could see the hillside dotted with homes. "It might not be much of a town, but people seem to be living here." Just then, a young girl of Annie's age tripped gaily down a path and on ahead of them. Dressed in a ruffled dimity dress, every passing horse hooked to a rig or under a saddle, sent clouds of fine dust toward her. "Sister, I sure wouldn't want to wear such a fine dress as that in this place."

"Dearie, don't you wear your best dress when you go to town?" Mary smiled.

"Sure I do," Annie answered readily, "but this isn't really a town."

"To us, it might not be, but to many of these people, it is the only one town they have ever seen. The lady who passed us in Lower Town and spoke to me has not been out to the railroad once in twenty-three years, she tells me."

Annie could not imagine anyone living here that long from choice, but refrained from saying so.

Annie's two week stay was over in the morning. She must be gotten up to DeLamar to go on the stage. That meant early rising. Mary would not ask John to go after his refusal to meet her. Nor would John offer to go. He was a bit miffed over the girl's outspoken criticism of him always working that tunnel when it didn't bring in any money.

"It sure is cool enough this morning to walk fast." Annie was a bit impatient of Mary's steady gait. "Do you know, Sister, now that I'm going home, I want to get there as fast as I can."

"I understand, Dear. That was the way I felt when we started back home from way down in Nevada. And that meant two whole weeks of slow traveling."

"I'd die if I was that long getting home." The town was not yet astir. Not seeing the stage in sight, she added, "What if that old stage has gone off and left me?"

Mary peeked through the store window to see the clock. "We are just early, Dear. You still have ten minutes to wait before it will come to get the mail sacks and any passengers. I hope Jimmy Burch or Mr. Lyons will come a second early so I can buy an orange or some fruit for your lunch. Just sandwiches and cookies are hardly enough."

Annie had seated herself now that she knew she had to wait, and was gazing at the homes with a new interest. The fingers of light in the sky reflected on many a windowpane. White ruffled curtains billowed at the open windows. The light rain of yesterday not only settled the dust, but every shrub, bush and tree was green, as if freshly washed in the morning dew. "Do you know—this might not be such a terrible place after all."

"Who says this isn't an A-1 mining town?" Dr. Tom, just back from a night vigil, nodded to Mary.

"This sister of mine hasn't been too favorably impressed until now. You haven't met Annie before, have you Dr. Thomas?"

After introductions, Annie continued to eye the tall man talking so easy like. After his next teasing remark about her not liking their town, she retaliated, "Are you married or just married to this place?"

"Annie, Child," gasped Mary in embarrassment.

"Put it this way." Dr. Tom was enjoying this. "I'm not married, but I have hopes."

"I expect I was rude to ask you that. Mother tells me I shouldn't. But I like to see what funny answers people give me. Not long ago, I asked a man why he never got married so he would have some youngsters of his own to tease. Max Thorn is a friend of ours, but he makes me pretty mad sometimes. What do you suppose he said was the reason why he never got married?" Annie knew she had this good natured man's interest by the way he smiled. "He said those he wanted, he couldn't get. And those he could get, the devil himself wouldn't have."

"That sounds very much like what Max would say," Mary had to smile. She was ill at ease, knowing she should be at home this very minute. The cow needed to be milked and the children would be awake. John might get them both fed properly, but he would be disgruntled if he couldn't get at his work the instant he swallowed his breakfast.

"Sister, now that you got me up here where the stage can't possibly leave without me, you don't have to wait. You know I'm not afraid." When Mary hesitated, "If I'm old enough to come on the train and stage alone, I'm surely old enough to wait by myself."

"I have nothing pressing for the next few minutes, Mrs. Marcus," Dr. Tom said. "I will make sure this sister of yours climbs no hills and misses her stage; or forgets her luggage." He was seating himself comfortably.

Mary was glad to be able to be on her way home, knowing she was in good hands. She would have been some perturbed had she listened in on the conversation going on between Annie and Dr. Tom at this moment.

"So, you are not liking these hills as well as your sister does?"

"Oh, the hills are alright. Mountains, I would call them." She tried to be very adult. "I would have liked to climb some of them, but sister Mary is much too busy for such things. It makes me angry because she has to work so hard."

"Yes, I'm sure Mrs. Marcus works very hard. Perhaps you will be able to come again and help her?"

"I fear not." This was said in the tone of mature judgment. "I have my own life to think of. I do not approve of Mary making a living for her family and letting her husband dig around in that tunnel all the time." This slip of a girl was talking like a wise old man.

Dr. Tom was full of mirth, but his face never gave it away. "Do you think it probable that John Marcus might find enough gold so his wife would never have to wash other people's clothes? Not even her own?"

"That would be a miracle." The brown head with its perky straw hat gave a negative shake. "Father says those things are not apt to happen." Very resigned was her tone. The next second, seeing the stage swing into view, she was all child again. "I would like to ride on the seat by the driver. Do you suppose he would let me?"

"We might ask him and see." Dr. Tom could get in a good grin now.

"Are you good at hanging on?" was Ed Wheeler's query at her request.

"Oh, yes. I can hang on like anything. No danger of me tumbling off." At any other time, she would have been dancing in her glee, but she remembered she was a grown up young lady. "Oh, botheration," as she stood ready to climb to the high seat. "I promised Sister I would buy my own orange." She would have dashed into the store on the heels of Jimmy Burch, but Dr. Tom's strong hand detained her.

"Allow me to do that little service for you." Very courtly, he bowed as he came back with two oranges and several pieces of gum.

Annie opened her purse to pay for them, and seemed surprised when he waved her money aside. "All aboard," called Ed from the top of the rig, as he finished anchoring the sacks of mail and picked up the reins. It was Dr. Tom who helped Annie to her seat. She might be hanging on as they rolled away, but one hand waved at him.

Jimmy Burch, soured on the world in general this morning, looked at the doctor and doubled up with laughter.

"What's so funny?"

"Oh, what a girl." Doc fished in his pocket for change to pay for the gum and oranges. "She is going to make more than one male turn his head for a second look."

"I fail to see anything so very attractive. She isn't half the woman Mrs. Marcus is."

"Nor is this girl half as old." Another chuckle. "Give her time, Man, give her time." He knew Jimmy was impatient to lock the door and be off, so he stepped outside. "I would say this Miss Annie hasn't reached her teens yet. What will she be like eight to ten years from now?" Jimmy kept step with him as he headed toward the hotel and breakfast. "You hungry too?" he asked jovially. Not for the world would he ask Jimmy why he was leaving home at meal time. He was sure Laura Burch and the babe were still in town. Some gossips would be stirring if she had left again.

"Doc, do you suppose there is anyone who could pound some sense into Laura's head? She's clean daffy over this moving to Boise City business."

"Don't look to me." Dr. Tom was sure Jimmy would wish that job off on him if he could. "I like you both, but would make the worst referee possible. You and Laura will have to set down some evening and talk this thing over—preferably when neither one of you are angry, and the room is cozy and warm. Settle it peacefully be…"

"I naturally expected this was all settled," Jimmy cut in. "Isn't that what every man takes for granted?"

"It don't always work out that way." Dr. Tom was treading

lightly. "Now, if lovers would take some bright moonlit stroll and talk over such seemingly unimportant things, like where we'll live and how..."

That calm advice was too much for Jimmy. "You just remember all your fine spiel when Helen Orchard begins her campaign, telling you where she'll live and where she won't." Jimmy went on in the restaurant.

Dr. Tom watched him go, then went in for his own meal. Jimmy's taunt stung. *I had it coming alright.* He would not whimper over that. *I would be pleased to know where Helen wants to live.* As much as he loved her, that little trait, never expressing her likes or dislikes, had him worried. *Is it possible that she doesn't want to go to England for this last year of finishing school, and is just going to please her parents?* He wished he knew.

Chapter Twenty Seven

WONDER WHAT IS TROUBLING John now, Mary asked herself as he became more irritable. He had lately worked for Mr. Smith for a week. *But I've heard no blasting.* Being much too busy to do much worrying, it surprised her a bit when he stomped into the house demanding, "I've got to have some money."

"I have no money." She looked up from the washboard and met his dark scowl. "What's wrong?"

"I said I had to have some money—that's what's wrong," he snapped.

"I told you this morning that I had no money." She went on rubbing.

"But you have ways of getting money for anything you want." He was flaying himself to anger.

"Only over this washboard, John Marcus. And that isn't spent for anything but what we have to have to live. Not for what I want or you want."

"You didn't have to have that sewing machine to live," he flung at her.

"We have to have clothes, don't we? It's much cheaper to make the children's clothes than it is to buy them." She tried to hold her temper.

"Where did you get the money to buy that?" was his taunt.

"I had no money for that, and if I remember right, I explained it to you at the time. Mrs. Howard, not being able to see enough to use the machine any longer, wanted to sell it for the $10. I knew it was worth that amount. It was her own suggestion to take a pound of butter a week until it was paid for. And I'm sure lucky those twenty weeks will be up in January, for the cow will be going dry the next month. She freshens early in the spring."

"You get cash for the rest of the butter you sell. I said I have to have money." His look was belligerent, as if he would gladly slap her to make her fork over the money she did not have.

She gave him stare for stare. "Every dollar you earn goes up in smoke. I've never dictated to you ab…"

"I have earned money this time," he shouted at her, "but Smith, damn him to hell, went away and never paid me." At her slowness in saying anything, he rasped out, "Believe me, if there was any other way, I wouldn't come crawling to you." He meant

269

this to sting.

Mary dried her hands and went to the cellar for the butter crock, and carried it to the kitchen so John could see for himself. It held but the two molds of butter. These she wrapped very carefully, first in wet cheese cloth, then in paper; and put both in a paper sack, folding the top down very neatly. With a pencil from the high shelf, she wrote on the package, *Please pay Mr. Marcus,* and signed her name. "Mr. Lyons at the Post Office will pay you the $1 for these two pounds. I doubt anyone else would pay more."

This is all wrong, she told herself, going back to her washing, *after spending all this effort and heartache in trying to force John to earn his own blasting money.* She sensed he was desperate. *I surely don't know when he's ever going to wake up to any sense of responsibility.* A heavy ache was in her heart. *I do hope he takes that butter to Mr. Lyons, for they depend on my supplying them.*

The last pieces of the wash were being hung on the line when she saw John hurrying into the yard from town. He still looked out of humor, but he carried a few sticks of powder. He stopped short on seeing her at the line. "Can you fix me a sandwich or something? I'm not taking time to come to the house for dinner." As she hesitated, he urged, "Anything that's cooked is alright."

"That's the question. There is very little cooked." She brought out a loaf of bread, as well as butter and part of a glass of jam. While she hunted for paper for wrapping and a sack to carry it in, John cut huge slices of bread and spooned jam between them, not even bothering to spread butter.

"Long about noon, that damned fat-headed Butch is liable to be down here thinking he's going to take the cow for that bill we owe him." He stuffed the food into the sack. "It's up to you to see he don't."

"What are you talking about? The cow doesn't belong to us. No one can take her for our debts."

"Sure, I know that. You don't have to shout at me. I tried to tell that old fool how it was, but he wouldn't take my say so. So now you tell him." He was on his way out as he finished speaking.

It was a jolt to know she had shouted. She was a bit thankful that the children were not in where they could hear it. She was so troubled over this new threat that she was hardly aware of the passing minutes. Anything threatening the cow was tragic. The thought of having to face, let alone explaining to that disagreeable man, made her shiver with distaste. *This is what I get for being so full of pride,* as she thought of the day she had gone to pay him. *Surely there must have been some way to make him give me a receipt that day for the money I would have paid him.*

The children, coming in and seeing the food on the table, asked, "Is we hungry?" It did not seem like meal time with Mother sitting there saying nothing, not working.

"No Dearies, it isn't quite dinner time. But Mother will fix ours early so we can have a good nap." She wrapped the rest of the loaf to keep it from drying. *I must make sure these two are asleep, not to hear that ugly talk.* Never once did she doubt her ability to keep the butcher from taking the cow.

The early lunch went off very well, but the two stalled about the nap question. If she had not been in this northwest room, she never would have heard the faint creak of the gate as it was closed. He already had the cow and saddle horse on the outside and was mounting as she reached the road and grabbed the cow's halter. "You cannot take this cow. She is not ours." Mary was being dragged right along as she clung to the strap.

"Bah, I no talk to wimen," he shouted, trying to pull the cow along faster. "John Marcus say come get cow. I take her. You owe me for meat."

Knowing she could be trampled and hurt easily, she let go and managed to not fall, except to her hands and knees. Too stunned now to even care about those scraped and stinging smarts, she lay on the couch in the cool dining room. The children were now still. They must have gone to sleep after all. *The cow is gone.* She tried to accept that as a fact.

Why does something like this always have to happen in the first few months of pregnancy? Still pretty much shaken to think coherently, *I am sure I still could have saved her by finding some way to pay that bill.* The only possible way she could think of was to get word to her father or to borrow that amount from Jimmy Burch. *I have paid more than twice that much on our store bill,* she reminded herself. But to be indebted to Jimmy personally was as distasteful as burdening Father more.

Working hard all the morning, eating no lunch, and now this

jolt, she was physically, as well as mentally ill. Sharp twinges came and went. In a discouraged stupor, she lay still until she could feel able to get up. The ringing of the telephone close to her head there on the wall aroused her, but it rang several times before she realized the three long rings meant this place. Very painfully, she got up and reached down the receiver. "Yes, this is Mrs. Marcus," she told the strange voice, who identified himself as Sheriff Black.

"Mrs. Marcus, what I want to learn is this. Did you willingly let one Adale Weinberger take your milk cow for a debt this day?" he asked.

"I certainly never let him take the cow willingly. I would call it by force that he took her, trying to knock me down at the same time. He would not listen when I told him the cow did not belong to us, but to my father."

"Did I understand you to say the cow doesn't belong to you people?"

"That's right. My father owns this cow and pays taxes on it. He just loaned her to us." There was a pleased chuckle on the line.

"That's another black mark against Weinberger then." He sounded a bit pleased. "But saying the cow did belong to you people, do you know your rights in this case?"

"I'm not sure just what you mean. We do owe him a bill, but he claims we owe him $41.50, when it should be only $39.00 bec..."

"Your rights in this case, Mrs. Marcus," he was fast to tell her, "is this: No one can take the only milk cow from a family without their consent."

"Then why did he come for her in the first place? Mary was trembling with relief.

Another chuckle. "I haven't figured that out myself yet. He says Marcus told him to come get the cow. Butch may know his hamburger, but he knows very little about American law. I'll see that he brings your cow back."

"Oh, no. I fear for him to bring her back. He might harm her. He was yanking her along much too fast as he took her away." She was all but pleading.

"Don't worry. I'm coming right along with him to see that he does no harm. I rather think after this clash, he'll be one scared

Dutchman."

"He won't leave us alone until he is paid, and that I cannot do right now. Believe me, if I could pay him and never ever have to see him or speak to him again, I would be only too pleased."

There was a snicker. "So, I'm not the only one he effects that way. How many chickens do you have and are willing to let go of?"

"Not near enough, I fear. I have about three dozen hens, and the fryers are not very large yet. We ate the few early ones. I doubt there would be more than ten or twelve big enough."

"Hens seem to bring the best price in this man's town. Around $1 a piece. Would you want to pay him that way?"

"Yes, oh yes. Any way to get settled with him." Mary leaned against the wall to steady her reeling senses, concluding that some of this dizziness could be from hunger. Still fearful of eating, she poured herself milk and sat sipping the tepid drink. She felt a bit more steady with that bit of nourishment.

The table was cleared, the floor swept, and she was out bringing the clothes in from the line when Weinberger's wagon stood at the big barnyard gate, leading the cow. At any other time, Mary would have laughed to herself over the sheriff sitting on his horse and not opening the gate, which he could have done without dismounting. Weinberger climbed from his rig, opened the gate, then climbed back up to his seat, and was driving through to the hen house when the sheriff made him stop, walk back, and close the gate. Yanking the tie rope loose, he led the cow back to the shade of the corral and turned her free. Only knowing that Sheriff Black was watching him kept him from venting his spleen on the animal.

"John Marcus go to jail, not me. He say come get cow. You owe bill. You gotta pay," he shouted as he backed the wagon around.

"You gotta shut that big mouth of yours," the sheriff imitated his tone, "or you won't get paid. One more peep out of you, and you'll go back without a feather." With a motion of his quirt, he directed Weinberger to open up the crates. "Now you stay in the wagon. Mrs. Marcus will hand out the chickens she can let you have. Remember, I'm doing the counting." As Mary entered the hen house from the fenced yard door, he asked, "What is the bill supposed to be?"

"It should be $39.00, but he claims $41.50. Three times he sent spoilt meat down to us. Once he agreed to deduct the amount of those." A maddened growl came from the man in the wagon. The sheriff merely looked his way and it subsided. Mary caught the tame hens without much trouble for several minutes, but then they got aroused and put to flight. Twenty hens had been handed out when the sheriff stopped and felt the body of a bright red combed hen. He said, "This is a laying hen, or I miss my guess." He looked about the fluttering fowls. "There looks to be four or five more of them laying hens. When you catch one of 'em, put 'em out here in the yard with the little chicks." He turned the one he held lose.

It was a few seconds before Mary caught another. A rooster came close to the sheriff's feet. He caught it and handed it up to the butcher. There was a pause before it was taken from his hand. "That's twenty-one, and this is twenty-two." On went the count to thirty-nine. The crates now held thirty-six hens and fryers, and three roosters. "That's it, Weinberger."

"Thirty-nine it is—only." He still stood as if expecting more.

"That's it." Sheriff Black closed the hen house door after Mary came through. "Now, write her out, Weinberger." He stepped closer to the wagon.

"Thirty-nine only, no pay me. She lie. I no send bad meat."

Suddenly Mary found herself without fear of this man. His saying she lied was like a challenge. With contempt in every word, she flung at him, "You cannot look me in the eye and say you didn't send us meat unfit for food. Nor can you say I did not come to your stinking shop to pay you. Four years last June, I came an…"

"I no see money." He shouted her down.

"It wasn't safe to let you see it. I was alone and couldn't make you correct that bill. Nor would you give me a receipt. I would not stand there and take your abuse."

"You lie. You lie. I no touch you." He was beside himself in fury, but stopped short when Sheriff Black made a motion to climb into the rig.

"The lady never said you touched her. Looking at you and listening to you talk is abuse in capital letters. I said write out that receipt or put your name on that bill and hand it over." The man was slow to comply. "You've got all the pay you are going to get.

And that's more chicken than you are going to have in another half minute." He made for the crates as if he would tear them open.

"I no write good." His hands were unsteady, it's true. He was trying to hand the smudged greasy paper into the other man's hand.

"You can write the simple words, *Paid in Full*." The Sheriff stood over him until he did, still refusing to accept the bill. "Sign your name and date it." Laboriously the man wrote his name. "I said date it. Are you so dumb you don't know this is September 10, 1906?" At long last, Sheriff Black stepped free from the rig to let it roll on its way. As the gate creaked on being closed, a stiff brimmed hat went into the air. "Phew! That's the hardest days work I've done in many a year." Mopping his brow and putting his hat back on, he grinned, "If I were you, Mrs. Marcus, I'd frame that piece of paper. And ever you hear tell you can't get blood from a turnip, you'll have proof it can be done."

David and Margaret were circling around the house to come close to Mama, their questioning eyes never leaving the man's face. Mary moved toward them, then bethought of hospitality. "Would you care for a cool glass of milk or buttermilk? I just finished churning before noon."

"I could sure go for a glass of sweet milk. Lew Walker, the livery stable man, is the one that goes for buttermilk."

"Yes, I know." Mary smiled for the first time all day, seeing her two offspring hoisted to the saddle. Steadied by one firm hand on two small legs, reins gripped close to the slick neck as he walked along. "I believe this is the children's first horseback ride." She pumped the water hydrant in the yard to wash her hands. The horse edged closer to drink. "Why, you thirsty horse, I'll go get a tub so you can drink right."

Coming from the cellar with the pitcher of milk, man, horse and little riders were headed that way along the east side of the yard. "Nice and shady here. I'll bring glasses out here." That was not all she brought. A plate of cookies found their way to the porch. Neither child wanted to come down from their seat, but accepted a cookie to eat while still there.

"I've been in hopes Jimmy Burch would see his way clear to add a meat department to his store," the man said as he took the milk from her. "I know it will mean an extra building and ice house, but I see no other way of DeLamar getting rid of Weinberger. A town of that size means a living for only one meat shop. So there is not much chance of someone new coming in to run competition. That guy may know his meats, like I say; sometimes I think he knows 'em just too dang well. That's how he gets by with all he does. But there's plenty complaints off and on." He downed half the milk in one drink. "Do you know, most women would be peppering me with questions, wanting to know how I came in on this, and such."

"I guess I'm just too relieved over the outcome to ask. And besides, I have to put all this behind me and forget about it." Her words held meaning but for herself alone. "I have to go on living, you understand, but there is one question I would like to ask—can a married man sell a home without the wife's consent?"

"She would have to sign the deed or it would be *no sale*." He was studying this young woman with her serious face meeting his gaze, her troubled eyes were questioning. "Seeing how you don't ask, I'll tell you. Butch was trying to sell the cow to Lew there at the livery stable, even before he got her home. So Lew came hot-footing it to me. As he said there was something rotten in Denmark, and he didn't think it was limburger cheese either." He now finished the milk and set down the glass, shaking his head to the offer of more. "That Lew sure likes his buttermilk." He smiled and set the two tots to the porch with a nod to Mary. The sheriff led his horse away, out through the front gate and was soon out of sight between clumps of willows.

While she cooked supper, Mary tried to come to an understanding of John's action. "I see the cow is still here, alright," was John's opening remark as he came in. "I knew you would be a match for him." He said it half admiringly. His words brought back all the hurt and anger of this day nearly over. Her eyes blazed at him, then she ran from the room, grabbing the milk pail in her flight. There was no trusting herself to speak—she would not quarrel before the children. It was a bit too early to milk, so she pulled an armload of the poorest turnips for the cow and took her time about milking. With the clean cloth from the line, she went around the back of the house to the cellar to strain the milk. It was there that John cornered her. "I want to know what all this fuss and bother is about that you'll not speak to me." He ended on an injured tone. "What have I done?"

"I could tell you of a lot of things you haven't done, John Marcus, but the one thing you did this day is enough for all time to come. You told that contemptible man to come get the cow. Don't you ever, ever try saying you didn't."

"I told him to come get her if he dared. There is a difference there." John was getting a bit angry himself. "I couldn't make him understand anything. He's rode my neck about long enough; hounding me for money when I had none."

"To save your precious neck, you put him on mine." With every word, acid dripped. "If you couldn't handle him, how did you think I could?"

"You are the one that wears the pants in this family, it seems. You handle the money," he flung at her. The two sleepy children were coming to the porch, whimpering in their unhappy state. He did not dare say more or detain her longer.

This night, John's hopes of a better understanding of all this trouble were dashed. His bed was left to him alone. Mary went to bed in the spare room with both children tucked in beside her. She did not expect to do much sleeping—there was too much unhappiness to mull over. *Now that I know where the sore point is, what can I do about it?* She was more than sure John would not have paid that meat bill if he had been able to get the money this day. *I doubt we would even have food enough if I didn't wear the pants, as he so contemptibly said.* All this rankled.

Breakfast was on the table and the children were eating when he came to the kitchen. He timed his leaving the house for work at the time Mary would be coming from the barn. "Mary, I want to know what the children are jabbering about a man taking the cow away and another man bringing her back."

"If you want to know, go ask the sheriff. He's the one that got her back."

"What's the sheriff got to do with it?" John was uneasy. "Did you call him in on it?"

"I did not call him. What he knows, I can only guess, but a deaf man could not help hearing Butch yell about how you told him to come get the cow. He wasn't the one going to jail, but you were. Was that why you hid yourself in your nice little tunnel until the fireworks were over yesterday?" This was pure vitriol. The hand he tried to stay her with, she struck hard.

The armed truce in this home continued on. Work was the

only solace to either one of them. There was always plenty of that for Mary, and preparing for winter was added work. The only brightness in John's gloom was the lure of gold. Somehow, he had to strike something good to make amends to Mary.

There is just one bright ray in all this, Mary thought as she snatched in the nearly dry clothes from the line against the threatening rain. *John won't trouble me asking for money. I might even dare to keep some at the house. I'm going to have to commence saving up for this next spring's payment.* She was sure there would be nowhere near enough cabbage for that amount of kraut. The rattle of a wagon coming down the rocky grade came to her. *That can't be Father coming from that direction; this is almost too early for him to come anyway. That rig sounds like a light one, or it's unloaded.* She well knew that Father would not be coming empty. Then the rawboned team and patched canvas-covered wagon came into view and stopped at their gate.

With the last armload of clothes still clutched to her, she walked a few steps toward the angular man ambling along the west porch. "Howdy, Ma'm." He tipped his worn, greasy-band hat. "We are strangers in this part of the country, just traveling through, and we'd like a place to sleep and eat." His voice was a half whine.

"It is but two miles to DeLamar. Right on up this creek, you cannot possibly miss the road." Mary had walked more to the front of the house to direct them.

The man was forced to retreat his steps. "Our team is about played out, as you can see. We'd like it if we could stop here for the night. Looks so you have room enough?"

"We aim to pay you sumpen," the gaunt faced woman peering out from the wagon told her. "Our beds got damp in all these rains we been hittin'." Her speech had almost as much of a whine as her husband's. Two half grown boys poked their untrimmed heads below the canvas.

"We have a big house, that is true," Mary was very firm in her voice, "but we do not have extra bedding to sleep people. I'm sorry about your beds being damp, so the best thing would be for you to try making those two miles."

Slowly, the man shook his head. "Can't do it. Anything to hinder us camping anywheres long where it's grassy?" His was a pleading whine now.

"We cannot stop you from camping anywhere outside our fences, but do you know about the creek water being full of cyanide? Your team cannot be allowed to drink it. That small trickle of water coming down the gulch there from the north and out under that little bridge is good water. You are welcomed to get water for camp to use from the hydrant here in the yard," Mary relented. Only too clearly could she remember being in the same predicament more than once. "It is not possible to loan you dry bedding throughout, but I can let you have a pair of double blankets for the night. They are nice soft wool. Sleeping in those, you'll hardly be aware of the dampness, for they are heavy ones."

Only this day, she had aired them out for the coming winter use. While carrying those clean smelling blankets to hand over the fence to the waiting hands, she thought, *I will need to give them a good washing perhaps, for these people look rather dirty and bedraggled.* From her garden, she brought carrots and turnips aplenty for their supper. Their appreciation overflowed. As a last act of the Good Samaritan, she brought a loaf of bread and a lard pail of milk from the cellar. A cautious instinct made her snap the padlock shut on that door as she came out.

The clamor they made over the pail of milk made her know it was a treat they didn't often have. "You are welcomed to the milk, but I would like the pail to be left in the morning right here on the fence beside the blankets." She tapped the picket fence as she spoke, thinking this way, they wouldn't have to come in the house and give John the chance to be surly with them. "It seems like I never have enough of these handy tin pails."

John came home from work late. He was again helping someone sink a shaft above DeLamar. When he saw the campers, he complained about them the first thing. "What in the devil is that outfit camping on us for?"

"I was under the impression that the fence was on the line of our holdings. I fail to see how we can control all the ground outside."

"I suppose you gave them permission to camp there?"

"As a matter of fact, I did." She continued to dish his supper for him.

"Pretty crumby looking outfit, they look to me. What will you do if you wake up in the morning and find they've stole you blind?"

Mary did not answer. She had no intention of arguing with him. She soon went to bed and to sleep, with the pleased warm thought that she was in truth being a friend to man.

Chapter Twenty Eight

NO FLICKERING LIGHT OF a campfire greeted Mary's eye as she dressed in the pre-dawn and made her way to the kitchen to build fires and start breakfast. No time now to walk through the yard to bring in her blankets. *They sure pulled out early, and I never heard them.* Quickly she washed, the dash of cold water on her face from cupped hands. *I must have been sleeping for keeps.* She was very much awake now.

It was a nuisance to go back to the house for the key as she went to the cellar for milk and cream, as well as bacon. *I haven't locked this since the Palmer family left here.* Not until John, with his lunch, had left for work did the time come to go for the blankets she knew would be draped over the fence. *I'll wash them first thing this morning.* She stopped short—there was nothing on that fence except the lard pail turned bottom side up on a picket, the wire-bail missing. Not satisfied but what those warm, soft wooly blankets were somewhere about, she went out the front gate and walked the distance to the campsite. The blackened place of the cook fire of last night was stone cold.

Stunned by this new calamity, she made her way back to the house and then to milk. The loss of that much bedding with thoughts of winter coming was frightening. *Now what can I do?* She could ask that question, but knew she herself was the one who would need to think out the answer. Sheriff Black in DeLamar was the only one she could think of who would have authority to get those blankets back. She tried ringing the store as soon as she went back to the house. No answer. It still lacked several minutes of seven. She strained the milk and got the children their meal before DeLamar answered to those two long rings. It was Jimmy Burch's voice she heard. "Jimmy, I hate to bother you, but could you get the sheriff for me?"

"Sure Mrs. Marcus, I can send for him. It might save time if you could tell me what you are wanting him for."

"Some campers paused for the night close beside our place. I felt sorry for them because their bedding was damp, and loaned them two woolen blankets. They left sometime before daylight, but forgot to leave me my bedding."

"What kind of an outfit was it?" Jimmy was much interested and listened to Mary's description as best she could give, then

281

assured her, "I believe that is them pulling through town here just as I gave out the mail sacks. Stop your worrying now; they haven't much of a start. You'll get your bedding okay."

The thought of how much trouble she might be causing those poor people came as she hung up the silent receiver. *I could have told Jimmy I only wanted what is mine.* Going about her work, she still puzzled over anyone forgetting to leave loaned things. *Here I thought they were appreciative, and they do a trick like this.* She would not say they were stealing.

Noon came and she had lunch ready. Jimmy Burch rode in with a bulky bundle tied to the back of his saddle. As he carried it into the house for her, she saw that it was two new wool blankets from the store. "Oh, I didn't want other blankets. I just wanted my own back." It was all but a cry. "Wouldn't they let the sheriff have them?" The rough scratchy feel of this coarse wool was disagreeable to her hand.

"Oh, they tried to give them back fast enough when I caught up with them, but who would want to touch anything that filthy outfit had once slept in." Jimmy brushed his hands as if to free himself from any contamination.

"Why, oh why, did you go to all this trouble yourself?" Mary was heartsick for sure now.

"Oh, I wasn't running any risk." Jimmy, thinking she worried him being in some danger, showed her the small, lightly tarnished badge he wore. "I was deputized once when Black had to be gone. I only had to flash the sight of this to make them come to terms. That outfit has tangled with the law before; they weren't wanting any more. In no time, they were trying to buy off and at the same time, trying to unroll those ragged bundles they call beds. At first, they offered $5; then $10. When their ante got up to $16, the price of the two best blankets in the store, I took it. And I thought *good riddance to bad rubbish.* They won't be hanging around these hills now."

It was plain to see Jimmy was proud of the way he had handled the whole affair. Mary could not tell him she would oh-so-gladly exchange the blankets, filth and all. *I haven't found much that good soap and water along with sunshine won't make clean.* But she could not say that to this fastidious man, eyeing her so anxiously. "You are not looking so good, Mrs. Marcus, have you been ill?"

"Just too busy to figure out if I'm sick or just lazy. You haven't had lunch with all this running around on our account. Would you care to join the children and I?"

"I would be glad to. Have you heard I'm without my cook again? Laura went out on the stage yesterday morning, vowing she and the baby are staying in Boise for the winter. Now that they are dropping the city part after Boise, I thought it might make a difference, but it hasn't yet." His smile at his own wit was a wry one.

Mary tried to talk of other things than his matrimony status. She spoke nary a word about her and John's rift on the same troubled sea. If Jimmy knew anything about the cow deal, he never once mentioned it. He was being the very same friendly fellow who had done so many nice things for the Marcus family. "I was talking to Baers at the hotel the other day, and he asked about the prospects of you having kraut for him this year. I made a mental note to ask you the next time I seen you."

"I fear I won't have but the one barrel and perhaps a keg for our own use. So many of the plants I put out last spring didn't live. I've not figured out all the reason yet."

"Cabbages seem to be scarce this year. They are selling for 25¢ a head right now. I believe Baers expects so, and will be willing to pay more for his barrel of kraut, say something like $20. I doubt he could get it for less than that."

"Thanks for the tip. He'll have to pay at least that, or I'll sell the cabbage without all that extra work. If he should ask you again, you can let him know if he wants the barrel for the $20, well and good, I'll make it for him. But he might have to find some way of getting those barrels sent down to me. You wouldn't happen to have a good sized kraut cutter in the store, would you?"

"Not a good sized one, I'm sure—just little dinky slaw shredders. They wouldn't be much force when it comes to making a barrel of kraut, I fear."

"It would be pretty slow work. Father brought his last year, but I thought if I could find a cutter, I would get the kraut made before he came this year, there being only about one fourth the amount."

"Ten chances to one, they would be having one at the hotel. I'll make sure Baers sends it along with the barrels, and I'll see that those kegs come down too."

The reaction that set in after Jimmy left and the children were down for their nap was of a different type. Back and forth her thoughts swung, first to her and Johns' trouble, then to Jimmy's problems. *I'm even more certain everyone has plenty of crosses to bear.* And she was more lenient in her judgment of John. *He had those campers sized up right, and I didn't. How can he be so wise in some things, yet so oblivious to other things?* There was no answer to this question. To keep from thinking so much, she spread out the length of dress goods Mother had sent her when first she knew of her having the sewing machine. *I'm going to have to get me a dress made. I can hardly get into any I have.* While cutting, she gave all her thoughts to it, but once she was ready for the stitching, her mind could wander again.

She was planning the work far ahead to be able to get everything done before winter came or Father should show up. The dress was stitched and ready for hemming the next afternoon. While trying it on to measure for the hem, she heard barrels and kegs tumbling to the front yard from a passing rig. *I can't go out like this.* They drove on before she was changed back into her other dress. She found a kraut cutter, well packed, with papers in one of the kegs. *That means I can get busy on that kraut.*

October was here and Father could be coming any day soon. She had the cabbages pulled, and part of them trimmed, ready for cutting. Her worry now was that Father might guess about the estrangement between her and John. It might be a very little worry, but it was there. Two nights later, on coming home from work late as usual, John found her busy cutting kraut. "So, you don't intend to let your dad in on such work?" he asked while washing for his meal.

"Not if I can help it." She cleared her hands of shreds to dish up his food.

"Don't you think he likes doing such things?" Mary was looking pale these days, and he wondered if she was sick. His biggest worry was what would he do if she got down sick.

"Maybe he does, but Father isn't as young as he tries to make out. He must often get too tired, but he is not one to give up as long as there is work to be done. He can't sit down and let others do it." Back to the cutting she went.

John finished his meal just as she picked up the heavy pounder and commenced that tiresome work. "Here, give that to me," taking the worn-smooth wooden stick from her hands. "You have no business doing this part. It's all the same as hard work when you keep it up very long."

Midnight came and Mary was still cutting. Too weary to stand erect as she dumped the pan full of pale green shreds into the barrel, she leaned on the edge. "It isn't full yet, and I just can't do any more to…" She was weeping in her exhaustion.

"Why do you want to kill yourself this way?" John thundered at her while helping her to bed. It was to her rightful place beside him, he steered her this night. Mary was much too worn and weary to make objection. It was rather soothing to have him scolding and fretting over her.

Her feet were so swollen in the morning, she had to wear slippers, so she did her kraut-cutting seated. Pounding in the keg was easier because it was lower. She then dipped the bruised mass into the barrel until it was full enough. Now came the surprise— she could not lift the heavy rock to weigh it down. *Oh botheration! Now I have to hunt up two or three smaller ones to do the trick.* The kraut had to be weighted down—there was no thought of not getting it done. Filling the keg could be left until evening.

Father Williams came this night, just as the Marcus Family finished their supper. The weary slump as he ate his meal told plainly of his hard trip. "The road's just soft enough in places that I had to drop the trail wagon on several steep pitches." Then came the knowledge that he had been three days making the trip.

"No wonder you are worn to a frazzle, Father." Mary hurried about waiting on him. "In the morning, John can feed and water those teams, and you just sleep in for once in your life." She was glad the cabbage and keg was not out in sight."

"A good night's rest will put me to rights, Daughter." He was not liking the weariness of this girl of his. He was sure something was wrong, but he must remember to go slow. In this home, he was the outsider.

No sooner had she built the fire in the morning, than Father was up and dressed. "You just can't stay in bed after the cock crows." She was feeling much better.

"So you think you are the only one who can be all done-in at night, yet come up fresh as a daisy by morning?" Playfully, he pinched her cheek as if that would bring back the rosiness.

"Maybe I did think that you had overstepped your endurance for once. John is dressing. You let him care for the team anyway. Please do that."

"Alright, Daughter. We'll compromise—you tell me where the milk pail is." Mary smiled at Father tricking her this once, all the while she was rushing about to get breakfast. *I like to milk, but I also like to cook meals in an orderly fashion. I do wish John would take it into his head to learn to milk.*

"Is the lady of the house against eating breakfast this early in the day?" Father teased as Mary was still busy and not seated to eat with him and John. She set more cakes for them, right from the griddle.

"It isn't that. I just need to have John's lunch ready for him. He thinks he has to go to work whether or not I have it ready." As she turned the cakes, they made a hissing sound.

"If you can leave that hay unloading until tonight," John said, "I can help with it. Bleso will be pretty mad if I don't show up this day."

"I might leave the one wagon, but I want the other one to do some scouting about, see where best to cut posts, and the easiest spot to haul them from. Riding part of the way might beat walking all the way." He turned to greet the two rosy-cheeked children coming into the warm room to dress, their small arms hugging their clothes.

"Can I goes with you?" two year old Margaret wanted to know.

"That's no way to talk," David, close beside her, reproved. "Grandpa won't want a baby-talking girl following him around."

Not for anything would Grandpa laugh. "Now, I rather think I would like a baby girl about Margaret's size, and her older brother tagging me about." A twinkle came to his eyes. "Do you suppose we could talk Mother into riding with us?"

David tried to dress quickly and still keep his eye on Mother, but he was all thumbs. Mother smiled, "Tend to your dressing, Son. Now I might consider going if you will allow me to take along a pail and basket, so if we find some elderberries, I can pick them. I haven't found the time to go after any. How about me fixing a lunch and taking it along?"

"A picnic then it is." Father accepted another cup of coffee. "That's providing you sit down and eat a good meal now." As the two tots climbed to their seats and commenced their meal, he asked David in mock seriousness, "Do you think we should let Mother take along a pail to gather berries in?" He waited for the nod of the serious faced boy.

As soon as those two swallowed their food, they raced outdoors to see what all camp was on the wagons. Mary was still eating, so Father stayed put so she would. "Tell me, is David always that serious?"

"Just about. Oh, he has his playful times, but he is just enough older and wiser than Margaret that he thinks he is grown up by comparison. It is funny—he will be five in the spring. I cannot see myself sending him to school in the fall—those two miles for him to go alone. I will be a nervous wreck by night."

Father smiled broadly. "Where have I heard that before?"

"Oh, I'm sure all parents must feel that way. Perhaps you and Mother did when I started to school. I just can't remember you showing any worry. But then, I only had a mile to walk. I believe he would be safe enough, but it's the sudden changes of weather here, especially during spring and autumn here in these hills, that give me the most worry. I shall not send him more than the two or two and a half months each season. I want to have a book here at home so he can go right on with his lessons. He learns easily, and would not be much behind his class, no matter how much he has to stay out."

"Yes. The sudden changes of weather would be a worry. It might be well to wait until he is past six to start him in school. Now I know just the proper Christmas present for that boy—one of those big ship barometers. I bought myself one last year, and at Christmas time, my sister Annie sent me another one. We have no use for two, so I'll just send David the one I bought. They are quite reliable for storm indications." He knew by Mary's pleased smile that this would be a very acceptable present.

"But you are not the only one having worries about sending a child to school. Mother and I are faced with a more serious problem in sending Annie away from home for high school."

"That is right. Annie will be through the eighth grade this year. Will it have to be Caldwell for her or is there a high school closer?"

"None close, but that is only half the trouble. As you know, her whole thought is for music. Caldwell has a good teacher in piano, but we've not found a home with a piano where she can board and do her practicing on. To send her to one of the academies in Boise might be the best plan, but that is nearly twice the distance, and we would not be able to see her except at holiday time. Your cousin Silvia wrote, urging us to let Annie come to Springfield for the full school year and be a companion to her husband's niece. They took her in to rear since she was orphaned."

"Oh no, Father. How can you and Mother let her go so far away?"

"That's what we've been asking ourselves lately," he said with all but a catch in his steady voice. "We know Silvia and her mate can well afford giving this niece a home and all the accompaniments. They live close to good schools—it is an ideal place for Annie, and she wants to go. The thought of that fine piano to play is looming big, I know. The expense of her trip both ways would not be as much as boarding would be in Caldwell or Boise."

"I know you are right, Father." Mary was thoughtful while she scraped and stacked the dishes. "It struck me as impossible at first, Silvia not having children of her own and loving them like she does. That would be the nicest place for Annie, as long as she has to be away from home. If it just weren't so far away from us all." A rueful smile came. "Sometimes two thousand miles are no farther than sixty—I'm up here and can do nothing to help."

"I wouldn't say that, Daughter. You can write your usual cheery letters. We'll send them on to Annie when you can manage only the one. You and I know the gap between Snake River Flats and Springfield, Illinois is not bridged in one short week, or by one letter."

"Forgive me for not writing lately, Father. I'll have to tell you what happened to knock the props right out from under your eldest."

"We were sure something had gone wrong," he assured her.

"Something did. And it was all my own doing. I have no one to blame but myself." Mary started to wash dishes now, sure that she could keep Father resting while she told him all about the loss of the blankets. Not for the world would she mention other troubles or misunderstanding. Anyway, that was all past and done with. "You remember those two fine wool blankets you and

Mother insisted were mine? Well, I haven't got them anymore." Then in great detail, she told of their loan and the outcome.

"How come you thought it needful to be that kind to strangers?"

"Well, to tell you the truth, it dates back to those two years and more that the Marcus family traveled hither and yon. More than once, we had damp bedding and were befriended by people on the way. Most people living out in the hinterlands are kind and hospitable. Once in awhile, we found the other type of people. About the end of the first year, we pulled into a ranch home to ask permission to camp close there because of water. John went to the barn to talk with the man. I saw the woman coming to the house with a milk pail, so I followed her right in. She did ask me in when I rapped, but when I asked to buy some milk for David, even a cupful, she cut me off short—telling me she had no milk for sale. Poor David had not learned to like malted milk yet, and he was hungry and whimpering for milk, seeing her strain it. I had most of that $40 you had sent me of the lease money, but do you suppose she would let me have even a cupful for my hungry boy? Not her. Yet she poured at least a pint of the warm milk into a pan for a big fat tom cat." Mary brushed away a tear this remembrance brought. "From then on, I taught David to like the malted milk and health cracker so he might never be hungry again."

Father nodded his head in understanding, then smiled as he asked, "Is that accounting for the many glasses of milk you give out for free?"

"No, not altogether. Every one of these timber haulers, and others who pass here, are always hauling things down for us. They claim it is no trouble, but I'm sure it often is a bother. They stop to fill their water sacks and get a drink. Most of the people in DeLamar are friendly."

"It is nice to have friends and neighbors. It'd be a poor life without them."

"We have the friends, but for neighbors, the two miles distance seems to be a barrier. When I go to town, I'm in a hurry. I have to rush right back. I've never been able to call on the few ladies that I have met, or who have gotten down here. Of course, most of those coming this far have come to buy milk, cream, or butter. I'll have to tell you about a woman who came last spring, real early before the cow freshened. She was the new mine engineer's wife, and had come from a big city in the east. Very pompously, she told me who she was and where I was to deliver both milk, cream and butter on certain days of the week. When I finally got a word in edgewise to tell her I had no milk for sale, she looked at me in her most haughty manner and said, "You have a cow, haven't you? I shall expect the delivery to be made." Really, Father, I had a hard time making that woman understand there is a time in every cow's life when she doesn't give milk."

Father smiled with her. "And I'm sure you haven't been bothered with her much since?"

"Oh, no. She didn't stay in DeLamar long, but went back east."

"That is what I meant—people of that type are not apt to stay long in these surroundings."

"Father, I've wanted to ask you something. Jimmy Burch's wife, Laura, thinks I'm a bit peculiar, or touched in the head, to like living in these hills. Is there something really wrong with me?"

Father smiled. "The only wrong thing I can see is you being imbued with the courage, self reliance, and ambition of your forefathers and mothers—those who ventured into new country–the real pioneers. They had to be unafraid of work and able to cope with hardships."

"Thanks for the assurance that your eldest is not some freak of nature." She laughed at him getting restless to get about his work. "Now I'm ready to help you unload the one wagon of hay."

"And I'm telling you, you should not do such heavy work." Father meant it.

"Oh, I've watched you enough to know one doesn't have to do heavy lifting to upend those bales to slide down that plank." She led the way to the barn, uncovering the long rows of green onions along the way.

"What are you going to do with all your fresh garden stuff?" He was eyeing not only the onions, but the rows of lettuce. "Those onions will hardly keep over the winter. I have a sack of dry ones on the load for your winter use."

Mary laughed. "I was in hopes you could tell me some way of fixing these to keep. John and the children like them to eat just as they are now, but I know after the first hard freeze, they are not going to be so good."

"Some could be taken up with plenty of earth and fixed in a window box. But that would be room for only a fraction of them. They might keep green and fresh in the cellar for a short while; the same way with the lettuce. Have you tried selling it?"

"No, I haven't, and that is a good idea, for there is sure plenty and then some."

"After our picnic today, we might take a sashay up town and see if anyone wants garden sass. Do you suppose the restaurant would be supplied?"

"They might not be at the hotel. Mr. Baers is a nice man to deal with, and they feed a good many men, I understand. He is the one I've made the barrel of kraut for."

Late in the afternoon, as they rode into DeLamar, the children napped. "They are worn out for sure. And here I'm feeling rested, riding in this comfortable spring seat instead of walking. And what a big basket of elderberries we did find. From now on, until storms come, I must spend part of the day gathering rosehips for jam if I find nothing else."

Mr. Baers pricked up his ears the second he heard her mention green onions. "Sure, I'll buy 'em. The cook has been yapping for green stuff. There hasn't been many peddlers up lately; maybe because of the rains. How many bunches did you say you had?"

"Any amount you want, or I can tie. You name them." Mary was happy to find a sale for them.

"Maybe fifty bunches at a time. Say, why go to all the trouble of tying them? More work for you as well as the cook. Just take the handful, about a dozen in a bunch, I believe; chop the roots off and part of the tops; stand 'em up in a box; count 'em that way. They bring about $.05 a bunch if they are good and fresh, which I know yours will be. Do you have any cabbage, beets or turnips? Cabbage seems the scarce thing. I've been paying $1 a bushel for beets, carrots and turnips."

"I could let you have some turnips and carrots, and maybe as much as ten head of cabbage. Could you make use of lettuce? It is just extra nice and tender. I've got big bunches of it right now."

He shook his head *no*. "It doesn't keep too well. But say, it would be a good change from cabbage or onions. When you are coming up, you might bring along enough for one meal. I'll leave it to you the amount you think one hundred-fifty men would eat."

291

Mary was smiling when she climbed back into the wagon. "That is going to take some figuring—how much lettuce one hundred-fifty men will eat, and the price it should be. At this rate, I'm going to have that payment out of the garden yet. I must not sell even one of the beets though—they keep, or I can pickle 'em and can them."

Chapter Twenty Nine

RAIN, SLEET, AND SNOW alternated throughout the month of November. Not until December did the snow pile deep, driven into huge drifts within a few hours by a near-blizzard storm. Mary Marcus delayed going to milk until John came from his work in the tunnel. "I know you are nearly frozen, John, but before you take off your coat, will you help me to the barn? Then you can come back easy enough, and I believe I can make it back alone. The storm will just blow me back. It is getting there in the first place, I fear." She had lantern, milk pail, and a pan of peelings for the cow.

"You better leave that pan of stuff 'til another time." He put his arm through the bail and led the way, leaving Mary to shield the lantern with her coat as best she could. Expecting a deeper drift along the barn, he circled a bit away from that, then steered back to the stable door at the northwest corner. He needed all his strength to hold the barn door open so Mary could enter. Once inside the snug building, talking was possible. "Do you think you could make it back alone?" He sounded half doubtful.

"I think I can. If I don't show up in ten or fifteen minutes, you can come dig me out of a snow bank." It was easy to feel safe now that she was inside. She did not mind John going on back to the house, knowing he was cold after his much further battle. *Why, it's such a short distance to the house, if I head straight there, I can't possibly get lost.* She planned leave the lantern and take just the milk. *And I'll keep along beside the barn all the way. That will be half the distance to the yard fence.* No, Mary would not take chances on getting lost in this storm.

With the warm fire and the good smell of food ready to eat, the two happy children ate their supper. John was lulled into a sense of well-being and contentment. Fifteen minutes had passed when Mary burst into the washroom calling, "Come quick," she gasped out of breath. "There is a man out here."

"What you talking about?" For a second, he thought she was frightened by the pull and tug of the storm.

"He is close to the barn. I nearly stumbled over him." She could catch her breath now. She lifted the pail of milk to the sink, put a match to a candle for the children to see by, and took the lamp to the washroom window while John pulled on his coat. Out into the storm they went again, guided by the faint glow behind them. The light was of no help once out of its range. The east corner of the barn was the best guide, once they reached that. Seconds seemed like hours before they had the unconscious man between them and headed toward the house. Coming up against the yard fence, several feet short of the gate, was another delay until the feeble light from the window could direct their steps. Getting their burden up the steps and to the porch was the hardest, for now there were no steps—nothing but a drift of snow to wallow through. They dragged the helpless form into the washroom.

Once the snow was cleared so she could close the door to shut out the storm, Mary naturally expected they would take the man to the kitchen. And here was John leaving him to lie on the cold floor, telling her to bring a blanket while he pulled off the snowy outer clothes. Getting off the shoes was the worst. "Fold the quilt and put 'er down beside him," he directed her, then motioned for her to help lift the rather short man onto it. "Can you commence rubbing his feet? He's still alive. Rub hard–don't be afraid to hurt him. We've got to get circulation." John was busy rubbing hands, arms and shoulders. David and Margaret, wide-eyed with wonder, stood in the kitchen door looking on. "We don't want much warmth in here." He spoke quickly. "Maybe we should stop rubbing and get 'im to bed. Put the coffee pot where she's hot. We'll try some of that soon."

Mary had been rubbing so hard, her own hands burned from the friction as soon as she stopped. She made short work of getting the two children to bed, although David would not be going to sleep very soon with his questions unanswered. But she dared not take the time to explain. "The man has been out in the snow too long and cannot talk yet, so we don't know his name yet. Daddy is rubbing him to make him feel better, and Mama must go to help." She hurried back, bringing a cup of coffee as she did so.

"Shall I try giving this to him with a spoon, or do you think I should work some more on his feet?" John was busy at those cold extremities.

"You can try it. Go 'er slow." The man's wrinkled throat seemed to move. "Looks like he managed that alright." John continued to massage the chilled limbs and left her to spoon in the hot coffee.

Both Mary and John wore their coats, leaving the room very cold. Mary knew nothing about taking care of frost-bitten people, but John ministrations were sure. She remembered him once telling her about how he helped his uncle revive a man they found half frozen. That man had to have one foot cut off afterwards. She hoped that wouldn't happen in this case.

Mary left the cold room long enough to go strain the milk. John let her take his place when she returned, but paused to give the man's upper limbs a brisk rub. "This part of him seems to be getting some feel to it, but those feet are still needing a lot of rubbing." He stood up, then paused, "You haven't eaten anything yet either. I'll snatch a bite, then relieve you so you can eat."

After eating some food, Mary's brain commenced to function better. "It is hardly eight o'clock yet," she informed John as she came back. "Do you think there might be someone in the store?"

"What good will that do?" The two miles between here and town couldn't be negotiated this night.

"I wasn't meaning to ask Dr. Tom or anyone to try coming down tonight, for I'm sure they never could make it. But I thought Doc could tell us the very best things for us to do."

"Try telephoning, if you want to." John was a bit miffed at Mary thinking he didn't know what to do. "The line may be down."

Mr. Lyons was the one answering her ring. As soon as she asked for Dr. Thomas, she could hear him calling. Evidently Dr. Tom was right there in the building. It was a relief to hear that steady voice, but he sounded perplexed. "I fear one could hardly make it unless this storm abates, and then only in daylight."

"Oh, I didn't want you to attempt to come," Mary was quick to tell him. "I just wanted you to tell us the best things to do for him." Then she listened to his instruction as best she could. The storm made the line noisy. After a crackle on the line, Dr. Tom's voice was heard no more.

"I believe the line must have blown down while I was talking," she told John. "But what I could hear, Dr. Tom said to do the very things you have been doing all along. He said hot soup, as well as coffee, as soon as he can swallow. There is a cupful of chicken broth left from yesterday. Shall I heat that next?" John nodded, and she put it on the stove, adding some water, for it was very rich.

By morning, the sun peeked through the top of the windows. The swirl of storm had left even the east windows nearly covered with snow. David and Margaret, clothes in arms, came to the slightly warm kitchen. "Where's Mama?" They were puzzled to find Daddy asleep in his chair, coffee cup still in his hand.

He awoke with a start as they asked again. "She's asleep in the other bedroom, but you mustn't wake her. You two dress there by the fire. I'll build it up, then I better get a path shoveled to the barn." But first, he needed to make a path to the woodhouse since they had burned up all the wood.

Mary was awake and cooking breakfast before the path to the barn was half way completed. John was out of sight in a drift when she called him to care for the half conscious man. The bright sunshine was dazzling in all this whiteness. She picked up the shovel to work those few minutes until he was back. "See, I'm not making my path nearly as wide as you are—just wide enough for me to get through. The quicker I can get to the barn, the quicker I can get that poor cow relieved of her milk. Shall I try some gruel for the sick man?" John was slow about answering, so she clarified, "Gruel is the thinnest kind of mush fixed with milk so he can almost drink it."

"Might be alright." John was busy shoveling away now.

Mary would not stop the work to get more answers. That came after John finished the path and she had come in with the milk. He was just through with his meal. "The man is doing alright, don't you think?"

"As far as I know about such things, he is. Of course, he's a pretty old man to stand such a freeze and come out of it alive. Sometimes he acts like he is conscious. A little while ago, he tried to talk. Sounded like he said *Jack*."

"Maybe that's his name. I'm thinking about making potato soup for our dinner today. I already have a baked Indian meal pudding in the oven. He should be able to eat both." She got up late this day; it was noon before Mary realized it. *Why, here it is twelve o'clock, and I've not started dinner.* Donning coat to go to the cellar, from the porch she watched a moving figure emerge between mounds of snow covered willows. "I think that must be Dr. Tom coming." She opened the door enough to call. *I want something more than potato soup for a meal,* she was thinking.

She picked up the last squash and carried it out atop her potato pan.

"Let me relieve you of that load." Dr. Tom, freeing his feet from snow shoes, carried in the huge green bumpy squash. "I haven't seen one of these in such a long time, I didn't think they grew them anymore."

"They cannot grow them up in these hills," Mary explained as she led the way into the kitchen. "My parents grew this down on the Flats. I see this one must have gotten bruised in hauling, in spite of being buried in a box of grain."

"Knowing the telephone line was out of commission, and I should get in practice with webs, I came down to see if I could be of any assistance." Off came his outer coat, mittens and cap. "Do I look more natural now?" he asked David, who was eyeing him so very seriously. Rubbing his hands together to warm them the faster, he followed John to the washroom.

Mary hurried about, putting wedges of the bright orange squash to steam; dicing the bacon, and cooking the kettle of soup. She paused to bring John's shrunken underclothes for the sick man. Then as she saw they were fixing to take him to the bed in the northeast room, she brought out a rubber sheet packed away with the baby things. Dr. Tom took it, and spread it very smooth beneath the man's hips, as John raised him. "This may not be needed," he smiled and winked at the helpless man, "but it's good to be on the safe side."

Mary could hear the male voices. *I would like to be in on that talk, so to learn how better to care for this man.* But there were the children to keep from bothering, and the meal to have ready. When at last the two came to the kitchen to wash and make ready to eat, Mary was busy fixing a tray of food. "Will this be about right as to amount of food?" she asked. She held out the baking pan covered with a napkin, a bowl of steaming soup, a mound of golden squash with its well of melting butter; coffee and the still-warm pudding.

"I would say it will be a plenty." Doctor went on drying his hands. "Mr. Jack should feel like a new man to get all that good food on the inside." Seeing that she was about to move on, he stopped her. "Just a moment. I have something here that might help him to drink his coffee." From his kit, he brought out a glass drinking tube, rinsed it at the faucet, and then placed it on the makeshift tray. "I doubt that soup will go through it unless it is strained, but it's handy for liquids, you'll find. Just so the patient is awake and rational, there is no danger of him biting down too hard on it."

Over their own meal, Dr. Tom explained to John, "I expect Mr. Jack won't be wanting anyone to feed him for long. His hands are going to be painful and sore for some time, but he'll be trying to use them. His feet are much more frost bitten. It may be some time before he will be able to walk on them. Make sure his feet are smeared well, night and morning, with the ointment I will leave. By the way, you will need to keep them well bandaged to keep the ointment from getting onto the bedding. The stain never comes out."

Mary, coming for more coffee, heard this part. "Would loose socks made of muslin and just tied around his ankles be more comfortable? They would protect the bedding."

"They might be better. The healing is sometimes retarded if too snuggly wrapped. A mitten-like affair on his hands might be a good idea. They will need some care too. He is going to be in quite some misery and often not able to sleep; or let you people sleep. So, I will leave some quieting tablets." He counted out the tiny pellets into a small envelop. "Now, have you a safe place to put these where the sick man cannot reach them…or others?" He glanced at the two alert children watching him. "I would not want anyone younger than ten tasting one of these."

Mary, at last seated to eat her meal, heard the men talking. Their voices receded. Then she felt herself lifted up as if she were falling. Flinging out her hand, she found nothing, and became frightened. "Where am I?" she cried.

"I think you need to finish your nap, Mrs. Marcus," Dr. Tom and John kept right on carrying her to bed.

When she next awakened, David and Margaret were talking to her. "Mama, the sick man is calling to Daddy and I can't wake him up." David could not understand everyone sleeping all the time this way.

"Mama will awaken Daddy, Sonny," she told the worried lad. But this was no easy thing to do. Long minutes passed before John was fully aware of what was needed. While he cared for the sick man's needs, Mary built up the fire to start the evening meal. "How would you two Dearies like a bowl of mush and milk for your supper?" She was planning something easy to cook, but still something one and all could eat.

"I like applesauce better," David informed her.

"Oh, we all can have applesauce too, with some cookies."

The boy's face clouded at the mention of cookies. "Maybe, we better not have cookies." He fidgeted about for a moment. "There hain't many cookies now, Mama. Sister got hungry and when you and Daddy was asleep, I gave her some cookies and milk to keep her still." Another little pause. "And I ate some too."

"That is fine, Sonny. Mama did have one nice sleep." She saw the jar was indeed all but empty. "Perhaps you and Sister will not be very hungry for supper. How would some nice buttered toast go with your applesauce?" Both brown heads nodded.

This past twenty-four hours was but an indicator of their round-the-clock vigil for the next week. The two weeks following were less strenuous. Christmas day was the occasion of Jack Wilson's first meal at the table. John drew him out in the small rocker, tipped back so his sore feet would be free from the floor. He could feed himself very well by now. "Did that old saw bones tell you when I could be going under my own power?" was Jack's first question as soon as they had him seated the right distance from the table.

Mary laughed at him. "Dr. Tom didn't say, but I expect the new year won't be too old before you will be trying to walk." She served him roasted chicken, dressing, mashed potatoes and gravy—the same as the rest of her family. "I thought these tiny pickled onions might taste good with our meal. And we can eat the baked apples with our meal instead of for desert for once. Enjoy this creamed cabbage, for it is the very last head. From now on, it will have to be kraut."

"And I'm a Dutchman when it comes to kraut," Jack told her. She found him not fussy about food, eating whatever she served him except the pickled beets once. Thinking he might like them unpickled, she had asked and received an impish grin. "I never could eat the bloody things," was his response.

Mary ate her meal slowly this day, enjoying the rest. All the food was on the table except the pie. The coffee pot was within reaching distance. Seeing John pour cream over another baked apple, she came alert. "Save room for your pie."

"Too late now," bemoaned John. "I'll have to eat mine for

supper."

"It's got whipped cream on top," whispered David, not understanding anyone turning down such a treat.

"I know, but I have no room for pie." He smiled at the tiny serving Mary was cutting for the two children. "Now, don't you two eat it all up." Her own wedge of pie was not much bigger. The one she would have dished for Jack was a regular size, but the old fellow stopped her.

"You'll have to earmark my hunk of pie for my supper too, Mrs. Marcus." He was eyeing the pumpkin pie. "What I'm wondering is, how did you come to have squash and pumpkins up here in these hills. Looks like it would be too short a season for vine stuff."

"My parents grew them on Snake River Flats. Yes, it is much too cool up here for such things. Father comes each fall and brings us hay for the cow, and brings many things besides. No matter how careful he is though, squash seems to get bruised and will not keep too long. This pie was made from dried pumpkin—that keeps forever."

As the holidays neared, Mary was quite concerned over not making even one present. Her eyes would close in sleep every time she sat down at the sewing machine. David's new shirt and Margaret's dress were still unfinished. *I may as well not have worried. I might have known the folks would be sending them something nice.* She thought about how pleased David had been with his red topped boots and red socks to match. Margaret's knit hose were blue; her dress a blue plaid. John's socks were of the grey wool, as usual. The two pair of fine white woolen ones had been marked for Jack Wilson, as were some underclothes and two woolen shirts. A slip was pinned to those, stating "I'll be glad if someone can wear these and get some good out of them. Father says they are too tight in the neck for him."

Their present to Mary had been beautiful bedroom slippers. *They are too pretty to wear. I will keep them to look at,* was her verdict as she unwrapped them. She continued to wear the felt ones she had made from two old hats until soon after New Years. Jack started hobbling about, and would get his white socks so very soiled, she gave him the felt slippers to wear, and now needed to wear her new fancy ones. She and John were sure it would be weeks before Jack would be able to wear shoes.

They had been surprised to learn that Jack was but fifty-five years old—he had seemed much older at first. His story was soon told once he was able to talk. He had been born in western Kansas, but kept drifting further west. He had worked over much of this state, ranching and herding sheep, but these particular hills were new to him. He had hired out to feed sheep at a ranch south of Reynolds, but missed the turn soon after leaving Reynolds. "For once in my life, I was lost—completely turned around," he had admitted. What he didn't say right then, was the fact that he had not been too sober. Later, he told Mary in confidence, "I'm alright as long as I have no money. Most work I know how to do, or can learn to do, but let payday roll around, and I'm broke again and hitting the road. So I say, money is no good for me. I'd even call it a curse. If it hadn't been for you good people finding me and caring for me, I'd be dead and buried, where maybe I ought to be. All a fellow needs out of life is the food he eats, and enough clothes to wear. From now on, I'm staying shy of money. To me it's a curse."

As Jack was able to hobble out of doors, he relieved Mary of all chores. The cow was dry now, ready to freshen. He kept the barn very clean, and was just as careful with the cow's feed and grain for the chickens as Mary herself. Coming back to the house this cold blustery March night after doing the chores, he surprised Mary by saying, "Now if that cow of yours was an old ewe, I'd say she was liable to lamb before morning."

"I expect she might at that." Mary smiled at his funny ways of saying things. "I could look up the date, but I expect you have her all snug and warm in the barn where no harm can come to her or her calf."

"Yeah, I cleaned out her manger and put all the stems and such down for her bed. Been batting down all the knot holes. I don't think enough breeze can get in to chill a new calf."

This night she explained to John as they made ready for bed, "With the cow fresh, it would be the proper time for you to learn how to milk. In less than a month, I won't be able to. I fear I cannot get up and down on the milking stool right now without help."

Each frosty morning and slushy evening, she followed John to the barn thereafter. Always, it wound up the same way: The patient cow would become impatient, holding up her flow of milk until Mary's knowing hands took over the task. She disparaged of John ever learning. *He doesn't want to, is most of the trouble.* Old Jack had never once said he could milk, and surely his now crippled fingers were not in any shape for milking, but several times she had noticed him rubbing and massaging his fingers as if to limber them. The first evening she was a few minutes slow in going to milk, she could not find the milk pail. She was more than sure she had hung it to sun on the cross beam of the clothes line. It was not there. Back to the house she went to look for it. From the porch, she could see Jack coming from the barn with pail in hand, full of milk. "I just had to try out these old juicers to see if they'd work." He was happy to know they did. He was walking much more straight.

The next morning, Jack not only milked, but he strained it and handled the heavy crocks without mishap. He washed the strainer and pail and put those to sun. That evening, Dr. Thomas was called. On the stroke of midnight, Susan Mary Marcus was ushered into this quiet household without much fanfare. "I'm sorry, Doctor. You always have to bathe my babies." Mary was weary and spoke slowly.

"Think nothing of it, Mrs. Marcus. I rather like to bathe them. We are taught to do that in our training. By the time I have them good and clean and dressed, I'm pretty sure they are all right. But Daughter can wait her turn." He had smeared her with oil and wrapped her warm. "It is you and your needs that come first."

"I don't want to be disturbed. I just want to sleep and sleep."

"I promise not to disturb even one of your dreams. Go right ahead and sleep." Deftly, he drew her on the sheet to one side of the bed and made up the half with the clean sheets she had ready at hand. John and he now lifted her back. She was covered warmly. Not a word was spoken. She was not aware of them leaving the room with the babe.

"Pretty fine girl you have here, Marcus." He was busy washing and putting the small garments on the tiny mite. "Can't say she's any finer than the one you already have, but she'll run her a close second. This one has more of David's features. I wonder if she will be as serious as he is." He looked up at the two men watching him handle the babe. "Either one of you ever try caring for one this small?"

"I was always afraid to try it," John told him, reaching down to touch her.

"Never had occasion to try it," old Jack smiled up at him. "But I'm good at mothering lambs. Suckled many a one on other ewes. Helped them steal their grub 'til their own mothers would take over, or find new ones for 'em." Jack grimaced at his misshapen hands. "I'd be afraid to try tackling a babe of that size now. I might drop her or stick pins in her." He took the cup of coffee from John's hand, but asked, "That's right—who is going to care for the Missus and the little widget?"

John said nothing, but drank his coffee, so Dr. Tom took over the questioning. "Mother and Babe might be alright the rest of the night, but come morning, they will need care," he told them as he accepted his coffee. To John, he spoke plainly. "Your wife should have several days of rest. I mean by that, she should not have to worry about the bathing of this new babe, much less the care of the other two. Have you any way of getting a woman in to care for her from DeLamar?"

John shook his head. "That's the worst of it. I haven't."

"Have either you or your wife spoken for anyone to come?" Dr. Tom was determined not to leave this patient without proper care this time.

"Mary talked some of trying to get Grandma Blatchey to come down—she's the one who took care of her when David was little. But Mary hasn't got up town all winter."

"And you cannot leave her very well in the morning. Do you want me to send Mrs. Blatchey down? Or someone else if she is not available?"

"That's putting you to a lot of bother, Doc," he finished his coffee, "but maybe that would be the best way." Each one of the three men was thinking about bed and sleep about now. Dr. Tom was soon on his way back to town.

Chapter Thirty

WATERING THE CABBAGE PLANTS in the window box, Mary was dismayed to see how tall and spindly they were growing. *I think I shall have to transplant them.* She wondered how she was going to spare the time to do so.

"I got her all turned over," old Jack told her as he came in from the raw spring day. "So now your garden can go in any time you wish." He took off his ragged gloves and rubbed his hands, which were still sensitive to any cold.

"I was just thinking these plants needed to be transplanted, but it is a bit early. They would need covering if they were set out," Mary fretted.

"I see you have a lot of boards nailed together. How would it do for me to string these plants in a row as long a distance as those V-shaped wooden tents will cover? Then as soon as the weather settles more, I could take up a plant with a small spade of dirt and put 'em where they should be, and they'll never know they've been shifted."

"That's a very good idea, Jack. I should be able to help you with all this work by tomorrow."

"Not so fast, there. I'm not wanting help—just asking for a bit of advice now and then. How many plants you figure might be in that box?"

"Might be 500. I planted the same amount of seed this year as last. Only about a fourth of them lived last year. I'm sure it was because I could not give them the care they needed." She smiled at David and Margaret coming in with red cheeks. "I see you have two helpers. If one gets in your way, she can come help me anytime. David has had the promise of dropping the larger seeds and the onion sets for us this year. Five years old, this boy will be tomorrow." She had thought it would help Jack if David would drop those seeds.

"Well, Ranchers, let's get busy." He patted the shoulders of both children, then turned back to ask, "Do you think it is too early to take the winter overcoats off those strawberry plants?"

"I know it can freeze most any night, but to give those berries a chance, we may have to uncover them. Since there is such a small patch, I believe we could cover them with the tarp and old horse blankets. It should be warm weather soon, this being the last day of April."

Sunny days commenced with the month of May, but the nippy nights still required protecting plants. As Mary helped to do this, she was surprised to find the strawberries in full bloom. "It looks as though this garden work is all getting done by magic," Mary smiled at Jack. In spite of his maimed fingers and feet, he had everything sown. The long straight rows were waiting for the cabbage plants.

"Yep. It must be spring around the corner." Jack was happy. "Heard the *bah bahs* today from up along the trail. Been thinking I might mosey up that way a little later and see if any bummers got left. Since you folks have plenty of milk, you could just as well raise your own lamb chops."

Mary could have told Jack about John's dislike of sheep at this time, but she was pressed for time, and she did not want to hurt this kind old man's feelings. *He is such a willing worker, and knows what to do and how to do it.* Jack had been accepted into this family as if he belonged here. Only Mary was aware of how many steps he saved her.

At supper time, Jack was missing. While milking, Mary remembered his mentioning about going to look for bummers. At full dark, Jack came in lugging seven lambs, two in a gunny sack over his shoulders.

"Sure crimping down right now." Jack lowered the lambs to the warm corner back of the range and hurried out for a box he had ready. "These bummers would have been finished off by morning without some warm milk on the inside of 'em." He would not take time to eat his own supper until each one of those bleating lambs was stilled by milk and warm sacks covering the box. Jack was happy about his find and assumed everyone else was.

John did all his grumbling to Mary in private, never once saying a word against the lambs to Jack. "What you letting him stink up the whole house with those stinking varmints for?"

"They won't be in the house, only tonight," Mary told him, thinking this would be the case. "Jack will build them a pen out in the sunshine tomorrow, and a place can be fixed in the barn for them to sleep at night."

Then came rain and no sunshine. Each morning for a week, Jack squinted at the lowering skies. "Doggonit! Looks like we could get a little sunshine mixed in with all this rain. Those bummers aren't doing good in the barn. Don't know if they'll make it through a real cold night." And this night, it was clearing and freezing by dark. Mary, helping spread more protection over the plants, relented—again her kitchen was a sheep-fold.

John was disgusted, not only with the smell, but with their bleating. It did not stop until they were well fed with warm milk, thoroughly warmed, and the lights put out. Then it became still. Mary heard Jack up once in the night fixing more fire. About three in the morning, when Susan let her know it was time to be nursed, Mary heard the faint bleating of a lamb. It persisted even after the contented babe was tucked back into her basket. *I'll never get to sleep with that noise.* She was more afraid it would awaken John. Slipping her feet into her slippers, she went to the half warm kitchen, lit a candle and built up the fire. The sound of discomfort was coming from the weakest lamb, the one Jack had put alone in a small padded box so the stronger ones would not trample it to death.

Guessing its bleating might be from hunger, Mary started to warm some milk for it, but there was no more milk. Jack must have fed it all. That would mean she would need to go back to their room, put on warm clothes, and go to the cellar. She was sure she could not possibly do that without awakening John. Fearing his displeasure, and in her compassion for this small helpless hungry creature, she felt her full breast contract sharply, wetting her gown with the drip. Down on knees beside the box, she let those drops fall into the mouth she held open to receive it. Getting to her feet again after long minutes in that trying position, she covered the now quiet lamb, closed the draft to keep the fire the better, and now made her way quietly back to bed. *This is one thing I've done that I shall never ever tell anyone.* But it was not that thought that kept her awake now—it was the fear she might have robbed her child of needed food. Soon, however the surging milk filled her breast again, and she slept.

The short summer season was passing. School time was near. Mary still had not made up her mind about David starting school this fall. Once, she had taken him through the wood yard and to the school house steps, telling him this was where he would one day come to learn to read. *He is so small to be going alone,* she thought, watching him hurry with his breakfast so to be out with

Jack. She was thinking this would be the day Annie would be starting east for her year of high school. "With Annie away from home, it is going to be much harder for Father to get away to bring the hay up to us. If I knew of some way to get that field west of the barn plowed and seeded, I believe that would grow enough hay for the cow."

Old Jack's wrinkled face spread into a smile. "I've been wondering how come you didn't have that in hay, and you such a good rancher at heart."

"Don't you go monkeying with those tailings," John warned her as he left the table. "We don't want any lawsuit on our hands when we have the place nearly paid for."

"What's this *tailings* business got to do with it?" Jack asked the second John left the house for the tunnel.

"I would have to go show you what it is and how it would interfere with plowing and fencing all the tillable ground. But I still believe there is a chance to grow enough hay on the rest. I'll tell you what I'll do. Just as soon as I can bathe Susan and get her down for her morning sleep, I'll go down there with you. No crime if I put off the wash an hour or two."

"We make quite a brigade," laughed Mary as Jack, David, Margaret and she headed down past the coral. The lambs, two-thirds grown, frolicked after them. "I believe all this fertilizer around the barn and here would help this field to grown more hay too," she said as they walked. When they reached the mounds of different colored earth, she explained to Jack. "These contain fine gold, and we don't own them. The heirs did not want to live here and were willing to sell the place on payments, which John and his partner, Tim Nichols, bought. But they retained ownership of these tailings. They wanted $5,000 cash for them, and of course, no one had that much money. So here they still are, spoiling our field. I really don't know if there is enough tailings left in these slurry ponds, or if they are exempted. If they are not, a fence could be run fairly straight along here."

Both she and Jack were sighting out the best angle for a fence. "These depressions are not nearly as deep as they were the first time I saw them," Mary explained, noting the weed filled ponds. "Guess the rain, snow and thaws are naturally filling them in. That was more than six years ago. I believe I can find out in town if these slurry ponds are exempted." Now as they walked along the width of the little valley, she tried to plan a trip to DeLamar into her busy day.

Jack called her attention to the large sage brush growing on the upper edge above the road. "That's a pretty good indication that it's good soil. Looks like it would pay to grub this off—give you your winters' wood partly, and add several feet to your ground to plow. It being watered from this high side, no trouble getting water on to it. What about this road? I've never seen a soul travel it."

"No one but us does, and that is only when Father comes in the fall to haul out posts. Mr. Kirtland, below us a few miles, has another road he travels. There is a road up over the ridge. I believe it must be the county road. They never have done any work on this road."

"If that's the case, and we can plow up this one, there'd be no question about you growing enough hay to feed a cow through the winter." Jack was already yanking out an armload of dead sage brush.

"I surely ought to be able to learn if it is a county road in town. I could go up there this day, right after noon while Baby naps, only I would need to hurry." She was moving fast now toward the house to get the washing started.

"Mama, you walk too fast," panted three year-old Margaret, trying to keep up.

"Sorry Dear, but Mama has to walk fast. Can you walk slower with David?" Then she saw that David was staying to help Jack. "You can come by yourself, can't you?" She was not sure if the child could make it alone. *I can let her try, but I must not get too busy to keep tabs on her.* From the porch, she saw the small tot trudging along, taking her own time. Then David, with his small arms full of wood, caught up with her. *My, that boy will feel big helping Jack clear that ground. And he'll be learning something useful. I believe I'll wait until spring to start him in school, as Father advised.*

By noon she had decided it would be better to wait until morning for her trip to town. The butter and cheese would be ready to take then. Now, as Jack went back to grubbing the brush, he took along a wheelbarrow of the fertilizer, scattering it as he went. Now David was doing likewise, taking a load in the express wagon. Mother's new fire shovel was used for his loading. Mary found it this evening, bent and battered beside the barn as she hurried to milk, and guessed how it came to be in such a sorry state. *Far be it from me to scold him. I hope I never dampen any of the initiative or ambition in that son of mine.* That night, David talked of nothing else at the supper table—he was so excited about helping Jack get in the winter's wood.

"What you going to be, Son, when you grow up—a wood cutter?" John asked.

"I'm going to be a sheep herder." David was as serious as if he was already grown.

Mary smiled. She could see the angry look on John's face. To stave off what she feared he might say, she said, "How odd our youthful ambitions look to us when we are adults. I well remember my childhood desire was to be a singer. I was many years older before I learned one had to have a voice for singing, which I failed to have. I would have been cruelly hurt at one time, had anyone told me I never could fulfill that desire of mine."

"I'm going to school next Monday, or maybe next spring, and learn to read everything I want to." David said this with mild defiance, as if he sensed his father's dislike of what he had said.

After the children were in bed, and Jack had gone to his room, Mary heard all of John's chagrin, just as she was sure she would. "Why take it so seriously? A boy not yet six is not knowing what he'll want to do at twenty-six. If you don't want him to be a herder of sheep, make sure you say nothing against it. He'll forget all about it if nothing is said. But any opposition is going to impress it more in his mind."

"You act as if you wouldn't mind if he did herd sheep," he taunted.

"There are many worse things he could be," she reminded the unreasonable man.

"I suppose you mean a prospector?" John angrily dropped his shoes. "No son of mine is going to be a crazy sheepherder."

"It looks to me as if a prospector, living off alone, would be just as lonesome and unnatural a life as any herder. But talk about people being crazy! I think we are—quarreling over what our small son will choose for his life's work when he grows up." With that comment, she marched off to bed ahead of him.

In DeLamar, she soon learned the road through their place was not a county road, but it took much more time to learn if those slurry ponds contained tailings and would be exempted. The man who handled the deal in the first place now lived in Boise. Mr. Lyons, the Post Master, was also a notary. He scratched his head and tried to think back. "I'm sure those papers were signed and witnessed right here before me. But as to the wording, I cannot recall if the ponds were mentioned. If the tailings were already shoveled out of them, they wouldn't be. I tell you what. You could ask John Knollen. He was one of the workmen there when the mill closed down. I believe he would know. He lives at the lower edge of town—that tin roofed cabin before the grade."

Mary thanked him and hurried on her way. She had never met Mr. Knollen, but had noticed this silver haired, slightly built man often about his cabin. His bright blue eyes were getting cloudy with age, but his mind seemed alert as he answered her inquiry. "Yes, it is true that I worked at the mill when it closed down, but my work was at the other end of the tram, so I could not say now if those ponds were cleared or not. But I would venture to say, there wouldn't be enough tailings left in them to be worth working it over."

"It is just the question of making our fence more straight if they are not valuable," Mary explained. "We want to plant all the ground possible to raise hay for our cow."

The dimmed eyes looked at her more closely. "Cow, did you say? Then John must be doing alright." His wrinkled face beamed with a smile. "Can't say how much hay those old ponds would grow, but you wouldn't be carting away any of the soil. I'd say, go ahead and make your fence as straight as you please. The only damage that could be done might be to the edge of your hay field some day if someone gets around to work those old tailings, say twenty years from now." Another smile and he detained her to ask after John and his work. "Is he still following that same lead vein? Tell him to stop in and see me when he can."

Mary assured him she would tell John. She liked this elderly man's appearance and would have liked to talk longer, but she was pressed for time. *And too, I do not want to tell him that John and I talk very little about his work. I expect that it is my fault because I do not understand this mining game.* She could have added that she found no time to learn about it.

David was still too busy hauling the small wagonloads of cut brush to fret over not starting school. It was Jack who was doing the worrying now. "I wish we had ten times that amount of fertilizer to plow under." He had it all clean in the corral and along the barn now. "Nights are getting cool enough to cool a carcass out pretty good. Whenever you want lamb chops, just say the word."

Mary had been wondering about those lambs and what Jack meant to do with them. She did not want to kill more chickens yet. "Lamb chops would taste pretty good about now, wouldn't they? I don't know if John will eat lamb, but Father sure likes it. I look for him to be coming in most any day after the first day of October. Will you be needing some help butchering a lamb?"

Jack gave her an odd look, then an impish grin. "Not so you could notice it. No, I don't need help." Nothing more was said about making meat of one of the lambs.

Mary had no way of knowing Jack had once worked as a butcher, and the dressing out of a lamb was but a few minutes work to him. The last night of September, he came in carrying heart, tongue, liver and skinned head. "I didn't know if you were used to cooking the heads or not, but figured I might as well skin it out ready while I was about it. Not a lot of meat on a lamb's head, but mighty tasty, what there is."

"I've never cooked a lamb's head, but I have pig, beef and veal heads aplenty. And you have this so nicely dressed, ready to be cooked. You must know all about this butchering. Do you want a meat sack or worn out sheet to put around the meat now?"

"Nope. No flies will be flying around this chilly night. Better to leave that meat carcass as it is 'til morning. One never wants to bother a freshly killed animal while it's still warm. I won't even split a lamb down the back 'til morning. More good meat is spoilt by handling it or wrapping sacks around it. My motto is *hands off*."

"You talk like Father does about butchering. We just won't mention what kind of liver this is in the morning," she half whispered, "and we'll see if John eats it."

John ate the tender liver, along with bacon, and made no comment whatsoever. The small heart, baked with dressing for dinner, vanished as did the tongue for the evening meal. Scrambled brains with eggs were for breakfast. The noon meal was beans, with the pressed meat from the head, for supper. "Whenever you want chops, cutlets, roast, or lamb stew, I'll cut it for you," Jack told her later. "Got it hoisted up well in the shed. The only thing that could get to it would be a magpie that could peck a hole in the sack. I been keeping tabs on 'em. If they start in on it, we might have to shift it to the cellar."

"Is it the neck that does not keep well, the same as on a beef or veal? But it seems to me there was some other part Father always brought in to use up first."

"Do you know, you are a smart young woman for your years?" Jack grinned. "A lot of gray haired folks never learn that about meat."

"Maybe they didn't have someone like my father and mother to teach them. I remember now, it was thin pieces of meat that Father cut out from the flank and brisket first for stews."

Jack nodded. "Are you aiming for a lamb stew or braised neck tomorrow?"

"Lamb stew would be good tomorrow. We have so many vegetables at this time of the year in the garden—everything except sweet corn, string beans, cucumbers and tomatoes. I wish there were some way we could grow those here." Mary was more than tired this night, and a bit depressed. On her trip to town in the morning, she had encountered Laura Burch in one of her most haughty moods. Without prelude, she had demanded that Mary take her weekly laundry home with her.

"My laundry is not hard to do, but I want it done right," had been her opening remarks. "I can assure you, it will not be as dirty and disagreeable as the miners' clothes you are in the habit of doing. But I pay well. I've been giving the woman $1.50 each week. There are never more than three changes of bed linens. There might sometimes be four tablecloths and napkins. Jim wants his shirts well starched. Daughter and my clothes are never starched. What I've been dissatisfied with is the clothes never being rinsed enough. The dark clothes and black hose are all covered with lint."

All the time the woman was talking, Mary had been doing some of her rapid calculations. *At least three hours of washing. Many more hours of ironing. In the same length of time, I can do a dozen men's washings, and that brings in twice as much.* "I'm sorry, Mrs. Burch, but I cannot possibly take on any more laundry than I already have." She tried to sound regretful. She was truly sorry on Jimmy's account, for he had done so much for the

Marcus family, and he was standing by now with a strange look on his face while his wife flounced from the store in the vilest of moods. "I'm sorry…" she commenced as her eye caught his.

"Think nothing of it," Jimmy cut in. "I told Laura you already had more work than you should do. There is no reason in the world why the laundry can't be done right in our own home. We have a good machine; stationary tubs with a good drain. Hot and cold water with the turn of a tap. If she is not pleased with Mrs. Smith's work, there are others wanting those hours of work." He gave a shrug. "Seems the aristocrats of Boise send their laundry out now days, and are never bothered with the untidy mess."

As tired as Mary was this night, when thinking back over Jimmy's expressive shrug, she smiled. *If I had been a good Christian, I could have told Jimmy or his wife, all the rinsing in the world wouldn't take all the lint from black hose if they are washed and rinsed in the same water after the white things.* She had had no chance to tell Laura anything and was sure she would not have been thanked for her pains. *Seems odd. Any sensible homemaker would know that. Now, if they were living down on the desert like we did for awhile, and had to measure out the amount of water to be used, there would be some excuse for saving on water.* She thought about how she had learned to leave all hose turned wrong side out while washing them so there would be less lint to show, or be brushed off.

Two evenings later, Father drove in. Mary went out with lantern in hand, and spied the washing machine securely tied atop the lead wagon. "Father, what do you mean buying us a washer?" she scolded the instant he swung down to the ground.

"This isn't a new machine, Daughter. It is the one I bought Mother the year after we came to the Flats. With Annie gone, she has owned up to not being able to run it without it giving her quite a pain through her chest. So, I'm unloading it onto you so she will not be using it at all." Later, while walking to the house, he remarked, "You remember how Mother always liked one of those funnel-shaped suction type hand washers—one she used in the tub or boiler to pummel the clothes? Well, I found one of those last time I was in Caldwell. I try to be around to do the most of that work."

The only thing unloaded this night was Father's bedroll and a box of apples, eating those and visiting until bedtime. It was hard work to get the two older children to bed after Grandpa came. Mary went in later to see that they were well covered, and came back with a half eaten apple. "Guess Margaret was going to be prepared for a lunch, should she wake up."

Breakfast and daylight brought many more surprises. Father handed down boxes and crates for Jack and then to John to carry. "Now this lug of fresh prunes I see are dripping. You'd better take them right to the kitchen. They need to be canned or made into jam the first thing." To Mary, he explained, "Mother washed those prunes before she packed them, and there has been no dust this trip, so you can just tumble them right into the kettle. It was an experiment, to see if they would haul. They were ripe, but fairly firm when I started." The basket he reached down to Mary was light in weight. "I'm sure these grapes made it alright. There's a lot of cut up paper around them."

Then came a flat box of tomatoes and a lug of cucumbers. These Mary hugged in her arms, and rushed to the house to hide her filled eyes. "Now this box of pears are heavy." Father was pleased to see John reach for it ahead of the older man. "They are the hardest and greenest looking pears I ever saw, but the man that grows them claims they are pretty good eating once they ripen. Put them in the darkest corner of the cellar and forget about them—say two-three weeks."

Jack carried the big squashes while John shouldered the hundred pound sacks of potatoes. The last thing to be handed out was a sack of seed, and it was to Jack's gnarled hands it went. "You'd better guard this well. It's enough to sow that hay field coming up."

Jack beamed with excitement. "Then I better tote this right to the house. It's not safe in the barn. I've seen more than one mouse in there." The bales of hay were stowed away by noon. Jack was still excited about the hay field and talked of not much else at the table. "Been just about the right amount of rain to make plowing easy."

"How you going to plow—with a shovel?" John sounded disgruntled. There was something going on here that he knew nothing about.

"Nope," grinned Jack. "I been trying to sharpen that plow point and tighten up the old plow so it'll hold together."

Father noticed how John was left out of the plans, so he

sought to include him. "You have a small forge here, and are used to sharpening steel. You might give us a few pointers on how to get that point in shape."

"I never worked on a plow—to sharpen or use it," John said shortly.

Father smiled. "I know you are good at post cutting. Will you exchange work with me? You get out my load of posts, and Jack and I here can spell each other plowing that ground and getting it sown. You can pick whichever team you wish. Or if it makes no difference to you, we might switch teams each day." He feared John would refuse.

"I need no team to bother with to cut posts," John spoke sourly.

"In that case, we get more fertilizer hauled down from the dairy below town. Which do you want to do," he asked Jack as he left the table, "do the hauling or start that plow going?"

"I'll start the plow out on that upper edge where I grubbed the brush. It's new ground and shouldn't need much fertilizer. And then I want to get the feel of a plow handle again. It's been a long time since I turned a furrow."

Chapter Thirty One

THE SLEET STORM WAS getting stronger and Mary was glad David was already home from school this disagreeable May day. Jack struggled in, facing the stinging ice with a sack over his shoulder. He had gone for more lambs. *I wish he wouldn't. I can hardly stretch the milk to feed what he already has found.* She opened the door for him.

"Sure devilish weather." He dug the sleet from his ears. "Afraid I couldn't make it with too many, so I only picked up four ewe bah-bahs. I think they'll make it alright, as soon as I can get them warmed up and some milk on the inside of 'em."

"Lucky you didn't bring in anymore," Mary chided. "This milk question is getting critical." She was opening one of the few remaining cans of milk. "This canned stuff is going to make our lamb chops come pretty high."

Jack nodded as he bent over to force the warm diluted milk into the chilled mouths. "Let's see, how old is that calf about now—six weeks isn't he? He hasn't been cut short of his milk, so he should make pretty good veal. The weather is still cold enough, heaven knows."

"Perhaps that would be the best way." Mary handed him more milk for the next feeble lamb. "It's sure something how quick the warm milk revives them." The first one fed was already trying to frisk about.

"Yeah, they can be half dead and a cupful of milk inside their wrinkled hides will bring 'em out of it. Get these ones warmed up good—I'll cart 'em out to the shop. That makes a pretty snug place for 'em with that old stove stoked up good."

This evening, the calf became veal. Bringing in the skinned head, heart, tongue and liver, Jack told her, "Unless it turns extra warm during the day time, that veal will keep good hung right there in the barn. Should it come hot days, we'll wrap 'er up good and bury it deep among the bales of hay. That will be just as cool as that old sawdust in the icehouse. Just so we remember to hang 'er out at night, it works fine."

Mary was often surprised at the resourcefulness of this man. Now the only disagreeable thing about the lambs was John's harping about them being penned in at one end of the shop. "Why say so much about it?" she asked him. "You still have plenty room to sharpen your drills. And it won't be for long. Jack will putt them in one corner of the barn soon so they can have more room to frisk about."

"Yeah, and stink up that place," he said angrily.

"That won't bother you otherwise." Mary said this knowing that John never went near the barn.

Jack was more than busy from then on. First there was the ditch to be re-dug. It had not been used for so many years, it was trampled full. As soon as he had the dam in the gulch stream to bring water to the field, as well as to the garden, he commenced on the fence about the hay ground. A break in the ditch around the knoll in front of the house had caused him a day's delay. "If there are no more breaks, I might get that fence finished by time to cut hay." He was drinking his fill of water at the sink. "I'll be working on this end of that fence–if you are wanting to make that trip to town this afternoon, I can keep my weather eye out for the two little ones."

Mary hurried to be on her way. It was June and the days were quite warm. *And this is the month Dr. Tom is supposed to be married. I wonder if Miss Orchard is home from England yet.* Mary expected to hear all the latest from Jimmy Burch as usual, but what she heard made her unhappy.

"Yes," commenced Jimmy, "this camp is all agog over Helen Orchard ditching Doc and marrying some guy with a title. But I say he's better off finding out now than after the knot was tied. If it takes a Coat of Arms to make her happy, just what kind of a life would she and Doc lead?"

"Not a very happy one, I fear. If he had no inkling of it before, it must have been quite a shock."

"Guess that was where most of the hurt was," Jimmy stated sagely. "Of course, he imagines himself madly in love with that girl. But she, with her nose in the air most of the time, didn't deem it good manners to even write Doc the news. He had to hear it from others. At first, he did not believe it. He went to Orchard himself and asked if she considered him so low on the scale of human beings that he could not be informed." Jimmy shook his head in concern. "Orchard, as you know, is so dignified, he supposed Helen had at least the grace to write Doc. And when it came out that she hadn't, it did look bad for the Orchard tribe. Then this business of her sister, Leatha Orchard, throwing herself into Doc's arms, figuratively speaking. She casually claimed she is the one that loves him; that Helen never did. I can't see where that is going to help."

"Why, she is only a slip of a girl." Mary could hardly believe all this. "She cannot be more than sixteen...and a stormy one at that."

"That's right. But she went about her conquest like a full grown woman—vowing she'll marry Doc any day he says; defying her parents to stop them and all that kind of talk."

"I cannot see Dr. Thomas eloping with a temperamental child. She is no more like her sister than if they were no kin." Mary spent no more time gossiping. There was more work waiting for her at home than she could possibly get done.

None of this talk would she pass on to John. To do so, she would have to tell where she heard it, and for some reason, he seemed to be sore at Jimmy Burch lately. *Oh, I know Jimmy has many of the failings of a vain person. He likes to gossip like an old woman, but I doubt he would tell things that are not true. And where would this family be without his help and friendship?*

John was unhappy these days. The work in the tunnel was going too slow. Mary still had to smile, remembering Jack's refusal to help in that work. With much diplomacy, for him, John talked about the work not being too strenuous. "You could easy catch on to it. Two pair of hands will make it go much faster."

Old Jack had waited until John had finished his spiel, then in his slow drawl said, "Do you know, John, I'd be plumb lost below the surface. Of course, I'll be lost anyway when I get planted six feet under, but then I won't be worrying about it. The other fellows will be doing the digging, not me." Wisely, he had spoken about all the work he had to finish on the fence, and to keep the water running, besides helping with the garden.

Mary had but changed her dress and commenced her work when Jack came through the kitchen for a drink. "Do you know, I wish you weren't so all fired busy."

She took the hint. "And here you are needing help changing those lambs to fresh grass and you wouldn't holler at me to come help?" She dried her hands on her apron while hurrying out. It was her chore to steady the two long wooden gate panels. He would wire them together, then unwire one side of the lamb pen, and swing out that panel. As the lambs rushed to eat the fresh grass, Jack would enclose them again by putting another long section in place. "My, they make short work of that grass." Mary watched for a second more. "They could mow a lawn off in a hurry, but I believe we'd better not try it because the children need the yard to play in."

"Do you think there is enough green stuff outside here to do 'em 'til I can get that hay fenced in sheep tight? Then we can turn 'em loose."

"School will soon be out. Do you suppose David could herd them around like he wants to?"

"Sure he can, but we're needing a dog to train right along with 'em." No more was said about the need of a dog. Friday afternoon, Jack was missing from his fence work. Mary guessed he might have gone to town for new shoes, which he needed badly. She had written out the order for those shoes, knowing Jack would not trust himself with the money.

When David came from school, Jack walked along with him wearing the new shoes, and was loaded down with laundry to be done. David carryied a third grown shepherd pup.

"He's mine, Mama. Jack gave him to me." He could hardly talk for all his excitement. "He's a sheep dog, and comes from a real sheep camp. But Jack won't tell me how much he had to pay for him."

Mary could see the twinkling eyes of the happy man. "David Son, when we are given a present–something nice like this fine puppy–we don't want to ask how much had to be paid for it. For no matter what the price of him, you like him, and are happy to have him. Since he's yours, you will be the one to see that he is fed twice a day, at least while he is small. And water, so he can get a drink whenever he wants it. A box will be needed in the woodshed for him to sleep in until he gets used to this place."

"But I want him to sleep with me, and go to school with me every day." He saw Mother's disapproving look. "Some of the other boys at school let their dogs follow 'em right to school. "Course the teacher don't like it and makes 'em put 'em outside."

"I expect they do, Son, but those boys live much closer to the school. If their dogs got tired of waiting around outside, they can trot on home. But your puppy is much too young, and he doesn't know this is his home yet. He might follow someone else and you would lose him. Have you named him yet?"

"His name is Gibson." David held the pup with one arm and tried to find a crumb left in his lunch box. "Is there one drop of milk for him?"

"I expect there isn't," cut in Jack, "but from now on, there is going to be. Those bummers are not going to need so much milk with you and Gibson letting 'em out to get more grass. And, my boy, don't forget—a sheep dog's place is with the sheep. This one will like you well enough if you are the one to feed him, but he'll feel right at home and less lonesome if his sleeping box is fixed right in the barn where the *bah bahs* were penned for awhile."

Gibson the pup grew fast. His innate knowledge of his life's work was surprising. "Mother, when I swing my arm out like Jack does, he goes out around the sheep, just like I told him to."

Mary smiled at the happy boy. It pleased her to hear him call her Mother instead of Mama. "They learn real fast, I'm sure." She was sure David considered himself nearly grown up, herding these dozen and a half lambs.

As the fence neared completion, Jack confided to the faithful boy, "I've got to get her done. When it comes time to cut that hay, it's going to take all hands and the cook to put her up. No one will have time to wrangle the woolies. We'll just have to turn 'em loose."

"Will Mother have to cut hay?" David wanted to know.

"I hope not, but she might have to ride along with you on the loaded wagon hauling 'er in. I doubt you're tall enough to reach the Jacob staff yet."

David didn't understand what Jack meant, but he did know that hauling meant horses. "Will Grandpa come up with his horses to haul in the hay?"

"Most too far for your Grandpappy to be coming. Besides, he has hay and grain of his own to cut and haul. Down there on the Flats where it's so much warmer, alfalfa grows so fast he has to cut it three to four times in the season."

"Where will we get some horses?" The boy puzzled over this.

He was not the only one trying to figure out this question. Mary had talked it over with Jack. He seemed sure they could handle it themselves if it were possible to rent a team, mower and hay rack. The wagon here would do with the tires tightened up. And it was possible to do without a rake, although it would take longer. She was sure Jack was thinking John would help. She was also sure that John did not intend to do so. *So my figuring must include a man's wages, unless I take a man's place.* She had helped Father haul hay in Illinois. She could handle a team well, but that left mowing, raking and pitching the hay. *Jack may know how to do all those things, but he cannot do it alone.*

Mary had $26 put aside to rent a team and mower. *I'd better not wait until the last day to learn if that can be done.* So this first day of July, she hurried to town to see what could be done. Jack was rolling rocks down to fill some of the bigger gaps below the wires where the two girls played. He was to keep an eye out for them. She pulled an express wagon stacked high with clean laundry. *I think I'll stop at the dairy first. I believe they always have a team there in the summer. And I'm sure they will need a rack, for they haul their own hay in from their ranch some place.* The first thing that caught her eye as she traveled the short distance from this road onto the private road was a wagon with a new hay rack standing in the yard. She had met Mr. Lewis; it was his wife who answered her knock. She was as short and broad as he was tall and skinny. He appeared behind her.

"Yes, we have a team and we have a mower and hay rack," he told her, but seemed to hesitate over renting them out. Instead, he commenced to ask her questions. "How many days you figuring it will take you to put up that patch of hay?"

"Jack Wilson, the elderly man who lives with us, says it would be at least two days to cut it, and nearly a day to rake it."

The gaunt man nodded. "Likely two days to haul it in, not being too far a distance from the barn. That would be five days perhaps. Like I say, we haven't a rake up here, but I think I know where I can borrow one. The blacksmith has one out back of his shop these several years doing no one any good. As I understand it, a team brings about $5 a day with a driver. I don't like to rent the team without my son handling 'em. They belong to him, really, and he is needin' the work. While he has never done much haying, he handles the team well and I have no fear but what he can do the mowing and raking, if this man Wilson you speak of, is willing to show him how."

Mary could see the big strapping lad of sixteen or so cleaning out the stable. "And how much would the rent of the machinery be?"

The man thought for a moment. "Five dollars a day for boy

and team. We'll let the use of the machinery go in on that, free of charge. The boy will be learning something useful. Another year and I think he'll be doing some ranching. Better let me know a few days ahead of time when it will be dry enough to get in to cut it. He'll need to sharpen sickles and have things greased. He just as well use this wagon—the rack's already on and it will save hoisting it off onto another wagon."

Mary was jubilant. "Shall I pay you now or later?"

"Better pay the boy when the job is finished."

Hurrying home, she felt so free of worry. *I feel rich, already having money enough to pay for the haying. I guess that is why I splurged and bought those firecrackers.* These she would keep as a surprise for them perhaps. She found two wet girlies when she arrived back home. Susan's lips were blue. "Margaret, you shouldn't let so much cold water run on Sister. She is too little. She cannot tell you when she is cold. See how blue her lips are? And her little hands are like frogs." Mary stripped off the wet clothes and hugged her to warm her while carrying her into the house and dry clothes.

The day was warm enough, but that water never was warm. David was nowhere about. That meant he was staying out with the sheep while they were bucked up in the shade of the brush somewhere. He was as faithful to his charge as Jack was to getting the fence fixed. Soon, Susan seemed none the worse for her experience, playing just as lively as ever. As soon as she was free of the house, she was out trying to pump the hydrant herself.

As they finished dinner, Susan's head nodded in sleep above her plate. Mary washed her soiled face and hands free of food, and put her down for her nap. Margaret, fearing that would be her fate, soon began to be very busy, teasing to go with Jack to help him roll rocks down to the fence line.

Jack looked not at all pleased. "I'd like your help alright, but I fear you might step on a rattlesnake."

"You don't be 'fraid, Jack," Margaret told him earnestly as she took his hand. "I won't step on no little snake and hurt it."

Jack could not trust himself to speak. Mary's warning look stopped John. "Do you know, Mother needs some help picking peas in the garden, and Margaret is about the best little pea picker I have. And we need radishes pulled too—how about it?"

"Can I walk with Jack a little ways first?" Margaret knew she was balked about the rock rolling deal—Jack never would let her help him do it.

"You can go a little ways. When Jack says it is far enough, you must scamper back and take a little rest." As soon as the child was out of hearing distance, John could hold his anger no longer.

"Why don't you tell her rattlesnakes will bite? A good scare is the only thing that's going to keep her from getting bit."

"When she sees one and how they act will be the proper time to tell her and warn her about that one kind of snake. They're the only kind that are harmful around here. I'm not going to have her afraid, like I was, of every snake that crawled. David got his lesson yesterday," Mary laughed, but she did not feel gay. "David and the pup happened along where Jack was sending those rocks down grade. The snake was on the prod, and the pup wanted to be in on the kill. Jack whipped him with his hat to make him stay away. And was David ever mad to think Jack would whip his dog!"

"Yes, and that boy will be getting bit one of these days. Then who will you blame but yourself?" John did not think this was the right way.

Mary was not too worried about rattlesnakes. She had never seen but two around the place in all her travels gathering cherries and berries that first year, and none since then.

The evening of July third, while washing for supper, David asked, "Mother, are we going to have firecrackers tomorrow?"

"What would anyone want to spend money for such things?" cut in John. "They just go bang and are done for."

Mother could see the crestfallen look. "Yes, you are to have firecrackers. I have two packets of them—one for you and one for Margaret; Susan is much too small to handle them. Besides, she will be asleep at the best time to shoot them tomorrow evening, just as it gets dark a little. I believe small men and girls like to hear the boom of caps and powder, just as well as some grownups do." She went right on dishing the meal.

"Can we have a picnic too?"

"Why go off on a hillside to eat your meal just so someone can get bit by a rattler? I say no to that." John was in a vile mood. Mary's rebuff was not lost on him.

Mary counted to ten before she spoke. "This nice green yard

would make a good picnic place. We wouldn't have any distance to carry our food. And besides, my special treat for all of us tomorrow would not be easy to carry."

"Will it be a cake?" Margaret almost whispered this guess.

"There will be a cake, yes, but the real surprise will be ice cream. I looked to make sure there was enough of that snow we buried in the ice house early last spring to freeze it with, and there was just about enough.

***

Life in the Marcus household seemed to run more smoothly the short while until the hay was ready to cut. John came from the tunnel at noon, and seeing the Lewis boy eating his meal with them after mowing the half day, guessed that Mary must have hired him. He said nothing, having no chance, but at supper time, he demanded, "What you paying that lunkhead?"

The unfairness of his asking, after letting her know he would not help with the hay, rankled deep. "Are you wanting to know so you can pay him for doing the work you should be doing?" She did not wait for an answer, but went to milk in a great hurry.

Old Jack, sensing the strained relations, was uneasy. "Doggonit, Man. The Missus didn't hire the lad. She just asked to rent the team and the mower and things we had to have to get the hay up. Mr. Lewis wanted the boy to do the handling of the team so he'd be learning about putting up fodder."

Before the hay was cured enough to be hauled and put in the barn, John was helping someone work his claim, so he was gone early and home late. Mary did not know if it was some more exchange work.

Summer passed quickly. By September, it was time for David to start school. "But who is going to herd my sheep?"

"Well, now," Jack drawled, "haying is over with and there's not a great deal of work piled up. I expect Gibson and I might be able to wrangle those woolies and get some winter's wood too."

October came, finding Mary feeling gloomy; Father would not be coming this autumn. Mary was so busy in the washroom rinsing the last tub of clothes, she did not hear the first rap on the kitchen door. She couldn't see who it was until she answered the louder knock. "Why, Max Thorn. This is a surprise." It had been more than six years since she had seen him, and he looked not a day older. She put out her hand to shake before she remembered he never did shake hands with her, but he surprised her by doing so now.

"How are you?" he asked, then spying Jack coming through the washroom, "Here's the guy I want to see."

Mary, seeing the two greet each other, guessed they were at least slightly acquainted. "Max, have you had dinner?"

"Sure have. I made that man Baers at the hotel feed me the best he had. I really should make him board me for a week or a month, playing such tricks."

Jack poked him in the ribs. "I see you have Williams' wagon and team. Did you by any chance come fixed to haul down about fifteen lambs?"

"I can do 'er if you can help catch 'em and load 'em. By the way, Mary, your dad sent up a few sacks of spuds and boxes of apples."

"The loading of those woolies is the easiest thing in the world," Jack told him. "I got 'em trained. All you have to do is back your wagon down into the creek somewheres. I'll hoist one end of that little bridge to the wagon bed and they'll walk right up into it."

"But before we do that little act, I want you two to listen to my tale of woe. You're not the only ones who have lambs on your hands and not knowin' what to do with them. I have 150 all cut out and trailed to a ranch over the hill from DeLamar. They were not ready to ship when I sold the rest. And then Baers wanted them for meat at the hotel and the boarding house he furnishes with grub. The man on the ranch where I delivered them was to dress 'em out for him, but the poor chap had to hustle his wife out to the railroad yesterday for some hospital care. That leaves me in the soup unless I can dispose of those lambs. But Baers is in a hotter kettle of soup, for he has been depending on those lambs for meat."

Jack grasping his need before Mary did. "How many did he say he wanted dressed at a time?"

"About twenty-five a week. I knew you could do it, and at that rate, you would be rid of 'em before winter set in."

"But we have no way of delivering them." Mary pondered.

"Oh, they'll come for them. You don't need to worry about that. Baers bargained to pay that fellow $1 a head to dress 'em out. He'll pay that to you. Ten chances to one, they won't bother with liver, heart and the like, so you'll have that much more gain. What's the verdict?"

"This will be Jack's work. He's the one to say," Mary answered.

"I say yes to the dressing 'em out," Jack stated, "but nix to handling any money. We don't get along good together. If Mrs. Marcus here can see any use for a hundred-fifty bucks between now and Christmas, we'll take on the deal."

"How can I say no," Mary appealed to them both, "when that means this place will be paid for before the year is out?" She turned to wash her hands at the sink to hide a tear. "Now I'm going out to see all the things those generous parents have sent." Her voice was husky. The two men were already making tracks along the porch.

Quickly they unloaded everything just inside the yard fence. "I'll be trotting them to the cellar later; Max is in a hurry to be on his way back," Jack told her as she broke open an apple box. They gave her no time to ask questions of them. Fastening back the slat in the top of the box, she went to the house to halve an apple for the girls. *Now I wonder who was at the bottom of all this.* She remembered that she wrote to Father about her dislike of seeing those ewe lambs made into meat. *Yes, and a week or so ago, Jack was up along the sheep trail, talking to some herder. I wonder now if that was one of Max Thorn's bands of sheep.*

Chapter Thirty Two

"I'VE NEVER SEEN SUCH a backward spring," Mary said, cleaning the mud from her shoes in the washroom before coming into the kitchen. Both men at the table looked toward her, it being so unusual for Mary to complain about the weather. She was overly tired, having washed for more than three hours. The bit of sun peeping through the clouds had fooled her into hanging the clothes out, only to have to snatch them in again just now to keep them from whipping to pieces in the sudden squall of sleet.

"What can you expect for the middle of April?" John asked.

"We sure could stand a mite of sunshine," joked Jack, "without the moss on our backs crackin."

"Aren't you going to eat your dinner?" John asked Mary as she washed food from Susan's hands and face and was taking her to nap.

"Not now. I think a little rest might do me more good than food." The bedroom was chilly, her outer clothes were damp, and she was uncomfortable and out of sorts. Slipping off dress, shoes and hose, she crawled into bed to rest. As she became warm and more comfortable, she thought *I could enjoy this if I didn't have to crawl out in a few minutes.* As soon as she relaxed, she was asleep. When next she opened her eyes, the room was in shadows. David stood beside the bed looking worried.

"Are you real sick Mother? Jack says you are. Dad says you're just tired and don't have sense enough to know it," the boy repeated.

His look of concern made her speak to reassure him. "Mother isn't sick, Son, just very tired. And I knew I was tired, so I rested—but I shouldn't have done so all afternoon. Change your school clothes, Sonny, you will need to feed the chickens and gather the eggs and maybe help Jack with the chores." She pulled on a fresh housedress, but her feet had to be slipped into those same clammy, cold shoes. "What do you mean, letting me sleep away half a day this way?" she scolded Jack as she came to the kitchen where he was busy whittling out tops for the two girlies.

"Jack wouldn't let us wake you up, Mama." Margaret told her. "He said he wouldn't make us one more top ever if we did."

Jack's wrinkled face brightened into a smile. "Now if you'd just make that a daily habit, it might do you some good."

"But I cannot possibly do all my work in half days," she got in before all three children began talking to her at once.

John, dumping an armload of wood into the wood box, added to the noise and confusion. "Hush, all of you!"

Mary saw the hurt look on each child's face and tried to sooth their feelings. She hugged all three, saying, "I just can't hear what is said when you all talk at once. Now, let it be just one at a time." They were much too surprised to talk for a second. "Did I hear someone say they were hungry? How about a glass of milk and a cookie all around?"

Margaret pulled away half laughing. "Susan and me had cookies and milk. Jack gave us 'em. One, two, three," she counted on her fingers.

"Then you two won't be very hungry. David, having the long walk perhaps, is the only one." She set out his lunch while thinking aloud. "Now I have to plan what we'll have for supper. Sleeping all afternoon when I should have been cooking and baking! I should have put beans on to cook at least. I sure miss having potatoes in the spring after they are all gone."

"Mama, Mama, can we have hominy?" Margaret was very fond of the hulled corn she had made last fall. Only a few of the many jars she had canned were left now.

"I like rice with lots of raisins better than any old hominy." David was the rice eater. It was always his choice.

"Say, Youngsters, do you know what my favorite supper was when I was about your size?" Jack called. "It was good ole cornmeal mush with milk. Might have been because milk was such a treat to us about then." He was cleaning up his whittling mess.

"We have that a lot of times for breakfast," Margaret reminded him.

Mary took a hand now. "Sure we do sometimes, but for a whole week now, we have eaten rolled oats or whole wheat cereal. Let us treat ourselves to a supper of cornmeal mush and milk. We have brown sugar to put on it for anyone who likes that best. What we don't eat tonight, I'll slice and fry for breakfast in the morning. You children all like it that way with syrup." She guessed Jack's suggestion had been to save her work, but then too, he did like the mush, she remembered. The children ate it well enough. John ate it, but grumbled about it. Mary didn't much care how she displeased him this evening. His dig about her not having any sense stacked up with his constant thoughtlessness, in her mind. *He growls about me working so hard, yet never once lifts his hand to make my work easier.*

Old Jack was the thoughtful one, helping her in so many ways. *Sometimes I wonder how I did it all alone before he came.* He fussed over her working so hard. It was his sharp eye that saw her misery the week after she walked to town to consult Dr. Tom. While busy at work this day, she thought about that wasted trip. *All Doc did was confirm my suspicion that a newcomer is on the way.* Her mouth grimaced. *It's all very easy for him to tell me not to work so hard and to rest more.* Bitterness settled when she recalled John's reply to her suggestion. *What you talking about, me getting some two bit job and let all the work I've put in go for nothing?* he had demanded, *and just when something good is about to show. Of course, you'd have to know something about quartz to understand what that upper vein is showing. With even a few dollars for powder, I could get 'er opened much faster...* On and on he had talked in glowing terms until she had buried her aching head in the pillow to shut out the words.

Thinking about it more calmly today, *I believe he has thought along those lines so much, he actually believes all he says.* To herself, she could admit that her talk with Dr. Tom had helped her morale. He assured her that she would lose her resentment once her babe arrived. "You have welcomed your other children and loved them. It will be the same with this one. You are not the only mother-to-be who has felt her burdens beyond her strength. Your problem is to shove this burden of making a livelihood on to the rightful shoulders, while you bear the little ones." *That was all very good advice, but he just doesn't know John Marcus,* was her concluding thought now.

Jack spent every non-storming day spading and planting the garden so he would be free as soon as he heard the bleating of sheep on the trail. He considered last year a profitable one. He had picked up ewe lambs mostly—eighteen of them sent to the Flats with one of Max Thorn's bands as they moved down in the fall. They had safely wintered along with the other fifteen head in Dad William's feed lot, fence rows and ditch banks. "I gotta remember we have a heifer calf this year," he muttered to himself as he scouted the trail for more bummers. "Can't make veal outta that heifer in order to feed more *bah bahs*."

Then came the evening when Jack failed to return by dark. Mary was worried. "He might have fallen down and hurt himself and can't get up. He packs such loads of wood in when he finds no lambs."

"More than likely, he's gone off the water wagon and is roaring-eyed by now," was John's response.

"He has no money, and he has said more than once, he is alright until a bit of silver burns a hole in his pocket." Mary could not feature Jack bumming drinks to get drunk, or leaving the lambs he had found for her to feed. She gave them their milk this night. They drank fairly well. Mary milked the cow, and after getting the children to bed, she put on a jacket and walked up the road toward the sheep trail. She could just see the lighter roadway along the smooth race track, as this swung further away from the noise of the stream. She thought she could hear a shuffling sound. Standing still, she heard it again. *That could be Jack, not able to make his feet track.* She was fearful, but called out, "Is that you, Jack?" She thought he tried to answer her. "Are you hurt?" This time, she heard the muffled words, "No." Again came the shuffling sound, but closer. Now she could hear his heavy breathing. Not until he was beside her could she make out the heavy sheep on his shoulders, weighing him down. "Here, let me help carry it."

"No, I'm going to make it," gasped Jack. "She's got a hurt leg. Don't want to shift her around none." The first rock they came to around the point, he paused to rest, then could talk easier. "You can get the lantern and have the gate opened for me, if you want to."

The light of the lantern made it easier traveling, but Jack was too exhausted to talk until he eased his burden down in the workshop. He rested on the littered grounds, with a steadying hand still on the ewe to keep her from getting up. "Couldn't find a thing wrong with her, but that snag on her leg," he said as soon as he could talk. "Looks like one bone might be broken, but I think a small splint and soft padding might fix it up if I can keep her from floundering around and breaking the other bone."

"Then shall I get you something to use for splints?" She waited for his nod, and then was away to the house. From the cellar, she brought thin boards from an apple box, and tore a strip of cloth from a stout dish towel. She dug out a handful of cotton from a ragged quilt she had lately washed. The last thing was the coffee pot from the just-warmed stove. John was mad because she didn't tell him what was wrong. *If he wants to know so badly, he can come see for himself,* was her thought as she hurried to the shop.

Jack drank coffee from the pot. Mary broke the thin wood strips to the right length over her knee, ready for him. Now it was her hands keeping the ewe from getting up while Jack's more knowing ones splinted the leg. "There. That should do the trick. Didn't have a doggone thing along with me to fix her up. Didn't dare leave her out tonight. She would have been coyote meat before morning for sure. Plenty of lambs there too, but couldn't bring them and her. She's worth more than any three lambs if she makes it, for she will suckle that many and save on the milk deal."

As they made it back to the house and John learned a hurt ewe was the cause of all this commotion, he was even more angry and stomped off to bed.

The next morning, Jack was still weary, but by noon, he was again up along the trail, bringing back two bummers. "These were all I could find alive. And this big one is a wether at that. He's a big fellow. Must have been one of the first drops." Jack took two lambs from the gunnysack, showing them to Susan. "We'll see if she'll own either one of 'em." There was no doubt about the ewe disclaiming any relationship to the smaller lamb, but accepted the bigger one, letting him nurse. Deftly, Jack went to the other side and put the smaller one to steal his meal with him as a guard.

Now came time for the dam to be put in. Some mornings the ice covered every puddle at the edge of the stream. *I hope Jack won't bring in any more lambs. I want a little milk left to cook with,* was Mary's thought, but Jack was missing at supper time after working on the dam most of the day. "Looks like he would be done with tromping the brush and sod in that dam. Even with rubber boots, that must be pretty cool on his feet."

"So he's off after more sick sheep, is he?" A hurt animal or a sick one was all the same to John, having no interest in any of them.

It was not quite fully dark when Jack showed up with a heavy sack over his shoulder. "I got more lambs alright," were his first words as Mary went to meet him. "I know you said we had all we

had milk for, but I brought their feed bags right along with 'em."
Jack was having trouble keeping his pants up—his suspenders
were attached to twisted shoe laces about the necks of two ewes.
"These doggone buggers never were taught to lead or drive in
harness." He put down the sack of lambs now and snaked the two
sheep along to the corral. With them safe inside, he could relax.
"Part of the distance, they pulled me right along after 'em, which
was alright as long as I could keep 'em headed in the right
direction."

"Can't you tell by the tags in their ears who they belong to?"

"Sure. And we'll let the owner know they are here. But if I
hadn't bothered to bring 'em in, they would have been coyote bait
by morning. Not many sheep men are going to go back for just
two ewes unless they happen to be close by. But if they do come
for 'em, say two months from now, they'll still pay for the bother,
for they'll have fed the four lambs that long."

"But there are only two bummers in this sack," David said as
he helped Mother carry it.

"I know, but that isn't saying I can't find two more most any
day soon."

Mary marveled at this man's energy. The more she worked,
the more he found to do that was helpful to her. He ran the hand
washing machine a few hours each day, which was the biggest
help. He had taken over all the garden work. *And still I'm tired
and never seem to get rested.*

***

School was out in June. Margaret, nearing six, went with
David the last day and talked of nothing else but what she would
do when she went to school in the fall. As July neared, the
children dug into the rotting sawdust and found no snow. There
would be no ice cream for July 4th, and they lamented that fact.
Mary was much too worn and tired to get ice from town. The 3rd
came with no preparation for any celebration, and she felt guilty.
All her strength and energy had gone into the laundry these past
weeks because that brought in cash money. *And it is money I have
to have,* she reminded herself. The haying had cost $30 last year,
and Jack seemed to think it would be more this year, for it was a
heavier stand.

I have enough to pay for the haying, and Grandma Blatchey, but not for Dr. Tom. And I haven't near enough baby clothes. Those she decided could wait. Bestirring herself now, she went to the west porch and called David from where he rested in the shade of the barn beside Jack and the dog, watching the small band of lambs and the three ewes feeding on the hillside. "Son, would you like to go up town for these few things I've written down? There are four sacks of laundry ready to go up. I have pinned the price of them on each one. It will come to $1.40, and that is more than enough to pay for a dozen oranges and that many lemons. And I have written down coconut, but if they haven't any at the store, you can get some chocolate. That would make us a nice cake. Whatever money is left over, you may have to buy firecrackers, sparklers, or whatever you like. But I wouldn't buy those great big firecrackers, Son. You could get hurt with those, and besides, they cost so much more, you would only get just a few bangs."

"Is that all written down here?" Eight year old David could read fairly well and was trying to read it all now.

"I just put down the lemons and oranges, and the coconut or chocolate. And below that, I stated you were to have the remaining money for yourself."

"Will the strawberries be ripe for tomorrow? I like a shortcake best."

"I fear not. They were pretty green the last time I looked at them, but we will have a shortcake when they do ripen."

Sometime later, Mary missed Susan and could not see her playing in the yard. Jack and the dog were meandering up toward the sheep. Finding Margaret, she asked, "Where is Susan?"

"I don't know," going on with her own play.

"Well then, you'd better look for her. Sister might get lost."

"She hasn't lost Mama. She knows where she is," Margaret told her.

Mary hid her smile, but could not go on about her work until the three year old tot was found in the hen house, playing with the baby chicks.

There was little else for Mary to smile about during the month of July. Rain came to interfere with the haying. There were long delays getting it into the barn. The hot days of August seemed to sap her strength all the more. Then came the day Jack hurried to the tunnel, meeting John just as he was emerging. "On your toes, Man," called the old fellow. "It's lambing time at the house."

For a second, John did not understand what he meant. "The baby isn't due for two months yet."

"None the less, your wife's in labor right now, or I miss my guess." He was backtracking right behind John, who was now hurrying.

"Has anyone had sense enough to telephone for the doctor?"

"You should be the one to see to that," Jack snapped back. "I was getting supper, her not feeling like it. When I saw what was happening, I came after you." It was hard to talk and hurry, so he said no more.

John, suddenly fearful, went directly to the telephone and put in a call for Dr. Tom, and thus was not able to answer the questions that were asked of him, as to the closeness or severity of the pains. At Dr. Tom's insistence to know those things, he dropped the receiver and went to the bedroom to find out from Mary. She was not able to talk at that moment, so he rushed back and reported, "She's bad enough that she can't talk, Doc."

"I'll be down as soon as I can make it. Shall I bring the same woman with me?"

John hardly remembered answering him, so looked up with a bit of surprise when Grandma Blatchey walked in with Dr. Tom half an hour later.

"Say, you youngsters," called Jack with concern. "Come to the kitchen and finish the meal you have on your plates, or I'll have to throw you to the howling coyotes." The children were not afraid of Jack's dire threat, but were terrified at Mother being sick.

Grandma, seeing the children were trying to dodge into the sick room, took a hand. Kindly, but firmly, she led all three back to the kitchen. "Sure your Mama is sick, but she will soon be better if you just stay here and do what this kind man says. If you don't bother none, Dr. Thomas can have her well faster. Here are some peppermints for each of you who eats your supper." From her apron pocket, she took a handful, giving them to Jack.

Margaret and Susan were soon asleep, lulled there by Jack's stories. They were in bed before Grandma brought out the well-wrapped small bundle in the basket. David stood tense, his eyes questioning each one as they came out.

Dr. Tom, scrubbing up at the sink, noticed the look. "Do you want to see your new baby brother? Now is that what you have been waiting up for?" He tried jollying the serious chap. At his nod, Grandma turned back a corner of the blanket for a mere peek.

David hardly looked at the tiny red face, but kept his eyes on Dr. Tom. "Can I see my mother before I go to bed?"

"Sure, Boy. You can peek in on Mother, but she is asleep just like this brother of yours, and you and I wouldn't want to awaken her, would we? But she'll be awake in the morning, much sooner than you if you stay up much later." Dr. Tom did not like those over bright eyes. "I see you haven't eaten your mint. They are good, but I have a nice little candy for you." He brought out a mild sedative. "This is such a small one, you won't have to chew it even. Now a little drink of water, then maybe the mint will taste better." Seeing Mother so sound asleep was not very reassuring, but it helped and he let his father take him upstairs for bed.

The worried doctor was still shaking his head as he helped Grandma hurry along with the oiling and dressing of the frail mite beside the warm stove. "Don't attempt to bathe him—just a bit of a rub with oil in your warm hand. Be sure to have him where it is warm to diaper him. We'll give him every chance we can." He looked up at John coming into the room. "That means plenty of warmth around this fellow. Hot water bottles, if you have them. If not, bottles or jars filled with hot water."

Old Jack scurried to the cellar for jars, and carefully warmed them, then filled and screwed the covers on tight. Dr. Tom tested each one as he tucked them about the babe in the blanket. "You three understand that the less this one is handled the better? It would be well not to change his clothing unless they're wet or soiled, and warm those before you put them on." Most of this talk did not register with John. Mary, not hearing any of it, was the one shocked when the feeble life flickered out in her very arms a few days later.

Old Jack hurried into the dark tunnel mouth, calling loudly to John. His own voice echoed back until he was not sure John heard or answered. Again he called, then he saw the dim gleam of the headlamp coming toward him. "The babe has died."

"Died. What do you mean?" John thought he hadn't heard right.

"The babe, Hugo." Jack turned to hurry out of the gloom. "You knew he didn't have much of a chance to live from the start."

"I knew no such thing. Why wasn't I told?" His voice was strained as they left the tunnel for the bright sunlight.

"Dr. Tom the same as told you that first night. Don't you remember?" Jack quit talking as he couldn't keep up with John's fast gait.

Mary had known this child was not as strong as her other three, but attributed it to his being premature. Now, as she lay in the warm but shaded room, still too stunned to weep, her mind flitted back to Dr. Tom's caution about her constant over work. Then another thought lodged. *They must not send word to Father and Mother. Their coming now will not help my little son, or bring him back to life. And such a hard, hurried trip could harm Mother with her heart condition.* She was sure her parents would come had they heard. She denied her own longing for their comforting presence. *Father, with his busy summer's work could ill afford to leave. They've had enough sorrow with Annie not coming home this summer vacation.*

John thought her decree to not let her parents know was unnatural. What was unnatural to Dr. Tom was her dry eyes and calmness in talking. "I would not heed your advice to take it easy, Doctor. In my foolishness, I considered only myself and the needs of the rest of my brood. I never once thought I was robbing my unborn son of the strength he needed to live. Now I feel like a murderer." With this wail of anguish, the tears broke through. Grandma moved about quietly.

The passing of the tiny babe after its few days of life left its mark on the Marcus family. For all of Dr. Tom's talk about science and medicine still did not explain why one child should be born frail and another strong. Every friend attended the simple burial in the cemetery so close at hand. Most of them called at the house and brought flowers, gifts of cooked food, and offers to aid in any way needed. Few of them reached the quiet, shaded room where Mary lay in her grief and self reproach. Grandma Blatchey had stayed on a few days longer at Dr. Tom's insistence.

Mary thanked her for the extra days of rest as she paid her. *But I might have been better off up and busy; I wouldn't have had so much time to think,* was her thought as she took up her duties anew. David and Margaret needed clothes to start school soon; Susan was fast outgrowing hers; there was little time for grieving. But still, the smudges did not fade from below her eyes. John, considerate and kind the first few days, became ill of humor. Her continued sleeping alone on the couch was a reminder that she would not forgive him over the cow misunderstanding.

John was impatient, but gave her time. *She'll get over this crazy notion she has if I give her time.* Her decision that she would not be both wife and breadwinner had been stated in a calm, quiet voice. She had no intention of quarreling, but she expected some understanding on John's part. When she found none, it hurt all the more.

Dr. Tom fell into the habit of riding downstream whenever possible. It was he who noted Mary's wane color and listlessness, and proposed a trip.

"Any trip is out," was Mary's short answer. "I still haven't half enough money to pay what we owe you."

"Why worry about that? I'm not. Neither do I need it. But you do need a change of scenery. I don't mean a long or expensive trip. I know you well enough that you would never consider it. But go somewhere. You've never seen the big city of Reynolds or Silver City."

"My curiosity about those places will have to wait until I can afford a trip to see them." Then came the longing to see her parents. "The only place I would want to go is down to the Flats, and that is out of the question—too far, too expensive. And besides, the two would miss the first part of school."

"The two missing school for a week or two is of small account, and such a trip need not be expensive. This time of year, people often drive to Boise Valley to can fruit. They go out nearly empty and would be glad to give you and the children a ride."

"Don't tempt me this way," the homesick Mary implored. "But I cannot go now—there is so much sewing, and the garden to tend." She shook her head as if that would stop this longing.

Jack came in just then. Dr. Tom appealed to him, "How are we going to persuade this good woman to take the trip to see her folks? *Shanghais* or kidnap—which do you say will work best?"

"Pair of hobbles might work 'til we could load her into a rig to get her off bed-ground." Jack grinned at Mary and then the doctor.

"You find the hobbles, Jack, I'll find the rig." Dr. Tom left after that sally.

Chapter Thirty Three

MARY HAD OFTEN IMagined the pleasure of a trip home for a visit, never guessing it would be on such short notice that she would be leaving. Day before yesterday, Dr. Tom had jokingly told Jack he would find the rig to haul her off bed-ground. Early the next morning, he had telephoned that Clyde Hendricks and his wife were only too glad to give her and the children a ride right to her parents' door as they went to the Boise Valley to put up fruit. They planned to make the trip that far in one day, so they wanted to start early, say five o'clock.

Now at this early hour, after a sleepless night, Mary tucked the lap robe about Susan and David to keep off the morning chill. Margaret was wedged between Mr. Hendricks and his wife on the front seat of this two-seated hack. These people were strangers to her. From what Mary could see of the team in the early dawn, the horses were not especially large, but she figured they must be pretty strong at the rate they were traveling—and upgrade at that.

"Mother, when will it be light enough so I can see?" David asked the moment they passed through DeLamar.

"It'll be another hour before we'll be on high enough ground to see anything," Mr. Hendricks told him. "It should be light enough by then. Along here, all there is to see is Jordon Creek and the hills that hem us in."

"I've never seen this part of the road either, Son. The only time I came over this road, it was nearly dark." She understood all about David's wish to see this new country—so close to their home, yet he had never traveled it. They had left the ravine and were climbing the first rim of barren hills when the sun came out in all its glory, making dew drops sparkle on the scrub brush and dry grass for a short moment before it dried up. David turned about in the seat to look back the way they had come, waking up Susan, who promptly wanted something to eat. "I've been expecting that," Mary tried to smile and act like a normal mother going with her children for a long delayed visit to her first home in the state, "so I came prepared." She reached for two sandwiches from the lunch box, breaking each in half for each child. Wrapping the paper well about the lower half of the sandwich, she passed one to Margaret. "Dear, be careful now— don't get any of your food smeared on other people's clothes."

338

Still having the rest in her hand, she commenced to nibble at it herself. *I must have been hungry. Maybe that was what made me feel so all in.* "Goodness me, here I am eating away and never once asked you people if you would have a sandwich. I put in plenty for all."

"Thanks just the same, but we are not hungry yet," Mrs. Hendricks said. "We really did eat a fair breakfast in spite of it being so early. I made up a lunch too. Long about noon, we'll stop to rest the team for a little while, and we may all want to snack."

"My brood did not eat enough to bother with fixing the meal. I believe it is getting warm enough to shed my coat." Mary hoped the cool breeze created by their speed of travel would keep her awake. What little dust there was in places had no time to swirl up and bother them.

"We should make it to the top spring by noon." Clyde Hendricks sounded very much awake.

Mary wondered how he could be—she was herself so drowsy, tired, thirsty and depressed. She suspected the spring he mentioned was the one where she and John had paused for a drink when they returned nine years previously. It had been such an odd place to find a spring—not a tree or shrub of any kind about it; not even green grass—out in the hot sun, and yet the water was so cold it made one's teeth ache to drink much of it.

By the time they reached this patch of dark mud so close to the wheel track, Mary was in a sorry state of exhaustion. For a moment, she was not sure she dared climb from the rig for fear she would never make it back into it again. Mr. Hendricks' long arms reached out to the tiny bowl shape in the center of that mud where the water bubbled up constantly, clear and pure. Being on the level here, there was no place for the water to drain away, causing a miry mud about it. Mrs. Hendricks gave each child a drink, then brought Mary a cup. Mary said, "You shouldn't wait on me this way. You must be every bit as tired as I." After the refreshing water, she did climb down and help spread the lunch.

David watched the man give each horse but one small sip of water, and then a cupful of grain in their feedbags. "Don't the horses like the cold water either?" he asked.

"They like it too well—that's the trouble with 'em." Then explained to the serious boy how too much cold water, or too much grain when they are so warm could founder them. "It isn't the fast travel that hurts 'em so much, as it is not taking care of 'em afterwards."

"Will you give 'em water to drink down at Grandpa's tonight?"

"Not very much until they have cooled off for awhile. If I did, I might never get 'em off bed ground."

David's eyes opened wide. "Were you a sheepherder?" The grownups laughed.

"Nope, never did wrangle the woolies—about the only job in these hills I haven't tackled. What made you think I was a herder?"

David was too shy after their laughter to say anything. Mother came to his rescue. "I think it is because you use some of the same expressions that Jack Wilson does, and he was once a herder. Won't you people have a jar of milk with your lunch?"

"Wouldn't that be robbing the kiddies?" he asked as he took the milk.

"Not at all. I have a dozen of these small jars with milk in them. I wanted the jars down there to put jam or jelly in. I just thought they were a good thing to carry milk in." With milk and food staying her, Mary felt better. A few minutes walking about woke her up. *I'd better not go to sleep from now on. I'm apt to fall out of the rig,* knowing it was mostly downgrade.

Again, the team was treated to a cupful of water and they were off.

Margaret tried to stay awake. "Mama, Mama, will Grandpa have some apples soon as we get there?"

"I expect he will have." Mary tried to smile again. "If there are none in the house, they will be soon picked when he sees this apple-starved tribe coming."

"Have your folks a fruit ranch?" Mrs. Hendricks asked, hopeful of their not having to travel further in the Boise Valley.

"No, not a fruit ranch. Just a family orchard they planted the first year they came to the Flats. It was nine years ago last spring. Some of the trees have done very well, but I doubt they have any fruit for sale." Mary was sure she read the woman's thoughts right. To keep herself awake, she told about finding the little tree of seedling apples by the racetrack in Wagontown that first autumn. "Something must have happened to the tree in the two and half years we were gone, for I never found it again."

"I expect some camper might have chopped it down for tent pegs."

The sun set further down in the west, bothering Mr. Hendricks' eyes on some of the curves. "Now if it wasn't so hazy, we could get a good look at the Flats from about here." On trotted the team. He used the whip instead of the brake. "We've made pretty good time," was his verdict as the sun slipped out of sight. "Can't be more'n ten–twelve miles from here on in."

"I believe they call it eleven miles," Mary aroused her interest enough to say.

"Less than three hours and we should be there." He showed his weariness too. The shadow of night and the haze gave the Flats below them an eerie look.

Mary watched for some landmark about her folks' place so she could point it out to the children, but it was too dark now. And it was a chore to keep the two girlies from sliding off the wagon when it tipped forward down the steep grade. Neither child's feet were touching anything to brace themselves, so Mary held each girl in an arm and braced with her feet. It was a trying position. *Will I be able to hold out?* were her weary thoughts. "When we reach the foot of the grade, you turn sharply to your left. I'm sure that part of the road is not changed. It is less than two miles from there to my people's ranch. It will be the second one. A few years ago, someone took up land on the east side of them."

"How many years since you have been home?" Mrs. Hendricks asked.

"Nine years last June."

"Where was I, Mama. Was I with you?" Margaret clamored.

"You weren't even born yet," David wiggled around to say in disgust.

A chuckle from the man, "I expect, Young Lady, you were but a twinkle in your daddy's eye about then. Say, how old are you anyway? You must be old enough to be thinking about going to school."

"I been to school already: One day yesterday and another last year. I'm most six and now I can go to school all the time. David is eight and he's been going to school two whole years."

"Not two whole years, Silly." David had to set her straight on that. "I just go little pieces of a year—'til the snow comes, then in the spring after it is most all gone. No time at all and school is out.

341

As soon as I get big enough to make me some snow shoes, I'm going to go every day."

Mary feared the two would commence quarreling. She thought they must be so very tired. She was sure they couldn't be hungry since only lately they'd finished eating the last cookie. To forestall any squabbles, she commenced to talk, telling of her first trip out from Caldwell on a freight wagon—how fearful her sister, Annie at Margaret's age, had been of the steep grade down to the river and ferry boat. Then she told of the weary child saying she didn't think they measured the miles right here in Idaho.

"That's pretty cute," chuckled Hendricks. "A kiddy of six thinking that."

"Will Aunt Annie be there when we get to Grandpa's?" Margaret asked.

"No Dear. Aunt Annie is in school a long long ways from home. Don't you remember Mother reading you her letter saying she was going to school of a different kind all summer just so she could learn more music?"

"Is your sister aiming to teach music?" the woman wanted to know.

"I doubt Annie is planning to teach music. It is just the love of music that makes her want to learn all she can—in the shortest time possible." Both girlies were asleep as they reached more level ground. As the road smoothed out, David slept too. Mary wished she could, but well knew they could hit a rock or drop into a badger hole, and it could be quite a jolt. To her, those two miles were endless. No one talked; all were too tired.

The old dog barked his welcome as they turned into the lane. Father stepped to the front gate, figuring it was a neighbor stopping, either calling on them or just bringing the mail. Then he recognized his daughter. "Mother, come see who is here," he called loudly to the form silhouetted in the doorway against the lamp light. "Mary and the children have come. Mother, light us a lantern." All three children came awake. "Here, Daughter, let me carry that heavy child. All who are able to walk—come on to the house." He didn't know his eldest daughter doubted her ability to walk right now. "I'll get the lantern and come back to help you with your team," he said over his shoulder as he entered the house.

Mother Williams had the lantern by then. She struck a match, but was too dazed to put it to the turned-up wick. Father took it from her hands and completed the job. "Steady, Mother, steady now." His calm voice did just that to her. In the next second, she was out to the steps trying to help Mary mount them. Mr. Hendricks and wife assisted Mary, their steadying hands keeping her from faltering until she was lowered to the couch.

The three children could not understand their Mother crying and laughing at the same time—nine years of longing was in this greeting. This strange woman, who talked like Mama but hardly looked like her, was crying just as much. David and Margaret knew this must be Grandma. It was Susan's frightened wail and Mama's tears that brought a pause. "Goodness me," Grandma was the first to speak. "Such an old crying ninny—carrying on so and scaring little folks this way the very first time they come to see me." She tried to hug all of them at once. Susan wanted nothing to do with her. "Don't blame you a bit. Such a thoughtless old woman as I am. Just you relax a moment, Daughter. Lady, you make yourself right to home. I'm going to get about the quickest supper you ever saw. Do some hungry children want an apple to stay them until dinner is ready? A few pretty good eating ones are here in the kitchen." She was already moving in that direction.

She had a fire built and food from the cold room put on the stove by the time the two men were back to the house. Father hurried and washed. "What can I do, Mother, that will be the most help?"

"If you want to set the table first, then peel and slice the peaches, I'd appreciate it. I have everything on getting hot, but this cold chicken. It's so nicely pressed, I think it will slice and be better cold." The flustered woman was trying to do two things at once. "I'll make tea—that is the quickest. We'll need milk and cream from the cooler. That can be the last minute." In spite of confusion, a hearty meal was on the table in a matter of minutes.

Mary would have preferred to lie where she was rather than going to the table for food, but knew it would worry Mother the more. She even accepted a cup of tea and sipped it. "I never knew tea could taste so good." In other words, she had never liked tea. Mother had forgotten that, but Mary found that the hot drink was reviving her. "I didn't think I was hungry either, but I find I am."

"There is plenty of milk, remember," Mother said. "I made tea because it was quicker, but if any of you want a cup of coffee, just say the word. With hot water in the teakettle, I can make it in a jiffy."

"No, no—this tea is plenty for us," both Mr. and Mrs. Hendricks said.

"There is going to be no visiting tonight." Grandma's graying head nodded in emphasis. "You tired people are going to tumble right into bed. We'll double up on the talking spree come daylight." She set about to make the couch up with bedding.

"Mother," Mary all-but-whispered. "The children and I can sleep in one bed if..."

"Stuff and nonsense, Child! How much rest would you get then? Besides, there are plenty of beds. We'll give those good folks Annie's room, and you and the two girlies take the sleeping porch. It has two beds out there, and don't let me catch you having one of those little ones in bed with you. This couch is the nicest kind of a bed for a boy the size as David. It's all made up and ready." Away she hurried to light more lamps.

At the breakfast table, all commented on how well they slept. "I put one over on all of you." Mary was determined to act naturally. "I put in two night's sleep all in one. That's what the excitement of this visit did for *Yours Truly*." She would blame it all onto that. Never would she say that John's attitude toward her coming had anything to do with her wakeful nights. "When I went to bed, I was sure it would take a week of sleep to put me back in harness again. And now I feel like I could do the biggest load of wash, and pick and husk a bushel of sweet corn. And I could eat half that amount myself!" Both parents smiled at her. "Remember, there are only two things I want to do while home these few days. One is to eat all the green corn I can eat, and to take a salt shaker out to the tomato patch and eat one right from the vine. And I'm liable to snitch a cucumber to eat that way too."

"We have plenty of all three—you just snap to it," Father beamed.

"Those are the things I miss most up in the hills where they can't be grown. I believe it was last year, I spoke to a lady in town and mentioned missing the green corn. She claimed she didn't like corn on the cob. Then I learned she had never eaten any right from the patch. All she knew about corn on the cob was what she could buy from the peddlers—and you can imagine what they would be like after being picked more than two-three days."

344

"Perhaps that's why I've never cared for green corn," Mrs. Hendricks said. "I've always preferred the canned corn better. It is sweeter. Now that creamed corn you served us last night was the best I ever ate."

"What made it so good," Mary told her, "was being picked one minute, cut from the cob the next, and put to cook right then. Every hour lapsing between the time it leaves the stalk and cooking, it loses some of its sweetness and flavor. I've learned that green peas lose their taste nearly as fast."

"Just how are you and the children getting home again?" Clyde Hendricks asked as they were ready to be on their way.

"Father will take us to Caldwell or Murphy to catch the stage. It might be before the week is up. He'll be so glad to get rid of us."

"We figure on being loaded going back, or we would be glad to take you. It'll take at least two days on the return trip with a load."

"Don't you worry about us getting back. We are only too glad for the ride down."

Soon the couple was on their way with a small basket of fruit to eat as they went. They had declined the offer of a lunch being put up for them, stating they would be in Caldwell by one o'clock at least. "And I'm sure they will be, the way that team of theirs eats up the miles," Mary told Mother as she rushed about trying to do all he work at once.

Not until the following day did Susan feel acquainted enough to get two feet distance from her mother. "I never realized what a mama's girl she was until now." Mary was husking out another bushel of corn. "Did you decide if you want this for drying or canning, Mother-of-Mine?"

"We'll dry this. We mustn't spend all the time you are here canning. Neither must we fill those drying racks so full we can't put more of those harvest apples to dry. I do believe they are the nicest ever. They never turn dark like other kinds do. What peaches we have, we should can for you to take back."

"What we don't eat, you mean?" Nearly a full grown smile came to Mary's face. She lifted the large kettle of corn to the hot stove and turned the teakettle of boiling water over them to blanch the ears a few minutes before cutting the corn from the cob. "Mother, did you hear the latest joke about what the Englishman who told his friends about us Americans when he went home?" She swept up her litter while she talked. "He said Americans were funny people—what we couldn't eat, we canned; and what we couldn't can, we preserved."

Mother laughed. "I expect our ways would seem odd to them, just as their ways do to us. Father says you have Cornish people up your way. Do you find them good neighbors?"

Mary shook her head. "I think they would be if we lived right next door perhaps, but the two miles distance is a barrier to neighbors as we used to know in the east. All the different nationalities in DeLamar seem kind enough."

"Then there are others besides Cornish?"

"Oh, yes. A few from about every country on the globe—mostly from Europe, though. There is one family—I don't know their name or nationality for sure—the woman talks so very broken I cannot understand her very well. But she makes the most beautiful handmade lace. She trims all her underclothing with it. Nice wide lace will be on the bottoms of her under-drawers. She is a large woman, and it takes a hundred pound flour sack to each leg, and you how some of the printing never will bleach out. So about every time I go to town, I get a laugh for myself. On her clothesline will be hung those drawers of hers—one leg reading *DeLamar Mines and Milling Company*, while the other half may say *Silver City Supply Company* in big black print above that beautiful lace."

Mother laughed heartily. "That would look funny. Is it because they are so very poor that she uses such material?"

"I believe they are anything but poor. Her husband and two sons are in the mines. They earn pretty good wages. I might have to use flour sacks for a lot of things, but I'm not going to trim them with lace."

Their short stay was about over. On the last afternoon, Mary snatched all the curtains down and got them in water while Mother was out of the house. "So, Daughter tricked you with that washing and ironing did she?" Father chuckled.

"It isn't fair, their going back so soon—I'm not a third visited out." Mother was beating up dumplings to drop in the kettle of bubbling chicken. "Don't expect I would be if they stayed a month." she said ruefully, determined she would save her tears until after they were gone. *From the looks of Mary, she's had more than enough gloom.*

"Don't think for a minute that I'm talked out either." Mary was hanging the fresh crisp curtains up as fast as she finished each one. "But there is such a thing as children having to go to school. Jack will have that churn full of cream and be wondering what to do with the rest. I've yet to see him stumped at knowing what to do, but he never has churned." Mary had been so blue and discouraged when she left her home, none too sure she wanted to go back, but now she had that part straightened out in her mind. That was her home—the place she had worked so hard to pay for. She could make a living for herself and her children just the same as she had been doing. *I have been pretty weak-minded to think I might saddle my family onto Father and Mother.*

"I've tried to let you two do most of the talking," Father said at the table, "knowing I would have my chance tomorrow. Do you think you want to do some shopping in Caldwell? If so, we'll start a bit earlier is all."

"No shopping, Father Dear," Mary answered lightly. She was not letting him know she had just enough money to get the four of them back home by rail and stage. "You know, these grandchildren of yours have never seen a train."

The haze was still with them on the morrow so one could not see a long distance. "I was wishing it would be clearer so the children could get a good look at the Flats like I did the first time I paused at this spot," Mary told her father as they paused on the rim above the river to rest the team. "I can see enough to know ten years has made a lot of changes in the Flats. Several new homes every which-way I look. We can see the water in the artificial lake, you say. I'm so glad of that. I've wanted to ask you if they had trouble with the water seeping away too much. You remember that was what Max Thorn was afraid would happen? He said the ground was pretty porous."

"They had to use quite a bit of cement in some of the ditches; still, in places water gets away from them. You should have seen Caldwell mid winter—every cellar and basement in town was full of water, and it was several inches deep in most streets for a day or so."

"Was it from this lake dammed up way out here?" Mary could just see it.

"Indirectly. See, the water from the Boise River coming to fill this big lake is brought by canals and is flumed across low spots and small streams. The ice broke one of those and let all the water pour down that small stream meandering through town. The heavy snow melt had already filled it capacity. There was nothing dry and dusty about this valley or the Flats for awhile last winter."

"This road has changed along here. Do the fences and the square turns make it much farther?"

"Not much, I believe, but there's little direct roads left. They did some grading, but the water doesn't run off too well. It may take plenty of gravel before we have a real good road all the way for wet weather."

"I can see Caldwell has grown. You say they have cement sidewalks?"

"Along several blocks, and they are now talking of surfacing some of the main business streets. That should help the mud of winter and dust of summer." He drew rein at the railroad crossing. A section of freight cars were traveling under their own momentum along the switch.

All three children were eyeing it. "Mama, Mama, where is the horses?" Susan wanted to know.

Grandfather chuckled. "Maybe it is about time theose grandchildren see the choo-choo train. It's getting near dusk now; I doubt those automobiles will be out now, but we have two to three of them around here. They say Boise has several now."

"They would be a curiosity for the children to see." She was not much interested herself, a mite hungry about now and weary from the long ride.

With the children in bed at the hotel, it was their time for a real talk. "Daughter, I don't believe you've said how your hay crop is doing?"

"Better each year, just like you said it should. But I still fear to stretch it to feed that those lambs and the three ewes. We might be able to, except for the heifer calf. She is such a nice little animal, we shouldn't stunt her. That's another thing I've wanted to ask your advice about: Jack is all for sending those sheep down like he did last fall, but I worry about the trouble and expense to whoever has to tend them."

"The trouble doesn't worry me, but I have learned that a small bunch of ranch sheep put into a herd that way does cause the herder plenty of worry sometimes. They have a tendency to split off from the herd. I have been giving this question some thought. According to Max, if a pack burro was dropped off at your place before the heavy storms come, Jack could get that small bunch down here by himself. It should take him about a week—about 45 miles. His bed and food would be all he'd need to bring. And if the heifer leads good, I'm wondering if she could be tailed to the pack animal."

"She leads well. She's so much of a pet, I believe she would just follow Jack—or the lambs even." Mary smiled a wry one. "For all the talk about sheep and cattle not being on speaking terms—it isn't that way with the heifer. She likes the petting and attention of whoever is out with the lambs. My biggest fear is that the cow will not bring a calf in the spring."

"She might not." Father nodded his head. "She's getting old, but she might give milk through next summer. By fall, I'd say we need to have another cow in view for a milker. I can help you buy her if need be. This one should fatten up quick. We can either make beef of her for your own winter's use or sell her to someone else to eat."

Mary did not have to think long. "It would have to be someone else to eat her."

Chapter Thirty Four

"MAMA, MAMA, WHAT DAY will Jack get home?" Margaret was dancing in her excitement. "Will he be here by Friday?" Mary hardly had the letter opened when the happy child commenced to ask, as she had with every letter for the past month.

"No, Dear, he won't be here that soon. The lambs are too small to travel yet. But Grandpa writes that Jack will be starting home in a week's time if no bad storms happen about then."

"Oh, goody goody. Jack is coming home and bringing lots of baby lambs," said the seven year old. Susan, not to be left out, sang and danced about too. "When he starts, will he come fast like we did?"

"Goodness no. It will take him a whole week to come. The mama sheep have to eat along the way, and the lambs can't walk very fast."

David was thoughtful. "He could be here for my birthday."

"If there are no storms, he might make it here by the first day of May."

"How many little lambs will Jack bring?"

"It's hard to tell, Dear. You and David must change your school clothes and commence your chores."

David came back in the kitchen fastening his shoes. "Did Grandpa write how many lambs there are?"

"So he did, Son. Let's see if you can you figure how many lambs there might be after the chores are finished."

David's share of the work was done in a whiz. With paper and pencil, he commenced his figuring, talking as he put down the numbers of lambs taken down last October. "Jack butchered one lamb for us to eat before he left, and you sold three to that man in town, and Jack killed 'em for him. So that left nineteen and the three ewes went down. But there were more than that many already down to Grandpa's."

"That is right, Son. Do you remember how many were sent down last year? I mean fall before last, and then the first year too?"

"It was eighteen that Jack put in with all those other sheep, wasn't it? And when they went down in Grandpa's wagon, there were only fifteen." The boy figured, "Fifteen and eighteen make thirty-three, and that added nineteen and three makes fifty-five altogether."

"That is correct, David." She paused her work to stand beside him. "One easy way to figure out the number of lambs is to make those numbers into groups. See, look at it this way: The lambs going down are two year olds, and so on. Now the yearlings don't have lambs this spring, but the two year olds did. Also those fifteen three-year olds did."

"I know now." The boy made his pencil fly. "That would be thirty-three lambs this year."

"You are forgetting the three ewes Jack picked up, and those two Grandpa bought from another rancher. Remember, they all had lambs. Grandpa wrote there were five pair of twins."

"That would be forty-three lambs. If I add all these numbers together, would that be the count?"

"It would—if you have down the number of ewe lambs from the first few sent down. Remember those roly-poly lambs last fall when we were there? They were almost as big as the mother sheep."

"There was eleven of 'em, but Grandpa wasn't going to keep all of 'em, he said."

"No, only six of them were ewe lambs, I believe. He planned to sell the five."

"Yeah, and he was going to buy two or three buck sheep, I 'member. Will those ones with horns come too?"

"No, they'll stay there to eat the grass on the ditch bank." Mary continued fixing supper leaving David with his adding.

"Mother, is One hundred thirty-nine the number Jack will bring?" Mother nodded he was right.

The girls coming in heard David's answer. "A hundred thirty nine lambs—oh, goody, goody. What a lot of 'em." She put the few eggs into Mother's hands. "There was more eggs, but a hen is setting on 'em. I let her be so she'll hatch off some baby chickens." She had not liked the hen pecking her hands.

"I will need to go get them. It is much better to put a full nest of eggs under a setting hen all at one time instead of letting the other hens lay their eggs in there day-to-day, Dear. We want them all to hatch out nearly at the same time."

David asked, "Who do most of the sheep belong to?"

"Well, Son, I would say it must be a company affair. Jack picked up most of them. Our cow furnished the milk to feed them.

Grandpa gave us the cow in the first place. Most the time, I milk her. You and Jack have done the herding. Grandpa fed them all this time. So a big part of them should belong to him, don't you think?"

David nodded. "Lucky they don't belong to Dad, or he'd just sell 'em or kill 'em."

"He'd do no such thing, Silly." It was Margaret's chance to use David's favorite expression. "Dad wouldn't touch those sheep with a ten foot pole. He said so."

Mary went outside without comment. *I'll be glad if he doesn't say worse than that in front of the children.* What he said to her in private might hurt, but she knew now she had a defense. Last time he spouted off about the stinking varmints, he said he would kill them or sell them to get rid of them. She had told him in no uncertain terms they did not belong to him—he wasn't paying taxes on them. "If you are wise, John Marcus, you won't try to dispose of them in any way." She was sure he remembered the sheriff bringing the cow back. "I will promise you one thing. If and when your work brings in a livelihood for this family, I'll see that the sheep are sold so they need never bother your sensitive nostrils."

"I can sell this damned place and not have to put up with the stink."

"Not without my say-so." She had often wondered how and when she would have to take this stand.

"What kind of a fool are you? Don't you want the money you've put in on it? I'll split even with you."

"Half of it," mocked the angry woman, her eyes blazing at the injustice. "You better think twice before you try selling this place. You could get into a peck of trouble. I'm signing no deed. This is a home for our children—a roof over their heads."

"But there is no chance for me to get a good start around here."

"Other men have no trouble making a living for their families. I notice you always land a job when you can't get blasting material any other way."

"What you trying to do?" John was angry too now. "Run me off without a cent after all my years of work on this place?"

"All your work—has it made this place one cent more valuable? Have you paid one dollar on it except when the team was sold? And I had to connive to get that payment out of it."

"You're forgetting I was to feed Tim for what he put in on it."

"And you've paid that grocery bill?" She knew she had him trapped.

"Alright, I'll leave. Just walk off and leave you the whole thing, if that is what you want."

"It isn't a question of what I want. I can't stop you from leaving. Nor would I try. If your children mean nothing to you, that would be the quickest way to let them know you don't care whether they have a home, food or care."

Not until afterwards did she realize she had said the one thing that gave John pause in his threat to leave, for he did care for his youngsters. But never having had to think of their support, it was not natural he would be thinking of it now.

***

May 1st, Mary hurried to ice David's cake before he and Margaret got home from school. *It will be a little bit of a surprise for him if I can get it put out of sight.* Having no present for him, and fearing Jack might not make it this day, she hurried to the cellar with the cake. Hearing the sheep bells as soon as they drifted over the knoll in front of the house, she rushed out to swing wide the big gate. She waved to Jack and hurried back to her work. David had left the corral poled out, ready for the band for the last week.

Jack corralled the sheep and came to the house before the school children arrived. "You are looking much better than you did last fall," was his greeting to Mary.

"I am better. So busy I haven't any time to be anything but well—so many washings to do, but I haven't all the garden planted yet. I expect if the truth was told, in the back of my mind was the thought that if I didn't get it done, Jack would soon be home to help." She smiled. "I know you must be weary. Rest yourself in that easy chair until supper time, unless you want to stretch out on the couch."

"Mite tired." He flopped in the chair. "But it wasn't too bad a trip—good weather all the way. I was able to help your dad with his garden until the lambs got to taking up more of my time. Sure a nice place your folks have down there. Did you know they insist on me doing that again—bring the woolies down in the fall, feed 'em and help lamb, get 'em sheared, and bring 'em up again.

353

Your dad claims he is putting down all the cost of feeding and shearing and such. And then the sale of the wool—he says it just about balances as to expenses." Jack sounded doubtful.

"I have no doubt that Father puts down all the figures, but with wool selling for $.15 a pound, I'm not sure just which way the scales are tipping. Knowing that father of mine, I say you and I might have to do a little bookkeeping ourselves."

"So you know what wool is selling for? The price of sheep hasn't dropped much." Jack's tiredness was showing.

"Here's hoping it won't. How many bummers did you find on your way up?" she joked.

"Only three," sighed Jack. "One ewe lost her lamb, so I gave her two to take her mind off her troubles. Oh, I have to see that she lets 'em eat yet. She and the three are still wearing strips of my red bandana so I can spot 'em easy. That third lamb gets his meals anywheres I find a full breadbasket. He seems to be holding his own. He might be putting one over on me and stealing part of his own grub."

"Did you hear the folks say if they expected Annie home as soon as her school is out?"

"They are still hoping she will." Jack drank the glass of buttermilk she proffered.

"Just think. Sister Annie is a grown woman, now at seventeen this spring. I cannot make it seem real."

"Mama, Mama," gasped Margaret running ahead of Susan who had gone to meet them. "David says not one of those lambs belong to me." She was so hurt, she failed to notice Jack.

The kindly old man reached out and turned the child to face him and his quizzical grin. "Now, just who does that young man think they belong to?"

"He says they belong to you and him 'cause you two do most the herding. Mama too 'cause she milks the cow. And to Grandpa, for he feeds 'em hay in the winter time." She was quite out of breath now.

"You know something, Young Lady? The very next bummers I find running around loose are going to wear a bright red daub of paint right on their rumps. That will be your brand. We'll just fool Mr. David. Say, where is that big sheep man anyway?"

"Oh, he went right to the corral to count them." Away she flew to tell her news.

***

Life at the Mills House took on more life and meaning for the children now that Jack and the sheep were home. The bells jingled and Gibson, the dog, remembered them, although he hardly left the sheep to romp or play anymore. Within a week's time, nine bummers wore a bright red patch of paint. She told Jack, "This is all we can possibly feed. The cow is giving less milk than I thought she would." She was helping Jack feed the sheep. "I expect every one of these are ewe lambs?"

"Sure thing," Jack smiled. "That's why I've had to make so many trips for 'em. Don't think that gal is quite old enough to understand giving her a lamb, then turn around and make it into chops."

Jack was happy, and so were the three youngsters. John was more unhappy, and life was becoming more of a nightmare to Mary. *I have to make my word good. I said I would not be both wife and breadwinner in this family.* To be a wife would mean more mouths to feed. *And I have all I can fill and clothe now.* No matter how she looked at it, the experience of last year loomed big. *Never could I forgive myself to have another frail babe die. That was terrible, but to live and never be strong could be worse.* She understood all this, but could not feature John seeing it in the same light. *I have to wake him up to be a man's responsibility to his family. If he wants a wife, he'll figure it out given time.*

So, she bided her time, hoping for such a miracle. John expected her to be normal. In health, she was, but not in agreeing to his ideas. "Sometimes I wonder why you came back last fall," he demanded more than once, "you being this fed up with me."

"I've wondered that myself," she had retaliated. By his surprise at their return, and his remarks afterwards, she guessed she feared they weren't coming back.

June was passing and July almost here. *That means haying too,* was her thought. She would need to help the two girlies watch the sheep during the days when the hay would be shocked and hauled. *David handles a pitchfork pretty well, but maybe it would be better to hire a man, let David look after the sheep, and I keep up my work on the laundry.*

Her mind was full of plans on how she would handle the work as she walked to DeLamar to learn the chances of finding a hired hand. The express wagon was loaded with clean laundry. Nestled among the sacks to keep cool were two pints of butter and a quart of buttermilk. She stopped at the livery stable to hand this to Lew.

"The sight of that jar when I'm good and thirsty is good for sore eyes." His mild blue eyes smiled at her while he drank the jar empty. "I sure wish you had more butter for sale—I'd buy a pound just for myself alone. The wife won't eat ranch butter." He wiped his mouth and handed her a quarter.

"I'm sorry too that I haven't more butter, but my worst fear is being without milk entirely very soon unless I can find another milk cow. Father told me last fall, if this one doesn't freshen this spring, to fatten her and sell her. I know little of where to look for another cow or even where to sell this one."

"I'll keep my ear out for someone with a milk cow. It's easy enough to sell a beef animal—Baers at the hotel would be your best bet. He furnishes the grub for that boarding house up close to the mines."

Mary thanked him and hurried on her way to Upper Town. Jimmy Burch was not too busy at the moment, so she asked him to give her the figures on their bill, and the money in cash from the laundry for this past month. "I have to be prepared to pay for the haying next month, and I might not be up town again before then." She fingered the $52 in bills Jimmy handed her. "If I could leave this applied on our account as it should be, that balance of $79.03 would be down where I could see over it in another month or so. My fondest hope is to have it paid before the year is out."

"I hardly understand how you manage so well." Jimmy looked at her much too admiringly. "Permit me to say, you are a wonderful woman."

Mary knew her face was flushing. "Oh, this business of managing," she told him glibly, "is just a matter of subtraction." To his puzzled air, she added, "I still make out three grocery lists. First, I write down all the things we should have, then things we can get along without and still get by. When I subtract the second from the first, the answer is just the necessities, and that is what I buy." She hurried away with her few purchases, mostly to get away from Jimmy's overtures. *I wish he wouldn't make such a point of being so very nice to me; I don't want to hurt his feelings by being rude, but others must notice how he singles me out with all that attention. I don't like it.*

So deep in thought was she that her name had to be spoken

more than once before she was aware of it. "Did you call to me, Mr. Knollen?" she asked, stepping toward the frail man with the breeze ruffling his white hair.

"Yes, Mrs. Marcus, and it is kind of you to come back. You see, I'm not as spry as I once was." He seated himself again beside his cabin wall. "I would have come down to see John myself if I were able. I wondered if you would give him the word that I find myself down to rock bottom, and wondered if he could manage to pay me a little on the loan." To her look of concern, he hurried to assure her. "I'm don't expect he can pay the whole $100 at once, but a few dollars every now and then would help me out."

Not knowing of this borrowed money floored her for a second. "Do you remember the date of the loan, Mr. Knollen?" She took out her account book and pencil, not for a moment doubting that John borrowed from his kindly old man.

"I have the date down in my ledger." He painfully tried to get to his feet. Mary stopped him with a hand on his arm. "Just to the day, I can't say, but it was the spring of 1901 when he was fixing to be married and had to make the payment on the place."

With hand in pocket, Mary separated one of the folded bills from the others and handed out a $5 bill. "This is not very much, Mr. Knollen, but it is a start to pay this off. I can promise you at least a dollar or two every week until it is paid." She was sorry to leave him so forlorn. *If I happened to have had that amount with me, I fear I would have just handed it over.* She was sure John never would think it needful to go to work for wages to pay it. *But I'm going to have the satisfaction of telling him about it and see what he says.*

"What does the miser think I've got to pay with?" roared John as soon as she told him. "Him down to rock bottom—that's a laugh! He's always had money salted away."

Mary had wisely closed the swinging door going into the rest of the house. She hoped Jack couldn't hear him. "Could it not be that he has loaned out all his money just like he did to you? I really believe the man is broke, just like he says."

"Him broke?" John refused to even consider such a possibility. One angry word led to another until they were quarreling. When Mary asked him if he borrowed that money, John flared again. "Sure I borrowed it. The old fool all the same as offered it to me. Some folks are so damned glad to see a man get married, they'll loan him anything they've got—knowing what a hell of a lot of misery he's getting into." He putt on his shoes, then went for his better coat.

Mary was frightened, and tried to stop him from leaving. "Where are you going this time of night?"

"What do you care where I go or when I come back? You've made it plain enough this long while." With that blast, he left. Through the opened door, she heard the sound of his footsteps as he crossed the bridge, the hollow sound like an echo of all their differences for the past decade. With no thought of sleep now, she lowered herself to the east porch. *The odd thing is, I do care.* She tried to shake her mind free of that thought. *I can't for the life of me see why I should.* She had stood alone in so many things without his help or understanding, she could not fathom feeling any regret.

He's blaming me, and I'm blaming him. After more long minutes of dismal thoughts, *It's true, just like he says. I knew he was a prospector and nothing more when I married him. Poor childish me didn't realize he had no intention of growing up and assuming any responsibility.* More probing into her own thoughts. *If I had been older and wiser, would all this have happened? I wonder if it would have made a difference had we waited that year like Father suggested.* Somehow she could not see where she would have been smart enough to set him on the right track of being a wage earner before marriage. *I naturally expected that every male knew how to earn a livelihood.*

Much later, *Has my blindness and my dogged determination to make a go of it been part of the reason of it all?* To think that she was some to blame caused her to act. In a matter of minutes, she crossed the bridge and walked in the moonlight toward town. *I hope I meet him on his way home.* She had no clear thought of what she would do if she didn't.

Mary was not too worried about him drinking too heavily. *He never has but the one. The lack of money would be a factor there.* Somehow, she did not rule out his drinking this night. *He sounded desperate enough for most anything.*

The only places with lighted windows at this time of night were the saloons and the neat cottage just this side of the first one. Mary had been slow to learn the character of this house, half hidden by the mammoth rose bushes beside the swept walk through the green lawn. Several times she had caught sight of the sarcastic woman who sat that day atop the woodric about this yard. It had solved one riddle for her: *I disliked her before I knew what her business was.* Mary stopped walking on the opposite side of the road. She hid in the shadow where her hope of meeting John was fading. Men tramped along the noisy board walk in the warm night. Voices mixed in jest and shouts mingled with song and music coming from the half hidden cottage. A familiar voice called a goodnight as Jimmy Burch came down the walk and out through the gate. There was no mistaking Jimmy with his special way of walking. Those that didn't like him called it a strut.

Still safe in the gloom, she waited until he had wondered out of sight. *If Laura won't live with him, I guess he has the right to do as he pleases,* was her thought. Then she saw John Marcus emerge from the half-swing doors, headed away from the saloon. She was glad he was here to walk home with her, and started to retrace her steps along the path, but John was not going home— his unsteady legs were taking him along the short walk through the crowding roses.

Chapter Thirty Five

HOW SHE WALKED HOME, or in what way she spent the rest of the night was never clear to Mary afterwards. She felt as if some part of her had died. The early morning light found her huddled on the couch in the dining room. Chilled from the lack of enough covering, force of habit made her build the fire and put on breakfast. Jack would need his before he went out with the sheep. She was certain her eyes had never closed, hearing every tick of the clock and stir from Jack's room. She realized why she must have come to this uncomfortable place to rest, afraid to awaken the girlies if she crawled in with them. Never again would she sleep on the extra bed in the same room with John Marcus. His none-too-sure steps on the walk, down the hall, and to the bedroom were like a death knoll to her hopes. She had not looked to see what time it was. *Our life together is over.*

What might be the next move, or who would make it, did not become clear. After setting the table and leaving the food on the edge of the stove handy, she fled the house. There was work she could do in the garden until milking time. Jack caught sight of her when she went from one to the other. "Don't you ever take time to eat any more?" he called. He was on his way to let the sheep out of the corral, and she need face no one. She went back to the garden again after straining the milk in the cellar. *Alone I can fight this out.* She feared Jack's sharp eyes. Any word of sympathy would be her undoing.

The children must have swallowed their meal on the run, they were in such a hurry to catch up with Jack. Margaret did take time to call her. "Dad says he's sick, and don't want any breakfast." and away she raced.

It was nearing mid day and she should have dinner ready. *With a cloudy day, the sheep won't be bucking up much. Jack will be going right back.* Now she must hurry with this meal. The empty coffee pot and the extra used cup was the evidence that John had been up and drunk coffee. Thinking he had gone back to bed, she stayed clear of those rooms. Not until noon when the children scampered back for food did she learn that he was not in bed.

"When did Daddy get up," asked Margaret after going to see how he was. "Was he real sick, Mama?"

"I was working out in the garden all forenoon, Child, so I cannot say." She was sure Jack gave her an inspecting look. Even the children seemed to be looking at her as if there was something tell-tale in her face. "You four go ahead and eat. I should have had my washing on the line so it will have a chance to dry before it decides to rain. I'll put it to soak right now."

In her hurry, a nasty sliver imbedded itself in her right hand as she moved the wooden bench. *Of all the stupid things to do.* The pain of it made her wince. *I've wished for a pair of tweezers more than once. This time, there is no way of getting that piece of wood out.* A wave of bitterness assailed her as she thought of the uselessness of all her skimping. *What earthly good has it done me?*

The worst of this little painful accident, it bothered so in her work. *I might better take the time to go have Dr. Tom take it out.* She didn't like that idea, but the thought of a swollen useless hand like she once had known sent her toward DeLamar. The pain in her hand and up her arm was nothing to the anguish she felt nearing this place where she had walked last night. The tiny fear that she might see or meet John was present. *He will think I'm spying on him.* On she marched to Dr. Tom's office without seeing any one she was well acquainted with. The office was still locked, which meant he was out on call. Going to the store to wait and ask for their mail, she came face to face with Jimmy. He was more than startled at her drawn look.

"You are ill, Mrs. Marcus. Let me help you over to Doc's office." He was tried to assist her.

"He's not in his office yet. A nasty sliver in my hand is nothing to be alarmed about." She still had no idea of how her face mirrored her shattered life.

"At least take this seat and relax until he does come. I believe he's not back from lunch yet." Jimmy brought her a drink of water. "Would you take a sip of wine if I rustle some up?"

"No," she managed to say. The water would hardly go down; how could she drink anything else. Jimmy continued to fuss over her while he watched for Dr. Tom to come. When Jimmy spied him, he called out, but Mary was already out the door and crossing the road to meet him halfway.

"Because I have part of a plank in my hand is no reason why everyone should think I'm sick." Dr. Tom's hand automatically helped her up the steps.

"Very painful is it?" He eyed the hand and guessed it had lately happened. "Better be prone while I work on it—might be nasty to dig out. I'll freeze it so the pain will be more bearable."

Guessing the hurt hand had not caused those deep circles about this woman's eyes, he probed much deeper than the piece of rotting wood, which he now had out. "Just what are you trying to do—work twenty four hours a day? I would say you've forgotten what a good night's sleep was." He got no response until he had the thermometer ready.

"I'm not sick, Doctor." The glass tube went under her tongue and she was afraid to talk. Mary tried to make her mind go blank so those knowing eyes watching the rise and fall of her chest could not probe into the sick void beneath.

Dr. Tom was thoughtful, true; neither pulse, respiration or temperature were bearing out any bodily illness. "Might be wise if tubs and washing machine were smashed. Right sure you wouldn't take the laundry to Jordon Creek then. I better put a bug in your husband's ear." He tried to bring this out jovially.

"I have no husband." Her startled look was because she had not intended to say this. Dr. Tom was the one person she could talk to without restraint, but she had not wanted to do so. Without food for more than twenty-four hours, and weak with hunger as well as mental strain, she was trapped. The whole sordid episode came tumbling out—all the pent up torment over this age old question. "I stood right on the other side of the street and saw him." She knew he held compassion toward her; she didn't want sympathy; nor were his first words kind.

"Woman alive! You stood there and let him go in without raising a hand to stop him? Why didn't you create a regular fish wife scene?"

That sounded like reproof. Mary tried to hurry away from his sight since he thought so ill of her to think she could go screaming after a man who had spurned her like John Marcus had.

"You little realize how weak we poor males are sometimes." With that, he let her go. Several things he was prepared to say; some advice might have helped; but right now, she wanted none.

***

362

Dr. Tom wasn't in a good frame of mind. His emotions were entangled in the lives in this mining camp and the few, isolated families close by. It was a repertoire of ills, ups, and downs of the people. Right now, it was a question of his own inner turmoil. Leatha Orchard, now home, was a puzzle in her new role of sophistication. Her tempestuous loyalty, open candor, and ardent demand for love and approval had been taxing. Now that that side of her character was subdued, he missed them. *This leaving her free until she is of mature mind has its disadvantage. I no longer know what she is thinking or wishing.*

Leatha, a full bloom vivacious young lady now, attractive in her dark coloring, found it pleasing to her vanity to be the ruling power in the social life of this small place. Few males measured up to the Orchard's standard. Her presumption of Dr. Tom as an escort was not challenged. The only flaw in her conquest was Dr. Tom's lack of ardor. She wanted him to be the wooer, the all-conquering lover. His complacency irked her, letting her jealousy have full sway.

The cooling breeze of a threatening rain was pleasing. Dr. Tom, about to be free of this routine office work, welcomed the change in the atmosphere, then he remembered this was the evening of Leatha's planned picnic. *She will be unhappy about that,* was his thought as he saw her trip across the dusty street toward his steps. "Come in, come in. You have been much in my thoughts. The impending weather isn't very kind to your plans, I fear."

"And you fail to appear very down hearted over the cancelled outing."

His smile went for naught as she pouted. "Step inside and I will cry on your shoulder." No move was made to comply. "Leatha, really, I'm sorry, but this isn't the last day of summer— it's not yet August. There's time for several picnics."

"I doubt I will have another free evening before I leave for the coast"

Dr. Tom wondered why all the crowded plans for one short summer. *It must be of her own planning.* He reasoned, "The black storm cloud is swinging to the north. It might miss us yet."

"Even if it doesn't, the picnic is out. I cannot round up everyone at this late hour."

"In that case, will you ride with me should the rain pass us up?" He would not have been at all surprised had she refused.

"Yes, if you have a moderate ride in mind. I do not care to be lame for the dance tomorrow night."

"Not very far. I should call at Wagontown for a second." She seemed glad of his asking her to go with him. *I'd better remember to do more of the asking. We might come to a better understanding.* "Alright, you can expect me on my black charger very shortly." A tag-end patient ended their dialogue.

Leatha was ready when Dr. Tom arrived, becomingly attired in the very latest riding habit. "We should do this more often," he said as he gave her a hand to mount. This was his idea of good relaxation—a fast cantor with lively company. Instead of being talkative, she was pensive. Gone were all her Tom-boyish ways. Once they were beyond the last straggling shanty, they slowed to a walk. "I must be very earthy to enjoy storms and the upheaval of the elements the way I do."

"What I love is the thunder of the sea and roar of the breakers as they smash on shore. It's deafening, but I enjoy it. I like the feel of the salt spray even. That is why Mother and I plan to stay at the beach as much as we can. Why don't you take your vacation next month and join us?"

"Now, if this vacation stunt was as easy to come by as it is to talk about, I would be right there. Having half promised my sister I would make the trip to see her, it is more apt to be the lake shore of Superior where I'll wind up in September. She's all the family I have, and it is impossible for her to come see me." Dr. Tom wondered if he imagined her cooling interest as soon as he did not fall in-line with her plans. "Have you forgotten the plans we used to have about a half day's jaunt to see those falls south of here? Sunday would be an ideal day for that. How about it?"

"That would take some thinking about." An airily wave of her hand could mean it was of small moment instead of any deep consideration.

As they came to the Marcus home, Leatha said, "You said you were to stop but a moment. I prefer not to dismount and go in."

"Oh, but I want you to come in. I'd like you to meet Mrs. Marcus—you'll like her." His hand on her elbow was compelling. Seeing small Susan eyeing them from the porch, Dr. Tom said, "Hi there. How are you this day?" The bashful child was not apt to say much with a stranger here. The flash of red in

Leatha's cheeks could mean a flare of anger at his insistence in taking her up this noisy board walk to meet someone she didn't care about at this moment. "Is Mama home?"

Susan nodded, then overcame her shyness, "Mama made some lemonade. Do you want some?" Susan held the screen door open for them when Mrs. Marcus came into the hall.

"I wondered who Susan was talking with. Do come in. It is true we do have lemonade. Would you two accept a glass?" Mary had seen Leatha Orchard several times, but never had been introduced until now. In neither look nor action would she take notice of the rudeness this young lady was displaying. She was not like her sister Helen in the least. "Margaret has hurried cold drinks out to our hay men," Mary told Dr. Tom as he accepted a glass. "Sort of a bribe to help them get those last two loads of hay in the barn before night fall."

"I expect the threatening storm would give you people concern." He was studying Mary's poised air, as if she was taking life more calmly than the last time he saw her. "Are you sure they are going to make it?"

"If a wheel doesn't come off or one of the crew doesn't take French leave," Mary answered.

Dr. Tom didn't want to hurry away. Neither was he pleased to have Leatha so haughty. "Just how big a crew do you have?"

"Just Jack, the Lewis' son, Gale, and one man I hired. That leaves David free to look after the sheep. I was afraid I would fail to be much of a herder."

"That would be the first thing I knew of you to fail at." He flashed her an understanding smile as they were leaving.

"I've failed miserably at several things." There was the hint of bitterness in her words.

As soon as they were out of sight of the paint-peeling house, Leatha lashed out, "I was under the delusion you had an errand at that place."

"I had one very important to my peace of mind. I wanted to know how that patient was bearing up under all the work she finds to do." He was sure this girl riding within arm's distance was burning with anger and resentment, but for what reason, he was in the dark. *Surely I should expect her to meet a friend of mine the same as she expects me to meet hers.*

"She in no way looked ill to me. From now on, I hope you

don't expect me to make sick calls with you. It would be much more mannerly on your part to refrain from insisting on me going to such people's homes."

"Leatha, what is the meaning of all this ill humor? We'd better talk this over." He had come up against many of her tantrums in the past, but this time he was going to address it. Her saddle horse stopped the instant his hands pressed her arms, her hands firmly gripping the reins. "Let us get this settled right now. I want to know what breach of good manners there was in asking you to meet Mrs. Marcus. I consider those people my friends. When you wish me to meet your friends, you have every right to expect me to be courteous to them, yet you were not courteous to Mary Marcus just now."

"Why should I be, pray tell?" She responded with insolence.

"Because I consider them friends would be reason enough. The fact that she is not in your social group should have no bearing on the question. She is a worthwhile person. A good woman."

"A good woman!" All her pent up jealousy made Leatha lash out. "You call her a friend of yours. And tell me she is such a good woman." This was nearly a scream as she fought to loosen his grip on her arm. "She murdered her own child and you call her good?"

"What utter nonsense are you talking about?" He still would not loosen his grasp. He had never before noticed how this slim girl resembled her father.

"The whole town knows all about it. How she confessed to you that she caused its death. Will you deny that?"

Dr. John Thomas was the one that was angry now. "You, Leatha Orchard, are a full grown adult now, and so full of pride. Surely you can't believe such small town gossip—just because it happens to please you to believe it. Mary Marcus no more caused her babe's death than you or all your friends. She might have said something in self censor because of all her hard work, but I didn't expect the babe to live the night through."

Releasing her arm, Dr. Tom said, "You are now as free as God's free air." He gathered up his reins and eluded the slash of her quirt.

"I despise you, John Thomas. I never want to speak to you again." Failing to strike him seemed to goad her all the more. "I hate you. I hate you," screamed the girl as she dashed up the road.

Dr. Tom reined his horse down and gave no heed to pursuit. His horse circled twice in its wish to follow. *That settles something,* he told himself as he kept his mount at a walk. At the fork of the road, he took the hill road for three miles so he would come into town from near the opposite direction. *It might be a novelty for her not to find me plodding along in her wake, should she get over her mad and race back to make amends. I'm sure no one else has ever held her and made her listen to anything unpleasant before in her life.*

He was so depressed, he did not want to repeat it. "What a lucky break this came now instead of after we were married," he said out loud as if to impress it more on his own mind. *What a hell on earth would our life together have been.* On the slow, lonely ride home, he did a lot of thinking. *It could be I'm just not the type to care greatly for another person.* Never had he doubted his love for Helen Orchard, but that had ceased to keep him awake nights. That might have been due to Leatha and her avowed undying love.

He made sure it was dark before he zigzagged down the steep hillside into Upper Town and left his horse at the livery stable. He ate a tasteless meal at the restaurant, it being after regular hours for the hotel. He drank a couple glasses of beer he didn't want, and played a couple games of pool before calling it a day. As he began to climb the steps to his rooming house, a dark shadow emerged from underneath and clutched him about the knees. "Why are you here, Leatha?" He could not take another step unless he loosened her arms by force. "Do you want to add a post script to your denouncement of me?"

"No, no. Can't you see why I'm here?" wailed the unhappy girl just above a whisper. "What a beast you must think me. How can you ever forgive me?" As no answer came, she cried the more. "I cannot go on living unless you forgive me."

His hand touched her soft hair as she stepped up to him. "No use torturing yourself this way. Just be glad we found out how miserable our life together would have been before it was too late." He kept his voice low.

Her hands clung to his. "Come with me where we can talk," she pleaded.

He stood in the path beside her. "I will escort you home now."

The narrow path along the hillside required they walk single file. He did not touch her, and soon, she led the way. There were two ways to go once beyond the next house. The main path angled down to the foot of those 100 steps leading up to the Orchard Home perched on its private point. The upper trail would bring them out nearly level with the house and yards. The path was at a slant, and not easy to travel in the dark, but this was the way she led. "We can talk here," stopping just short of her own brightly lighted home.

"There is nothing to talk about. The decision of this afternoon stands. There can be no other way."

"No, no, you cannot mean that. I cannot go on living with you. I love you. Is that so hard to understand?" A heavy sigh was his only answer. "How can I humble myself more than begging your forgiveness?"

"My forgiveness is freely given, Leatha. I can even understand where you are not to blame for your attitude toward other people, which only makes it clearer how unsuited to each other we really are."

"When you belong to me alone, I promise you, I will never be jealous of you again this way." Her tears were very wet on his hands below her bowed head.

"Jealous?" he questioned her. "Why should you be so unreasonable over my friendship with other people? You have friends, and those you admire. What would you think if I were to put on such a scene?

"You do not love me," was her cry. "If you loved me one little part as much as I care for you, you would understand how I feel. How I go wild when you take others' side against me. No one must come between us." She was wailing now.

Dr. Tom had never realized how much jealousy governed her life. As she became calmer, he tried to reason with her. "Your resentment over my interest toward patients and friends makes this day but a foretaste of what our life together would have been."

"No, I will never act like that again," interrupted the sobbing girl.

"Yes, Leatha, you would. Perfect love is supposed to cast out fear. Yours and my regard for each other only multiplies fear."

"I promise I'll never be that foolish again. To show you I have changed, I will go with you and apologize to that woman any day you say."

"No, Leatha. That would not help in the least. I believe you are sincere in your wish to make amends, but before you finished your apology, your tone would imply that Mary Marcus was a person who did not matter to you."

"Of course she doesn't. Why should she? Be sensible about this. I was rude, and I'm sorry about that, and offered to do what I can, but you and I cannot be expected to pal with all the people in this camp. We deserve a better life than that—a place big enough where you could have a good practice, and we could be surrounded by people of our own level; where we both would have friends. I know you will love Seattle—that's where I want us to go on our honeymoon; so you can see the place. If you love me, you will want to live where I will be the happiest. Father will help you buy a really good practice. He has already said as much."

Jimmy Burch had insisted more than once that Leatha Orchard was a *managing* woman. Dr. Tom had not believed him, knowing Jimmy was a pessimist because of his own marital rifts, but now it was so clear. "So, at this late hour, the bridegroom is to be told where he would have lived?"

The sarcasm in his voice was not lost on Leatha. "No, oh no, that isn't the way to look at it. I just want us to live some place where both of us would be happy. Isn't that what love means—to make someone happy? Isn't it common sense to look toward the future and what you want out of life?"

"The sensible thing now is to take you home." He was nudging her in that direction.

Bracing herself to stop them, she now faced him. "Do you mean this is goodbye?"

"It has to be. I'm not going to let you in for a lifetime of regret and unhappiness. No matter how you feel about it now, some time you will thank me." He was not sure she would walk that short stretch of level, gassy lawn. Each step was halting, as if she might balk.

Mr. Orchard himself came to the door and opened the screen to his ring. "I am glad to find you still up, and turn this girl over to your care and protection. Leatha has had rather a shocking encounter." He had no intention of saying more. How Leatha chose to explain would be her affair. Neither would he linger after his briefest *goodnight.*

Much to his surprise, he slept sound that night. The weight of doubt that had been bothering him a good while was rolled away. A loud rap on his door awoke him at the first light of dawn. Expecting this was some hurry up call, he wasted no time in getting on slippers. He was still tying his robe about him as he opened the door. This was no sick call. Mr. Orchard moved in without a word, closing the door carefully.

"Dr. Thomas, you seem surprised. Did you think I would let this misunderstanding continue without raising my hand to stop it? When my daughter's happiness is at stake, I will risk much." Never had this man seemed more imposing.

"Married to me would mean only unhappiness for Leatha. I honestly tried to make that plain to her last evening." Dr. Tom was aware of his unshaven, rumpled hair and a worn robe. He folded his arms, confident of his convictions.

"How can you be so sure of this? Leatha loves you very much. She has never been seriously interested in anyone else. Am I to understand at this late date that you never cared for her?"

"Because I do care is the reason I won't alter this decision. Leatha is very attractive and desirable. It would be easy to do as she wishes now—marry her and start a life together, but I'm not that much of a cad to spoil her chances of a happier life."

"Do you mind telling me why you disapprove of a better location, say in a place the size of Seattle?"

"If I remember correctly, Mr. Orchard, but a few short years past, I made you a promise at your request. I was to leave Leatha free of all entanglement until she was of adult mind to be able to choose her life. Yesterday, she did so. And I will abide by the choice—knowing that it is the right choice. All this wish to be in Seattle or any place else would not make for happiness. You, being a man of good judgment, must be aware of this."

Nothing more was said. Mr. Orchard left as quietly as he had entered. *I wonder if this is the first time he failed to do whatever his daughter asked.* While shaving, a thought came to him, *Orchard may very well oust me from my place in this town.*

Chapter Thirty Six

DELAMAR BUZZED WITH CONJECTURE for more than the usual nine days of the rift between Leatha Orchard and Dr. Tom. She left hurriedly with her mother for the coast, and then on to England to visit her sister, Helen. Now, after nearly two years, the question was not settled as to who jilted whom. Dr. Tom would be the last one to make a statement. Jimmy Burch's incessant prying had kept him on guard for some time. Now, after all these months, there was a let up.

Life at the Marcus home had settled into the pattern of a house seemingly whole, but divided none the less. John Marcus, knowing only the lure of gold, was more convinced than ever that only a real strike and sudden wealth could redeem him in Mary's eyes. Again this spring, he worked hard to earn the needed cash to buy powder, leaving home early and retuning at dark. Mary, busy in the garden, paused to ready Father's letter when the children came from school. "Hurry, Mama, tell us when Jack and the lambies will be here," Margaret lamented before Mary could get the envelop opened. "I want to know so bad. David just put it in his pocket and wouldn't let me touch it."

"It is best never to open other people's letters, Dear. Stop your dancing about until I can learn what Grandfather has written." She glanced again at the date—May 2, 1913. The post mark was not legible. "This was written a week ago, and Jack was ready to start the next morning if no storm came that night." Mary thought for a moment. "But that was the night it snowed and rained so hard here—don't you remember how cold and wet it was the next day when you went to school?"

"I bet he started the very next day, though." David was very sure of it.

"Goody, goody–then he will be here tomorrow night maybe. How many baby lambs will I have this year?" Margaret was impatient.

"Figure that yourself. You're not a baby," was David's taunt.

"Son," admonished Mother, "can you tell her how you would go about finding the answer to that problem?"

"That's easy. She knows there are nine ewe lambs old enough to have lambs this spring, and they won't be having any twins."

"But Jack branded ten more lambs for me last year," Margaret reminded him.

"And do you know something, Missy? Only seven of those were ewe lambs to keep, and they aren't having lambs this year."

"Why did Jack kill those three lambs of mine, Mama?"

"I thought I explained that to you, Child. They were the kind we killed for meat. They would not be the ones to have little lambs, so why keep them? Besides, you had to have new shoes for school, and a coat and warm clothes for winter. They just about paid for those things. Remember, we killed and sold several others at the same time?"

"When those seven have lambs, will those others have some more?" Margaret was in a hurry for her number to equal the like number David was claiming.

"Silly, of course they will—next year."

"Mister Smarty, I bet you don't know how many lambs Jack will bring." She was eager to find something David didn't know.

"Just the same, I can figure it out."

"Before you do so, all three of you change your school clothes and do your chores. Susan, I believe can feed and water the chickens and gather the eggs. Margaret, you might get supper for us."

"Who is going to pack in the wood?" David wanted to know.

Before Mother could speak, Margaret piped up, "Getting wood is boy's work. Jack said so."

"Hush your fussing. We'll settle that question later. Right now, do what is expected of you. I have burned very little fuel this warm day and not washing. I believe one good big armload as you come in from chopping it, Son, will be all that is needed for the night." She read the rest of her letter in a hurry. There was still much work to done in the garden before sundown. *In fact, I won't be able to work out here too late. I will need to drop my hoe the second that daughter calls supper. There will be quite a lesson in arithmetic as well as geography.*

David ate fast so he could be at his bookkeeping. "'Member, Mother, Jack had 141 that first year he come back when we thought it would be 139. That was 45 lambs. When I add Margaret's nine lambs, that still won't make it come out right, for Jack only took down 39 lambs." His figures were smudged and hard to read.

"That would be right, Son, for I believe 16 of those were

wethers—butchered and sold here. But he did take down all 96 ewes. Yet there were but 91 to bring lambs next spring. Do you know how that came about?"

"Sure. Grandpa sold those old ewes and bought bucks. And there were 100 percent lambs just the same, so Jack brought back more than 220 last spring. And he took down almost as many last fall."

"That was because we did not butcher them here. I believe Grandfather wrote they sold all the meat animals, and he bought nearly the same number of ewe lambs."

"But that's only 140 to have lambs this spring then."

"And that will be quite a few, won't it?"

All 'em counted together makes more than 360. That will be a lot."

"Do you know that this year, Jack is also bringing back something of far more value than several lambs?" She had all their attention at once. None could think there could be anything more worthwhile than those lambs.

"Is it the burro that packs Jack's bed and grub?" David was sure that must be important, for otherwise he could not make the trip.

"Not the burro, though he is valuable too. It is the heifer-calf Jack took down two and a half years ago nearly. She is three years old now, and a fine big cow. She'll soon be a milk cow."

"Has she a tiny calf, Mama?" Susan wanted to know. The event of a new calf less than two months ago had been something special to her.

"Not yet, but I expect she will find one as soon as she gets here. David, I want you to be the one to water her, give her salt, and handle her so she'll be used to you. When she freshens, you'll be the one to milk her."

"Can I milk her all alone?" It bothered him he could never manage to strip the cow they now had.

"If she is as easy a milker as her mother was, you'll be able to. This one you have been learning on is a hard milker."

"I can milk her every bit as good as David can." Margaret wanted in on this. "Why can't I milk the heifer?"

"Milking is boys' work. You know Jack said that too."

"Now stop fussing for a second. I want all of you to learn to milk, but let it be one at a time. It is better for the cow. I know

Jack thinks it is boys' work, but that is because he was reared in one of these western states, and he had no sisters, I believe. So he and his brothers learned to milk. Their mother would have been much too busy—cooking, washing and sewing for that large family."

"But you do the milking," cut in Margaret, "and Daddy doesn't, yet he was born in Colorado."

"Which is true. But your father never owned a cow—didn't even live on a ranch so he could learn. That makes a big difference. It is the same way with which country you were born in whether it is men's or women's work to do the milking. Some places, women and girls do all the milking, and let the men do the heavier work. In some countries, they have few cattle. What animals do you think they milk?"

"Goats." David had learned about that in his reading.

"Not only goats, but sheep and camels. And there are places where they milk reindeer. That is up in the far north where those animals can survive. I'm sure that would be a man's work, though there might be some that are gentle."

"You know something?" David was pensive. "Jack said once there was a baby near starving and they didn't have any milk for it, but a mama burro had a baby and one of the men milked some of that burrow's milk and fed that baby and it didn't hurt it none."

"Of course it wouldn't hurt the baby. I believe most all milk must be good. There might be some that have a different taste that we would not like, not being used to it, but think how fat and healthy little animals get on their mother's nurse. When I was your age, I can remember my grandmother telling the same thing happening to a hungry little one and they milked one of the mares. That is a mama horse that has a colt. Then a few years later, I learned that in some country where they have lots and lots of horses and no cattle, they milk them just like we do our cow, only they would not give as much milk as a cow will."

"You still haven't said if it is girl's work to chop the wood and bring it in." That work wasn't to Margaret's liking.

"No, I haven't come to that yet. Sawing and chopping wood isn't easy. Carrying it in is easier, even Susan can be doing that most of the time. If Margaret gets our meals for us and spends some of her time learning to sew and wash, David can take care of the wood. When it comes to getting the winter's big supply, your dad will have to stop his mine work long enough to help with that."

"When I get big, I'm not going to work in any mine," David stated. "I'm going to have a ranch just like Grandpa's, only I'm going to have a saddle horse to ride."

Mary smiled. "I must have been about your age when my greatest wish was for a saddle horse."

"Didn't you have one to ride?" David was puzzled because Grandpa seemed to think of everything else.

"Not until I was grown. See, in the east, there were not so many saddle horses. We had driving horses instead. But the first six months I lived in this state, I had the loan of a pretty good saddle animal and I learned to ride."

"Couldn't you have bought it and had it all the time?"

"The horse was not for sale, Margaret." The door opened, and John coming home for supper put an end to further discussion. "If you have homework, Son, you'd better get at it. Susan and I will clear away these dishes while you make sure your father's supper is hot before you dish it," she told Margaret.

The next evening, just before supper time, Jack arrived. The meal was left to tend itself as each excited child dashed out to help corral the sheep. "How many lambs are there," chorused all three.

The tired old fellow grinned at Mary before answering. "Now, I can't say right off hand, seeing I haven't counted them for a week. Been too busy getting 'em here all in one bunch. But when I started, your Grandpap figured we were one lamb short of 100 percent crop." He untied the leg-weary cow from the burro's tail. "I was afraid this one was going to give me a calf before we made it home."

"I know how many lambs there is then." David reached for the cow's rope. "There must be 139 instead of 140."

"Not so fast, Son," Mary cautioned. "See how leg weary she is and heavy with calf? Let her move slowly. As soon as you have her tied in the barn, we'd better eat supper. Jack, you must be more than hungry and more than tired." She moved along beside him and the girls toward the house.

"Jack, did every one of my big lambs have a little one?" Margaret had waited as long as she could to ask.

The wrinkled, sun-tanned face screwed up in pretended

thought. "I believe every last one of 'em did. If we find any that don't have lambs, we can find orphans for 'em, now can't we?"

"Can I go with you so I can find me a lamb?" Susan felt left out.

"Sure. Come Saturday when you don't have school, all three of you can scout out to find bummers. Ought to have plenty of milk around here soon." He saw John enter the kitchen from the other door. "Hi. How goes the mining world?"

According to John, things were looking good and the conversation was not all about lambs. Knowing he had powder, caps and fuses enough to last for a month is what fed John's enthusiasm.

David was very thoughtful as he went to the barn to help with the work there. "Mother, do you think there is any other kind of work Dad will ever do but prospecting and sinking shafts?"

"I'm afraid not, Son. A dozen years ago, I thought any able bodied man could learn to do more than one kind of work and take pride and pleasure in doing it. But now I'm not so sure. This prospecting must be like the work men do on boats. Those that follow the sea never seem content to work on land any more. Some of them leave their families for a year at a time, just so they can do that kind of work." She did most of the milking this evening, leaving the boy free to pet and curry the heifer.

"I'm going to learn to pitch hay this summer. Last year, Jack said I wasn't tall enough, but he can't say that now. I'm near as tall as he is. I gotta learn sometime. Jack is getting plenty old. I think I'd better help him take those sheep down this fall so to learn that trail." He sounded so grown up for an eleven year old. Then the next moment, he spoke like the child he still was. "Do you know something? I think this heifer kinda likes me."

The days got busier as they lengthened and became warmer. As long as school was open, Mary planned the laundry so the children could take back a few loads each day. The cent she paid them for each small package they carried was an inducement. In fact, she needed to limit Margaret's load always. *I believe that girl would try to carry them all, just to earn the money.*

This day, she planned to go herself. *I want to pay that last $5.00 to Mr. Knollen—then I will feel freer.* Only she found that she felt sad, not free. The frail man was unsure of his step as he tottered from the cabin and thrust the yellowed page from his ledger into her hand instead of trying to write his name. *Makes me wish I had more money to give him,* was her thought as she trudged on to Upper Town with her burden.

On her trip to town the next day, there were men about the cemetery. Knowing they must be busy digging a grave, she wondered idly who passed away. At noon, the men came to their well for water to drink, and she took fresh buttermilk out to them.

"Frightful hard digging, it is," spoke one as he accepted the glass. "An' the hottest day so far this season." He mopped his streaked face.

"Who is it that has passed away?" Mary asked as the last man took his.

"Old man Knollen. And it's a sad day for all of DeLamar. Weren't a finer guy than him. Everyone liked him. And it was rotten whiskey that killed him."

"And is Dr. Tom hopping mad," said another. "Less than two years ago, he warned the bunch of us not to be so free with the bottle, but to slip Knollen grub, fuel and the things he needed."

"Yeah, none of us gave him that rot gut," said the first man. "Somehow he got a five spot, and he got two fifths. If old Hank had been hoppin' bar, he might have handled it differently, lettin' him carry away only the one."

As soon as the men were back to their toil, Mary Marcus was on her way to town. *I must let Dr. Tom know it was me who paid Mr. Knollen that money so he won't blame someone else.* The only stop she made was to hand Lew his jar of buttermilk, but there was no way to get away without hearing Lew's version of Mr. Knollen's death.

"Do you know—I think that old fellow got tired of livin' and sorta planned it all just that way. We all know Knollen never was much of a goose hound. I kinda think Doc thinks the same thing, but of course, he wouldn't say it."

Mary hurried on as soon as she politely could. "Come in, Mary Marcus. I must say, you fail to look ill this day. Are looks deceiving?" was Dr. Tom's greeting.

"I'm not sick, Doctor, and have no big troubles to unload on your shoulders this day, except I wanted you to know it was me that gave Mr. Knollen the $5, so you wouldn't think some of the men had carelessly done so. It was the last few dollars of a loan made more than a dozen years ago."

"Sit down and relax, even for a minute. That's better now. Let us talk this thing over. I take it you got the idea was riled over all this." He shook his head slowly. "The men were upset, not me. Sometime back when the kind old fellow came near death from too much drink, I suggested the men not be too free with their bottles—it would be better to get him food and necessities of life. But I did not say then, and will not now, that he drank that much for this very purpose." Dr. Tom was relaxed. "Because everyone liked him, they would have gladly furnished him with a living, but John Knollen wanted no charity. As I understand it, he had always been on the other end of the giving. I am sure it's harder for people like him to be on the receiving end."

"I just feel terrible that I was the means of him doing away with himself. I felt awfully sorry for him when I paid him that money—he seemed so weak then."

"Don't feel that way about it. You merely repaid money once borrowed. If all those he helped through his long life had done the same, he might still be breathing. Just be happy your debt is paid. You are in no way to blame with how he spent his money. So forget it. How goes life in general at the Mills House—busier than ever, I dare say?"

"That is right. We didn't have enough lambs in the bunch to suit Jack and the children, only something like 140, so they still go out scouting for more bummers. The last count I had was 17 orphans."

"That Jack is quite a guy. I hear sheep and wool have come up a bit in price. I expect there is nothing that would please Jack more than to see you the sheep queen of these hills."

"And that is something I never could be, of course." Mary now was ill at ease. There was something she wanted to ask Dr. Tom, but didn't know how to go about it. So instead, she visited for some moments before broaching the subject.

"Dr. Tom, there is something I have wanted to ask you for some time. You can tell me it's none of my business, but then Jimmy Burch connected my name with yours and Leatha Orchard's misunderstanding, as if I was in some way mixed up in it. It set me to thinking I might have said something to cause trouble. I sure hope not."

There was quite a hearty laugh from the man. "Leave it to that Jimmy to hatch up something farfetched. Of course, you are not in the least way responsible for Leatha's and my affairs. I won't say her rudeness that day wasn't an eye-opener to me, for it was. And she was very contrite afterwards over it. She was all for apologizing to you later." A broad smile crossed his face. There is no sting in the remembrance of that unhappy day.

"I suppose since neither us saw fit to explain the true state of affairs, the gossipers would have to come up with some answer to the riddle—from the sublime to the ridiculous. While the real reason was simple, they would overlook that. I simply figured out I would make a very poor puppet—one of those dolls dressed in different costumes and yanked about by a string." An amused smile was his reward for all his pantomime. "I was always under the impression that the less said the sooner things were forgotten. Could be I was wrong in this case."

"You were as far as Jimmy Burch is concerned." A slight grimace. "I believe that man wants to be in on all the tidbits more than anyone I know."

"Sometimes you and I have very much the same thoughts." Dr. Tom allowed himself this much range of comment.

"And I'm thinking it will be much more profitable for me to be home and to work than bothering you. My work never does itself while I'm off gadding or blabbing," was her parting wit.

Chapter Thirty Seven

MARY GATHERED UP HER few purchases and the roll of papers Father never failed to send. Along with the many sacks of laundry, she had a pretty good load, but she hurried away while Jimmy Burch was busy. *I don't want him offering to drive me home* was her thought now. *I will have to stop and tell Lew that I cannot take back those empty milk jars like I had planned. I'm sure the children will prefer to carry them instead of these dirty, smelly clothes.* She had paused to tell the livery man about her change in plans, when she caught sight of the heads of Jimmy's driving team rounding the curve coming from Upper Town. "Can I use your private foot-bridge?" She was half way the length of the stable while still asking.

Lew still sat on his heels against the barn with an amused grin on his tanned face when Jimmy paused. There never had been any real liking between these two men, although they spoke amicably enough. They did just that for a minute or two. Jimmy finally got fidgety, and asked. "Didn't I see Mary Marcus here just the instant before I reached here?" Lew squinted up at him without answering. "If I remember right, she had a load of heavy bundles. I'm driving down the creek, and could just as easy give her a lift with that load."

"The way she hot-footed it through the stable and across the foot bridge the instant she saw your team poke their noses in sight—it don't look like she was wanting a lift." Lew was enjoying this.

"Would she be over visiting your wife?" A bit of red mantled his face.

"She never has that I know of." Lew's manner was obtuse.

"Can you kindly tell me where she went so I can offer her the courtesy?"

"I have no way of knowing where she went. The way it looks to me is that woman doesn't like all the yakity-yakity that gets spread around this damn gossipy camp. Did you ever stop to think of that?" He watched the flush of anger spreading down to Jimmy's white collar.

Jimmy could see no wrong in being friendly with an old friend, and being as helpful as he knew how to be. He had ceased to consider himself a married man since Laura persisted in living in Boise these many years. *Dame rumor* had it that Mary Marcus did not consider herself a wife either. To his way of thinking, they were free to do as they wished. If he could once be sure where he stood in this woman's esteem, he would gladly file for divorce.

It was not to his liking to have this nincompoop chewing his every last straw and passing judgment on his actions and intent. Jimmy wheeled his team about and headed back the way he came, not wanting to give Lew the satisfaction of an answer.

This was something Mary was not apt to ever hear about. She would have been very thankful, had she known it this day, for she was at her wit's end to know how to discourage Jimmy's attention without being rude. *It isn't so much what he says as it is the way he says it. It's never anything to get mad about—in fact he is always the perfect gentleman—just too much so, I guess.* The path on this side of the stream was anything but easy to travel. *If I had known it was this steep and brush-grown, I don't know that I would have tackled it this day with such a heavy load.*

Having to pause and rest often, Mary was able to keep tabs on the rigs going along the road on the opposite side. In places, she had a good view of the road, yet she was screened by the brush. Not seeing Jimmy's grays, she wondered if he had guessed she had given him the dodge. *Maybe he'll take the hint without me having to tell him in so many words that his attention is unwelcome.* Resting several minutes before leaving the path to come down to the last bridge, she heard sheep bells. *Now, that could be Jack coming. Also, it could be any one of a dozen different bands of sheep on that trail.*

Nearing home, she heard the bells again. *They sound as loud here as they did back there.* Mary knew this would be the direction Jack would take if it was their sheep. Feeling sure it must be Jack, she hurried faster. *I'd better have the chores done and supper going. If the children hear those sheep bells, they won't be home 'til the band comes in.* Going to the wood house for chips to build the fire, she was sure now it was their sheep nearing home. She hurried to gather eggs and feed the hens. *Eight eggs! That means eggs for breakfast in the morning.* Then she was off to the cellar on a trot for cream to add to the dried corn she had soaking and cooking most the day. She hunted until she found the last glass of chokecherry jelly she had hidden. This she slipped into her apron pocket and reached for a jar of pickled

beets. *Pshaw! I don't want that. Jack doesn't like beets.* She
carried the last jar of sauerkraut to the house instead, putting this
to simmer with shreds of bacon.

"Mama! Mama! Jack and the sheeps have come," called
Susan racing along the porch and in the open door. "Come see
'em, Mama. There is so many lambs--little and big ones. More an'
two, three hundred of 'em." There was nothing to do but go to the
porch and see them dotting the greening hillside. "Hain't there
lots of 'em?"

"Yes Dear, there is getting to be a good sized band. Better
than 500 all told." She had been doing some rapid figuring
herself. David and Margaret were riding the burro and waved to
her. Then she caught sight of Jack seated. He was resting to let the
sheep feed a while yet. "Susan, how about you and I surprise
those two by getting in all the wood and chips before they get
here?"

"Then can I go help drive 'em in the corral?"

"Yes, you can help do that; we'll have plenty of time. Notice
how Jack is resting and letting them eat the grass? They must be
very hungry." Mary and Susan hurried to gather kindling, then
Mary went to milk the cow. Margaret was the milk-maid this year,
but Mother was sure the ten year old girl would forget this once.

For some unexplained reason, John came home early and
chaffed at the delayed supper. "Looks like you would get those
youngsters in here to help you a little," he told her, watching her
rush around with still no meal on the table. Seldom did he speak
directly to her, so this in itself was a novelty.

"Oh! They do help—really well; all the time. But this is an
occasion for them—something like the gala the Swiss Villages put
on when their herds come down from the mountains. Only it is the
other way around for us."

She could not make out the disparaging remark he made about
the *stinking varmints* as he lit another match, picked up the roll of
papers, and went into the other room to read. What he said did not
trouble her anymore—just so he did not say such things in the
children's hearing. And she had to admit he was better about
remembering that lately.

"Oh! Mother, I forgot about to milk." Margaret burst into the
room. "Susan just now told me you did the milking."

"I was afraid you might forget, but the poor cow didn't. By

the time I commenced, she was dripping a steady stream of milk. How are you, Jack?" She smiled at the weary old man limping in. "I shouldn't need to ask, when I can see you are just worn to a frazzle. Sit right down here." Mary pushed the easy chair for him to drop into. The next second, she placed a bowl of warm water on a chair for him to wash without moving. "Now you don't need to stir a step. I'll have supper on the table in no time, and we can bring it right to you." She placed soap and towel handy.

The excited noise of the happy children filled the room. Their many questions interfered with the tired man eating his meal. "David, Margaret and Susan—not one more question until after supper. I know how you want to know all about the trip—I do too. I also want to know all about how Grandpa and Grandma are, but I'm not going to ask Jack until after he has eaten. In fact, I think it a good plan to wait until morning."

"Oh, but Mama we'll be in school and can't ask him then." That was too much for Margaret, who needed to know about everything.

"I am a bit tuckered out—that's a fact," nodded Jack.

After the meal, Mary noticed that Jack could hardly hobble into the next room. She hurriedly set the two girls to washing the dishes. "David, I have a job for you." When the tall lanky boy came back to the kitchen, she put the big white washbowl into his hands. "This warm soapy water will feel good on Jack's tired sore feet. You see if he won't let you help him get his shoes and socks off, and let his feet soak awhile." She turned to get the bottle of rubbing alcohol to take in, with a towel and a clean pair of soft white socks.

"Mother you should see the bottoms of his feet—they are all raw." David paled at the thought of how sore they must be.

"Then you won't want this bottle. I'll find the ointment and some soft pieces for bandages. Just let them soak as long as he'll let them, Son. Don't attempt to dry them—the rubbing will hurt. I'll be in soon to help you fix them up."

"Jack is not going to be able to walk on those feet for a week at least. I'm staying home from school and herd those sheep." Mary could see his maturity in saying this, and nodded.

"Pretty near like old times," was Jack's comment as Mary seated herself on the floor and commenced to smear the ointment on a piece of cloth for each foot before wrapping the bandages.

"How many years ago was that, anyway? My mind is a bit fuzzy tonight. I can't seem to think straight."

"It will be eight years this winter. No wonder you can't think straight, Jack, you are so over tired. Don't you try walking on these feet. Let John and David push your chair into your room. You and I know from past experience that these sore feet will heal much faster if you stay off of them." Carefully, she pinned the last bandage.

"Tain't right for the boy to stay out of school," muttered the weary man as David moved the light weight chair and him toward the bedroom.

"Won't bother my studies one bit. Sis can bring my books home and I can get those old lessons every night before I go to bed. You'll see." He was surprised that Jack needed help to get his clothes off.

Mary scooted the girls to bed, and soon climbed the stairs herself. She was not worried about David having to stay out of school; he seemed to have no trouble making up his work. She was sure that she herself could herd the sheep, but that would trouble Jack the more. Besides, she must be around the house to have meals cooked and wait on him, or he would be up and doing for himself.

In the morning, it was Margaret that balked at the arrangement. "If David is going to stay out of school to herd 'em today, then I get to tomorrow." She loved to find excuses to not go to school. Not until she was assured she could take her turn on Saturday and Sunday did she go willingly.

While Margaret, with Susan's help, herded the sheep the two days, David with his mother's help, rolled more rocks into the small gulch stream, and tramped in the dam so water would be ready for garden and field. "I always thought I could put this dam in if I had to," David told her as he sat down to empty his boots of water before walking to the house. "I've watched Jack do it enough to know how. But the hardest work is keeping the ditch cleaned out so the water won't break it."

"We must remember, Son, to take the band out directly north from the corral and bring them in that way at night. Since the ditch there is more on the level, they won'kick in so many rocks and loose soil like they do along this knoll."

"Mom, with Jack laid-up this way, we better not bother about any bummers this year, do you think?"

"Might be just as well we didn't. Having only the one cow, we won't have a great surplus of milk, even after that calf gets made into veal. What we do have can always be made into cottage cheese and sold or eaten like we used to. There need be no waste."

Mary was glad this little job was done, though it had taken most of Sunday to finish it. "I wonder if should sell that calf unbutchered, then Jack won't think he has to do that job. I want to keep him off those feet until they are healed, but we could use that meat now."

"If I knew how, I'd tackle that job." David was slow to offer. "But I'm not sure I could even kill that calf." His face showed repulsion with the thought. "Are you still glad you sold that other cow for a beefer last fall?"

"Yes Son, I'm glad. I still think it was wise; that wasn't a good buy I made. With her drying up so early like she did, she wouldn't have been a profitable cow to winter through. We would hardly have had enough hay to winter them both. And we must always have some extra hay on hand, for there might be a late snow in the spring or an early one in the fall, and the sheep might have to be fed a day or two." It was turning real cool now. The gathering clouds could mean snow just as easily as it could rain.

The ground was white by the time Mary and David got the sheep that evening. Jack, still unable to walk, was fretting. "Now you just stop your worrying," Mary told him sternly. "What I want to ask you is this—if the storm gets worse, should we open up the barn and the shed and let them go under shelter?"

The troubled man shook his head. "They might better be in the corral. There won't be any hungry lambs then. The barn won't hold more'n half, an' that shed bein' as open as it is, they're sure to pile up in a corner. They're going to get wet, sure. But that hain't hurtin' 'em. You say you have plenty hay, and that's what's going to count if this lays on for a few days."

"You and I know it can do just that. That is another reason why you must stop this fretting. I want you to be clear headed to tell us the best thing to do. At the rate it is coming down right now, I would say none of the children will be going to school on the morrow. That means there will be four of us to feed them. We could hand feed each of those lambs individually if need be." She got no answer from Jack.

At nine o'clock, Mary and David, lanterns in hand, made the rounds. "Look at those big flakes coming down." The boy admired them in the lantern light.

"That means it is getting warmer, Son." She was surprised at how little the sheep seemed to mind the snow. The ewes were placidly chewing their cud. At midnight, she went out alone and reported back to Jack. "The snow seems to be falling straight down—no wind at all."

"That's good," said the old fellow. "No danger of 'em piling up tonight. How deep would you say it is right now?"

"Not more than three or four inches. It's packing down as it falls—it seem so, anyway,"

"Yeah, it could be raining by morning." Jack settled in for a sleep.

Daylight showed a white world. A foot of snow was on the ground and it was still snowing. Mary and the children shoveled long paths, putting the hay out on the white shelf above it. The snow powdered the hay as fast as they strew it along. The hungry animals ate it well. Mary could see some of the precious feed getting trampled underfoot and wasted. *But that must be expected,* she told herself.

By nightfall, with the sheep back in the corral after their second feeding, the skies were clearing and it was getting cold. Again Mary sought Jack's advice. "I know you have said big sheep can stand a lot of cold if they are dry and have enough to eat. But these are wet and that corral is wet. Should we scatter enough hay so they can bed down? Wouldn't it help the lambs more?"

"The hay on the inside of their paunches helps 'em more." He shook his gray head. "You would be surprised how much cold those lambs can stand with their stomachs full of milk and their mothers to huddle against. Sometimes I believe they can stand just about as much as the shorn ewes. They'll have to be fed tomorrow, remember. Should be some bare ground by night if no more snow comes." As Jack predicted, tiny patches of ground poked through the next evening.

"Yup, they'll be able to find some feed by tomorrow, but they'll wanta scatter then." Jack was more than troubled. "They're always a bother after being penned up for a few days with feed. With the snow covering part of the ground, they'll just ramble in search of more grass."

"There you go fretting again. I say stop it! We have come through so far without the loss of even one lamb. I figure to go out with David tomorrow just so they won't have any chance to get away from us. I'll set the girlies to baking and cooking so there will be plenty of food. Do you know, we have eaten nearly double the amount of food these last few days? Of course everyone has been working."

"Everyone but me," lamented the old fellow. "Still I eat like a horse. Hungry all the time seems like."

"You have been working that brain of yours overtime I'd say." Smiling, she fluffed up his pillow. "And I know that is the hardest kind of work. Could you stand a glass of milk and a sandwich or handful of cookies if there are any left?"

His face brightened. "I sure could handle that all right. Must have had a powerful lot of wrinkles to fill out. Don't you come toting in that sack—let some of the others do it. Tain't right for you to be waiting on me hand an' foot this way again."

"Just feet this time, Jack. Your hands are okay." She was pleased she could jolly him out of his worries.

The second morning, Margaret was again stalling about going to school. "I can't see any use of going today. There is only this one day this week."

"More reason you should go, Dearie. You haven't opened your books once. You have four days of lessons to makeup, remember. Better bring your books back again tonight to study some over the weekend. Do not try to bring down any laundry, but do stop with this letter, and then bring home any mail there might be. There should be a letter from Grandpa. He and Grandma will be worried about this snow. That is why I want this letter to be sure to be mailed—letting them know we didn't lose one lamb."

Mary had let David leave alone with the sheep this morning, saying, "I'll be along with our lunches later. I must get some washing done and on the line first. We are out of towels, and Jack will need his clothes most anytime now, so I'd better get them clean. I will leave dinner partly ready so your father can get it easily for him and Jack. Do be careful now," had been her parting advice.

Now, as she climbed the slopes in the warm mid-morning sun, she found three ewes and their lambs in a fold of the hills. *Maybe they are but the tag-end of the herd,* was her first thought as she edged them on before her. But on topping that rise and seeing the distance between them and the band, *This must be what Jack meant about their scattering.* Knowing it would bother David if he knew he had accidentally left these behind, she was hoping she could get them back into the herd without him knowing about it.

David, perched atop the ridge, had already seen her and the moving lighter dots ahead, and guessed what had happened. Walking at an angle, he came to meet her. "Gee, Mother, did I leave those?" He could not see how that could happen when he had tried to be so careful.

"They must have found that choice spot of feed and just preferred to stay right there out of sight instead of coming on with the band. I rather expect that is the easiest way to lose a small bunch. Jack knows sheep pretty well and he said they would scatter badly after being penned up and fed. Ten chances to one, he has had them pull just such tricks on him more than once. That is how he learn, Son. I put our lunches up separately again, so you can be on one side of them and me on the other, and we can eat when we want." She smiled as she saw the hungry boy wolf down a fat sandwich.

I'm glad I put those two extra ones into his package, she told herself as she slowly climbed on.

From the top of the ridge, she had a good view. This balmy spring day was pleasant. She hunted up a flat rock to sit on since the ground was so wet still. *What's that saying Sherman was supposed to have said? More rain, more snow and mud; the more grass grows.* This was the first time she had ever been to the very top of this barren ridge. In her ramblings for chokecherries and elderberries her first autumn here, she had never expected to find any this high. *But I do believe that wild rose bush just below me here is that same one I reached that terrible windy day just before that storm. The same day we had to kill Roan Cow.* She turned her thoughts away from the sad aftermath of that storm. *I want to think only pleasant thoughts this nice spring day. Just look at everything turning green. Why, there are even wild flowers right under my feet.* She had needed to look closely to tell they were flowers, they were so tiny. A few hundred yards' walk, and she could look east and see the mining dumps dotting the top of the hills above DeLamar. To the north, a higher ridge blocked any long view the same as to the west. This was a more gradual slope, and in a few places, she could see the faint line, which was the road they had traveled as they left on their travels to Nevada, Arizona and California. *Yes and we came back over that same road, more happy to get back than we had been to leave.*

As she seated herself to eat her lunch, she thought of all the mountains she had expected to climb when first she came here. *I expect this is about as high a point I'll ever spend the time or energy to climb, so I'd better enjoy it.* She did not bemoan her lot, but realized there were many things that didn't work out as planned. *I didn't imagine then that my marriage would be the way it is either. I guess one can't have everything. I have good children.* They were a solace to her. *I know I can make a living for them until they are able to do so for themselves. We are almost out of debt except to Father and Mother. I don't know if I'll ever feel square with them for all they have done.*

Then came the thought of the need to hire a man to help Jack take the sheep to the Flats in the fall. *It is either that or let David stay out of school. Of course he is all for that. He wants to learn the trail, and I know he will be learning it, as well as how to better handle sheep in driving them. But it would be the week going down, and another week before he would get back perhaps, for I wouldn't want Father to make a hurry-up trip into Caldwell the very next day to speed him home.*

I suppose the reason why I hesitate to buy him a saddle horse is the fact that Father would have another animal to feed. And then, for all the good it would do, David would be riding down with the sheep when he would be needed the most. Maybe I will have to do like Mother always says when she is in doubt—don't cross all the bridges that aren't yet built in this state. Glancing down at the sheet of newspaper she had wrapped about her lunch, she saw the account of more proposed bridges across Snake River. *Let's see. They already have one new one, but that isn't where it helps Father. I know it would be more pleasant for those living on the Flats to have a bridge to drive across instead of depending on the ferry. When the wind prevents the boat landing on one side or the other, it's no fun to sit and wait by the hour. I know, because that happened once when Father and I were crossing.* That had been the time she had gone in to own to buy her wedding things.

There is one thing I must remember from now on—Margaret

cannot stay out of school. It is so hard for her to go back after missing even a day or two. I wonder if I was that way when I was her age, but school was so close for me, there was never the need to miss. I don't like the idea of all three going every day regardless the weather, but I do think they'll have to have snow shoes all around. We'll try it this year.

With the price of sheep and wool up, we can afford good light-weight webs for the children. Jack thinks the fighting and talk of war over in Europe is a factor in the better price. I don't like to think we are gaining at other people's miseries. My, it must be heart sickening to the Cornish people in town to know their relatives and friends are in the thick of it.

Then came another disturbing thought. *There are several people in town and scattered through these hills, that were born in Germany. It is going to be as bad or worse for them.* All this war news was disturbing, but it filtered in so slowly up in these hills that it seemed far away. Little did most of them guess how soon the sinking of the *Lusitania* would be flashed all over the world, and then the speculation of how soon the USA would be drawn into the conflict, filling the newspapers and the minds of mankind.

Chapter Thirty Eight

THIS COLD RAW OCTOBER day, Mary Marcus admitted to everyone that she was tired. The mad rush to get Jack and David off with the sheep in good shape had taken its toll. "Now that they are on their way, perhaps we can settle down to something like our regular routine again." She told Margaret after they had hurriedly snatched the last of the clothes from the line.

"What I don't like is having to do David's chores and my own too." Margaret did not mind working as long as she felt everyone else was doing their work. David had gone last fall, so she could see no reason why she shouldn't have been the one to go this year. "How long did you tell David he could stay down this time?"

Her mother was almost too tired to talk. "I didn't say as to the number of days, my Dear."

"What if he don't come home for two whole weeks like last year?" To the eleven year old girl, that was an endless time. As she received no response from Mother, she considered all the nice things David might be in on. "I suppose he'll get to ride in Mr. Simmon's automobile again—the one that took him to Caldwell so Grandpa didn't have to make the trip. Someday I'm going to have enough money to go down to Grandpa and Grandma's place all by myself and stay all summer like they asked me to." She paused long enough to take the stack of folded towels and put them away.

"Last year David brought home a gramophone and flashlights for all of us. I wonder what he'll bring this time."

"A saddle horse," piped up Susan. "He said that is what he's going to buy."

"Silly, he can't buy a saddle horse. They cost lots of money. And besides, he'd have to leave it down there for Grandpa to feed."

Margaret gave a weary sigh after each armload of clothes. "It's the same as it was last year: Work, work all the time. We won't have any more dressings than we had last year, no pretty curtains up to our windows like other people do."

Mother roused herself enough to say. "With a bit more practice on the sewing, Dear, you will be able to make curtains. We'll get the material as soon as you finish piecing that last dozen blocks for your quilt. Remember we need more bedding. The quicker you finish those few blocks, the sooner we'll be able to get it made into a warm quilt." She did not add that it had been this way for more than fourteen years. Necessary things had to come before those they could do without.

A week later, after a full day's washing, Mary found herself exhausted again. *I'm pretty lazy when I can't do an ordinary day's work.* "Margaret, before you take off your jacket, take this basket and bring in all the clothes that are dry from the line, please. I'm afraid it will rain any minute. Susan, those chickens need both feed and water, I'm sure. Be careful when you gather the eggs so you won't break them." She saw that the child was none too keen about doing this regular chore, so she held out as an inducement, "Afterwards, you might cook supper if you like."

"Why can't Margaret cook supper? I want to play."

"Sister has the cow to milk, and before supper, she has to put away clean clothes that don't have to be ironed; and to make up all the beds. I pulled every one of them apart, and washed some of the blankets even." The child was slow to comply. "Run along now, Dear, those chick-biddies will be hungry and going to bed without their supper—it's getting dark."

"Two-three drops of rain just now wet my face." Margaret came in lugging the basket of fresh smelling clothes.

"Then you and I had better snatch in the rest before it gets worse." Mary had trouble getting to her feet and dumping the basket onto the couch where she had been seated. "It isn't good for clothes to whip all night in any kind of a storm." She needed to hurry, yet every fiber of her body wanted to rebel.

"What I don't like about this," nimble fingered Margaret was getting the half damp clothes off just as fast as Mother, "is having to hang 'em up again in the washroom." Together they carried the heavy burden in just ahead of the first real downpour.

"We got in just in time." Mary was at the door to take the pail of eggs from Susan as she dashed in. "Oh my, both you girlies were out with your school shoes on—you'll have to think to do so without being told. It seems when I get so tired, I can't remember everything."

"Mama, can we have eggs for supper? I found a whole nest full. Can I cook 'em all by myself?"

"Yes. We can have eggs for supper, but they take so little time to cook, they should be done the very last thing. We'll leave them up here safe until the rest of the meal is planned."

Susan understood what that meant and asked excitedly. "Can we have mashed potatoes, turnips and maybe applesauce?" These were her favorite foods to eat.

"That means a lot of peeling, Dear," said Mother as she built the fire.

"And I don't peel very good yet," lamented the child. "I peel 'em all too thick."

"We can have the applesauce. I can manage to peel those for you, and I'll show you again how to peel the turnips. How about having nice baked potatoes this once? Pick out enough of the same size, Dear. Take a good sized pan so you can bring all of them from the cellar at once." As she eased her spent body into the chair close to the kitchen table, she saw Margaret with a scowl on her face, going about the disagreeable work of hanging up those half dry clothes. "Don't bother with those now, Honey; they won't hurt now that they are in out of the storm. Some of them may be just right to iron. After supper I might feel like sorting them out. And Susan likes to hang up clothes for me. You'll have plenty to do getting all the beds made up. As you go to each room, take an armful of clothes to put away."

"You going to sleep in Jack's room all the time, Mama?"

"I doubt I could make it up the stairs tonight. Remember how tired I got last year for a little while after David and Jack left? But I got over it. I wish I would hurry up and do so now." She didn't worry about herself, but feared she was expecting too much of the children, and sought ways to make their work lighter.

After the evening meal, Mary forced herself to tend to the baskets of clothes waiting in the washroom, steadying the chair and Susan as she hung some of them on the high line over her head. "Now you can hop down, Dearie—that is the last big piece. All the rest are small things, and they can be put on the rack. You won't need to shake them—the wind has already done that for us." She left the 8 1/2 year old girl to finish this task and went back to the kitchen to wash the dishes. She had let Margaret iron, which was good experience for her. As Mary struggled to stand upright at the sink doing the dishes, she sighed, "I sure don't care to get this tired again right soon."

John put down his newspaper enough to ask, "Was anyone with a whip at your back making you work that hard?" His tone was too sarcastic to be thought concern for her well being.

"Necessity has the keenest lash, I believe," was her retort as she quit the room. There were more clothes to be folded. *Right now I don't care if they ever get done.* She went to bed.

Each day brought its added burdens: Soap to be made before winter set in; the last of the garden vegetables to be dug and stored. So worn was she now that she was glad there wasn't extra cabbage to be made into sauerkraut. *I must be lazy when I object to that bit of added work.*

By Thanksgiving, Mary was still not rested. *If Dr. Tom is in town, I believe I'll ask him for some ambition pills.* She could think in jest, but not smile about it. *I'm not sick. I don't have an ache or a pain anywhere. I would look silly reciinge all my imaginary ills to a stranger.* She had heard that another MD had come to take Dr. Tom's place while he was gone these months for a short course of studies. *It's nice for Dr. Tom that he can get away, but DeLamar must miss him.*

The change in DeLamar was not only Dr. Tom being gone— all the unmarried workers had been laid off. Some thought it was but temporary; others were of the opinion it was the forerunner of a general shut-down. "About out of ore," voiced some. "Oh, they have ore aplenty," Jimmy Burch had assured her the one time she had gone to town all fall, "but it is too low a grade to pay them to work it unless they can get cheaper power. The water question is bothersome still. This fighting across the pond is putting a big crimp in the finances to build the tunnel that was expected to drain away a lot of that water. Several million has been spent, and still hardly two-thirds the distance covered. If that were completed, and all those pumps didn't have to operate, they would have less overhead expenses."

This all sounded quite reasonable to her, but she couldn't have been less interested, the way she felt right now. The newspapers were so full of war news, she decided not to read anymore. *It's just too depressing, and there's nothing I can do to help or hinder it spreading.*

By Christmas time, Margaret and David were doing the laundry coming down from DeLamar. They were fewer, but their wish to earn some money for Christmas buying, and Mary's inability to get them done often, had made the shift. Now as March came, they were still doing the laundry on Saturday.

Faithfully, Margaret pressed out the shirts under Mother's supervision. None of them noticed that Mother talked less and less. Seeing her own clothes washed, ironed, mended and ready to put on was getting to be a rarity.

"This is not a nice April fool's joke," stormed Margaret. "I can't find one clean dud to put on. I'm not going to school with dirty clothes on."

"If you knew you had nothing clean, why didn't you wash some?" was her father's surprising question. "I've seen you do the washing as if you knew how."

"I do know how," snapped the girl. "And I'm going to stay home and do it this very day." She rather expected Mother to object to that, and was relieved that she didn't.

David, trudging to school alone through the mud this raw cold day, wondered why Mother said nothing against the girls missing school. Susan had seen her chance to skip too, with her promise to do all the dishes while Margaret did the washing. *Mother has been tired all winter,* was the puzzled boy's thought. *But from the amount of dirty clothes Margaret found, it don't look like Mother has washed for a month. So that can't be why she is so tired.* He could not understand all this. Once beyond the racetrack, he still had to take the path along the stream. The mud clung to his boots, but that was better than trying to find footholds in the packed snow. The sun was slow to melt on the north slope.

David was tired himself with the load of laundry he was bringing. It was a relief to be free of it upon reaching the store. He stood about for a moment, hoping that new clerk would take the hint to pay him for those packages. Jimmy Burch always did, but he was out to Boise just now. David fingered the plaid shirt he wanted to buy should the clerk take the hint. The one he had on wasn't very dirty, but it was getting too ragged to wear to school. As he left the store, a gang of boys was clustered about the bridge where the roiling water of the swollen stream lapped the planks.

"Betcha she goes out by night," was the verdict of one youth.

"Nah, no such luck," another said, thinking of the lark it would be if the bridge went out and they might not have school. To David, this appeared a near tragedy. *If it's out, I'll have to climb up above the mill, and all the same as crawl over that slope of ice to get home. It will take me 'til after dark to make it.* But at four o'clock, and the stout bridge still stood in spite of the water splashing at the planks, David heaved a sigh. *No need for me to have worried, I might have known they wouldn't have been building a weak bridge in the first place.*

There were no sacks of dirty clothes to pack down. The roll of papers and one letter from Grandma was all he could have. Jimmy still was not back, nor did David get paid. *I think that clerk is rather dull,* was his thought as he headed home. And home somehow seemed brighter and more cheerful as he came in this evening. Margaret was bustling about the kitchen; the clothes rack in back of the stove was filled with washed clothes to dry the faster; the lines in the washroom were likewise draped, and all the lines out of doors filled.

The good smell of a fresh baked cake greeted him. "I baked a cake all by myself." Susan squealed in defense as she tried to keep Margaret from dipping into the icing bowl she was cleaning out. "And I frosted it too." She gave the spoon another lick. "You have to pack in all the wood 'cause Bossy Cow hasn't had her calf yet, so you don't have to milk."

David said he expected to. He put the letter and roll of papers into Mother's hand. She took them without comment, and laid them on the small shelf above the sink, which was odd.

"Hurry up, Mother, and open the letter." Margaret, peeling the last of the small potatoes, was impatient. "I want to know when Aunt Annie is coming to visit us. Please hurry and read it to us."

"Cut it out, Sis." David could see Margaret's urgency troubled Mother. "The letter is Mother's; it's got her name on it. She will open it when she gets good and ready, and read it to us when she wants to and not before." David was worried, seeing her walk about aimlessly. He had not realized how sharp had been his voice. He went to the barn first to do those few chores. True, the cow still had no calf, but she needed hay and water and the barn cleaned. The meal was ready by the time he dumped his armload of wood in the box.

The only one talking much was Susan. Mother's silence had come on so gradually, none noticed it now. It was the same way with her not eating. She sat at the table, yet no food passed her lips. Often Mother had eaten her meals on the fly or after they had gone to school of a morning. Margaret was still miffed over the letter not being opened. After the meal and the two girls washed the dishes, Margaret's resentment took the form of clattering the dishes more as she washed them. "Are you aiming to break 'em so you won't have to wash 'em?" This was unexpected from Father, who seldom reproved them. He had come to the sink, then reached down for the paper to read.

Margaret said nothing, but she was less noisy. David had no studies to do, but he wished he did have. Life was not the same anymore. Mother sat so still, just smoothing out one of his ragged shirts with her hands as if she were thinking about patching it. Going to her and taking it from her hand, David said, "I don't think there is any use in you patching that. It's rotten and won't stay sewed. If they'd of paid me for that laundry today, I was in mind to get me a new shirt." As Mother said nothing, David was reminded that Mother did not talk about what they would buy in front of Father. It was generally more pleasant not to. *But I must remember to ask her before I leave in the morning.*

The family went to bed early this night, and most of them to sleep at once. None knew if Mother slept. In the morning, David awoke with a start. He could not believe he had been called, yet here it was getting late. He was still buttoning his shirt as he hurried to the kitchen. There was no fire going. Rushing through the cold dining room, he called. "Did you oversleep, Mother?" The door was not quite closed, and he could see the two girls stirring in the big bed. "How about you two rustle up some breakfast, and let Mother rest some more? I'll build the fire for you." He peeked in on Mother in the single bed, but he could not say for sure if she was asleep or not.

Once out at the barn, he did the chores in a hurry, not wanting to be late for school. *I'll not bother to take off my boots; have to wear 'em to school through that mud anyway.* He would carry his shoes along with him just like he did yesterday, but he did pause to clean the worst of the soil from them before coming in now. It was here on the west porch that Susan found him.

"Mama won't talk to me," sobbed the hurt child. "She won't say a word when we ask her something." David's dirty footgear was forgotten as he rushed past Susan and on to the bedroom. The early morning light was dawning. Margaret, in wide-eyed terror, was asking Mother over and over if she was sick.

"Stop badgering her, Sis. Can't you see she is sick and not able to answer?" He spoke crossly. To Father coming to the doorway he demanded, "Can't you do something? Call Dr. Tom. I know he'll come down. I just know he will." Fear was freezing him all up on the inside.

John Marcus had but little more experience in the case of sickness than these children of his. He was just as fearful, but was determined to not show it and add to their fright. The small alarm clock by the bed told it was not yet eight o'clock. "I don't suppose there is anyone in the store yet, but you can try telephoning 'em." John Marcus had used the telephone but once, but neither of the children had become familiar with its use.

David continued to ring the two long rings until the store did answer. It was the new clerk, and David, so fraught with fear by now, could only tell him to have Dr. Tom call Wagontown as soon as possible.

The morning passed with the household moving about in hushed dread. There was no thought of food at noon; the food Margaret had cooked in the morning was still uneaten. Father just sat there beside the bed, like he couldn't talk either.

The crying girlies, huddled in the kitchen, was too much for David, who was afraid he would be crying too. "I can't stand waiting for that telephone to ring when it don't. That dumb clerk maybe never told Dr. Tom. I'm going up there and tell him myself." As he said this, he wondered if he could walk that far, he felt so weak on the inside. Thinking it might be because he had not eaten, he grabbed a dish for some cold, mushy cereal with syrup, and gulped it down. He was soon on his way.

When John Marcus learned that David had gone, he berated himself for not thinking of to do so. *The trying to do something would be better than just sitting here doing nothing.* Those half-opened eyes were too much for him, and he went to the wood house and chopped wood furiously until the wood box was more than full. Then he was back at his post, watching for some sound or movement that would tell him Mary was conscious. He knew she must be still alive for there was a heartbeat and her hands were no colder than they had been. He looked up questioningly as David's white face came in, but it was Margaret following him who asked, "When will Dr. Tom come?"

"I don't know." The dispirited boy could hardly talk. "I couldn't find him. Nor could anybody tell me for sure where he was at, or I would have gone there. Guess he is somewheres a baby is being born."

"Then how is he ever going to know Mother is sick?" Margaret thought what a slim chance there was of Dr. Tom hearing about Mother, now that David was down here.

"I wrote two notes and tacked 'em on his doors, one at his office and one at his room. That landlady sure made me mad—she tried to stop me from doing that." David was in deep gloom. "She didn't like it 'cause my feet was all dirty. Said she'd tell him herself, but I went ahead and left the note anyway. She might forget, just like that dumb clerk did. Anyway, he wouldn't say for sure he told Doc."

David was afraid he was going to be sick, so he hurried to the barn, but there were no chores to be done. The cow's manger was full of hay and her stall was all cleaned. *She is supposed to be loose at a time like this.* He remembered Mother telling him that last spring when she calved, so he unsnapped the rope and left her free. She in turn rubbed her hornless head against his side while he petted her. "I don't know what you are wanting unless it's water." He picked up her bucket and went to the hydrant in the yard and filled it. This she soon emptied, and he again filled it. This she did not touch, but he left it for her to drink later. "Guess it must have been water you wanted." *Must have been Dad that fed you. He'd not think about water perhaps, but Sis would if she had been the one.* He could not remember his father ever having tended the cow before. Dreading to go back to the house and that endless waiting, yet fearing more to not be near and know how Mother was, he moved his wooden legs along the path, now dim in the gathering dusk. With an effort, he mounted the steps. As he opened the door, he heard Father's voice. Not until he was in the dining room and saw him did he realize he was answering the telephone.

"Yes," was his first word; then came, "No. I don't know what's wrong." Another short pause. "She hasn't spoken, so how would I know?" Fumbling, he put the receiver back in place, too stunned at Dr. Tom's anger, acting like John was to blame for her being sick.

"Is he going to come right away?" Margaret had to know that right now. Father was not answering, just walking back to the bedroom. She turned to David who looked very sick himself. "Do you think he'll come now that he knows?" David managed a nod before he rushed out of doors. The fresh air stayed the sick feeling in his stomach as he sat on the steps. Both girls followed him out, hoping he would say something to them.

After awhile he did just that. "Doc will come about as soon as he can. 'Course, there may be other sick people too. And that path is so slippery he can't ride too fast, but he'll get here." David pinned all his faith on that. The three of them stayed there until the chill of the night sent them indoors.

Chapter Thirty Nine

ONE LOOK INTO THOSE bleak faces stayed any anger Dr. Tom might have. John Marcus seemed more dazed than the children, moving away slowly to let him close; not speaking until questioned. The briefest examination told him he was none too soon. He had work to do, and fast. Just what had brought Mary Marcus to this state, he might learn later, or at least piece together the cause. There was no time now. Tersely, he barked his requests for water, spoon and hot water bottles. "If you have no hot water bottles, fill jars with hot water," he snapped. "Better put bricks or soapstone to heat. We'll need plenty of warmth about her." He was pleased to see John stir enough to do as directed.

It was Margaret who brought the first things asked for. With fingers still pressed to that thready, irregular pulse, he asked, "When did Mary take sick?"

"This morning when we got up, Mother wouldn't talk to us." It was half a cry.

This did not add up right, to Dr. Tom's thinking right now. "How long since she has eaten or drunk water?"

John, back in the room with two fruit jars of hot water, spoke. "I don't know that." He wondered if either of the children did.

"I'm sure Mother did not eat much supper last night." David paled again.

"And she didn't eat any dinner either." This was Margaret trying to remember. "She said she wasn't hungry the night before, don't you remember?" She appealed to David.

Dr. Tom was counting the seconds until time to give more stimulants. "Can any of you recall when she first complained of not being well?"

"She never said she was sick—just tired." David wondered if that meant Mother was sick all that time. His face whitened at the thought.

The Doctor was watching his patient, but he had glanced up. "About how long ago since she first mentioned being tired?"

"I noticed it when I came back after helping Jack take the sheep down to the Flats."

"But she was tired like that the year before and got over it." Margaret could not see where this being tired would make Mother sick now.

"Have you milk, broth or an egg handy?" He was massaging her throat now.

"I found one egg today." Margaret would have gone for it, but Dr. Tom stopped her.

"If there be but the one, Child, bring it to me very carefully. Also a cup or glass, a fork and another spoon." When these things came, he stopped rubbing her throat enough to break the egg and beat it just enough to liquefy, but no froth. "We'll see if some of this raw egg will slip down easy like." Slowly he spooned dribbles into her placid mouth. Much more massaging was needed to get even a small amount swallowed. "Next we will try coffee. It wouldn't be a bad idea to make a pot of coffee, John. I could do with a cup myself. I didn't stop long enough to eat supper."

This was something John knew how to do. He not only made coffee, but fried bacon, then cooked the cold potatoes. Margaret came out and set the table. Very neatly, she arranged everything on the new white oil cloth that covered table. David had bought that oil cloth with his share of the laundry money only last week. She put out bread, jam, and stewed prunes. The last slice of cake graced the center. But Dr. Tom did not come for several minutes after he was told it was ready. John had poured a cup of coffee, and knowing it was getting cold, sat down and tried to drink it himself.

"He's listening with that thing he puts in his ears," reported Margaret. "He says he'll come as soon as he hears her heart beat better."

Susan came into the lighted room, trying to find the right place on her own sturdy wrist with her fingers, like she had noticed Dr. Tom doing to Mother's. He loomed up just back of her. "Yes, I'll be glad of that coffee now," seeing the table ready. "And here you have a meal all fixed! Well I'm sure I can use that too. How about the rest of you—have you eaten?"

"Just coffee," answered John short like, wondering at how the man could expect he could eat.

"Better make it thicker than that, Man. There is more food here than I can eat; fall to and eat something. How about you girlies? Remember we all have to eat plenty. We are going to be busy taking care of your mother to get her well."

John tried to catch Doc's eye to learn if he was hopeful just for the children's benefit. When at last he did, he was not sure. Dr.

Tom ate rather quickly, taking his own cup of coffee back to the sickroom with him, along with one for the patient.

"Mother doesn't care much about coffee." The tense boy had trouble leaving the chair so Dr. Tom could sit there.

"Perhaps not, but we are giving it like medicine. Did you know that coffee will make your heart beat a tiny bit faster? And anything we know that will help your mother, we'll try." While he fed her coffee slowly, he explained to John, "This is the one thing you will have to do; others might be too impatient, and she could easily strangle. See how it is? When there is no muscle movement here in the throat, give no more until that is swallowed." Gently, he kneaded her throat. When he listened to the same irregular heartbeat, but his face cleared a bit. He might be mistaken, but he believed there was a bit more tone there. "Better get paper and pencil, and write down some of these things. It is now 9:30 and she has taken the bit of coffee. In fifteen minutes, it'll be time for these drops here." He tapped the tumbler he had measured the medicine into, diluted with water, covered it with a sheet of paper and weighted it down with the spoon. "I have written down the amount and how often. At ten o'clock we'll try a bit more of the egg; another half hour, more liquid. The idea is to get all the liquid down that we can."

Seeing David standing about so tense, Dr. Tom thought to give him something to do. "David, some chicken broth would be good for Mother. Do you think you could pick out a good hen to dress out?" Doc's keen ear heard that sharp intake of breath, and it was he who carried the slim youth to the cool porch just in time. After the violent retching had stopped, the two men carried him into the house, held him the short minute it took Margaret to spread a worn blanket over the couch. "Now we'll need more blankets to keep him warm. Slip off his outer clothes, John." He knew he'd better work fast to give the hypo needed while the two girls scurried for more bedding. As he finished the ordeal, he said, "Some more jars filled with hot water about this boy wouldn't be a bad idea."

"I better do that." John feared the girls might burn themselves in their haste.

"Alright," Dr. Tom spoke, then turned to Margaret tucking the bedding about David. "Will you now clear everything from the table, wipe the oil cloth clean and dry, and bring it to me? We'll

403

need that to protect your mother's bed." Before the table covering was brought to him, he had the full bed free of its bedding. On went the oil cloth, then a sheet, then another folded lengthwise across the bed. At his nod, Margaret understood and tucked in the other end, the same as he was doing. "Do either of you know where your mother's clean gowns are?"

Susan crowded past him to pull out the lower dresser drawer. "The only ones she's got are these pretty ones she won't ever wear." The child fingered the thin fancy garment's lace and ribbon trimming.

The tall weary man stooped to look. "They wouldn't be very warm, for sure, but this will be fine." He brought out the short dressing gown of soft trench flannel. *Now to get the two out from underfoot while I and John work.* "Do you happen to know where there would be worn sheets or blankets?" As the girls left and John came in, Doc directed him. "We need to shift your wife to that more comfortable bed, and we must do it with the least movement to her." While he spoke, he tore the faded housedress she had on along each side and snipped each sleeve and shoulder open. As she was lifted to the fresh bed, the lower half of the worn dress dropped away. The dressing sack served as a hospital gown on her hind side, only Doc didn't even try to fasten it at the neck.

Stethoscope in hand, he gave no heed to Margaret standing with her armload. "She tolerated that fair, but no more moving her about." He handed the now cooling jars to John. "These can be refilled; more warmth is needed." Now, as he turned to go see how David was, he took note of the patient girl's waiting. "How many did you find?"

"Two sheets and three cotton blankets." Susan still held the candle they had used to light their way.

"Fine. Now if you two can cut or tear those all in quarters, it will help. Then you'd better think about bed." The boy was quiet as Dr. Tom expected he would be, but his feet and hands were still too cold to suit him, so he wedged the jars closer to him. He could hear the cloth being ripped in the kitchen, so he joined the girls and picked up one section and folded it into fourths. "It's about right. Now I'll help you in with those jars," he said to John. Back in the sick room, he explained to him about the pads. "I believe the girlie said there were five of those she was tearing up. That will mean twenty of these pads. Whether you try washing any soiled ones will be up to you, but I advise you to make sure the damp ones are washed and dried, or you might find yourselves short soon. Now, you raise her hips very carefully, just enough for me to smooth this pad under them."

Later he went on talking. "You'll have to be the one lifting her so, and have Margaret do the smoothing out of the pad. Make sure it is free from wrinkles as much as possible, so not to make sores." He rumpled the brown hair as Margaret placed the folded pads on the foot of the unmade bed. "This girl will blossom into a good nurse, but nurses must sleep part of the time."

John was fearful, all this being so new to him. "Doc, should I try to bathe her?"

"Only just what is necessary, and make sure the water and cloth are warm, real warm in fact. Dry and comfortable is the main thing."

"How come her bed wasn't even a mite damp?" This puzzled John as he gathered up the ragged dress and rumpled sheet.

"No moisture in her body," was the short answer.

John wanted to ask a lot of questions, but went off to make coffee instead. *Where the heck is that tea kettle all of a sudden?* He could not find it, so turned on the faucet for hot water. Just as Dr. Tom came into the room thinking the coffee should be ready, the two girls came in from out of doors. Susan had the lantern in hand; Margaret had the now empty tea kettle in one hand, and a nice plucked hen in the other.

"I see these two homemakers don't know when to call it a day either." Not until the fowl was drawn, washed, cut up and put to cook did the two girls climb the stairs.

At midnight when coffee was again made, Dr. Tom would not drink any. "I've got to get a little sleep, say from now 'til three o'clock. Then you take your turn."

"I'm not a bit sleepy. I'm sure I couldn't sleep." John reassured.

"I know," nodded Doc. Laying his watch down and picking up the alarm clock, "I'll take this to get me up. Shall I roll into your bed in the other part of the house?" He waited only for John's nod, then turned at the door. "That hen is beginning to smell good already. Another hour, I'd say try a little of the broth instead of coffee."

"Doc, do you think David will be all right when he wakes

405

up?"

"I believe he will be. But the quieter that young man can be kept for the next few days, the better for him."

"But what would make him sick like that? I've never known him to be sick before in his life."

"I rather expect he has never had such a shock before. Undoubtedly, it was somewhat of a shock to see his Mother unable to speak or to say what was wrong. While he may have been puzzled by her behavior these several months, he is so young with nothing to gauge by, I rather think he is blaming himself for not knowing."

"David is not to blame in not knowing," John was quick to defend.

"Certainly he isn't. But he is just the sort of chap who would think he might be—knowing someone should have been looking out for her." Dr. Tom took himself off to bed before he said anything more cutting.

John Marcus tried hard not to think, yet that was all there was to do most of the time for the next three hours. The persistent thought about his responsibility in this case kept creeping in. *Doc acts like I was to blame. Sure I seen her walking about aimlessly and not talking, but how was I to know that meant she was sick?* He shoved the unwanted coffee aside, spilling some. *How was I to know she was sick if she didn't tell me so?*

The worst to bear now were those half closed eyes, as if they too might be asking what he was going to do now if she never spoke again. For the first time in his life, John Marcus stood alone. The prop he had leaned upon these more than fifteen years, was fragile. He grasped at the delusion everything would be alright the moment Mary could speak, then he remembered Doc's warning that she is not apt to be rational if she can. *How much longer can this go on? And how am I going to stand it?* None could answer that question.

The sound of the alarm from the distant room came faintly to the sick room. In no time, Dr. Tom was there listening. No matter how closely he watched, John could not read his expression. "I spilt a couple spoons of those medicine drops, but I believe I got the right amount down. Do you want broth or coffee next?"

"Broth. Then you hit the hay for the next three hours." John brought the cup and would have waited to see if it was swallowed better, but he was waved away. He was sure he could not sleep, but realized he was dead on his feet. Off came his shoes, and he covered himself with the still warm bedding where Doc had rested. When next he realized anything, Doc was shaking him awake. "Up with you, Man. I hate to do this, but I've got to be on my way shortly, and there are several things we have to iron out before I leave."

The gray of early dawn made the kitchen half light; a candle or lamp was unneeded. Coffee was just now coming to the boil. "I thought this might be a bracer for you," Doc said as he set the pot aside. "A cup of it might get me back to town in better shape."

"Has there been any change?" Now that he had the question out, he was more frightened than ever of what the answer would be.

"No apparent change." Doc shook his head. "It's early yet. Her pulse is a bit better, I would say. Swallowing not quite so slow. Still, you must use caution, remember. With the amount of fluids we have managed to get down, her body functions should be taking over anytime now. I wish it were possible to stay even a half day more, but there are several sick ones in town. The question to settle now is this: Do you know of anyone capable to come in here and relieve you part of the time?" Doc was sure the answer would be *no* even before it was spoken. "There will have to be another adult—the children are too young for such a grave responsibility. This caring for your wife is a 24 hour a day job. I might even say her life depends on that constant care. Perhaps you can stay awake another day and part of a night. Would her mother be able to come?"

"I don't believe so. She can't ride long distances."

David pushed the swinging door open a little. Seeing only Father and Dr. Tom alone, he came in in his underwear. "I can't find my clothes. Tell me, is Mother going to be all right?" He appealed to first one then the other.

"We sure hope she will be, Boy. I believe her pulse is some stronger. The big question right now is finding someone to care for her. You and your Father haven't had a lot of experience along that line, and I fear the girls are a mite too young, wouldn't you?"

"Maybe Aunt Annie would come. Grandmother wrote how she took care of her and made her get well." David shivered close to the stove.

On first thought, Dr. Tom remembered this Aunt Annie as a very young girl. Then came the realization that that was nearly ten years ago when he had chatted with her while she waited for the stage. "Now, she just might be the very best person to make your mother get well in a hurry. Could you suggest the quickest way to get word to her?"

"The mail takes several days sometimes." John was not hopeful.

"The ranch next to Grandfather's has a telephone. Their name is Simmons, and they have an automobile too. And I bet if one was to call 'em, they would go right over and tell Grandfather right now. Maybe he would hire Mr. Simmons to bring Aunt Annie right to Caldwell in that automobile so she could get on the stage right today." David was getting excited over the plan, his face losing some of its pallor.

Dr. Tom was already writing some of this down rapidly. Then he questioned David closer for names, distances, and whether Caldwell was central for those scattered telephones. The boy was not too sure about that. "Never mind, I'll be able to learn that from Silver City. And if I hurry, I might catch Mr. Lyons as he gives out the mail sacks and get that call in early. I'll call you as soon as I learn any news. I will come back by evening at least."

After Doc was gone, Margaret came downstairs with Susan at her heels. When she heard that Aunt Annie was to be called, she had a sudden thought. "If we knew what Grandma wrote in that letter, we'd know if Aunt Annie is on her way up to see us, or already gone back east."

David still thought they should not open Mother's letter, but his father said it was right to do so. From it, they learned Annie had not left, but was still planning to come to see them before she went back to Illinois. "Then she's sure to come when she knows Mother is sick." David hurriedly pulled on a coat to go to the barn.

John went to the sick room. His hard, callused fingers could not detect any change in Mary's pulse, nor could he tell in the shaded room if her eyes were as listless. *Maybe it's just looking so much at them, hoping those lids will move that they seem more closed than before.* It had been hard for the girls to refrain from asking their Mother to talk to them. *I guess I'm just like 'em. I want to do the same thing.* The room was chilly, so he went to the washroom for his coat. David was back from the barn, sitting pensively.

"Did the calf come?" Margaret paused her breakfast-getting long enough to ask.

"Yes, it came sometime last night, an' I don't know for sure all I'm supposed to do now." John knew he would not be of much help to him, so went on back to the sick room.

"All you have to do, Silly, is to put the calf in the pen so it can't suck the cow." There was no uncertainty with Margaret.

"It looks like he's already sucked her. And that cow don't like me touchin' her calf—just shakes her head at me every time I go near."

"Of course she don't want you to take her calf away. She wouldn't hurt anyone, she's just trying to bluff you. You tend to breakfast then I'll go with you."

Margaret was glad to quit the house. She couldn't learn anything from Father; now she would try David. "Did Dr. Tom say what kind of sickness Mother has?"

"No, he didn't say what kind, but he did say she had been getting sick a long time. It's why she didn't eat, and when she didn't eat, she got more sick."

"You're as bad as Father not knowing what ails her." Margaret was now peeved. "Did Dr. Tom say when Mother would get?"

"How can anybody tell that? Not even a doctor always knows. Some folks get well in a hurry, some take a long time. Others don't..." David stopped talking. He had been just old enough when the baby died to know something about death.

"You think Mother might be sick a long time? If she is, I won't go back to school anymore this spring." She sounded more pleased than worried over that thought. She had not caught what David's words might imply. "Do you think Aunt Annie might get here tonight?"

"If Dr. Tom can get Grandfather on the telephone soon enough, she will be." David opened the barn door almost fearfully, glad that Margaret dodged ahead of him. Boldly, she walked in, giving no heed to the tossing head, and snapped the rope to the halter.

"Now she can't bother us while we wrestle this calf into the pen." She already had the lively fellow half way there. "It's a bull calf. I was wishing she'd have a heifer so we could keep it. Looks like there is still lots of milk. Guess he just couldn't hold all of it. We better milk her out good. Do you want to do that, or do you want me to?" She could not understand David leaning against the stall this way.

"I'm not afraid to milk her." He squatted down on his heels. "But I am still sorta jiggly on the inside."

"Then I'll milk her and feed it to the chickens–most of it anyway. I guess I'd better save a little to warm and feed the calf if he gets to bawling too much. We don't know how much he got." Margaret was busy milking away and talking at the same time. "How do you suppose Aunt Annie will get down here from town if she does come tonight?"

"There will be someone to bring her, I guess—either Lew at the livery barn or maybe Jimmy Burch if he's back—he has two good saddle horses."

"You can just as well go back to the house. I can feed and water this cow just as good as you can." Margaret wanted to do something nice for David.

He made no move to leave, but settled in more comfortably. "I wish this calf had come several days ago. Then the milk would be good to use now when Mother needs some milk."

"I wish so too. Was that the first thing Dr. Tom asked for?"

"Just about the best thing we could give her, he said once. Do you think the dairy would let us have some milk for Mother?"

"I don't know as they'd give it to us, but they'd probably sell us some."

"The store clerk never has paid me for that last laundry, so I haven't any money. I could walk the rest of the way into town to see if they'd pay me, but if they didn't, I wouldn't be any better off."

"I'll let you have some money to buy milk for Mother. I'll get it for you just as soon as I get to the house, but you better eat some breakfast 'fore you go so you won't get sick on the way." Margaret would part with her precious horde of money for Mother—just don't let anyone else try to beg or borrow those few dollars.

Chapter Forty

NOW THAT HER MOTHER was well again, Annie was free to admit she was happy to be home, and was enjoying these nice early spring days. "I'm sure there is no place where the first part of April can sometimes be as nice and sunny as Snake River Flats," Annie stopped her happy song to tell Mother, as she came in from feeding her setting hens.

"I see you added that *sometimes.* To be truthful, you would need to, for it isn't always this nice a weather time of the year. You must get out more and enjoy it too. No need for you to hunt up all the work I have had to let slide these many weeks."

"Why, I am enjoying it all." Annie danced about opening all the doors. "I'm letting the sun shine in on me while I work. You must remember, Mother of mine, your youngest is a mature woman now, and I believe I will have to do and act as I think best." Annie saw her mother's serene face cloud over. "Why that look?" Annie hugged her and nibbled at her ear in fun. "*Yours Truly* is thinking about cleaning this house from top to bottom this very week, whether you approve or not. I want to get it out of the way before I go up to visit Mary and her flock. If I leave it, you would try to do it."

"No I won't." Mother said firmly, drawing away to put away her feed pan. "I promise you, I won't tackle cleaning. You go on up and visit Mary. I would feel much easier in my mind if you did. I don't quite understand not hearing from her for near a month now. I know Father is worried too."

"It isn't like Mary to let so many days go by without sending some word. Even as busy as she always is, she would manage a letter or card. If we fail to get a word this next mail day, poor Jack is liable to start out with those sheep—lambs dropping along the trail. He seems to think that Mary is bedfast or has broken arms when she doesn't write."

"I know Dear. I feel sorry for Jack. Never having any family of his own, he has naturally adopted Mary and her family; and it frets him in not knowing how they are. You just plan your trip and go."

"The quicker I go, the sooner I can be back. The road may still not be open between DeLamar and Mary's, just like Jack says, but the children go every day to school the last we heard, so

411

there must be a path at least. With a good flashlight, I could make it at night, even if there is no one to be hired with saddle horses."

"All I mind is the thought of you going that two miles alone about midnight." Mother would not name her other worries. Not hearing from Mary was to the fore of her mind now, of course. But tucked away and seldom brought out for discussion was Annie's unrest. Annie herself made no secret of her indecision. *Mother, I don't know where my niche in life is—whether I should go back to Springfield or look for some work closer here.* She was aware that Mother and Father would much prefer her to be closer to them. *I like my work there; it is pleasant in the music store. But the wages are not very good. I see now I could have prepared to teach one branch of music, but one has to live and learn.* She had sighed and then tossed it off with a laugh.

Mother, in her years of wisdom, had guessed that Annie, like every normal healthy young woman, had visions of a home, husband and babies of her own some day. This career business was a side issue until Mr. Right came along. But last week, Annie had tried to pin Mother down with questions of how would she know her mate when she did run across him. "Oh! You'll recognize the right one, whatever his name may be, when he happens along." Mother was sure of this. She was sure also that Annie had yet to meet the one that would claim any lasting interest in her thoughts. *Annie is whole of heart and fancy free. That is why she is having such a time deciding where she will go right now.*

They could hear the noise of their neighbor' automobile before he turned into their driveway. Mr. Simmons' smooth tanned face registered concern as he rapped at the open door. "This is too nice a spring morning to bring worried news to you good people," was his opening remark as both women came forward. "A Dr. Thomas of DeLamar just got a call through to me asking if I would bring you people word. A Mrs. Mary Marcus is very ill. Can her sister come to care for her?"

"We have been worried about not hearing from her." Annie was already untying her apron. "Is that all of the message?" She seemed to think there should be more.

"That was the message he said to bring. He had me repeat it so he was sure I had it correct. Then he suggested that I bring you to Murphy this day in time for the noon stage if possible. I can do

412

that if it is possible to start very soon. That road, being what it is, one must take time over it."

"I can be ready in a very few minutes. While I pack, will you step to the barns and repeat the message to Father?" She knew she had to forestall Mother from hurrying out to do so. Jerking out both suitcases, she handed the smaller one to Mother. "The larger one will hold all the clothes. You fill this with whatever you can think of." She wanted to give Mother something to do—this sudden shock wasn't easy on her.

Annie donned a sensible gray suit and perky blouse, and tucked the housedress she had just shed into the suitcase when Father came in. He pulled out the few worn bills his pocketbook contained. "I have only $23 here, Daughter, but that will take you up there, I'm sure, and I'll send more as soon as I can make it to Caldwell."

"I can loan you some money right now, Williams," spoke up the waiting man.

Mother had closed the suitcase cover on a side of bacon, several pints of butter and apples. She reached for her cracked teapot and emptied the contents. "No need of borrowing, thank you just the same." Into Annie's hand she put a stack of silver dollars and half dollars. "About $9 or $10 there. It's heavy, so use it to buy your ticket, Child."

After Annie's hurried kiss on her cheek, Mrs. Williams turned to her husband, who was slipping on his coat. She knew what he had in mind without his saying. "I'm glad you are headed to the telephone to learn what more you can."

"Yes, Mother. It might take awhile to get through, so don't you be uneasy if I'm late." He patted her shoulder as he kissed her wrinkled cheek.

The top was up, but the side curtains were off. "Can you tie your head up good? Or shall I take the time to put on the curtains?" was all Mr. Simmons asked.

"Don't worry about me. A little breeze won't hurt me." Annie was already knotting the scarf about her head. Nothing more was said until the auto slowed to let Father Williams off as they passed the next lane.

"I'll come over to Mr. Simmons each forenoon after chore time, Annie, so you call me here if possible." The pat of his hand on her shoulder as he hopped from the running board was his goodbye.

It was a full two hours later before Father Williams trudged back home, meeting Mother in their own lane, pretending to look for stray hen nests, but he was not fooled by that pretense. "I never did get Dr. Thomas on line, Mother. So then I telephoned Wagontown. It was David who answered, and the poor chap was all at sea in knowing what is wrong. But he assured me that Dr. Tom says his mother's pulse was a little stronger this morning." Father chose his words carefully, not letting it slip that Mary was not able to speak.

"I, for one, am glad Annie is on her way to care for our Mary. If good nursing will make her well, she'll get it. The more I think of it, Father, her family would be in a bad way with Mary herself sick. I doubt John is very handy about a sick person, and the children are much too young."

"I guess you are right about that, Mother." He could see why Dr. Thomas called for help. "The Marcus family might manage most any calamity with Mary at the wheel, but with her helpless, they are in a bad way."

"Will you try calling again this evening, Father?" She wondered if she could ride that mile distance.

"Not in the evening; it's too hard to get through to DeLamar. The telephone is in the store, and they are more apt to be closed after supper. And I doubt we could learn much except from Dr. Thomas himself." As they neared the house and found Jack waiting for any news, Father said, "About the time I think Mr. Simmons will be back, I'll walk over to his house. It could be that some word got through. We'll at least know if Annie made connections with the stage in time."

"With Dr. Tom on the job, he's going to pull Mary through if any such thing is possible." Old Jack had every confidence in that, and tried to put his fears aside. "But between you and me and the gatepost, Williams, I'm glad Miss Annie is going to be there to help out on the job."

David Williams timed going to reach his neighbor's house just as Simmons drove down the lane ahead of him. "I could have been back sooner," he told Williams, "but I waited at Murphy while a Mr. Burch put through a call to Dr. Thomas to learn what he could. Miss Annie said she had met Mr. Burch, and she asked him if he knew of Mrs. Marcus sickness. He knew nothing about

414

it, for he had been in Boise the past week on business. He was just then headed home. He's a rather short man, but can he move fast and get things done in a hurry. In no time at all, he had that call put through and the doctor called away from his meal. And from all I could gather, by the big words that was used, your daughter is suffering from some sort of a nerve exhaustion, or general breakdown. While she is very ill, the doctor would not say she was in any immediate danger. But I was under the impression he was glad someone was on their way up there to care for her.

"And if care is what she needs, Annie will give it. She seems to have a knack for it. I won't try to put in another call today, but I will trouble you good people by hanging around each 'forenoon for an hour or so to get any word Annie may be able to get down to me, if that's amenable to you. I'm not when I can repay you for all you have done for us this day..."

"Forget it, Williams. I haven't done one thing more than you would do for me or any other neighbor if you were the one that had a machine and we didn't. What good is an automobile, but to get a person someplace faster than he could otherwise?"

Annie was not especially hungry—so concerned for Mary, but she made herself eat a good lunch at Murphy while waiting for the stage. *Mary is in need of care and more care to get well. Dr. Tom made that plain. I'm going to eat all I can to be in the best shape possible.* She could still remember how hungry she had gotten the first time she had come travelled this road. *And I had a pretty good lunch along with me too. This time I have nothing except those apples Mother poured into that suitcase, and I'm not going to ask the driver to untie it now that he has it all loaded and tied down.*

Ed Wheeler, the same stage driver that she remembered from ten years ago, was the one who swung to the seat after Jimmy Burch helped her to the seat just back of the driver; then Mr. Burch was beside her. One other passenger rode beside the driver.

"I see they haven't a different rig than when I made this trip before."

"The old coach was about to fall apart. This hack might be more open to the weather, but I really think it more comfortable." Jimmy was finding this friendly, alert young woman very pleasant company. He remembered Dr. Tom had thought that when she was a mere slip of a girl. *I couldn't see it then, but I can now.*

415

There was much to converse about on the smoother stretches of road when conversation was possible. When they stopped to change teams toward the top of the hill, Annie walked about to relieve the tension. Jimmy kept step with her, chatting the while. She asked about the health and well being of his family.

"Miss Williams, I'm not one to sail under false colors. I have no family. The woman that might still bare my name, and the daughter I fathered, have chosen to live in Boise these many years. We have grown so far apart, I no longer think of them as my family. This past week, I settled questions about their support, which in all fairness, I will do. But I also think it only fair to me to give my freedom legally. As I understand life, every normal man is entitled to a home companion and children if he is able to support them. I have been denied the fulfillment." Jimmy would have liked to hear her thoughts on the question of divorce, but there was no time; they needed to retrace their steps—Ed Wheeler held his reins at the ready.

"During the supper stop in Silver City, we might get a call through and learn how Mrs. Marcus is," Jimmy told her as he handed her into the seat.

"Thanks for that suggestion. I may act upon it, but my sole thought now is, I must hurry." The fast pace of the team as they started suited her mood. Once over the summit, they traveled faster on the downgrade. "At this rate of speed, it looks like we should be in DeLamar before 11 o'clock tonight."

"Yes it would seem so from the good condition of the road on the hill. But once we strike the lower stretch, it means plowing through mud hub-deep in places. There would have been a way to shortened this trip for you, if I had presence of mind at Murphy, to have someone meet the stage as we hit the stream. We could have been in DeLamar at the same time we will be in Silver City. How thoughtless of me not to think of that," he berated himself.

"Surely this worry of mine isn't yours, Mr. Burch. You have been most kind for all you have done, and I do thank you. I well remember the evening I came in by stage before and wondered how I would ever walk that two miles distance with Sister. I was so weary. And you were so kind to drive us down in your rig. I never will forget that kindness."

A smile played about Jimmy's lips. "If I recall right, you said you would remember me in your prayers. I only wish it were

416

possible to convey you as easily this nigh, but it will need to be horse back now. The last lap of your journey is still a sloped, icy snow bank."

"And not a bit of snow along here." Annie tried to figure that out, knowing they were several hundred feet higher here than the road between DeLamar and Wagontown.

"This side lies toward the south," Jimmy explained, "where the sun makes short work of the snow hanging on. But that mile of road along the opposite side is where the sun never hits. About the only thing that will melt it off in a hurry is a good rain. The harder it rains, the quicker the road will be opened."

"Then once I arrive, I won't care if heavy a rain storm comes." Annie responded. "I wonder how the road came to be built in the first place along that side of the stream?"

Jimmy looked at her more admiringly in the early dusk. "You are a wide awake young woman, Miss Williams. I asked that question after my first year in these hills too, but have yet to receive a satisfactory answer. I've spent much time and thought advocating for the change in this road. The county thinks the mining company should be the one footing such an expense, and vice versa; the mining interest, knowing it is a county road, thinks they should be the ones to change it and make it useable more months of the year. Right now I cannot see either side making a move."

Annie nodded as if understanding some of it. "Father explained how the government is trying to collect for all the timber the mines have cut and used these many years. That must look like a terribly big sum for them to have to pay. Was it a half a million or only a quarter?"

"I can't see them paying, whatever the amount. To them, Public Domain means just that: free to whoever wants to use it. The trees were cut all these years without hindrance and without much being said. I'm not defending the right or wrong of this question. Of course the mining interest thinks it is unjust. As I see it, they are more apt to fold up and quit operation."

"And would that mean DeLamar would become a ghost town? What would that do to your business?"

"I would need to hunt a new location—a town with a payroll, or at least a large enough place to call for more business." The rig was now in the rutted, muddy road headed upstream, and talking was not easy. He might have said he already had property bought in the valley.

"When one thinks about it, it hardly seems possible that a place the size of DeLamar could just vanish and be no more."

"It has happened many times over in mining country, even here in these hills. Did you hear about the town that was once just below Silver City? Some claim there were between four and five thousand people there. Now there is nothing to show there was ever a town there. The same as the top of the mountain above town—a thriving town was once built there. The only thing left to tell the tale is a few depressions where there were cellars dug. A still bigger town once flourished on West Mountain—a sawmill, and a brewery was there. While there is not a house left standing, there is more evidence of a settlement at one time. Huge sawdust piles are still there."

It was after eight o'clock when the stage pulled into Silver City. Jimmy knew where to find the person in charge of the small telephone exchange in the cubbyhole off the hotel lobby. Soon he was talking to Dr. Tom while Annie waited. *I wish he would let me talk. While I know Mr. Burch means well, he sounds too demanding with his questions,* was her thought as he hung up, taking her arm to steer her toward the dining room. "Tell me, did you learn anything at all?"

"Nothing, except Mrs. Marcus seems to be holding her own. No real change, Doc said. We must stow away as good a meal as possible to find at this late hour," he said as he seated her and signaled the girl coming through the nearly empty room.

They both were glad for the food and hot coffee brought to them. They were not much behind Ed Wheeler as he finished his meal and went out into the chilly night. As the last tug was hooked, Annie took her seat and then Jimmy followed. Annie was weary, and the sound of the wheels cutting through the frozen mud in places, added its noise to the horses' hooves plodding along. Staying awake was a problem for Annie. She could not recall the next two hours that passed so slowly.

As the rig stopped to unload mail sacks, a man leading two saddle horses came forward. "You must be Mrs. Marcus' sister. Dr. Tom had me ready these two horses—said I was to see that you got there safe."

"That was a good idea, Lew." Jimmy was taking over. "Sure

saves the time it would take me to saddle my two. And as I promised to deliver Miss Williams to her journey's end, I can relieve you of the ride down and back again." Lew might not like the way Mr. Burch was handling this, but he was sure he could say but little.

In no time, they were mounted and away they rode side by side until they were below town. "The trail from here on is single file. Perhaps I should go first, then there will be no question of your mount following. Both are surefooted—you need have no fear of slipping or falling. And there's such a small amount of brush, you won't be bothered with that. But there are a few big boulders where the trail swings around—be careful you are not scraped on those. If you need to rest or are fearful, all you have to do is to call."

Annie wished she had enough sense to have slip her suit skirt off before leaving DeLamar. Never intended as a riding habit, it was much too narrow to even be comfortable. *Why didn't I have sense enough to bring along my old divided skirts.* While her woolen suit was warmly lined, her legs from knees down had no protection except the fine, black silk hose. *If it was light enough for me to see, I would get off and walk; I would keep warmer I'm sure.*

Chilled and miserable, Annie was glad of the help to dismount. *Why, I can hardly walk, I'm so cold,* was her thought, but she was determined to not speak of it. The east door into the dining room seemed to was opened as if waiting for them, so they moved toward it instead of going in through the front hall. The room was warm with a fire in the fireplace. The only ones in sight in the dim lit room were David on the worn couch, and Dr. Tom. It was him her eyes sought. "Can I go to Sister now?"

He nodded his assent and guided her into the sickroom. John moved aside to let her close. Her cry of, "Mary Dear," was not loud, but it seemed so in the silent house. She wanted to gather her close, but feared to, so she kissed her.

"Annie," gasped the half conscious woman in a whisper.

"Yes Dear, it's Annie." Down on knees, she strained close to her. "I have come to take care of you…" Someone was lifting her bodily to her feet and walking her from the room. This frightened her when she realized it was the doctor. "Did I do something wrong?" she asked before they reached the kitchen door.

"You did just right," Dr. Tom told her while he stopped and nudged David prone again and covered him. "Young Man, it is time you went to sleep. You've heard your mother speak—that is good news enough, I would say for one night." To Jimmy Burch he said, "Go out and have a cup of coffee. I'm sure John has some made from the smell." He let Jimmy take the shaken girl the rest of the way while he saw that David swallowed another sedative. Instead of him going to the kitchen to explain more, he went back to the sickroom and relieved John.

From his silent withdrawn way, Annie had little hope of learning much. Her hand went to John's shoulder in compassion. "John, can you tell me anything? It seemed Doctor Tom wanted me to go right in there, then he hurried me right out again?"

"Doc has warned us not to try talking to Mary—guess that's why." He went on drinking the coffee he had already poured; it was plenty cool now.

"We are not to ask her anything then, just let her tell us her wants?"

"She hasn't spoken a word for more than two days—not 'til she said your name just now." The man seemed sunken into deep gloom. As he downed his coffee, he went back to watch beside Mary.

The warm drink relieved the chilled girl. When Dr. Tom appeared some minutes later, she was again poised and ready to question him. "Can you now tell me the dos and the don'ts in caring for my sister? I shall try in every way to carry out your orders. I might find it easier if I understand some of the whys."

Dr. Tom poured himself coffee and seemed in no hurry to answer. "The don'ts in this case are easy told. Do not speak or ask Mrs. Marcus anything. At present, she is not able to make her wants known. You must use your judgement of what is needed; what will make her the most comfortable. The less moving, fuss or bother, the better. In other words, do nothing to tire her. She can swallow without much difficulty now: Broth, milk, raw eggs and such liquids are all she can get down. That's the help she needs right now. My advice is for you to take the next four hours for a rest."

"Oh, I couldn't sleep, Doctor. I want to commence learning to do things right while you are still here to correct me."

"I'll be here until daylight. John has had his sleep—he just awoke as you came, so we two will manage while you get some rest. One thing you will find out soon enough: When one of you are awake, the other must sleep so to be able to carry on. Whether it will be four or six hour intervals, you and John can settle that between you. Now to bed with you." He had hardly noticed Jimmy, and was too weary to do any talking right now. "You take the bed in the west room; I'll call you around five. I need to be alert for an hour now and might get some shut-eye after that." He hoped Jimmy would take himself home as soon as the door closed after the girl.

Chapter Forty One

NOW IN THE GRAY of early dawn, Annie tried to think where she was. Why was someone persistently shaking her shoulder? "I have to leave shortly, Miss Annie." It was Dr. Tom.

That brought her awake immediately. "Why have you let me sleep so long?" Quickly alert to where she was and to her responsibility, "I'll be out at once," she said as the tall form left through the washroom to the kitchen. She put on shoes, suit skirt, and blouse. She had slept in her other clothes, not knowing where there were gowns. Washing her face at the faucet in the kitchen and smoothing back her hair with her wet hands took but a minute. John was slumped in weariness by the stove.

"Now to bed with you." Dr. Tom back from the sickroom was all but propelling John along. "Don't let that bed get cold." With the kitchen door closed, he poured coffee for both of them. "Better take a bracer. You'll be on your own now. Better let John sleep 'til noon if possible. He's had it most the time since midnight. I had to get in my forty winks. I've been jotting down some of the things you might want the answers to. I don't look for any sudden change. It will be the steady routine of getting all the liquids down her possible. Those jars filled with hot water about her are for the added warmth. When it is necessary to change pads, you be the one to lift her hip—just what is needful—while Margaret spreads the dry one smooth."

He stood up, cup in hand. "Because of the uncertainty of where and when you can catch me by phone, I'll try calling here a couple times during the day." He took one last look at both patients, then was off on the now frozen trail.

As morning dawned, Annie quietly oriented herself in the sickroom. Mary was lying just as she had at midnight. It still was not bright enough to read the chart or the instructions Dr. Tom had handed her. Tip-toeing through the dining room to the kitchen, David awoke. "Aunt Annie, I couldn't tell you last night that I am so glad you came." It was almost a whisper. "Not one of us knows how to take care of Mother."

"And I'm glad it was possible for me to come, and so soon, Child." She hugged the boney lad hard. "Can't you sleep a bit more if I'm still?"

"No, I'm going to get up. Can you tell me if Mother is

422

better?" He reached for his pants while talking.

"Bless you, Boy. I've only gotten up myself—I hardly know if she is better. I should start breakfast; we can talk a bit better in the kitchen. She had just put more wood on the fire when David was out there, huddling about the stove as if he were cold.

"Didn't Dr. Tom say if she was better?"

"I'm sure he thinks she is some better, for he mentioned about her swallowing better without difficulty. But I slept so late, I didn't have time to ask any questions. I'm still in the dark as to how your mother got sick or how long she's been ill. Maybe you can fill me in on those things?" She let down the oven door to make it warmer for the shivering boy.

"I guess Mother has been sick a long time, only none of us knew it. Doc said that was why she didn't eat or talk much. Not eating made her worse."

"If she was a long time getting sick, David, we must remember it takes just as long or longer for her to get well. We can't expect Mother to be bright and perky, ready to talk and laugh for several days yet. It is like a nice long rest she must take now before she will feel like talking to anyone. We'll feed her all the good food we can, just as fast as she is able to eat it; we won't bother her with questions or talk. Just let her rest; some of us must be around close, should she want something."

Hurriedly, Annie put rolled oats to cook before going back to the sickroom. When next she came out, the two girlies were down, chatting in subdued tones. Annie had read Dr. Tom's instructions, understanding most of it, but still puzzled over the last line. It didn't make sense to her, *Keep the other patient as still as possible.* As she had not heard of anyone else being sick, she thought she would ask Dr. Tom when he called. She commenced to find nourishing liquid to give Mary.

In the doctor's list of possible things to be given her was thin gruel. Now she hunted for a sieve or strainer. Finding neither, she used a square of cheesecloth to force the hot cereal through. "Now for milk or cream?" she asked the children as a group, while she sugared the gruel sparingly.

"All the milk there is, is that covered in this bowl," David told her while the girls started their breakfast. "Guess there's not much cream left on it, for we skimmed it off yesterday so Dad could give it to Mother. That lady up at the dairy where I went to buy the milk yesterday said cream would make Mother well if we fed her enough of it." David was slow in his speech. He did not seem to be eating at all.

"We're going to have lots of milk pretty soon ourselves," Margaret interposed. "Tain't good yet—the calf only came yesterday morning. I'm going to give David some more money, and he'll go up to buy more milk this morning."

Annie tasted the blue looking skimmed milk to make sure it was sweet, which it was. "That will be fine, Children, but let me know before you go, David, for I want to send for one or two things for your mother too. You'd better eat some breakfast, Boy. That is going to be quite a walk. If I remember right, the dairy is close to town." She was none too sure how much nourishment this gruel would have, so she was more than glad to think of richer milk soon. When she came back to the kitchen after spooning it into Mary's mouth, Margaret counted some change into David's hand. "Never mind figuring out the right change, Child. I'm going to give David money to buy a piece of beef to make good broth." She handed the lad a five dollar bill. "If you have the milk to bring, you cannot possibly pack down much else, but we do need the meat if possible. I have written down several other things here for Mr. Burch. I'm sure he means to bring down my suitcases somehow, and perhaps he will be kind enough to bring down these articles too. Now don't you attempt to try packing all of them."

Seeing the gaping pockets of the worn coat the boy was putting on, "David, if you want to open the smaller of those two suitcases of mine, they aren't locked, you will find some pints of butter, and I believe one of those would slip right into one of your coat pockets. I'm also sure Grandmother put apples in that same case. Take two or three to eat if you like, but it won't be long before they'll all be brought down." There was plenty to keep her busy, giving no time to worry over the thin serious lad tramping away in the frosty morning. Back in the kitchen, making herself eat a bowl of cereal and coffee minus cream, Margaret came in from the barn, "Do you know if there is another egg, Child?"

"I just found the one day before yesterday. That was the first one they laid for a long time, but maybe they will lay one today. What will he do if he can't find any fresh meat in town?" Margaret's mind was with David and his errand.

"In that case, we will need to kill another hen for broth. I see there isn't a bit of broth left on this one, so we need to use up the meat of the chicken today. Your mother cannot eat it, but we all can. It might be a good idea to kill another and get it to cooking this morning before David gets back. Can you pick out a good fat one for me?"

"I can kill it, and dress it out ready to cook," boasted the girl. "But don't ask David to kill no chicken, Aunt Annie. That was what made him sick the other night."

Annie knew there were people who would not kill a chicken, but she could not see why that should make David sick. He, who had spent his life here where the killing and dressing out of one's own meat was common. "Alright, I'll try to remember." The more Annie thought about these things, the more they didn't add up right. Questioning the girl more, she was now sure that David was the other patient Dr. Tom had advised her to keep as quiet as possible. It was with a heavy heart she went back to sit beside Mary.

What can I do? she asked herself. *I cannot leave Mary and go after David myself. I would have to awaken John, and he's supposed to sleep. Margaret could go up to pack the milk and meat, but he is too far ahead to overtake him.* No, the more she thought of it, the more worried she was. It was hard to sit still this way and not try to do something, so she wandered back to the kitchen where the two girls seemed busy.

"Oh, look what I've done!" lamented Margaret, her hand stayed from cutting up the hen she was getting ready to cook. "I killed a laying hen, and just when we need eggs for Mother." The girl was ready to cry over this calamity.

Annie looked. Sure enough, the white shell of an egg was showing. "You must not feel bad about this, Child." Deftly, she garnered the egg. "There was never a time we needed one more than we do right now. Haven't you heard about people chasing hens around the barn to make them lay an egg faster because it was needed right then?" She could see the humor in this case escaped the girl, so she said no more and was soon beating that still-warm egg and adding it to the last of the blue milk.

"I wish David would hurry up and get home." Margaret fretted as she went about her disagreeable work. "What if he gets sick on the way going up there?"

Those were Annie's thoughts about now. "I'll give your mother this, and you finish putting the hen to cook, then we'll plan what is best to do. Either you will need to go and meet David, or we will awaken your father."

David came before Margaret was ready to set out, but he did not come afoot—Jimmy Burch brought him. Annie rushed out to lend a hand as Jimmy helped the pinched faced youth from the saddle. "Doc says this boy needs to be put to bed and made to stay there." He could see the unshed tears as Annie walked on the other side of David. Between them, they took David to the couch. "He also said there were small tablets left to give him every so many hours." Margaret stepped up on a chair to reach them on the clock shelf.

Annie managed to bear up long enough to minister to David and mutely leave Margaret beside her mother, then sailed out of doors to where Jimmy Burch was unloading her suitcases.

"Tell me what is wrong with David," she cried, bursting into tears. "I didn't even know he was sick until after he left." She was sobbing too hard now to talk.

"Don't grieve this way, Miss Williams. You'll be making yourself sick. All I know is, Doc said it was some kind of a shock affecting the boy. He was pretty sick just as he got there to the store and handed me your list. Someone went for Doc right then. At first he wasn't going to let him come home at all, but put him to bed somewheres right there. But that wasn't suiting David, of course, so the next best thing was to bring him on horseback." Jimmy gripped her firm shapely hands in sympathy. "You must not weep this way. You didn't know he was sick. You're not to blame yourself in the least. Doc was pretty mad, of course, when he found the boy had walked those two miles. Perhaps there is no lasting harm done if he is kept quiet now. I took no time to scout the town for beef—we had none at the store of course. But I did bring a jar of malted milk and found one can of pineapple at my home. The gallon of milk David was carrying in a pail, I turned into a jug, the better to pack it down. I can promise you someone will bring beef or fresh meat of some kind for the sick before nightfall." This pleasant young woman was calm now and trying to draw her hands free. "Remember, my Dear Girl, you are no further from me than that telephone on the wall in there. All you have to do is give that crank two long twists, and I'll be here. I will be only too glad to bring down anything you need."

"Oh, how kind you are. I will never be able to thank you as it is." Wiping her eyes, she reached for the jug of milk. "I can pack this in as I go." She was sure the man would have stopped her from lifting even that much had he been quick enough.

David was still awake when she tiptoed in. "I don't like to take those pills you gave me," he told her. "They just make me go to sleep, and I want to stay awake and eat an apple."

Poor Annie now was in a quandary. She did not know what the boy should eat, or if at all. "I tell you what, David Boy, you can have an apple just as soon as Dr. Thomas says you can have one. You take a little nap now. I'll put one right here where you can look at it. As soon as we find out about you eating one, I can scrape it and feed it to you that way. Do you know that is what I did for Grandmother this winter when she was sick?"

It was comforting to feel Jimmy Burch's presence now in all these perplexities, though he did not know the answers anymore than she did. He stayed several minutes while she surveyed the supplies to learn what more was needed. "I don't find even one potato, but then I guess they use more beans than potatoes up here in the hills. If you have eggs, and there is any safe way of bringing them down, we should have a couple of dozen until these hens decide to give us more. Oh, we do need yeast cakes." She doubted there was bread to be bought already baked in DeLamar, so would not trouble to ask.

Jimmy well knew how to make his adoration appreciated. And being sincere in this case, Annie responded to his friendship and helpfulness. It was with regret that she saw him ride away after eleven o'clock. The next moment as she entered the house, she uttered a dismaying cry. "Oh' my, poor father is waiting for me to telephone him." She turned the crank on the wall phone close to David's couch, but he seemed too drowsy to arouse. Annie was so weak with regret at having kept Father waiting so long, she could hardly speak calmly when the connection was made and she recognized his familiar voice. "Oh Father, forgive me for not phoning sooner. I expect you have been waiting for hours. Mary recognized me when I arrived last night, and she spoke my name, so we must take that as good news until I can give you better. I hope that will be tomorrow or soon." She now waited for the question she knew Father would be asking, then answered. "Do not make a special trip into Caldwell for money. I have enough to do for another week or two. I will try to write some kind of a letter this very day. John is asleep now for six hours; soon he will be awake and I'll sleep. In that way, one of us is always there to care for Mary. Bye for now, don't you worry, Father Dear. I'll be more prompt tomorrow." She would not say one word about David being sick until she knew herself how bad he was. Only Dr. Thomas could tell her that. She questioned John as soon as he awoke and learned that he knew but little.

Making Margaret promise to awaken her at once should David waken, she dropped off to sleep. When next she came to, the girl was patiently shaking her shoulder ever so gently. "Aunt Annie, you have to wake up. Doc Tom can't stay long, and he says Dad has to go to sleep now. You was sound to sleep."

Annie patted the hand on her shoulder. "It is right that you should awaken me, only you should shake me harder. My, how rough your hands are, Child. You must put something on them so they won't get sore," she told the waiting girl while she dressed.

"I know. We got some mutton tallow I can rub on my hands, only I don't like the smell of it. It stinks."

"Here is something that smells good; maybe it will do just as well." Annie put her jar of fine hand cream into those rough, red hands before leaving the room. She went out to where the doctor and John sat in the kitchen, fearful of censor, but determined to learn the worst, waiting only until John went on his way to bed before asking. "Having pulled one terrible mistake this day by letting David go before I knew he was the other patient, you must put me straight on this: What to do and how to care for him? What he can eat and such things?"

Dr. Tom was still weary from long hours and very little sleep these last few nights, but he was keenly alert to this young woman's poise and wholesome charm. *No wonder Jimmy Burch was falling for her.* "It might take as much as a week's rest and quiet to do the trick. And here is the rub—he is not liking the cure. It will have to be opiates, I fear, unless you can prevail upon him to rest several days, then only give the sedatives at night to make sure of sleep."

"Have you the time to tell me what would be the best foods for him? And what to avoid?" Margaret came into the room now, rubbing the fragrant cream into her rough hands vigorously.

Susan, a few feet behind her, was doing the same. "David wanted to eat an apple before he went to sleep at noon. Would a scraped raw apple harm him?"

"A baked one might be the better deal at first. A soft or semi-soft diet of easily digested foods is alright. It needs to be nourishing, and the goal here is to get him to eat enough. That scraped apple you spoke of might be an idea—he would be taking it slow. You are going to have to be the judge of what he will eat and how often. We want no more nausea. Milk might be the best borne; if it cannot be retained, then try strained soups and fruit juices sipped slowly."

"Then school is out? He said he wanted to go for sure tomorrow for some examination."

"No school for at least a week; then we'll talk about it."

"I can go on to school and get his books tomorrow when I go after milk." Margaret offered. "Then maybe he'll stay in bed better and read them." She sniffed the fragrance of her hands.

"You do that, Girlie. If you haven't got too big of an armload, stop at the office. I believe I have a couple of books that might interest him. I'll try to come each evening. In case I cannot, I will phone." Soon he was on his way back to DeLamar.

Annie ate a supper of biscuits. Margaret had fixed cold chicken and coffee before the two girls went up to bed early this night. Annie commenced the pattern that would be their life for the next two weeks. Then came the change: Mary could speak sometimes, and not always in a rattled voice. Annie figured anything was better than that silent stare with half-closed eyes. David need no longer be confined to bed, but they learned through bitter experience that it was the only way to keep him still. Most evenings, Dr. Tom or Jimmy Burch came. They seemed to alternate their comings by common consent, bringing the mail, fresh meat, and any needful article, as well as more books for David.

As soon as the need for night vigils passed, Annie commenced her campaign to move Mary to the west bedroom. The room was much larger and could be warmed enough to bathe her comfortably. First, she asked Dr. Tom, and he admitted that moving the patient need not be harmful if planned for, so there would be no fuss or bother. "Only make sure she is in accord with this shift," was his advice. Now as he came this mid-day, the three of them carried their patient to the massive bed in the shaded west room. What a different looking room this was: Not only was it warm, there were white ruffled curtains to give a cozy feel, something it never had before Miss Annie came to this house.

Dr. Tom continued to sit beside the patient and check the stronger, but still irregular, pulse for several minutes before he sought out Annie in the kitchen where she was beating up custards to bake for supper. "Our patient stood the trip very well, I came to report." There was a twinkle in his eyes. "Between you and Jimmy Burch's work and shopping, you have that room looking like an enchanted castle."

"Thanks for the compliment. I think it looks very nice myself. I fear I would never have gotten it all done if Mr. Burch had not helped. He went to so much trouble to measure those windows for the right size curtains, and knew just where to phone for them. He even came yesterday evening and helped me put up the rods and hang them. Both girls worked like beavers all day, scrubbing and cleaning the room to have it ready." Annie was bone-weary from all this extra work, but she knew the satisfaction of accomplishment.

"My curiosity is how you won her approval to be moved in the first place?" He liked to watch this capable girl at her work.

"Oh, I was very careful with my approach to the subject." Annie was smiling as she answered him. "What really did the trick was my telling her how much easier it would be for me to care for her. Would it be better to wait until nearly night before I bathe her?"

"The time to do so is up to your convenience, but make it of short duration so as not to weary her. Do you know that you are a wonderful nurse? You claim you have had very little experience, so you must have a natural aptitude. How is our other patient doing? Eating half enough yet?"

"Just about half enough is right." Annie knew her face flushed at his unexpected praise. "We have plenty of milk, and the hens are laying enough finally. David will oblige me by drinking an eggnog mid afternoon and before bed time. But as to eating other food, I must confess, I must be a poor nurse or a worse cook."

"You might try the third enriched drink mid-forenoon." In a much lower tone he continued, "If he downs three of those, and they are made with half cream, he'll gain some weight."

Annie was finding herself wider awake each day now, her night's rest not always broken. She was too busy to think about what direction her life's work might take, or what might be her special niche. In fact, she was happy. Jimmy's open adoration was pleasant; the heavy demands on her thoughts left no time to consider the deeper question of her own feelings. She was humming a bit of a song as she beat up the foamy drinks for both patients this day. John, downstairs now from his afternoon nap, came into the kitchen frowning. "Getting caught-up on your sleep?" she asked him with a smile.

"Guess I must be. I couldn't sleep with that yapping going on below me. Do you think it is a good thing for those two to be in there talking a blue streak that way? Mary couldn't go to sleep if she wanted to."

"I was only leaving them there the few minutes it takes me to fix these. I'll be scattering them and their noise out of there pronto." Away she sailed handing David his tumbler first. "This is made a new way, Boy—with just the whites of the eggs. See how high it piles up? That is the way Grandmother wanted hers made. I want you to drink every last drop, then tell me which way you like it best."

"Hi, you two?" she called to gain the attention of the two excited girls making up for lost time in talking to Mother. "How about you two find us some wood? I want to know which is the best wood-picker-upper anyway." She knew they would vie with each other in that work. As they left, taking their noise with them, she made a wide flourish with the drinking tube as she put it to Mary's lips. "I do believe these tubes are the handiest gadgets. You can sip just as slow as you like and not have to be raised up and down." Annie made sure Mary was alert. Once she had not done this, and a tube had been broken. Luckily her mouth had escaped any cut. "I don't care how slowly you take this, as long as you take it all." She could see Mary turning her mouth away from the tube.

"The girls say I have been in bed more than three weeks. That can't be possible. I knew when you put me to bed in here—wasn't that about a week ago?"

"That's right. A week ago yesterday. Now how about a long drag on this foamy stuff? Like I told David, these are made a new

431

way and I want your opinion." Annie wished now she hadn't allowed the girls in here.

Dutifully, Mary took a sip, then was ready with more questions. "Why am I in bed in the first place? I'm not sick. I don't feel a pain anywhere. Why can't I move my feet like I want to?"

"I can tell you why your feet won't track." Annie made a show of secrecy. "You haven't as yet drunk enough of these fancy drinks. Now, how about another long draw on this peace pipe?" On and on went the ordeal to get enough nourishment down Mary.

As Mary's mind cleared, and she realized she had been sick a month, she still fretted over that lost time. "Why worry over it, Sister mine?" Annie teased. "That first two weeks was just suspended-animation anyway. That is why you don't remember it. You were having such a nice quiet rest, you wouldn't arouse to tell us about it."

"But what made me sick in the first place? That is what I can't understand—for the life of me, I can't remember getting sick."

"You'll have to ask Dr. Tom some of those questions. This big sister of yours is not smart enough to answer them. I feel so much larger than you now—I must outweigh you by fifty pounds. How about me giving that tired back of yours a brisk alcohol rub about now?" She intended to extend that rub the full length of her limbs, like she had the last few days, whenever she could get Mary to consent to being rubbed.

Two days later when Dr. Tom came to call, Mary's first question was. "When can I get up?"

"That's the way I like to hear my patients talk." He was happy at the progress Mary Marcus had made. She moved her hands well by now. "How well can you handle those feet of yours?" He flipped up the bedding to watch the slow, halting movement. "Not fast enough for any foot race yet," he joked, "but I'll tell you what we will do. John and I will lift you to a chair while this good nurse of yours gives your bed a shaking up."

In a few minutes she was lifted back. "I-guess-I'm-not-half-as-strong-as-I-thought." There was a pause between each word she had spoken. Never had the bed felt as good as it did now.

Before Dr. Tom left, he cautioned both John and Annie, "If she gets too restless, you can prop her up in bed to a sitting position, and even turn her so her feet will dangle over the side of the bed for a few minutes. But do remember to not loosen your hold on her for one second, for she could get a nasty fall. She cannot handle her body yet, much less walk. Be on your guard, for she might attempt it."

Chapter Forty Two

NOW EACH DAY, ALL could see Mary's progress toward recovery. Then came the day when she was lifted into a blanket-covered rocking chair, well covered, and John and Dr. Tom went sailing away with her. "Hang on tight now." Out they went through the front hall and along the west porch in the warm afternoon sun. "This is where you should spend most of your time each sunny afternoon," he said. "Now how is that?" he asked as he and John steadied her on her feet for the first time.

Mary didn't speak, trying to get the feel of her feet under her. "Why, my feet don't feel like they are there." There was a catch in her voice. "I can't move them at all." She was glad when they lifted her back into the bed again.

"You need feet with wheels on them for awhile," Dr. Tom teased, "a wheelchair, in other words. I think I have at last traced down the one we did have in DeLamar. Now all we have to do is find someone with a rig to go for it."

"I, a woman not quite thirty-five years old, and going in a wheelchair? I don't like the idea." Mary sounded hurt.

"Of course you don't like it. Neither do we. But you must be out in the sunshine. That will help you more than any one thing, except food. You'll need some power of locomotion. Will you see to it that John pulls you and your comfortable chair out in the sun just like I did, half a dozen times a day?" He waited a second for her to answer, then finished. "Each time, stay a minute longer. Just so you don't tire yourself."

"I will see that she is in the sun." John nodded his head to emphasize his meaning.

Dr. Tom noticed how lacking in bounce Annie seemed this day. He wondered if she was overdoing it. Always before, she had a sparkle in her eyes, or a ready smile. There was no smile on that serious face this day. The two patients were doing so well, yet this girl was unhappy, so he engaged her in conversation as far as the gate. He was in no hurry to mount and be away. Annie made no effort to talk. He tapped her white knuckled hands as they gripped the picket, "What's wrong with these patients of ours? I have the impression they are doing fine' I believe David might tackle school any day now."

"Oh, they both are doing well, I believe. David is eating much better."

"Then these worry wrinkles have nothing to do with our patients?" He pretended to smooth out lines along her forehead with the tip of his finger.

"In a way I'm worried about Mary, but I hardly know how to put it into words. For the life of me, I cannot think what I have for her to think ill of me." Her eyes filled with tears ready to spill over. "I would not hurt Mary for anything in the world."

"Of course you wouldn't. We all know that, and your sister does too. But remember, she is still pretty weak and little things can look as big as mountains when one is very low like she has been." His strong but smooth hands covered hers and eased them from the rough wood. "Can you tell me about it? I might be able to help you get a different view on the subject."

"We were doing the washing yesterday—they are pretty big loads; we were all helping. I made sure John did all the heavy lifting, so the girlies wouldn't be. I think sometimes they do too much for their ages and size." The tears were spilling now. "Later, when I went in to care for Mary, she spoke almost sarcastically about John helping me wash—as if he was doing it just to please me, and she was jealous over it." Annie was really crying now.

Dr. Tom startled her by laughing. "That's the best news yet." More mirth. Then to her hurt look, he explained. "I did not think Mary Marcus had that much spunk yet—now I have hopes of her full recovery." Another short laugh while he dried her tears away. "Do you know that jealousy is rather a human failing? It can crop up in the most unexpected times and places, and really throw the best of us when we are off guard. But I rather expect it was more the irony of John helping you do the wash than any real jealousy on your sister's part. Look at it from this angle: There he was being helpful, even though the three kiddies were helping too, when all these years he has never helped her, no matter how much she needed it."

Annie's eyes were clearing, almost snapping. "Do you mean he never helped her at all?" This was unbelievable.

"I believe that is right. She was so capable for so long that she rarely needed help. And she was also too proud to demand it when she did need it; and he would not offer to help." Dr. Tom liked to see the play of changing thoughts on this girl's face.

"What shall I do? The washing has to be done. It is much too big for me to do alone and still give Mary the care she should have." There was a bit of a catch in her voice. "I cannot bear to have her feeling hurt towards me."

"I tell you what. Next wash day, you just set the bunch of them at it. Advise them, but don't stay out there. Go busy yourself caring for your sister—you might even make a joke of training her husband for her."

"You make everything so understandable. I do believe that was what ailed Sister." Her hands were quick to grasp his hands in the same manner as he had held hers.

He knew he should hurry toward town, but it was much more pleasant here talking to Annie. "Have you heard about the wife who was considered to be in a hopeless decline, slowly dying, because she lacked interest in the fight to live? That is until someone hit onto the bright idea of flirting outrageously with the husband. That made the sick woman so furiously jealous that she got well, just to thwart the budding romance." He smiled into the still too serious face. "The ironic part of that story is supposed to be the wife never believed it had been a hatched up plan, so she never would forgive her husband."

"We are not going to do that to Mary," she said, freed from her hurt and worry.

"No, we are not. No need to. Mary Marcus has many reasons to make the fight back to health. And from now on, she is going to surprise us all by the speed in which she does it. She'll be walking in another week, I think." He had to pry himself away, and as he rode up the wet but opened road, he thought about how he did not blame Jimmy Burch for being so infatuated. *If I were but a few years younger, I'd give Jimmy a race.* Then he fell to wondering if Jimmy had a ghost of a chance.

Back in the house and taking up the busy routine again, Annie thought of Jimmy Burch too, but for a very different reason. *Why does John Marcus act the way he does every time Mr. Burch comes? Surely he must know the many kind things that thoughtful man has done for all of us. Sometimes I wonder if we could have gotten the necessary food and things to care for Sister properly without his help.* Annie was ready to give Jimmy full credit for all he had done and was still doing. *But I wish he hadn't insisted last night I give careful thought to the big question he is going to ask me one of these days.* A proposal of marriage was what he meant, she was sure of that now. *And I tried to make him understand that my answer would have to be* no *a month from now, the same as it would be now.*

Annie had no strong conviction on the question of divorce; she had not given it much thought. That it was legalized in most states, she knew, and any thought on the subject would be in general—not for any certain case. *If Mr. Jimmy Burch wants to free himself from the woman who refuses to live with him, that is his right and privilege. But I must make him understand that he should not do so thinking I'm going to marry him. But just how am I going to go about it when he has never come right out and said so in so many words?* All this was troubling Annie. *If Sister was well, I would ask her advice. And if she was well, I wouldn't be in this predicament—accepting all these favors when I'm sure what my answer is going to be.*

Two days later as Annie brought the mid morning drink, she found Mary trying to walk with the aid of a chair back to steady herself. "Here you are, Sister mine. You down this, and you might walk a mite steadier. I do believe these between-meal drinks are doing the trick."

"They ought to be doing something. I've sure drunk enough of them to floor a mine shaft or sink a battleship."

"Are you really getting so tired of them, Mary? I have tried to change them each time and flavor them differently."

"Of course I'm tired of them. I always did prefer my milk straight–unflavored anyway. I think I'll give Dr. Tom an earful the next time he is down. For the life of me, I cannot see what is the difference if I take eggs and milk together or separate." Mary commenced to drink the tumble of foamy drink without relish, even though Annie had given so much care to fix it.

"That's right. There might not be a bit of difference whether you drink 'em or eat 'em. I'll give you just plain milk next time, and you eat one extra egg at mealtime until we learn differently." She was going to make sure the milk was half cream just the same as she had been using in the fancy drinks. "I wish there was more sunshine. Looks like it should be, here it is May."

"Nasty weather for Jack to be trailing the sheep for sure." Mary handed Annie the empty glass. "I'm glad Father could hire a man to help Jack instead of David making that long trip down and then back. He must be growing too fast—he's so thin and not too full of pep." She was commencing to notice such things, but was not told of David's illness.

"I'm glad too." Not for the world would Annie say that she was the one making clear to Father the need for someone other than David to help trail those sheep. "I wonder how close Jack can be now?"

"Not knowing for sure what day they started, it's only guesswork as to their arrival." Mary was tired now after her effort to walk, and had to settle back in bed much against her will. "Many times I've wished for a few extra hours of sleep, and now I'm so sick and tired of all this resting business, I could scream."

Annie gave her an impish smile. "Just go ahead and scream, Sister. It won't bother me while I give those legs of yours a good rubbing. And no one else is within hearing distance; at least I haven't seen John back yet. I expect he'll trundle in that wheelbarrow piled high with wood by supper time." She had learned quite a bit about massaging by now, and set about the task. She was sure Mary would not do any screaming. On the other hand, she would not have been frightened had that happened. *For Mary to be still half helpless must be galling to her. I guess I would be the same way if I had to depend on others for every little thing.*

In another three days, Mary was walking more steadily, but still needed the cramps massaged away afterwards. Annie was busy doing so and chatting away when suddenly, Margaret and Susan burst into the room all out of breath. "Oh, Mother and Aunt Annie!" gasped Margaret. "We walked along the sheep trail where Jack will bring the sheep over. Susan got tired and I had to come home with her 'cause she cried." It was plain the girl was disgruntled over that fact.

"And I suppose David kept right on along that trail?" Mary was sure of this before either girlie nodded. "That means he won't be home 'til dark or later, sheep or no sheep. You two had better change your school clothes and get at the chores early so you can do his too." This sounded more like Mary, although only natural to the two girls. Out in the kitchen, Annie and John faced each other with a half smile, for this was good news.

Then John scowled, "David has no way of knowing that Jack and the sheep will get in tonight. That young man will keep walking 'til he's worn out and ready to drop, then be back in bed again." He put on coat and hat.

Annie was pretty sure he was going after the boy. "Do you want to take a sandwich or pocketful of cookies along with you?"

"Might be a good idea at that." Impatiently he waited for the food Annie wrapped. Margaret wanted to go along with him, but he would not let her. "No use you tramping all over kingdom come too. Who will milk the cow if you go?" Pocketing the lunch, he told Annie. "Don't look for us 'til we get here."

"Dad don't know a thing about driving sheep," Margaret confided to her aunt while buttoning her shoes in the kitchen. She was peeved at not being allowed to go along. "He's never once touched a one of 'em."

"Daddy can learn, can't he?" Annie tried to jolly her out of her peeve. She was sure John's concern now was for David's well-being, not the sheep, but Margaret was too young to understand that.

It was nearing night fall before the sheep poured down toward the barnyard and corral, much too dark to see David perched on the saddle horse. John was not sure if the young fellow understood why he insisted David ride the horse, but he was sure Jack knew about David being sick, and left him to explain to his helper. It was true that John had never before taken interest in the sheep, but this night, he helped corral them because there was need of the extra man. And for the first time in his life, he could see them as valuable—representing money and a way of livelihood. Old Jack's talk of the price of wool, and what this bunch of sheep would bring in hard cash right this day if they wanted to sell them, helped John Marcus understand.

Supper had been one long exciting meal. Looking now at Mary on the couch where she was forced to rest after eating, Annie thought she should pack her off to bed whether she wanted to go or not. It had been pitiful to see how happy Jack was to be back, and his pleasure at seeing Mary walk her few slow steps. David tried to get Jack to get his shoes off while he went for the washbowl of warm water, but John took an unexpected hand. "I say to bed with you, Young Man. I can pack in that water just as well as you can." He took the heavy white bowl from his hand, and commenced to fill it.

Annie could see that David didn't think this was fair, so she stopped clearing the dining room table long enough to scold, "Listen! All three of you children. It is more than bed time. Mother is going there right this minute if I have to pack her in on my back. Jack surely is weary enough to hit the hay the second he gets his tootsies soaked a short while. Now scatter." She made a wide swing with her arms as if flaying them out of her way. None were amused by the antic this night; they did not want to miss any of the excitement. With John busy, Jack and Mary much too weary, Annie did not realize just how near spent this silent woman was until she attempted to get her up from the couch. "Up, up with us!" she called in fun, trying to help her sister, but waited until John had put the too-full bowl of water down before she called for his aid. "We are going to need some brawn and muscle, John." They lifted Mary into the light rocker and took her back to the bedroom that way; no word was spoken as the two lifted her to the bed. "I think I can manage now." Annie's heart was heavy with misgivings, *What if she has over-taxed her strength? What will it do to her?*

Annie berated herself for not getting Mary to bed earlier despite the joyous homecoming. *I was soft-hearted when I should have been the other way.* She took off Mary's slippers and covered her warmly. *I'll not disturb her to get that dressing gown off.*

"I'm not near as tuckered out like I was last year," Jack said as Annie went back to the warm pleasant room to finish putting the food away. "When that sleet storm rolled down on us the first night out, I was sure glad we were still low along the foothills—really still on the Flats. Dad Williams and his neighbor Simmons could come out in that Ford truck and pick up the stragglers. They must have taken back a dozen at least. Most of 'em would never stood the gaff to make it here. That Simmons is a good neighbor. Guess he is to have part of those bummers for lawn mowers." The old fellow dried his feet and shuffled off to bed. Neither John nor Annie would voice their worries, hoping that morning would find Mary rested and back on the road to recovery again.

But morning brought no word from Mary's mute lips. John was beside himself with fears the second Annie mentioned this fact. "You go sit beside her and try to get this coffee down, while I see to the children's breakfast. We'll put the catch on the hall door so none of them can come in from that direction. I'll head

440

'em off from the kitchen." They especially did not want David to know his mother was worse.

Susan was the one to give trouble this morning, offering several excuses why she had to talk to Mama before she went to school. "You cannot do so this once," Annie told her firmly. "Mother was up much too long last eve, and she became overtired, so she is going to sleep as long as she wants this morning." David directed a suspicious look at Aunt Annie guarding the washroom door so that nine year old Susan could not pass. "Daddy is in there now to keep everyone out so Mother can sleep. I bet he wouldn't even let me go in there." This ruse worked, so soon all three, with lunch boxes in hand, were headed toward school.

Old Jack was eating his meal. On seeing that Annie ate nothing, he sensed something was wrong. "Tell me the truth—I'm past being a kid, remember. Is Mary worse?" His hand was trembling and giving him trouble with his cup. He wished his helper on the trail had not left last night. Undoubtedly he would already be headed back to Max Thorn's ranch.

"Don't fret so, Jack. I won't try to fool you. Mary is worse. And I'm going to call Dr. Tom and find out if her getting overtired last eve would have caused this very thing." She thought perhaps John should be consulted on this question, so went to ask him. He was reluctant to leave Mary's bedside long enough to come to the kitchen, but nodded in agreement that she should call Dr. Tom. Jimmy Burch was not yet at the store, and the clerk was not sure where he could find the doctor this time of the morning, but he would see what he could do.

This uncertainty did not suit John. He knew what happened before when they relied on that same clerk, so he Old Jack's urging to go find the doctor himself. "I tell you, John, the only way to learn for sure how the land lays is to ask Doc point blank if Mary is getting well. He won't lie to you, and it's your right to know as I see it." Jack was in no hurry to get those sheep out of the corral this once, knowing he could leave with Mary in this condition.

"That is how she was the two weeks when first I came," Annie explained to ease his fears. "Sometimes I wondered if she would ever talk again; but she did, and has been more like herself every day lately."

Annie's watch was difficult, counting Mary's slow breaths. She was getting better at keeping her finger tips on that variable pulse. Again she filled jars with hot water and tucked them about Mary's feet and lower limbs—not that they were so very cold. *Neither are they warm,* was her thought.

John found Dr. Tom in DeLamar. He had just talked to Annie by phone, and said that while no relapse could be viewed lightly, neither should it be considered with such alarm. "I told Annie to keep her quiet and feed her those nourishing drinks, just like we did at first. I will be down sometime before night." This was too much for John to endure in this present state.

"You can cut out all your explaining, as far as I'm concerned, Doc. What I want to know is this: Is Mary getting well, or isn't she?" demanded John.

"As yet, I see no reason why your wife will not recover, given time to do so." Dr. Tom was cautious in what he said.

The doc's composure was an affront to John's tense nerves. "You are not telling me straight! Is Mary getting well?"

"This is a setback for sure, and she may have more than one of them unless you and Miss Annie can guard her from overtaxing her strength. You'd better sit down, John, and I'll see if I can put it in plain words." John slumped onto a bench. "There is no need for me to say low close to death Mary Marcus was, not much over a month ago. You are aware of just how ill she was. And she has made a wonderful comeback—part way; but she cannot endure on her own. This is where you two caring for her have to use your heads."

"In other words, Mary is never going to be well again?"

That question nettled Dr. Tom. "If you mean, will your wife be strong enough to take up her life where she left off, earning a livelihood for the Marcus family over a washboard, I would say no—she is not apt to be that well again. Her abounding strength and ambition just about depleted her." He paused for a second to let this soak in. "On the other hand, there is no reason why your wife cannot be well enough to enjoy a fairly comfortable life and live out her allotted years—providing you take over the burden of providing for your family. In short words: Your wife's very life depends on how you measure up to your responsibilities." Doc knew he was laying this on plenty thick.

"But what can I do about it now? I know nothing about

sheep. All the work I've ever done is mining—and they're all closing down." The helplessness of the man was not faked.

"Haven't you ever worked for wages?" Doc was still grim.

"Some, but not much. And I'm stuck here. And where are the wages to be had?"

"True, the DeLamar Mining Co. has been laying off men right and left, but there is work to be had. Right now the new outfit that is sinking the shaft up above the Old Big Eye is crying for men."

Doc was relieved to see a patient come in. He did not want to overplay his hand with John, but it was the first time he had been so direct with him. *I know it's a pretty big pill for him to swallow all at once. Whether he downs it or spits it out is up to him now.*

***

Old Jack let the herd graze on the partly barren hillside close above the race track. This small triangle between the place, road and the designated sheep trail was hardly big enough to feed them this half day, but the worried man was determined to learn first-hand what the doctor had said. In this, Jack was unsuccessful. John was a long time in coming back, and had little to say when he came. As quiet as ever, John hardly made known the fact that this relapse of Mary's was not to be considered defeat. The poor old fellow was more than worried when he returned with the sheep this night. After corralling them, he made for the house. Dr. Tom's saddle horse was tied at the front gate, and Jack was primed with his questions, only to find Doc busy explaining to the three youngsters why they must not bother going into their mother's room. "I know how much you want to go in and see Mother and ask her even one little question to hear her speak. But Aunt Annie knew best when she said *no*. You must mind your Auntie and let Mother rest. And pretty soon, Mother will be walking about and talking to us again." David was too woebegone to be convinced. "We all can remember what it was like when Mother could not talk for so many days. None of us wants that to happen again. That is why we must let her rest now. Your Aunt Annie is a Jim Dandy nurse—if I were ever sick, she is just the kind of a nurse I would want to make me take my pills and stay still."

A faint flicker of a smile appeared on Margaret's face at the thought of a doctor ever being sick and having to stay in bed. David's fears abated some. Doc nodded to Jack and shook hands

443

with him. "I would say you are getting younger every year."

It was not to the old man's liking to ask the questions he wanted to before these children, so he would catch Doc as he was leaving. The conversation became more general for a little while. Margaret told of her dad going to work in the morning. Annie flitted about getting the meal ready between her trips into the sick room. John was out hauling in the wood he had already cut, according to Susan. It was Annie who followed Dr. Tom out to the porch as he left. She wanted to know how long to keep Mary isolated from all noise. To keep Annie from darting back inside, Dr. Tom held her hand firmly while they talked.

"You two gotta excuse me," Jack said as he opened the door and bumped them as he closed it again behind him. "I have to know the lay of the land around here. Did all my jolly homecoming last night do this harm to Mary?" He was pitiful in his concern.

"No permanent harm done, Jack, I fully believe, but it showed us how much farther that woman has to climb before she can be on her own." He put his hand on the stooped shoulder in compassion, but to do so, he had to drop Annie's hand. Until then, he had not realized he still held it. He was sure Jack had noticed this by the sly dig he gave him in the short ribs.

"But Mary will get well if we give her time enough?" pleaded Jack.

"If we give her time enough. Yes. Do you, by any chance, know how to make Mary Marcus be a lady of leisure for the next several weeks?"

Jack did not know the answer to that. Annie had already gone back to her patient, and John was coming in with his last wheelbarrow load of wood. There wasn't much chance for another word with Annie, so Doc soon left.

Chapter Forty Three

THE MONTH OF MAY was half gone. This was payday for John Marcus, and he came into the office just as Dr. Tom was ready to call it a day. He fingered some bills into two piles on the desk. "I want to pay you some on what we owe you. All I've earned won't be near enough I know, but here is $40. I'd give you all of it, but David has to have shoes, as well as the girls." John was weary and ready to rest for a moment.

"This is more than what your bill comes to, I believe." He added up the calls. "It should be $38.25."

"Maybe that's what I owe since Mary got sick, but we owe you from earlier." John could not understand this anymore than he could understand that dumb clerk at the store where he got his check cashed. He had wanted to pay some on their bill there, but that fellow couldn't find any account in the name of Marcus.

Dr. Tom turned the account book around for him to read. "As you see, this is the only account on my books unpaid under the name of Marcus."

"Who paid the rest of 'em?" John shot back.

"If you have the time to look back through this ledger, and a couple more like them, you will see where a dollar was paid here and two dollars there—whenever those precious dollars could be stretched beyond the basics."

John did not look up for several minutes; neither could one say he was reading. Certainly he never turned a page. "Do you know if Mary paid the store bill too?"

"You'd better ask her that question. I have no way of knowing. Here, don't forget your change," he said as John was about to leave the silver on the desk. "Buy some fruit or a big box of candy for that wife of yours now that she is making such great strides in getting well again. How goes the job these days?"

"Alright as far as a job goes, but I quit it today."

"Oh...what was wrong about it?"

"Nothing wrong with the job only it was a short one—wouldn't be more than another week of it. And Mary is fretting 'cause that garden isn't in. You said yourself she wasn't to do any worrying. Jack can't tend to it and herd those sheep. He's a pretty old man, when you come right down to it."

"So Mrs. Marcus is doing some worrying?" asked Doc as if he

had not heard this from Annie. The two had rejoiced over that good news.

"I'd sure call it frettin.' And the noise of the younguns seem bother her. Annie thinks they should go down to their grandparents for a while. Guess these last few weeks of school are not so all fired important."

"It might be a good change for them. We can't expect children to understand the need to be quiet all the time." Not for all the world would he tell this man the real reason Annie suggested the children's stay at the Flats. In his mind's eye, he still could see Annie Williams' animated face as she explained to him only forty-eight hours ago how the children were losing respect for John Marcus. "And it is not right they lose that," Annie had insisted. "While he has a lot of faults, goodness only knows, he still is their father. But oh, my heart bleeds for those poor kiddies. They are so at sea and can't understand all this. They know much more about the work to be done, and how to go about doing it. Of course, John doesn't know the first living thing about feeding chickens or making a garden. When they want to start something, he is sure to stop them. That means confusion and hurt feelings on their part. The only thing I can see to help this situation is to send them down to stay with Father and Mother for awhile. The change will do them good. They will be learning many things, and not unlearning what they already know."

And I second the motion heartily, Dr. Tom reminded himself as he mounted the steps to his room. *I see no harm, but good coming from this change, as long as their mother was agreeable to them going. And wonder of wonders, she was. It could be that Mary Marcus is more observant than we think she is yet. She may see how unhappy the children are since their father has been trying to be the head of that house.* Dr. Tom had some sympathy for the man trying to do something he had never before known he was supposed to do. *That poor girl has her hands and heart full trying to keep that household on an even keel.* He would like to have an excuse to ride down this evening, but he refrained, knowing that Jimmy meant to go.

Now that the days were warm, Mary spent all her time out in the sunshine. With the children gone, the house seemed unnaturally quiet. For two days now, she had walked to the knoll in front of the house. Jack, coming back to the house mid

446

forenoon, saw her there and came that way. "Sure lucky it's getting warm enough for those woollies to hit the shade so I can help John on that garden. Don't believe the man knows a damn thing about making a garden."

"I'm sure he doesn't," was all Mary said before the man started on. Then she spoke with more interest. "I can see the sheep from here, Jack. I'm not worth a cent for anything else, but I can at least watch them."

"That might be alright for you to watch 'em from here," Jack paused to tell her, "but you better not let me catch you taking one step closer. If you see 'em leave the brush or some varmint disturb their cud-chewing siesta, you just call out. Some of us is sure to hear you." With that, he went on down to where John worked in the garden plot back of the barn. Strawberries had been in this spot until last year, but were now started in a new bed. This ground had worked up nicely and John had spaded it deep, now covering the last row of seed.

"You are too late. I got 'er finished," he called out to Jack.

One look at the rows all going in the wrong direction for irrigation, Jack burst out angrily, "You damned fool—you're no Mormon! You can't make water run uphill." Flaying the air with his hands, he stomped about, squinting at the slope of the plot to see if there would be any way to water it from such an angle. "Hells bells it can't be watered good in a month of Sundays." So angry had he been, that he didn't realize John had left until Annie spoke to him.

"What's all the shouting around here?" Annie smiled, though she feared the unpleasantness between the two men, who seemed to never understand each other, might reach Mary on her hilltop.

"Look how that fool man has made the rows." Then he noticed John was not there. "Now where in tunket has that dimwit run off to?"

"He had the ax over his shoulder as if he was going to cut wood." She wanted to laugh at the old fellow's disgust. "Looks like he means to let you make the garden from now on."

"Why couldn't he've left it alone in the first place—all this waste to make it right now." His face was loosing some of its flush, as he scratched his head while puzzling about it.

"In raking it all down and making the rows the way they need to go," Annie laughed now, "you might have a nice mixture of plants for sure."

"But think of the cost of more seed and the trouble to go get 'em." Jack could not calm down.

"I can pay for the seed if you want to go get it. I would go myself, but I have bread ready to bake." Annie went back to the house and the work waiting for her. She was not sure if Jack would go before noon or later, but she got a bill from her purse and had it ready with a slip of paper to write down the needed things. Soon Jack came in and she handed him the money. "I started to write down the list of seeds, then realized you knew better than I what was needed and what grows best up here. After you get those, with what money is left, I wish you would get us a fair-sized chunk of beef. That is about the only thing I can think of that we need right off hand."

A pan of rolls was baked by noon when dinner was ready. As she took them from the oven, John came in with a huge armload of cut wood. "'Gee, but am I glad to see that. I was wondering how I was going to get all this bread baked without wood."

"Where is the rest of 'em?" asked John as he made ready for dinner.

"Mary is still up on the knoll sunning herself—watching the sheep she says. I was up there talking to her not long ago. I'm going to surprise her by taking her meal up to her, and she won't have to walk down yet. You go ahead and eat; I'll be back pronto." Picking up the baking pan she used to carry Mary's meal, away she went.

"I think these rolls are still hot and fit to eat," panted Annie as she put the makeshift tray on her sister's lap, then flopped to the ground beside her. "Now I want you to eat every crumb. Don't let me catch you feeding one bite to rock chucks or ground squirrels."

"You shouldn't go to all this extra work, Annie." Mary uncovered the dish of steaming beans and a mound of fresh cottage cheese on the plate beside the butter and rolls, and another small plate that held a wedge of raisin pie. "You brought such a lot. How can I eat it all? I can't say I'm hungry. I just didn't feel like moving out of my tracks enough to come down to the house."

"That is all the more sign you need more food under your belt. I'll be back later for these dishes." Away she flew down the steep slope and in to eat her own meal.

"Does it take Mary and Jack both to keep tabs on those

sheep?" John was nearly finished with his meal.

"Oh, Jack has gone to town to get more seed. What you or I would plant would never grow. They'd be slanted the wrong way or the wrong end up," Annie joked while dishing a good helping of beans to her plate.

"How much money did you give Jack?" John demanded.

For a second, Annie thought of refusing to answer that question. It was her own money. "What difference does it make how much I gave him? But as a matter of fact, I don't mind telling you that I gave him the smallest bill I had."

"About enough for the old cuss to get drunk on," was John's comment.

Annie, not being aware of Jack's curse with drink, had not thought of such a thing. "He surely can't have too big a spree on $5. My only hope is that he doesn't come home unsteady on his pegs, or Mary will be out trying to round up those sheep in his stead." She was now thinking to have everything done so she could trot up those hillsides in place of Mary if need be.

John never said what he would do, but about three o'clock in the afternoon, when Annie was up visiting with Mary, they noticed him sauntering off toward the sheep as they commenced to leave the patches of shade. "There goes your new herder," Annie tried to joke. But there was no smile on Mary's face.

Annie had figured out there might be danger of Jack going on a binge. *That would be a worry for Mary for sure,* was her thought on the way back to the house. *So the best thing to do is to learn who in the big* City of Gold *could get Jack headed home before he gets into trouble.* She would hardly know how to find him herself should she go up there. *I don't want to ask Jimmy Burch, so that means I shall need to trouble Dr. Tom. He is so good and willing to help in every way needed. I hate to bother him, but perhaps he can refer the task to the sheriff. I can at least find out who would be the proper one.*

Just as she feared, Jimmy Burch answered the call, and when she asked to speak to Dr. Thomas, he commenced his wise-cracking. "Now look here, my Dear Lady. Why is it only to that tall sawbones you'll talk?" Annie knew by that remark that Dr. Tom must be right there in hearing distance.

"When did you hang out your shingle, Dr. Burch?" She was not sure he had heard this until his dismaying "Ouch" was heard over the line.

When Dr. Tom came on the line, Annie told him, in as few words possible, what she feared had happened, and asked the best way to get the erring man back on the water wagon again.

"Let me ask you one question: What would happen to the Marcus household should Jack be in no shape to come home at once?"

"I believe John can get those sheep into the corral tonight, but he sure can't milk the cow." Annie told him.

Doc cut in to say, "Thanks for that reminder. Now don't worry, I'll have the wayward Jack back there by milking time." With that, he hung up the receiver.

Annie was fated to never hear the little tiff going on in the store as Dr. Tom started to leave. Jimmy, hearing just enough of the conversation to guess what was wanted, made a wise crack, "It must be something different for you, this being a bouncer instead of a qualified M.D." A laugh then. "It is good you have the reach of arm for the job."

This was not the first time he had felt Jimmy's barbed wit. He had no wish to quarrel with him, but could not refrain from one jab as he left. "Even the dumbest of bouncers have to know enough to keep their mouth shut sometimes." Doc walked away fast now. He entered the first saloon and was about to ask if Jack was there, but realized he did not know Jack's last name. He paused at his office long enough to gather a few drugs to help him, should he be successful in his search in Lower Town.

At the very last saloon, he found Jack—dead to the world. This would be the first place Jack would hit as he came into town. Borrowing a beer mug from the barman, Doc mixed a drink for Jack, and with the help of onlookers, got it down him. Doc then hustled him out ast to the livery stable across the street. "Guess a bit more poison added to this water won't hurt," Dr. Tom told Lew with a grin as the two of them held Jack as he bent over the railing of the foot bridge.

Lew wanted to laugh at Doc keeping this man retching so, and yet keeping himself from getting bespattered. "Looks like you've had plenty of experience to know how to do it right."

Dr. Tom did not mind Lew's ribbing. "Just a few times wouldn't you say?" They commenced to walk the sick man about between them. As soon as he became sober enough to fight back,

Doc said, "Fight all you want, Man. The more you fight, the quicker you'll sober up. Snap out of it, Jack. Who is going to round up those sheep tonight or milk that cow? How is there going to be fresh milk for Mary Marcus this night? Can John milk that cow?" On and on he hammered that idea home until the sodden brain cleared, and Jack began to curse—the thickened words running together before speech became understandable.

"That fool can't milk. Never gots to learn. Help me to my feet, Doc, an' head me straight. I'll walk this jag off." As soon as the unsteady man was on his feet, he started weaving downstream. The two men watched him go until he was out of sight.

"He might just make it at that," voiced Lew as he chewed on a straw.

"To be on the safe side, I believe I'd better have my horse saddled and trail along behind. He might fall down and not be able to get to his feet without help." Not for anything would he admit he wanted to see Annie Williams.

Mary and Annie helped corral the sheep, and Annie had just finished milking the cow when they heard voices and a horse step on the bridge. "That must be Jack and someone bringing him home." Annie put the pail of milk into John's hand to carry. "You just let on that Mary milked that cow tonight. I bet Jack will never let her down again." Away to the house the girl flew before Dr. Tom and Jack came in sight of the barnyard. John and Mary slowly trudged to the west porch. Quickly, Annie washed and was busy putting cold supper on the table when Dr. Tom came in with a grin.

"Another patient for you, I fear, but plenty of black coffee might be the cure in this case."

"Thanks for the tip, Doctor. I'll make a quick fire with this sagebrush and put coffee on right now. How am I ever going to thank you for all this trouble you went to? Will you join us for a cold supper? Oh, I'll make enough coffee so you may have some if you prefer the hot drink instead of cold buttermilk."

"Buttermilk for me, if you have plenty." Every time he looked at this spirited young woman, he found something more to admire about her. Without fuss or bother, she built the fire with the pungent brush; in short order, she had the coffee pot in the hottest place.

"Talk about plenty of buttermilk. You should have seen the

quarts of milk I churned this day, thinking it was cream. I'm that dumb." With a wry face she uncovered the mold of fresh butter. "I believe there isn't more than a pound of butter, and this full pitcher of buttermilk," she said with mirth.

"You might be like the *city miss* I heard about. She and her chum moved to the country for the summer, and she was not too impressed with country life. Some of their friends were extolling the good points of the country, and asked her how she liked the abundance of fresh cream, milk and butter. *Yes,* she admitted, *the milk and cream were alright, but when I churn the milk, no butter comes off it—just curds and whey."*

Annie could laugh with him over that. "I must be that very city gal."

"Why not be truthful," Mary was in the washroom and heard the joke, "and say you have fed all the cream to me instead of churning it?" Mary was slow in her walk as she came—washed and ready to eat. Then came John, still carrying the pail of milk. Jack followed behind.

Black coffee was Jack's only intake, and he soon left the table for bed. The four of them sat on and chatted by candle light for several minutes. *I never realized John Marcus could or would talk this much,* was Dr. Tom's thought. Then came the knock that he had somehow expected: Jimmy Burch proffered two slim letters and a roll of papers as his excuse for coming.

"Won't you come in?" Annie did the honors certain that John would never act the part of a host toward Jimmy Burch. Mary still had a ways to go before she would be her old hospitable self. "We had a cold snack this night for supper, is it too late for you to join us?" Annie could see John leave the kitchen, lighting a lamp to read the roll of newspapers.

"I just came from the dinner table, thanks." But later he accepted a glass of buttermilk as he took a seat with the others. Somehow the easy jovial talk was lost this evening. Soon Mary went to bed.

"I should by all means help with these dishes to pay for my meal, but fear I shall have to be like the beggar and eat and run." Dr. Tom had no intentions of trying to out-stay Jimmy, and wanted him to know it.

"If you are not in too big a rush, Doc, I'll ride along with you." Jimmy made sure he kept Doc waiting a short minute while he spoke to Annie alone before following him out and mounting his horse. He cantered the short distance to overtake Dr. Tom, who was already in motion. Jimmy knew this man well enough that he himself would have to start the conversation. He waited until the rocky part of the road was reached where they needed to travel slowly. "Doc, I guess I must have made a double-ringed ass of myself this afternoon." He waited for a comment but none came. "It didn't come out quite like I meant it to. I was trying to make a joke, whether you believe that or not. I'm sorry if you took it otherwise." He paused again, but was no wise expecting a comment now. "I'm sure you have no idea just how much Annie Williams means to me. I have all the same as staked out a claim to her thoughts for the next two weeks. She is to give me my answer then."

"I doubt I was ever considered a claim jumper." There was acid in his tone. Doc touched his horse with his heel and rode on faster. He was getting tired of Jimmy's presuming ways.

By bedtime, he was disgusted with himself for letting Jimmy rile him. *It will be very easy to stay away from the Mills House for the next two weeks. Then for sure, Jimmy can't think I'm pulling any fast ones on him.* He found the next three days to be the longest he ever remembered.

There were no young folks left in DeLamar now with the mine playing out. Doc found none free to go fishing with him when he could get away. He was about to call a truce and see if Jimmy was in a fishing mood the third day, when that stony faced fellow passed him by as if he wasn't there. *Now that guy saw me alright. If he doesn't want to speak, it is alright too. But I'm sure not going to beg him to go fishing.* After the few sick calls were made, time again hung heavy on his hands. *Jimmy owes me nothing; nor I him. To the devil with him! He can think what he jolly well pleases. He will anyway.* And with that, he went for his horse and rode down the creek.

I have so little to do—I wonder how long the mining company will keep me on. Doc knew, of course, that as long as they had any men working, he would still be under contract. The day very pleasant, light travel over this road created no dust, and it was still warm enough for the locust to buzz their presence. His saddle horse did not mistake them now for rattlesnakes, as it once had. *I wonder if Jimmy got his answer and it was a* no. *That could account for his vile mood.* Doc's ride had been mellow and thoughtful, but the second he caught sight of Annie Williams in the doorway of the Mills House, he became alert at once.

"How goes everything here?" He sensed something was amiss.

Annie had just taken a pan of cookies from the oven and took a moment to find a safe place for the hot pan. "I'm sure everyone is as well as can be expected." She tried to sound natural, but the penetrating look from Dr. Tom indicated she had failed, "Come in if you wish. I believe some of the family will be here about noon."

Now what could have happened in three short days to change this spirited young woman so? Dark circles around her eyes told their tale of no sleep. He hesitated to pry, so spoke of the first thing coming to mind. "Are you really able to bake five dozen cookies all at once?" He glanced at the square pan with its eight rows of nicely browned rounds.

"It's a big oven, and this pan just fits." Annie was carefully removing the baked cookies from the pan ready for the next batch that was cut and ready.

"How is our patient walking these days, and where might she be tramping now?" He made a play as if to snitch one of those warm cookies, but no smile came to her troubled face.

"Mary insisted she go watch the sheep this forenoon. I think it very foolish of her to stay out all day."

"Does she take along a hearty lunch, or walk back for her meal?"

"She said she is not coming back today; I rather think she took a sandwich." Gone was all pretense of concern.

How two such fine women and loving sisters can hurt each other, as these two, is beyond me. Dr. Tom recalled Annie's woebegone face of a short while back. "You just turn your back while I swipe a dozen of these cookies and half this pitcher of milk. If Mary Marcus insists on doing a man's work, she is going to have to eat like a farm hand." While wrapping the fresh cookies for him, he filled a small jar with milk. Annie would not rise to his bait of conversation.

Doc rode his horse part of the distance, then walked behind the fresh sheep tracks that led ever upward toward the steeper slopes. It was now mid-day, and he guessed the sheep must be resting among the rocks and scant brush, as non were in sight. He spied a lone figure seated on the ridge. As he climbed toward her, the dog Gibson trotted down to meet him. Mary walked slowly along the ridge, but didn't leave her place of lookout.

"It's a steep climb from that direction," was Mary's greeting as Dr. Tom came close enough for speech. As he seated himself to rest, and she saw the milk and food he was taking from his pockets, she scolded. "Why did you think you had to bring me more lunch? I brought a sandwich with me."

"I learned at the house what you had, but it isn't half enough food for you. Even the poorest shepherd will bring more than that."

"I fear I'm not a very competent herder; I can't say yet if I'm the worst, but I can set up here and make sure none wanders over this ridge. Gibson minds well. All I have to do is swing my arm and he's out and pushing them back. But I do believe he is like me—getting old and lazy."

"Yes. I can see you are lazy." Dr. Tom's smile was infectious. "Pretty bad case of it." He was very much at ease with Mary Marcus. She looked well these days—a good tan on hand and arms; a hat shielded her face, but a tint of color showed on her cheeks. "This nomad's life seems to agree with you—if you can remember to rest lots, and not push yourself. But there must be times when you won't be able to stop and rest, should these woolies, as Jack calls them, take a notion to travel where you don't want them to go."

"That's where I'm trying to make my head save my heels. I'm getting good at figuring what direction these sheep will start out next, and Gibson and I wander that way. I wish I were as good at guessing what is troubling that dear sister of mine. She seems so unhappy, it worries me."

"I was about to ask you that question, thinking you would have some inkling."

"So you noticed it too? I thought she might be homesick, but she says not. This morning she commenced to talk about me selling this place and moving away, as if that was easy to do or I wanted to. She sure has me baffled." Mary's sigh was deep.

Chapter Forty Four

"WHAT'S THAT OLD ADAGE, *the course of true love never runs smooth?*" Watching Mary's hat shake thoughtfully, he added, "Jimmy Burch seems badly out of sorts this fine summer day too."

"I know," said Mary. "Jimmy was hurt because I would not use my influence to persuade Annie to think more favorably of him as a future mate." She had no intention of saying more about the unpleasant scene of yesterday. Some of it was not clear to her yet. "Annie's unhappiness cannot be due to her refusal of Jimmy. She talked about it the night before with me, and was somewhat ashamed that she had allowed herself to even considering his proposal. No. It can't be that. When she said *no* to Jimmy, she meant just that."

"And the gentleman in question accepted the answer as final?" Dr. Tom asked himself that question as much as he was asking Mary Marcus.

"I doubt it." Her grimace showed displeasure. "Being acquainted with Jimmy for the past fifteen years, I would say it is hard for him to accept defeat." It was several seconds before she went on, as if no thought of time. "She could be homesick, and feels she should not leave me. That is the only explanation I can think of in her insistence that I sell this place. If you get the opportunity, make it plain to Annie that it is safe to leave me on my own. While I may not have the will yet to work like a sane human, I'm sure I won't starve or let the others."

"Any advice coming from me might not be acceptable." Doc could see the roof gable of their house below, and thought of Annie's unhappy face. He did not care to get involved in something he knew nothing about.

"I believe you are about the only one here who would have much weight with Annie. She thinks very highly of you and your advice. A few weeks back, Annie was quite unhappy for a day or two and then she came up smiling. She admitted that some little question had troubled her, and when she talked it over with you, all the answers came clear. That is Annie's only fault—she is too conscientious; lets little things hurt her."

"Do you suppose she will feed me, should I happen back looking hungry?" He grinned down at the upturned face that still did not have its customary smile in place.

"You might have to mention the fact." There was a slight grin to her lips as she said this.

Guess I timed it about right, was his thought at seeing old Jack leave the house to clean ditches, and John with his axe glinting in the sun, evidently after more wood. His rap at the kitchen door startled the girl emptying a dishpan of water into the sink at that moment. She seemed dismayed to see anyone, knowing there were tell-tale tears on her cheeks. As her shoulder came up to brush them away, he brought his handkerchief into play. "You haven't got half of them." This girl might be only homesick, but never had he seen such a tense stony grief as this. "Wanting to go home?" he asked, as his fingers tipped up her chin ever so slightly. She tried to turn her face to better wipe her eyes. "And afraid to leave your sister?"

"No, I am not homesick." She drew away from Tom, putting away the pan and hanging up the towel. There were no more tears as she turned to face him. "It is true that I think it best not to leave my sister here. She is far from strong enough to do the hard work she has been forced to do all these years. The only sensible thing for her to do is to sell this place and go where life can be easier for her."

"You might be right about all of that. The only drawback is that Mary Marcus considers this home. With the bunch of sheep they now have, I wonder if she will need to go back to the hard work over the washboard. Come sit down and let's talk this over." He did not guide her to the stool beside the cleared table, but was glad to see her take that. On his favorite perch atop of one corner of the sought after table, he was above her and looking down on the brown head that bent forward under its load of woe. "While any life in these hills cannot be called easy, many people like it. I'm aware of the hardships your sister has endured, and I can agree whole heartedly—she is entitled to an easier way of life from now on. It seems John Marcus is showing some evidence of learning this little game of life. Of course he is going to be awkward, never having shouldered the responsibility before."

"Life for Mary will never be easier or happier as long as she lives here, or pretends to live with John Marcus." There was meaning in this statement.

"On the other hand, if this is her choice, you and I must bow to it. We might differ with her as to what would be the best way. Still, when all is said and done, what she and John Marcus decide they want is the final answer. Given time, the seemingly worse mismatched husband and wife have ways of working out their own difficulties." He patted Annie's shoulder consolingly.

Up came the bowed head. "Mary hasn't lived as John's wife for more than five years." To Annie, this was proof of the hopeless situation.

"Perhaps so. But she also has stayed here—not leaving; neither has John. There must be some bond of affection there, wouldn't you say?"

More sorrow showed in the eyes meeting his. "John Marcus is not a man to be forgiving her—ever!"

"Forgiving her?" Dr. Tom was taken aback. "What does he have to forgive? Unless it is because she didn't kick him out years ago and make him support his family."

"John knows about Jimmy Burch being her lover." This was agonizing to admit.

"Who filled your mind with such rot?" He gripped both her shoulders as if he would shake the admission from her. "Anyone telling you that is either lying or trying to mislead you as to the truth."

"John Marcus himself told me." Annie could say no more.

"And no one knows better than John how false accusations can be." Dr. Tom was troubled over what was behind all this. He could not fathom John Marcus deliberately telling such a lie. "I can't imagine why John would make such a charge. If he has half the brain I think he was blessed with, he knows that is not true. More likely, his wife refused to be a wife to him so there would be no more frail babies that might not live, or that she was not able to support. That's the most tangible reason why. Mary would be the last person to welcome a lover." As he said the word *lover*, a thought came to him, but before he could put that thought into words, Annie spoke.

"Surely John would not say that if he didn't believe it to be true." No one could be that low to do such a trick in her opinion.

"I'm not so sure of that. If John was riled enough, and his jealousy worked overtime, as it undoubtedly has all this time, he might say things far wide of the truth. Did you think of that?"

"John was angry, I'm sure. He has never liked Jimmy Burch

coming to see me. I guess he was jealous to see Jimmy ride up the knoll to talk to Mary." Remembering John's accusation came flooding back. "He couldn't have said such a thing and known it was a lie." Tears were gathering again.

"Are you sure John Marcus even knows the meaning of the word *lover*? The more I think about his limited schooling and reading, the more I wonder if he might have confused *admiration* or *affection* with that word, *lover*. It is surprising how simple the man is in some ways."

Annie considered this view point. She had been so crushed in spirit to think her sister, whom she had idolized, could fall so short from the pedestal she had been placed. "Surely John would not say that just to make me suffer so, that I might marry Jimmy Burch. I never said he need not worry on that score." Her voice faltered before going bravely on. "Even yesterday, when John came out to the porch where we stood talking, he was so nasty to Jimmy. I wouldn't give John the satisfaction to know what I had just told Jimmy—I didn't think John Marcus had any right to act that way. I'm of age and capable of thinking for myself. And that is what I told John Marcus later, after he and Jimmy had their little tiff. I must say, Jimmy acted very well. He told John that he had given me the honor of asking me to be his wife, and he hoped other people would let us settle the question without outside influence."

"Go on." Doc made the pressure of his hands felt the more. All this was becoming clearer. "Was that when John made the accusation?"

Annie nodded then lifted her wet face. "Jimmy said he was going to speak with a calm and sensible person. He wasn't halfway up to where Mary sat when John turned on me, saying he guessed I would think twice about marrying Jimmy Burch when I knew he had been Mary's lover these last five years. That made me furious, and all I could think of was the injustice of him saying such a thing about his wife. And when I told him that, he said Mary had not been his wife all this time." Only Doc's strong hands kept her upright now, and they were letting her lean forward as the weeping commenced with abandon.

"Weep all you want, Little Woman." One hand held hers, the other touched the smooth coils of her soft hair, then patted her heaving shoulder. "And let your tears wash away all the hurt. All this has been one huge misunderstanding somehow." For long minutes of consolation, she wept, her tears increasing. Doc spoke in calm tones. "Think of it this way—John Marcus may be different in his upbringing and outlook on life, but he is very much the normal male. If he, for one moment, thought his wife preferred someone over him, he would have been long gone from this place." He shifted his position to hold her more comfortably. "Jimmy Burch, like most of the population in DeLamar, has great admiration for Mary Marcus and her fight to make a living for her family. In Jimmy's position, it was possible for him to do many things to help her, but that is a far cry from being her lover."

He was sure the girl was not hearing what he said—her weeping became more hysterical. "You have cried enough, Annie Girl. Go wash away the hurt of all time." He shook her to give her pause in her sobbing. Knowing of her constant work and care these several weeks, and not half enough sleep at times, and this hurt on top of it all made him tender toward her. He was thought a sharp slap or splash of cool water might bring her out of it, but he continued to cradle her in his arms.

Was it her suffering or her nearness that was affecting him? "Stop it," he said in stern tones; the immediately smoothed back the tumbled hair from her face. "Don't grieve this way, Annie Dear." For long moments he held her, her tears wetting his coat— deep sobs wracking her whole body. The fragrance of her hair was intoxicating as his lips brushed her hair and then her salty temple. Not until her hands pushed against his chest was he aware of her will to be free. Only then did he realize she was not now weeping. How long a time this had been, he could not have said. "Let me hold you longer," he whispered. His arms tensed in their longing to hold her again; his lips burned for the feel of hers.

She drew back not in anger, but in surprise. Jack's heavy footsteps sounded on the porch as he came up the west steps. Annie stepped away and nodded to the kind old fellow ambling in. "What did you think of that automobile passing here a few minutes ago? We are getting on the map for sure. First time one of those buzz-wagons made it up here that I know of." Jack helped himself to a big drink of water. "There's several of 'em dodging around down on the Flats nowadays. I been wondering how long before some adventurous cuss would tackle these hills, so history has been made this day." He stopped to fill his pipe, which he rarely smoked.

Doc fell into conversation with the old gentleman. "So it has. How long do you suppose before you and I will learn how to dodge all the high centers there are on these roads?" Jack grinned at him, expecting that he had seen the automobile, yet Doc had not even heard it. "Do you think it's smashed any bridges between here and town?" was his sally as he walked out along the east porch. He did not walk fast, and tarried a second at the front hall door hoping to see Annie. There was no chance of Jack leaving soon, and he guessed she would not show her red swollen eyes to anyone. *I would feel plenty foolish if she refuses to see me, should I knock.*

Just what he would say, he had not thought out, but the fear she would not come to the door kept him from making the try. *I could not blame her any,* he told himself as he mounted and rode away. Once around the willow clumps and out of sight of the house, he rode slower. His jumbled emotions were hard to sort out. *I would not hurt Annie for the world.* The kiss lingered on his burning lips. *When my hard mouth is sore, what must hers be?* Then came the next dismaying thought, *What manner of beast must she think me?*

Leatha Orchard's image came to mind. He had not thought of her in months. The contrast of his sentiments toward her and what he now felt for Annie Williams promoted the thought, *Sometimes I wonder if Leatha will ever know real happiness.* He imagined Leatha in England, and away from his present need and hunger for the girl he had just mauled. *Annie must be more than disgusted with me,* feeling sure this was the reason she had pulled away to search his face. *What other reason could there be for her refusal to stay in my arms? She must have known how much I want her? For one short moment I had the craziest hallucination that she welcomed and responded to my lips.* The next second she pushed herself free.

The most manly thing to do would be to go back and apologize, I'm sure. But if she came within reaching distance of my arms... What could I say after repeating such caveman tactics? That he had offended! And that thought drove him on instead of turning back. He was so deeply entrenched in his bachelorhood role, living where marriageable young women were scarce, he was convinced he was not destined to have a wife and family ever. *I must be getting foolish ideas now that I'm near the forty mark.*

As he neared town, he thought of Jimmy and his disappointment. *He is only two years younger than I, and having failed once, he's all for trying it again. Mary thinks he has not accepted Annie's turndown as final. That is where Jimmy and I differ: I won't need to be told no. If I mean anything to Annie at all, I can catch on; if not, I will be scarce around the Mills House from now on.*

***

Old Jack had climbed the slopes later in the afternoon, soon after the sheep commenced their browsing. That left Mary free to go to the house, but she seemed to be in no hurry; instead, she chatted with Jack for some little time. On her ridge top, she had heard the foreign sound of the automobile, but had caught no sight of it. She guessed what it must have been, for she had not seen anything that looked like an airplane in the sky. "They must be making the automobiles better. I read where they are traveling everywhere in them." She folded up the newspaper she had brought out with her to read. "I wonder if the one today had to have help up that steep hill between here and Reynolds? I judged it came from that direction"

"Must have. It seemed to have a lot of pull to it. It's sure a noisy thing when you are close to it. No wonder they frighten horses." Jack was full of talk, but he had no chance of saying more now. Mary was picking her way down slope, and he needed to head in another direction.

Annie had put cold compresses on her eyes to take down the puffiness, then found that the wet towel covering her burning lips felt good. With the bowl of water close to the bed where she could wring the towel out often, she soon got relief. Having slept none the night before, she dropped off quickly. Mary's step into the shade-drawn room awakened her. "Oh, my! And here I've been to sleep." Her mouth felt odd as she tried to talk. Laying aside the nearly dry towel, she came to her feet.

"Do you have a headache Annie?" Mary noticed the cloth and water handy. "Just go on relaxing—no need of you getting up."

Chapter Forty Five

THE DINNER WAS TURNING out just as Dr. Tom expected it would with Jimmy monopolizing the conversation. He had to admit, Jimmy was good at these social graces. It was plain he was out to impress Annie, and perhaps John Marcus too. For more than two hours, the six of them sat at the table, talking, telling funny stories, and doing knife, fork and tumbler tricks. The conversation turned to places Annie had never been, including camping.

"Camping for fun might be fun," Mary told her, "but camping as a way of living is far from it. Sometimes it can be right down disagreeable. If it rains, or dirt commences to blow, there is no place like home."

John was hearing about Mary's dislike of their nomad life for the first time. He was learning a few other things this day. *Now take Doc, Annie, Mary and old Jack all talking to Jimmy, and seemingly enjoying it. And I'd say not one of 'em fooled by his smooth talk.* He had noticed how first one, then another had differed with him on many subjects.

"My dear young lady, we must make amends at once and see that you do go camping." Jimmy was very gallant in his talk. "The weather is at its very best the first of June. There should be good fishing still, perhaps on Deer Creek, which is not very far distant. All those in favor of a short camping trip, please say *aye* or forever hold your peace." Jimmy stood on tip toe with his right hand raised. None answered. The smiles were general.

"Just because I haven't been camping, or fishing either, is no reason why I must go this summer," Annie appealed. "There is always another year. Sister here has never been fishing; another season and she might stand such a trip better." Annie had no intentions of being put in Jimmy's debt any more than she already was.

The subject was dropped for other topics until just before Jack left to go tend the sheep. "Why in tunket can't you take these two gals on a little camping trip?" he asked John. "Couldn't come at a better time—nothing to do around here for a week at least but milk that cow and wrangle the woolies. I can do that and keep that water running too. Kept myself alive many a year on my own cooking. I 'kin go it again. 'Course, it won't be as good a grub as I been stowing away here for some time." He grinned, while putting a slice of cake in a bit of paper and chucking it in his pocket.

"It looks to me as if you good people are set for a camping trip." Jimmy was pleased with how it was working out. "Like I wanted to say before, there is the whole camping equipment—tent, folding chairs, three-four cots and cooking gear—all stored away doing no one a bit of good. I would be more than glad if someone would use them. The light camp wagon has extra springs so it is a comfortable ride. The wheels might need greasing—it's been some time since it has been used. You can always find a team to haul it wherever you choose to camp. I tell you what. If you make it somwheres along Deer Creek, Doc and I will ride over the first night and bring the team back to town so you'll not have them to bother with them until you need them to haul you back."

John cast no vote against this plan, thinking Annie might want to go. Mary had not been agreeable to his censor of trying to bust up Annie and Jimmy's romance. *I still don't know how it is going to pan out.* Then he remembered Doc had mentioned more than once that a short trip of most any kind would be a benefit to Mary.

Mary, thinking Annie might enjoy camping, did not veto the plan. Annie at this moment was all at sea, not knowing if those strong fingers gripping her hand below the table were trying to convey some special message or not. One thing sure, it was sending chills up her spine. Fearing her flushed face might betray all this exultation, she turned to face him. "I fail to hear Dr. Thomas consenting to come eat fish with us. Perhaps he fears we won't catch any." Somehow, it mattered to her if he was not going to be in on this camping deal.

"I'll be there." He gave an extra press of the hand before freeing hers. "Neither am I an expert fisherman, but I am a first rate flunky about camp. And to prove it, I shall wash these dishes." Deftly, he untied Annie's apron and donned it. "Then I must trot along." He would not try to out-stay Jimmy.

Monday was a busy day at the Mills House and Tuesday started out that way. Early forenoon, John walked to town for team and rig, arriving back just before noon expecting they would be ready to load and start at once. "Here I'm all steamed up and ready to be off, and we have to stop and eat," he grumbled.

Annie heard it, and came storming in and shaking him by the shoulders. "Don't you let me hear one more growl. Mary is hungry. I'm hungry. Jack is here and ready to eat, and you should be hungry, for you had breakfast an hour early. It is not going to take one moment longer to eat our meal here than at camp." This might have been said mostly in fun, but Annie meant it too. She did not intend to let John spoil Mary's trip.

He did no more growling in her hearing. Dinner smelled good; he looked over the three elderberry pies not long from the oven. "How is Jack going to eat all those pies?"

"We'll leave him one. Two go with us if I have to pack them in my lap. I could eat a quarter section of one right now, but I know they are much too hot. I was hoping to get them baked early so they would be cool, but that cream liked to have never churned—just because I was in a hurry, I expect." She yanked the coffee pot back just as it bubbled from the spout. "The box of groceries are packed and ready to be loaded if you want to. No, maybe it will be good to leave it until the last thing—the milk, cheese, and butter are there; it won't be good to have them in the hot sun—though I have wet towels around them." Annie was thinking on the run, making sure they were taking everything needed and leaving plenty for Jack.

She sliced bread for dinner while she talked. "I believe there will be plenty of bread for you, Jack. I made all the extra milk up into cheese, and we will take a big part of that with us. We also are taking along the morning's milk—one crock of last night's milk is all you will find in the cellar. That means you are not going to have to wash milk pans or crocks for several days." She was smiling while rushing about.

"Better slow down there, Miss Annie, or you'll never wait to ride in that rig. You'll be running ahead of the team to get there faster," grinned Jack.

"I guess I am pretty excited. Remember, this is my first camping trip. I believe the meal is ready to eat. I'll go call Sister." She started for Mary's and her room by way of the dining room. With a deft move, Jack blocked her way. He was sure Mary was on her way through the washroom.

"You are not doing that right for a real camper. When you have the meal ready, sing out real loud, *Grub is piled. Come and get it before I throw it out.* They'll come a running and it will save you lots of steps."

Mary, in the kitchen by now, smiled with Annie over Jack's coaching. "Lucky the washing, ironing and scrubbing were finished yesterday, or Annie would have been crowding all that work in this half day."

"Something like her sister used-to-was," joked Jack before drying his face.

"Just like her," came from John unexpectedly.

"I am so slow and pokey now," lamented Mary. "It doesn't seem possible I ever hurried about like Annie.

"You should make a rip snorting good fisherwoman. They are supposed to move slow and cautious so as not to scare the trout." Jack was getting as much pleasure out of this trip as if he were included.

The team proved to be a fair driving team, but there were a few spots where they could travel at no more than a slow walk. Annie thought of Jack's joke about her running ahead of the team. That was just what she wanted to do. Making herself relax a bit, she intended to enjoy this trip, come what may. "This side of the mountain is so different—even the flowers are of a different kind and color than on the north slope. Look at those sunflowers, so bright yellow. There was hardly one in bloom on the other side. Did you say, Sister, that you never have been on this road before?"

"That is right. I never have. I thought I was going to come over here fishing once—that was when David was just a wee babe. He must have been but three weeks old, for it was the day before we left on our travels. John was none too sure about how that team he had gotten the week before would perform, so he thought it good that David and I weren't along." Mary stopped talking. She suddenly remembered that John had come fishing that day solely because she mentioned being hungry for some fish. And he had brought back nearly a dozen.

She remember that must have been the same day she had leased the place to Max Thorn. And mixed with the good feeling that security brought was the guilty feeling that John would never approve. In trying to ignore John's jealous ranting when he learned about it, she started to talk of other things. "That was fourteen years ago. It doesn't seem possible that David is that old, but he is; and Margaret will be twelve this autumn. How time flies." She wondered if John was also thinking of that time, for Annie was having a hard time getting any conversation out of him.

"I bet we've traveled more than three miles already," Annie said, then turned to Mary. "That would leave one more mile. Do you think you can stand it, Sister?"

"I think so, if it no further."

"You are tired, Mary, I know. I have been wishing we had fixed you bed of sorts—one of those cots put up perhaps in the back of the wagon so you could have been resting. Sister, do you remember how Max Thorn fixed that bed on top of the load for Mother when first we came? I was just a kiddie, but I remember it as if it were yesterday. And he made some sort of a nest for me to curl into. I have seen Max just once since I have been back—while Mother was so sick, he came one evening to see her." Annie laughed happily. "He made it plain that he came to see Mother. He said I was too much the city girl. He is a funny guy. I do believe he doesn't look a day older than the first time I saw him." Annie could get no conversation with either one of them on this subject, so she switched direction. "Are you sure you know where this camp is they we're talking about?"

"I know about where it has to be. This morning, Doc said it was right where this road meets with the one coming from DeLamar. No danger of missing it.; we'll be sighting it soon—can't be more than a quarter of a mile now." True to expectations, the slope of the hill was becoming less steep. On their left, they could see the road angling from the top down and joining this road right at a clump of tall cottonwoods.

"Isn't it beautiful?" Annie lookied up into the canopy of leaves as John stopped the rig in the shade. "There are different kinds of trees here." The backdrop along the stream was crowded with water beach and willows, while on the hillside leading down to this place, held a scattering of juniper instead of pine and fir. "And here is a fresh spring right where we want it. Someone has even built a table." Her eye kept tabs on John helping Mary to the ground; then she worried as he let her ease to lie prone. "Oh, Sister Mine, I'll have a cot fixed for you in no time." When it was ready, Mary refused to be lifted to it.

"Just let me be. I will be alright in an hour or two. Stop your worrying. I've rested on ground before, and not always this clean or shaded. Now go on with your fishing. I need no waiting on; nor did I come to spoil anyone's fun." She did let Annie put a pillow under her head, then pretended she was asleep.

John finally went fishing, but Annie still puttered about camp putting all the food stuff in the safest and handiest places. Below the spring in the shallow water was a wooden box. Into this she set the jugs of milk, a crock of cheese, and another with the butter. Small jars of cream were tucked in too. To be doubly safe, she turned the wooden box they had brought things in over the top. There was no place for the pies except on the camp table. In no time at all, a line of ants trailed across the white cloth covering. Grabbing up a dipper of water, she did battle with them, but as soon as the table runner dried, back they came. She built up a fire and used hot water as fast as they started up the rough legs. "I'll keep right on scalding as fast as you come, you pesky varmints." Her talking aroused Mary.

"For goodness sake, who are you doing battle with?" Mary asked as she got up.

"Ants! Whole armies of them. I've been scalding them right and left and still they come. They are determined to eat those pies and I'm just as determined they are not going to." Splash went another cup full of water.

"Grease of any kind smeared on the table legs will stop them, but it is mean about getting onto clothing. I learned that down in the desert when there was no water. Do you suppose we can find four tin cans around that will hold water? We can set the table legs in those to stop them." The cans were found and soon the pies were safe. "But we must have John swing one of these wooden boxes from a limb, so to have other things safe, for ants will bother sugar, flour, bacon and raisins—even bread if they can get at it. And we must remember to have everything well covered at night or the magpies will have their breakfast before we are up."

"Not very nice neighbors around our pretty camp, I would say." As dusk came on, Annie listened for some sound along the grade on the hillside above them. First came the snap of brush close at hand as John came toward camp in the growing dark. "How many fish did you catch?" she asked as soon as he came in sight. She heard his answer of seven, just as she heard the first roll of small rocks set in motion by the horses' hooves. "I hear them coming, don't you?"

John nodded as he knelt in the firelight to dress out the fish. They were fair sized ones, and Mary admired them as she washed them for him.

"I'll get the skillet on and we will have them frying before they get here. The beans are already baked; I just have to heat them and everything else is ready. We can have supper in short order."

The sound of the rocks and the ping of a horses' shoe on rock came every few seconds until the two cantered the last few yards on the more level road. Dr. Tom brought a wrapped package to the table as soon as he swung from the saddle. "Oh ho, and here I was afraid of your fishing ability and brought steaks. The magpies might like these." He was smiling as he gave them into Annie's hands.

"If I can prevent it, those sassy birds are not getting one little mite of these. We haven't so many fish, but what each one of you might want a steak also. Just think—we can broil them right over the coals."

"No steak for me," boasted Jimmy eyeing the ready food. "Not when I see good baked beans, a gallon or two of cottage cheese, and deviled egg salad. You even gathered watercress." Jimmy was getting in a smile too.

"If you have a cool place to keep these, they might be alright until tomorrow."

"And we eat those when you are not here to enjoy them?" Annie was scandalized at such a thing.

"The road is still opened, and I might make it over tomorrow about this same time—if I should be invited, that is." He knew Jimmy would be fuming and wrangle himself an invitation.

"Of course you are invited." Annie turned away quickly so none would guess how happy she was. "I'll wash this crock that held the cheese; that should make a safe place. And down in that cold water, they will keep. And I will weight the whole thing down with rocks so even a bobcat can't get them, should he come around. While I do that, will the best coffee maker please measure the coffee into the pot."

John reached for the coffee and dipped out several tablespoons full, then quickly pulled the pot to a cooler spot as it bubbled over. "Expect I may be the worst maker of the brew, but I

Effie Sutton

want to eat sometime before midnight."

But it was midnight before the group about the campfire broke up and the two visitors climbed the hill, trusting to the sure footedness of their mounts. "I know you must be dead tired, Sister Dear," Annie fussed over Mary to get her ready for bed before the last flicker of light should be gone, "but it was fun wasn't it?" she whispered.

"Of course it was nice with everyone visiting. Why should I be weary? I have been resting here on this cot for the past two hours, and hardly did a tap of work since we got here." Mary was weary, but got little sleep; Annie was much too excited to sleep; but it was John who grumbled in the morning about not sleeping.

"I'm going to cut me a good soft bed of boughs before dark tonight. To the devil with all their cots—they can have 'em." This day, he went hunting instead of fishing. Three young sage chickens and a cottontail were dressed out.

"Shall we cook the rabbit for the three of us this noon, and run the chance these birds will keep?" Annie asked Mary, knowing she was well versed in such things.

"I'm pretty sure they'll keep. That water those crocks are setting in is really cold. With no sun striking the place, they can't get very warm."

That night after their fine steak supper, Mary slept well. Thursday evening, they dined on the sage hens. Friday, John went fishing again, but with only five to his credit, he managed to get another rabbit—a young snowshoe this time, so they dined well.

As they sat about the fire this night, Dr. Tom spoke up. "No wise fair for you people to be feeding us two big eaters every night, so tomorrow evening, I bring the meal already prepared."

"And I say that would not be fair for you to go to all that trouble." Annie wanted to say something. Jimmy had his eye on her, so she dared not let her hand be held by the one waiting in the shadow to grasp it.

"No bother to me." Dr. Tom shifted his position. "I have already asked the cook at the hotel to roast me a couple of chickens. He makes a very good potato salad, so that is to be included. Oh, I will allow you to gather some cress to garnish it." He smiled and patted Annie's hand. "I will even let you make the coffee."

"If Sawbones is going to be piggish as all that," Jimmy was

470

quick to take advantage of the opening, "not letting me help, Sunday will be my day. How about a picnic dinner? We can bring the team and wagon over as we come in the forenoon, and it is possible to drive down on the other side of this stream for about two miles. The road is real smooth and can be taken at a trot. There's a fair camping place there where we can eat our picnic, or we can pack things down to the falls that is a mile below. I do want Miss Annie to see those falls. There should be plenty of water going over them this time of the year. I will bring something so we can measure that drop. I have guessed it to be better than 200 feet. Others have guessed it much less. A few will have the height at 250. We will measure it and have the question settled for all time."

Dr. Tom was sure that Jimmy's insistence on Sunday being his day had a double meaning. More than once, Jimmy had informed him he was still expecting a favorable answer to his suit. *I am not afraid of Annie changing her mind, and I can afford to wait until that guy wakes up to the fact that he hasn't a chance,* was his way of looking at things this night, with a warm hand creeping into his. "Mrs. Mary, are you sure you are in favor of such a jaunt? Don't let anyone stampede you into anything, remember."

"If the road is smooth like Jimmy says, and it is only two miles, I can stand that ride down in the forenoon and back in the late afternoon. But I will not attempt to go to the falls. I stood the trip well for two-thirds of the distance as we came. If I had been wise, I would have gotten out of the rig, rested an hour, and walked on in. Walking does not seem to bother me as long as I take it slow."

"Glad to hear that," beamed the doctor. "Just make sure you take everything slow for the next few months and you will be alright."

Saturday evening was a gay one. Supper was eaten rather early, being already prepared when it was brought. Later, after singing themselves hoarse, they roasted the marshmallows Dr. Tom had brought along. "These sticky gooey things almost call for more coffee," John remarked as he washed his hands, "but guess I better not brew any, or I won't get to sleep until it comes daylight." It was now nearing midnight, so all of them voted against more coffee.

On Sunday, a light breeze kept the heat from being too uncomfortable. It was eleven o'clock when they pulled away from the camp, crossing the stream and heading down on the opposite side. The ride was quite comfortable. They could have traveled faster had they wished. The two on horseback rode on either side, and all chatted more or less. The only fly bothering anyone this day was Annie's refusal to borrow Dr. Tom's horse to ride with Jimmy, as he had hoped. She had a very legal excuse, for she had no divided riding skirts with her. As they neared this camp site, Annie became curious as to why they had driven those two rough miles up this creek instead of the one they were on. "Why, this camping place looks nearly as good as the one above. Tell me why we didn't come down here, instead of going those two rocky miles?"

"How would you get down here?" John was quick to ask her.

"Surely there must be some way. It is such a short distance from the road above to that patch of trees." Annie did not think the hillside could be too steep.

"Alright, when we get down there, you pick out the road, and we'll come this way when we go home." John was commencing to enjoy this.

The closer they came to the place, the steeper the ground became. Not only that, the whole was strewn with boulders the same color as the earth, and they were all sizes. Annie could see the joke was on her and laughed. "I have never seen such a rocky place; but still, it looks like there is a trail through that jumble."

"That is Paul Bunions' potato patch. He'd have to walk through it when he planted it, wouldn't he?" So seldom did John joke anymore that it was enjoyed all the more for that reason.

As soon as they commenced to unload the picnic lunch, it was plain that Jimmy had spared no expense on this. There was a great array of pickles, olives and relishes, with finished cheeses and cold meats of all different kinds; crackers and rich cookies; oranges, bananas and a can of pineapple slices. This Jimmy opened first with a new fangled can opener just to show them how it worked. He then hunted out the coffee to make. "There is just a cupful of coffee in this muslin bag. Wouldn't you say that is about right for this big pot, Miss Annie?" He wanted her attention and used every ruse to gain it. "We can drop it right into the water this way and not be bothered with the grounds then."

Next came the new gallon thermos jug filled with lemonade. "Oh, by the way, I forgot to mention this spring water is not very good. It must be surface water—tastes a bit like alkali. It's never cold. I prefer not to drink it myself, so I brought the jugs of water. This thermos jug is supposed to keep things either hot or cold for several hours. I filled it half full of ice when I made it this morning, so it should be a good cool drink." Proudly, he poured each a cupful. All the rest of them were relishing the drink, but not Jimmy when he came to drink his. "Why, there is not a bit of ice in this. It's hardly cool enough to drink." He set his down, "I am not pleased with this at all."

"I would take it right back to the store I bought it from." Dr. Tom mimicked a shrill voiced woman, "and I would demand my money back."

Neither John, Mary, nor Annie had ever heard him mimic before, and they laughed at the comical way he pulled it off. Jimmy had to laugh along with them, but his face was red. "I'll do better than that. It will be shipped right back to the company at their expense, with a nice little wire telling them what I think of their product."

The subject was dropped after that and the rest of the meal was eaten in fairly good humor. When it came to the trip to the falls, only Annie and Jimmy were ready to go. Jimmy was plainly pleased that none other wanted to go. Not so with Annie—she would not ask Mary to make that walk, though she had hoped she might. John had said flatly he was not going, and now Dr. Tom could not be enticed. "Why don't you come? You said you have never seen them." Jimmy had her by one hand trying to hurry her away, while she still clung to the hand she had taken in her plea for him to come too.

"Some other time." He tryed to make his hand and eyes tell her something. Seeing her hurt look, he stage whispered in a childish tone, "I am afraid of *snaddle rakes*." His acting was comical, but Annie could not smile very heartily as she let go of his hand and left.

Chapter Forty Six

A SHORT DISTANCE FROM the camp site, the trail narrowed to a mere path, winding around boulders, skirting willows, and dodging sagebrush. Annie was pleased that it was not wide enough for them to walk side by side. Jimmy had to stop trying to assist her every step of the way. Still hurt over Dr. Tom's refusal to come with them, she walked on ahead of Jimmy, and rather fast at that. But she was giving heed to stir up as little dust as possible because the fine light colored soil contained some alkali, and it smarted the eyes.

In a few places, the trail swung back to the small stream, and there were stepping stones on which they could have crossed, but always there was this line, cut deeply by cattle, leading down on this side, so Annie kept on. The willows got much smaller along the water's edge, then nothing but tiny whips. The sagebrush got even more scant until there was none; the terrain was barren. The midday sun was dazzling, and one needed to shade the eyes.

Now on the quietness came an indefinable noise, coming so gradually, one was hardly aware of it until it filled the air. "Swing right," Jimmy called to her, and his voice sounded odd because of the noise. She paused for a second, about to step up on the slight rise in front of them where the trail ought to lead, only there was no trail. Instead, it swung sharply to the right, away from the stream. "I want you to *view* the falls, My Dear," Jimmy was beside here now, taking her arm, "not tumble over them." They were going north some distance before the path angled down and around, and they headed back in the right direction. The ground fell away at every step here, and Annie was almost glad of Jimmy's steadying hand. As they worked their way along this rough going, the noise increased in volume until it was a deafening roar.

Still, there seemed no water in sight the few times she dared look up from each careful step. Now far below, she could see the surging boil of the water in the small stream. *How can that mist make it feel so cool up here?* was her thought as they inched their way along the ledge. "Oh!" was her startled expression as they came within sight of the sheet of falling water, so very close at hand. Lucky for her, Jimmy did have a good grasp on her arm then. In another moment, he was urging her back the way they had come. There was no such thing as making oneself heard. Neither could one get a good view of the falls from along here. Jimmy had brought her to this point, half the distance of the drop, knowing it was possible to be close to the water falls before one caught sight of it.

"Now, we can make ourselves heard." Jimmy led her down the easier trail, swinging far from the turbulence. "We will cross the stream below here, and come up on the other side so you can have a really good view. Are you getting weary and care to rest first?" He was more than solicitous.

"No rest needed. I came to see the falls, remember?" She wondered if there was a bridge somewhere close for them to cross, but figured that would be unlikely, knowing there were no roads at all to this place. *Not even a tree growing this far down to have a log to walk on.* It soon became a better trail along the stream and it was losing its boil. Around another few curves, it became the same placid stream it had been above; then came the shallow place with stepping stones for easy crossing. Once over, Annie pulled away from his supporting hand. "Thanks for keeping me from tumbling from that perch when I first saw that water right beside me, but I do not need help along this good path."

"You might not require a helping hand, My Dear, for you choose to be one very independent young lady. But think of the pleasure it gives me to be of assistance. It is much more pleasant to walk side by side and talk. Soon, we will be back where it is not possible to talk." But Annie would not tarry for any talking. From this distance, the falls did not seem too impressive, but the closer they came to them, the more the roar increased. A rainbow glinted in the mist churned at the foot. Jimmy was again leading her, and this time, around a rocky point and into the cove close to the water's edge. The sun did not strike in this sheltered nook, cooled by the water spray about it. It was quite chilly here. Jimmy now took a reel from his wide pocket and anchored it with rocks as close to the falls as he could get. Next he scrambled up the bluff, letting the tape billow out with the current of air, until he was on top and walking back to the brink of the bluff and falls on that side. Reeling in the tape until it was nearly perpendicular, with a nod to Annie below, he started back down the steep rough going. Not until he was near did she notice that he still held the tape with his fingers at a certain place.

She had loosened the end, fastened it in the wet cove and inched her way out again by the time he was down to the creek level. Jimmy held the tape for her to read the 217 foot mark, then he slowly rewound the tape. Annie had seated herself here to look some more at the narrow sheet of water poring over that drop. She had never seen any big falls, but knew this would be but a tiny trickle beside Niagara Falls. *And still, it is two thirds its height.* She would have liked to have stayed here for long moments, but decided not to and commenced to climb the easy trail back upstream. She guessed this would have been the better way down in the first place.

Getting away from the noisy roar so they could talk was suiting Jimmy well, only Annie did not care to rest and talk. "You know, I do appreciate your bringing me to see this sight, but I do need to get back. I'm not at all sure how that sister of mine is standing this trip; she will not always say when she is tired. I still have to judge by how she acts." She would have gone on, but his hand stopped her, which she did not like. She tried to loosen his grip.

"Let us talk for just a little while then. Surely you will grant me that much time. We haven't had a moment to get better acquainted the past two weeks. It's always others taking up your time or interfering. The one big point in bringing you down here today was to have you alone so we could talk, for only in so doing can we understand each other better."

"There can be nothing more to talk about. I have tried to be very honest about all this. I gave you my answer just as soon as I knew my own mind. And you must believe me when I say no one else influenced me, one way or another. Please loosen my hand."

"Sit beside me so we can talk, and I will. Here, close—not way off there on another rock," he pleaded. "This is large enough for both of us. I cannot think you are afraid of me. You've shown no sign of being so until just lately. So how can I but think John's boorish attitude has influenced you? That was the reason I refused to accept any answer then. You haven't had the time to think all this through calmly, not with all the work you have been forced to do. Now that Mary is on the mend and needs less of your time, take another two weeks to study the question."

"With all the time and thinking there is, my answer has to be no." Annie couldn't understand a man refusing to accept two *no's.*

"Dear Girl, and I will continue to call you that, for you are dear to me and always will be, you do not seem to realize just how much I love you, or how happy you and I could be. My life will be spent in making you happy. Would that not be better than yoked to someone who does not care for you?"

"Won't you understand me when I say, I cannot marry you?" Annie was now getting riled.

"I do understand, Annie Dear, that you think yourself somewhat interested in Dr. Tom. Others have gone there too, but they got nowhere. None of them seemed to realize Doc is a dedicated man. A few years back, Leatha Orchard was madly in love with Doc, and crazy with jealousy over his caring so much for Mary Marcus."

Annie was flaying him with her one free hand until he caught that too and held her powerless. "How dare you say such things about my sister!" she screamed at him. "Do you want me to utterly despise you?"

"I mean only respect to Mary Marcus. She has never encouraged men to fall in love with her. Yet more than one has, and it did them no good." Jimmy used his strength of hands to hold her while he pleaded. "Your sister may not even be aware of Doc's adoration. I sometimes think she isn't. It is nearly killing me to see you fall for him when I know it can only lead to heartbreak for you. That is my only excuse in telling you this."

Whatever reaction Jimmy thought she might make, it was not this quiet withdrawing of her hands the second he loosened his grip. Her face might be a shade paler, but her eyes snapped as she looked him over with disdain. "You say you love me so much." She could see him brighten at those words. "I am glad to know that, for in that way, I can be sure of what my regard for Dr. Thomas really is. It cannot be love, for one definition could not possibly cover both." Recklessly, she was off and up the trail. All of Jimmy's hurrying and trying to talk to her did him no good. When he would have taken her hand the next chance to do so, she struck his hand hard. After that, he tried no more.

Annie expected he would puzzle out her meaning, given time. Right now, her one and only thought was to get back to the others.

Dr. Tom was the first one to see them coming. He had not done much resting, so ill at ease over turning down Annie's plea

477

for him to go with them. *I wish I had, but Jimmy would have been nasty and would have made another session possible to get her alone. Hope that man has sense enough to take a no this time.* From the rate they were coming, it was plain this was no amiable stroll. On Annie came, and flopped down beside Mary as if tired after her walk. She was more than tired, for she had walked fast, and all upgrade at that. Jimmy didn't come on to where they rested, but stopped to tighten the cinch of his saddle. Doc figured this was a dead giveaway that Jimmy at last knew that no meant *no.*

"Was the falls worth the walk to see them?" Mary asked as she fanned Annie's face with her hat as she lay close beside her on the blanket. None of the others could hear the answer she gave. Jimmy called as he mounted his horse, "Can you manage bringing the team back, Doc? I should be back at the store right now. I just thought of a telephone call that is supposed to come in." He hardly waited for Dr. Tom to wave him on before he was off, letting his horse pick his footing through the rocks. Once on the road, he lost no time.

"Rides like he feared some of us were going to stop him." There was a hint of humor in John's voice as he commenced to load the picnic things into the wagon. "I take it everyone is in favor of heading back to camp."

"I am." Mary got to her feet and stepped free of the blanket.

"Miss Annie is tired after her long walk. I will just roll her up, load her in the wagon, and let her sleep," Doc ventured. Stooping to catch the heavy blanket by one side, Annie was up and away before he could stop her. "More awake than I thought she might be." He was sure Annie was avoiding meeting his eyes. Neither would she allow her hand to touch his as they carted things to the wagon.

John was already hitching the tugs. While helping Mary into the wagon, Annie nimbly climbed in. "I see you have your own ideas of how to be assisted." There might be banter in his tone, but his eyes were not merry.

Annie, being herself so hurt, could see it reflected here. "Forgive me. I did not mean to be rude and not accept your kindness." Impulsively, she put out her hand and touched his hair just before he donned his hat. Snatching it back with a rueful laugh, "I must still be half tomboy and the other half gabby."

478

John released the brake and they were on their way.

Annie pretended to sleep all the way there on the folds of bedding, so busy mapping out her life from this moment on that she took no stock of what John and Mary were talking about. First, she must school herself to feel no emotion to prove that she could do this.

Sedately, she allowed Dr. Tom to help her from the wagon at camp. No lingering handclasp was to follow, though.

"There is no earthly for you to take this team back to town tonight," Mary told Dr. Tom as he handed her down. "John would only have to walk over there for them in the morning."

John heard this and a bit of glow came, thinking Mary was concerned over his walk of two miles. Dr. Tom asked, "Then you are not enjoying your camping?" He failed again to catch Annie's eye. "I expect you prefer your own more comfortable bed."

"I have enjoyed it, yes. But there is a limit to this doing nothing–more than two months of it for me. It's about time for me to earn my salt."

"How are we going to keep this team here all night without keeping them tied up all the time?" John asked. "We haven't any hobbles."

"We can picket them out with their halter ropes until dark. There are several nice grassy spots around close, and we can watch them. That will be three to four hours for them to eat. And then in the morning, we can do the same while we eat breakfast and break camp. In that way, they are not going to be too hungry."

When John came back from staking them out, he saw Dr. Tom climbing the grade toward town. "How come? Wouldn't Doc stay and eat supper with us?" "He said he wasn't a bit hungry." Annie spoke without interest, as she arranged the food stuff from the picnic lunch so neither flies nor ants could bother it. She didn't think she could eat anything. Feeling John's eyes on her, she tried all the more to appear care-free.

***

Jimmy Burch wasn't around when Dr. Tom arrived back last evening; nor did he see him this morning. He thought nothing of that—he wasn't in the habit of asking about Jimmy. He did not learn until evening what most of the town already knew. "What do you know, Doc, about all this excitement in town—Jimmy Burch kept the wires hot to Boise last evening early?" was Lew's first question as Dr. Tom went for his horse right after supper this night. "It don't make sense to me—Jimmy doing all that telephoning, and then burning up the road to get to the railroad. Did I hear you say what you knew about it?"

"Not a thing, Lew. Not a thing. I was gone all day yesterday. Wasn't aware anything out of the ordinary had taken place.

'Yeah, an' I know you, Doc. If you did know, you would never let on. Now it's different with me. I get a kick out of the funny things people will do. Jimmy was so hot and bothered, trying to get that wife of his to file for a divorce, and the day after those papers got filed, he rushes over there like mad to stop 'em. Don't make sense to me. Just between you, me and the hitching rack, Doc, I don't care either way the cat jumps, but if I was Jimmy, I'd of set that Laura dame out on her behind a long time ago."

"Oh now, Lew, you and I cannot say what we would do if we were in Jimmy's shoes. Now, if you will make my horse ready for me, I thought I would drop in on Aleck, and I want daylight to find that path. Can't say I can do a mite of good going—he still will not move into town here so someone can care for him better. Ned Miller does the best he can for him, I know, but I have the feeling that Ned should be in bed and have someone caring for him." Dr. Tom considered this a safe subject for gossip.

"Beats all how Aleck hangs on. Anyone else having miner's con as bad as he has, they'd been dead and decently buried long ago. Maybe that fresh air and out-of-doors living they are making such a holler about is what has kept Aleck alive this long. That cabin sure lets in plenty of air. I can sorta understand he not wanting to be moved away. That shack has been home to him for about a quarter of a century. Maybe he won't last 'til the snow flies this year, but then we have been thinking that for the last two–three years. To have to move him against his will would be bad. Could be, we might all have to be on the move if this camp closes down like it is shaping up to do."

"Could be. You remember that old saying about there being but two things one can be sure of—death and taxes?" Doc made his getaway the second Lew had his horse ready. The shortcut up to Aleck Norton's claim and cabin led through the chaparral on the north face of the hill. The call there might not take very long. The trail then out to the forks of the road was plainer. He intended to go on down to the Mills House before coming back.

A lamp was still lit in the dining room, so that meant someone was up. It was Mary, still folding clothes. "Oh, I thought you were Annie. Come in Doctor. Annie is around here someplace. I expect that you met John taking the rig back as you came down."

"No, I didn't—must have missed him before I came onto the road at the forks. I was up to Aleck Norton's cabin."

"It was late afternoon before the washing was all finished, so then we ate supper before John started out. He and Annie have been so busy this day. Looks like I should help a little bit. This business of having no pep or even any interest in things isn't to my liking. It frightens me sometimes, the way I feel. Why, it would be so easy for me to just set down and not move even enough to feed myself. I shouldn't be that way, for I'm not a bit sick."

"Perhaps new scenery, different people, or some interesting hobby is all you need now." Dr. Tom was placing great store in seeing Annie this night, and she not being about the house did not bode well.

"A trip is out of the question. I would like to see the faces of the children walking in, but they seem so satisfied down on the Flats, all having jobs, I doubt they want to come home until school time. As for hobbies, I never had time to think about one. I wouldn't know how to go about acquiring one." She pulled the last pair of socks together.

"They tell me it is the easiest thing in the world to do. Just single out something you like to do. If it's knitting baby booties, just knit; if it is collecting butterflies, fix you a net and go bug hunting. Really, there is rather a wide range of floral and plant life in these hills. That is what I will go for if I am not kept busy from now on. There are such different formations of rock to gather and study. Even mining has its fascinating side."

Mary's laugh was too cynical to be called amused. "No thanks. I think I have had enough mining. I think I heard Annie now—that laugh of mine must have scared her. She might think I've suddenly gone loco."

"You did not hear me out, Mrs. Mary. I do not mean the digging and blasting. That part just spells hard work—but the

481

legends and the old miner's lore might be interesting. According to one of the oldest stories in these hills, is that the whole length of this stream has been placer mined but for two exceptions—and those two spots are the cemetery in Silver City and your own fenced door yard."

"I understand most of the placering was done by the Chinese." Mary was not much interested.

"That is right. And it was one of those last Chinese who told me about it. He is the old laundry man living up the gulch above town. He seems sure there is a pocket of coarse gold, just about where this house stands. They all know the ground is rich in that one spot in Silver City. This ground, being patented land and by a mining man at that, none came in and dug up his door yard."

"And you think I should start doing just that for pastime?" Mary wanted to say something amusing. She was a bit worried about Annie not coming in.

"John might want some exercise. Where is Jack, by the way? Doesn't he get in before real dark?"

"Jack ate dinner with us at noon, then at three, he drank coffee and with some sandwiches in his pocket, and a blanket over his shoulder, he started out. He said he would camp wherever the sheep bedded down, come night fall. He will head them back in this direction tomorrow, and as soon as they buck up, he'll come in for breakfast."

"Jack's quite a guy." Dr. Tom had come to see Annie. Now that Jimmy's little drama was over, there would be no unpleasantness from that source. Sure in his own mind of his intentions, he had wanted to feel the clasp of her hand to assure him he was not imagining her regard toward him. But he was forced to ride back this night without even a glimpse of Annie.

"Who's there?" John thought he heard a noise close by on the rocky point, like a loose rock dislodged by a foot. His heart missed a beat, thinking it could be Mary.

"It's me," answered Annie coming down to the roadway. "I want to talk to you for a moment, John—to learn what you think about Sister being well enough now to get by alone, with what help you can give her. I really do need to leave."

"I was just talking to Doc up the road a ways. He says Mary is doing okay. Only she shouldn't be doing the washing and heavy work yet. Is that what he told you?" He naturally expected that

482

she and Dr. Tom had been talking.

Annie ignored the question. "Then, can I go away with an easy mind in knowing you will help her with the washings and heavy work?"

"Sure, I can do that. But why all the rush all of a sudden?" Annie's face was not clear in the moonlight. He was not sure if she had been crying. "I thought you liked it here a little bit, and was interested in Doc some..."

"Who told you that?" demanded the distraught girl.

"Nobody told me anything. I've got eyes, haven't I?" He was sure she was crying now, yet not making a sound. As she said nothing, he went on more gently. "Of course, what you want to do is your own business. I wouldn't want to hold you here when you wasn't wanting to stay, and I don't know as I'm very good at saying what I want to. But I am understanding all you have done for us. Not sure we could have pulled Mary through if you hadn't come. Don't know if I can ever make it up to you in anyway. It bothered me when I was afraid you might be falling for Jimmy's smooth talk. Not that I have so much against the guy, but I thought you ought to know about him always trying to make love to Mary. I guess I was somewhat of a heel to butt in that way. Then when I thought you might be liking Doc, that was okay by me. He's a pretty white guy. Some older than you, but I do—"

"That is not why I am leaving!" Annie cut in.

"No?" John asked doubtfully. "Then are you letting Jimmy's jibe talk stampede you?"

"That isn't the way of it. I have the most valid of reasons, John. The one I care for does not care for me."

"I kinda thought he did. Has Doc said he didn't, in so many words?"

"One does not need words always to prove what you know in your own heart."

"I suppose not. But I'm not liking it to turn out this way. Mary is going to be unhappy over—"

"Mary must not know!" Annie was desperate in her concern. "Sister must never be unhappy for one moment over me. Surely she has had enough unhappiness to be spared this. You owe me nothing, John. For what little I have done, I'm only glad that it was possible for me to come and help out. But I do want your promise that you will not tell Mary this."

John felt trapped. "Have you told her you are wanting to leave?"

"Not a word. I wanted to talk to you first, and now my courage is gone."

"Maybe I can help you out in that." He wanted to do something.

"Oh, if you only would." Annie turned away as he started on to the house.

John did not formulate a plan or words. To him, there was only one course left open. As he entered the dining room where Mary was reading, she looked up. "Oh, I thought you were Annie at first. She has been out ever so long. Did you see her as you came in?"

"Yes, I talked to her for a minute." John was short in his words.

"I'm rather worried about Annie. She seems unhappy. Do you think she is homesick and thinks she should not leave me?"

"Something like that. She wants to go home anyway." Afraid he might say more than he should, John took himself off to bed.

Mary was still awake when her sister came in quietly to bed. "Oh, Annie Sister, did you think me some selfish imbecile not capable of any understanding about you wanting to go home?"

"You are not selfish, Dear," Annie told her, returning her quick hug. "To tell you the truth, I am the selfish one, staying on and on when it really has not been necessary—just having a good time, when I should be home."

"I know. Mother was only just back on her feet when you had to rush up here on a moment's notice. You have worked so hard, and done so much all the time you have been here. I know you have spent a lot of money too on this family. I can see to Father paying you back as soon as the lambs and wool are sold, but what about your fare home?"

"I have enough for that, Mary. You must not worry about me. I really have plenty to pay my fare all the way to Caldwell. But I am trying to decide if I want to go there direct—Father is haying now, and he is too busy to have to make a trip in for me. I have a notion to stop over in Murphy and telephone Mr. Simmons. I could hire him to come for me; in that way, I could be home in less time and sorta surprise Father and Mother."

"Sister, you must put the call through in the morning to learn what day they could best come to meet you so there's no need wait around. Murphy can be a very hot, disagreeable place to wait this time of the year. If you could get the call in early enough, David might be at the house and I could hear his voice." She would not say how homesick she was for the children.

"I smell coffee." Annie came awake with a start, thinking she had overslept. "Why, it is only six. John must be in a hurry to be up this morning." Seeing Mary getting up too, she scolded, "No need for you to get up, Sister. He may have his breakfast already cooked. Can't you rest some more if I go away and you be still?" Mary got up and dressed quickly.

"What's your big rush today?" Annie asked John as soon as they reached the kitchen.

"Couldn't sleep. Figured I might as well be up. Don't like Jack sleeping out with only a blanket this way. He's a pretty old man for such stunts." He poured coffee into his own cup, then reached for two more and filled those ready for Mary and Annie. "He might get sick or fall and break a leg, and no one the wiser for awhile. And those sheep would scatter from hell to breakfast." He was unaware of any change in his thinking.

Chapter Forty Seven

"HI THERE, DOC," ED Wheeler called from the back of the stage as he tucked the canvas over Annie Williams' suitcases. "Do you always get out this early?"

"Not unless I am called out or haven't yet gone to bed, like today—full twelve-hour session of it." Then Doc noticed Annie in the front seat. "What is the meaning of this?" dropping his bag and stepping closer. "Are you leaving and not even letting an old friend know?"

"And were you expecting I could stay forever?" She made her tone bantering.

"No, I could not expect that." Somehow he had been thinking she might. Ed was now lugging out the mail pouch and would be ready to leave the second it was loaded. Annie's gloved hands held her purse, and she made no move to shake Doc's hand. He gripped hers hard, purse and all. "I don't like your going, remember. Will you write to me sometimes?" Somehow, he must not let her leave without some link to hold onto. The rig swayed as Ed swung his bulk to the seat. He was grinning and Doc knew he should step free and not hinder the U.S. Mail departure. At last came Annie's answer, "If you wish, I will write. In that way, I will know how Mary is, perhaps," determined to make this goodbye impersonal.

"Nice morning, this." Mr. Lyons said, locking the door. He wondered at Dr. Tom, with his bag at his feet, standing as if he was in doubt of what to do after the stage left.

"Yes, it is nice weather," Doc aroused himself to say. He guessed he must look uncertain standing there, so he picked up his bag. "I'm just debating if I want breakfast more than I do bed. Do you think the early birds would object to me eating beside them with my feathers untrimmed?" He rubbed his unshaven chin." As the stage left, he crossed the street, dumped his bag in the office, and continued down to the restaurant, not that he was especially hungry. Neither did he care to be alone with his gloomy thoughts. They were none brighter by evening. To him, Annie's leaving spelled only one thing—he meant nothing to her. The thought kept him from sleeping or relaxing, although he had plenty chance for both. He tried to consider Annie's conduct from different perspectives. She was much too serious to go in for love making if

486

she did not mean it. She had not objected to his caresses that day in the cellar. But did she have a chance to object? *There was no caveman stuff making her hand reach out to mine around the campfire.* Yes, he had that consolation, but it was not helping him much.

I never saw John around this morning. I wonder, did Annie lug her luggage up? Later came another disturbing thought: *Why had neither of the Marcus' mentioned Annie leaving?* And he had talked to both of them. That thought hurt too, for he considered them his friends. By nighttime, he was in an agitated state—about ready to leave this place, contract or no contract. Finding another location did not worry him—from the sound of the war news these days, there was a place for every able-bodied M.D. *The way I feel right now, I would welcome a change,* was his one thought as he climbed the steps and entered the room that had been home to him for more than ten years.

To pick up and leave would have been easy. The hard part was staying and fulfilling his contract to the DeLamar Mine and Milling Company. Yet, knowing they were more than likely to cancel said agreement any day now, was the unfairness to him. He was aware that Mr. Orchard's trip east this spring had been to unload some of this property. None were sure just yet about the outcome. *I can understand him and Mrs. Orchard being worried about their two daughters in England, but it looks to me like that would not be a very pleasant place for them to head for now.*

The memory of either Helen or Leatha brought no hurt now, but the thought of Annie leaving did. His evening meal was unceremoniously interrupted by word brought to him that he was wanted at his office at once. Jean Keller had been thrown from her horse, and had a broken arm. The messenger was walking back with him and trying to tell him all the details as they went. "Horse stepped in a badger hole. That Jean is a tough one. Rode all the way in." Dr. Tom caught that much.

He knew Jean Keller by sight, but not as a patient. *That Jean is too ornery to get sick,* he remembered someone saying. She was seated on the office steps waiting for him, in torn shirt, overalls, and boots, minus her Stetson hat. He guessed her to be in plenty of misery the way she held the useless arm, so his first thought was for a hypo to ease the pain. This, she refused. "I'm no panty-waist. Get on with the setting of my bones." Her natural high pitched voice was shrill. He would not have been surprised if she commenced her usual cursing. To her credit, she did not, especially with a broken humerus mid way between elbow and shoulder, and a fractured collar bone.

When at last splints and bandages, as well as much tape, were in place, Jean caught sight of herself in the mirror. "I'll be damned, Doc, if you haven't rigged me out to look like a mummy." Her short hair, graying at the temples, was tousled still from her fall. She insisted on getting her torn shirt on her unbandaged arm, cursing because it could not be buttoned at the neck. Out she stomped as if she intended to ride back to her homestead this night. Dr. Tom had used some strong language himself on learning that was her intention. Not yet sure if she would go to the hotel or attempt that four mile ride, Doc walked on past the hotel and was relieved to see her at the front desk.

He found Jean Keller and her accident the topic of conversation at the saloon. "The funny part is her pretending she is a man by dressing like one, out drinking some, and out cussing most, while all the time that voice of hers gives her away," claimed one man at the bar.

"I heard once somewheres, the reason why she dresses as a man was 'cause she damned near got killed getting tangled up in skirts in a runaway rig." This opinion, Dr. Tom had heard before from others.

"Don't believe all you hear, Feller," Lew interjected. "I won't say that wasn't true, but it never happened since Jean hit these hills, for she rode in on the stage wearing men's britches." Lew liked to talk, but he gave heed to finishing his beer and getting home now.

After a few mediocre games of pool, Doc paused to drink a nightcap with his opponent. "Hey there, Doc," Ed Wheeler hailed him in jovially. "How about having a drink with me?"

Dr. Tom held up his half filled glass. "Thanks, Ed, for the offer. Another time I might take you up on that. This one will have to do me tonight—I'm still subject to call." He wondered how many times he had said this in the years he had been in this town. When first he came, he had asked some of the persistent ones how they would like him setting their broken bones and seeing double; or delivering their new son and think there were twins. It had been some time since anyone had taken offence at his turning down the offer of a drink, but Ed Wheeler acted like he was offended this night. That puzzled Doc. While Ed might be quarrelsome when he was drunk, he had not been in from his run long enough to be so well oiled as that. He knew Ed would not drink while on duty.

Ed moved closer with his refilled glass. "Ya know, Doc, I've always kinda liked you until today. Held to the idea you tended to your own knitting," Ed was near over-playing a pretended drunkenness, "and didn't make other people drop too many stitches. What I don't like is big he-men making nice little girls cry."

Doc's reaction was sudden. "And I have had respect for you 'til now. Don't make me lose it." Every word was like a threat, and Dr. Tom stomped out.

Ed rubbed his head as if to clear it. "Now, what in the devil did I say to rile Doc? I meant no disrespect, named no names. I was just trying to jolly Doc a bit."

"You must have hit a sore spot somewheres, Ed," the bartender advised.

"I sure as hell must have." He gulped the rest of his drink. "Never knew Doc couldn't be kidded before, but he was sure sorer than hell at me just now." And to forget this, Ed was out to get drunk as speedily as possible, having only so many hours to sleep it off before his morning start.

For a week, Dr. Tom made himself stay away from Mills House. With Annie not there, it held no attraction for him, but the answers to his questions might be found there. He found Mary on the east porch, churning. "And how is this nice summer weather treating you?" he asked.

"Cannot complain about the weather, as of now," she told him, reaching into the kitchen for another chair. He had already seated himself on the porch, and was letting his feet dangle. "But I could do some grouching over not having half the strength or ambition I should have." Her weariness showed as she seated herself again. "We were beginning to think you had forgotten you had friends down this way."

"And I have been wondering if you people were my friends." He forced a smile as he said this. "I was thinking it's not one bit friendly, not letting me in on the secret of Miss Annie's planned departure. I would have liked to have been in the know, and given

Annie a small party."

"We did not know it ourselves until after you were here that evening. I didn't, at least. John might have had some inkling of it, for she was quite determined that she should leave. Guess she had talked it over first with him. Poor Sister...so upset in thinking I'm still the half invalid."

"I had a very short note from her today. Never a word of why she needed to hurry away. I do believe she can write the nicest letter, and give out the least information of anyone I know. Would you happen to know if she is planning on going east soon?"

"That I do not know either. We had a letter also. John went for the mail early this morning. A very newsy letter it was, about the rest of the folks and life in general on the Flats, but not what her plans are. But she did add a post script that she would write more as soon as she was sure where she would be. So I know by that, Annie is not planning to stay at home." Mary was slowly twirling the dasher to gather the butter now. "And too, she wrote wanting us to leave the children down there until school time. All three have jobs. David is driving a team to haul hay on a slip for Mr. Simmons. They are neighbors of my parents. Margaret drives derrick horse at that one place, and her grandfather's. Guess she will be hired to milk Grandfather's cows and do his chores between cuttings. Susan is water girl, and earns 10¢ an hour."

"I expect those three have big plans for all their wealth?" Dr. Tom felt he should carry part of the conversation load.

"David has a saddle horse about paid for; next comes a saddle. Margaret is having Grandfather bank hers, and not a peep yet as to what she intends to do with it. Susan has bought the whole catalogue out, twice over I'm sure."

"Hi there," John's greeting broke in on their laughter. He came out through the kitchen, but stopped for a drink of water at the sink first. "Warm enough for you, Doc? He mopped his face as if he had been working, but never said what he had been doing.

"Would a glass of buttermilk interest either one of you men?" Mary asked as she rolled the churn on its edge kitchen-ward.

"Sounds good to me," John answered. He seemed to have little to say. The two men accepted the drinks when Mary brought them. Dr. Tom was not talkative either. Looking out at this east yard in the early dusk, it looked different somehow. Not until he walked along the porch and headed home did he figure out what made the yard look different. The currant bushes that grew along the side fence were dug up.

The news of John Marcus' placer mine a few days later set the town of DeLamar astir. It came on the heels of news via the grapevine that DeLamar Mining and Milling Company was not going to start up with a bigger crew, like had been talked about. A week later, as Dr. Tom went for his horse to ride downstream, he heard Lew's version of all the other claims being staked about the old Mills property. "Those suckers are just out their filing fees, the way it looks to me, Doc. As I understand it, coarse gold like that is washed in pockets like. All that ground outside that fenced yard has been turned over more 'an once in the past fifty years."

"That could be the way of it, Lew." Doc was in a hurry to be on his way. He had some news of his own, which had nothing to do with gold—coarse or fine. It was astonishing how fast that green grassy yard was getting torn up. An old rocker-type washer was already in use, just below the wood house. Part of what had once been garden was wet and muddy. A new ditch in back of the cellar was bringing the water from the gulch to it. There were two men working with John—all three had waved as he rode close by, so he guessed he was acquainted with all of them, but they were so bespattered with mud, he could not have named them. Going back to the front gate and tying his horse, he went along the porch.

"Safer for you here," smiled Mary as she brought out chairs. "You're not nearly so apt to get a mud bath from this distance, and still one can see most of the excitement."

"Looks as if you have plenty of that around here. What I want to know is, how are you standing all this hubbub?" He eyed her closely.

"Just letting it slide over my head. I cook what is the easiest and quickest to fix whenever John can tear himself away from that rocker or the digging long enough to eat. Jack is generally hungry enough to eat when first he comes in after the sheep hit the brush—along about nine o'clock. But I do declare, I believe he gets a little of the gold fever himself before he is ready to go out again at three. I've seen him monkeying about, helping them build a sluice box or something. The two men helping John bring their lunch, but they like coffee to go with it. Really, I have the coffee pot on most of the time."

491

The men appeared to be shutting down for the day. "It's a wonder they haven't rigged up some light so they can work two shifts."

"Don't you dare suggest it," Mary was quick to say. "If they did that, there would be no sleeping around this place."

"Are you already sorry you started all this?" He was sure she had in some way used the hint he had given her.

"I have news for you, Dr. Tom." This was said with meaning. "There happens to be only one miner in the Marcus family, and that isn't this old lady." She made it plain that she took no honors for this discovery.

"Perhaps I have news for you." He said this in the same tone she had used. "Last night's stage brought me a letter from one Dr. Stewart of Seattle, asking for a recommendation for one Annie K. Williams, who had lately been enrolled as a student nurse in the hospital he heads."

"I heard from Mother and the children too today, and they wrote that Annie had gone to Seattle, hoping to become a nurse. I would say she would make a very good one." Mary's hands moved as if she were tired. "Do I understand you would give her a good recommend?"

Dr. Tom was not sure if Mary was asking this seriously or was trying to be humorous. "Now, just how shall I word my letter? Should it be something like this? *Dear Sir: I am sorry to inform you, one Annie K. Williams is by far too young and flighty to know her own mind; much too good looking and full of life to settle down to the exacting duties of a nurse; signed by one W. J. Thomas, M.D.*" He pretended to be writing while talking. "Or should it be something along this line? *Dear Sir: You may not be aware as yet just how lucky you are to have Annie K. Williams sign for training in your old hospital. But I should come kick your teeth in for stealing her away from this young state, as we are in need of good nurses too.*"

Mary was laughing now. "I am sure you have no idea how funny you can make ordinary words sound. I was sure you would give her a good letter."

"Why could she not have asked for that letter before she left? Surely she knew me well enough to know I would have been glad to write her the best of recommendations, and assisted her in any way possible. If that was the work she wanted to go into, why would she be unhappy about it? That's what I cannot understand." This last had slipped out unguarded in his own unhappiness.

"I cannot see Annie unhappy in any work she would choose to do, but she would be the very last person to talk about it until she had been accepted, or it was all settled one way or the other." Mary stopped visiting long enough to bid the two workmen goodnight as they came close to the porch and picked up their lunch kits. As John came along on his way to turn the gulch water back to run on the hay field, Mary got up. "I'd better close up this kitchen to keep what warmth there is inside. There's plenty of muck to wash off every night." As she came back to her chair, she laughed, "If it wasn't for Jack bringing in armloads of wood each morning as he comes, I'm not sure I would have enough to cook with." She chuckled, "I fear our hay field is getting robbed of water somewhat."

"It's about July when you turn the water off, is it not?"

"Yes, in another week. I hope the men we find to put up the hay this year won't catch the gold fever too."

John was close enough on his way back to hear this. "Is it necessary to bother with cutting that hay?" he asked as he hitched his tired body to the porch edge.

"Of course it is. We still have a cow to feed through the winter, and a couple of times, we have been glad of some extra hay to feed the sheep when late or early snows have come."

John wagged his head in mock unbelief. "Living in the middle of a placer mine, and she still wants to bother to cut hay." A little laugh came.

"What is the extent of your pocket of gold, do you think?" Doc asked.

"Hard telling yet," answered John. "You see, this is all new to me as a hard rock miner, so I'm having to learn this as I go along. Don't know as I would have ever stumbled onto there being enough to make a color anywheres in this yard if I hadn't been helping Mary dig up those half dead currant bushes. I panned some of that, and you should have seen the ring around—just about a complete circle. One needed no magnifying glass to see that coarse stuff. Then I panned some from all over the yard. On the west side, I hardly got a color. On this side, it was varying in spots, but the front walk seems to be the dividing line."

"In that case, you will only have half your house moved." Doc was trying to joke with Mary sitting so very quietly there, saying nothing now.

"It will need to be very rich ground to pay to move any of it. The cellar cannot be moved—it being built of rock. When one figures the cost of tearing it down and rebuilding it, that much gold could hardly be under it.

"I'm not worried about digging it out from under the house," John said. "It being a frame building, with care, one can jack it up and keep it somewhat level. It would have to have a new foundation, of course, but the way things look now, that cellar is setting on mighty rich ground." John went on in the house to wash, and soon, Dr. Tom took himself back to town.

Mary was having her troubles. Often she found herself without wood to bake bread, and most of the time, without water to do any washing. They needed the water from the hydrant to supplement the water from the gulch, and that would drain the tank at the spring. The first time she mentioned this, John bundled up the laundry and sent it up by one of his helpers, who said his wife would be glad of that work. And at the mention of not being able to bake bread for the lack of wood, the same man had assured that his wife made good bread. From then on, he brought down two loaves of bread every other day. There was just no jarring any of them loose to go get wood.

The haying took a long time to get done. Mary insisted that John hire two men for that job so that Jack did not have to help. She dared not attempt doing any of it herself. "It keeps me busy doing nothing," she complained to Jack. "Here I am, doing no washing because there is no water; no ironing or baking because no one but Jack has time to get wood to keep a fire going." She sounded half peeved. "Water can't be spared for the garden that got planted, so we eat out of tin cans. It's funny what a difference those grains of yellow makes in people's lives."

"It does for a fact," Jack nodded, "but you better change your ways or you and I are going to bat if I once more see you out lugging in wood. Lucky it's summer time so you won't freeze. If they don't get all this gold leached out of this yard before cold weather, you or I will have to smash that rocker and boxes so some of 'em can take time off to get wood up."

The month of August was nearly ended when John admitted

494

to Mary that just the cleanup was left. "There is plenty of work to be done around here, goodness only knows. But why pay the men to do something I can do myself, like filling in and such. Think I better lay 'em off tomorrow night, and next morning, settle up with 'em."

That night over the super table, he remarked, "We've about shot our wad. It was just a pocket like we expected it might be from the first. Still, we haven't done too bad." John was bone weary, working like a slave for nearly ten weeks. And it was like him to not say how much they had made. Mary thought she had an idea of what the take had been from comments John had made at times. And knowing what the men's wages were, she could have guessed pretty close to how much richer the Marcus family was, but here was the catch—that money in the bank at DeLamar was in John Marcus' name, not hers. She never thought of it being connected to her—she had not helped earn it. At first, she thought John might ask her to put the men's time down, but he had done it himself, after his own fashion. He used a stub of a pencil and a worn time book, which he carried in his pocket.

John had not offered her money or asked if she needed any. He never had done so before, for the simple reason he had never had it to give. For fifteen years, it had been the other way around. Habits like that are hard to break. The milk, butter and cream had been used lavishly all summer—none had been sold. For this length of time, Mary had been without money.

It bothered her now. She was not only homesick to see the children, she knew they should be here so she could get them ready for school. All three of them would be needing clothes. They had been gone nearly four months. It seemed they had slipped away from her completely in that time. If she had had the money, she would have sent it for their fare. She had mentioned they should be sent for, but John had not said a word about it. The only way she could see to it, Jack would need to dress out a few lambs and sell those. Yet, that would add more work for Jack and getting them to town for sale was not as easy as it used to be with wood and timber haulers passing.

Things were changing, and she was not able to change with them. Hardly a day passed, but what an automobile went by. Often, they needed to stop for water for their radiators, and a few times, it was rather embarrassing to have to tell them there was

495

none. *It's nearly as bad as it was on the desert sometimes,* was her thought. In some of the children's letters, they had hinted about wanting to stay down there and go to school. This was not pleasing to their mother, but the more she heard about the slim chance DeLamar had of having more than one teacher this coming school year, the more she could see it would be better for David to stay there at Mr. Simmons like he wanted to. He would get $10 a month for doing chores, and could still go to school. He would be in the ninth grade this year. *But if David does that, it will mean just the two girls going alone through the snow and storms.* This was not to Mary's liking either.

Mary was not happy these days. There seemed no way of planning for all her brood to please everyone. *I wonder if it is like this in all families as they commence to grow out of babyhood?*

Chapter Forty Eight

MARY WAS NOT LIKING these sleepless nights. In fact, they worried her a bit. This morning, she had to force herself to get up. *That cow has to be milked. It is not right for her to wait 'til nine when Jack gets here. Nor is it right that Jack has to do my work, as well as his own,* she kept telling herself while dressing. Once up, the struggle was getting easier. *But never did I have a harder time prying my lazy carcass out of bed.*

John had coffee made and was about ready to eat his breakfast. "Didn't find much bread, but I'm not taking time to make biscuits. I want to get to town early to catch those fellows and get everything settled up. If you are going to milk first before you eat, I'll happen out and pack the milk in."

Mary finished washing and drying her hands and face with nothing to say, but she thought she might mention this *not sleeping* to Dr. Tom, should he come down. Milking didn't make her feel any worse. *Guess it was all in my head, this not feeling good.* The pail of milk was heavy, and she was glad John reached for it when she came to the steps.

"Thought I would get there at the right time, and I didn't. Shall I take it on to the cellar for you?"

"It might be safer for you to. I feel none too secure walking those planks somehow." She followed him through the house and out to the east steps.

"They are safe enough." He went along their springy lengths at a fast clip, put the milk just inside the screened door, and turned to come back. Mary was still not venturing on the planks yet. "This is about the first filling in I'd better do." The depth below this walk meant nothing to him. As he went past her and up the steps to be off, he asked, "Can you walk it?"

"If I cannot walk it, I guess I can creep." She moved slowly along the two planks now with her eyes closed so as not to be dizzy. *I wonder what he would say if I told him I was scared to death every time I have to walk those planks?* She finished straining the milk and remembered to take both cream and milk, so as not to have to make any more trips this day.

Mary was not hungry, but did make herself drink some milk and eat some cereal. John had evidently cooked himself an egg and ate the small amount of bread. *I should have had my wits about me and told John what groceries we are short on so he could bring them down.* It was possible to put in a call to the store and give them the order for John. *That would be a pretty big load if he brought down all the food stuff we're short on.* Carefully scanning what food stuff there was, she decided they could get by another day. There was not another stick of wood in the wood box, and it was nearing eight o'clock, so she need hurry to find some and not let Jack see her doing it. His old eyes were plenty sharp. In finding wood, she found a hen's nest full of eggs. That would make Jack's breakfast much easier.

"We have no bread and very little flour, Jack," she told him the second he came, "but we do have plenty of corn meal and eggs. How do corn cakes along with your eggs sound?"

"Sounds good to me. I suppose you and John ate your meal so long ago, you have forgotten about it?" Jack was busy washing to the tune of Mary beating up the cake batter.

"Long enough for me to think I might eat a corn cake. No telling when John will be back for a meal. He might be more than a half day getting settled up with the men." The cakes sizzled as she turned them. "I will let you pour your own coffee. I am trying to get this syrup pitcher cover soaked loose. It looks like it hasn't been off in a month. What a slack housekeep I'm getting to be." She dropped more round yellow pools on the hot griddle, and still could not budge the encrusted cover. "We will have to go camp-style and dip our syrup right from the pail."

"That's the ticket, I say—don't dirty one more dish than you have to. Saves on the dishwashing, you know." Jack was enjoying his meal. "What we going to do around here for excitement now that the placer mine has petered out?"

"I haven't given it a thought. I know there is a lot of work and fixing to do before this place looks livable again. It might take from now 'til snow flies to get ready for winter." Mary was making out a fair meal now.

"Yes, I guess it will at that. What has Miss Annie had to say about missing out on all this fun around here?"

"She has written very little about anything except her work, and that she likes. I know she must be very busy. There is plenty of studying to do. I wish Annie were not so far away. I would so like to go see her sometime. She wrote once that she would have two weeks off each year, but that is a long time 'til next June when her first vacation comes."

"Why, next June will be here before we know it. The big question is, where will we be?"

"Life may be uncertain, but if I'm alive next June, I expect to be right here, the same as I am now." Mary stacked the few dishes and covered the food stuff. "Our tank at the spring won't be drained now. I believe I will splurge by washing, there being about enough fire to heat the water in the tank here. While I have a good fire going, I should be thinking about getting something baked ready for your night lunch. The only thing I can think of is brambleberry tarts. There are raisins, a few walnuts; flour enough for the pastry. No shortening except butter, but that makes them all the better. Those will carry well in your coat pocket." She sighed from weary thinking.

"I should have made out a list of the things we need. John might have brought them down. Do you know, we haven't a dry bean on the place?"

Jack stopped filling the washing machine a moment to ask, "Do you want me to go get grub for you?"

"No, you don't need to if you can get along on cornbread, ham and pan gravy for your afternoon meal. I just mentioned having no dry beans, for we used to depend so much on them."

Jack gathered more wood to make sure she had enough, and he happened around at the proper time to empty and fill the tubs and machine for her. It was a small wash, for which she was thankful. By the time the clothes were flapping on the line, she had commenced to tire, and it was an effort to make the tarts and have Jack's meal ready for him. Much too weary now to care about food herself, she sat toying with a tart. *I have to wait until Jack is gone before I go to bed to rest. The poor old fellow will think I'm sick again.* So she sat there, neither eating nor talking—just thinking. And her thoughts were not happy thoughts.

"There, I've eaten an extra tart, so there's no need to take any," Jack joked as he got up from the table.

"Oh, but you need something for a snack long about bedtime," Mary aroused herself to say. "If you can stand to eat them, you'd better take several, they being so small. How would a jar of milk do to drink with them?"

"That wouldn't be a bad idea at all. Sometimes it is a devilish long ways for a drink. A hunk of cornbread and slab of ham might not go a begging either." In the end, Jack went away with a fair lunch. After he was gone and she could go to rest, it seemed almost too big an effort to make it to the bedroom.

Mary's body might be resting, but her mind was not. The longer she laid there, the more tense she became. *All the trouble with me is, for so many years I had to plan for us to be able to live. Now, I cannot live without planning, and I don't know what to plan on. I'm all at sea.*

Before another hour passed, she was wishing she had not washed. *If I had not done so, I would be able to scout around to see if there is a chokecherry or elderberry to be found.* Anything would be better than just lying here stewing this way, so up she got. The clothes were mostly dry and she brought those in, folded and put away those not needing ironing.

I used to be able to think clearer when I was out gathering berries. I'd better commence to do so and get those cobwebs jarred loose. Still toying with the idea of starting out, she heard John's step on the plank bridge, not aware that she had been waiting impatiently for that very sound these several hours. From force of habit, she went to the wood box to build the fire, thinking he would want dinner. There was but little wood in the box. The clock said four o'clock.

"I didn't think I'd be gone all day when I left this morning." He was drinking water. "Sure lots of figuring to do. Still some for us to do." He laid a pocket full of papers on the table—most of them looked like legal sheets. "Had dinner yet?"

"I ate a little when Jack did at three. The food is all cold now. I could fix you something to eat, but you will need to get some wood first." She lifted the cloth that covered the food.

"I'm not wanting to eat. I had a pretty good meal at the hotel long about noon. Doc insisted I eat with him. He claimed all the free meals had always been coming the other way." Slowly, he sorted out the papers.

"Were there any letters at all?" She was anxious to know, and he was so slow in telling.

"A letter from the youngsters. It was addressed to me, so I opened it. Guess it was really for both of us." More sorting was going on, but no move to give her the letter.

This was maddening. *Can't he see I'm half crazy with worry over them while he just sits there figuring away?* For long

500

moments, she was too tense to speak. After awhile, she managed to ask, "Are they alright?"

"Sure they are alright." He looked up rather surprised, then did some more figuring. "Do you know how many washings that woman done for us?"

Such an ordinary question as this did much to restore reasoning power at this moment. "It has been all of two months, at least, so it must be eight or more washings. I marked it down on the calendar when the first one went up. I can look it up."

"Don't bother. It's paid anyhow. She had down nine washings, and she charged $3.50 for the washing of 'em, and a buck for the ironing each time. Was that too much?"

A faint touch of humor in this. "Never before have I figured from the paying angle. It has always been from the receiving end. Four dollars and fifty cents seems like a lot for each week's laundry, but that means your mucky work clothes too, so I think that price is about right."

"It don't seem like we could have gotten away with sixty-two loaves of bread." He was checking a long list of markings. "That is a devil of a lot of bread."

"Most of our meals all these weeks have been more on the lunch style, and that takes more bread." Mary's tension was easing and she could talk with more ease.

Putting aside another slip, "The men are paid. Doc is paid, and I settled up with the store. What do you figure our grocery bill for these two and half months was?"

"It would easily be more than $100, for we had those hay men to feed, and eating out of cans instead of the garden is more expensive."

"You guessed it pretty close. It was $110. Say, those guys that put up the hay charged $75. For that amount, we could have bought three ton and not had all that bother."

"As it is, we have twice that much hay in the barn." She was on familiar footing now.

"How do you know how much hay is in there?"

"I learned to figure hay before I was Margaret's age." To keep from being so tense again, she rested her elbows on the table, with head in hands. She was preparing to sit it out until he gave her the children's letter, or tell her what was in it.

"Like I say, we've some figuring to do now, and it isn't hay.

Our little wad is made. All in a pile at the bank until we decide how it should be split up. Have you any guess as to how much we cleaned up? Guess I should say how much we have after all the expenses have been paid."

"I wouldn't venture to say." This was not what she was waiting for.

"So, I'll tell you. It's a few hundred more than $6,000." He erased one figure and put down another, then jotted down others.

Mary could not take her eyes away from that work-scarred hand with the so new pencil doing this unfamiliar work. *Does he expect me to ask him what he is going to do with his money?* She was thinking about the many times when John had such great plans, if he could but find $5,000 in ready cash. In those days, it would have been borrowed money. Now, he had it in cash and it wasn't borrowed. Idly, she wondered what he would do with his money, but to ask him was not her way. She and John, who had lived together at least in the same dwelling, for more than fifteen years, were further apart—needing to, yet not able to share their thoughts or plans. Yet, in many ways, they were back right where they started out. Just the two of them standing alone—thoughts tied together.

John shoved the smudged sheet of paper toward her. "Look at this, and say what you think of it."

She brought her gaze to rest on the irregular writing. The figures were easy to read and not too long a column—all ending with double zero. "I don't know that I understand this. You have all our names down. Also, Annie's and Jack's."

"That's it. I figure we owe Annie something for all she did for us when you were sick. You say she won't be earning any money 'til she is through there two-three years from now. I thought $500 might help her out so she can come home, or up here, or wherever she wants to on her vacations each year. And she won't have to be calling on your dad for it. You and I know, Jack is one who can't handle money, but still, he might need it pretty bad sometime. The only way I can think of is to put it in the bank so he can't get it without Dad Williams' say so. In that way, if we weren't around handy to look out for him, there still would be cash for him should he get sick and need, say $500." John made a ring around those two names with his pencil.

"At first, I was thinking I wouldn't put the $1,000 to David's name, he feeling most of the sheep belong to him, which is alright too. But him being the older, he's going to be the first one wanting to go to college or branch out for himself maybe. So I changed my sights, and say $1,000 for each one of 'em." Another loop enclosed those three names. "Take away $4,000 from $6,000, leaves $2,000, the way I figure it. And I'll split that even with you. You can do with yours what you want, and I'll do the same with mine." He acted as if he expected her to say something. As she remained mute, he went on. "The safest place for the kid's money, I think, will be either a bank in Boise or Caldwell. DeLamar is not apt to have a bank for long—that camp is folding for sure. Doc says his contract is out next month, then he's going east for another *refresher course,* he called it."

That news jarred Mary into speech. "It will not seem right with Dr. Tom gone and a strange doctor in his place."

"The worse part of it is, they don't aim for another doctor to come. The company isn't going to hire anyone. And it isn't safe for us to have to depend on a doctor getting here from Silver City or Reynolds. It's alright this time of year when roads are good, but not winter time."

Mary could understand some of his worry about some of them getting sick, after she herself had caused them so much trouble this spring.

"Aren't you going to say what you think of the idea?" John asked.

"I...I can't seem to grasp all this at once. To put the money in the bank for the children's education is the very nicest thing you could do. And I know how much $500 is going to mean to Annie. While Jack might not ever need the money as long as we are able to look out for him, the way you have it planned is good." Then she was in deep thought, an aching void to fill. Longing for the children, she now spoke of them. "All three children must be about grown out of their clothes. They'll be needing new ones for school."

"I expect they will," John said absent mindedly.

After another pause, Mary ventured out in speech. "If you mean I can use some of that money, I want to buy each one of them good warm school clothes for this winter."

"I mean that $1,000 is for you to do with just as you want to, but you are not buying the kid's school clothes with it. I said there was a bit more over the $6,000. In fact, there is $400, and that should be enough to outfit this whole family with clothes."

Mary thought this over for awhile. "If I'm to use it just as I want, then I know right now what I shall do with it. I will pay off the $1,000 loan Father has against their place. I did not know they had any such debt as that hanging over their heads until Sister accidentally let it slip one day. And I am very sure their helping us so much all these years has been the reason."

"That is your business what you do with your money. I'm not saying what you aim to do with it isn't right, but you don't have to tell me. See?

"But I wanted to tell you." The saying of this surprised her as much as it did John.

"And I guess I'll have to tell you what I'm going to do with my money." He picked up one of the tarts, munching away, but toyed with the pencil. "Pretty good eating."

"And those are what you'll be eating for supper—that or cold cornbread and milk. There isn't wood enough to even heat up the lone can of pork and beans."

"We that low on grub? I should have asked you this morning what we needed. Too big a hurry to get settled up and know where we stood." He flipped a crumb from his hand as he picked up the pencil again. "Well, you haven't asked me what I'm going to do with mine."

"Should I have? I thought you were meaning neither one of us need tell."

"But I have to tell you." He paused as if he weren't real sure how to say the rest, then hurried to say it all. "Because I'm taking you south to a warmer climate just as soon as winter sets in. Doc says that would be the best thing that could happen to you. On that much money, you and I won't be living like any millionaires, but we should be able to see some country around Arizona and California. I always did want to look that Death Valley over, and as I understand it, winter time is the only time one ever wants to get caught there."

He was hoping Mary would say something so he would know what she thought of this trip he had planned. He continued to eat another tart slowly.

Her first reaction was negative. *No use talking. I am not going off and leaving the children all winter; nor my home locked up.*

Then on second thought, she remembered this house had gotten along without her for two and a half years once, and had been here when they came back. The children had been away from her all this time and even wanting to stay away. Then came a disturbing thought: "Have you been writing to the children about staying down there and going to school?" she demanded.

John nodded. "I had to find out how they liked the idea." There seemed to be nothing more to say. He handed her the crumpled letter now.

Carefully she smoothed it out and read the three short letters all written on the one large sheet. David sounded very adult about the proposed trip—approved of it and thought it would do Mother much good. He was glad he could keep his job and still go to high school. Margaret's reason for wanting to stay and go to school on the Flats was for a very different one: She would ride to school every morning and night instead of walk, and it would be in an automobile. Mr. Simmons took his children to school and would let them all ride. Susan made some proviso in her agreement to stay: Mama and Daddy had to be there at Grandpa and Grandma's for Christmas. Mary folded the letter and put it back in the envelope, but still held it in her hand.

"Well, I guess I better get you some wood." John got up quickly now, sure that Mary would make no comment. He went out through the washroom and toward the barn, hoping to find some broken boards so he could be back to the house soon. Failing to find anything else, he would go cut sagebrush.

Mary spread the cloth back over the tarts and went to the east door, looking at the torn up yard. All this did not seem to be her home any more. The cellar stood alone like an island in a sea of debris. The earth underneath was shorn away on three sides. The woodhouse and old ice house were there no more. The best of the lumber from those was piled in a rough heap waiting to be fashioned into another woodhouse. The picket fence still stood, although in a few places it had been necessary to prop it up. No grass was left on this side of the house—nothing but scooped out holes. A small pipe extended out, close to the last of their digging. Water still dripped from it; no one had bothered to turn it off.

Reaching in for her warm jacket, Mary walked along the uneven porch, still jacked up above the dugout places, out the front gate and toward the gulch. The rocky path was more worn;

even the rocks were dust coated. Many feet had trod this path in the past weeks. Of all those staking claims, none were now on the job. They had found nothing. Much to her surprise, she found a newly built head gate in the ditch, making it easy to turn the water either to the hay field or for their placer work. She lowered the gate—not that it made any difference, but it would stop the drip of the water in the yard washing away more soil. It was shady and comfortable here in the gulch—a good place to rest and think things out.

She found a place where she was screened by some willows, but then she didn't expect to be disturbed anyway. The longer she sat there thinking, the more relaxed she became. All the problems she had been worrying about lately seemed to have been settled for her, without her help. This was a new experience, and she was nowise sure she liked it. *Makes life rather meaningless to have no say-so or be in on the planning.* She had not said she would go on the trip, and was now trying to think up reasons why she should not.

Having slept but little for several nights, she was getting much too drowsy to think now. How long she slept, she did not know. Something woke her, and she sat up, surprised to find it nearly dark. She was cramped from lying in the one position, a bit chilly. What had awakened her, she did not know until the call came again, echoing back from the rocky sides of the narrow gulch. It was John calling. She could now hear him on the uneven path as he came closer. She answered, "Here I am."

He could not discern her through the willows in the dusk, but followed her voice. His fright made his voice incoherent. His relief in finding her sent him stumbling on to scoop her up, as if he would carry her away at once. Strength failing him to lift her far in this awkward way, he sat down, crushing her to him. "Don't ever frighten me again this way," he cried as soon as he could speak. "Don't ever do it, Mary. I can't stand it—not knowing what had happened to you or where you were." He was savage in his caress. "I called and called, and no answer." This was a sob.

"I didn't hear you 'til just at last," Mary found breath to say. "I must have been asleep." John's rough cheek caressed hers softly, but his arms were like bands of steel.

"Don't ever go away again, and I not know where." It was all he could think to say. Mary, not drawing away, calmed him somewhat. She seemed content to be cradled this way in his arms, and a feel of completion filled him. Mary was all his. Fate, for once was kind to John Marcus, letting him have this short space of time to enjoy before Mary remembered the cow that hadn't been milked.

Mary shivered in the cool night air. "It's getting cold, Honey." He tried to wrap her the more in his arms to shield her, not wanting to lose this moment.

Mary said languidly, "Maybe we better go to the house and build a fire."

"I got up a pretty good jag of wood to heat that can of beans." A half laugh with a catch to his breath. "That was before I found you gone, and went off the bean myself." Another catch in his throat, "I never knew before just how crazy one can get."

As always, reviews are highly valued, and Judy Hudson, as editor and publisher, would love to hear your response to *White Wool and Yellow Gold.* She may be contacted at HudsonCounsel@aol.com or through her blog, UntetheredVoice.com